The Fifth
WEXFORD
Omnibus

The Fifth
WEXFORD
Omnibus

incorporating
MEANS OF EVIL
AN UNKINDNESS OF RAVENS
THE VEILED ONE

Ruth Rendell

BCA
LONDON · NEW YORK · SYDNEY · TORONTO

incorporating
MEANS OF EVIL
First published by Hutchinson and Co (Publishers) Ltd 1979
© Kingsmarkham Enterprises Ltd 1979

AN UNKINDNESS OF RAVENS
First published by Hutchinson and Co (Publishers) Ltd 1985
© Kingsmarkham Enterprises 1985

THE VEILED ONE
First published by Hutchinson Ltd 1988
© Kingsmarkham Enterprises Ltd 1988

Photoset in Sabon by
Speedset Ltd, Ellesmere Port, South Wirral
Printed and bound in Great Britain by
Mackays of Chatham PLC, Chatham, Kent

MEANS OF EVIL
and Other Stories

To Jane Bakerman

Means of Evil

'Blewits,' said Inspector Burden, 'parasols, horns of plenty, morels and boletus. Mean anything to you?'

Chief Inspector Wexford shrugged. 'Sounds like one of those magazine quizzes. What have these in common? I'll make a guess and say they're crustacea. Or sea anemones. How about that?'

'They are edible fungi,' said Burden.

'Are they now? And what have edible fungi to do with Mrs Hannah Kingman throwing herself off, or being pushed off, a balcony?'

The two men were sitting in Wexford's office at the police station, Kingsmarkham, in the County of Sussex. The month was November, but Wexford had only just returned from his holiday. And while he had been away, enjoying in Cornwall an end of October that had been more summery than the summer, Hannah Kingman had committed suicide. Or so Burden had thought at first. Now he was in a dilemma, and as soon as Wexford had walked in that Monday morning, Burden had begun to tell the whole story to his chief.

Wexford, getting on for sixty, was a tall, ungainly, rather ugly man who had once been fat to the point of obesity but had slimmed to gauntness for reasons of health. Nearly twenty years his junior, Burden had the slenderness of a man who has always been thin. His face was ascetic, handsome in a frosty way. The older man, who had a good wife who looked after him devotedly, nevertheless always looked as if his clothes came off the peg from the War on Want Shop, while the younger, a widower, was sartorially immaculate. A tramp

9

and a Beau Brummell, they seemed to be, but the dandy relied on the tramp, trusted him, understood his powers and his perception. In secret he almost worshipped him.

Without his chief he had felt a little at sea in this case. Everything had pointed at first to Hannah Kingman's having killed herself. She had been a manic-depressive, with a strong sense of her own inadequacy; apparently her marriage, though not of long duration, had been unhappy, and her previous marriage had failed. Even in the absence of a suicide note or suicide threats, Burden would have taken her death for self-destruction – if her brother hadn't come along and told him about the edible fungi. And Wexford hadn't been there to do what he always could do, sort out sheep from goats and wheat from chaff.

'The thing is,' Burden said across the desk, 'we're not looking for proof of murder so much as proof of *attempted* murder. Axel Kingman could have pushed his wife off that balcony – he has no alibi for the time in question – but I had no reason to think he had done so until I was told of an attempt to murder her some two weeks before.'

'Which attempt has something to do with edible fungi?'

Burden nodded. 'Say with administering to her some noxious substance in a stew made from edible fungi. Though if he did it, God knows how he did it, because three other people, including himself, ate the stew without ill effects. I think I'd better tell you about it from the beginning.'

'I think you had,' said Wexford.

'The facts,' Burden began, very like a Prosecuting Counsel, 'are as follows. Axel Kingman is thirty-five years old and he keeps a health-food shop here in the High Street called Harvest Home. Know it?' When Wexford signified by a nod that he did, Burden went on, 'He used to be a teacher in Myringham, and for about seven years before he came here he'd been living with a woman named Corinne Last. He left her, gave up his job, put all the capital he had into this shop, and married a Mrs Hannah Nicholson.'

'He's some sort of food freak, I take it,' said Wexford.

Burden wrinkled his nose. 'Lot of affected nonsense,' he said. 'Have you ever noticed what thin pale weeds these health-food people are? While the folks who live on roast beef and suet and whisky and plum cake are full of beans and rarin' to go.'

'Is Kingman a thin pale weed?'

'A feeble – what's the word? – aesthete, if you ask me. Anyway, he and Hannah opened this shop and took a flat in the high-rise tower our planning geniuses have been pleased to raise over the top of it. The fifth floor. Corinne Last, according to her and according to Kingman, accepted the situation after a while and they all remained friends.'

'Tell me about them,' Wexford said. 'Leave the facts for a bit and tell me about them.'

Burden never found this easy. He was inclined to describe people as 'just ordinary' or 'just like anyone else', a negative attitude which exasperated Wexford. So he made an effort. 'Kingman looks the sort who wouldn't hurt a fly. The fact is, I'd apply the word gentle to him if I wasn't coming round to thinking he's a cold-blooded wife-killer. He's a total abstainer with a bee in his bonnet about drink. His father went bankrupt and finally died of alcoholism, and our Kingman is an anti-booze fanatic.

'The dead woman was twenty-nine. Her first husband left her after six months of marriage and went off with some girl friend of hers. Hannah went back to live with her parents and had a part-time job helping with the meals at the school where Kingman was a teacher. That was where they met.'

'And the other woman?' said Wexford.

Burden's face took on a repressive expression. Sex outside marriage, however sanctioned by custom and general approval, was always distasteful to him. That, in the course of his work, he almost daily came across illicit sex had done nothing to mitigate his disapproval. As Wexford sometimes derisively put it, you would think that in Burden's eyes all the suffering in the world, and certainly all the crime, somehow derived from men and women going to bed together outside the bonds of wedlock. 'God knows why he didn't marry her,' Burden now said. 'Personally I think things were a lot better in the days when education authorities put their foot down about immorality among teachers.'

'Let's not have your views on that now, Mike,' said

11

Wexford. 'Presumably Hannah Kingman didn't die because her husband didn't come to her a pure virgin.'

Burden flushed slightly. 'I'll tell you about this Corinne Last. She's very good-looking, if you like the dark sort of intense type. Her father left her some money and the house where she and Kingman lived, and she still lives in it. She's one of those women who seem to be good at everything they put their hands to. She paints and sells her paintings. She makes her own clothes, she's more or less the star in the local dramatic society, she's a violinist and plays in some string trio. Also she writes for health magazines and she's the author of a cookery book.'

'It would look then,' Wexford put in, 'as if Kingman split up with her because all this was more than he could take. And hence he took up with the dull little school-meals lady. No competition from her, I fancy.'

'I daresay you're right. As a matter of fact, that theory has already been put to me.'

'By whom?' said Wexford. 'Just where did you get all this information, Mike?'

'From an angry young man, the fourth member of the quartet, who happens to be Hannah's brother. His name is John Hood and I think he's got a lot more to tell. But it's time I left off describing the people and got on with the story.

'No one saw Hannah fall from the balcony. It happened last Thursday afternoon at about four. According to her husband, he was in a sort of office behind the shop doing what he always did on early-closing day – stock-taking and sticking labels on various bottles and packets.

'She fell on to a hard-top parking area at the back of the flats, and her body was found by a neighbour a couple of hours later between two parked cars. We were sent for, and Kingman seemed to be distraught. I asked him if he had had any idea that his wife might have wished to take her own life and he said she had never threatened to do so but had lately been very depressed and there had been quarrels, principally about money. Her doctor had put her on tranquillisers – of which, by the way, Kingman disapproved – and the doctor himself, old Dr Castle, told me Mrs Kingman had been to him for depression and because she felt her life wasn't worth living and she was a drag on her husband. He wasn't suprised that she

12

had killed herself and neither, by that time, was I. We were all set for an inquest verdict of suicide while the balance of the mind was disturbed when John Hood walked in here and told me Kingman had attempted to murder his wife on a previous occasion.'

'He told you just like that?'

'Pretty well. It's plain he doesn't like Kingman, and no doubt he was fond of his sister. He also seems to like and admire Corinne Last. He told me that on a Saturday night at the end of October the four of them had a meal together in the Kingmans' flat. It was a lot of vegetarian stuff cooked by Kingman – he always did the cooking – and one of the dishes was made out of what I'm old-fashioned enough, or narrow-minded enough, to call toadstools. They all ate it and they were all OK but for Hannah who got up from the table, vomited for hours, and apparently was quite seriously ill.'

Wexford's eyebrows went up. 'Elucidate, please,' he said.

Burden sat back, put his elbows on the arms of the chair, and pressed the tips of his fingers together. 'A few days before this meal was eaten, Kingman and Hood met at the squash club of which they are both members. Kingman told Hood that Corinne Last had promised to get him some edible fungi called shaggy caps from her own garden, the garden of the house which they had at one time shared. A crop of these things show themselves every autumn under a tree in this garden. I've seen them myself, but we'll come to that in a minute.

'Kingman's got a thing about using weeds and whatnot for cooking, makes salads out of dandelion and sorrel, and he swears by this fungi rubbish, says they've got far more flavour than mushrooms. Give me something that comes in a plastic bag from the supermarket every time, but no doubt it takes all sorts to make a world. By the way, this cookbook of Corinne Last's is called *Cooking for Nothing*, and all the recipes are for making dishes out of stuff you pull up by the wayside or pluck from the hedgerow.'

'These warty blobs or spotted puffets or whatever, had he cooked them before?'

'Shaggy caps,' said Burden, grinning, 'or *coprinus comatus*. Oh, yes, every year, and every year he and Corinne had eaten the resulting stew. He told Hood he was going to cook them

13

again this time, and Hood says he seemed very grateful to Corinne for being so – well, magnanimous.'

'Yes, I can see it would have been a wrench for her. Like hearing "our tune" in the company of your ex-lover and your supplanter.' Wexford put on a vibrant growl. ' "Can you bear the sight of me eating our toadstools with another?" '

'As a matter of fact,' said Burden seriously, 'it could have been just like that. Anyway, the upshot of it was that Hood was invited round for the following Saturday to taste these delicacies and was told that Corinne would be there. Perhaps it was that fact which made him accept. Well, the day came. Hood looked in on his sister at lunchtime. She showed him the pot containing the stew which Kingman had already made and she said *she had tasted it* and it was delicious. She also showed Hood half a dozen specimens of shaggy caps which she said Kingman hadn't needed and which they would fry for their breakfast. This is what she showed him.'

Burden opened a drawer in the desk and produced one of those plastic bags which he had said so inspired him with confidence. But the contents of this one hadn't come from a supermarket. He removed the wire fastener and tipped out four whitish scaly objects. They were egg-shaped, or rather elongated ovals, each with a short fleshy stalk.

'I picked them myself this morning,' he said, 'from Corinne Last's garden. When they get bigger, the egg-shaped bit opens like an umbrella, or a pagoda really, and there are sort of black gills underneath. You're supposed to eat them when they're in the stage these are.'

'I suppose you've got a book on fungi?' said Wexford.

'Here.' This also was produced from the drawer. *British Fungi, Edible and Poisonous.* 'And here we are – shaggy caps.'

Burden had opened it at the *Edible* section and at a line and wash drawing of the species he held in his hand. He passed it to the chief inspector.

'Coprinus comatus,' Wexford read aloud, '*a common species, attaining when full-grown a height of nine inches. The fungus is frequently to be found, during late summer and autumn, growing in fields, hedgerows and often in gardens. It should be eaten before the cap opens and disgorges its inky*

14

fluid, but is at all times quite harmless.' He put the book down but didn't close it. 'Go on, please, Mike,' he said.

'Hood called for Corinne and they arrived together. They got there just after eight. At about eight-fifteen they all sat down to table and began the meal with avocado *vinaigrette*. The next course was to be the stew, followed by nut cutlets with a salad and then an applecake. Very obviously, there was no wine or liquor of any sort on account of Kingman's prejudice. They drank grape juice from the shop.

'The kitchen opens directly out of the living-dining room. Kingman brought in the stew in a large tureen and served it himself at the table, beginning, of course, with Corinne. Each one of those shaggy caps had been sliced in half lengthwise and the pieces were floating in a thickish gravy to which carrots, onions and other vegetables had been added. Now, ever since he had been invited to this meal, Hood had been feeling uneasy about eating fungi, but Corinne had reassured him, and once he began to eat it and saw the others were eating it quite happily, he stopped worrying for the time being. In fact, he had a second helping.

'Kingman took the plates out and the tureen and immediately *rinsed them under the tap*. Both Hood and Corinne Last have told me this, though Kingman says it was something he always did, being fastidious about things of that sort.'

'Surely his ex-girlfriend could confirm or deny that,' Wexford put in, 'since they lived together for so long.'

'We must ask her. All traces of the stew were rinsed away. Kingman then brought in the nut concoction and the salad, but before he could begin to serve them Hannah jumped up, covered her mouth with her napkin, and rushed to the bathroom.

'After a while Corinne went to her. Hood could hear a violent vomiting from the bathroom. He remained in the living room while Kingman and Corinne were both in the bathroom with Hannah. No one ate any more. Kingman eventually came back, said that Hannah must have picked up some "bug" and that he had put her to bed. Hood went into the bedroom where Hannah was lying on the bed with Corinne beside her. Hannah's face was greenish and covered with sweat and she was evidently in great pain because while he was there she

15

doubled up and groaned. She had to go to the bathroom again and that time Kingman had to carry her back.

'Hood suggested Dr Castle should be sent for, but this was strenuously opposed by Kingman who dislikes doctors and is one of those people who go in for herbal remedies – raspberry leaf tablets and camomile tea and that sort of thing. Also he told Hood rather absurdly that Hannah had had quite enough to do with doctors and that if this wasn't some gastric germ it was the result of her taking "dangerous" tranquillisers.

'Hood thought Hannah was seriously ill and the argument got heated, with Hood trying to make Kingman either call a doctor or take her to a hospital. Kingman wouldn't and Corinne took his part. Hood is one of those angry but weak people who are all bluster, and although he might have called a doctor himself, he didn't. The effect on him of Corinne again, I suppose. What he did do was tell Kingman he was a fool to mess about cooking things everyone knew weren't safe, to which Kingman replied that if the shaggy caps were dangerous, how was it they weren't all ill? Eventually, at about midnight, Hannah stopped retching, seemed to have no more pain, and fell asleep. Hood drove Corinne home, returned to the Kingmans' and remained there for the rest of the night, sleeping on their sofa.

'In the morning Hannah seemed perfectly well, though weak, which rather upset Kingman's theory about the gastric bug. Relations between the brothers-in-law were strained. Kingman said he hadn't liked Hood's suggestions and that when he wanted to see his sister he, Kingman, would rather he came there when he was out or in the shop. Hood went off home, and since that day he hasn't seen Kingman.

'The day after his sister's death he stormed in here, told me what I've told you, and accused Kingman of trying to poison Hannah. He was wild and nearly hysterical, but I felt I couldn't dismiss this allegation as – well, the ravings of a bereaved person. There were too many peculiar circumstances, the unhappiness of the marriage, the fact of Kingman rinsing those plates, his refusal to call a doctor. Was I right?'

Burden stopped and sat waiting for approval. It came in the form of a not very enthusiastic nod.

16

After a moment Wexford spoke. 'Could Kingman have pushed her off that balcony, Mike?'

'She was a small fragile woman. It was physically possible. The back of the flats isn't overlooked. There's nothing behind but the parking area and then open fields. Kingman could have gone up by the stairs instead of using the lift and come down by the stairs. Two of the flats on the lower floors are empty. Below the Kingmans lives a bedridden woman whose husband was at work. Below that the tenant, a young married woman, was in but she saw and heard nothing. The invalid says she thinks she heard a scream during the afternoon but she did nothing about it, and if she did hear it, so what? It seems to me that a suicide, in those circumstances, is as likely to cry out as a murder victim.'

'OK,' said Wexford. 'Now to return to the curious business of this meal. The idea would presumably be that Kingman intended to kill her that night but that his plan misfired because whatever he gave her wasn't toxic enough. She was very ill but she didn't die. He chose those means and that company so that he would have witnesses to his innocence. They all ate the stew out of the same tureen, but only Hannah was affected by it. How then are you suggesting he gave her whatever poison he did give her?'

'I'm not,' said Burden frankly, 'but others are making suggestions. Hood's a bit of a fool, and first of all he would only keep on about all fungi being dangerous and the whole dish being poisonous. When I pointed out that this was obviously not so, he said Kingman must have slipped something into Hannah's plate, or else it was the salt.'

'What salt?'

'He remembered that no one but Hannah took salt with the stew. But that's absurd because Kingman couldn't have known that would happen. And, incidentally, to another point we may as well clear up now – the avocados were quite innocuous. Kingman halved them *at the table* and the *vinaigrette* sauce was served in a jug. The bread was not in the form of rolls but a home-made wholemeal loaf. If there was anything there which shouldn't have been it was in the stew all right.

'Corinne Last refuses to consider the possibility that

17

Kingman might be guilty. But when I pressed her she said she was not actually sitting at the table while the stew was served. She had got up and gone into the hall to fetch her handbag. So she didn't see Kingman serve Hannah.' Burden reached across and picked up the book Wexford had left open at the description and drawing of the shaggy caps. He flicked over to the *Poisonous* section and pushed the book back to Wexford. 'Have a look at some of these.'

'Ah, yes,' said Wexford. 'Our old friend, the fly agaric. A nice-looking little red job with white spots, much favoured by illustrators of children's books. They usually stick a frog on top of it and a gnome underneath. I see that when ingested it causes nausea, vomiting, tetanic convulsions, coma and death. Lots of these agarics, aren't there? Purple, crested, warty, verdigris – all more or less lethal. Aha! The death cap, *amanita phalloides*. How very unpleasant. The most dangerous fungus known, it says here. Very small quantities will cause intense suffering and often death. So where does all that get us?'

'The death cap, according to Corinne Last, is quite common round here. What she doesn't say, but what I infer, is that Kingman could have got hold of it easily. Now suppose he cooked just one specimen separately and dropped it into the stew just before he brought it in from the kitchen? When he comes to serve Hannah he spoons up for her this specimen, or the pieces of it, in the same way as someone might select a special piece of chicken for someone out of a casserole. The gravy was thick, it wasn't like thin soup.'

Wexford looked dubious. 'Well, we won't dismiss it as a theory. If he had contaminated the rest of the stew and others had been ill, that would have made it look even more like an accident, which was presumably what he wanted. But there's one drawback to that, Mike. If he meant Hannah to die, and was unscrupulous enough not to mind about Corinne and Hood being made ill, why did he rinse the plates? To *prove* that it was an accident, he would have wanted above all to keep some of that stew for analysis when the time came, for analysis would have shown the presence of poisonous as well as non-poisonous fungi, and it would have seemed that he had merely been careless.

'But let's go and talk to these people, shall we?'

* * *

18

The shop called Harvest Home was closed. Wexford and Burden went down an alley at the side of the block, passed the glass-doored main entrance, and went to the back to a door that was labelled *Stairs and Emergency Exit*. They entered a small tiled vestibule and began to mount a steepish flight of stairs.

On each floor was a front door and a door to the lift. There was no one about. If there had been and they had had no wish to be seen, it would only have been necessary to wait behind the bend in the stairs until whoever it was had got into the lift. The bell by the front door on the fifth floor was marked *A. and H. Kingman*. Wexford rang it.

The man who admitted them was smallish and mild-looking and he looked sad. He showed Wexford the balcony from which his wife had fallen. It was one of two in the flat, the other being larger and extending outside the living-room windows. This one was outside a glazed kitchen door, a place for hanging washing or for gardening of the window-box variety. Herbs grew in pots, and in a long trough there still remained frost-bitten tomato vines. The wall surrounding the balcony was about three feet high, the drop sheer to the hard-top below.

'Were you surprised that your wife committed suicide, Mr Kingman?' said Wexford.

Kingman didn't answer directly. 'My wife set a very low valuation on herself. When we got married I thought she was like me, a simple sort of person who doesn't ask much from life but has quite a capacity for contentment. It wasn't like that. She expected more support and more comfort and encouragement than I could give. That was especially so for the first three months of our marriage. Then she seemed to turn against me. She was very moody, always up and down. My business isn't doing very well and she was spending more money than we could afford. I don't know where all the money was going and we quarrelled about it. Then she'd become depressed and say she was no use to me, she'd be better dead.'

He had given, Wexford thought, rather a long explanation for which he hadn't been asked. But it could be that these thoughts, defensive yet self-reproachful, were at the moment uppermost in his mind. 'Mr Kingman,' he said, 'we have

19

reason to believe, as you know, that foul play may have been involved here. I should like to ask you a few questions about a meal you cooked on October 29th, after which your wife was ill.'

'I can guess who's been telling you about that.'

Wexford took no notice. 'When did Miss Last bring you these – er, shaggy caps?'

'On the evening of the 28th. I made the stew from them in the morning, according to Miss Last's own recipe.'

'Was there any other type of fungus in the flat at the time?'

'Mushrooms, probably.'

'Did you at any time add any noxious object or substance to that stew, Mr Kingman?'

Kingman said quietly, wearily, 'Of course not. My brother-in-law has a lot of ignorant prejudices. He refuses to understand that that stew, which I have made dozens of times before in exactly the same way, was as wholesome as, say, a chicken casserole. More wholesome, in my view.'

'Very well. Nevertheless, your wife was very ill. Why didn't you call a doctor?'

'Because my wife was not "very" ill. She had pains and diarrhoea, that's all. Perhaps you aren't aware of what the symptoms of fungus poisoning are. The victim doesn't just have pain and sickness. His vision is impaired, he very likely blacks out or has convulsions of the kind associated with tetanus. There was nothing like that with Hannah.'

'It was unfortunate that you rinsed those plates. Had you not done so and called a doctor, the remains of that stew would almost certainly have been sent for analysis, and if it was harmless as you say, all this investigation could have been avoided.'

'It was harmless,' Kingman said stonily.

Out in the car Wexford said, 'I'm inclined to believe him, Mike. And unless Hood or Corinne Last has something really positive to tell us, I'd let it rest. Shall we go and see her next?'

The cottage Corinne had shared with Axel Kingman was on a lonely stretch of road outside the village of Myfleet. It was a stone cottage with a slate roof, surrounded by a well-tended pretty garden. A green Ford Escort stood on the drive in front of a weatherboard garage. Under a big old apple tree, from which the yellow leaves were falling, the shaggy caps, immediately recognisable, grew in three thick clumps.

She was a tall woman, the owner of this house, with a beautiful, square-jawed, high-cheekboned face and a mass of dark hair. Wexford was at once reminded of the Klimt painting of a languorous red-lipped woman, gold-neckleted, half covered in gold draperies, though Corinne Last wore a sweater and a denim smock. Her voice was low and measured. He had the impression she could never be flustered or caught off her guard.

'You're the author of a cookery book, I believe?' he said.

She made no answer but handed him a paperback which she took down from a bookshelf. *Cooking for Nothing, Dishes from Hedgerow and Pasture* by Corinne Last. He looked through the index and found the recipe he wanted. Opposite it was a coloured photograph of six people eating what looked like brown soup. The recipe included carrots, onions, herbs, cream, and a number of other harmless ingredients. The last lines read: *Stewed shaggy caps are best served piping hot with wholewheat bread. For drinkables, see page 171.* He glanced at page 171, then handed the book to Burden.

'This was the dish Mr Kingman made that night?'

'Yes.' She had a way of leaning back when she spoke and of half lowering her heavy glossy eyelids. It was serpentine and a little repellent. 'I picked the shaggy caps myself out of this garden. I don't understand how they could have made Hannah ill, but they must have done because she was fine when we first arrived. She hadn't got any sort of gastric infection, that's nonsense.'

Burden put the book aside. 'But you were all served stew out of the same tureen.'

'I didn't see Axel actually serve Hannah. I was out of the room.' The eyelids flickered and almost closed.

'Was it usual for Mr Kingman to rinse plates as soon as they were removed?'

'Don't ask me.' She moved her shoulders. 'I don't know. I do know that Hannah was very ill just after eating that stew. Axel doesn't like doctors, of course, and perhaps it would have — well, embarrassed him to call Dr Castle in the circumstances.

21

Hannah had black spots in front of her eyes, she was getting double vision. I was extremely concerned for her.'

'But you didn't take it on yourself to get a doctor, Miss Last? Or even support Mr Hood in his allegations?'

'Whatever John Hood said, I knew it couldn't be the shaggy caps.' There was a note of scorn when she spoke Hood's name. 'And I was rather frightened. I couldn't help thinking it would be terrible if Axel got into some sort of trouble, if there was an inquiry or something.'

'There's an inquiry now, Miss Last.'

'Well, it's different now, isn't it? Hannah's dead. I mean, it's not just suspicion or conjecture any more.'

She saw them out and closed the front door before they had reached the garden gate. Farther along the roadside and under the hedges more shaggy caps could be seen as well as other kinds of fungi Wexford couldn't identify – little mushroom-like things with pinkish gills, a cluster of small yellow umbrellas, and on the trunk of an oak tree, bulbous smoke-coloured swellings that Burden said were oyster mushrooms.

'That woman,' said Wexford, 'is a mistress of the artless insinuation. She damned Kingman with almost every word, but she never came out with anything like an accusation.' He shook his head. 'I suppose Kingman's brother-in-law will be at work?'

'Presumably,' said Burden, but John Hood was not at work. He was waiting for them at the police station, fuming at the delay, and threatening 'if something wasn't done at once' to take his grievances to the Chief Constable, even to the Home Office.

'Something is being done,' said Wexford quietly. 'I'm glad you've come here, Mr Hood. But try to keep calm, will you, please?'

It was apparent to Wexford from the first that John Hood was in a different category of intelligence from that of Kingman and Corinne Last. He was a thick-set man of perhaps no more than twenty-seven or twenty-eight, with bewildered, resentful blue eyes in a puffy flushed face. A man, Wexford thought, who would fling out rash accusations he couldn't substantiate, who would be driven to bombast and bluster in the company of the ex-teacher and that clever subtle woman.

He began to talk now, not wildly, but still without restraint, repeating what he had said to Burden, reiterating, without putting forward any real evidence, that his brother-in-law had meant to kill his sister that night. It was only by luck that she had survived. Kingman was a ruthless man who would have stopped at nothing to be rid of her. He, Hood, would never forgive himself that he hadn't made a stand and called the doctor.

'Yes, yes, Mr Hood, but what exactly were your sister's symptoms?'

'Vomiting and stomach pains, violent pains,' said Hood.

'She complained of nothing else?'

'Wasn't that enough? That's what you get when someone feeds you poisonous rubbish.'

Wexford merely raised his eyebrows. Abruptly, he left the events of that evening and said, 'What had gone wrong with your sister's marriage?'

Before Hood replied, Wexford could sense he was keeping something back. A wariness came into his eyes and then was gone. 'Axel wasn't the right person for her,' he began. 'She had problems, she needed understanding, she wasn't . . .' His voice trailed away.

'Wasn't what, Mr Hood? What problems?'

'It's got nothing to do with all this,' Hood muttered.

'I'll be the judge of that. You made this accusation, you started this business off. It's not for you now to keep anything back.' On a sudden inspiration, Wexford said, 'Had these problems anything to do with the money she was spending?'

Hood was silent and sullen. Wexford thought rapidly over the things he had been told – Axel Kingman's fanaticism on one particular subject, Hannah's desperate need of an un-specified kind of support during the early days of her marriage. Later on, her alternating moods, and then the money, the weekly sums of money spent and unaccounted for.

He looked up and said baldly, 'Was your sister an alcoholic, Mr Hood?'

Hood hadn't liked this directness. He flushed and looked affronted. He skirted round a frank answer. Well, yes, she drank. She was at pains to conceal her drinking. It had been going on more or less consistently since her first marriage broke up.

'In fact, she was an alcoholic,' said Wexford.

'I suppose so.'

'Your brother-in-law didn't know?'

'Good God, no. Axel would have killed her!' He realised what he had said. 'Maybe that's why. Maybe he found out.'

'I don't think so, Mr Hood. Now I imagine that in the first few months of her marriage she made an effort to give up drinking. She needed a good deal of support during this time but she couldn't, or wouldn't, tell Mr Kingman why she needed it. Her efforts failed, and slowly, because she couldn't manage without it, she began drinking again.'

'She wasn't as bad as she used to be,' Hood said with pathetic eagerness. 'And only in the evenings. She told me she never had a drink before six, and after that she'd have a few more, gulping them down on the quiet so Axel wouldn't know.'

Burden said suddenly, 'Had your sister been drinking that evening?'

'I expect so. She wouldn't have been able to face company, not even just Corinne and me, without a drink.'

'Did anyone besides yourself know that your sister drank?'

'My mother did. My mother and I had a sort of pact to keep it dark from everyone so that Axel wouldn't find out.' He hesitated and then said rather defiantly, 'I did tell Corinne. She's a wonderful person, she's very clever. I was worried about it and I didn't know what to do. She promised she wouldn't tell Axel.'

'I see.' Wexford had his own reasons for thinking she hadn't done so. Deep in thought, he got up and walked to the other end of the room where he stood gazing out of the window. Burden's continuing questions, Hood's answers, reached him only as a confused murmur of voices. Then he heard Burden say more loudly, 'That's all for now, Mr Hood, unless the chief inspector has anything more to ask you.'

'No, no,' said Wexford abstractedly, and when Hood had somewhat truculently departed, 'Time for lunch. It's past two. Personally, I shall avoid any dish containing fungi, even *psalliota campestris.*

24

After Burden had looked that one up and identified it as the common mushroom, they lunched and then made a round of such wineshops in Kingsmarkham as were open at that hour. At the Wine Basket they drew a blank, but the assistant in the Vineyard told them that a woman answering Hannah Kingman's description had been a regular customer, and that on the previous Wednesday, the day before her death, she had called in and bought a bottle of Courvoisier Cognac.

'There was no liquor of any kind in Kingman's flat,' said Burden. 'Might have been an empty bottle in the rubbish, I suppose.' He made a rueful face. 'We didn't look, didn't think we had any reason to. But she couldn't have drunk a whole bottleful on the Wednesday, could she?'

'Why are you so interested in this drinking business, Mike? You don't seriously see it as a motive for murder, do you? That Kingman killed her because he'd found out, or been told, that she was a secret drinker?'

'It was a means, not a motive,' said Burden. 'I know how it was done. I know how Kingman tried to kill her that first time.' He grinned. 'Makes a change for me to find the answer before you, doesn't it? I'm going to follow in your footsteps and make a mystery of it for the time being, if you don't mind. With your permission we'll go back to the station, pick up those shaggy caps and conduct a little experiment.'

Michael Burden lived in a neat bungalow in Tabard Road. He had lived there with his wife until her untimely death and continued to live there with his sixteen-year-old daughter, his son being away at university. But that evening Pat Burden was out with her boy friend, and there was a note left for her father on the refrigerator. *Dad, I ate the cold beef from yesterday. Can you open a tin for yourself? Back by 10.30. Love, P.*

Burden read this note several times, his expression of consternation deepening with each perusal. And Wexford could precisely have defined the separate causes which brought that look of weariness into Burden's eyes, that frown, that drooping of the mouth. Because she was motherless his daughter had to eat not only cold but leftover food, she who should be carefree was obliged to worry about her father, loneliness drove her out of their home until the appallingly late

25

hour of half-past ten. It was all nonsense, of course, the Burden children were happy and recovered from their loss, but how to make Burden see it that way? Widowhood was something he dragged about with him like a physical infirmity. He looked up from the note, screwed it up and eyed his surroundings vaguely and with a kind of despair. Wexford knew that look of desolation. He saw it on Burden's face each time he accompanied him home.

It evoked exasperation as well as pity. He wanted to tell Burden – one or twice he had done so – to stop treating John and Pat like retarded paranoiacs, but instead he said lightly, 'I read somewhere the other day that it wouldn't do us a scrap of harm if we never ate another hot meal as long as we lived. In fact, the colder and rawer the better.'

'You sound like the Axel Kingman brigade,' said Burden, rallying and laughing which was what Wexford had meant him to do. 'Anyway, I'm glad she didn't cook anything. I shouldn't have been able to eat it and I'd hate her to take it as criticism.'

Wexford decided to ignore that one. 'While you're deciding just how much I'm to be told about this experiment of yours, d'you mind if I phone my wife?'

'Be my guest.'

It was nearly six. Wexford came back to find Burden peeling carrots and onions. The four specimens of *coprinus comatus*, beginning to look a little wizened, lay on a chopping board. On the stove a saucepanful of bone stock was heating up.

'What the hell are you doing?'

'Making shaggy cap stew. My theory is that the stew is harmless when eaten by non-drinkers, and toxic, or toxic to some extent, when taken by those with alcohol in the stomach. How about that? In a minute, when this lot's cooking, I'm going to take a moderate quantity of alcohol, then I'm going to eat the stew. Now say I'm a damned fool if you like.'

Wexford shrugged. He grinned. 'I'm overcome by so much courage and selfless devotion to the duty you owe the taxpayers. But wait a minute. Are you sure only Hannah had been drinking that night? We know Kingman hadn't. What about the other two?'

'I asked Hood that when you were off in your daydream. He

26

called for Corinne Last at six, at her request. They picked some apples for his mother, then she made him coffee. He did suggest they call in at a pub for a drink on their way to the Kingmans', but apparently she took so long getting ready that they didn't have time.'

'OK. Go ahead then. But wouldn't it be easier to call in an expert? There must be such people. Very likely someone holds a chair of fungology or whatever it's called at the University of the South.'

'Very likely. We can do that after I've tried it. I want to know for sure *now*. Are you willing too?'

'Certainly not. I'm not your guest to that extent. Since I've told my wife I won't be home for dinner, I'll take it as a kindness if you'll make me some innocent scrambled eggs.'

He followed Burden into the living room where the inspector opened a door in the sideboard. 'What'll you drink?'

'White wine, if you've got any, or vermouth if you haven't. You know how abstemious I have to be.'

Burden poured vermouth and soda. 'Ice?'

'No, thanks. What are you going to have? Brandy? That was Hannah Kingman's favourite tipple apparently.'

'Haven't got any,' said Burden. 'It'll have to be whisky. I think we can reckon she had two double brandies before that meal, don't you? I'm not so brave I want to be as ill as she was.' He caught Wexford's eye. 'You don't think some people could be more sensitive to it than others, do you?'

'Bound to be,' said Wexford breezily. 'Cheers!'

Burden sipped his heavily watered whisky, then tossed it down. 'I'll just have a look at my stew. You sit down. Put the television on.'

Wexford obeyed him. The big coloured picture was of a wood in autumn, pale blue sky, golden beech leaves. Then the camera closed in on a cluster of red-and-white-spotted fly agaric. Chuckling, Wexford turned it off as Burden put his head round the door.

'I think it's more or less ready.'

'Better have another whisky.'

'I suppose I had.' Burden came in and re-filled his glass. 'That ought to do it.'

'What about my eggs?'

27

'Oh, God, I forgot. I'm not much of a cook, you know. Don't know how women manage to get a whole lot of different things brewing and make them synchronise.'

'It is a mystery, isn't it? I'll get myself some bread and cheese, if I may.'

The brownish mixture was in a soup bowl. In the gravy floated four shaggy caps, cut lengthwise. Burden finished his whisky at a gulp.

'What was it the Christians in the arena used to say to the Roman Emperor before they went to the lions?'

'*Morituri, te salutamus,*' said Wexford. '"We who are about to die salute thee."'

'Well . . .' Burden made an effort with the Latin he had culled from his son's homework. '*Moriturus, te saluto.* Would that be right?'

'I daresay. You won't die, though.'

Burden made no answer. He picked up his spoon and began to eat. 'Can I have some more soda?' said Wexford.

There are perhaps few stabs harder to bear than derision directed at one's heroism. Burden gave him a sour look. 'Help yourself. I'm busy.'

Wexford did so. 'What's it like?' he said.

'All right. It's quite nice, like mushrooms.'

Doggedly he ate. He didn't once gag on it. He finished the lot and wiped the bowl round with a piece of bread. Then he sat up, holding himself rather tensely.

'May as well have your telly on now,' said Wexford. 'Pass the time.' He switched it on again. No fly agaric this time, but a dog fox moving across a meadow with Vivaldi playing. 'How d'you feel?'

'Fine,' said Burden gloomily.

'Cheer up. It may not last.'

But it did. After fifteen minutes had passed, Burden still felt perfectly well. He looked bewildered. 'I was so damned positive. I *knew* I was going to be retching and vomiting by now. I didn't put the car away because I was certain you'd have to run me down to the hospital.'

Wexford only raised his eyebrows.

'You were pretty casual about it, I must say. Didn't say a word to stop me, did you? Didn't it occur to you it might have been a bit awkward for you if anything had happened to me?'

'I knew it wouldn't. I said to get a fungologist.' And then Wexford, faced by Burden's aggrieved stare, burst out laughing. 'Dear old Mike, you'll have to forgive me. But you know me, d'you honestly think I'd have let you risk your life eating that stuff? I knew you were safe.'

'May one ask how?'

'One may. And you'd have known too if you'd bothered to take a proper look at that book of Corinne Last's. Under the recipe for shaggy cap stew it said, "*For drinkables, see page 171.*" Well, I looked at page 171, and there Miss Last gave a recipe for cowslip wine and another for sloe gin, both highly intoxicating drinks. Would she have recommended a wine and a spirit to drink with those fungi if there'd been the slightest risk? Not if she wanted to sell her book she wouldn't. Not unless she was risking hundreds of furious letters and expensive lawsuits.'

Burden had flushed a little. Then he too began to laugh.

After a little while they had coffee.

'A little logical thinking would be in order, I fancy,' said Wexford. 'You said this morning that we were not so much seeking to prove murder as attempted murder. Axel Kingman could have pushed her off that balcony, but no one saw her fall and no one heard him or anybody else go up to that flat during the afternoon. If, however, an attempt to murder her was made two weeks before, the presumption that she was eventually murdered is enormously strengthened.'

Burden said impatiently, 'We've been through all that. We know that.'

'Wait a minute. The attempt failed. Now just how seriously ill was she? According to Kingman and Hood, she had severe stomach pains and she vomited. By midnight she was peacefully sleeping and by the following day she was all right.'

'I don't see where all this is getting us.'

'To a point which is very important and which may be the crux of the whole case. You say that Axel Kingman attempted to murder her. In order to do so he must have made very elaborate plans – the arranging of the meal, the inviting of the two witnesses, the ensuring that his wife tasted the stew earlier

29

in the same day, and the preparation for some very nifty sleight of hand at the time the meal was served. Isn't it odd that the actual method used should so signally have failed? That Hannah's *life* never seems to have been in danger? And what if the method had succeeded? At post-mortem some noxious agent would have been found in her body or the effects of such. How could he have hoped to get away with that since, as we know, neither of his witnesses actually watched him serve Hannah and one of them was even out of the room?

'So what I am postulating is that no one attempted to murder her, but someone *attempted* to make her ill so that, taken in conjunction with the sinister reputation of non-mushroom fungi and Hood's admitted suspicion of them, taken in conjunction with the known unhappiness of the marriage, *it would look as if there had been a murder attempt.*'

Burden stared at him. 'Kingman would never have done that. He would either have wanted his attempt to succeed or not to have looked like an attempt at all.'

'Exactly. And where does that get us?'

Instead of answering him, Burden said on a note of triumph, his humiliation still rankling, 'You're wrong about one thing. She *was* seriously ill, she didn't just have nausea and vomiting. Kingman and Hood may not have mentioned it, but Corinne Last said she had double vision and black spots before her eyes and . . .' His voice faltered. 'My God, you mean. . . ?'

Wexford nodded. 'Corinne Last only of the three says she had those symptoms. Only Corinne Last is in a position to say, because she lived with him, if Kingman was in the habit of rinsing plates as soon as he removed them from the table. What does she say? That she doesn't know. Isn't that rather odd? Isn't it rather odd too that she chose that precise moment to leave the table and go out into the hall for her handbag?

'She knew that Hannah drank because Hood had told her so. On the evening that meal was eaten you say Hood called for her at her own request. Why? She has her own car, and I don't for a moment believe that a woman like her would feel anything much but contempt for Hood.'

'She told him there was something wrong with the car.'

'She asked him to come at six, although they were not due at the Kingmans' till eight. She gave him *coffee*. A funny thing to drink at that hour, wasn't it, and before a meal? So what happens when he suggests calling in at a pub on the way? She doesn't say no or say it isn't a good idea to drink and drive. She takes so long getting ready that they don't have time.

'She didn't want Hood to drink any alcohol, Mike, and she was determined to prevent it. She, of course, would take no alcohol and she knew Kingman never drank. But she also knew Hannah's habit of having her first drink of the day at about six.

'Now look at her motive, far stronger than Kingman's. She strikes me as a violent, passionate and determined woman. Hannah had taken Kingman away from her. Kingman had rejected her. Why not revenge herself on both of them by killing Hannah and seeing to it that Kingman was convicted of the crime? If she simply killed Hannah, she had no way of ensuring that Kingman would come under suspicion. But if she made it look as if he had previously attempted her life, the case against him would become very strong indeed.

'Where was she last Thursday afternoon? She could just as easily have gone up those stairs as Kingman could. Hannah would have admitted her to the flat. If she, known to be interested in gardening, had suggested that Hannah take her on to that balcony and show her the pot herbs, Hannah would willingly have done so. And then we have the mystery of the missing brandy bottle with some of its contents surely remaining. If Kingman had killed her, he would have left that there as it would greatly have strengthened the case for suicide. Imagine how he might have used it. "Heavy drinking made my wife ill that night. She knew I had lost respect for her because of her drinking. She killed herself because her mind was unbalanced by drink."

'Corinne Last took that bottle away because she didn't want it known that Hannah drank, and she was banking on Hood's keeping it dark from us just as he had kept it from so many people in the past. And she didn't want it known because the fake murder attempt that *she* staged depended on her victim having alcohol present in her body.'

Burden sighed, poured the last dregs of coffee into Wexford's cup. 'But we tried that out,' he said. 'Or I tried it out, and it doesn't work. You knew it wouldn't work from her

31

book. True, she brought the shaggy caps from her own garden, but she couldn't have mixed up poisonous fungi with them because Axel Kingman would have realised at once. Or if he hadn't, they'd all have been ill, alcohol or no alcohol. She was never alone with Hannah before the meal, and while the stew was served she was out of the room.'

'I know. But we'll see her in the morning and ask her a few more questions.' Wexford hesitated, then quoted softly, ' "Out of good still to find means of evil." '

'What?'

'That's what she did, isn't it? It was good for everyone but Hannah, you look as if it's done you a power of good, but it was evil for Hannah. I'm off now, Mike, it's been a long day. Don't forget to put your car away. You won't be making any emergency trips to hospital tonight.'

They were unable to puncture her self-possession. The languorous Klimt face was carefully painted this morning, and she was dressed as befitted the violinist or the actress or the author. She had been forewarned of their coming and the gardener image had been laid aside. Her long smooth hands looked as if they had never touched the earth or pulled up a weed.

Where had she been on the afternoon of Hannah Kingman's death? Her thick shapely eyebrows went up. At home, indoors, painting. Alone?

'Painters don't work with an audience,' she said rather insolently, and she leaned back, dropping her eyelids in that way of hers. She lit a cigarette and flicked her fingers at Burden for an ashtray as if he were a waiter.

Wexford said, 'On Saturday, October 29th, Miss Last, I believe you had something wrong with your car?'

She nodded lazily.

In asking what was wrong with it, he thought he might catch her. He didn't.

'The glass in the offside front headlight was broken while the car was parked,' she said, and although he thought how easily she could have broken that glass herself, he could hardly say so. In the same smooth voice she added, 'Would you like to see the bill I had from the garage for repairing it?'

'That won't be necessary.' She wouldn't have offered to show it to him if she hadn't possessed it. 'You asked Mr Hood to call for you here at six, I understand.'

'Yes. He's not my idea of the best company in the world, but I'd promised him some apples for his mother and we had to pick them before it got dark.'

'You gave him coffee but had no alcohol. You had no drinks on the way to Mr and Mrs Kingman's flat. Weren't you a little disconcerted at the idea of going out to dinner at a place where there wouldn't even be a glass of wine?'

'I was used to Mr Kingman's ways.' But not so used, thought Wexford, that you can tell me whether it was normal or abnormal for him to have rinsed those plates. Her mouth curled, betraying her a little. 'It didn't bother me, I'm not a slave to liquor.'

'I should like to return to these shaggy caps. You picked them from here on October 28th and took them to Mr Kingman that evening. I think you said that?'

'I did. I picked them from this garden.'

She enunciated the words precisely, her eyes wide open and gazing sincerely at him. The words, or perhaps her unusual straightforwardness, stirred in him the glimmer of an idea. But if she had said nothing more, that idea might have died as quickly as it had been born.

'If you want to have them analysed or examined or whatever, you're getting a bit late. Their season's practically over.' She looked at Burden and gave him a gracious smile. 'But you took the last of them yesterday, didn't you? So that's all right.'

Wexford, of course, said nothing about Burden's experiment. 'We'll have a look in your garden, if you don't mind.'

She didn't seem to mind, but she had been wrong. Most of the fungi had grown into black-gilled pagodas in the twenty-four hours that had elapsed. Two new ones, however, had thrust their white oval caps up through the wet grass. Wexford picked them, and still she didn't seem to mind. Why, then, had she appeared to want their season to be over? He thanked her and she went back into the cottage. The door closed. Wexford and Burden walked out into the road.

The fungus season was far from over. From the abundant

33

array by the roadside it looked as if the season would last weeks longer. Shaggy caps were everywhere, some of them smaller and greyer than the clump that grew out of Corinne Last's well-fed lawn. There were green and purple agarics, horn-shaped toadstools, and tiny mushrooms growing in fairy rings.

'She doesn't exactly mind our having them analysed,' Wexford said thoughtfully, 'but it seems she'd prefer the analysis to be done on the ones you picked yesterday than on those I picked today. Can that be so or am I just imagining it?'

'If you're imagining it, I'm imagining it too. But it's no good, that line of reasoning. We know they're not potentiated – or whatever the word is – by alcohol.'

'I shall pick some more all the same,' said Wexford. 'Haven't got a paper bag, have you?'

'I've got a clean handkerchief. Will that do?'

'Have to,' said Wexford who never had a clean one. He picked a dozen more young shaggy caps, big and small, white and grey, immature and fully grown. They got back into the car and Wexford told the driver to stop at the public library. He went in and emerged a few minutes later with three books under his arm.

'When we get back,' he said to Burden, 'I want you to get on to the university and see what they can offer us in the way of an expert in fungilogy.'

He closeted himself in his office with the three books and a pot of coffee. When it was nearly lunchtime, Burden knocked on the door.

'Come in,' said Wexford. 'How did you get on?'

'It's not fungologist or fungilogist,' said Burden with triumphant severity. 'It's *mycologist* and they don't have one. But there's a man on the faculty who's a toxicologist and who's just published one of those popular science books. This one's about poisoning by wild plants and fungi.'

Wexford grinned. 'What's it called? *Killing for Nothing?* He sounds as if he'd do fine.'

'I said we'd see him at six. Let's hope something will come of it.'

'No doubt it will.' Wexford slammed shut the thickest of his books. 'We need confirmation,' he said, 'but I've found the answer.'

'For God's sake! Why didn't you say?'

'You didn't ask. Sit down.' Wexford motioned him to the chair on the other side of the desk. 'I said you'd done your homework, Mike, and so you had, only your textbook wasn't quite comprehensive enough. It's got a section on edible fungi and a section on poisonous fungi – *but nothing in between.* What I mean by that is, there's nothing in your book about fungi which aren't wholesome yet don't cause death or intense suffering. There's nothing about the kind that can make people ill in certain circumstances.'

'But we know they ate shaggy caps,' Burden protested. 'And if by "circumstances" you mean the intake of alcohol, we know shaggy caps aren't affected by alcohol.'

'Mike,' said Wexford quietly, '*do* we know they ate shaggy caps?' He spread out on the desk the haul he had made from the roadside and from Corinne Last's garden. 'Look closely at these, will you?'

Quite bewildered now, Burden looked at and fingered the dozen or so specimens of fungi. 'What am I to look *for*?'

'Differences,' said Wexford laconically.

'Some of them are smaller than the others, and the smaller ones are greyish. Is that what you mean? But, look here, think of the differences between mushrooms. You get big flat ones and small button ones and . . .'

'Nevertheless, in this case it is that small difference that makes all the difference.' Wexford sorted the fungi into two groups. 'All the small greyer ones,' he said, 'came from the roadside. Some of the larger whiter ones came from Corinne Last's garden and some from the roadside.'

He picked up between forefinger and thumb a specimen of the former. 'This isn't a shaggy cap, it's an ink cap. Now listen.' The thick book fell open where he had placed a marker. Slowly and clearly he read: '*The ink cap, coprinus atramentarius, is not to be confused with the shaggy cap, coprinus comatus. It is smaller and greyer in colour, but otherwise the resemblance between them is strong. While coprinus atramentarius is usually harmless when cooked, it contains, however, a chemical similar to the active principle in Antabuse, a drug used in the treatment of alcoholics, and if eaten in conjunction with alcohol will cause nausea and vomiting.*'

35

'We'll never prove it.'

'I don't know about that,' said Wexford. 'We can begin by concentrating on the one lie we know Corinne Last told when she said she picked the fungi she gave Axel Kingman *from her own garden.*'

Old Wives' Tales

They looked shocked and affronted and somehow ashamed. Above all, they looked old. Wexford thought that in the nature of things a woman of seventy ought to be an orphan, ought to have been an orphan for twenty years. This one had been an orphan for scarcely twenty days. Her husband, sitting opposite her, pulling his wispy moustache, slowly and mechanically shaking his head, seemed older than she, perhaps not so many years the junior of his late mother-in-law. He wore a brown cardigan with a small neat darn at one elbow and sheepskin slippers, and when he spoke he snuffled. His wife kept saying she couldn't believe her ears, she couldn't believe it, why were people so wicked? Wexford didn't answer that. He couldn't, though he had often wondered himself.

'My mother died of a stroke,' Mrs Betts said tremulously. 'It was on the death certificate, Dr Moss put it on the death certificate.'

Betts snuffled and wheezed. He reminded Wexford of an aged rabbit, a rabbit with myxomatosis perhaps. It was partly the effect of the brown woolly cardigan and the furry slippers, and partly the moustache and the unshaven bristly chin. 'She was ninety-two,' Betts said in his thick catarrhal voice. '*Ninety-two.* I reckon you lot must have got bats in the belfry.'

'I mean,' said Mrs Betts, 'are you saying Dr Moss was telling untruths? A doctor?'

'Why don't you ask him? We're only ordinary people, the wife and me, we're not educated. Doctor said a cerebral haemorrhage,' Betts stumbled a little over the words, 'and in plain language that's a stroke. That's what he said. Are you

37

saying me or the wife gave Mother a stroke? Are you saying that?'

'I'm making no allegations, Mr Betts.' Wexford felt uncomfortable, wished himself anywhere but in this newly decorated, paint-smartened house. 'I am merely making inquiries which information received obliges me to do.'

'Gossip,' said Mrs Betts bitterly. 'This street's a hotbed of gossip. Pity they've nothing better to do. Oh, I know what they're saying. Half of them turn up their noses and look the other way when I pass them. All except Elsie Parrish, and that goes without saying.'

'She's been a brick,' said her husband. 'A real brick is Elsie.' He stared at Wexford with a kind of timid outrage. 'Haven't you folk got nothing better to do than listen to a bunch of old hens? What about the real crime? What about the muggings and the break-ins?'

Wexford sighed. But he went on doggedly questioning, remembering what the nurse had said, what Dr Moss had said, keeping in the forefront of his mind that motive which was so much more than merely wanting an aged parent out of the way. If he hadn't been a policeman with a profound respect for the law and for human life, he might have felt that these two, or one of them, had been provoked beyond bearing to do murder.

One of them? Or both? Or neither? Ivy Wrangton had either died an unnatural death or else there had been a series of coincidences and unexplained contingencies which were nothing short of incredible.

It was the nurse who had started it, coming to him three days before. Sergeant Martin brought her to him because what she alleged was so serious. Wexford knew her by sight, had seen her making her calls, and had sometimes wondered how district nurses could endure their jobs, the unremitting daily toil, the poor pay, the unsavoury tasks. Perhaps she felt the same about his. She was a fair, pretty woman, about thirty-five, overweight, with big red hands, who always looked tired. She looked tired now, though she hadn't long been back from two weeks' holiday. She was in her summer uniform, blue and white print dress, white apron, dark cardigan, small round hat and the stout shoes that served for summer and winter alike. Nurse Radcliffe. Judith Radcliffe.

'Mr Wexford?' she said. 'Chief Inspector Wexford? Yes. I believe I used to look in on your daughter after she'd had a baby. I was doing my midwifery then. I can't remember her name but the baby was Benjamin.'

Wexford smiled and told her his daughter's name and wondered, looking at the bland faded blue eyes and the stolid set of the neck and shoulders, just how intelligent this woman was, how perceptive and how truthful. He pulled up one of the little yellow chairs for her. His office was cheerful and sunny-looking even when the sun wasn't shining, not much like a police station.

'Please sit down, Nurse Radcliffe,' he said. 'Sergeant Martin's given me some idea what you've come about.'

'I feel rather awful. You may think I'm making a mountain out of a molehill.'

'I shouldn't worry about that. If I do I'll tell you so and we'll forget it. No one else will know of it, it'll be between us and these four walls.'

At that she gave a short laugh. 'Oh, dear, I'm afraid it's gone *much* further than that already. I've three patients in Castle Road and each one of them mentioned it to me. That's what Castle Road gossip is at the moment, poor old Mrs Wrangton's death. And I just thought – well, you can't have that much smoke without fire, can you?'

Mountains and molehills, Wexford thought, smoke and fire. This promised to be a real volcano. He said firmly, 'I think you'd better tell me all about it.'

She was rather pathetic. 'It's best you hear it from someone *professional*.' She planted her feet rather wide apart in front of her and leant forward, her hands on her knees. 'Mrs Wrangton was a very old woman. She was ninety-two. But allowing for her age, she was as fit as a fiddle, thin, strong, continent, her heart as sound as a bell. The day she died was the day I went away on holiday, but I was in there the day before to give her her bath – I did that once a week, she couldn't get in and out of the bath on her own – and I remember thinking she was fitter than I'd seen her for months. You could have knocked me down with a feather when I came back from holiday and heard she'd had a stroke the next day.'

'When did you come back, Nurse Radcliffe?'

'Last Friday, Friday the 16th. Well, it's Thursday now and I was back on my district on Monday and the first thing I heard was that Mrs Wrangton was dead and suggestions she'd been – well, helped on her way.' She paused, worked something out on her fingers. 'I went away June 2nd, that was the day she died, and the funeral was June 7th.'

'Funeral?'

'Well, cremation,' said Nurse Radcliffe, glancing up as Wexford sighed. 'Dr Moss attended Mrs Wrangton. She was really Dr Crocker's patient, but he was on holiday too like me. Look, Mr Wexford, I don't know the details of what happened that day, June 2nd, not first-hand, only what the Castle Road ladies say. D'you want to hear that?'

'You haven't yet told me what she died of.'

'A stroke – according to Dr Moss.'

'I'm not at all sure,' said Wexford dryly, 'how one sets about giving someone a stroke. Would you give them a bad fright or push an empty hypodermic into them or get them into a rage or what?'

'I really don't know.' Nurse Radcliffe looked a little put out and as if she would like to say, had she dared, that to find this out was Wexford's job, not hers. She veered away from the actual death. 'Mrs Wrangton and her daughter – that's Mrs Betts, Mrs Doreen Betts – they hated each other, they were cat and dog. And I don't think Mr Betts had spoken to Mrs Wrangton for a year or more. Considering the house was Mrs Wrangton's and every stick of furniture in it belonged to her, I used to think they were very ungrateful. I never liked the way Mrs Betts spoke about her mother, let alone the way she spoke *to* her, but I couldn't say a word. Mr Betts is retired now but he only had a very ordinary sort of job in the Post Office and they lived rent-free in Mrs Wrangton's home. It's a nice house, you know, late Victorian, and they built to last in those days. I used to think it badly needed doing up and it was a pity Mr Betts couldn't get down to a bit of painting, when Mrs Wrangton said to me she was having decorators in, having the whole house done up inside and out . . .'

Wexford cut short the flow of what seemed like irrelevancies. 'Why were the Bettses and Mrs Wrangton on such bad terms?'

The look he got implied that seldom had Nurse Radcliffe come across such depths of naivety. 'It's a sad fact, Mr Wexford, that people can outstay their welcome in this world. To put it bluntly, Mr and Mrs Betts couldn't wait for something to happen to Mrs Wrangton.' Her voice lingered over the euphemism. 'They hadn't been married all that long, you know,' she said surprisingly. 'Only five or six years. Mrs Betts was just a spinster before that, living at home with Mother. Mr Betts was a widower that she met at the Over-Sixties Club. Mrs Wrangton used to say she could have done better for herself – seems funny to say that about a woman of her age, doesn't it? – and that Mr Betts was only after the house and her money.'

'You mean she said it to you?'

'Well, not just to me, to anybody,' said Nurse Radcliffe, unconsciously blackening the dead woman to whom she showed such conscious bias. 'She really felt it. I think she bitterly resented having him in the house.'

Wexford moved a little impatiently in his chair. 'If we were to investigate every death just because the victim happened to be on bad terms with his or her relations . . .'

'Oh, no, no, it's not just that, not at all. Mrs Betts sent for Dr Moss on May 23rd, just four days after Dr Crocker went away. Why did she? There wasn't anything wrong with Mrs Wrangton. I was getting her dressed after her bath and I was amazed to see Dr Moss. Mrs Wrangton said, I don't know what you're doing here, I never asked my daughter to send for you. Just because I overslept a bit this morning, she said. She was so proud of her good health, poor dear, never had an illness in her long life but the once and that was more an allergy than an illness. I can tell you why he was sent for, Mr Wexford. So that *when Mrs Wrangton died* he'd be within his rights signing the death certificate. He wasn't her doctor, you see, but it'd be all right if he'd attended her within the past two weeks, that's the law. They're all saying Mrs Betts waited for Dr Crocker to go away, she knew he'd never have just accepted her mother's death like that. He'd have asked for a post-mortem and then the fat would have been in the fire.' Nurse Radcliffe didn't specify how, and Wexford thought better of interrupting her again. 'The last time I saw Mrs Wrangton,'

41

she went on, 'was on June 1st. I had a word with the painter as I was going out. There were two of them but this was a young boy, about twenty. I asked him when they expected to finish, and he said, sooner than they thought, next week, because Mrs Betts had told them just to finish the kitchen and the outside and then to leave it. I thought it was funny at the time, Mrs Wrangton hadn't said a word to me about it. In fact, what she'd said was, wouldn't it be nice when the bathroom walls were all tiled and I wouldn't have to worry about splashing when I bathed her.

'Mr Wexford, it's possible Mrs Betts stopped that work because she knew her mother was going to die the next day. She personally didn't want the whole house re-decorated and she didn't want to have to pay for it out of the money her mother left her.'

'Was there much money?' Wexford asked.

'I'd guess a few thousands in the bank, maybe three or four, and there was the house, wasn't there? I know she'd made a will, I witnessed it. I and Dr Crocker. In the presence,' said Nurse Radcliffe sententiously, 'of the legatee and of each other, which is the law. But naturally I didn't see what its *provisions* were. Mrs Wrangton did tell me the house was to go to Mrs Betts and there was a little something for her friend Elsie Parrish. Beyond that, I couldn't tell you. Mind you, Mrs Parrish won't have it that there could have been foul play. I met her in Castle Road and she said, wasn't it wicked the things people were saying?'

'Who is Elsie Parrish?'

'A very nice old friend of Mrs Wrangton's. Nearly eighty but as spry as a cricket. And that brings me to the worst thing. June 2nd, that Friday afternoon, Mr and Mrs Betts went off to a whist drive. Mrs Parrish knew they were going. Mrs Betts had promised to knock on her door before they went so that she could come round and sit with Mrs Wrangton. She sometimes did that. It wasn't right to leave her alone, not at her age. Well, Mrs Parrish waited in and Mrs Betts never came, so naturally she thought the Bettses had changed their minds and hadn't gone out. But they had. They deliberately didn't call to fetch Mrs Parrish. They left Mrs Wrangton all alone but for that young boy painter, and they'd never done such a thing before, not once.'

42

Wexford digested all this in silence, not liking it but not really seeing it as a possible murder case. Nurse Radcliffe seemed to have dried up. She slackened back in the chair with a sigh.

'You mentioned an allergy. . . ?'

'Oh, my goodness, that was about fifty years ago! Only some kind of hay fever, I think. There's asthma in the family. Mrs Betts's brother had asthma all his life, and Mrs Betts gets *urticaria* – nettle rash, that is. They're all connected, you know.'

He nodded. He had the impression she had a bombshell yet to explode, or that the volcano was about to erupt. 'If they weren't there,' he said, 'how could either of them possibly have hastened Mrs Wrangton's end?'

'They'd been back two hours before she died. When they came back she was in a coma, and they waited *one hour and twenty minutes* before they phoned Dr Moss.'

'Would you have signed that death certificate, Len?' said Wexford to Dr Crocker. They were in the purpose-built bungalow that housed two consulting rooms and a waiting room. Dr Crocker's evening surgery was over, the last patient packed off with reassurance and a prescription. Crocker gave Wexford rather a defiant look.

'Of course I would. Why not? Mrs Wrangton was ninety-two. It's ridiculous of Radcliffe to say she didn't expect her to die. You expect everyone of ninety-two to die and pretty soon. I hope nobody's casting any aspersions on my extremely able partner.'

'I'm not,' said Wexford. 'There's nothing I'd like more than for this to turn out a lot of hot air. But I do have to ask you, don't I? I do have to ask Jim Moss.'

Dr Crocker looked a little mollified. He and the chief inspector were lifelong friends, they had been at school together, had lived most of their lives in Kingsmarkham where Crocker had his practice and Wexford was head of the CID. But for a medical practitioner, no amount of friendship will excuse hints that he or one of his fellows have been negligent. And he prickled up again when Wexford said:

'How could he *know* it was a stroke without a post-mortem?'

43

'God give me patience! He saw her before she was dead, didn't he? He got there about half an hour before she died. There are unmistakable signs of stroke, Reg. An experienced medical man couldn't fail to recognise them. The patient is unconscious, the face flushed, the pulse slow, the breathing stertorous with a puffing of the cheeks during expiration. The only possible confusion is with alcoholic poisoning, but in alcoholic poisoning the pupils of the eyes are widely dilated whereas in apoplexy or stroke they're contracted. Does that satisfy you?'

'Well, OK, it was a stroke, but aren't I right in thinking a stroke can be the consequence of something else, of an operation, for instance, or in the case of a young woman, of childbirth, or in an old person even of bedsores?'

'Old Ivy Wrangton didn't have bedsores and she hadn't had a baby for seventy years. She had a stroke because she was ninety-two and her arteries were worn out. "The days of our age",' quoted the doctor solemnly, ' "are threescore years and ten, and though men be so strong that they come to fourscore years, yet is their strength then but labour and sorrow." She'd reached fourscore years and twelve and she was worn out.' He had been pacing up and down, getting heated, but now came to sit on the edge of his desk, a favourite perch of his. 'A damn good thing she was cremated,' he said. 'That puts out of court all the ghastliness of exhumation and cutting her up. She was a remarkable old woman, you know, Reg. Tough as old boots. She told me once about having her first baby. She was eighteen, out scrubbing the doorstep when she had a labour pain. Indoors she went, called her mother to fetch the midwife and lay down on her bed. The baby was born after two more pains, and the daughter came even easier.'

'Yes, I heard there'd been another child.' Wexford saw the absurdity of referring to someone who must necessarily be in his seventies as a child. 'Mrs Betts has a brother?' he corrected himself.

'*Had.* He died last winter. He was an old man, Reg, and he'd been bronchial all his life. Seventy-four *is* old till you start comparing it with Mrs Wrangton's age. She was so proud of her good health, boasted about never being ill. I used to drop in every three months or so as a matter of routine, and when I'd ask her how she was she'd say, I'm fine, Doctor, I'm in the pink.'

'But I understand she'd had some illness connected with an allergy?' Wexford was clutching at straws. 'Nurse Radcliffe told me about it. I've been wondering if anything to do with that could have contributed to...?'

'Of course not,' the doctor cut in. 'How could it? That was when she was middle-aged and the so-called illness was an asthmatic attack with some swelling of the eyes and a bit of gastric trouble. I fancy she used to exaggerate it the way healthy people do when they're talking about the one little bit of illness they've ever had ... Oh, here's Jim. I thought I'd heard his last patient leave.'

Dr Moss, small, dark and trim, came in from the corridor between the consulting rooms. He gave Wexford the very wide smile that showed thirty-two large white teeth which the chief inspector had never been able to precisely define as false, as crowns or simply as his own. The teeth were rather too big for Dr Moss's face which was small and smooth and lightly tanned. His small black eyes didn't smile at all.

'Enter the villainous medico,' he said, 'who is notoriously in cahoots with greedy legatees and paranoid Post Office clerks. What evidence can I show you? The number of my Swiss bank account? Or shall I produce the hammer, a crafty tap from which ensured an immediate subarachnoid haemorrhage?'

It is very difficult to counter this kind of facetiousness. Wexford knew he would only get more fatuous pleasantries, heavy irony, outrageous confessions, if he attempted to rebut any of it or if he were to assure Moss that this wasn't what he had meant at all. He smiled stiffly, tapping his feet against the leg of Crocker's desk, while Dr Moss elaborated on his fantasy of himself as corrupt, a kind of latter-day William Palmer, poison-bottle-happy and ever-ready with his hypodermic to gratify the impatient next-of-kin. At length, unable to bear any more of it, Wexford cut across the seemingly interminable harangue and said to Crocker:

'You witnessed her will, I understand?'

'I and that busybody Radcliffe, that's right. If you want to know what's in it, the house and three thousand pounds go to Doreen Betts, and the residue to another patient of mine, a Mrs

45

Parrish. Residue would have been about fifteen hundred at that time, Mrs Wrangton told me, but considering her money was in a building society and she managed to save out of her pension and her annuity, I imagine it'll be a good deal more by now.'

Wexford nodded. By now Dr Moss had dried up, having run out, presumably, of subject matter and witticisms. His teeth irradiated his face like lamps, and when his mouth was closed he looked rather ill-tempered and sinister. Wexford decided to try the direct and simple approach. He apologised.

'I'd no intention of suggesting you'd been negligent, Dr Moss. But put yourself in my position . . .'

'Impossible!'

'Very well. Let me put it this way. Try to understand that in my position I had no choice but to make inquiries.'

'Mrs Betts might try an action for slander. She can count on my support. The Bettses had neither the opportunity nor the motive to do violence to Mrs Wrangton, but a bunch of tongue-clacking old witches are allowed to take their characters away just the same.'

'Motive,' said Wexford gently, 'I'm afraid they did have, the straightforward one of getting rid of Mrs Wrangton who had become an encumbrance to them, and of inheriting her house.'

'Nonsense.' Momentarily the teeth showed in a white blaze. 'They were going to get rid of her in any case. They would have had the house to themselves in any case. Mrs Wrangton was going into a nursing home.' He paused, enjoying the effect of what he had said. 'For the rest of her days,' he added with a touch of drama.

Crocker shifted off the edge of the desk. 'I never knew that.'

'No? Well, it was you who told her about a new nursing home opening in Stowerton, or so she said. She told me all about it that day Mrs Betts called me when you'd gone away. Sometime at the end of May it was. She was having the house decorated for her daughter and son-in-law prior to her leaving.'

'Did she tell you that too?' asked Wexford.

'No, but it was obvious. I can tell you exactly what happened during that visit if it makes you happy. That interfering harpy, Radcliffe, had just been bathing her, and when she'd dressed her she left. Thank God. I'd never met Mrs Wrangton before. There was nothing wrong with her, bar extreme old age and her blood pressure up a bit, and I was rather narked that Mrs Betts had called me out. Mrs Wrangton said her daughter got nervous when she slept late in the mornings as she'd done that day and the day before. Wasn't to be wondered at, she said, considering she'd been sitting up in bed watching the World Cup on television till all hours. Only Mrs Betts and her husband didn't know that and I wasn't to tell them. Well, we had a conspiratorial laugh over that, I liked her, she was a game old dear, and then she started talking about the nursing home – what's it called? Springfield? Sunnyside?'

'Summerland,' said Dr Crocker.

'Cost you a lot, that will, I said, and she said she'd got a good bit coming in which would die with her anyway. I assumed she meant an annuity. We talked for about five minutes and I got the impression she'd been tossing around this nursing home idea for months. I asked her what her daughter thought and she said . . .'

'Yes?' prompted Wexford.

'Oh, my God, people like you make one see sinister nuances in the most innocent remarks. It's just that she said, You'd reckon Doreen'd be only too glad to see the back of me, wouldn't you? I mean, it rather implied she wouldn't be glad. I don't know what she was inferring and I didn't ask. But you can rest assured Mrs Betts had no motive for killing her mother. Leaving sentiment apart, it was all the same to her whether her mother was alive or dead. The Bettses would still have got the house and after her death Mrs Wrangton's capital. The next time I saw her she was unconscious, she was dying. She did die, at seven-thirty, on June 2nd.'

Both Wexford's parents had died before he was forty. His wife's mother had been dead twenty years, her father fifteen. None of these people had been beyond their seventies, so therefore Wexford had no personal experience of the geriatric problem. It seemed to him that for a woman like Mrs Wrangton, to end one's days in a nursing home with companionship and good nursing and in pleasant surroundings

47

was not so bad a fate. And an obvious blessing to the daughter and son-in-law whose affection for a parent might be renewed when they only encountered her for an hour or so a week. No, Doreen Betts and her husband had no motive for helping Mrs Wrangton out of this world, for by retiring to Summerland she wouldn't even make inroads into that three or four thousand pounds of capital. Her pension and her annuity would cover the fees. Wexford wondered what those fees would be, and remembered vaguely from a few years back hearing a figure of twenty pounds a week mentioned in a similar connection. Somebody's old aunt, some friend of his wife. You'd have to allow for inflation, of course, but surely it would cost no more than thirty pounds a week now. With the Retirement Pension at eighteen pounds and the annuity worth, say, another twenty, Mrs Wrangton could amply have afforded Summerland.

But she had died first – of natural causes. It no longer mattered that she and Harry Betts hadn't been on speaking terms, that no one had fetched Elsie Parrish, that Dr Moss had been called out to visit a healthy woman, that Mrs Betts had given orders to stop the painting. There was no motive. Eventually the tongues would cease to wag, Mrs Wrangton's will would be proved, and the Bettses settle down to enjoy the rest of their lives in their newly decorated home.

Wexford put it out of his head, apart from wondering whether he should visit Castle Road and drop a word of warning to the gossips. Immediately he saw how impossible this would be. The slander would be denied, and besides he hardly saw his function as extending so far. No, let it die a natural death – as Mrs Wrangton had.

On Monday morning he was having breakfast, his wife reading a letter just come from her sister in Wales.

'Frances says Bill's mother has got to go into a nursing home at last.' Bill was Wexford's brother-in-law. 'It's either that or Fran having her, which really isn't on.'

Wexford, from behind his newspaper, made noises indicative of sympathy with and support for Frances. He was reading a verbatim report of the trial of some bank robbers.

'Ninety pounds a week,' said Dora.

'What did you say?'

'I was talking to myself, dear. You read your paper.'

'Did you say ninety pounds a week?'

'That's right. For the nursing home. I shouldn't think Bill and Fran could stand that for long. It's getting on for five thousand a year.'

'But . . .' Wexford almost stammered, '. . . I thought a couple of years ago you said it was twenty a week for what's-her-name, Rosemary's aunt, wherever they put her?'

'Darling,' said Dora gently, 'first of all, that wasn't a couple of years ago, it was at least *twelve* years ago. And secondly, haven't you heard of the rising cost of living?'

An hour later he was in the matron's office at Summerland, having made no attempt to disguise who he was, but presenting himself as there to inquire about a prospective home for an aged relative of his wife. Aunt Lilian. Such a woman had actually existed, perhaps still did exist in the remote Westmorland village from which the Wexfords had last heard of her in a letter dated 1959.

The matron was an Irishwoman, Mrs Corrigan. She seemed about the same age as Nurse Radcliffe. At her knee stood a boy of perhaps six, at her feet, playing with a toy tractor, was another of three. Outside the window three little girls were trying to coax a black cat from its refuge under a car. You might have thought this was a children's home but for the presence of half a dozen old women sitting on the lawn in a half circle, dozing, muttering to themselves or just staring. The grounds were full of flowers, mauve and white lilac everywhere, roses coming out. From behind a hedge came the sound of a lawn mower, plied perhaps by the philoprogenitive Mr Corrigan.

'Our fees are ninety-*five* pounds a week, Mr Wexford,' said the matron. 'And with the extra for laundry and dry-cleaning, sure and you might say five thousand a year for a good round figure.'

'I see.'

'The ladies only have to share a room with one other lady. We bath them once a week and change their clothes once a week. And if you could please see to it your aunt only has synthetic fabrics, if you know what I mean, for the lot's popped in the washing machine all together. We like the fees a month in advance and paid on a banker's order, if you please.'

'I'm afraid I don't please,' said Wexford. 'Your charges are more than I expected. I shall have to make other arrangements.'

'Then there's no more to be said,' said Mrs Corrigan with a smile nearly equalling the candlepower of Dr Moss's.

'Just out of curiosity, Mrs Corrigan, how do your – er, guests meet your fees? Five thousand a year is more than most incomes would be equal to.'

'Sure and aren't they widows, Mr Wexford, and didn't their husbands leave them their houses? Mostly the ladies sell their houses, and with prices the way they are today that's enough to keep them in Summerland for four years or five.'

Mrs Wrangton had intended to sell her house, and she was having it re-decorated inside and out in order to get a better price. She had intended to sell the roof over the Bettses' heads – no wonder she had implied to Dr Moss that Doreen Betts would be sorry to see the back of her. What a woman! What malevolence at ninety-two! And who could have said she wouldn't have been within her moral as well as her legal rights to sell? It was her house. Doreen Wrangton might long ago have found a home of her own, ought perhaps to have done so, and as Doreen Betts might have expected her husband to provide one for her. It is universally admitted to be wrong to anticipate stepping into dead men's shoes. And yet what a monstrous revenge to have on an uncongenial son-in-law, a not always co-operative daughter. There was a subtlety about it that evoked Wexford's admiration nearly as much as its cruelty aroused his disgust. It was a motive all right, and a strong one.

So at last he had found himself in Castle Road, in the Bettses' living room, confronting an elderly orphan and her husband. The room was papered in a silvery oyster colour, the woodwork ivory. He was sure that that door had never previously sported a shade lighter than chocolate brown, just as the hall walls had, until their recent coat of magnolia, been gloomily clothed in dark Lincrusta.

When the two of them had protested bitterly about the gossip and the apparent inability of the police to get their priorities right, Doreen Betts agreed without too much mutiny to answer Wexford's questions. To the first one she reacted passionately.

'Mother would never have done it. I know she wouldn't, it was all bluff with her. Even Mother wouldn't have been that cruel.'

Her husband pulled his moustache, slowly shuffling his slippered feet back and forth. His angry excitement had resulted in a drop of water appearing on the end of his nose. It hung there, trembling.

Doreen Betts said, 'I knew she didn't mean to go ahead with it when I said, Can I tell the builders to leave the upstairs? And she said, I daresay. That's what she said. I daresay, she said, I'm not bothered either way. Of course she wouldn't have gone ahead with it. You don't even get a room to yourself in that place. Ninety-five pounds a week! They'll put you to bed at eight o'clock, Mother, I said, so don't think they'll let you sit up till all hours watching TV.'

'Quite right,' said Harry Betts ambiguously.

'Why, if we'd known Mother meant to do a thing like that, we could have lived in Harry's flat when we got married. He had a nice little flat over the freezer centre in the High Street. It wasn't just one room like Mother went about saying, it was a proper flat, wasn't it, Harry? What'd we have done if Mother'd done a thing like that? We'd have had nowhere.' Her husband's head-shaking, the trembling droplet, the fidgety feet, seemed suddenly to unnerve her. She said to him, distress in her voice, 'I'm going to have a little talk to the officer on my own, dear.'

Wexford followed her into the room where Mrs Wrangton had slept for the last years of her life. It was on the ground floor at the back, presumably originally designated as a dining room, with a pair of windows looking out on to a long narrow concrete terrace and a very long, very narrow garden. No re-decorations had been carried out here. The walls were papered in a pattern of faded nasturtiums, the woodwork grained to look like walnut. Mrs Wrangton's double bed was still there, the mattress uncovered, a pile of folded blankets on top of it. There was a television set in this room as well as in the front room, and it had been placed so that the occupant of the bed could watch it.

51

'Mother came to sleep down here a few years back,' said Mrs Betts. 'There's a toilet just down the passage. She couldn't manage the stairs any more except when nurse helped her.' She sat on the edge of the mattress, nervously fingering a cage-like object of metal bars. 'I'll have to see about her walking frame going back, I'll have to get on to the welfare people.' Her hands resting on it, she said dolefully, 'Mother hated Harry. She always said he wasn't good enough for me. She did everything she could to stop me marrying him.' Mrs Betts's voice took on a rebellious girlish note. 'I think it's awful having to ask your mother's consent to marry when you're sixty-five, don't you?'

At any rate, he thought, she had gone ahead without receiving it. He looked wonderingly at this grey wisp of a woman, seventy years old, who talked as if she were a fairy princess.

'You see, she talked for years of changing her will and leaving the house to my brother. It was after he died that the nursing home business started. She quarrelled outright with Harry. Elsie Parrish was in here and Mother accused Harry in front of her of only marrying me to get this place. Harry never spoke a word to Mother again, and quite right too. I said to Mother, You're a wicked woman, you promised me years ago I'd have this house and now you're going back on your word. Cheats never prosper, I said.'

The daughter had inherited the mother's tongue. Wexford could imagine the altercations, overheard by visitors, by neighbours, which had contributed to the gossip. He turned to look at the framed photograph on a mahogany tallboy. A wedding picture, *circa* 1903. The bride was seated, lilies in her lap under a bolster of a bosom hung with lace and pearls. The bridegroom stood behind her, frock coat, black handlebar moustache. Ivy Wrangton must have been seventeen, Wexford calculated, her face plain, puffy, young, her figure modishly pouter-pigeon-like, her hair in that most unflattering of fashions, the cottage loaf. She had been rather plump then, but thin, according to Nurse Radcliffe in old age. Wexford said quietly, apparently idly:

'Mrs Betts, why did you send for Dr Moss on May 23rd? Your mother wasn't ill. She hadn't complained of feeling ill.'

She held the walking frame, pushing it backwards and

forwards. 'Why shouldn't I? Dr Crocker was away. Elsie came in at nine and Mother was still asleep, and Elsie said it wasn't right the amount she slept. We couldn't wake her, though we shook her, we were so worried. I wasn't to know she'd get up as fit as a flea ten minutes after I'd phoned for him, was I?'

'Tell me about the day your mother died, Mrs Betts, Friday, June 2nd,' he said, and it occurred to him that no one had yet told him anything much about that day.

'Well . . .' Her mouth trembled and she said quickly, 'You don't think Harry did anything to Mother, do you? He wouldn't, I swear he wouldn't.'

'Tell me about that Friday.'

She made an effort to control herself, clenching her hands on the metal bar. 'We wanted to go to a whist drive. Elsie came round in the morning and I said, if we went out would she sit with Mother, and she said, OK, of course she would if I'd just give her a knock before we left.' Mrs Betts sighed and her voice steadied. 'Elsie lives two doors down. She and Mother'd been pals for years and she always came to sit with her when we went out. Though it's a lie,' her old eyes flashing like young ones, 'to say we were always out. Once in a blue moon we went out.'

Wexford's eyes went from the pudding-faced girl in the photograph, her mouth smug and proud even then, to the long strip of turfed-over garden – why did he feel Betts had done that turfing, had uprooted flowers? – and back to the nervous little woman on the mattress edge.

'I gave Mother her lunch and she was sitting in the front room, doing a bit of knitting. I popped down to Elsie's and rang her bell but she can't have heard it, she didn't come. I rang and rang and I thought, well, she's gone out, she's forgotten and that's that. But Harry said, Why not go out just the same? The painter was there, he was only a bit of a boy, twenty, twenty-two, but he and Mother got on a treat, a sight better than her and I ever did, I can tell you. So the upshot was, we went off and left her there with the painter – what was he called? Ray? Rafe? No, Roy, that was it, Roy – with Roy doing the hall walls. She was OK, fit as a flea. It was a nice day so I left all the windows open because that paint did smell. I'll never forget the way she spoke to me before I left. That was the last thing she ever said to me. Doreen, she said, you ought to be lucky at cards. You haven't been very lucky in love. And she laughed and I'll swear Roy was laughing too.'

You're building an edifice of motives for yourself, Mrs Betts, reflected Wexford. 'Go on,' was all he said.

She moved directly into hearsay evidence, but Wexford didn't stop her. 'That Roy closed the door to keep the smell out, but he popped in a few times to see if Mother was all right. They had a bit of a chat, he said, and he offered to make her a cup of tea but she didn't want any. Then about half-past three Mother said she'd got a headache – that was the onset of the stroke but she didn't know that, she put it down to the paint – and would he fetch her a couple of her paracetamols from the bathroom. So he did and he got her a glass of water and she said she'd try and have a sleep in her chair. Anyway, the next thing he knew she was out in the hall walking with her walking frame, going to have a lay-down on her bed, she said.

'Well, Harry and me came in at five-thirty and Roy was just packing up. He said Mother was asleep on her bed, and I just put my head round the door to check. She'd drawn the curtains.' Mrs Betts paused, burst out, 'To tell you the honest truth, I didn't look too closely. I thought, well, thank God for half an hour's peace to have a cup of tea in before she starts picking on Harry. It was just about a quarter to seven, ten to seven, before I went in again. I could tell there was something going on, the way she was breathing, sort of puffing out her cheeks, and red in the face. There was blood on her lips.' She looked fearfully at Wexford, looked him in the eye for the first time. 'I wiped that clean before I called the doctor, I didn't want him seeing that.

'He came straightaway. I thought maybe he'd call an ambulance but he didn't. He said she'd had a stroke and when people had strokes they shouldn't be moved. We stayed with her – well, Doctor and I stayed with her – but she passed away just before half-past.'

Wexford nodded. Something about what she had said was wrong. He felt it. It wasn't that she had told a lie, though she might well have done, but something else, something that rang incongruously in that otherwise commonplace narrative, some esoteric term in place of a household word . . . He was checking back, almost there, when a footstep sounded in the hall, the door opened and a face appeared round it.

'There you are, Doreen!' said the face which was very pretty considering its age. 'I was just on my way to – Oh, I beg your pardon, I'm intruding.'

'That's all right,' said Mrs Betts. 'You can come in, Elsie.' She looked blankly at Wexford, her eyes once more old and tired. 'This is Mrs Parrish.'

Elsie Parrish, Wexford decided, looked exactly as an old lady should. She had a powdery, violet cashew, creamy smell, which might equally well have been associated with a very clean baby. Her legs were neat and shapely in grey stockings, her hands in white gloves with tiny darns at the fingertips, her coat silky navy-blue over blue flowery pleats, and her face withered rose leaves with rouge on. The bouffant mass of silvery hair was so profuse that from a distance it might have been taken for a white silk turban. She and Wexford walked down the street together towards the shops, Elsie Parrish swinging a pink nylon string bag.

'It's wicked the way they gossip. You can't understand how people can be so evil-minded. You'll notice how none of them are able to say how Doreen gave Ivy a stroke when she wasn't even there.' Mrs Parrish gave a dry satirical laugh. 'Perhaps they think she bribed that poor young man, the painter, to give Ivy a fright. I remember my mother saying that fright could give you a stroke – an apoplexy, she called it – or too much excitement or drinking too much or over-eating even.'

To his surprise, because this isn't what old ladies of elegant appearance usually do or perhaps should do, she opened her handbag, took out a packet of cigarettes and put one between her lips. He shook his head when the packet was offered to him, watched her light the cigarette with a match from a matchbook with a black shiny cover. She puffed delicately. He didn't think he had ever before seen someone smoke a cigarette while wearing white gloves. He said:

'Why didn't you go round and sit with Mrs Wrangton, that afternoon, Mrs Parrish?'

'The day she died, you mean?'

'Yes.' Wexford had the impression she didn't want to

answer, she didn't want to infer anything against Doreen Betts. She spoke with care.

'It's quite true I'm getting rather deaf.' He hadn't noticed it. She had heard everything he said, in the open noisy street, and he hadn't raised his voice. 'I don't always hear the bell. Doreen must have rung and I didn't hear. That's the only explanation.'

Was it?

'I thought she and Harry had changed their minds about going out.' Elsie Parrish put the cigarette to her lips between thumb and forefinger. 'I'd give a lot,' she said, 'to be able to go back in time. I wouldn't hesitate this time, I'd go round and check on Ivy whether Doreen had asked me or not.'

'Probably your presence would have made no difference,' he said, and then, 'Mrs Betts had told the builders not to do any work upstairs . . .'

She interrupted him. 'Maybe it didn't need it. I've never been upstairs in Ivy's house, so I couldn't say. Besides, when she'd sold it the new people might have had their own ideas, mightn't they? They might have wanted to do their own decorating.'

They were standing still now on the street corner, he about to go in one direction, she in the other. She dropped the cigarette end, stamped it out over-thoroughly with a high heel. From her handbag she took a small lacy handkerchief and dabbed her nostrils with it. The impression was that the tears, though near, would be restrained. 'She left me two thousand pounds. Dear Ivy, she was so kind and generous. I knew I was to have something, I didn't dream as much as that.' Elsie Parrish smiled, a watery, girlish, rueful smile, but still he was totally unprepared for what she said next. 'I'm going to buy a car.'

His eyebrows went up.

'I've kept my licence going. I haven't driven since my husband died and that's twenty-two years ago. I had to sell our car and I've always longed and longed for another.' She really looked as if she had, a yearning expression crumpling the roses still further. 'I'm going to have my own dear little car!' She was on the verge of executing a dance on the pavement. 'And dear Ivy made that possible!' Anxiously: 'You don't think I'm too old to drive?'

Wexford did, but he only said that this kind of judgement wasn't really within his province. She nodded, smiled again, whisked off suprisingly fast into the corner supermarket. Wexford moved more slowly and thoughtfully away, his eyes down. It was because he was looking down that he saw the matchbook, and then he remembered fancying he had seen her drop something when she got out that handkerchief.

She wasn't in the shop. She must have left by the other exit into the High Street and now she was nowhere to be seen. Deciding that matchbooks were in the category of objects which no one much minds losing, Wexford dropped it into his pocket and forgot it.

'You want Roy?'

'That's right,' said Wexford.

The foreman, storekeeper, proprietor, whatever he was, didn't ask why. 'You'll find him,' he said, 'doing the Snowcem on them flats up the Sewingbury Road.'

Wexford drove up there. Roy was a gigantic youth, broad-shouldered, heavily muscled, with an aureole of thick curly fair hair. He came down the ladder and said he'd just been about to knock off for his tea break, anyway. There was a carmen's café conveniently near. Roy lit a cigarette, put his elbows on the table.

'I never knew a thing about it till I turned up there the next day.'

'But surely when Mrs Betts came in the afternoon before she asked you how her mother had been?'

'Sure she did. And I said the truth, that the old lady'd got a headache and asked for something for it and I'd given it her, and then she'd felt tired and gone in for a lay-down. But there was no sign she was *dying*. My God, that'd never have crossed my mind.'

A headache, Wexford reflected, was often one of the premonitory signs of a cerebral haemorrhage. Roy seemed to read his thoughts, for he said quickly:

'She'd had a good many headaches while I was in the place working. Them non-drip plastic-based paints have got a bit of a smell to them, used to turn *me* up at first. I mean, you don't want to get thinking there was anything out of the way in her

57

having an aspirin and laying down, guv. That'd happened two or three times while I was there. And she'd shovel them aspirins down, swallow four as soon as look at you.'

Wexford said, 'Tell me about that afternoon. Did anyone come into the house between the time Mr and Mrs Betts went out and the time they got back?'

Roy shook his head. 'Definitely not, and I'd have known. I was working on the hall, see? The front door was wide open on account of the smell. Nobody could have come in there without my seeing, could they? The other old girl – Mrs Betts, that is – she locked the back door before she went out and I hadn't no call to unlock it. What else d'you want to know, guv?'

'Exactly what happened, what you and Mrs Wrangton talked about, the lot.'

Roy swigged his tea, lit a fresh cigarette from the stub of the last. 'I got on OK with her, you know. I reckon she reminded me of my gran. It's a funny thing, but everyone got on OK with her bar her own daughter and the old man. Funny old git, isn't he? Gave me the creeps. Well, to what you're asking, I don't know that we talked much. I was painting, you see, and the door to the front room was shut. I looked in a couple of times. She was sitting there knitting, watching cricket on the TV. I do remember she said I was making a nice job of the house and it was a pity she wouldn't be there to enjoy it. Well, I thought she meant she'd be dead, you know the way they talk, and I said, Now come on, Mrs Wrangton, you mustn't talk like that. That made her laugh. She said, I don't mean that, you naughty boy, I mean I'm going into a nursing home and I've got to sell the place, didn't you know? No, I said, I didn't, but I reckoned it'd fetch a packet, big old house like that, twenty thousand at least, I said, and she said she hoped so.'

Wexford nodded. So Mrs Wrangton had intended to go ahead with her plans, and Doreen Betts's denial had either been purposeful lying to demolish her motive or a post-mortem white-washing of her mother's character. For it had certainly been black-hearted enough, he thought, quite an act it had been, that of deliberately turning your own daughter and her husband out of their home. He looked back to Roy.

'You offered to make her tea?'

'Yeah, well, the daughter, Mrs Betts, said to make myself and her a cup of tea if she wanted, but she didn't want. She asked me to turn off the TV and then she said she'd got a headache and would I go to the bathroom cupboard and get her aspirins? Well, I'd seen Mrs Betts do it often enough, though I'd never actually . . .'

'You're sure she said aspirins?' Quite suddenly Wexford knew what it was that had seemed incongruous to him in Mrs Betts's description of her mother's last afternoon of life. Doreen Betts had specified paracetamol instead of the common household remedy. 'You're sure she used that word?' he said.

Roy pursed his mouth. 'Well, now you mention it, I'm not sure. I reckon what she said was, my tablets or the tablets for my head, something like that. You just do say aspirins, don't you, like naturally? I mean, that's what everybody takes. Anyway, I brought them down, the bottle and gave them to her with a glass of water, and she says she's going to have a bit of shut-eye in her chair. But the next thing I knew she was coming out, leaning on that walking frame the welfare people give her. I took four, Roy, she says, but my head's that bad, I reckon it's worse, and I'm ever so giddy. Well, I didn't think much of that, they're all giddy at that age, aren't they? I remember my gran. She says she's got ringing in her ears, so I said, I'll help you into your room, shall I? And I sort of give her my arm and helped her in and she lay down on the bed with all her things on and shut her eyes. The light was glaring so I pulled the curtains over and then I went back to my painting. I never heard another thing till Mrs Betts and the old boy come in at half five . . .'

Wexford closed *Practical Forensic Medicine* by Francis E. Camps and J. M. Cameron and made his way back to Castle Road. He had decided to discuss the matter no further with Mrs Betts. The presence of her husband, shuffling about almost silently in his furry slippers, his feet like the paws of an old hibernating animal, rather unnerved him. She made no demur at his proposal to remove from the bathroom cabinet the prescription bottle of pain-killing tablets, labelled: Mrs I. Wrangton, Paracetamol.

Evening surgery had only just begun. Wexford went home

for his dinner, having sent two items away for fingerprint analysis. By eight-thirty he was back in the surgery building and again Dr Crocker had finished first. He groaned when he saw Wexford.

'What is it now, Reg?'

'Why did you prescribe paracetamol for Mrs Wrangton?'

'Because I thought it suitable for her, of course. She was allergic to aspirin.'

Wexford looked despairingly at his friend. 'Now he tells me. I'd rather gathered it. I mean, today I caught on, but you might have told me.'

'For God's sake! You *knew*. You said to me, Nurse Radcliffe told me all about it. Those were your words. You said . . .'

'I thought it was asthma.'

Crocker sat on the edge of his desk. 'Look, Reg, we've both been barking up the wrong trees. There was asthma in Mrs Wrangton's family. Mrs Betts has nettle rash, her brother was a chronic asthmatic. People with asthma or a family history of asthma are sometimes allergic to acetylsalicylic acid or aspirin. In fact, about ten per cent of such people are thought to have the allergy. One of the reactions of the hypersensitive person to aspirin is an asthmatic attack. That's what Mrs Wrangton had when she was in her forties, that and haematemesis. Which means,' he added kindly for the layman, 'bringing up blood from an internal haemorrhage.'

'OK, I'm not bone ignorant,' Wexford snapped, 'and I've been reading up hypersensitivity to acetylsalicylic acid . . .'

'Mrs Wrangton couldn't have had aspirin poisoning,' said the doctor quickly. 'There were never any aspirins in the house. Mrs Betts was strict about that.'

They were interrupted by the arrival of smiling Dr Moss. Wexford wheeled round on him.

'What would you expect to be the result of – let me see – one point two grammes of acetylsalicylic acid on a woman of ninety-two who was hypersensitive to the drug?'

Moss looked at him warily. 'I take it this is academic?' Wexford didn't answer. 'Well, it'd depend on the degree of hypersensitivity. Nausea, maybe, diarrhoea, dizziness, tinnitus – that's ringing in the ears – breathing difficulties, gastric haemorrhages, oedema of gastric mucosa, possible rupture of the oesophagus. In a person of that age, consequent upon such a shock and localised haemorrhages, I suppose a brain haemorrhage . . .' He stopped, realising what he had said.

'Thanks very much,' said Wexford. 'I think you've more or less described what happened to Mrs Wrangton on June 2nd after she'd taken four three hundred milligram tablets of aspirin.'

Dr Moss was looking stunned. He looked as if he would never smile again. Wexford passed an envelope to Crocker.

'Those are aspirins?'

Crocker looked at them, touched one to his tongue. 'I suppose so, but . . .'

'I've sent the rest away to be analysed. To be certain. There were fifty-six in the bottle.'

'Reg, it's unthinkable there could have been a mistake on the part of the pharmacist, but just supposing by a one in a million chance there was, she couldn't have taken forty-four tablets of aspirin. Not even over the months she couldn't.'

'You're being a bit slow,' said Wexford. 'You prescribed one hundred paracetamol, and one hundred paracetamol were put into that bottle at Fraser's, the chemist's. Between the time the prescription was made up and the day before, or a few days before, or a week before, she died, she took forty tablets of paracetamol, leaving sixty in the bottle. But on June 2nd she took four tablets of aspirin. Or, to put it bluntly, some time before June 2nd someone removed those sixty tablets of paracetamol and substituted sixty tablets of aspirin.'

Dr Moss found his voice. 'That would be murder.'

'Well . . .' Wexford spoke hesitantly. 'The hypersensitivity might not have resulted in a stroke. The intent may only have been to cause illness of a more or less severe kind. Ulceration of the stomach, say. That would have meant hospitalisation for Mrs Wrangton. On the Welfare State. No exorbitant nursing home fees to be paid there, no swallowing up of capital or selling of property. Later on, if she survived, she would probably have been transferred, again for free, to a geriatric ward in the same hospital. It's well-known that no private nursing home will take the chronically sick.'

'You think Mrs Betts . . . ?' Dr Moss began.

'No, I don't. For two good reasons, Mrs Betts is the one person who wouldn't have done it this way. If she had wanted to kill her mother or to make her seriously ill, why go to all the trouble of changing over sixty tablets in a bottle, when she had only to give Mrs Wrangton the aspirins in her hand? And if she had changed them, wouldn't she, immediately her mother was dead, have changed them back again?'

'Then who was it?'

'I shall know tomorrow,' said Wexford.

Crocker came to him at his office in the police station.

'Sorry I'm late. I just lost a patient.'

Wexford made sympathetic noises. Having walked round the room, eyed the two available chairs, the doctor settled for the edge of Wexford's desk.

'Yesterday,' Wexford began, 'I had a talk with Mrs Elsie Parrish.' He checked the doctor's exclamation and sudden start forward. 'Wait a minute, Len. She dropped a matchbook before we parted. It was one of those with a glossy surface that very easily take prints. I had the prints on it and those on the paracetamol bottle compared. There were Mrs Betts's prints on the bottle, and a set that were presumably Mrs Wrangton's, and a man's that were presumably the painter's. And there was also a very clear set identical to those on the matchbook.

'It was Elsie Parrish who changed those tablets, Len. She did it because she knew that Mrs Wrangton fully intended to retire to Summerland and that the first money to go, perhaps before the house was sold, would be the few thousands of capital she and Doreen Betts were to share. Elsie Parrish had waited for years for that money, she wanted to buy a car. A few more years and if she herself survived it would be too late for driving cars. Besides, by then her legacy would have been swallowed up in nursing home fees.'

'A nice old creature like that?' Crocker said. 'That's no proof, her prints on the bottle. She'll have fetched that bottle often enough for old Ivy.'

'No. She told me she had never been upstairs in Ivy Wrangton's house.'

'Oh, God.'

'I don't suppose she saw it as murder. It wouldn't seem like murder, or manslaughter, or grievous bodily harm, changing tablets over in a bottle.' Wexford sat down, wrinkled up his face. He said crossly, dispiritedly, 'I don't know what to do, Len. We've no way of proving Mrs Wrangton died of aspirin poisoning. We can't exhume her, we can't analyse "two handfuls of white dust shut in an urn of brass". And even if we could, would we be so inhumane as to have a woman of – how old is Elsie Parrish?'

'Seventy-eight.'

'Seventy-eight up in court on a murder charge. On the other hand, should she be allowed to profit from her crime? Should she be permitted to terrorise pedestrians in a smart little Ford Fiesta?'

'She won't,' said Crocker.

Something in his voice brought Wexford to his feet. 'Why? What d'you mean?'

The doctor slid lightly off the edge of the desk. 'I told you I'd lost a patient. Elsie Parrish died last night. A neighbour found her and called me.'

'Maybe that's for the best. What did she die of?'

'A stroke,' said Crocker, and went.

Ginger and the Kingsmarkham Chalk Circle

'There's a girl downstairs, sir,' said Polly Davies, 'and she says someone's taken her baby out of its pram.'

Chief Inspector Wexford had been contemplating a sheet of foolscap. On it, written by himself in the cause of crime prevention, was a politely worded request to the local authority, asking them to refrain from erecting scaffolding around their rented property a full nine months before building work was due to commence. Because of the scaffolding there had already been two burglaries and an assault on a young woman. He looked up from the paper, adjusted his thoughts and sighed.

'They will do it,' he said. 'Leave their babies about I mean. You'd never find them leaving their handbags outside shops.'

'It was outside her flat, sir, not a shop, and the thing is, whoever took the baby left another one in its place.'

Slowly Wexford got up. He came round the desk and looked narrowly at Polly.

'Constable Davies, you have to be pulling my leg.'

'No, sir, you know I wouldn't. She's a Mrs Bond and she says that when she went downstairs to fetch in her pram, her baby had gone and another one been put there.'

Wexford followed Polly down to the ground floor. In one of the interview rooms a girl was sitting at the bleak, rectangular, plastic-topped table, drinking tea and crying. She looked about nineteen. She had long straw-coloured hair and a small childish face, naive and innocent and frightened, and she was wearing blue denims and a tee-shirt with apples and oranges and cherries printed all over the front. From her appearance one would not have supposed her to be a mother. But also in the room was a baby. The baby, in short white frock and woolly coat and napkin and cotton socks, slept in the uneasy arms of Detective Constable Loring.

It had occurred to Wexford on the way down that women who have recently had babies are, or are said to be, prone to various kinds of mental disturbance, and his first thought was that Mrs Bond might only think or only be saying that this child was not hers.

'Now, Mrs Bond,' he began, 'this is a strange business. Do you feel like telling me about it?'

'I've told it all,' she said.

'Well, yes, but not to me. Why not start by telling me where you live and where your baby was?'

She gulped. She pushed the teacup away. 'Greenhill Court. We're on the fifth floor. We haven't got a balcony or anything. I have to go all the way down in the lift to put Karen out in her pram. She's got to have fresh air. And when she's there I can't watch her all the time. I can't even see her from my lounge on account of it looks out over the car park.'

'So you put her out in the pram this afternoon,' said Wexford. 'What time would that have been?'

'It was just on two. I put the pram on the grass with the cat net on it, and when I went to fetch it in at half-past four the cat net was still on it and the baby was asleep but it – it wasn't Karen!' She made little whimpering noises that exploded in a sob. 'It wasn't Karen, it was that baby he's holding!'

The baby woke up and also began to cry. Loring wrinkled up his nose and shifted his left hand from under its buttocks. His eyes appealed to Polly who nodded and left the room.

'So what did you do?' said Wexford.

'I didn't even go back upstairs. I got hold of the pram and I pushed it and I started to run and I ran all the way down here to you.'

65

He was touched by her childish faith. In real or imaginary trouble, at time of fear, she ran to those whom her sheltered small-town upbringing had taught her to trust, the kindly helmeted man in blue, the strong arm of the law. Not for her the grosser cynical image her city-bred contemporaries held of brutal and bribable policemen.

'Mrs Bond,' he said, and then, 'What's your first name?'

'Philippa. I'm called Pippa.'

'Then I'll call you that if you don't mind. Describe your baby to me, will you, Pippa? Is she dark or fair? How old is she?'

'She's two months old – well, nine weeks. She's got blue eyes, she's wearing a white frock.' The voice broke and trembled again. 'And she's got the most beautiful red-gold hair you've ever seen!'

Inevitably, Wexford's eyes went to the child in Loring's arms whom this description seemed perfectly to fit. He said gently to Pippa Bond, 'Now you're quite sure you aren't imagining all this? No one will be angry if you are, we shall understand. Perhaps you worried or felt a bit guilty about leaving Karen out of your sight for so long, and then when you came down you got a feeling she looked rather different from usual and . . .'

A wail of indignation and misery cut across the rest of what he had to say. The girl began to cry with long tearing sobs. Polly Davies came back, carrying a small square hand towel from the women's lavatory. She took the baby from Loring, laid it on its back on the table and undid the big safety pin above its naval. Pippa Bond flinched away from the baby as if it were carrying a disease.

'I'm not imagining it,' she shouted at Wexford. 'I'm not! D'you think I wouldn't know my own baby? D'you think I wouldn't know my Karen from *that*?'

Polly had folded the towel cornerwise. She moved a little so that Wexford could see the baby's waving legs and bare crotch. 'Whoever this baby is, sir, it isn't Karen. Look for yourself – it's a boy.'

Trevor Bond was fetched from the Stowerton estate agent's where he worked. He looked very little older than his wife.

Pippa clung to him, crying and inarticulate, and over her bent head he cast despairing eyes at the policemen.

He had arrived in a car driven by a young woman he said was his sister-in-law, Pippa's sister, who also lived at Greenhill Court with her husband. She sat stiffly at the wheel, giving Pippa no more than a nod and what seemed like a shrug of exasperation when she came out of the police station with Trevor's arm round her. Susan Rains, her name was, and a quarter of an hour later it was she who was showing Loring and Sergeant Martin just where the pram had stood on the lawn between the block of flats and the main road from Kingsmarkham to Stowerton. While this thin red-haired girl castigated her sister's negligence and put forward her own theories as to where Karen might be, Dr Moss arrived with sedation for Pippa, though she had become calmer once she understood no one would expect her to have charge of the changeling boy.

His fate was removal to a Kingsmarkham Borough nursery for infants in the care of the local authority.

'Poor lamb,' said the chidren's officer Wexford spoke to. 'I expect Kay will be able to take him in Bystall Lane. There's no one to fetch him, though, they've got ten to bath and get to bed down there.'

Young Ginger, Wexford had begun to call him. He was a fine-looking baby with large eyes, strong pudgy features, and hair of a curious pale red, the colour of a new raw carrot. To Wexford's not inexperienced eye, he looked older than the missing Karen, nearer four months than two. His eyes were able to focus firmly, and now they focussed on the chief inspector, a scrutiny which moved the baby to yell miserably. Young Ginger buried his face in Polly's boyish bosom, crying and searching for sustenance.

'You don't know what they're thinking, do you, sir?' Polly said. 'Just because we can't remember anything about when we were his age we sort of think babies don't feel much or notice things. But suppose what they feel is so awful they sort of block it off just so as they won't be able to remember? Suppose it's dreadful pain being separated from your mother and not being able to say and – Oh, I don't know, but does anyone think of these things, sir?'

'Well, psychiatrists do,' said Wexford, 'and philosophers, I expect, but not many ordinary people like us. You'll have to remember it when you have babies of your own. Now take him down to Bystall Lane, will you?'

A few minutes after she had gone Inspector Burden came in. He had heard the story downstairs but had not entirely believed it. It was the part about putting another baby in Karen's place that he couldn't believe, he told Wexford. He hadn't either, said Wexford, but it was true.

'You can't think of a reason why anyone would do such a thing,' said Burden. 'You can't think of a single reason why even a mentally disturbed person would do such a thing.'

'I suppose,' said Wexford, 'that by "you" you mean yourself or "one" because I can think of several reasons for doing it. First of all, you've got to take some degree of mental disturbance for granted here. Well-adjusted normal people don't steal other people's babies, let alone exchange them. It's going to be a woman. It's a woman who's done it because she wants to be rid of that particular child, yet she must have a child. Agreed?'

'Right,' said Burden. 'Why?'

'She has to show it to someone else,' Wexford said slowly, as if thinking aloud, 'someone who expects to see a baby nearer in age and appearance to Karen Bond than to young Ginger, or who expects a baby of Karen's sex. She may be a woman who has several sons and whose husband was away when the last one was born. She has told him he has a daughter, and to bear this out because she's afraid of him, she has to have a girl to produce for him. On the other hand, she may not be married. She may have told a boy friend or ex-boy friend the child is younger than it is in order to convince him of his paternity.'

'I'm glad you mentioned mental disturbance,' said Burden sarcastically.

'She may simply be exhausted by looking after a child who screams incessantly – young Ginger's got a good pair of lungs – so she exchanges him for a baby she believes won't scream. Or she may have been told that Ginger has some illness or even hereditary defect which frightened her so she wanted to be rid of him, but she still has to have a baby for her husband or mother or whoever to see.'

68

Burden seemed to be considering this inventiveness with reluctant admiration but not much conviction. He said, 'So what are we going to do about it?'

'I've taken everyone in the place off what they were doing and put them on to this. We're getting on to all the hospitals and GPs, the Registrar of births, and the post-natal and baby clinics. I think it has to be someone local, maybe even someone who knew the pram would be there because she'd seen it there before.'

'And seen the baby who was in it before?' asked Burden, quirking up an eyebrow.

'Not necessarily. A pram with a cat net over and whose occupant can't be seen implies a very young baby.' Wexford hesitated. 'This is a hell of a lot more worrying,' he said, 'than a run-of-the-mill baby-snatching.'

'Because Karen Bond's so young?' Burden hazarded.

'No, not that. Look, Mike, your typical baby-snatcher loves babies, she yearns for one of her own, and that's why she takes someone else's. But this one's *got* a baby of her own and one she dislikes enough to hand him over to a stranger. You can pretty well take it for granted the ordinary baby-snatcher will care for a child almost extravagantly well, but will this one? If she doesn't care for her own child, will she care for a substitute? I say it's worrying because we can be certain this woman's taken Karen for a purpose, a use, and what happens when that use is over?'

The block of flats in which the Bonds lived was not one of those concerning whose vulnerability to break-ins Wexford had been drafting his letter, but a privately owned five-storeyed building standing on what not long ago had been open green meadows. There were three such blocks, Greenhill, Fairlawn and Hillside Courts, interspersed with rows of weatherboarded town houses, and each block was separated from the main road to Stowerton only by a strip of lawn thirty feet deep. On this turf, a little way in from the narrow service road, Karen Bond's pram had stood.

Wexford and Burden talked to the porter who had charge of the three blocks. He had been cleaning a car in the car park at the relevant time and had noticed nothing. Wexford, going up in the Greenhill lift, commented to Burden that it was unfortunate children were forbidden to play on the lawns. They would have served as protection for Karen or at least as witnesses. There were a good many children on this new estate which was mainly occupied by young couples. Between two and four-thirty that afternoon the little ones had been cooped up in small rooms or out for walks with their mothers, the older ones at school.

Mrs Louise Pelham had fetched her son and her next-door neighbour's two sons home from school, passing within a few feet of Karen's pram. That was at a quarter to four. She had glanced into the pram, as she always did, and now she said she remembered thinking Karen looked 'funny'. The baby in the pram had seemed to have a bigger face and redder hair than the one she had looked at when she passed on her way to the children's school half an hour before. Wexford felt that there was a real lead here, a pinpointing of the time of the substitution, until he learned that Susan Rains had been with Mrs Pelham before him and told her the whole story in detail.

Susan Rains and her sister Pippa had each been married at the age of eighteen, but Pippa at twenty already had a baby while Susan, seven years older, was childless. She was without a job too, it appeared, and at three years short of thirty was leading the life of a middle-aged houseproud gossip. She seemed very anxious to tell Wexford and Burden that, in her opinion, her sister was far too young to have a child, her brother-in-law too young to be a father, and that they were both too irresponsible to look after a baby. Pippa, she said, was always bringing Karen round for her to mind, and now Wexford, who had been wondering about the two folded napkins, the plastic spoon and bottle of concentrated orange juice on Mrs Rains's spotless kitchen counter, understood why they were there.

'Are you fond of babies, Mrs Rains?' Wexford asked, and got an almost frightening response.

Hard lines bit into Mrs Rains's face and her redhead's pale eyes flashed. 'I'd be an unnatural woman if I wasn't, wouldn't I?' What else she might have said – a defence? An explanation? – was cut off by the arrival of a woman in her late forties whom she introduced in a mutter as her mother. It was left to

Wexford to find out that this was Mrs Leighton who had left Pippa in a drugged sleep and Trevor trying to answer Sergeant Martin's second spate of questions.

Mrs Leighton was sprightly and not too concerned. 'Well, babies that get taken out of prams, they always turn up safe and sound, don't they?' Her hair was dyed to a more glorious red than her daughter's natural shade. She was on her way to babysit for her son and daughter-in-law who had a six-month-old son, and she had just looked in on Pippa to collect the one pound twenty she owed her for dry-cleaning. Imagine what she'd felt, the whole place full of policemen and Karen gone. She really thought Trevor or Susan might have phoned her, and now she was in two minds whether to go and babysit for Mark or not. 'But she's bound to turn up OK, isn't she?' she said to Wexford.

Wexford said they must hope so, and then he and Burden left the two women to argue between themselves as to which was the more important, keeping a promise to the son or commiserating with the daughter.

The world, or this small corner of it, suddenly seemed full of babies. From behind two doors on the ground floor came the whimpers and low peevish grizzlings of infants put unwillingly in their cots for the night. As they left by the glass double doors, they passed on the step an athletic-looking girl in sweater and denims with a very small baby clamped to her chest in a canvas baby carrier. The car park was filling as men returned home from work, some of them commuters from London, and among them, walking from a jaunty red sports car, a couple swinging between them a baby in a shallow rush basket. Wexford wondered just how many children under the age of two lived in those flats and small neat houses. Nearly as many as there were adults, he thought, and he stood aside to let pass a girl pushing twins in a wide push-chair.

There was very little more that he could do that night beyond embroiling himself in another discussion with Burden as to the reason why. Burden put forward several strange suggestions. Having previously declared that he couldn't think of a single motive, he now posited that the baby-snatcher was due to have her own baby immunised against whooping cough on the following day. She had read in the newspaper that this could cause brain damage but was too diffident to refuse the immunisation, so planned to substitute someone else's baby for her own.

'The trouble with you unimaginative people,' said Wexford, 'is that when you do fantasise you really go crazy. She wants to protect her child from what's something like a one in a million chance of brain damage, but she doesn't mind entrusting him to the care of strangers who might do him far more harm.'

'But the point is she knew they wouldn't do him harm. She'd know that what's happened is exactly what must happen, that he'd be brought to us and then put in the care of the local authority.' Burden waited for some show of enthusiasm and when he didn't get it he went home. For three hours. At eleven that night he was destined to be called out again.

But not on account of Karen Bond.

In normal circumstances Sergeant Willoughby, going off duty, wouldn't have given a second glance at the Ford Transit parked under some overhanging bushes at the foot of Ploughman's Lane. But the sergeant's head, like those of most members of the Mid-Sussex Constabulary, was full of thoughts of missing children. He saw the van as a possible caravan substitute, and his mind went vaguely back to old tales of infants stolen by gypsies. He parked his scooter and went over to investigate.

The young man sitting in the driving seat switched on the ignition, put the van into gear and moved off as fast as he could on a roar of the engine. There was no real danger of his hitting Sergeant Willoughby, nor did that seem to have been his intention, but he passed within a yard or so of him and swung down the lane towards the town.

The nearest phone was in the sergeant's own home in Queen Street, and he went quickly to it.

But the Ford Transit turned out to have had nothing to do with Karen Bond. It was the getaway car for two men who were taking advantage of the absence of a Kingsmarkham stockbroker and his wife to remove a safe from their home.

Ploughman's Lane was Kingsmarkham's millionaire's row, and Stephen Pollard's house, pretentiously named Baron's Keep, by no means the smallest or most modest house in it. It was a nineteen-thirties palace of red brick and leaded lattices

72

and neo-Tudor twisty chimneys. All the windows on the ground floor had stout bars to them, but there were no bars on the french window which led from the largest of the rear bedrooms on to a spacious balcony. When Burden and Loring got there they found signs that two men had climbed up to this balcony, ignored the thief-proof locks on the french window, and cut the glass neatly out of its frame with a glass cutter.

Where the safe had been in the study on the ground floor was now a gaping cavity. This room was said to be a precise replica of some writing room or den or hidey-hole of Mary Queen of Scots in Holyrood Palace, and the safe had been concealed behind a sliding door in the linenfold panelling. The thieves had chipped it out of its niche with a cold chisel and removed it bodily. Burden thought it must have been immensely heavy, which explained the need for having the van nearby.

Although the weather was dry, a long wet spell had only just ended. Deeply indented footprints, one set of a size eight shoe, the other of a size twelve, had ground into the flowerbed under the balcony. These same prints crossed the rear lawn to where there was a gate in the tall wattle fence, and alongside them went parallel grooves about two inches apart.

'I reckon,' said Burden, 'they had a set of those wheels people have for pushing heavy luggage along. That's what they used. The sheer cheek of it!'

Loring shone his torch. 'They rested it down here, sir, in front of the gate. Must have been a bit of a blow when they found their motor gone and they had to keep on wheeling.'

In vain they searched the lane, the ditches and the copse which bordered the lane on one side. They didn't find the safe and no fingerprints were found on the window ledges or in the study at Baron's Keep. The thieves had worn gloves.

'And Big Feet,' said Burden in the morning, 'should have worn snow shoes. There aren't going to be many villains about with great plates of meat like that.'

'I'd think of Lofty Peters first thing,' said Wexford, 'only he's inside.'

'Well, he's not actually. He came out last week. But we were round at his place, knocking him up at midnight and waking all the neighbours, and there was no doubt where he'd been all evening. He was blind drunk, smashed out of his mind. I reckon this lot came down from London. Old Pollard's been shooting his mouth off around the City about his missus's diamonds and this is the outcome.'

'The van was nicked,' said Wexford. 'I've just had a call from the super at Myringham. They found it ditched on the edge of a wood with the licence plates missing.'

'What a lively time we are having,' said Burden, and he looked out of the window at the geraniums on the forecourt and the shops opening, striped awnings gradually being unfurled, shoppers' cars moving in, the July sun spreading a great sheet of light and warmth across the Pomfret Road – and a little figure walking through it in unseasonable black. 'My God,' he said, 'I don't believe it, not another one!'

Wexford got up and came over to the window. The small stout man in the black cassock was now on the forecourt, walking between the geranium tubs. In his arms was a bundle that was undoubtedly a baby. He was carrying the baby very confidently and securely as might be expected in one who so often performed the sacrament of baptism. Wexford watched him in silence, craning out to follow the priest's progress under the overhanging canopy and through the swing doors into the police station.

He said in a distant speculative voice, 'You don't suppose, do you, Mike, that this is the latest craze? I mean, we've had wife-swapping, are we going to have baby-swapping? Maybe it's something that bored young housewives are going to take up instead of going to evening classes or playing with their deep freezes.'

'Or maybe there's a maniac on the rampage who gets his kicks from changing them all round and confusing their mums.'

'Musical babes,' said Wexford. 'Come on, let's go down and see.' They descended to the foyer in the lift. 'Good morning, Father. And who might this be?'

The priest in charge of the Catholic church of Our Lady of Loretto was leaning against the long parabola-shaped counter behind which the station sergeant, Sergeant Camb, presided. The sleeping baby in his arms was swathed, indeed tightly cocooned, in a clean pale blue cellular blanket. Only its face,

74

fragile yet healthy-looking, and one hand were exposed. Thick dark lashes rested on the rose-leaf skin, but otherwise the child was fair, eyebrow-less and with fine downy hair as bright as a new copper coin. Holding it with tender firmness, Father Glanville looked round from his conversation with the sergeant to give Wexford a mystified grin, while Polly Davies stroked the baby's tiny fingers with her own forefinger.

'Your guess is as good as mine, Mr Wexford. I went over to the church just before nine and when I came back this little one was on the front steps of the presbytery. My lady help, Mrs Bream, had come in by the back door and hadn't even noticed him.'

'You found him just like that?' said Wexford. 'Just wrapped in that blanket and lying on the doorstep.'

'No indeed. He was wrapped in this blanket inside a cardboard box. The cardboard box,' said Father Glanville, smiling, 'is of the kind one sees in grocery supermarkets. This particular one has printed on it: Smith's Ready Salted Crisps, Ten Family Packs.' He added rather anxiously, 'I'm afraid I haven't brought it with me.'

Wexford couldn't help laughing. 'Well, don't throw it away. It's very likely a vital piece of evidence.' He came closer to the child who slept on regardless of the talk and the four large alien presences. 'You brought it straight here?'

'I brought *him* straight here,' said Father Glanville with the faintest note of reproof in his voice. Wexford reflected that he ought to have known the priest would never refer to any human soul, however youthful, however unknown and un-identified, as 'it', and then he said:

'I suppose he is a he? Blue blankets don't necessarily denote maleness, do they?'

The three men, for some obscure reason known to none of them, turned their eyes simultaneously on Polly Davies. And she, somehow recognising that to ascertain gender was her peculiar function, gently took the baby out of Father Glanville's arms, turned away and began unwrapping the blue blanket. The baby woke up and at once began a strenuous crying. Polly re-wrapped the blanket, set the child against her shoulder, her hand pressed against the four-inch wide back.

'This is a little girl, sir.' She put the baby's cheek against her own. 'Sir, don't you think it's Karen Bond? I'm sure it is, it must be.' Her voice had a catch in it. To her own evident horror, there were tears coming into her eyes. 'To think someone just dumped her, someone else's child, on a doorstep, in a cardboard box!'

'Well, the someone couldn't have left her in a better place, could she?' said Wexford with a grin at the priest. 'Come now, Constable Davies, this is no way for a liberated woman to go on. Let us pull ourselves together and go and phone Mrs Bond.'

Trevor and Pippa Bond arrived together, having again been brought to the police station in Susan Rains's car. The young husband was plainly terrified that the child would turn out not to be theirs, that their journey would prove to have been a cruel and vain awakening of hope, and for this reason he had tried to persuade his wife not to come. But she had come. Nothing could have kept her away, though she was fuddled and dazed still from Dr Moss's sedatives.

But once she saw the baby the muzziness left her and the glazed look went out of her eyes. She seized her in her arms, crushing her until Karen cried out and struggled with all her nine-week-old energy. Inscrutably, Susan Rains watched the little drama, watched her sister throw the blue blanket on to the floor, shuddering as she did so, watched the tears run down her cheeks on to the baby's head. Pippa began frenetically examining the white frock, the matinée jacket, the minute socks, as if hunting for visible germs.

'Why don't you burn the lot?' said Susan very coolly. 'Then you won't have to worry.'

Trevor Bond said quickly and awkwardly, 'Well, thanks very much, thanks a lot. I'll just see these girls of mine home and then I'll get off to the office. We've got a lot on our plates, always have this time of the year.'

'I'll take them back, Trev,' said Susan. 'You get off to work. And I'll phone Mother.'

'I'd let Dr Moss have a look at Karen if I were you,' said Wexford. 'She seems fine and I'm sure she is, but better be on the safe side.'

They went on their way. Susan Rains walked a little behind

76

the others, already marked for her role as the eternal aunt. Wexford's thoughts went to her nephew, her brother Mark's child, though he didn't know why he should think of him just then, and then to young Ginger, that grass orphan, down in Bystall Lane. He picked up the blanket – young Ginger's blanket? – and examined it, coming to the conclusion at the end of a few minutes' scrutiny of its texture and its label, that it was made of pure wool, had been manufactured in Wales, was old but clean and had been mended in one corner by someone who was no tyro when it came to handling a darning needle. From its honeycombing he picked a quantity of hairs. Most of these were baby hair, very fine red-gold filaments that might (or then again might not) all have come from the same child's scalp, but among them were a few coarser longer hairs that were clearly from a woman's head. A red-headed woman. He was thinking about the two red-headed women he had encountered during the time Karen was missing, when there came a knock at the door.

Wexford called, 'Come in,' and Sergeant Willoughby first put his head round the door, then advanced a little sheepishly into the office. Behind him came Burden.

'The young chap I saw driving that van last night, sir,' said Willoughby, 'I knew his face was familiar, I knew I'd seen him before. Anyway, I've remembered who he is. Tony Jasper, sir. I'm certain of it.'

'And am I supposed to know who Tony Jasper is?'

Burden said quickly, 'You know his brother. His brother's Paddy Jasper.'

'Paddy Jasper went up north.'

'That's what they said,' said Burden, 'and maybe he did, but his girl friend's back living round here. You know Leilie Somers, he's lived with her on and off for years, ever since she left Stowerton Secondary Modern when she was sixteen.'

'D'you know where she's living?'

'In one of those flats over the shops in Roland Road,' said Burden.

Roland Road was in Stowerton, running behind and parallel to the High Street. Wexford's driver took him and Burden along the High Street to reach it and, looking out of the window, Wexford saw Pippa Bond's mother walking along, shop-window-gazing and pushing a pram that was higher and grander than her daughter's and of a rich dark green colour. Its occupant was presumably her grandson. Mrs Leighton was also dressed in dark green and her dyed hair looked redder than ever.

The car turned left, then right into Roland Road. The row of shops, eight of them, was surmounted by a squat upper floor of aimlessly peaked roofs and, on its façade, a useless adornment of green-painted studs and beams. The block had been put up at approximately the same period as Baron's Keep, the time which Wexford called the Great Tudor Revival. He remarked to Burden that the whole face of urban and semi-rural Britain would have been changed immeasurably for the better if architects in the third and fourth decades of the century had revived the Georgian instead of the Elizabethan. Think of it, he said, long elegant sash windows instead of poky casements, columns instead of half-timbering and pediments instead of gables. Burden didn't answer him. He had given a push to the door between the newsagent's and the pet food shop, and it gave under his hand and swung inwards.

The passage was rather dark. At the foot of the stairs was a pram from which a young woman was lifting a baby. She turned round as the light fell on her and said:

'Oh, hallo, I was just coming back to shut that. Were you wanting something?'

Burden was inspired. He said, remembering Leilie Somers's character, guessing at her hopes and fears, 'We're looking for Mrs Jasper.'

The girl knew at once whom he meant. 'Leilie's door's the one on the right at the top of the stairs.' The baby on her hip, she parked the pram a little way down the passage, pulled and fastened the cover up over it.

'Do you know if her husband's at home?'

Her reply came guilelessly up to them as they mounted the steep stairs: 'Not unless he's come back. I heard him go out at just after eight this morning.'

At the top there was a door to the left and a door to the right. Burden knocked on the right one, and it was so rapidly opened that it was apparent Leilie Somers had been listening behind it. And she wanted them inside the flat just as fast. Her neighbour was steadily coming up the stairs and Leilie knew better than to let her hear the law introducing itself or see warrant cards flashed. She was a thin little person of twenty-eight or nine with a pinched face and hennaed hair. Throughout her whole youth she had been the mistress of a man who lived by robbery and occasionally by violent crime, and she had herself been in the dock. But she had never come to adopt, as other such women adopt, an attitude of insolence or truculence towards the police. She was always polite, she was always timid, and now as Wexford said, 'So you've moved back to your old stamping ground, Leilie,' she only nodded and smiled nervously and said yes, that was right, she'd moved back, managed to get this flat which was a piece of luck.

'And Paddy with you, I gather.'

'Sometimes,' she said. 'On and off. He's not what you'd call *living* here.'

'What would I call it then? Staying here for his holidays?' Leilie made no answer. The flat seemed to consist of a living room, a bedroom, a lavatory and a kitchen with covered bath in it. They went through to the living room. The furniture in it was ugly and cheap and old but it was very clean and the woodwork and walls were fresh white. The room had been re-decorated perhaps only the week before. There was still a lingering smell of paint. 'He was here last night,' said Wexford. 'He went out around eight this morning. When's he coming back?'

She would be rid of the man if she could be. Wexford had that impression now as he had received it from her once before, years before. Some bond she couldn't break bound her to Paddy Jasper, love or merely habit, but she would be relieved if external circumstances could sever it. Meanwhile, she would be unremittingly loyal.

'What did you want to see him for?'

Two can play at that game, thought Wexford, answering questions with another question. 'Where was he last evening?'

'He was here. He had a couple of pals in playing cards and for a beer.'

'I don't suppose,' said Burden, 'that one of these pals was by any chance his little brother Tony?'

Leilie looked at the rug on the floor, up at the ceiling, then out of the window so intently that it seemed there must be at least Concorde manifesting itself up in the sky if not a flying saucer.

'Come on, Leilie, you know Tony. That nice clean-living young Englishman who did two years for mugging an old lady up in the Smoke.'

She said very quietly, now staring down at her fingers, "Course I know Tony. I reckon he was here too, I don't know, I was out at my job.' Her voice went up a bit and her chin went up. 'I've got an evening job down the Andromeda. Cloakroom attendant, eight till midnight.'

A sign of the times, was what Wexford called the Andromeda. It was Kingsmarkham's casino, a gambling club in a spruced-up Victorian house out on the Sewingbury Road. He was going to ask why an evening job, what had happened to her full-time work – for at the time of his last encounter with Leilie she had been a stylist at Mr Nicholas, the hairdresser's – when his eye fixed itself on an object which stood on one end of the mantelpiece. It was a baby's feeding bottle with dregs of milk still in it.

'I didn't know you had a baby, Leilie,' he said.

'He's in the bedroom,' she said, and as if to confirm her words there sounded through the wall a reedy wail which quickly gained in volume. She listened. As the cries grew shrill she smiled and the smile became a laugh, a burst of laughter. Then she bit her lip and said in her usual monotone, 'Paddy and them were here babysitting for me. They were here all evening.'

'I see,' said Wexford. He knew then beyond a doubt that Paddy Jasper had not been there, that his friends had not been there, but that on the other hand they, or some of them including Jasper and his brother, had been up in Ploughman's Lane robbing Baron's Keep. 'I see,' he said again. The baby went on crying, working itself up into a passion of rage or misery. 'Is Paddy the child's father?'

She came the nearest to rudeness she ever had. 'You've no right to ask me that, Mr Wexford. What's it to you?'

No, maybe he had no right, he thought. That ninety-nine out of a hundred policemen would have asked it was no reason why he should. 'It's nothing to me,' he said. 'I'm sorry, Leilie. You'd better go and see to him, hadn't you?'

But at that moment the crying stopped. Leilie Somers sighed. In the flat next door footsteps sounded and a door slammed. Wexford said, 'We'll be back,' and followed Leilie out into the passage. She went into the bedroom and shut herself in.

Burden let them out and closed the front door. 'That's her second child, you know,' he said as they went down the stairs. 'She had a kid by Jasper years ago.'

'Yes, I remember.' Wexford recalled Father Glanville's implied admonition and said carefully, 'Where is he or she now?'

'She's a baby batterer, is Leilie Somers. Didn't you know? No, you wouldn't. The case came up when you were ill and had all that time off.' Wexford didn't much like hearing his month's convalescence after a thrombosis described as 'all that time off' but he said nothing. 'I was amazed,' said Burden severely, 'to hear you apologising to her as if she were a decent respectable sort of woman. She's a woman who's capable of giving a helpless baby a fractured skull and a broken arm. Those were her kid's injuries. And what did Leilie get? A suspended sentence, a recommendation for psychiatric treatment, all the nonsense.'

'What happened to the child?'

'He was adopted,' said Burden. 'He was quite a long time in hospital and then I heard that Leilie had agreed to have him adopted. Best thing for him.'

Wexford nodded. 'Strange, though,' he said. 'She always seems such a gentle meek creature. I can imagine her not knowing how to cope with a child or being a bit too easy-going or not noticing it was ill, say, but baby-battering – it seems so out of character.'

'You're always saying how inconsistent people are. You're always saying people are peculiar and you never can tell what they'll do next.'

'I suppose I am,' said Wexford.

He sent Loring to keep the Roland Road flat under observation, and then he and Burden went to lunch in the police station canteen. Polly Davies came up to Wexford while he was eating his dessert.

'I looked in at Bystall Lane, sir, and saw young Ginger. They

81

said, did we think of making other arrangements for him or were they to keep him for a bit?'

'My God, they haven't had him twenty-four hours yet.'

'That's what I said, sir. Well, I sort of said that. I think they're short-staffed.'

'So are we,' said Wexford. 'Now then, I don't suppose anyone saw Karen Bond being put on that doorstep?'

'I'm afraid not, sir. No one I've spoken to, anyway, and no one's come forward. Mrs Bream who housekeeps for the priest, she says the cardboard box – the Smith's Crisps box, you know – was there when she came at nine only she didn't look at it. She thought it was something someone had left for the father and she was going to take it in once she'd got the kitchen cleared up and his bed made. Father Glanville says he went out at ten to nine and he's positive the box wasn't there then, so someone must have put it there in those ten minutes. It looks like someone who knows their habits, the father's and Mrs Bream's, doesn't it, sir?'

'One of his flock, d'you mean?'

'It could be. Why not?'

'If you're right,' said Wexford dryly, 'whoever it was is probably confessing it at this moment and Father Glanville will, of course, have to keep her identity locked in his bosom.'

He went off up to his office to await word from Loring. There, sitting at his desk, thinking, he remembered noticing in Susan Rains's flat, honoured on a little shelf fixed there for the purpose, a plaster statuette of the Virgin with lilies in her arms. The Leightons were perhaps a Catholic family. He was on the point of deciding to go back to Greenhill Court for a further talk with Susan Rains when a phone call from Sergeant Camb announced the arrival of Stephen Pollard.

The stockbroker and his wife had been on holiday in Scotland and had driven all the way back, non-stop, all five hundred and forty miles, starting at six that morning. Wexford had met Pollard once before and remembered him as a choleric person. Now he was tired from the long drive but he still rampaged and shouted with as much misery as Pippa Bond had shown over the loss of her baby. The safe, it appeared, had contained a sapphire and platinum necklace and bracelet, four rings, three cameos and a diamond cross which Pollard said were worth thirty thousand pounds. No, of course no one knew he had a safe in which he kept valuables. Well, he supposed the cleaning woman did and the cleaning woman before her and all of the series of *au pair* girls, and maybe the builders who had painted the outside of the house, and the firm who had put up the bars.

'It's ludicrous,' said Burden when he had gone. 'All that carry-on when it's a dead cert his insurance company'll fork out. He might as well go straight back to Scotland. We're the people who've got the slog and we'll get stick if those villains aren't caught, while it won't make a scrap of difference to him one way or the other. And I'll tell you another thing that's ludicrous,' he said, warming to a resentful theme. 'The ratepayers of Sussex could have the expense of young Ginger's upbringing for eighteen years because his mother's too scared to come and claim him.'

'What shall I do about it? Hold a young wives' meeting and draw them a chalk circle?'

Burden looked bewildered.

'Haven't you ever heard of the Chinese chalk circle and Brecht's *Caucasian Chalk Circle*? You have to draw a circle in chalk on the ground and put the child in it, and of the mothers who claim him the one who can pull him out of the circle is his true mother and may have him.'

'That's all very well,' said Burden after a pause, 'but in this case, it's not mothers who want him, it's he who wants a mother. No one seems to want him.'

'Poor Ginger,' said Wexford, and then the phone rang. It was Loring on his radio to say Paddy Jasper had come into Roland Road and gone up the stairs to Leilie Somers's flat.

By the time Wexford and Burden got there Tony Jasper had arrived as well. The brothers were both tall, heavily built men but Tony's figure still had a youthfully athletic look about it while Paddy had the beginnings of a paunch. Tony's otherwise handsome appearance was ruined by a broken nose which had never been put right and through which he had difficulty in breathing. The repulsive and even sinister air he had was partly due to his always breathing through his mouth. Paddy and he were sitting facing each other at Leilie's living-room table.

They were both smoking, the air in the room was thick with smoke, and Tony was dealing a pack of cards. Wexford thought the cards were the inspiration of the moment, hastily fetched out when they heard the knock at the downstairs door.

'Put the cards away, Tone,' said Paddy. 'It's rude to play when we've got company.' He was always polite in a thoroughly offensive way. 'Leilie here,' he said, 'has got something in her head about you wanting to know where I was last evening. Like what sort of time did you have in mind?'

Wexford told him. Paddy smiled. Somehow he managed to make it a paternal smile. He was stopping a few days with Leilie, he said, and his son. He hadn't seen much of his son since the child was born on account of having this good job up north but not a chance of accommodation for a woman and a kid, no way. So he'd come down for his holidays the previous Saturday and what does he hear but that Leilie's got this evening job up the Andromeda. Well, she'd taken Monday night off to be with him and done an exchange with another girl for Tuesday, but when it got to last night she couldn't very well skive off again so he said not to worry, he'd babysit, him and Tony here, and they'd have some of their old mates round. Johnny Farrow and Pip Monkton, for a beer and a hand of solo.

'Which is what we did, Mr Wexford.'

'Right,' said Tony.

'Leilie put Matthew in his cot and then the boys came round and she got us a bite to eat. She's a good girl is Leilie. She went off to work about half seven, didn't you, love? Then we did the dishes and had our game. Oh, and the lady next door came round to check up if four grown men could look after baby OK, very kind of her, I'm sure. And then at half eleven Pip went off home on account of his missus being the boss round his place, and at quarter past twelve Leilie came back. She got a lift so she was early. That's right, isn't it, love?'

Leilie nodded. 'Except you never did no dishes.'

Wexford kept looking at the man's huge feet which were no longer under the table but splayed out across the cheap bright bit of carpet. He wondered where the shoes were that had made those prints. Burnt, probably. The remains of the safe, once they had blown it open, might be in any pond or river in the Home Counties. Johnny Farrow was a notorious peterman or expert with explosives. He turned to Leilie and asked a question perhaps none of them had expected.

'Who usually looks after the baby when you're working?'

'Julie next door. That girl you were talking to when you came earlier. I used to take him to my mum, my mum lives up Charteris Road, it's not very far, but he started getting funny in the evenings, crying and screaming, and he got worse if I took him out and left him in a strange place.' Wexford wondered if she was giving him such a detailed answer to his question because she sometimes left the baby unattended and thought she might be breaking the law. He remembered the other boy, the one with the fractured skull and broken arm, and he hardened towards her. 'Then Mum had to go into hospital, anyway, she only came out yesterday. So Julie said to leave him here and she'd pop in every half hour, and she'd hear him anyway if he cried. You can hear a pin drop through these walls. And Julie never goes out on account of she's got a baby of her own. She's been very good has Julie because I reckon Matthew does cry most evenings, and you can't just leave them to cry, can you?'

'I'm glad to inform you, my dear,' said Paddy with outrageous pomposity, 'that my son did not utter a squeak last evening but was as good as gold,' and on the last word he looked hard at Wexford and stretched his lips into a huge humourless smile.

Julie Lang confirmed that Paddy Jasper, Tony Jasper, Pip Monkton and Johnny Farrow had all been in the flat next door when she called to check on the safety and comfort of Matthew at eight-thirty. She had a key to Leilie's flat but she hadn't used it, knowing Mr Jasper to be there. She wouldn't have dreamt of doing that because it was Mr Jasper's home really, wasn't it? So she had knocked at the door and Mr Jasper had let her in and not been very nice about it actually, and she had felt very awkward especially when he'd said, go in and see for yourself if I'm not to be trusted to look after my own child. He had opened the bedroom door and made her look and she had just glanced at the cot and seen Matthew was all right and sleeping.

'Well, I felt so bad about it,' said Julie Lang, 'that I said to him, perhaps he'd like the key back, and he said, yes, he'd been going to ask me for it as they wouldn't be needing my services any longer, thanks very much. He was quite rude really but I did feel bad about it.'

She had given Paddy Jasper the key. As far as she knew, the four men had remained in the flat with Matthew till Leilie got back at twelve-fifteen. By then, anyway, her husband had come home and they were both in bed asleep. No, she had heard no footsteps on the stairs, not even those of Pip Monkton going home at eleven-thirty. Of course she had had the television on so maybe she wouldn't have heard, but she was positive there hadn't been a sound out of Matthew.

Wexford and Burden went next to the home of Pip Monkton. Johnny Farrow's confirmation of the alibi would amount to very little, for he had a long criminal record for safebreaking, but Monkton had never been convicted of anything, had never even been charged with anything. He was an ex-publican, apparently perfectly respectable, and the only blot on his white innocent life was his known friendship with Farrow with whom he had been at school and whom he had supported and stuck to during Farrow's long prison sentences and periods of poverty-stricken idleness. If Monkton said that the four of them had been together all that evening babysitting in Leilie Somers's flat, Wexford knew he might as well throw up the sponge. The judge, the jury, the court, would believe Pip Monkton just as they would believe Julie Lang.

And Monkton did say it. Looking Wexford straight in the eye (so that the chief inspector knew he must be lying) he declared boldly that he and the Jaspers and Johnny had been in Roland Road, playing solo and drinking beer, until he left for home at half-past eleven. Wexford had him down to the police station and went on asking him about it, but he couldn't break him down. Monkton sounded as if he had learnt by heart what he had to say, and he went on saying it over and over again like a talking bird or a record on which the needle has got stuck.

When it got to six Wexford had himself driven to the Andromeda where the manager, who had an interest in keeping on the right side of the police, answered his questions very promptly. He got back to the station to find Burden and

Polly discussing the one relevant piece of information Burden had succeeded in finding out about Monkton – that he had recently had an extension built on to his house. To cover the cost of this he had taken out a second mortgage, but the costs had come to three thousand pounds more than the builder's estimate.

'That'll be about what Monkton's getting for perjury,' said Burden. 'That'll be his share. Tony drove the van, Paddy and Johnny did the job while Monkton covers for them. I imagine they left Leilie's place around nine and got to Ploughman's Lane by a quarter past. They'll have got the safe out in an hour and got to the gate in the fence with it by ten-thirty, which was just about the time Willoughby spotted the van. Tony drove off, ditched the van in Myringham, came back to Stowerton on the last bus, the one that leaves Myringham at ten past eleven and which would have got him to Stowerton High Street by ten to twelve. God knows how the others got that safe back. My guess is that they didn't. They hid it in one of the meadows at the back of Ploughman's Lane and went back for it this morning – with Johnny Farrow's car. Then Johnny blew it. They used the wheels again and Johnny blew it somewhere up on the downs.'

Wexford hadn't spoken for some minutes. Now he said, 'When Leilie Somers was charged with this baby-battering thing, did she plead guilty or not guilty?'

Rather surprised by the apparent irrelevance of this question, Burden said, 'Guilty. There wasn't much evidence offered apart from the doctor's. Leilie pleaded guilty and said something about being tired and strained and not being able to stand it when the baby cried. Damned disgraceful nonsense.'

'Yes, it was damned disgraceful nonsense,' said Wexford quietly, and then he said, 'The walls in those flats are very thin, aren't they? So thin that from one side you can hear a pin drop on the other.' He was silent and meditative for a moment. 'What was Leilie Somers's mother's maiden name?'

'*What*?' said Burden. 'How on earth do you expect me to know a thing like that?'

'I just thought you might. I thought it might be an Irish name, you see. Because Leilie is probably short for Eileen, which is an Irish name. I expect she called herself Leilie when she was too young to pronounce her name properly.'

Burden said with an edge of impatience to his voice, 'Look, do I get to know what all this is leading up to?'

'Sure you do. The arrest of Paddy and Tony Jasper and Johnny Farrow. You can get down to Roland Road and see to it as soon as you like.'

'For God's sake, you know as well as I do we'll never make it stick. We couldn't break Monkton and he'll alibi the lot of them.'

'That'll be OK,' said Wexford laconically. 'Trust me. Believe me, there is no alibi. And now, Polly, you and I will turn our attention to the matter of young Ginger and the Kingsmarkham Chalk Circle.'

Wexford left Polly sitting outside in the car. It was eight o'clock and still light. He rang the bell that had fetched Leilie down that afternoon, and when she didn't come he rang the other. Julie Lang appeared.

'She's upset. I've got her in with me having a cup of tea.'

'I'd like to see her, Mrs Lang, and I'll need to see her alone. I'll go and sit in my car for five minutes and then if she'll . . .'

Leilie Somers's voice from the top of the stairs cut off the end of his sentence. 'You can come up. I'm OK now.'

Wexford climbed the stairs towards her, Julie Lang following him. Leilie stood back to let him pass. She seemed smaller than ever, thinner, meeker, her hennaed hair showing a paler red at the roots, her face white and deeply sad. Julie Lang put her hand on her arm, squeezed it, went off quickly into her own flat. Leilie put the key into the lock of her front door and opened the door and stood looking at the empty neat place, the passage, the open doors into the other rooms, now all made more melancholy by the encroaching twilight. Tears stood in her eyes and she turned her face so that Wexford should not see them fall.

'He's not worth it, Leilie,' said Wexford.

'I know *that*, I know what he's worth. But you won't get me being disloyal to him, Mr Wexford, I shan't say a word.'

'Let's go in and sit down.' He made his way to the table where it was lightest and sat down in the chair Tony Jasper had sat in. 'Where's the baby?'

'With my mum.'

88

'Rather much for someone who's just come out of hospital, isn't it?' Wexford looked at his watch. 'You're going to be late for work. What time is it you start? Eight-thirty?'

'Eight,' she said. 'I'm not going. I couldn't, not after what's happened to Paddy. Mr Wexford, you might as well go. I'm not going to say anything. If I was Paddy's wife you couldn't make me say anything, and I'm as good as his wife, I've been more to him than most wives'd have been.'

'I know that, Leilie,' said Wexford, 'I know all about that,' and his voice was so loaded with meaning that she stared at him with frightened eyes whose whites shone in the dusk. 'Leilie,' he said, 'when they drew the chalk circle and put the child in it the girl who had brought him up refused to pull him out because she knew she would hurt him. Rather than hurt him she preferred that someone else should have him.'

'I don't know what you're talking about,' she said.

'I think you do. It's not so different from Solomon's judgement of cutting the baby in half. The child's mother wouldn't have that happen, better let the other woman have him. You pleaded guilty in court to crimes against your first son you had never committed. It was Jasper who injured that child, and it was Jasper who got you to take the blame because he knew you would get a light sentence whereas he would get a heavy one. And afterwards you had the baby adopted – not because you didn't love him but because like the chalk circle woman you would rather lose him than have him hurt again. Isn't it true?'

She stared at him. Her head moved, a tiny affirmative bob. Wexford leaned across to the window and opened it. He waved his hand out of the window, withdrew it and closed the casement again. Leilie was crying, making no attempt to dry her tears.

'Were you brought up as a Catholic?' he said.

'I was baptised,' she said in a voice not much above a whisper. 'Mum's a Catholic. Her and Dad, they got married in Galway where Mum comes from, and Dad had to promise to bring the kids up Catholic.' A sob caught her throat. 'I haven't been to mass for years. Mr Wexford, please go away now and leave me alone. I just want to be left alone.'

He said, 'I'm sorry to hear you say that because I've got a

visitor for you, and he'll certainly be staying the night.' He switched on lights, the living-room light, the light in the hall and one over the top of the door, and then he opened the door and Polly Davies walked in with young Ginger in her arms.

Leilie blinked at the light. She closed her eyes and lowered her head, and then she lifted it and opened her eyes and made a sort of bound for Polly, nearly knocking Wexford over. But she didn't snatch Ginger. She stood trembling, looking at Polly, her hands moving slowly forward until, with an extreme gentle tenderness, they closed over and caressed the baby's downy red-gold head.

'Matthew,' she said. 'Matthew.'

The baby lay in Leilie's lap. He had whimpered a little at first, but now he lay quiet and relaxed, gripping one of her fingers, and for the first time in their acquaintance Wexford saw him smile. It was a beautiful spontaneous smile of happiness at being home again with Mother.

'You're going to tell me all about it, aren't you, Leilie?' said Wexford.

She was transformed. He had never seen her so animated, so high-spirited. She was giggly with joy so that Matthew, sensing her mood, gurgled in response, and she hugged him again, calling him her lovely lovely sweetheart, her precious boy.

'Come on now, Leilie,' said Wexford, 'you've got him back without the least trouble to yourself which is more than you damn well deserve. Now you can give an account of yourself.'

'I don't know where to start,' said Leilie, giggling.

'At the beginning, whenever that is.'

'Well, the beginning,' said Leilie, 'I reckon was when Patrick, my first boy, was adopted.' She had stopped laughing and a little of the old melancholy had come back into her face. 'That was four years ago. Paddy went off up north and after a bit he wrote and said would I join him, and I don't know why I said yes, I reckon I always do say yes to Paddy, and there didn't seem anything else, there didn't seem any future. It was all right with Paddy for a bit, and then a couple of years back he got this other girl. I sort of pretended I didn't know about it, I thought he'd get tired of her, but he didn't and I was lonely, I was so lonely. I didn't know a soul up there but Paddy, not like I could talk to, and he'd go away for weeks on end. I sort of took to going out with other fellas, anyone, I didn't care, just for the company.' She paused, shifted Matthew on her knees. 'When I knew I was pregnant I told Paddy I wasn't having the baby up there, I was going home to Mum. But he said to stay and he wouldn't see the other girl, and I did stay till after Matthew was born, and then I knew he was carrying on again so I came back here and Mum got me this flat. I know what you're going to say, Mr Wexford!'

'I wasn't going to say a word.'

'You were thinking it. So what? It's true. I couldn't tell you who Matthew's father is, I don't know. It might be Paddy, it might be one of half a dozen.' Her expression had grown fierce. She almost glared at him. 'And I'm glad I don't know, I'm glad. It makes him more mine. I never went out with any other fella but Paddy till he drove me to it.'

'All right,' said Wexford, 'all right. So you lived here with Matthew and you had your job at the Andromeda and then Paddy wrote to say he was coming down, and on Saturday he did come. And you took Monday evening off work to be with him and exchanged your Tuesday turn with another girl – and so we come to Wednesday, yesterday.'

Leilie sighed. She didn't seem unhappy, only rueful. 'Paddy said he'd babysit. He said he'd asked Tony over and Johnny and a fella called Pip Monkton, and they'd be in all evening. I said he wasn't to bother, I could take Matthew next door into Julie's, and Paddy got mad at me and said Julie was an interfering bitch and didn't I trust him to look after his own child? Well, that was it, I didn't, I kept remembering what he'd done to Patrick, and that was because Patrick cried. Paddy used to go crazy when he cried, I used to think he'd kill him, and when I tried to stop him he nearly killed me. And, you see, Mr Wexford, Matthew'd got into this way of crying in the evenings. They said at the clinic some babies cry at night and some in the evenings and it's hard to know why, but they all grow out of it. I knew Mathew'd start screaming about eight and I thought, my God, what'll Paddy do? He gets in a rage, he doesn't know what he's doing, and Tony wouldn't stop him, he's scared of him like they all are, Paddy's so big. Well, I got in a real state. Mum'd come out of hospital that morning, she'd had a major op, so I couldn't take him there and go back there myself and hide from Paddy, and I couldn't take him to work. I did once and they made a hell of a fuss. I just couldn't see any way out of it.

'Paddy went out about eleven. He never said where he was going and I didn't ask. Anyway, I went out too, carrying Matthew in the baby carrier, and I just walked about thinking. I reckon I must have walked miles, worrying about it and wondering what to do and imagining all sorts of things, you know how you do. I'd been feeding Matthew myself and I'm still giving him one feed a day, so I took him into a field and fed him under a hedge, and after that I walked a bit more.

'Well, I was coming back along the Stowerton Road. I knew I'd have to go home on account of Matthew was wet and he'd soon be hungry again, and then I saw this pram. I knew who it belonged to, I'd seen it there before and I'd seen this girl lift her baby out of it. I mean, I didn't know her name or anything but I'd talked to her once queueing for the check-out in the Tesco, and we'd got talking about our babies and she said hers never cried except sometimes for a feed in the night. She was such a good baby, they never got a peep out of her all day and all evening. She was a bit younger than Matthew but it was funny, they looked a bit alike and they'd got just the same colour hair.

'That was what gave me the idea, them having the same colour hair. I know I was mad, Mr Wexford, I know that now. I was crazy, but you don't know how scared of Paddy I was. I went over to that pram and I bent over it. I unhooked the cat net and took the other baby out and put Matthew in.'

Until now quite silent in her corner, Polly Davies gave a suppressed exclamation. Wexford drew in his breath, shaking his head.

'It's interesting,' he said, and his voice was frosty, 'how I supposed at first that whoever had taken Karen Bond wanted her and wished to be rid of her own child. Now it looks as if the reverse was true. It looks as if she didn't at all mind sacrificing Karen for her own child's safety.'

Leilie said passionately, 'That's not true!'

'No, perhaps it isn't, I believe you did have second thoughts. Go on.'

'I put Matthew in the pram. I knew he'd be all right, I knew no one'd hurt him, but it went to my heart when he started to cry.'

'Weren't you afraid someone would see you?' asked Polly.

'I wouldn't have cared if they had. Don't you see? I was past caring for any of that. If I'd been seen I wouldn't have had to go home, I'd have lost my job, but they wouldn't have taken Matthew from me, would they? No one saw me. Did you say her name was Karen? Well, I took Karen home and I fed her and bathed her. No one can say I didn't look after her like she was my own.'

'Except for delivering her into the hands of that ravening wolf, Paddy Jasper,' said Wexford unpleasantly.

She shivered a little but otherwise she took no notice. 'Paddy came in at six with Tony. The baby was in Matthew's cot by then. All you could see was its red hair like Matthew's. I remembered what that girl had said about her never crying in the evenings, and I thought, I prayed, don't cry tonight, don't cry because you're in a strange place.' Leilie lifted her head and began to speak more rapidly. 'I cooked egg and chips for the lot of them and I went out at half seven. I got back at a quarter past twelve and she was OK, she was fast asleep and she hadn't cried at all.'

Wexford said softly, 'Haven't you forgotten something, Leilie?'

Her eyes darted over him. He fancied she had grown a little paler. She picked up Matthew and held him closely against her. 'Well, the next day,' she said. 'Today. Paddy went off out early so I thought about getting the baby back. I thought of taking her to the priest. I knew about the priest, when he went out and when the lady cleaner came, I knew about it from Mum. So I got on the bus to Kingsmarkham and just by the bus stop's a shop where they'd put all their boxes out on the pavement for the dustmen. I took a box and put the baby in and left her on the doorstep of the priest's house. But I didn't know how I was going to get Matthew back, I thought I'd never get him back.

'And then you came. I said Matthew was in the bedroom and just then Julie's baby started crying and you thought it was Matthew. I couldn't help laughing, though I felt I was going to pieces, I was being torn apart. And that's all, that's everything, and now you can charge me with whatever it is I've done.'

'But you've forgotten something, Leilie.'

'I don't know what you mean,' she said.

'Of course you do. Why d'you think I had Paddy and Tony and Johnny Farrow arrested even though Pip Monkton had given them all a cast-iron alibi? How do you think I know Pip will break down and tell me that tale of his was all moonshine and tell me as well just where the contents of that safe are now? I had a little talk with the management of the Andromeda this afternoon, Leilie.'

She gave him a stony stare.

'You've got the sack, haven't you?' he said. 'Work out your notice till the end of next week or go now. They were bound to catch you out.'

'If you know all about it, Mr Wexford, why ask?'

'Because I want you to say yes.'

She whispered something to the baby, but the baby had fallen asleep.

'If you won't tell me, I shall tell you,' said Wexford, 'and if I get it wrong you can stop me. I'm going to tell you about those second thoughts you had, Leilie. You went off to work like you said but you weren't easy in your mind. You kept thinking about that baby, that other baby, that good baby that never cried in the evenings. But maybe the reason she didn't cry was that she was usually in her own bed, safe and secure in her own home with her own mother, maybe it'd be different if she woke up to find herself in a strange place. So you started worrying. You ran around that glorified ladies' loo where you work, wiping the basins and filling the towel machines and taking your ten pence tips, but you were going off your head with worry about that other baby. You kept thinking of her crying and what that animal Paddy Jasper might do to her if she cried, punch her with his great fists perhaps or bash her head against the wall. And then you knew you hadn't done anything so clever after all in swapping Matthew for her, because you're a kind loving woman at heart, Leilie, though you're a fool, and you were as worried about her as you'd have been about him.'

'And you're a devil,' whispered Leilie, staring at him as if he had supernatural powers. 'How d'you know what I thought?'

'I just know,' said Wexford. 'I know what you thought and I know what you did. When it got to half-past nine you couldn't stand it any longer. You put on your coat and ran out to catch the nine-thirty-five bus and you were home, walking up those stairs, by five to ten. There were lights on in the flat. You let yourself in and went straight into the bedroom, and Karen was in there, safe and sound and fast asleep.'

Leilie smiled a little. A ghost of a smile of happy recollection crossed her face and was gone. 'I don't know how you know,' she said, 'but yes, she was OK and asleep, and oh God, the relief of it. I'd been picturing her lying there with blood on her and I don't know what.'

'So all you had to do then was explain to Paddy why you'd come home.'

'I told him I felt ill,' said Leilie carefully. 'I said I felt rotten and I'd got one of my migraines coming.'

'No, you didn't. He wasn't there.'

'What d'you mean, wasn't there? He was there! Him and Tony and Pip and Johnny, they were in here playing cards. I said to Paddy, I feel rotten, I had to come home. I'm going to have a lay-down, I said, and I went into the bedroom and laid down.'

'Leilie, when you came in the flat was empty. You know it was empty. You know Pip Monkton's lying and you know his story won't stand up for two seconds once you tell the truth that at *five to ten this flat was empty.* Listen to me, Leilie. Paddy will go away for quite a long time over this business. It'll be a chance for you and young Ginge – er, Matthew, to make a new life. You don't want him round you for ever, do you? Ruining your life, beating up your kids? Do you, Leilie?'

She lifted the baby in her arms. She walked the length of the room and half back again as if he were restless and needed soothing instead of peacefully asleep. In front of Wexford she stood still, looking at him, and he got to his feet.

'We'll come and fetch you in the morning, Leilie,' he said, 'and take you to the police station where I'll want you to make a statement. Maybe two statements. One about taking Karen and one about Paddy not being here when you came back last night.'

'I won't say a thing about that,' she said.

95

'It might be that we wouldn't proceed with any charge against you for taking Karen.'

'I don't care about that!'

He hated doing it. He knew he had to. 'A woman who knew what you knew about Paddy and who still exposed a child to him, someone else's child – how'll that sound in court, Leilie? When they know you're living with Paddy again? And when they hear your record?'

Her face had gone white and she clasped Matthew against her. 'They wouldn't take him away from me? They wouldn't make a what-d'you-call-it?'

'A care order? They might.'

'Oh God, oh God. I promised myself I'd stick by Paddy all my life . . .'

'Romantic promises, Leilie, they haven't much to do with real life.' Wexford moved a little away from her. He went to the window. It was quite dark outside now. 'They told me at the Andromeda that you came back at half-past ten. You'd been away an hour and there had been complaints so they sacked you.'

She said feverishly, 'I did go back. I told Paddy I felt better, I . . .'

'All in the space of five minutes? Or ten at the most? You were quickly ill and well, Leilie. Shall I tell you why you went back, shall I tell you the only circumstances in which you'd have dared go back? You didn't want to lose your job but you were more afraid of what Paddy might do to the baby. If Paddy had been there the one thing you wouldn't have done is go back. Because he wasn't there you went back with a light heart. You believed he could only get in again when you were there to let him in. You didn't know then that he had a key, the key he had taken from Julie Lang.'

She spoke at last the word he had been waiting for. 'Yes.' She nodded. 'Yes, it's true. If I'd known he had that key,' she said, and she shivered, 'I'd no more have gone and left that baby there than I'd have left it in the lion house at the zoo.'

'We'll be on our way,' he said. 'Come along, Constable Davies. See you in the morning, Leilie.'

Still holding Matthew, she came up to him just as he reached the door and laid a hand on his sleeve. 'I've been thinking about what you said, Mr Wexford,' she said, 'and I don't think I'd be able to pull anybody's baby, *any* baby, out of that circle.'

Achilles Heel

The walls of the city afforded on one side a view of the blue Adriatic, on the other, massed roofs, tiled in weathered terracotta, and cataracts of stone streets descending to the cathedral and the Stradun Placa. It was very hot on the walls, the sun hard and the air dry and clear. Among the red-brown roofs and the complexities of ramparts and stairs, different colours shimmered, the purple of the bougainvillaea, the sky blue of the plumbago, and the flame flash of the orange trumpet flower.

'Lovely,' said Dora Wexford. 'Breathtaking. Aren't you glad now I made you come up here?'

'It's all right for you dark-skinned people,' grumbled her husband. 'My nose is beginning to feel like a fried egg.'

'We'll go down at the next lot of steps and you can administer some more sun cream over a glass of beer.'

It was noon, the date Saturday, 18 June. The full heat of the day had kept the Yugoslavs, but not the tourists, off the walls. Germans went by with cameras or stood murmuring, '*Wunderschön!*' Vivacious Italians chattered, unaffected by the midsummer sun. But some of the snatches of talk which reached Wexford were in languages not only incomprehensible but unidentifiable. It was a surprise to hear English spoken.

'Don't keep on about it, Iris!'

At first they couldn't see the speaker. But now, as they came out of the narrow defile and emerged on to one of the broad jutting courts made by a buttress top, they came face to face with the Englishman. A tall, fair young man, he was standing in the furthest angle of the court, and with him was a dark-haired girl. Her back was to the Wexfords. She was staring out to sea. From her clothes, she looked as if she would have been more at home in the South of France than on the walls of Dubrovnik. She wore a jade-green halter top that left her deeply tanned midriff bare, and a calf-length silk skirt in green and blue with parabolas on it of flamingo pink. Her sandals were pink, the strings criss-crossed up her legs, the wedge heels high. But perhaps the most striking thing about her was her hair. Raven black and very short, it was cut at the nape in three sharp Vs.

She must have replied to her companion, though Wexford hadn't heard the words. But now, without turning round, she stamped her foot and the man said:

'How can you go to the bloody place, Iris, when we can't find anyone to take us? There's nowhere to land. I wish to God you'd give it a rest.'

Dora took her husband's arm, hastening him along. He could read her thoughts, not to eavesdrop on someone else's quarrel.

'You're so nosy, darling,' she said when they had reached the steps and were out of earshot. 'I suppose it's what comes of being a policeman.'

Wexford laughed. 'I'm glad you realise that's the reason. Any other man's wife would accuse him of looking at that girl.'

'She *was* beautiful, wasn't she?' said Dora wistfully, conscious of her age. 'Of course we couldn't see her face, but you could tell she had a perfect figure.'

'Except for the legs. Pity she hasn't got the sense to wear trousers.'

'Oh, Reg, what was wrong with her legs? And she was so beautifully tanned. When I see a girl like that it makes me feel such an old has-been.'

'Don't be so daft,' said Wexford crossly. 'You look fine.' He meant it. He was proud of his handsome wife, so young-looking for her late fifties, elegant and decorous in navy skirt and crisp white blouse, her skin already golden after only two days of holiday. 'And I'll tell you one thing,' he added. 'You'd beat her hollow in any ankle competition.'

Dora smiled at him, comforted. They sat down at a table in a pavement café where the shade was deep and a cool breeze blew. Just time for a beer and an orange juice, and then to catch the water taxi back down the coast to Mirna.

In Serbo-Croat *mirna* means peaceful. And so Wexford found the resort after a gruelling winter and spring in Kingsmarkham, after petty crime and serious crime, and finally a squalid murder case which had been solved, not by him in spite of his work and research, but by a young expert from Scotland Yard. It was Mike Burden who had advised him to get right away for his holiday. Not Wales or Cornwall this time, but the Dalmatian coast of Yugoslavia where he, Burden, had taken his children the previous year.

'Mirna,' said Burden. 'There are three good hotels but the village is quite unspoilt. You can go everywhere by water. Two or three old chaps run taxi boats. It never rained once while we were there. And you're into all this nature stuff, this ecology. The marine life's amazing and so are the flowers and butterflies.'

It was the marine life with which Wexford was getting acquainted two mornings after the trip to Dubrovnik. He had left Dora prone on an air bed by the hotel swimming pool, knowing full well that sunbathing was impossible for his Anglo-Saxon skin. Already his nose was peeling. So he had anointed his face, put on a long-sleeved shirt, and walked round the wooded point to Mirna harbour. The little port had a harbour wall built of the same stone as the city of Dubrovnik, and kneeling down to peer over, he saw that beneath the water line the rocks and masonry were thickly covered by a tapestry of sea anemones and tiny shells and flowering weed and starfishes. The water was perfectly clear and unpolluted. He could clearly see the bottom, fifteen feet down, and now a shoal of silvery-brown fish glided out from a sea-bed bush. Fascinated, he leaned over, understanding why so many swimmers out there were equipped with goggles and snorkels. A scarlet fish darted out from a rock, then a broad silver one, banded with black.

Behind him, a voice said, 'You like it?'

Wexford got up on to his haunches. The man who had spoken was older than he, skinny and wrinkled and tough-

100

looking. He had a walnut face, a dry smile and surprisingly good teeth. He wore a sailor's cap and a blue and white striped tee-shirt, and Wexford recognised him as one of the taxi boatmen.

He replied slowly and carefully, 'I like it very much. It is pretty, beautiful.'

'The shores of your country were like this once. But in the nineteenth century a man called Gosse, a marine biologist, wrote a book about them and within a few years collectors had come and divested the rocks of everything.'

Wexford couldn't help laughing. 'Good God,' he said. 'I beg your pardon, but I thought . . .'

'That an old boatman can say "please" and "zank you" and "ten dinara"?'

'Something like that.' Wexford got up to stand inches taller than the other man. 'You speak remarkable English.'

A broad smile. 'No, it is too pedantic. I have only once been to England and that many years ago.' He put out his hand. 'How do you do, *gospodine*? Ivo Racic at your service.'

'Reginald Wexford.'

The hand was iron hard but the grip gentle. Racic said, 'I do not wish to intrude. I spoke to you because it is rare to find a tourist interested in nature. With most it is only the sunbathing and the food and drink, eh? Or to catch the fish and take the shells.'

'Come and have a drink,' said Wexford, 'or are you working?'

'Josip and Mirko and I, we have a little syndicate, and they will not mind if I have a half an hour off. But I buy the drinks. This is my country and you are my guest.'

They walked towards the avenue of stout palm trees. 'I was born here in Mirna,' said Racic. 'At eighteen I left for the university and when I retired and came back here after forty years and more, those palm trees were just the same, no bigger, no different. Nothing was changed till they built the hotels.'

'What did you do in those forty years? Not run a boat service?'

'I was professor of Anglo-Saxon studies at the University of Beograd, Gospodin Wexford.'

'Ah,' said Wexford, 'all is made plain. And when you retired you took up with Josip and Mirko to run the water taxis. Perhaps they were childhood friends?'

'They were. I see you have perspicacity. And may I inquire in return what is your occupation?'

Wexford said what he always said on holiday, 'I'm a civil servant.'

Racic smiled. 'Here in Yugoslavia we are all civil servants. But let us go for our drinks. *Hajdemo, drug!*'

They chose a cluster of tables set under a vine-covered canopy, through which the sun made a gentle dappling on cobbles. Racic drank *slivovic*. The fiery brandy with its hinted undertaste of plums was forbidden to Wexford who had to watch his blood pressure. He even felt guilty when the white wine called Posip which Racic ordered for him arrived in a tumbler filled to the brim.

'You live here in Mirna?'

'Here alone in my *kucica* that was once my father's house. My wife died in Beograd. But it is a good and pleasant life. I have my pension and my boat and the grapes I grow and the figs, and sometimes a guest like yourself, Gospodin Wexford, on whom to practise my English.'

Wexford would have liked to question him about the political regime, but he felt that this might be unwise and perhaps discourteous. So instead he remarked on the stately appearance of a woman in national costume, white coif, heavily embroidered stiff black dress, who had emerged with a full basket from the grocer's shop. Racic nodded, then pointed a brown thumb to a table outside the shadow of the vines.

'That is better, I think. Healthier, eh? And freer.'

She was sitting in the full sun, a young woman with short black hair geometrically cut, who wore only a pair of white shorts and jade-green halter top. A man came out of the currency exchange bureau, she got up to meet him, and Wexford recognised them as the couple he had seen on the walls of Dubrovnik. They went off hand in hand and got into a white Lancia Gamma parked under the palms.

'Last time I saw them they were quarrelling.'

'They are staying at the Hotel Bosnia,' said Racic. 'On Sunday evening they drove here from Dubrovnik and they are

102

going to remain for a week. Her name I cannot tell you, but his is Philip.'

'May I ask how you come to be such a mine of information, Mr Racic?'

'They came out in my boat this morning.' Racic's dark bright eyes twinkled. 'Just the two of them, to be ferried across to Vrt and back. But let me tell you a little story. Once, about a year ago, a young English couple hired my boat. They were, I think, on their wedding journey, their honeymoon, as you say, and it was evident they were much in love. They had no eyes but for each other and certainly no inclination to speak to the boatman. We were coming into the shore here, perhaps a hundred metres out, when the young husband began telling his wife how much he loved her and how he could hardly wait to get back to the hotel to make love to her. Oh, very frank and explicit he was – and why not with only the old Yugoslav there who speaks nothing but his own outlandish tongue?

'I said nothing. I betrayed nothing in my face. We pulled in, he paid me twenty dinars and they walked off up the quay. Then I saw the young lady had left her bag behind and I called to her. She came back, took it and thanked me. Gospodin Wexford, I could not resist it. "You have a charming husband, madame," I said, "but no more than you deserve." Oh, how she blushed, but I think she was not displeased, though they never came in my boat again.'

Laughing, Wexford said, 'It was hardly a similar conversation you overheard between Philip and his wife, though?'

'No.' Racic looked thoughtful. 'I think I will not tell you what I overheard. It is no business of ours. And now I must make my excuses, but we shall meet again.'

'In your boat, certainly. I must take my wife over to Vrt for the bathing.'

'Better than that. Bring your wife and I will take you for a trip round the islands. On Wednesday? No, I'm not touting for custom. This will be a trip – now for a good colloquial expression – on the house! You and me and Gospoda Wexford.'

'Those very nice Germans,' said Dora, 'have asked us to go with them in their car to Cetinje on Wednesday.'

'Mm,' said Wexford absently. 'Good idea.' It was nine o'clock but very dark beyond the range of the waterside lights. They had walked into Mirna after dinner, it being too late for the taxi boats, and were having coffee on the terrace of a restaurant at the harbour edge. The nearly tideless Adriatic lapped the stones at their feet with soft gulping sounds.

Suddenly he remembered. 'Oh, God, I can't. I promised that Yugoslav I told you about to go on a trip round the islands with him. It'd look discourteous to let him down. But you go to Cetinje.'

'Well, I should like to. I may never get another chance to see Montenegro. Oh, look, darling, there are those people we saw in Dubrovnik!'

For the first time Wexford saw the girl full-face. Her haircut from the front was as spectacular as from the back, a fringe having been cut into a sharp peak in the centre of her forehead. It looked less like hair, he thought, than a black cap painted on. In spite of the hour, she wore large tinted glasses. Her coloured skirt was the same one she had been wearing that first time.

She and her companion had come on to the terrace from the harbour walk. They walked slowly, she somehow reluctantly, the man called Philip looking about him as if for friends they had arranged to meet here. It couldn't have been for a vacant table, for the terrace was half-empty. Dora kicked her husband's foot under the table, a warning against overt curiosity, and started to talk about her German friends, Werner and Trudi. Out of the corner of his eye, Wexford saw the man and the girl hesitate, then sit down at a neighbouring table. He made some sort of reply to Dora, conscious that it was he now who was being stared at. A voice he had heard once before said:

'Excuse me, we don't seem to have an ashtray. Would you mind if we had yours?'

Dora handed it to him. 'Please do.' She hardly looked up.

He insisted, smiling. 'You're sure you won't need it?'

'Quite sure. We don't smoke.'

He wasn't the kind to give up easily, thought Wexford, and now, very intrigued by something he had noticed, he didn't want to. Another prod from Dora's foot merely made him withdraw his own under his chair. He turned towards the other table, and to the next question, 'Are you staying long in Mirna?' replied pleasantly, 'A fortnight. We've been here four days.'

The effect of this simple rejoinder was startling. The man couldn't have expressed more satisfaction – and, yes, relief – if Wexford had brought him news of some great inheritance or that a close friend, presumed in danger, was safe.

'Oh, fantastic! That's really great. It's such a change to meet some English people. We must try and get together. This is my wife. We're called Philip and Iris Nyman. Are you Londoners too?'

Wexford introduced himself and Dora and said that they were from Kingsmarkham in Sussex. It was lovely to meet them, said Philip Nyman. They must let him buy them a drink. No? More coffee, then? At last Wexford accepted a cup of coffee, wondering what was so upsetting Iris Nyman that she had responded to the introduction only with a nod and now seemed almost paralysed. Her husband's extrovert behaviour? Certainly his effusive manner would have embarrassed all but the most insensitive. As soon as they had settled the question of the drinks, he launched into a long account of their trip from England, how they had come down through France and Italy, the people they had met, the weather, their delight at their first sight of the Dalmatian coast which they had never previously visited. Iris Nyman showed no delight. She simply stared out to sea, gulping down *slivovic* as if it were lemonade.

'We absolutely adored it. They say it's the least spoilt of the Mediterranean resorts, and that I can believe. We all loved Dubrovnik. That is, I mean, we brought a cousin of my wife's along with us. She was going on to holiday with some people she knows in Greece, so she flew to Athens from Dubrovnik on Sunday and left us to come on here.'

Dora said, 'We saw you in Dubrovnik. On the walls.'

Iris Nyman's glass made a little clinking sound against her teeth. Her husband said, 'You saw us on the walls? D'you know, I think I remember that.' He seemed just slightly taken aback. But not deterred. 'In fact, I seem to remember we were having a bit of a row at the time.'

Dora made a deprecating movement with her hands. 'We

just walked past you. It was terribly hot, wasn't it?'

'You're being very charmingly discreet, Mrs Wexford – or may I call you Dora? The point was, Dora, my wife wanted to climb one of the local mountains and I was telling her just how impractical this was. I mean, in that heat, and for what? To get the same view you get from the walls.'

'So you managed to dissuade her?' Wexford said quietly.

'Indeed I did, but you came along rather at the height of the ding-dong. Another drink, darling? And how about you, Dora? Won't you change your mind?'

They replied simultaneously, 'Another *slivovic*,' and 'Thank you so much, but we must go.' It was a long time since Wexford had seen his wife so huffy and so thoroughly out of countenance. He marvelled at Nyman's continuing efforts, his fixed smile.

'Let me guess, you're staying at the Adriatic?' He took silence for assent. 'We're at the Bosnia. Wait a minute, how about making a date for, say, Wednesday? We could all have a trip somewhere in my car.'

The Wexfords, having previous engagements, were able to refuse with clear consciences. They said good night, Wexford nodding non-committally at Nyman's insistence that they must meet again, mustn't lose touch after having been so lucky as to encounter each other. His eyes followed them. Wexford looked back once to see.

'Well!' said Dora when they were out of earshot, 'what an insufferably rude woman!'

'Just very nervous, I think,' said Wexford thoughtfully. He gave her his arm and they began the walk back along the waterside path. It was very dark, the sea inky and calm, the island invisible. 'When you come to think of it, that was all very odd.'

'Was it? She was rude and he was effusive to the point of impertinence, if you call that odd. He forced himself on us, got us to tell him our names – you could see she just didn't want to know. I was amazed when he called me Dora.'

'That part wasn't so odd. After all, that's how one does make holiday acquaintances. Presumably it was much the same with Werner and Trudi.'

'No, it wasn't, Reg, not at all. For one thing, we're much of an age and we're staying at the same hotel. Trudi speaks quite good English, and we were watching the children in the paddling pool and she happened to mention her grandsons who are just the same age as ours, and that started it. You must see that's quite different from a man of thirty walking into a café and latching on to a couple old enough to be his parents. I call it pushy.'

Wexford reacted impatiently. 'That's as may be. Perhaps you didn't notice there was a perfectly clean ashtray in the middle of that table before they sat down at it.'

'*What?*' Dora halted, staring at him in the dark.

'There was. He must have put it in his pocket to give him an excuse for speaking to us. Now that was odd. And giving us all that gratuitous information was odd. And telling a deliberate lie was very odd indeed. Come along, my dear. Don't stand there gawping at me.'

'What do you mean, a deliberate lie?'

'When you told them we'd seen them on the walls, he said he remembered it and we must have overheard the quarrel between himself and his wife. Now that was odd in itself. Why mention it at all? Why should we care about his domestic – or maybe I should say mural – rows? He said the quarrel had been over climbing a mountain, but no one climbs the mountains here in summer. Besides, I remember precisely what he did say up on the walls. He said, "We can't find anyone to take us." OK, so he might have meant they couldn't get a guide. But "there's nowhere to land"? That's what he said, no doubt about it. You don't land on mountains, Dora, unless you assault them by helicopter.'

'I wonder why, though? I wonder what he's up to?'

'So do I,' said Wexford, 'but I'm pretty sure it's not pinching ashtrays from waterside cafés.'

They rounded the point and came within sight of the lights of the Hotel Adriatic. A little further and they could see each other's faces. Dora saw his and read there much to disquiet her.

'You're not going to start detecting, Reg!'

'Can't help it, it's in my bones. But I won't let it interfere with your holiday, that's a promise.'

* * *

On Tuesday morning Racic's taxi boat was waiting at the landing stage outside the hotel.

'Gospoda Wexford, it is a great pleasure to meet you.'

Courteously he handed Dora into the boat. Its awning of green canvas, now furled, gave it somewhat the look of a gondola. As the engines started, Dora made her excuses for the following day.

'You will like Cetinje,' said Racic. 'Have a good time. Gospodin Wexford and I will have a bachelor day out. All boys together, eh? Are you quite comfortable? A little more suitable than that one for a lady, I hope.'

He pointed across the bay to where a man was paddling a yellow and blue inflatable dinghy. The girl with him wore a very brief bikini. The Nymans.

'If you could manage to avoid passing those people, Mr Racic,' said Dora, 'that would make me very comfortable indeed.'

Racic glanced at Wexford. 'You have met them? They have annoyed you?'

'Not that. They spoke to us last night in Mirna and the man was rather pushing.'

'I will keep close to the shore and cross to Vrt from the small peninsula there.'

For most of the morning there was no one else on the little shingly beach of Vrt, which Racic had told them meant a garden. The huddle of cottages behind were overhung with the blue trumpet flowers of the morning glory, and among the walls rose the slender spires of cypress trees. Wexford sat in the shade reading while Dora sunbathed. The dinghy came close only once, but the Wexfords went unrecognised, perhaps because they were in swimming costumes. Iris Nyman stood up briefly before jumping with an explosive splash into the deep water.

'Rude she may be,' said Dora, 'but I'll grant she's got a lovely figure. And you were wrong about her legs, Reg. Her legs are perfect.'

'Didn't notice,' said Wexford.

Josip took them back. He was a thin smiling brown man, not unlike Racic, but he had no English beyond 'thank you' and 'good-bye'. They hired him again in the afternoon to take them into Mirna, and they spent a quiet, pleasant evening drinking coffee with Werner and Trudi Muller on the Germans' balcony.

Wednesday came in with a storm at sunrise, and Wexford, watching the lightning and the choppy sea, wondered if Burden had been over-optimistic with his guarantee of fine weather. But by nine the sun was out and the sky clear. He saw Dora off in the Mullers' Mercedes, then walked down to the landing stage. Racic's boat glided in.

'I have brought bread and sausage for our lunch, and Posip in a flask to keep it cool.'

'Then we must eat it for our elevenses because I'm taking you out to lunch.'

This they ate in Dubrovnik after Racic had taken him to the island of Lokrum. Wexford listened with deepening interest to the boatman-professor's stories. How the ease and wealth of the city merchants had led to a literary renascence, how Dubrovnik-built ships had taken part in the Spanish Armada, how an earthquake had devastated the city and almost destroyed the state. They set off again for Lopud, Sipan and Kolocep, returning across the broad calm waters as the sun began to dip towards the sea.

'Does that little island have a name?' Wexford asked.

'It is called Vrapci, which is to say "sparrows". There are thousands of sparrows, so they say, and only sparrows, for no one goes there. One cannot land a boat.'

'You mean you can't get off a boat because the rocks are too sheer? What about the other side?'

'I will pull in close and you shall see. There is a beach but no one would wish to use it. Wait.'

The island was very small, perhaps no more than half a mile in circumference, and totally overgrown with stunted pines. At their roots the grey rock fell sheer to the water from a height of about ten feet. Racic brought the boat about and they came to the Adriatic side of Vrapci. No sparrows were to be seen, no life of any kind. Between ramparts of rock was a small and forbidding beach of shingle over which an overhanging pine cast deep shade. Looking up at the sky and then down at this dark and stony cove, Wexford could see that, no matter what its altitude, the sun would never penetrate to this beach. Where the shingle narrowed, at the apex, was a cleft in the rock just wide enough to allow the passage of a man's body.

'Not very attractive,' he said. 'Why should people want to come here?'

'They don't, as far as I know. Except perhaps – well, there is a new fashion, Gospodin Wexford, or Mister as I should call you.'

'Call me Reg.'

Racic inclined his head. 'Reg, yes, thank you. I like the name, though I have not previously encountered it. There is a fashion, as I mentioned, for nude bathing. Here in Yugoslavia we do not allow it, for it is not proper, not decorous. No doubt you have seen painted on some of the rocks the words – in, I fear, lamentable English – "No Nudist". But there are some who would defy this rule, especially on the small islands. Vrapci might take their fancy if they could find a boat and a boatman to bring them.'

'A boat could land on the beach and its occupants swim off the rocks on the other side in the sun.'

'If they were good swimmers. But we will not try it, Reg, not at our age being inclined to strip ourselves naked and risk our necks, eh?'

Once more they were off across the wide sea. Wexford looked back to the city walls, those man-made defensive cliffs, and brought himself hesitantly to ask:

'Would you tell me what you overheard of the conversation between that English couple, Philip and Iris Nyman, when you took them out in your boat?'

'So that is their name? Nyman?' He was stalling.

'I have a good reason for asking.'

'May I know it?'

Wexford sighed. 'I'm a policeman.'

Racic's face went very still and tight. 'I don't much like that. You were sent here to watch these people? You should have told me before.'

'No, Ivo, no.' Wexford brought out the unfamiliar name a little self-consciously. 'No, you've got me wrong. I never saw or heard of them till last Saturday. But now I've seen them and spoken to them I believe they're doing something illegal. If that's so it's my duty to do something about it. They're my countrymen.'

'Reg,' said Racic more gently, 'what I overheard can have nothing to do with this matter of an illegality. It was personal and private.'

'You won't tell me?'

'No. We are not old housewives to spend our time in gossip over the garden walls of our *kucice*, eh?'

Wexford grinned. 'Then will you *do* something for me? Will you contrive to let these people know – subtly, of course – that you understand the English language?'

'You are sure that what they are doing is against the law?'

'I am sure. It's drugs or some kind of confidence trick.'

There was silence, during which Racic seemed to commune with his sea. Then he said quietly, 'I trust you, Reg. Yes, I will do this if I can.'

'Then go into Mirna. They're very likely having a drink on the waterfront.'

Mirko's boat passed them as they came in and Mirko waved, calling, '*Dobro vece!*'

On the jetty stood a queue of tourists, waiting to be ferried back to the Adriatic or to the hotel at Vrt. There were perhaps a dozen people, and Philip and Iris Nyman brought up the end of the line. It worked out better than Wexford could have hoped. The first four got into Josip's boat, bound for Vrt, the next group into Mirko's which, with its capacity of only eight, was inadequate to take the Nymans.

'Hotel Adriatic,' said Nyman. Then he recognised Wexford. 'Well, well, we meet again. Had a good day?'

Wexford replied that he had been to Dubrovnik. He helped the girl into the boat. She thanked him, seeming less nervous and even gave him a diffident smile. The motor started and they were off, Racic the anonymous taxi-man, the piece of equipment without which the vehicle won't go.

'I saw you out in your dinghy yesterday,' said Wexford.

'Did you?' Philip Nyman seemed gratified. 'We can't use it tonight, though. It's not safe after dark and you've really got to be in swimming costumes. We're dining at your hotel with another English couple that we met yesterday and we thought we'd have a romantic walk back along the path.'

They were rather more dressed up than usual. Nyman wore a cream-coloured safari suit, his wife a yellow and black dress

111

and high-heeled black sandals. Wexford was on the alert for an invitation to join them for dinner and was surprised when none came.

Both the Nymans lit cigarettes. Wexford noticed Racic stiffen. He had learned enough about the man's principles and shibboleths to be aware of his feelings on pollution. Those cigarette butts would certainly end up in the sea. Anger with his passengers might make him all the more willing to fulfil his promise. But for the moment he remained silent. They rounded the point on to a sea where the sun seemed to have laid a skin of gold.

'So beautiful!' said Iris Nyman.

'A pity you have to go so soon.'

'We're staying till Saturday,' said Nyman, though without renewing his suggestion that they and the Wexfords should meet again. The girl took a last draw on her cigarette and threw it overboard.

'Oh, well,' said Nyman, 'there's so much muck in there already, a bit more won't do any harm,' and he cast his still-lighted butt into the ripples of melted gold.

They were approaching the hotel landing stage and Racic cut the motor. Nyman felt in his pocket for change. It was Wexford who got up first. He said to Racic as the Yugoslav made the boat fast:

'I've had a splendid day. Thanks very much indeed.'

He wasn't looking at them but he fancied the amused glance Nyman would have given his wife at this display of the Englishman's well-known assumption that all but cretins speak his language. Racic drew himself up to his not very great height. What accent he had, what stiltedness and syntactical awkwardness, seemed to be lost. He spoke as if he had been born in Kensington and educated at Oxford.

'I'm glad you enjoyed it, I certainly did. Give my regards to your wife and tell her I hope to see her soon.'

There was no sound from the Nymans. They got out of the boat, Racic saying, 'Let me give you a hand, madame.' Nyman's voice sounded stifled when he produced his twenty dinars and muttered his thanks. Neither said a word to Wexford. They didn't look back. They walked away and his eyes followed them.

'Did I do all right, Reg? I was moved by the foul contamination of my sea.'

Absently, still staring, Wexford said, 'You did fine.'

'What do you look at with such concentration?'

'Legs,' said Wexford. 'Thanks again. I'll see you tomorrow.'

He walked up towards the hotel, looking for them, but they were nowhere in sight. On the terrace he turned and looked back and there they were, walking hurriedly along the waterfront path back to Mirna, their new friends and their dinner engagement forgotten. Wexford went into the hotel and took the lift up to his room. Dora wasn't back yet. Feeling rather shaken, he lay down on one of the twin beds. This latest development or discovery was, at any rate, far from what he had expected. And what now? Somehow get hold of the Dubrovnik police? He reached for the phone to call reception but dropped it again when Dora walked in.

She came up to him in consternation. 'Are you all right, darling?'

His blood pressure, his heart, too much sun – he could tell what she was thinking. It was rare for him to take a rest in the daytime. 'Of course I am. I'm fine.' He sat up. 'Dora, something most peculiar . . .'

'You're detecting again! I knew it.' She kicked off her shoes and threw open the doors to the balcony. 'You haven't even asked me if I've had a nice day.'

'I can see you have. Come in, my dear, don't be difficult. I always like to think you're the only woman I know who isn't difficult.' She looked at him warily. 'Listen,' he said. 'Do something for me. Describe the woman we saw on the walls.'

'Iris Nyman? What do you mean?'

'Just do as I ask, there's a good girl.'

'You're mad. You *have* had a touch of the sun. Well, I suppose if it humours you . . . Medium height, good figure, very tanned, about thirty, geometric haircut. She was wearing a jade green halter top and a blue and green and pink skirt.'

'Now describe the woman we saw with Nyman on Monday.'

'There's no difference except for a black top and a stole.'

Wexford nodded. He got off the bed, walked past her on to the balcony and said:

'They're not the same woman.'

'What on earth are you suggesting?'

'I wish I knew,' said Wexford, 'but I do know the Iris Nyman we saw on the walls is not the Iris Nyman I saw in Mirna on Monday morning and we saw that night and we saw yesterday and I saw this evening.'

'You're letting your imagination run away with you. You are, Reg. That hair, for instance, it was striking, and those clothes, and being with Philip Nyman.'

'Don't you see you've named the very things that would be used to make anyone think they're the same woman? Neither of us saw her face that first time. Neither of us heard her voice. We only noticed the striking things about her.'

'What makes you think they're not the same?'

'Her legs. The legs are different. You drew my attention to them. One might say you set me off on this.'

Dora leaned over the balcony rail. Her shoulders sagged. 'Then I wish I hadn't. Reg, you never discuss cases with me at home. Why do it here?'

'There's no one else.'

'Thanks very much. All this about their not being the same woman, it's nonsense, you've dreamed it up. Why would anyone try and fake a thing like that? Come to that, *how* could anyone?'

'Easily. All you need is a female accomplice of similar build and age. On Saturday or Sunday this accomplice had her hair cut and dyed and assumed Iris Nyman's clothes. I mean to find out why.'

Dora turned her back on the sunset and fixed him with a cold and stony look. 'No, Reg, no. I'm not being difficult. I'm just behaving like any normal woman would when she goes on holiday and finds her husband can't leave his job at home for just two weeks. This is the first foreign holiday I've had in ten years. If you'd been sent here to watch these people, if it was work, I wouldn't say a word. But it's just something you've dreamed up because you can't relax and enjoy the sun and the sea like other people.'

'OK,' said her husband, 'look at it that way.' He was very

fond of his wife, he valued her and quickly felt guilt over his frequent enforced neglect of her. This time any neglect would be as if by design, the result of that bone-deep need of his to unravel mysteries. 'Don't give me that Gorgon face. I've said I won't let this spoil your holiday and I won't.' He touched her cheek, gently rubbing it. 'And now I'm going to have my bath.'

Not much more than twelve hours later he was walking the path to Mirna. The sun was already hot and there was a speedboat out in the bay. Carpet sellers had spread their wares in the market place, and the cafés were open for those who wanted coffee or – even at this hour – plum brandy.

The Bosnia, most of it mercifully concealed by pines and ranks of cypresses, looked from close to, with its floors in plate-like layers and its concrete flying buttresses, more like an Unidentified Flying Object come to rest in the woods than a holiday hotel. Wexford crossed a forecourt as big as a football pitch and entered a foyer that wouldn't have disgraced some capital city's palace of justice.

The receptionist spoke good English.

'Mr and Mrs Nyman checked out last evening, sir.'

'Surely they expected to stay another three days?'

'I cannot tell you, sir. They left last evening before dinner. I cannot help you more.'

So that was that.

'What are you going to do now?' said Dora over a late breakfast. 'Have a hilarious cops and robbers car chase up the Dalmatian coast?'

'I'm going to wait and see. And in the meantime I'm going to enjoy my holiday and see that you enjoy yours.' He watched her relax and smile for the first time since the previous evening.

The Nymans were at the back of his mind all the time, but he did manage to enjoy the rest of his holiday. Werner and Trudi took them to Mostar to see the Turkish bridge. They went on a coach to Budva, and the members of the taxi boat syndicate ferried them from Mirna to Vrt and out to Lokrum. It was in secret that Wexford daily bought a London newspaper, a day old and three times its normal price. He wasn't sure why he did so, what he hoped or feared. On their last morning he nearly didn't bother. After all, he would be home in not much more than twenty-four hours and then he would have to take some action. But as he passed the reception desk, Dora having

115

already entered the dining room for breakfast, the clerk held out the newspaper to him as a matter of course.

Wexford thanked him – and there it was on the front page. *Disappearance of Tycoon's Daughter,* said the headline. *Beachwear King Fears Kidnap Plot.*

The text beneath read: 'Mrs Iris Nyman, 32, failed to return to her North London home from a shopping expedition yesterday. Her father, Mr James Woodhouse, Chairman of Sunsports Ltd, a leading manufacturer of beachwear, fears his daughter may have been kidnapped and expects a ransom demand. Police are taking a serious view.

'Mrs Nyman's husband, 33-year-old Philip Nyman, said at the couple's home in Flask Walk, Hamsptead, today, "My wife and I had just got back from a motoring holiday in Italy and Yugoslavia. On the following morning Iris went out shopping and never returned. I am frantic with worry. She seemed to be happy and relaxed."

'Mr Woodhouse's company, of which Mrs Nyman is a director, was this year involved in a vast takeover bid as a result of which two other major clothing firms were absorbed into Sunsports Ltd. The company's turnover last year was in the region of £100,000,000.'

There was a photograph of Iris Nyman in black glasses. Wexford would have been hard put to it to say whether this was of the woman on the walls or the woman in Mirna.

That night they gave Racic a farewell dinner at the Dubrovacka restaurant.

'Don't say what they all say, Reg, that you will come back next year. Dalmatia is beautiful to you and Gospoda Wexford now, but a few days and the memory will fade. Someone will say, San Marino for you next time, or Ibiza, and there you will go. Is it not so?'

'I said I shall be back,' said Wexford, 'and I meant it.' He raised his glass of Posip. 'But not in a year's time. It'll be sooner than that.'

Three hundred and sixty-two days sooner, as Racic pointed out.

'And here I am, sitting in the *vrt* of your *kucica*!'

'Reg, we shall have you fluent in Serbo-Croat yet.'

116

'Alas, no. I must be back in London again tomorrow night.'

They were in Racic's garden, halfway up the terraced hill behind Mirna, sitting in wicker chairs under his vine and his fig tree. Pink and white and red oleanders shimmered in the dusk, and above their heads bunches of small green grapes hung between the slats of a canopy. On the table was a bottle of Posip and the remains of a dinner of king prawns and Dalmatian buttered potatoes, salad and bread and big ripe peaches.

'And now we have eaten,' said Racic, 'you will please tell me the tale of the important business that brought you back to Mirna so pleasantly soon. It concerns Mr and Mrs Nyman?'

'Ivo, we shall have you a policeman yet.'

Racic laughed and re-filled Wexford's glass. Then he looked serious. 'Not a laughing matter, I think, not pleasant.'

'Far from it. Iris Nyman is dead, murdered, unless I am much mistaken. This afternoon I accompanied the Dubrovnik police out into the bay and we took her body out of the cave on Vrapci.'

'*Zaboga!* You cannot mean it! That girl who was at the Bosnia and who came out with her husband in my boat?'

'Well, no, not that one. She's alive and in Athens from where, I imagine, she'll be extradited.'

'I don't understand. Tell me the tale from the beginning.'

Wexford leaned back in his chair and looked up through the vines at the violet sky where the first stars had begun to show. 'I'll have to start with the background,' he said, and after a pause, 'Iris Nyman was the daughter and only child of James Woodhouse, the chairman of a company called Sunsports Ltd which makes sports- and beachwear and has a large export trade. She married when she was very young, less than twenty, a junior salesman in her father's firm. After the marriage Woodhouse made a director of her, settled a lot of money on her, bought her a house and gave her a company car. To justify her company fees and expenses, she was in the habit of annually making a trip to holiday resorts in Europe with her husband, ostensibly to wear Sunsports clothes and note who else was wearing them, and also to study the success of rival markets. Probably, she simply holidayed.

'The marriage was not a happy one. At any rate, Philip

117

Nyman wasn't happy. Iris was a typically arrogant rich girl who expected always to have her own way. Besides, the money and the house and the car were all hers. He remained a salesman. Then, a year or so ago, he fell in love with a cousin of Iris, a girl called Anna Ashby. Apparently, Iris knew nothing about this, and her father certainly didn't.'

'Then how can you . . . ?' Racic interrupted.

'These affairs are always known to someone, Ivo. One of Anna's friends has made a statement to Scotland Yard.' Wexford paused and drank some of his wine. 'That's the background,' he said. 'Now for what happened a month or so ago.

'The Nymans had arranged to motor down as usual to the south of France, but this time to cross northern Italy and spend a week or ten days here on the Dalmatian coast. Anna Ashby had planned to spend part of the summer with friends in Greece so, *at Iris's invitation*, she was to accompany the Nymans as far as Dubrovnik where she would stay a few days with them, then go on by air to Athens.

'In Dubrovnik, after the three of them had been there a few days, Iris got hold of the idea of bathing off Vrapci. Perhaps she wanted to bathe in the nude, perhaps she had already been on the "topless" beach at St Tropez. I don't know. Philip Nyman has admitted nothing of this. Up until the time I left, he was still insisting that his wife had returned to England with him.'

'It was your idea, then,' put in Racic, 'that this poor woman's body was concealed on the isle of sparrows?'

'It was a guess,' said Wexford. 'I overheard some words, I was later told a lie. I'm a policeman. Whether they went to Vrapci on Saturday, June 18th, or Sunday, June 19th, I can't tell you. Suffice that they did go – in that inflatable dinghy of theirs. The three of them went but only two came back, Nyman and Anna Ashby.'

'They killed Mrs Nyman?'

Wexford looked thoughtful. 'I think so, certainly. Of course there's a possibility that she drowned, that it was an accident. But in that case wouldn't any normal husband have immediately informed the proper authority? If he had recovered the body, wouldn't he have brought it back with him? We're awaiting the results of the post-mortem, but even if that shows no wounds or bruises on the body, even if the lungs are full of water, I should be very surprised to learn that Nyman and, or, Anna hadn't hastened her death or watched her drown.'

Both were silent for a moment, Racic nodding slowly as he digested what Wexford had told him. Then he got up and fetched from the house a candelabrum, but thinking better of it, switched on an electric lamp attached to the wall.

'Any light will attract the insects, but there at least they will not trouble us. So it was this Anna Ashby who came to Mirna, posing as Mrs Nyman?'

'According to the manager of the hotel in Dubrovnik where the three of them had been staying, Nyman checked out and paid his bill early on the evening of the 19th. Neither of the women was with him. Iris was dead and Anna was at the hairdresser's, having her hair cut and dyed to the same style and colour as her cousin's. The police have already found the hairdresser who did the job.'

'They came here next,' said Racic. 'Why didn't they go straight back to England? And now I must ask, surely they did not intend to play this game in England? Even if the two women, as cousins, to a degree resembled each other, this Anna could not hope to deceive a father, close friends, Mrs Nyman's neighbours.'

'The answer to your first question is that to have returned to England a week earlier than expected would have looked odd. Why go back? The weather was perfect. Nyman wanted to give the impression they had both been well and happy during their holiday. No, his idea was to make sufficient people here in Yugoslavia believe that Iris was alive after June 19th. That's why he latched on to us and got our name and home town out of us. He wanted to be sure of witnesses if need be. Anna was less bold, she was frightened to death. But Philip actually found himself two more English witnesses, though, thanks to your intervention, he never kept the appointment to dine with them.'

'My intervention?'

'Your excellent English. And now perhaps you'll tell me what you overheard in the boat.'

Racic laughed. His strong white teeth gleamed in the

lamplight. 'I knew she was not Mrs Nyman, Reg, but that knowledge would not have helped you then, eh? You had seen the lady on the walls but not, I presume, her marriage document. I thought to myself, why should I tell this busybody of a policeman the secrets of my passengers? But now, to use an idiom, here goes. Reg, the lady said, "I feel so guilty, it is terrible what we have done," and he replied, "Everyone here thinks you are my wife, and no one at home will suspect a thing. One day you will be and we shall forget all this." Now, would you have supposed they were talking of murder or of illicit passion?'

Wexford smiled. 'Nyman must have thought we'd confer, you and I, and jump to the former conclusion. Or else he'd forgotten what he'd said. He has rather a way of doing that.'

'And after they left?'

'Anna was to travel on Iris's passport in the hope it would be stamped at at least one frontier. In fact, it was stamped at two, between Yugoslavia and Italy and again at Calais. At Dover Anna presumably left him and caught the first plane to Athens she could get. Nyman went home, reaching there in the night of the 28th, the precise date on which he and Iris had planned to return. On the following afternoon he told his father-in-law and the police that Iris was missing.'

'He hoped the search for her or her body,' said Racic, 'would be confined to England because he had incontrovertible proof she had stayed with him in Mirna and had travelled back with him to England. No one would think of looking for her here, for it was known to many witnesses that she left here alive. But what did he hope to gain? Surely, if your laws are like ours, and I believe all laws are alike in this, without her body it would be years before he could inherit her money or marry again?'

'You have to remember this wasn't a premeditated murder. It must have happened on the spur of the moment. So conceal the body where it may never be found or not found until it's beyond identification, announce that his wife has gone missing in England, and he gets the sympathy of his powerful father-in-law and certainly Iris's house to live in and Iris's car to drive. He keeps his job which he would have lost had he divorced Iris, and very likely gets all or some of her allowance

120

transferred to him. Anna gets her hair back to its natural colour – brown, incidentally – lets it grow out, returns home and they resume their friendship. One day Iris will be presumed dead and they can marry.'

Racic cut himself a slice of bread and nibbled at an olive. 'I see it all or nearly all. I see that, but for your presence here in Mirna, the conspiracy had every chance of success. What I don't see is, if this woman made herself look so much like this woman you saw on the walls, if she had the same hair and clothes – but I am a fool! You saw her face.'

'I didn't see her face and I didn't hear her voice. Dora and I saw her very briefly and then only from the back.'

'It is beyond my comprehension.'

'The legs,' said Wexford. 'The legs were different.'

'But, my dear Reg, my dear policeman, surely the leg of one brown-skinned slender young woman is much like the leg of such another? Or was there a mole perhaps or a protruding vein?'

'Not as far as I know. The only time I saw the true Iris Nyman she wore a skirt that covered her legs to mid-calf. In fact, I could see very little of her legs.'

'Then I am flummoxed.'

'Ankles,' said Wexford. 'There are two types of normal ankle in this world, and the difference between them can only be seen from the back. In one type the calf seems to join the heel with a narrowing but no distinct shaft. In the other, the type of beauty, the Achilles tendon makes a long slender shaft with deep indentations on either side of it beneath the ankle bones. I saw Iris Nyman's legs only from behind and in her the Achilles tendon was not apparent. It was a flaw in her appearance. When I first noticed Anna Ashby's legs from behind as she was getting off your boat, I observed the long shaft of the tendon leading up into the muscle of a shapely calf. She had no flaw in her legs, but you might call that perfection her Achilles Heel.'

'*Zaboga!* Beauty, eh? Only two types in the world?' Racic extended one foot and rolled up his trouser leg. Wexford's was already rucked up. In the lamplight they peered down at each other's calves from behind. 'Yours are all right,' said Racic. 'In fact, they are fine. In the beauty class.'

'So are yours, you old professor and boatman.'

Racic burst out laughing. '*Tesko meni!* Two elderly gentlemen who should know better, airing their limbs in an ankle competition! Whatever next?'

'Well, I shouldn't,' said Wexford, 'but next let's finish up the Posip.'

When the Wedding
Was Over

'Matrimony,' said Chief Inspector Wexford, 'begins with dearly beloved and ends with amazement.'

His wife, sitting beside him on the bridegroom's side of the church, whispered, 'What did you say?'

He repeated it. She steadied the large floral hat which her husband had called becoming but not exactly conducive to *sotto voce* intimacies. 'What on earth makes you say that?'

'Thomas Hardy. He said it first. But look in your Prayer Book.'

The bridegroom waited, hang-dog, with his best man. Michael Burden was very much in love, was entering this second marriage with someone admirably suited to him, had agreed with his fiancée that nothing but a religious ceremony would do for them, yet at forty-four was a little superannuated for what Wexford called 'all this white wedding gubbins'. There were two hundred people in the church. Burden, his best man and his ushers were in morning dress. Madonna lilies and stephanotis and syringa decorated the pews, the pulpit and the chancel steps. It was the kind of thing that is properly designed for someone twenty years younger. Burden had been through it before when he *was* twenty years younger. Wexford chuckled silently, looking at the anxious face above the high white collar. And then as Dora, leafing through the marriage service, said, 'Oh, I *see*,' the organist went from voluntaries into the opening bars of the Lohengrin march and Jenny Ireland appeared at the church door on her father's arm.

123

A beautiful bride, of course. Seven years younger than Burden, blonde, gentle, low-voiced, and given to radiant smiles. Jenny's father gave her hand into Burden's and the Rector of St Peter's began:

'Dearly beloved, we are gathered together . . .'

While bride and groom were being informed that marriage was not for the satisfaction of their carnal lusts, and that they must bring up their children in a Christian manner, Wexford studied the congregation. In front of himself and Dora sat Burden's sister-in-law, Grace, whom everyone had thought he would marry after the death of his first wife. But Burden had found consolation with a red-headed woman, wild and sweet and strange, gone now God knew where, and Grace had married someone else. Two little boys now sat between Grace and that someone else, giving their parents a full-time job keeping them quiet.

Burden's mother and father were both dead. Wexford thought he recognised, from one meeting a dozen years before, an aged aunt. Beside her sat Dr Crocker and his wife, beyond them and behind were a crowd whose individual members he knew either only by sight or not at all. Sylvia, his elder daughter, was sitting on his other side, his grandsons between her and their father, and at the central aisle end of the pew, Sheila Wexford of the Royal Shakespeare Company. Wexford's actress daughter, who on her entry had commanded nudges, whispers, every gaze, sat looking with unaccustomed wistfulness at Jenny Ireland in her clouds of white and wreath of pearls.

'I, Michael George, take thee, Janina, to my wedded wife, to have and to hold from this day forward . . .'

Janina. *Janina?* Wexford had supposed her name was Jennifer. What sort of parents called a daughter Janina? Turks? Fans of Dumas? He leaned forward to get a good look at these philonomatous progenitors. They looked ordinary enough, Mr Ireland apparently exhausted by the effort of giving the bride away, Jenny's mother making use of the lace handkerchief provided for the specific purpose of crying into it those tears of joy and loss. What romantic streak had led them to dismiss Elizabeth and Susan and Anne in favour of – Janina?

'Those whom God hath joined together, let no man put

asunder. Forasmuch as Michael George and Janina have consented together in holy wedlock . . .'

Had they been as adventurous in the naming of their son? All Wexford could see of him was a broad back, a bit of profile, and now a hand. The hand was passing a large white handkerchief to his mother. Wexford found himself being suddenly yanked to his feet to sing a hymn.

'O, Perfect Love, all human thought transcending,
Lowly we kneel in prayer before Thy throne . . .'

These words had the effect of evoking from Mrs Ireland audible sobs. Her son – hadn't Burden said he was in publishing? – looked embarrassed, turning his head. A young woman, strangely dressed in black with an orange hat, edged past the publisher to put a consoling arm round his mother.

'O Lord, save Thy servant and Thy handmaid.'

'Who put their trust in Thee,' said Dora and most of the rest of the congregation.

'O Lord, send them help from Thy holy place.'

Wexford, to show team spirit, said, 'Amen,' and when everyone else said, 'And evermore defend them,' decided to keep quiet in future.

Mrs Ireland had stopped crying. Wexford's gaze drifted to his own daughters, Sheila singing lustily, Sylvia, the Women's Liberationist, with less assurance as if she doubted the ethics of lending her support to so archaic and sexist a ceremony. His grandsons were beginning to fidget.

'Almighty God, who at the beginning did create our first parents, Adam and Eve . . .'

Dear Mike, thought Wexford with a flash of sentimentality that came to him perhaps once every ten years, you'll be OK now. No more carnal lusts conflicting with a puritan conscience, no more loneliness, no more worrying about those selfish kids of yours, no more temptation-of-St-Anthony stuff. For is it not ordained as a remedy against sin, and to avoid fornication, that such persons as have not the gift of continency may marry and keep themselves undefiled?

'For after this manner in the old time the holy women who trusted in God . . .'

He was quite surprised that they were using the ancient

form. Still, the bride had promised to obey. He couldn't resist glancing at Sylvia.

'. . . being in subjection to their own husbands . . .'

Her face was a study in incredulous dismay as she mouthed at her sister 'unbelievable' and 'antique'.

'. . . Even as Sarah obeyed Abraham, calling him Lord, whose daughters ye are as long as ye do well, and are not afraid with any amazement.'

At the Olive and Dove hotel there was a reception line to greet guests, Mrs Ireland smiling, re-rouged and restored, Burden looking like someone who has had an operation and been told the prognosis is excellent, Jenny serene as a bride should be. Dry sherry and white wine on trays. No champagne. Wexford remembered that there was a younger Ireland daughter, absent with her husband in some dreadful place – Botswana? Lesotho? No doubt all the champagne funds had been expended on her. It was a buffet lunch, but a good one. Smoked salmon and duck and strawberries. Nobody, he said to himself, has ever really thought of anything better to eat than smoked salmon and duck and strawberries unless it might be caviare and grouse and syllabub. He was weighing the two menus against one another, must without knowing it have been thinking aloud, for a voice said:

'Asparagus, trout, apple pie.'

'Well, maybe,' said Wexford, 'but I do like meat. Trout's a bit insipid. You're Jenny's brother, I'm sorry I don't remember your name. How d'you do?'

'How d'you do? I know who you are. Mike told me. I'm Amyas Ireland.'

So that funny old pair hadn't had a one-off indulgence when they had named Janina. Again Wexford's thoughts seemed revealed to this intuitive person.

'Oh, I know,' said Ireland, 'but how about my other sister? She's called Cunegonde. Her husband calls her Queenie. Look, I'd like to talk to you. Could we get together a minute away from all this crush? Mike was going to help me out, but I can't ask him now, not when he's off on his honeymoon. It's about a book we're publishing.'

The girl in black and orange, Burden's nephews, Sheila

Wexford, Burden's best man and a gaggle of children, all carrying plates, passed between them at this point. It was at least a minute before Wexford could ask, 'Who's we?' and another half-minute before Amyas Ireland understood what he meant.

'Carlyon Brent,' he said, his mouth full of duck. 'I'm with Carlyon Brent.'

One of the largest and most distinguished of publishing houses. Wexford was impressed. 'You published the Vandrian, didn't you, and the de Coverley books?'

Ireland nodded. 'Mike said you were a great reader. That's good. Can I get you some more duck? No? I'm going to. I won't be a minute.' Enviously Wexford watched him shovel fat-rimmed slices of duck breast on to his plate, take a brioche, have second thoughts and take another. The man was as thin as a rail too, positively emaciated.

'I look after the crime list,' he said as he sat down again. 'As I said, Mike half-promised . . . This isn't fiction, it's fact. The Winchurch case?'

'Ah.'

'I know it's a bit of a nerve asking, but would you read a manuscript for me?'

Wexford took a cup of coffee from a passing tray. 'What for?'

'Well, in the interests of truth. Mike was going to tell me what he thought.' Wexford looked at him dubiously. He had the highest respect and the deepest affection for Inspector Burden but he was one of the last people he would have considered as a literary critic. 'To tell me what he thought,' the publisher said once again. 'You see, it's worrying me. The author has discovered some new facts and they more or less prove Mrs Winchurch's innocence.' He hesitated. 'Have you ever heard of a writer called Kenneth Gandolph?'

Wexford was saved from answering by the pounding of a gavel on the top table and the beginning of the speeches. A great many toasts had been drunk, several dozen telegrams read out, and the bride and groom departed to change their clothes before he had an opportunity to reply to Ireland's question. And he was glad of the respite, for what he knew of Gandolph, though based on hearsay, was not prepossessing.

127

'Doesn't he write crime novels?' he said when the inquiry was repeated. 'And the occasional examination of a real-life crime?'

Nodding, Ireland said, 'It's good, this script of his. We want to do it for next spring's list. It's an eighty-year-old murder, sure, but people are still fascinated by it. I think this new version could cause quite a sensation.'

'Florence Winchurch was hanged,' said Wexford, 'yet there was always some margin of doubt about her guilt. Where does Gandolph get his fresh facts from?'

'May I send you a copy of the script? You'll find all that in the introduction.'

Wexford shrugged, then smiled. 'I suppose so. You do realise I can't do more than maybe spot mistakes in forensics? I did say maybe, mind.' But his interest had already been caught. It made him say, 'Florence was married at St Peter's, you know, and she also had her wedding reception here.'

'And spent part of her honeymoon in Greece.'

'No doubt the parallels end there,' said Wexford as Burden and Jenny came back into the room.

Burden was in a grey lounge suit, she in pale blue sprigged muslin. Wexford felt an absurd impulse of tenderness towards him. It was partly caused by Jenny's hat which she would never wear again, would never have occasion to wear, would remove the minute they got into the car. But Burden was the sort of man who could never be happy with a woman who didn't have a hat as part of her 'going-away' costume. His own clothes were eminently unsuitable for flying to Crete in June. They both looked very happy and embarrassed.

Mrs Ireland seized her daughter in a crushing embrace.

'It's not for ever, Mother,' said Jenny. 'It's only for two weeks.'

'Well, in a way,' said Burden. He shook hands gravely with his own son, down from university for the weekend, and planted a kiss on his daughter's forehead. Must have been reading novels, Wexford thought, grinning to himself.

'Good luck, Mike,' he said.

The bride took his hand, put a soft cool kiss on to the corner of his mouth. Say I'm growing old but add, Jenny kissed me. He didn't say that aloud. He nodded and smiled and took his wife's arm and frowned at Sylvia's naughty boys like the patriarch he was. Burden and Jenny went out to the car which had Just Married written in lipstick on the rear window and a shoe tied on the back bumper.

There was a clicking of handbag clasps, a flurry of hands, and then a tempest of confetti broke over them.

It was an isolated house, standing some twenty yards back from the Myringham road. Plumb in the centre of the façade was a plaque bearing the date 1896. Wexford had often thought that there seemed to have been positive intent on the part of late-Victorian builders to design and erect houses that were not only ugly, complex and inconvenient, but also distinctly sinister in appearance. The Limes, though well-maintained and set in a garden as multi-coloured, cushiony and floral as a quilt, nevertheless kept this sinister quality. Khaki-coloured brick and grey slate had been the principal materials used in its construction. Without being able to define exactly how, Wexford could see that, in relation to the walls, the proportions of the sash windows were wrong. A turret grew out of each of the front corners and each of these turrets was topped by a conical roof, giving the place the look of a cross between Balmoral castle and a hotel in Kitzbuehl. The lime trees which gave it its name had been lopped so many times since their planting at the turn of the century that now they were squat and misshapen.

In the days of the Winchurches it had been called Paraleash House. But this name, of historical significance on account of its connection with the ancient manor of Paraleash, had been changed specifically as a result of the murder of Edward Winchurch. Even so, it had stood empty for ten years. Then it had found a buyer a year or so before the First World War, a man who was killed in that war. Its present owner had occupied it for half a dozen years, and in the time intervening between his purchase of it and 1918 it had been variously a nursing home, the annexe of an agricultural college and a private school. The owner was a retired brigadier. As he emerged from the front door with two Sealyhams on a lead, Wexford retreated to his car and drove home.

It was Monday evening and Burden's marriage was two

days old. Monday was the evening of Dora's pottery class, the fruits of which, bruised-looking and not invariably symmetrical, were scattered haphazardly about the room like windfalls. Hunting along the shelves for G. Hallam Saul's *When the Summer is Shed* and *The Trial of Florence Winchurch* from the Notable British Trials series, he nearly knocked over one of those rotund yet lop-sided objects. With a sigh of relief that it was unharmed, he set about refreshing his memory of the Winchurch case with the help of Miss Saul's classic.

Florence May Anstruther had been nineteen at the time of her marriage to Edward Winchurch and he forty-seven. She was a good-looking fair-haired girl, rather tall and Junoesque, the daughter of a Kingsmarkham chemist – that is, a pharmacist, for her father had kept a shop in the High Street. In 1895 this damned her as of no account in the social hierarchy, and few people would have bet much on her chances of marrying well. But she did. Winchurch was a barrister who, at this stage of his life, practised law from inclination rather than from need. His father, a Sussex landowner, had died some three years before and had left him what for the last decade of the nineteenth century was an enormous fortune, two hundred thousand pounds. Presumably, he had been attracted to Florence by her youth, her looks and her ladylike ways. She had been given the best education, including six months at a finishing school, that the chemist could afford. Winchurch's attraction for Florence was generally supposed to have been solely his money.

They were married in June 1895 at the parish church of St Peter's, Kingsmarkham, and went on a six-months honeymoon, touring Italy, Greece and the Swiss Alps. When they returned home Winchurch took a lease of Sewingbury Priory while building began on Paraleash House, and it may have been that the conical roofs on those turrets were inspired directly by what Florence had seen on her alpine travels. They moved into the lavishly furnished new house in May 1896, and Florence settled down to the life of a Victorian lady with a wealthy husband and a staff of indoor and outdoor servants. A vapid life at best, even if alleviated by a brood of children. But Florence had no children and was to have none.

Once or twice a week Edward Winchurch went up to London by the train from Kingsmarkham, as commuters had done before and have been doing ever since. Florence gave orders to her cook, arranged the flowers, paid and received calls, read novels and devoted a good many hours a day to her face, her hair and her dress. Local opinion of the couple at that time seemed to have been that they were as happy as most people, that Florence had done very well for herself and knew it, and Edward not so badly as had been predicted.

In the autumn of 1896 a young doctor of medicine bought a practice in Kingsmarkham and came to live there with his unmarried sister. Their name was Fenton. Frank Fenton was an extremely handsome man, twenty-six years old, six feet tall, with jet black hair, a Byronic eye and an arrogant lift to his chin. The sister was called Ada, and she was neither good-looking nor arrogant, being partly crippled by poliomyelitis which had left her with one leg badly twisted and paralysed.

It was ostensibly to befriend Ada Fenton that Florence first began calling at the Fentons' house in Queen Street. Florence professed great affection for Ada, took her about in her carriage and offered her the use of it whenever she had to go any distance. From this it was an obvious step to persuade Edward that Frank Fenton should become the Winchurches' doctor. Within another few months young Mrs Winchurch had become the doctor's mistress.

It was probable that Ada knew nothing, or next to nothing, about it. In the eighteen-nineties a young girl could be, and usually was, very innocent. At the trial it was stated by Florence's coachman that he would be sent to the Fentons' house several times a week to take Miss Fenton driving, while Ada's housemaid said that Mrs Winchurch would arrive on foot soon after Miss Fenton had gone out and be admitted rapidly through a french window by the doctor himself. During the winter of 1898 it seemed likely that Frank Fenton had performed an abortion on Mrs Winchurch, and for some months afterwards they met only at social gatherings and occasionally when Florence was visiting Ada. But their feelings for each other were too strong for them to bear separation and by the following summer they were again meeting at Fenton's house while Ada was out, and now also at Paraleash House on the days when Edward had departed for the law courts.

Divorce was difficult but by no means impossible or unheard-of in 1899. At the trial Frank Fenton said he had wanted Mrs Winchurch to ask her husband for a divorce. He would have married her in spite of the disastrous effect on his career. It was she, he said, who refused to consider it on the grounds that she did not think she could bear the disgrace.

In January 1900 Florence went to London for the day and, among other purchases, bought at a grocer's two cans of herring fillets marinaded in a white wine sauce. It was rare for canned food to appear in the Winchurch household, and when Florence suggested that these herring fillets should be used in the preparation of a dish called *Filets de hareng marinés à la Rosette*, the recipe for which she had been given by Ada Fenton, the cook, Mrs Eliza Holmes, protested that she could prepare it from fresh fish. Florence, however, insisted, one of the cans was used, and the dish was made and served to Florence and Edward at dinner. It was brought in by the parlourmaid, Alice Evans, as a savoury or final course to a four-course meal. Although Florence had shown so much enthusiasm about the dish, she took none of it. Edward ate a moderate amount and the rest was removed to the kitchen where it was shared between Mrs Holmes, Alice Evans and the housemaid, Violet Stedman. No one suffered any ill-effects. The date was 30 January 1900.

Five weeks later on 5 March Florence asked Mrs Holmes to make the dish again, using the remaining can, as her husband had liked it so much. This time Florence too partook of the marinaded herrings, but when the remains of it were about to be removed by Alice to the kitchen, she advised her to tell the others not to eat it as she 'thought it had a strange taste and was perhaps not quite fresh'. However, although Mrs Holmes and Alice abstained, Violet Stedman ate a larger quantity of the dish than had either Florence or Edward.

Florence, as was her habit, left Edward to drink his port alone. Within a few minutes a strangled shout was heard from the dining room and a sound as of furniture breaking. Florence and Alice Evans and Mrs Holmes went into the room and found Edward Winchurch lying on the floor, a chair with one leg wrenched from its socket tipped over beside him and an overturned glass of port on the table. Florence approached him and he went into a violent convulsion, arching his back and baring his teeth, his hands grasping the chair in apparent agony.

John Barstow, the coachman, was sent to fetch Dr Fenton. By this time Florence was complaining of stomach pains and seemed unable to stand. Fenton arrived, had Edward and Florence removed upstairs and asked Mrs Holmes what they had eaten. She showed him the empty herring fillets can, and he recognised the brand as that by which a patient of a colleague of his had recently been infected with botulism, a virulent and usually fatal form of food poisoning. Fenton immediately assumed that it was *bacillus botulinus* which had attacked the Winchurches, and such is the power of suggestion that Violet Stedman now said she felt sick and faint.

Botulism causes paralysis, difficulty in breathing and a disturbance of the vision. Florence appeared to be partly paralysed and said she had double vision. Edward's symptoms were different. He continued to have spasms, was totally relaxed between spasms, and although he had difficulty in breathing and other symptoms of botulism, the onset had been exceptionally rapid for any form of food poisoning. Fenton, however, had never seen a case of botulism, which is extremely rare, and he supposed that the symptoms would vary greatly from person to person. He gave jalap and cream of tartar as a purgative and, in the absence of any known relatives of Edward Winchurch, he sent for Florence's father, Thomas Anstruther.

If Fenton was less innocent than was supposed, he had made a mistake in sending for Anstruther, for Florence's father insisted on a second opinion, and at ten o'clock went himself to the home of that very colleague of Fenton's who had recently witnessed a known case of botulism. This was Dr Maurice Waterfield, twice Fenton's age, a popular man with a large practice in Stowerton. He looked at Edward Winchurch, at the agonised grin which overspread his features, and as Edward went into his last convulsive seizure, pronounced that he had been poisoned not by *bacillus botulinus* but by strychnine.

Edward died a few minutes afterwards. Dr Waterfield told

Fenton that there was nothing physically wrong with either Florence or Violet Stedman. The former was suffering from shock or 'neurasthenia', the latter from indigestion brought on by over-eating. The police were informed, an inquest took place, and after it Florence was immediately arrested and charged with murdering her husband by administering to him a noxious substance, to wit *strychnos nux vomica*, in a decanter of port wine.

Her trial took place in London at the Central Criminal Court. She was twenty-four years old, a beautiful woman, and was by then known to have been having a love affair with the young and handsome Dr Fenton. As such, she and her case attracted national attention. Fenton had by then lost his practice, lost all hope of succeeding with another in the British Isles, and even before the trial his name had become a by-word, scurrilous doggerel being sung about him and Florence in the music halls. But far from increasing his loyalty to Florence, this seemed to make him the more determined to dissociate himself from her. He appeared as the prosecution's principal witness, and it was his evidence which sent Florence to the gallows.

Fenton admitted his relationship with Florence but said that he had told her it must end. The only possible alternative was divorce and ultimately marriage to himself. In early January 1900 Florence had been calling on his sister Ada, and he had come in to find them looking through a book of recipes. One of the recipes called for the use of herring fillets marinaded in white wine sauce, the mention of which had caused him to tell them about a case of botulism which a patient of Dr Waterfield was believed to have contracted from eating the contents of a can of just such fillets. He had named the brand and advised his sister not to buy any of that kind. When, some seven weeks later, he was called to the dying Edward Winchurch, the cook had shown him an empty can of that very brand. In his opinion, Mrs Winchurch herself was not ill at all, was not even ill from 'nerves' but was shamming. The judge said that he was not there to give his opinion, but the warning came too late. To the jury the point had already been made.

Asked if he was aware that strychnine had therapeutic uses in small quantities, Fenton said he was but that he kept none in

134

his dispensary. In any case, his dispensary was kept locked and the cupboards inside it locked, so it would have been impossible for Florence to have entered it or to have appropriated anything while on a visit to Ada. Ada Fenton was not called as a witness. She was ill, suffering from what her doctor, Dr Waterfield, called 'brain fever'.

The prosecution's case was that, in order to inherit his fortune and marry Dr Fenton, Florence Winchurch had attempted to poison her husband with infected fish, or fish she had good reason to suppose might be infected. When this failed she saw to it that the dish was provided again, and herself added strychnine to the port decanter. It was postulated that she obtained the strychnine from her father's shop, without his knowledge, where it was kept in stock for the destruction of rats and moles. After her husband was taken ill, she herself simulated symptoms of botulism in the hope that the convulsions of strychnine poisoning would be confused with the paralysis and impeded breathing caused by the bacillus.

The defence tried to shift the blame to Frank Fenton, at least to suggest a conspiracy with Florence, but it was no use. The jury were out for only forty minutes. They pronounced her guilty, the judge sentenced her to death, and she was hanged just twenty-three days later, this being some twenty years before the institution of a Court of Appeal.

After the execution Frank and Ada Fenton emigrated to the United States and settled in New England. Fenton's reputation had gone before him. He was never again able to practise as a doctor but worked as the travelling representative of a firm of pharmaceutical manufacturers until his death in 1932. He never married. Ada, on the other hand, surprisingly enough, did. Ephraim Hurst fell in love with her in spite of her sickly constitution and withered leg. They were married in the summer of 1902 and by the spring of 1903 Ada Hurst was dead in childbirth.

By then Paraleash house had been re-named The Limes and lime trees planted to conceal its forbidding yet fascinating façade from the curious passer-by.

The parcel from Carlyon Brent arrived in the morning with a very polite covering letter from Amyas Ireland, grateful in anticipation. Wexford had never before seen a book in this embryo stage. The script, a hundred thousand words long, was bound in red, and through a window in its cover appeared the provisional title and the author's name: *Poison at Paraleash, A Reappraisal of the Winchurch Case* by Kenneth Gandolph.

'Remember all that fuss about Gandolph?' Wexford said to Dora across the coffee pot. 'About four years ago?'

'Somebody confessed a murder to him, didn't they?'

'Well, maybe. While a prison visitor, he spent some time talking to Paxton, the bank robber, in Wormwood Scrubs. Paxton died of cancer a few months later, and Gandolph then published an article in a newspaper in which he said that during the course of their conversations, Paxton had confessed to him that he was the perpetrator of the Conyngford murder in 1962. Paxton's widow protested, there was a heated correspondence, MPs wanting the libel laws extended to libelling the dead, Gandolph shouting about the power of truth. Finally, the by then retired Detective Superintendent Warren of Scotland Yard put an end to all further controversy by issuing a statement to the press. He said Paxton couldn't have killed James Conyngford because on the day of Conyngford's death in Brighton Warren's sergeant and a constable had had Paxton under constant surveillance in London. In other words, he was never out of their sight.'

'Why would Gandolph invent such a thing, Reg?' said Dora.

'Perhaps he didn't. Paxton may have spun him all sorts of tales as a way of passing a boring afternoon. Who knows? On the other hand, Gandolph does rather set himself up as the elucidator of unsolved crimes. Years ago, I believe, he did find a satisfactory and quite reasonable solution to some murder in Scotland, and maybe it went to his head. Marshall, Groves, Folliott used to be his publishers. I wonder if they've refused this one because of the Paxton business, if it was offered to them and they turned it down?'

'But Mr Ireland's people have taken it,' Dora pointed out.

'Mm-hm. But they're not falling over themselves with enthusiasm, are they? They're scared. Ireland hasn't sent me this so that I can check up on the police procedural part. What do I know about police procedure in 1900? He's sent it to me in the hope that if Gandolph's been up to his old tricks I'll spot what they are.'

The working day presented no opportunity for a look at *Poison at Paraleash*, but at eight o'clock that night Wexford opened it and read Gandolph's long introduction.

Gandolph began by saying that as a criminologist he had always been aware of the Winchurch case and of the doubt which many felt about Florence Winchurch's guilt. Therefore, when he was staying with friends in Boston, Massachusetts, some two years before and they spoke to him of an acquaintance of theirs who was the niece of one of the principals in the case, he had asked to be introduced to her. The niece was Ada Hurst's daughter, Lina, still Miss Hurst, seventy-four years old and suffering from a terminal illness.

Miss Hurst showed no particular interest in the events of March 1900. She had been brought up by her father and his second wife and had hardly known her uncle. All her mother's property had come into her possession, including the diary which Ada Fenton Hurst had kept for three years prior to Edward Winchurch's death. Lina Hurst told Gandolph she had kept the diary for sentimental reasons but that he might borrow it and after her death she would see that it passed to him.

Within weeks Lina Hurst did die and her stepbrother, who was her executor, had the diary sent to Gandolph. Gandolph had read it and had been enormously excited by certain entries because in his view they incriminated Frank Fenton and exonerated Florence Winchurch. Here Wexford turned back a few pages and noted the author's dedication: *In memory of Miss Lina Hurst, of Cambridge, Massachusetts, without whose help this reappraisal would have been impossible.*

More than this Wexford had no time to read that evening, but he returned to it on the following day. The diary, it appeared, was a five-year one. At the top of each page was the date, as it might be 1 April, and beneath that five spaces each headed 18 . . . There was room for the diarist to write perhaps forty or fifty words in each space, no more. On the 1 January page in the third heading down, the number of the year, the eight had been crossed out and a nine substituted, and so it went on for every subsequent entry until March 6, after which no more entries were made until the diarist resumed in December 1900, by which time she and her brother were in Boston.

Wexford proceeded to Gandolph's first chapters. The story he had to tell was substantially the same as Hallam Saul's, and it was not until he came to chapter five and the weeks preceding the crime that he began to concentrate on the character of Frank Fenton. Fenton, he suggested, wanted Mrs Winchurch for the money and property she would inherit on her husband's death. Far from encouraging Florence to seek a divorce, he urged her never to let her husband suspect her preference for another man. Divorce would have left Florence penniless and homeless and have ruined his career. Fenton had known that it was only by making away with Winchurch and so arranging things that the death appeared natural, that he could have money, his profession and Florence.

There was only his word for it, said Gandolph, that he had spoken to Florence of botulism and had warned her against these particular canned herrings. Of course he had never seriously expected those cans to infect Winchurch, but that the fish should be eaten by him was necessary for his strategy. On the night before Winchurch's death, after dining with his sister at Paraleash House, he had introduced strychnine into the port decanter. He had also, Gandolph suggested, contrived to bring the conversation round to a discussion of food and to fish dishes. From that it would have been a short step to get Winchurch to admit how much he had enjoyed *Filets de hareng marinés à la Rosette* and to ask Florence to have them served again on the following day. Edward, apparently would have been highly likely to take his doctor's advice, even when in health, even on such a matter as what he should eat for the fourth course of his dinner, while Edward's wife did every-thing her lover, if not her husband, told her to do.

It was no surprise to Frank Fenton to be called out on the following evening to a man whose spasms only he would recognise as symptomatic of having swallowed strychnine. The arrival of Dr Waterfield was an unlooked-for circum-stance. Once Winchurch's symptoms had been defined as arising from strychnine poisoning there was nothing left for Fenton to do but shift the blame on to his mistress. Gandolph suggested that Fenton attributed the source of the strychnine to Anstruther's chemist's shop out of revenge on Anstruther for calling in Waterfield and thus frustrating his hopes.

And what grounds had Gandolph for believing all this? Certain entries in Ada Hurst's diary. Wexford read them slowly and carefully.

For 27 February 1900, she had written, filling the entire small space: *Very cold. Leg painful again today. FW sent round the carriage and had John drive me to Pomfret. Compton says rats in the cellars and the old stables. Dined at home with F who says rats carry leptospiral jaundice, must be got rid of.* 28 February: *Drove in FW's carriage to call on old Mrs Paget. FW still here, having tea with F when I returned. I hope there is no harm in it. Dare I warn F?* 29 February: *F destroyed twenty rats with strychnine from his dispensary. What a relief!* 1 March: *Poor old Mrs Paget passed away in the night. A merciful release. Compton complained about the rats again. Warmer this evening and raining.* There was no entry for 2 March. 3 March: *Annie gave notice, she is getting married. Shall be sorry to lose her. Would not go out in carriage for fear of leaving FW too much alone with F. To bed early as leg most painful.* 4 March: *My birthday. 26 today and an old maid now, I think. FW drove over, brought me beautiful Indian shawl. She is always kind. Invited F and me to dinner tomorrow.* There was no entry for 5 March, and the last entry for nine months was the one for 6 March: *Dined last night at Paraleash House, six guests besides ourselves and the Ws. F left cigar case in the dining room, went back after seeing me home. I hope and pray there is no harm.*

Gandolph was evidently basing his case on the entries for 29 February and 6 March. In telling the court he had no strychnine in his dispensary, Fenton had lied. He had had an obvious opportunity for the introduction of strychnine into the decanter when he returned to Paraleash House in pursuit of his mislaid cigar case, and when he no doubt took care that he entered the dining room alone.

The next day Wexford re-read the chapters in which the new information was contained and he studied with concentration the section concerning the diary. But unless Gandolph were simply lying about the existence of the diary or of those two entries – things which he would hardly dare to do – there seemed no reason to differ from his inference. Florence was innocent, Frank Fenton the murderer of Edward Winchurch. But still Wexford wished Burden were there so that they might have one of their often acrimonious but always fruitful discussions. Somehow, with old Mike to argue against him and put up opposition, he felt things might have been better clarified.

And the morning brought news of Burden, if not the inspector himself, in the form of a postcard from Agios Nikolaios. The blue Aegean, a rocky escarpment, green pines. Who but Burden, as Wexford remarked to Dora, would send postcards while on his honeymoon? The post also brought a parcel from Carlyon Brent. It contained books, a selection from the publishing house's current list as a present for Wexford, and on the compliments slip accompanying them, a note from Amyas Ireland. *I shall be in Kingsmarkham with my people at the weekend. Can we meet? AI.* The books were the latest novel about Regency London by Camilla Barnet; *Put Money in Thy Purse*, the biography of Vassili Vandrian, the financier; the memoirs of Sofya Bolkinska, Bolshoi ballerina; an onmibus version of three novels of farming life by Giles de Coverley; the *Cosmos Book of Stars and Calendars*, and Vernon Trevor's short stories, *Raise me up Samuel*. Wexford wondered if he would ever have time to read them, but he enjoyed looking at them, their handsome glossy jackets, and smelling the civilised, aromatic, slightly acrid print smell of them. At ten he phoned Amyas Ireland, thanked him for the present and said he had read *Poison at Paraleash*.

'We can talk about it?'

'Sure. I'll be at home all Saturday and Sunday.'

'Let me take you and Mrs Wexford out to dinner on Saturday night,' said Ireland.

But Dora refused. She would be an embarrassment to both of them, she said, they would have their talk much better without her, and she would spend the evening at home having a shot at making a coil pot on her own. So Wexford went alone to meet Ireland in the bar of the Olive and Dove.

'I suppose,' he said, accepting a glass of Moselle, 'that we

140

can dispense with the fiction that you wanted me to read this book to check on police methods and court procedure? Not to put too fine a point on it, you were apprehensive Gandolph might have been up to his old tricks again?'

'Oh, well now, come,' said Ireland. He seemed thinner than ever. He looked about him, he looked at Wexford, made a face, wrinkling up nose and mouth. 'Well, if you must put it like that – yes.'

'There may not have been any tricks, though, may there?' Paxton couldn't have murdered James Conyngford, but that doesn't mean he didn't tell Gandolph he did murder him. Certainly the people who give Gandolph information seem to die very conveniently soon afterwards. He picks on the dying, first Paxton, then Lina Hurst. I suppose you've seen this diary?'

'Oh, yes. We shall be using prints of the two relevant pages among the illustrations.'

'No possibility of forgery?'

Ireland looked unhappy. 'Ada Hurst wrote a very stylised hand, what's called a *ronde* hand, which she had obviously taught herself. It would be easy to forge. I can't submit it to handwriting experts, can I? I'm not a policeman. I'm just a poor publisher who very much wants to publish this re-appraisal of the Winchurch case if it's genuine – and shun it like the plague if it's not.'

'I think it's genuine.' Wexford smiled at the slight lightening in Ireland's face. 'I take it that it was usual for Ada Hurst to leave blanks as she did for March 2nd and March 5th?'

Ireland nodded. 'Quite usual. Every month there'd have been half a dozen days on which she made no entries.' A waiter came up to them with two large menus. 'I'll have the *bouillabaisse* and the lamb *en croûte* and the *médaillon* potatoes and french beans.'

'Consommé and then the parma ham,' said Wexford austerely. When the waiter had gone he grinned at Ireland. 'Pity they don't do *Filets de hareng marinés à la Rosette*. It might have provided us with the authentic atmosphere.' He was silent for a moment, savouring the delicate tangy wine. 'I'm assuming you've checked that 1900 genuinely was a Leap Year?'

141

'All first years of a century are.'

Wexford thought about it. 'Yes, of course, all years divisible by four are Leap Years.'

'I must say it's a great relief to me you're so happy about it.'

'I wouldn't quite say that,' said Wexford.

They went into the dining room and were shown, at Ireland's request, to a sheltered corner table. A waiter brought a bottle of Château de Portets 1973. Wexford looked at the basket of rolls, croissants, little plump brioches, miniature wholemeal loaves, Italian sticks, swallowed his desire and refused with an abrupt shake of the head. Ireland took two croissants.

'What exactly do you mean?' he said.

'It strikes me as being odd,' said the chief inspector, 'that in the entry for February 29th Ada Hurst says that her brother destroyed twenty rats with strychnine, yet in the entry for March 1st that Compton, whom I take to be the gardener, is still complaining about the rats. Why wasn't he told how effective the strychnine had been? Hadn't he been taken into Fenton's confidence about the poisoning? Or was twenty only a very small percentage of the hordes of rats which infested the place?'

'Right. It is odd. What else?'

'I don't know why, on March 6th, she mentions Fenton's returning for the cigar case. It wasn't interesting and she was limited for space. She doesn't record the name of a single guest at the dinner party, doesn't say what any of the women wore, but she carefully notes that her brother had left his cigar case in the Paraleash House dining room and had to go back for it. Why does she?'

'Oh, surely because by now she's nervous whenever Frank is alone with Florence.'

'But he wouldn't have been alone with Florence, Winchurch would have been there.'

They discussed the script throughout the meal, and later pored over it, Ireland with his brandy, Wexford with coffee. Dora had been wise not to come. But the outcome was that the new facts were really new and sound and that Carlyon Brent could safely publish the book in the spring. Wexford got home to find Dora sitting with a wobbly looking half-finished coil

142

pot beside her and deep in the *Cosmos Book of Stars and Calendars*.

'Reg, did you know that for the Greeks the year began on Midsummer Day? And that the Chinese and Jewish calendars have twelve months in some years and thirteen in others?'

'I can't say I did.'

'We avoid that, you see, by using the Gregorian Calendar and correct the error by making every fourth year a Leap Year. You really must read this book, it's fascinating.'

But Wexford's preference was for the Vassili Vandrian and the farming trilogy, though with little time to read he hadn't completed a single one of these works by the time Burden returned on the following Monday week. Burden had a fine even tan but for his nose which had peeled.

'Have a good time?' asked Wexford with automatic politeness.

'What a question,' said the inspector, 'to ask a man who has just come back from his honeymoon. Of course I had a good time.' He cautiously scratched his nose. 'What have you been up to?'

'Seeing something of your brother-in-law. He got me to read a manuscript.'

'Ha!' said Burden. 'I know what that was. He said something about it but he knew Gandolph'd get short shrift from me. A devious liar if ever there was one. It beats me what sort of satisfaction a man can get out of the kind of fame that comes from foisting on the public stories he *knows* aren't true. All that about Paxton was a pack of lies, and I've no doubt he bases this new version of the Winchurch case on another pack of lies. He's not interested in the truth. He's only interested in being known as the great criminologist and the man who shows the police up for fools.'

'Come on, Mike, that's a bit sweeping. I told Ireland I thought it would be OK to go ahead and publish.'

Burden's face wore an expression that was almost a caricature of sophisticated scathing knowingness. 'Well, of course, I haven't seen it, I can't say. I'm basing my objection to Gandolph on the Paxton affair. Paxton never confessed to any murder and Gandolph knows it.'

'You can't say that for sure.'

Burden sat down. He tapped his fist lightly on the corner of the desk. 'I *can* say. I knew Paxton, I knew him well.'

'I didn't know that.'

'No, it was years back, before I came here. In Eastbourne, it was, when Paxton was with the Garfield gang. In the force down there we knew it was useless ever trying to get Paxton to talk. He *never* talked. I don't mean he just didn't give away any info, I mean he didn't answer when you spoke to him. Various times we tried to interrogate him he just maintained this total silence. A mate of his told me he'd made it a rule not to talk to policemen or social workers or lawyers or any what you might call establishment people, and he never had. He talked to his wife and his kids and his mates all right. But I remember once he was in the dock at Lewes Assizes and the judge addressed him. He just didn't answer – he wouldn't – and the judge, it was old Clydesdale, sent him down for contempt. So don't tell me Paxton made any sort of confession to Kenneth Gandolph, not *Paxton*.'

The effect of this was to reawaken all Wexford's former doubts. He trusted Burden, he had a high opinion of his opinion. He began to wish he had advised Ireland to have tests made to determine the age of the ink used in the 29 February and 6 March entries, or to have the writing examined by a handwriting expert. Yet if Ada Hurst had had a stylised hand self-taught in adulthood ... What good were handwriting experts anyway? Not much, in his experience. And of course Ireland couldn't suggest to Gandolph that the ink should be tested without offending the man to such an extent that he would refuse publication of *Poison at Paraleash* to Carlyon Brent. But Wexford was suddenly certain that those entries were false and that Gandolph had forged them. Very subtly and cunningly he had forged them, having judged that the addition to the diary of just thirty-four words would alter the whole balance of the Winchurch case and shift the culpability from Florence to her lover.

Thirty-four words. Wexford had made a copy of the diary entries and now he looked at them again. 29 February: *F destroyed twenty rats with strychnine from his dispensary. What a relief!* 6 March: *F left cigar case in the dining room, went back after seeing me home. I hope and pray there is no harm*. There were no anachronisms – men certainly used cigar cases in 1900 – no divergence from Ada's usual style. The word 'twenty' was written in letters instead of two figures. The writer, on 6 March, had written not about that day but about the day before. Did that amount to anything? Wexford thought not, though he pondered on it for most of the day.

That evening he was well into the last chapter of *Put Money in Thy Purse* when the phone rang. It was Jenny Burden. Would he and Dora come to dinner on Saturday? Her parents would be there and her brother.

Wexford said Dora was out at her pottery class, but yes, they would love to, and had she had a nice time in Crete?

'How sweet of you to ask,' said the bride. 'No one else has. Thank you, we had a lovely time.'

He had meant it when he said they would love to, but still he didn't feel very happy about meeting Amyas Ireland again. He had a notion that once the book was published some as yet unimagined Warren or Burden would turn up and denounce it, deride it, laugh at the glaring giveaway he and Ireland couldn't see. When he saw Ireland again he ought to say, don't do it, don't take the risk, publish and be damned can have another meaning than the popular one. But how to give such a warning with no sound reason for giving it, with nothing but one of those vague feelings, this time of foreboding, which had so assisted him yet run him into so much trouble in the past? No, there was nothing he could do. He sighed, finished his chapter and moved on to the farmer's fictionalised memoirs.

Afterwards Wexford was in the habit of saying that he got more reading done during that week than he had in years. Perhaps it had been a way of escape from fretful thought. But certainly he had passed a freakishly slack week, getting home most nights by six. He even read Miss Camilla Barnet's *The Golden Reticule*, and by Friday night there was nothing left but the *Cosmos Book of Stars and Calendars*.

It was a large party, Mr and Mrs Ireland and their son, Burden's daughter Pat, Grace and her husband and, of course, the Burdens themselves. Jenny's face glowed with happiness and Aegean sunshine. She welcomed the Wexfords with kisses and brought them drinks served in their own wedding present to her.

The meeting with Amyas Ireland wasn't the embarrassment Wexford had feared it would be – had feared, that is, up till a few minutes before he and Dora had left home. And now he knew that he couldn't contain himself till after dinner, till the morning, or perhaps worse than that – a phone call on Monday morning. He asked his hostess if she would think him very rude if he spoke to her brother alone for five minutes.

She laughed. 'Not rude at all. I think you must have got the world's most wonderful idea for a crime novel and Ammy's going to publish it. But I don't know where to put you unless it's the kitchen. And you,' she said to her brother, 'are not to eat anything, mind.'

'I couldn't wait,' Wexford said as they found themselves stowed away into the kitchen where every surface was necessarily loaded with the constituents of dinner for ten people. 'I only found out this evening at the last minute before we were due to come out.'

'It's something about the Winchurch book?'

Wexford said eagerly, 'It's not too late, is it? I was worried I might be too late.'

'Good God, no. We hadn't planned to start printing before the autumn.' Ireland, who had seemed about to disobey his sister and help himself to a macaroon from a silver dish, suddenly lost his appetite. 'This is serious?'

'Wait till you hear. I was waiting for my wife to finish dressing.' He grinned. 'You should make it a rule to read your own books, you know. That's what I was doing, reading one of those books you sent me and that's where I found it. You won't be able to publish *Poison at Paraleash*.' The smile went and he looked almost fierce. 'I've no hesitation in saying Kenneth Gandolph is a forger and a cheat and you'd be advised to have nothing to do with him in future.'

Ireland's eyes narrowed. 'Better know it now than later. What did he do and how do you know?'

From his jacket pocket Wexford took the copy he had made of the diary entries. 'I can't prove that the last entry, the one for March 6th that says, *F left cigar case in the dining room, went back after seeing me home*, I can't prove that's forged, I only think it is. What I know for certain is a forgery is the entry for February 29th.'

146

'Isn't that the one about strychnine?'

'*F destroyed twenty rats with strychnine from his dispensary. What a relief!*'

'How do you know it's forged?'

'Because the day itself didn't occur,' said Wexford. 'In 1900 there was no February 29th, it wasn't a Leap Year.'

'Oh, yes, it was. We've been through all that before.' Ireland sounded both relieved and impatient. 'All years divisible by four are Leap Years. All century years are divisible by four and 1900 was a century year. 1897 was the year she began the diary, following 1896 which was a Leap Year. Needless to say, there was no February 29th in 1897, 1898 or 1899 so there must have been one in 1900.'

'It wasn't a Leap Year,' said Wexford. 'Didn't I tell you I found this out through that book of yours, the *Cosmos Book of Stars and Calendars*? There's a lot of useful information in there, and one of the bits of information is about how Pope Gregory composed a new civil calendar to correct the errors of the Julian Calendar. One of his rulings was that every fourth year should be a Leap Year except in certain cases . . .'

Ireland interrupted him. 'I don't believe it!' he said in the voice of someone who knows he believes every word.

Wexford shrugged. He went on, 'Century years were not to be Leap Years unless they were divisible not by four but by four hundred. Therefore, 1600 would have been a Leap Year if the Gregorian Calendar had by then been adopted, and 2000 will be a Leap Year, but 1800 was not and 1900 was not. So in 1900 there was no February 29th and Ada Hurst left the space on that page blank for the very good reason that the day following February 28th was March 1st. Unluckily for him, Gandolph, like you and me and most people, knew nothing of this as otherwise he would surely have inserted his strychnine entry into the blank space of March 2nd and his forgery might never have been discovered.'

Ireland slowly shook his head at man's ingenuity and perhaps his chicanery. 'I'm very grateful to you. We should have looked fools, shouldn't we?'

'I'm glad Florence wasn't hanged in error,' Wexford said as they went back to join the others. 'Her marriage didn't begin with dearly beloved, but if she was afraid at the end it can't have been with any amazement.'

147

AN UNKINDNESS
OF RAVENS

To Sonia and Jeff

1

She was a neighbour. She was an acquaintance of Dora's and they spoke if they met in the street. Only this time there had been more to it than passing the time of day.

'I said I'd tell you,' Dora said. 'I said I'd mention it. She had that strange look she sometimes has and, to tell you the truth, I was awfully embarrassed.'

'What did she say?' Wexford asked.

' "Rod's missing" or "Rod's disappeared" – something like that. And then she asked me if I'd tell you. Because of who you are, of course.'

Detective chief inspectors have better things to do with their time than waste it listening to the complaints of women whose husbands have run off with other women. Wexford hadn't been in the house five minutes before he decided that was what had happened. But she was a neighbour. She lived in the next street to his. He ought to be glad really, he thought, that it hadn't the makings of a case for him to investigate.

His house and this one had been built at the same time, in the mid-1930s when Kingsmarkham was growing out of being a village. And structurally they were much the same house, three bedrooms, two receptions, kitchen, bathroom and downstairs loo. But this was a home, comfortable and full of lovingly collected things and this was – what? A shelter to keep the rain off, a place where people could eat, sleep and watch television. Joy Williams took him into the front room that she called the lounge. There were no books. The carpet was a square surrounded by mustard yellow vinyl tiles and the furniture a three-piece suite covered in grainy mustard-coloured synthetic leather. The 1935 fireplace, which in his house had been replaced by one of York stone, accommodated an electric fire of complicated design, part Regency, part medieval, and with a portcullis effect at the front. Above it hung a mirror framed in segments of green and yellow frosted glass, a fine specimen of Art Deco if you liked that sort of thing. The only picture was a composition in coloured silver paper of two cats playing with a ball of wool.

'She's rather a colourless person,' Dora had said. 'Doesn't seem interested in anything and always seems depressed. I don't suppose living with Rodney Williams for twenty years has done much for her.'

Joy. Dora had said rather apologetically that it was a misnomer. She was a woman whose whole self had turned grey, not just her hair. Her features had once been good, were probably still good, only her awful complexion, lined, pitted, pinkish-grey, rough and worn, masked them. Apparently she was forty-five but she looked ten years more. Up until his arrival she had been watching television and the set was still on, though with the sound turned off. It was the biggest set Wexford had ever seen, at any rate in a domestic setting. He guessed she spent a fair proportion of her time watching it and perhaps felt uneasy when the screen was blank.

There was no seat in the room that did not face it. He sat on the end of the sofa at an angle, turning his back. Joy Williams's eyes flickered over the flashing figures of skaters taking part in some contest. She sat on the extreme edge of her chair.

'Did your wife tell you what I . . . ?'

'She said something.' He interrupted to save her the embarrassment he could see already mottling her nose and cheeks with dull red. 'Something about your husband being missing.'

Joy Williams laughed. It was a laugh he was to hear often and get to know, a harsh cackle. There was no humour in it, no gaiety, no amusement. She laughed to hide emotion or because she knew no other way of showing it. The hands in her lap stretched and clenched. She wore a very wide, heavily chased platinum or white-gold wedding ring with an even more ornate platinum or white-gold engagement ring containing amid the pits and pyramids a minuscule diamond.

'He went on a trip to Ipswich and I haven't seen him since.'

'Your husband's a sales representative, I think Dora said.'

'With Sevensmith Harding,' she said. 'The paint people.'

She need not have added that. Sevensmith Harding were probably the biggest suppliers to builders' merchants and home decorating retail stores in the south of England. Sevenstar matt and silk emulsion coated a million walls, he thought, between Dover and Land's End. He and Dora had just had their second bedroom done up in it, and if he wasn't much mistaken the paintwork in Mrs Williams's own hall was the newest shade in Sevenshine non-drip high gloss, Wholewheat.

'He covers Suffolk for them.' She began pushing the rings up and down.

'It was last Thursday he went – well, yesterday week. It's the twenty-third now, that must have been the fifteenth. He said he was going to Ipswich to stop the night and start first thing in the morning.'

'What time did he leave?'

'It was evening time. About six. He'd been home all afternoon.'

It was at this point that Wexford had his thought about the other woman. It would be a good three and a half hour run from Kingsmarkham to Ipswich even via the Dartford Tunnel. A salesman who was legitimately going to drive to Suffolk and could have started at four instead of six would surely have done so.

'Where did he stay in Ipswich? At a hotel presumably?'

'A motel. Outside Ipswich, I think.'

She spoke listlessly, as if she knew little about her husband's work and took no interest in it. The door opened and a girl came in. She stopped on the threshold and said, 'Oh, sorry.'

'Sara, what time did Dad go when he left?'

'Around six.'

Mrs Williams nodded. She said, 'This is my daughter Sara,' pronouncing the name so that the first syllable rhymed with 'car'.

'I believe you've a son too?'

'Kevin. He's twenty. He's away at university.'

The girl stood with her arms over the back of the yellow

plastic armchair no one was sitting in, her eyes fixed on her mother in a more or less neutral way, though one that tended towards the hostile rather than the friendly. She was very slender, fair, with the face of a Renaissance painter's model, small-featured with a high forehead and a secretive look. Her hair was exceptionally long, reaching almost to her waist, and with the rippling appearance hair has which is usually done in plaits. She wore jeans and a tee-shirt with a design on it of a raven and the letters ARRIA superimposed over it.

She picked up a photograph in a chrome frame off the only table in the room, a bamboo affair with a glass top almost hidden by the sofa back. Passing it to Wexford, she stuck her thumb at the head of the man sitting on a beach with a teenage boy and a girl who was herself five years before. The man was big, tall, but out of condition and running to fat around his middle. He had a huge domed forehead. His features, perhaps because they were dominated by this bare dome, looked insignificant and crowded together, the mouth a lipless slit stretched into a smile for the camera.

Wexford handed it back to her. She replaced it on the table, let her eyes linger on her mother for a moment, a curious, faintly contemptuous look, and walked out of the room. He heard her feet going upstairs.

'When did you expect your husband to come back?'

'The Sunday night, he said. I didn't think much about it when he didn't. I thought he'd stayed another night and he'd be back Monday, but he wasn't and he never phoned.'

'You didn't phone the motel yourself?'

She looked at him as if he had proposed to her some gargantuan and complex task quite beyond her capacity, writing a fifty-thousand-word thesis perhaps or devising a computer programme.

'I wouldn't do that. I mean, it's a long-distance call. I haven't got the number anyway.'

'Did you do anything?'

She laughed the dry humourless cackle. 'What could I do? Kevin was home for the weekend but he went back to Keele on the Sunday.' She spoke as if action in such a matter could only be taken by a member of the male sex. 'I knew I'd have been let know if he'd had an accident. He's got his name on him, his bank card and his cheque book and ever so many things with his name on.'

'You didn't phone Sevensmith Harding, for instance?'

'What good would that have done? He never went in there for weeks on end.'

'And you haven't heard a word from him since? For – let's see – eight days, you've had no indication where he might be?'

'That's right. Well, five days. I expected him to be gone the first three.'

He would have to ask it. After all, she had called him in. As a neighbour to confide in certainly, but primarily as a policeman. Nothing he had heard so far made him feel even a preliminary inquiry into Rodney Williams's whereabouts was called for. Looking at Mrs Williams, the house, the daughter, the set-up, he could only wonder with an unkindness he would never openly have expressed even to Dora why the man had stayed so long. He had run off with another woman, or run off *to* another woman, and only cowardice was holding him back from writing the requisite letter or making the obligatory phone call.

'Forgive me, but is it possible your husband could be –' he sought for a word and came out with a mealy-mouthed one he despised '– friendly with some other woman? Could he have been seeing another woman?'

She gave him a long, cold, unshocked look. Whatever she might say, Wexford could tell his suggestion had already crossed her mind and done more than cross her mind. There was something in that look which told him she was the sort of woman who made a point, a principle almost, of avoiding admitting anything unpleasant. Push it away, suppress it, get out of the habit of thinking, don't wonder or think or speculate, for that will make you unhappy. Don't think, don't wonder, turn on the telly and in mindless apathy stare at the screen until it's time for bed and the doctor's little Mogadon that comes on a permanent prescription you pick up at reception.

Of course, he might be doing her an injustice. All this was only in his imagination. 'It's just a possibility,' he said. 'I'm sorry I had to suggest it.'

'I don't know what he does when he's away days and nights

157

on end, do I? All our married life he's been away selling as much as he's been home. I don't know what floozies he's had and I wouldn't ask.'

The old-fashioned word suited the room and Mrs Williams's grey, Crimplene-clad, scurfy respectability. For the first time he noticed the thick sprinkling of dandruff, like a fall of flour, on the shoulders of her blouse. He had given her a solution which to most women would be the least acceptable, but she, he thought, was relieved. Did she suspect her husband of having been up to something *illegal* so that something *immoral* would be seen as a happier alternative?

You suspect everyone and everything, he told himself. You policeman!

'Do you think we ought to do anything?'

'If you mean by that should you report him as a missing person and the police take steps to find him, no, certainly not. The chances are you'll have word from him in the next few days. If you don't, I think your best course will be to see a solicitor or go to your Citizen's Advice Bureau. But don't do that before you've been on to Sevensmith Harding. The likelihood is you'll find him through them.'

She didn't thank him for coming. He hadn't even been home yet, he had called on her on his way home, but she didn't thank him or apologise for taking up his time. He looked back and saw her still standing on the doorstep holding the door, a very thin angular woman in fawn blouse and unfashionably cut dark green trousers with bell bottoms and a high waist. Her front garden was the only one in Alverbury Road with no spring bulbs out, not a narcissus to relieve the bit of lawn and the dark yew hedge.

It was a cloudy evening, bright as noonday still, April-cool. This little honeycomb of streets was like an orchard in springtime, puffs and clouds of pink and white blossom all over the gardens and drifts of petals already lying on the pavements. A great weeping cherry, pink as ice cream, had taken over his front lawn.

His wife was sitting in an armchair placed in much the same position at the same angle to the fireplace as the chair Joy Williams had sat in, in a room of the same size and proportions to the one he had just left. But there the resemblance ended. A

158

log fire was burning. It had been a cold winter and the spring was cold and protracted, frosts threatening nightly to nip that blossom. Dora was making patchwork, a bedspread in blues and reds, all shades of blues and reds in a multiplicity of patterns, and the finished part covered the long red velvet skirt of the housedress she had taken to wearing in the evenings because of the cold. Her hair was dark and plentiful. Wexford had told her she must be a gipsy to have hair still not grey at nearly sixty.

'Did you see Mike today?'

She meant Detective Inspector Burden. Wexford said no, he had been at court in Myringham.

'Jenny came in to tell me she'd had the results of the amniocentesis. The baby's all right, and it's a girl.'

'What's amniocentesis?'

'They stick something through the abdominal wall into the womb and take out a sample of amniotic fluid. The fluid's got cells from the foetus in it and they grow them like a sort of culture, I think. Anyway, the cells divide and they can tell if Down's Syndrome is present and spina bifida too. And of course they can tell the sex by whether the chromosomes come out XY or XX.'

'What a lot you know! Where did you pick up all that?'

'Jenny told me.' She got up and transferred the patchwork to the seat of the chair. 'They can't do an amniocentesis till the sixteenth week of pregnancy and there's always a risk of losing the baby.'

He followed her out into the kitchen. He was more than usually aware this evening of the warmth and light in his own house. It occurred to him that Joy Williams had offered him nothing, not even a cup of tea. Dora had opened the oven door and was looking critically at a steak and kidney pie that was almost ready on the top shelf.

'Do you want a drink?'

'Why not?' she said. 'Celebrate Jenny and Mike's healthy baby.'

'I'm surprised she took any risk,' he said when she had her sherry and he his Bell's and three parts water. 'She's very set on having this child. They've been trying for years.'

'She's forty-one, Reg. At that age there's also a much higher

159

risk of having a mongoloid baby. Anyway, all's well.'

'Don't you want to hear about your Mrs Williams?'

'Poor Joy,' said Dora. 'She was rather pretty when I first knew her. Of course, that was eighteen years ago. I suppose he's gone off with some girl, has he?'

'If you knew that I don't know what you roped me in for.'

Dora laughed. She had a rich throaty giggle. Immediately she said she knew she shouldn't laugh. 'He's such an awful man. You never met him, did you? There's something so secretive and deceitful about him. I used to think no one could be so obviously like that if they really had something to hide.'

'But now you're not so sure.'

'I'll tell you something I was scared to tell you at the time. I thought you might do something violent.'

'Sure,' he said. 'I've always been so wild and free with my fists. What are you on about?'

'He made a pass at Sylvia.'

She said it defiantly. Standing there in the long red dress, holding the sherry glass, her eyes suddenly wide and wary, she looked astonishingly young.

'So?' His elder daughter was thirty, married twelve years, and the mother of two tall sons. 'She's an attractive woman. I daresay men do make passes at her and no doubt she can take care of herself.'

Dora gave him a sidelong look. 'I said I was scared to tell you. She was fifteen at the time.'

The violent feelings she had predicted were there to hand. After all those years. His fifteen-year-old daughter! He resisted the temptation to bellow. Nor did he stamp. He took a sip of his drink and spoke coolly. 'And, like a good little girl, she came to mother and told her?'

Dora said flippantly, 'Sweet of her, wasn't it? I was touched. I think the truth was, Reg, she was scared stiff.'

'Did you do anything?'

'Oh, yes. I went to him and told him what her father was. He didn't know. I don't think there was ever much communication between him and Joy. Anyway, it worked. He made himself very scarce and Sylvia didn't baby-sit for them again. I didn't tell Joy but I think she knew and was disillusioned. Anyway, she didn't adore him any more the way she used to.'

'I was adored once,' Wexford quoted.

'And still are, darling. You know we all adore you. You haven't forfeited our respect, running after little girls. Can I have some more sherry?'

'You'll have to get it yourself,' said Wexford, opening the oven and taking out the pie. 'All this drinking and gossiping. I want my dinner.'

2

The firm of Sevensmith Harding had been founded in 1875 by Septimus Sevensmith who called himself a colourman. He sold artists' materials in a shop in the High Street in Myringham. Paints for exterior- and interior-decorating use came along later. After the First World War in fact, when Septimus's granddaughter married a Major John Harding who left a leg behind him at Passchendaele.

The first great house-building boom of the eighties and nineties was past and gone, the next due to begin. Major Harding got in on it. He began manufacturing in huge quantities the browns and greens dear to the hearts of builders creating the terraces and semidetacheds which were growing in branches and tentacles out of South London. And towards the end of the decade he brought out a daring shade of cream.

Already the company had been renamed Sevensmith Harding. It kept its offices in Myringham High Street, though the factory behind was soon to be moved to sites on distant industrial complexes. With the disappearance of its retail trade the shop as such also disappeared.

The world's paint industry enjoyed a steady growth during the 1960s and early 1970s. It is estimated that close on five hundred companies make paint in the United Kingdom but the bulk of the sales volume is handled by a few large manufacturers. Four of these manufacturers dominate the British Isles and one of them is Sevensmith Harding.

Today their paints, Sevenstar vinyl silk and Sevenstar vinyl matt emulsion, Sevenshine gloss and satin finish, are manufactured at Harlow in Essex, and their wallpapers, borders and coordinating tiles at Crawley in Sussex. The head offices in Myringham, in the centre of the High Street opposite the Old Flag Hotel, have more a look of solicitors' chambers or the establishment of a very refined antique dealer than the seat of paint makers. Indeed, there is scarcely anything to show that they are paint makers. The bow windows with their occasional pane of distorted glass that flank the front door contain, instead of cans of paint and display stands of delighted housewives with brushes in their hands, a *famille noire* vase of dried grasses on one side and a Hepplewhite chair on the other. But over the door, Georgian in style and of polished mahogany, are royal armorial bearings and the legend: 'By appointment to Her Majesty Queen Elizabeth the Queen Mother, Colourists and Makers of Fine Pigments'.

The company chairman, Jeremy Harding-Grey, divided his time between his house in Monte Carlo and his house in Nassau, and the managing director, George Delahaye, though he lived in Sussex, was seldom seen in the vicinity of Myringham. But the deputy managing director was a humbler person and altogether more on the level of ordinary men. Wexford knew him. They had met at the home of Sylvia's father-in-law, an architect, and since then the Gardners had once been guests at a drinks party at the Wexfords' and the Wexfords guests at the Gardners'. But for all that Wexford would not have considered himself on the kind of terms with Miles Gardner to warrant dropping in at Sevensmith Harding when he found himself in Myringham at lunchtime to ask Miles out for a drink and a sandwich.

A fortnight had passed since his talk to Joy Williams and he had virtually forgotten about it. He had dismissed it from his mind before he went to bed that same night. And if he had thought about it at all since then it had only been to tell himself that by now Mrs Williams and her solicitor would be settling things to her satisfaction or that Williams had returned home, having found like many a man before him that domesticity is the better part of economics.

But even if Williams were still missing there was nothing to justify Wexford's making inquiries about him at Sevensmith Harding. Let Joy Williams do that. He wouldn't be missing as far as his employers were concerned. No matter how complex a man's love life he still has to go to work and earn his bread. Williams earned it on too humble a level though, Wexford reflected, for it to be likely Miles Gardner had ever heard of him.

He and Burden had both been at Myringham Crown Court, witnesses in two separate cases, and the court had adjourned for lunch. Burden would have to go back to watch his case – a rather ticklish matter concerning the receiving of stolen goods – through to the bitter end, but Wexford's day, at least as far as appearing in court went, was over. As they walked towards the hotel Burden was silent and morose. He had been like this since they came out of court. If it had been anyone else Wexford would have supposed his mood due to the dressing down, indeed the scathing tongue-lashing, meted out to him by the alleged receiver's counsel. But Burden was impervious to such things. He had taken that sort of stick too many times to care. This was something else, something closer to home, Wexford thought. And now he came to think of it, this whatever it was, had been growing on Burden for days now, weeks even, a morose surly misery that didn't seem to affect his work but militated badly against his relations with other people.

He looked the same as ever. There was no sign of anxiety or care in his appearance. He was thin but he had always been thin. Wexford didn't know if it was a new suit he was wearing or last year's cleaned and the trousers nightly pressed in the electric press his wife had given him for Christmas. ('Like those things you get in swish hotels,' Burden had said proudly.) It was a happy marriage, Burden's second, as happy as his first. But almost any marriage Burden made would be happy, he had a gift for marriage. He was uxorious without making himself ridiculous. There couldn't be anything in his marriage that was bugging him. His wife was pregnant with a longed-for child – longed for by her at any rate. Burden had a grown-up son and daughter by his first marriage. Wexford considered an idea that came to him and then dismissed it as absurd and out of character. Burden was the last man to dread the coming child just because he was now in his mid-forties. That he would take in his stride.

'What's wrong, Mike?' he asked as the silence became oppressive.

'Nothing.'

The classic answer. One of the cases in which a statement means the precise opposite of what it says, as when a man in doubt says he's absolutely certain.

Wexford didn't press it. He walked along, looking about him at the old market town which had changed so much since he had first known it. A huge shopping complex had been built, and since then an arts centre, incorporating theatre, cinema and concert hall. The university term was three weeks old and the place was thronged with blue-jeaned students. But up at this end of the town, where preservation orders proliferated and buildings were listed, things were much the same. Things were even rather better since the local authority had woken up to the fact that Myringham was beautiful and worth conserving and had therefore cleaned and tidied and painted and planted.

He looked into the bow windows of Sevensmith Harding, first at the Hepplewhite chair, then at the vase. Beyond the dried grasses he could see a young girl receptionist talking on the phone. Wexford and Burden crossed the road and went into the Old Flag.

Wexford had been there once or twice before. It was not a place ever to be crowded in the middle of the day. The busy lunch trade went to the cheaper brighter pubs and the wine bars. In the smaller of the lounge bars where food was being served several vacant tables remained. Wexford was making for one of them when he caught sight of Miles Gardner sitting alone.

'Won't you join me?'

'You look as if you're waiting for someone,' Wexford said.

'Any congenial company that offers itself.' He had a gracious warm manner of speaking that was in no way affected. Wexford recalled that this was what he had always liked about him. 'They do a nice prawn salad,' Miles Gardner said. 'And if you can get here before one they'll send up to the butcher for a fillet steak.'

'What happens at one?'

'The butcher closes. He opens at two and then the pub closes. There's Myringham for you.'

Wexford laughed. Burden didn't laugh but sat wearing the sort of stiff polite expression that indicates to even the most insensitive that one would be happier – or less miserable – on one's own. Wexford made up his mind to ignore him. Gardner seemed delighted with their company and, having bought a round of drinks, began to talk in the easy rather elegant way he had about the new house he had just moved into which Sylvia's father-in-law had designed. It was a valuable gift, Wexford thought, to be able to talk to people, one whom you had only just met and the other a mere acquaintance, as if they were old friends whom you conversed with regularly.

Gardner was a small, undistinguished-looking man. His style was in his voice and manner. He had a much taller wife and two or three rather noisy daughters, Wexford remembered. From the new house and the time it had taken to get itself built, Gardner had moved on to talk of work, lack of work and unemployment, eliciting mild sparks of interest from Burden, at least to the extent of extracting monosyllables from him. Sevensmith Harding had battled against laying off workers at their Harlow factory and the battle had been won – allowing for the few redundancies which Gardner insisted had been acceptable to the men and women concerned.

'Yes,' said Burden. 'I daresay.'

Always reactionary, he had until a few years back threatened to become unbearably right wing and Blimpish, but Jenny had reversed the tide. Burden was far more of a moderate now. He did not, as he once would have, launch into a tirade against unemployment benefits, Social Security payments and general idleness. Or perhaps it was only this depression of his that made him forbear.

'The whole attitude towards work and employment and keeping one's job is changing, I find,' Gardner said. He began talking about what he thought gave rise to these new patterns and made it interesting enough. Or so Wexford thought. Burden, eating prawn salad rather too rapidly, kept looking at his watch. He had to be back in court by two. Wexford thought he would be glad to be rid of him for a while.

'Isn't what you're really saying,' he said to Gardner, 'that, in spite of the threat of unemployment and the inadequacy of unemployment benefits, men seem to have lost that craven fear of losing their jobs they had in the thirties?'

'Yes, and to a great extent, at any rate among the middle

166

class, lost the feeling they used to have that they had to stick in a hated job or career for the rest of their lives just because it's the one they went into at twenty.'

'Then what's brought this change about?'

'I don't know. I've thought about it but the answers I come up with don't satisfy me. But I can tell you that just as the fear has gone, and the respect for employers because they were employers, so has pride in one's job and the old loyalty to a company. My marketing manager is a case in point. Time was when you could say a man in that position would also be a responsible person, someone you could trust not to let you down. He'd have been proud – and yes, I'll say it, *grateful* – to be where he was and he'd have had a real feeling for the firm's welfare too.'

'What's he done?' said Burden. 'Decided to change his career in midstream?'

It was said acidulously but Gardner gave no sign of having noticed the edge to Burden's voice and replied pleasantly.

'Not so far as I know. He simply walked out on me. He's on three months' notice, or supposed to be. First we get a phone call from his wife saying he's sick, then not a word until a letter of resignation comes, very clipped and curt, and a note at the bottom –' Gardner looked almost apologetic – 'quite an *insolent* sort of note, saying he'd be in touch with our accounts department about his superannuation.'

'Had he been with you long?'

'All his working life, I gather, and five years as marketing manager.'

'At least you'll have no difficulty in finding a replacement in these hard times.'

'It's going to be a case of promotion for one of our best reps. That's always been Sevensmith Harding's policy. Promote rather than take in from outside. Only usually, of course, we're given a bit more time.'

Burden got up and said he must get back to court. He shook hands with Gardner and had the grace to mutter something about its having been good to meet him.

'Let me get you another beer,' said Wexford when Burden had left and been described (very much to his surprise) by Gardner as a 'nice chap'.

167

'Thanks so much. I don't suppose they'll sling us out before two-thirty, will they?'

The beer came, one of the 130 varieties of 'real ale' the Old Flag claimed to stock.

'It's not by any chance my neighbour Rodney Williams you'll be promoting, is it?'

Gardner looked up at him, surprised.

'Rod Williams?'

'Yes. He lives in the next street to me.'

Gardner said in a patient tone, 'Rod Williams is our former marketing manager, the one I was telling you resigned.'

'Williams?'

'Yes, I thought I explained. Perhaps I didn't say the name.'

'Somebody,' said Wexford, 'is getting hold of the wrong end of the stick here.'

'It's you,' said Gardner, smiling.

'Yes, I expect it is. Somebody has given me the wrong end of the stick. Am I to take it then that Williams wasn't one of your reps and didn't cover the Suffolk area for you?'

'He was once. He did once. Up till five years ago. We kept to our customary policy and when our former marketing manager took early retirement due to a heart condition, we promoted Rod Williams.'

'As far as his wife knows he's still a rep. That is, he's still spending half his time selling in Suffolk.'

Gardner's eyebrows went up. He gave a twisted grin. 'His private life is no affair of mine.'

'Nor mine.'

It was Gardner who changed the subject. He began talking about his eldest daughter who was getting married in the late summer. Wexford finally parted from him with a promise to be in touch, to 'get Dora to give Pam a ring and fix something up'. Driving home to Kingsmarkham, he thought for a while about Rodney Williams. There had been no room in his own marriage for alibis. He wondered what it would be like to have a marriage in which a permanent, on-going, five-year-long alibi existed as an integral part of life. Unthinkable. Unimaginable. He stopped trying to identify and thought about it with detachment.

What had happened perhaps was that five years ago

168

Williams had met a girl with whom he wanted to spend time without ending his marriage. Keeping his promotion a secret from his wife would have been a way of achieving this. Probably the girl lived in Myringham. While Joy Williams believed her husband was staying at a motel outside Ipswich he was in reality seeing this other girl, no doubt sharing her home and doing his nine-to-five job at Sevensmith Harding in Myringham.

It was the sort of situation some men chuckle over. Wexford wasn't one of them. And there was another aspect, one that few men would find funny. If Williams hadn't told his wife about his promotion he presumably also hadn't told her about the considerable increase in salary that went with it. Still, there was no mystery. Williams had written to the company. Joy had phoned with excuses. Back in Alverbury Road Williams was still perhaps managing to shore up a few fragments of deceit against discovery.

It was nine at night and he was still in his office, going through for the tenth time the statements he had taken for the preparation of a case of fraud against one Francis Wingrave Adams. He still doubted whether they would constitute a watertight case and so did counsel representing the police, though both knew he was guilty. On the final stroke of nine – St Peter's clock had a dead sound too, like St Mary Woolnoth's – he put the papers away and set off to walk homewards.

Lately he had taken to walking to and from work. Dr Crocker recommended it, pointing out that it was less than half a mile.

'Hardly worth it then,' Wexford said.

'A couple of miles' walk a day could make a difference of ten years' life to you.'

'Does that mean that if I walked six miles a day I could prolong my life by thirty years?'

The doctor had refused to answer that one. Wexford, though feigning to scoff, had gone some way towards obeying him. Sometimes his walk took him down Tabard Road past Burden's bungalow, sometimes along Alverbury Road where the Williams family lived, and there was an occasional longer route along one of the meadow footpaths. Tonight he intended

169

to drop in and see Burden for a final assessment of the Adams business.

But now he began to feel that there was very little left to say about this man who had conned an elderly woman out of £20,000. He wouldn't talk about that. Instead he would try to get out of Burden what was happening in his life to account for his depression.

The Burdens still lived in the bungalow Burden had moved into soon after his first marriage where the garden after twenty years and more still had an immature look and the ivy which tried to climb up the house had been ruthlessly cut back with secateurs. Only the front door changed. It had been all colours – Burden was a relentless decorator – but Wexford had liked the rose pink best. Now it was a dark greenish blue – Sevenshine Oriental Peacock probably. Above the door, now dusk had come, the porch light was on, a lantern of leaded lights in the shape of a star.

Jenny came to let him in. She was halfway through her pregnancy now and 'showing', as the old wives say. Instead of a smock she wore a full-sleeved, square-necked dress with a high waist, like the one the woman is wearing in Vermeer's *The Letter*. She had let her golden-brown hair grow and it hung to her shoulders. But, for all that, Wexford was shocked by her appearance. She looked drawn and dispirited.

Burden, having years ago agreed to stop calling Wexford 'sir', now called him nothing at all. But Jenny called him Reg. She said, 'Mike's in the living room, Reg,' and added in a way quite unlike her usual self, 'I was just going to bed.'

He felt constrained to say he was sorry for calling so late, though it was only twenty past nine. She shrugged and said it didn't matter and she said it in a way which seemed to imply that nothing much mattered. He followed her into the room where Burden was.

On the middle cushion of the three-seater settee Burden sat reading *Police Review*. Wexford would have expected Jenny to have been sitting beside him but she hadn't been. Beside a chair at the far end of the room lay her book face downwards and a piece of white knitting that had a look about it of the knitter's having no enthusiasm for her task. In a glass vase on the windowsill dying wallflowers stood in three inches of water.

'Have a drink,' said Burden, laying down his magazine. 'There's beer. There is beer, isn't there, Jenny?'

'I don't know. I never touch the stuff.'

Burden said nothing. He left the room, went out to the kitchen and came back with two cans on a tray. Burden's first wife would have said, and Jenny once would have said, that they must have glasses to drink the beer out of. Jenny, languidly sitting down, picking up book and knitting but looking at neither, said, 'You can drink it out of the can, can't you?'

Wexford began to feel awkward. Some sort of powerful angry tension that existed between these two seemed to hang in the air like smoke, to get in his throat and give him a choky feeling. He snapped the top off his beer can. Jenny was holding the knitting needles in one clenched hand and staring at the wall. He had no intention of talking about Francis Wingrave Adams in her presence. On other occasions like this he and Burden would have gone into one of the other rooms. Burden sat on the settee, wearing his half-frown. He opened the beer can with a sharp, rough movement and a spurt of froth shot out across the carpet.

Three months before Wexford had seen Jenny soothing and practical when her husband had dropped, not a spoonful of beer, but a bowl of strawberry mousse on the paler newer carpet of the dining room. She had laughed and told him to leave the clearing up to her. Now she gave a cry of real distress and jumped up out of her chair.

'All right,' said Burden. 'All right. I'll do it. It's nothing anyway. I'll get a cloth.'

She burst into tears. She put one hand up to her face and ran out of the room. Burden followed her. That is, Wexford thought he had followed her but he came back almost immediately holding a floorcloth.

'Sorry about that,' he said on his hands and knees. 'Of course it's not the beer. It's just any little thing sets her off. Take no notice.' He lifted an angry face. 'I've made up my mind I'm simply not going to take any notice any more.'

'But if she's not well, Mike . . .'

'She is perfectly well.' Burden got up and dropped the cloth onto the tiled kerb of the fireplace. 'She is having an ideal

171

trouble-free pregnancy. Why, she wasn't even sick. When I remember what Jean went through . . .' Wexford could hardly believe his ears. For a husband – and such a husband as Burden – to make that comparison! Burden seemed to realise what he had said and a dull flush crept across his face. 'No, honestly, she's perfectly fit, she says so herself. It's simply neurotic behaviour.'

Wexford had sometimes thought in the past that if every instance diagnosed by Burden as neurotic were taken as sound, almost the entire population would have to be tranquillised, not to say confined in mental hospitals. He said, 'The amniocentesis was all right, wasn't it? They didn't tell her something to worry her?'

Burden hesitated. 'Well, as a matter of fact they did.' He gave an ugly humourless laugh. 'That's just what they did. They told her something to worry her. You've hit the nail bang on the head. It doesn't worry *me* and I'm the child's father. But it worries her like hell and I'm the one who has to bear the brunt of it.' He sat down and said very loudly, almost shouting, 'I don't want to talk about it anyway. I've said too much already and I've no intention of saying any more. I feel like learning a formula to explain my wife's conduct and repeating it to people when they first come to the door.'

Wexford said quietly, 'You can do it extempore for it is nothing but roaring.'

He got a glare for that. 'I came to talk about Adams. Or are you too preoccupied with your domestic fracas to care?'

'I told you, I'm simply not going to take any notice any more,' said Burden, and they talked about Adams not very profitably for the next half-hour.

Dora was in bed when he got home, sitting up reading. While he undressed he told her about the Burdens.

'They're too old to have babies,' was all she would say.

'Flying in the face of nature, would you call it?'

'You'd be surprised, my lad. I might. And by the way, Rod Williams hasn't come back. I saw Joy and she hasn't heard a word.'

'But I had the distinct impression she'd phoned Sevensmith Harding,' Wexford began.

'You told her to, you mean. You told her to phone them and find out if they could tell her anything and she's going to.'

That wasn't what he had meant. He got into bed, sure now that he hadn't heard the last of the Williams affair.

3

For more than a couple of weeks now he had been keeping his eye on the dark blue Ford Granada parked outside his house in Arnold Road, Myringham. It had appeared there for the first time soon after Easter. Graham Gee couldn't see it from his front windows nor, because of the tall lonicera hedge, from his front garden. He saw it when he drove his own car out of the entrance to his garage each morning and when he drove it in each afternoon at 5.30.

At first (he told the police) he thought it might have something to do with the boy opposite, the teenage son of the people in the bungalow. But it was too respectable a car for that. Well, it was *then*. Dismissing that theory, he wondered if it belonged to some commuter who was using Arnold Road as a station car park. Arnold Road wasn't very near Myringham Southern Region Station, it was a good quarter of a mile away, but it was probably the nearest street to the station not clogged on both sides with commuters' cars.

Graham Gee began to see the presence of the Ford Granada outside his gate as the thin end of the wedge. Soon there would be a hundred rail travellers' cars parked in Arnold Road. He was not a commuter himself but a partner in a firm of accountants in Pomfret.

Arnold Road was known as a 'nice neighbourhood'. The houses were detached, standing in large gardens. There weren't any rough elements, there wasn't any trouble, except perhaps for the theft of dahlias from someone's front garden the previous autumn. So Graham Gee was surprised to notice one morning that the Granada's hub caps had gone. Perhaps they had always been gone though, he couldn't remember. Still, he knew the wheels hadn't always been gone. The car hadn't always been propped up on bricks. Dirty now, streaked with rain, it sat on its brick supports, looking as if it might after all be the property of the teenager opposite.

He still did nothing about it, though he knew by now that it was there all the time. It wasn't driven there in the morning and taken away in the evening. For a week now it hadn't been drivable. It took the smashing of a rear window to get him to do something.

The rear window had been broken, the front doors opened and the interior stripped. The radio had been removed, the headrests taken off the front seats, and something dug out of the dashboard, a clock perhaps. Though the boot was open, the thieves hadn't thought it worth their while to help themselves to the snow shovel inside. Gee phoned the police.

There was no need for the police to go through the procedure of tracing the driver through the Vehicle Licensing Department in Swansea, for the vehicle registration document was in the Granada's glove compartment along with a road map of southern England, a ballpoint pen and a pair of sunglasses.

Vehicle registration documents have named on them the 'keeper' of the vehicle, not its owner, a fact which was also of assistance to the police. This one listed the keeper as Rodney John Williams of 31 Alverbury Road, Kingsmarkham.

Why had Williams dumped the car in Arnold Road when Sevensmith Harding's own car park was less than a quarter of a mile away behind the company's High Street offices? That car park was never locked. It had no gates, only an opening in the fence and on the fence a notice requesting 'unauthorised personnel' not to park there.

'I don't understand it,' Miles Gardner said. 'Frankly, we've been wondering what to do about recovering the car but we don't know where Williams is. He didn't mention the car in his letter of resignation. Apparently, wherever he was when he first left, he's no longer with his wife, otherwise we would have tackled her. He's disappeared into thin air. It's a bit much really, isn't it? I gather the car's in a state, not much more than a shell?'

'The engine's still there,' said Wexford.

Gardner made a face. They were in his rather gloomy though luxurious office, a room not so much panelled as lined with oak, the decor dating from those between-wars days when hardwood was plentiful. None of your Sevenstar matt emulsion here, Wexford thought to himself.

There were more framed photographs than in the average elderly couple's living room. On Gardner's desk, placed to catch his eye every time he looked up, was a big one of tall Mrs Gardner and her three girls, all affectionate nestling and entwined arms. The walls were reserved for various groups and gatherings of men at company functions or on sporting occasions. One was of a cricket match with a tall gangling man going in to bat. Rodney Williams. The high forehead, slight concavity of features that would do doubt show more clearly in profile, the thin mouth stretched in a grin, were unmistakable.

Gardner looked at it dolefully.

'He was a lot younger then,' he said. 'The company had a crack team in those days.' He made as if to take the photograph down, angered no doubt by the sight of the permanently grinning Williams, but seemed to change his mind. 'The whole thing's extraordinary. He was very keen on cars, you know, one of those car men. You don't think anything's happened to him, do you?'

The euphemism that always signified death . . .

'If you mean some sort of accident, I don't know but I don't think so. It's more what has he been up to, isn't it?'

Gardner looked mystified.

'It looks to me as if he may have been up to something he shouldn't have been, he's been on the fiddle. Either he decided he'd made enough out of it and was going to call it a day or else something happened to make him think discovery was imminent. Now, the most likely place for him to have been cooking the books is here. Do you have any thoughts on that one?'

'He wouldn't have had the opportunity. He never went near any books, so to speak. Do you want me to have our chief accountant up? I mean, as far as I can see, any fiddle he was up to would have to be an expenses fiddle and Ken Risby would be the man to tell you about that.'

176

Gardner made a call on the internal phone. While they waited for Risby Wexford said, 'There is nothing small, portable but of considerable value he could have stolen? No cheque coming into his hands he could have falsified? No forgery he could have perpetrated?'

Gardner looked simply bewildered. 'I don't think so. I'm sure not. I mean, I should know by now. Good God, the man's been gone over three weeks.' He jumped up. 'Here's Ken now. He'll tell us.'

But Risby was not able to tell them much. He was a thin, fair man in his thirties, with a nervous manner, and he seemed as shocked by Wexford's suggestion as Gardner had been. You'd think the pair of them lived in a world where fraud had never been heard of, Wexford thought impatiently, and every businessman was a sea-green incorruptible.

'He was a mite heavy on his expenses sometimes but that's all, that's positively all. He never had the handling of the firm's money. What makes you think he's done something like that?'

'You think about it. Look at it for yourself. For five years the man's been lying to his wife about his position with his firm. What salary was he getting, by the way?'

'Twenty-five thousand,' said Gardner rather grudgingly.

More than Wexford had expected, £5000 more. 'And lying about that too. You can bet on it she thinks he was getting less than half of that. One day he tells her he's going to Ipswich, a place he doubtless hasn't set foot in for five years, and off he goes, dumps his company car in the street, and disappears. Apart from getting the lady he's in cahoots with to phone here and say he's ill and apart from writing his resignation he's never heard from again. And you ask me why I think he's been up to something? Tell me about the man. If he's not a man who'd steal or forge, is there some other disgraceful thing he might have done?'

They looked at him. Having no imagination, they didn't know and couldn't hazard a guess. Wexford had plenty of imagination and very little knowledge of marketing.

'For instance, he couldn't have been selling his paint of yours at prices over the odds and pocketing the difference? Something like that?'

Gardner, who had looked as if he would never smile again, burst out laughing.

'He never actually *sold* anything, Reg. It doesn't work like that. He never handled money. He never handled money in any shape or form.'

'You make him sound like royalty,' said Wexford. 'Anyway, will you, Mr Risby, have a good look at your books for me, please? Do a supplementary audit or whatever.'

'Really not necessary, I assure you, not necessary at all. I'd go into court at this moment and swear there's not a squeak of a discrepancy in my books.'

'I hope you'll never have to go into court on this matter, but don't count on it.' Risby's eyes opened wide at that one. 'And do as I ask and check the books, will you? And now,' Wexford said to Gardner, 'I'd like to see that letter of resignation Williams wrote to you.'

Gardner called his secretary in to find it. Wexford noticed he called her Susan, and what was less expected, she called him Miles. The letter was typed and by someone not accustomed to frequent use of a typewriter.

Dear Mr Gardner,
This is to give you notice of my resignation from Sevensmith Harding from today. I am afraid it is rather sudden but is due to circumstances beyond my control. I shall not be returning to the office and would prefer you not to attempt to get in touch with me.

> Yours sincerely,
> Rodney J. Williams

PS. I will contact the Accounts Dept. about my superannuation refund in due course.

Wexford said, 'Everyone in this office calls each other by their Christian names but Rodney Williams called you Mr Gardner? Is that right?'

'No, of course not. He called me Miles.'

'He doesn't in the letter.'

'I took that to be because he thought the occasion demanded something more formal.'

'It's a possibility. Don't you find it odd when a man on three months' notice gives you one day's? Wouldn't you have expected a more detailed explanation for common courtesy's sake than "circumstances beyond my control"?'

'Are you suggesting someone else might have written that letter?'

Wexford didn't answer directly. 'I'll take it with me if I may. Maybe have some experts look at that signature. Can you let me have a specimen of his signature? One we *know* is his?'

Nine separate sets of fingerprints had been found on and in the car. These would presumably include the prints of whoever had vandalised it. The others would be Williams's, Joy's, Sara's, Kevin's. Early days yet to ask these people to let him check their own prints against those in the car. A lot of hairs, fair and grey, had been on the upholstery. No blood, of course, nothing dramatic. There was one odd thing, though. On the floor of the boot, along with the shovel, were some crumbs of plaster the lab had identified as either Tetrion or Sevensmith Harding's Stopgap.

It took a few more days to get a verdict on the letter.

A manual portable machine, the Remington 315, had been used to type it. There was a chip out of the apex of the capital A on this machine, a similar flaw in the ascender of the lower-case t and a smudging of the head of the comma. As to the signature, it wasn't Williams's. The handwriting expert was far more categorical than such people are usually willing to be. He was almost scathing in his incredulity that anyone could for a moment have believed that the signature was made by Williams.

When Joy had told Dora of her intention to phone Sevensmith Harding she had followed this up with a request to 'send' Wexford round to her house once more. This time Dora had said in quite a sharp way that her husband wasn't a private detective and Wexford, of course, hadn't gone. But Williams's disappearance had stopped being a private matter. At any rate, he thought, he wouldn't be unwelcome at 31 Alverbury Road. The answer to a prayer, in fact. He walked round there in the evening, at about eight.

This time the girl Sara let him in. She spoke not a word but closed the front door after him, opened the living-room door, left him and went back upstairs.

Joy Williams was watching television. The programme was one of those contests in which teams of people go through

179

ridiculous or humiliating ordeals. Men in dress suits and top hats were trying to walk a tightrope over what looked like a lake of mashed potato. Just before the door was opened he had heard her laughing. She didn't turn the set off, only the sound. He thought she looked anything but pleased to see him. Her expression had very quickly become sullen.

Yes, she admitted, they had a joint bank account. Rod was away so much they had had to. Wexford asked her if he might see some recent bank statements.

She hunched herself, arms wrapping her thin body, right hand on left shoulder, left hand with the ugly showy rings on right. It was a habitual gesture with her which a psychiatrist might have said began as a way of protecting herself from assault. She had the green trousers on and a knitted jumper, its shoulders sprinkled with fallen hairs and dandruff.

'How often does your bank send you statements?'

'It's been once a month lately.' Her eyes strayed to the silent but tumultuous screen. A contestant had fallen into the mashed potato. 'They made a mistake over something and Rod complained, so they started sending statements once a month.'

Dr Crocker had told Wexford of a recent visit to one of his patients, a woman ill with bronchitis. The television had been on in her bedroom, all her six children sitting there watching it. When he tried to examine her she had protested angrily at his request that the set be turned off.

'I pull the plug out now without a by-your-leave,' said the doctor. 'If the TV's on or their video I don't ask any more, I pull out the plug.'

Wexford would have liked to do that. He would have done it if he had had just a fraction more evidence for disquiet over Rodney Williams. It was curious that Joy, who had come close to pestering Dora for his attention, was now making it plain she didn't want him there.

'Will you show me the statements?'

She turned her head reluctantly. 'OK, if you want.' He had put his request very politely as if she would be doing him a favour and she responded as if she was.

It didn't take long to find the statements. She wasn't going to miss more of her programme than she had to. As he began to

180

look at the statements she leaned across and summoned a little sound out of the television, so that shrieks, exclamations and commentary were just audible. He wondered what could possibly distract her, what real event or shock, and then he knew. The phone bell. Somewhere, elsewhere in the house, the phone began to ring.

She jumped up. 'That'll be my son. My son always phones me on Thursday nights.'

Wexford returned to the monthly bank statements. Each one showed the sum of £500 paid into the account more or less at the beginning of the month. A salary cheque apparently. Several objections to that one. Williams's salary had been £25,000 a year and there was no way £500 a month, even after all possible deductions, could amount to as much as that. Secondly, the sum would vary, not be a set round figure. Thirdly, it would be paid in on the same day of the month, give or take a day each way, not sometimes on the first and sometimes on the eighth.

It was evident what had been going on. Williams had another account somewhere into which his salary was paid. From that account he transferred £500 a month into the account he had jointly with his wife. If this was so, and it must be, it was going to be useless asking Joy, as he had intended, if her husband had drawn on their joint account since his disappearance.

Sevensmith Harding would make no bones about telling him where his other account was. The problem would be the intransigent bank manager refusing to disclose any inform- ation about a client's account. He looked at the April statement again. Five hundred pounds had been paid in on 2 April. No May statement had yet been sent to Mrs Williams as May was only half over.

She came back into the room, looking brighter and younger, her face more animated than he had ever seen it. She had been talking to her son, her favourite.

'I'd like you to give your bank a ring,' he said, 'and ask them if the usual five hundred was paid into the account at the beginning of the month. Will you do that?'

She nodded. He asked her to tell him about the last afternoon and evening Williams had spent at home. Rod had mowed the lawn in the afternoon, she said, and then he'd taken her shopping to the Tesco discount. She couldn't drive.

'We came back and had a cup of tea. Rod had a sandwich. He didn't want more than that. He said he'd get something on his way to Ipswich. Then he went upstairs and packed a bag and left. He'd be back on Sunday, he said.' She gave one of her dull laughs. 'And that was the last of him. After twenty-two years.'

'What did you do for the rest of the evening?'

'Me?'

'Yes, what did you do? Did you stay at home? Go out? Did anyone come here?'

'I went over to my sister's. She lives in Pomfret. I went on the bus. I had something to eat and then I went to my sister's.'

'And Sara?'

'She was here. Up there.' Joy Williams pointed to the ceiling. 'Studying for her A-levels, I suppose.' She made it sound an unworthy, even slightly disgraceful thing for her daughter to have been doing.

There was something wrong with this description of how the evening had been passed, something incongruous, only Wexford couldn't put his finger on what.

'I'd like to talk to Sara,' he said.

'Do as you like.'

She twisted round in her chair and looked fully at him, the television for the moment forgotten.

'She'll be in her bedroom but you can go up. She won't object.' The awful laugh came. 'Rather the reverse if I know her.'

182

4

So young Sara, who looked like one of Botticelli's girls, a Quattrocento virgin, had been caught in bed with a boy friend. Or not in bed, most probably. On the yellow plastic settee or in the back of a car. It was difficult with daughters. You knew what your enlightened principles were but things looked different when it was *your* daughter. Still, that hardly justified Joy's snide insinuation. Wexford, going upstairs, decided that as well as disliking what he knew of Williams, he didn't care for Mrs Williams either. Not that it mattered whether he liked them or not. It made no difference. Perhaps the woman did have some justification. She was going through a bad time; she, who was surely in the process of losing her man, would feel bitter towards a daughter gaining one. And the discovery of Sara and the boy might have been made very recently.

He knew which bedroom it was because music was coming from behind the door. Rock music of some kind, soft with a monotonous drumbeat. She must have heard his feet on the stairs by now. He had taken care to make a bit of noise, not difficult on the linoleum covered with thin haircord. He knocked on the door.

She didn't say, 'Come in!' She opened it herself. Wexford had often noted reactions to a knock at the door. They offered indications of character and motivation. The woman, for example, who calls out 'Come in!' is more open, relaxed and easy-going than she who opens the door herself. The latter will be cagey and reserved. In the thirty seconds or so before she opens the door, what has she put away in a drawer or hidden under a magazine?

He could see that Sara had created the room herself. What attractiveness it had had nothing to do with the furniture, carpet and curtains provided by her parents. It was the smallest bedroom. Wexford had had an extension built on to his house when the girls were little but this house remained as it had originally been. There would be a large front bedroom for the husband and wife, a slightly smaller back bedroom – in this case for the son – and a tiny boxroom no more than nine feet by seven for the daughter. She had put posters all over the walls, one of a red horse galloping in the snow from the Yugoslav Naive school of painting, another of a thin naked black man playing a guitar. Between them hung a tennis racket, a corn dolly and a montage of Tarot cards. Perhaps the most striking poster was the one that faced the door. A harpy-like creature with the head and breasts of a woman and the body, wings and claws of a raven, clutched at an unfurling ribbon on which was painted the name – acronym? – ARRIA. Wexford remembered the tee-shirt Sara had been wearing when first they met. The raven woman had a face like Britannia or maybe Boadicea, one of those noble, handsome, courageous, fanatical faces, that made you feel like locking up the knives and reaching for the Valium.

Bookshelves that looked as if put up by Sara herself held a paperback *Life of Freud*, Phyllis Grosskurth's *Havelock Ellis*, Fromm, Laing, Freud on the *Wolf Man* and *Leonardo*, Erin Pizzey and Jeff Shapiro on incest and child abuse, but not a single work of fiction. With her tiny radio providing background music, she had been sitting at a dressing table that doubled as a desk, swotting for an exam. It was evidently chemistry. The textbook lay open at a page of formulae.

'We're trying to find your father, Sara. I wouldn't exactly say he's disappeared but he's making himself very hard to find.'

She had fixed him with her grave contained look. He noticed her skin, creamy and smooth like velvet, with a gold dusting of freckles on her small nose. When she opened the door to him she had been holding a green felt-tipped pen in her hand. On the back of the other hand she had drawn a green snake. Teenagers had always drawn on their hands, they had done so when he was in his teens and when his daughters were in their teens, but now some sort of specific fashion for it had sprung up. To have black and red and green drawings on your hands and arms and body was the 'in' thing. Sara had drawn with her green pen a spotted snake, not curled round itself but stretched out and slightly undulant, its forked tongue extended.

'Have you any thoughts about where he might be?'

She shook her head. She put the cap on the pen and laid it down.

'Would you like to tell me about the last time you were with your father? Were you here when he left?'

She hesitated, then gave a nod. 'It was the second day of term after the Easter holidays. I was late home because I went to the library. They'd got a book in for me, a new book I'd put my name down for and they'd sent me a card to say it was in.' She lifted two books off the stack and handed him one from underneath. She was out to impress and the book was a learned work: Stern's *Principles of Human Genetics*. He didn't take much notice of that but he did look at the date stamp in the back. 'I rang the library to renew it,' she said defensively. 'I couldn't read it in three weeks. It's very difficult.' She smiled at last and became at once a beauty. 'I'm not saying it's too difficult for me but genetics is an abstruse subject. I've got my A-levels and they have to take priority.'

'You're interested in this sort of thing?'

'I've been offered a place in medical school, St Biddulph's.' Crocker had trained there, Wexford recalled. 'I shall get it, of course, but in theory it depends on my A-level results.' Her tone was such as to show she was in no real doubt that these would meet the standard. 'I have to get at least three Bs but an A and two Bs would be better.'

She must be a bright girl. A year or two back statistics had been published showing an excess of medical students and that at this rate there would be a surplus of forty thousand doctors by the end of the century. Medical schools were being instructed to raise their standards and cut their intake. So if Sara Williams had been offered a place at the highly prestigious St Biddulph's . . .

'Your mother and father must be proud of you.'

The sweeping glance she gave him told him he had said something stupid or at least wide of the mark.

185

'I can see you don't know my parents.'

'They'd prefer something else for you?'

'I could be a shorthand typist, couldn't I? I could be a nurse, I'd get paid while I was being those things, wouldn't I?' Her voice was full of scorn and anger. 'I can't be stopped, though. I'll get a grant anyway. I don't know what I'd have done in olden times.'

By 'olden times' he supposed she meant the days of his own youth when your parents paid for your education or you borrowed the money or worked your way. Things were different now. A father couldn't put his foot down with the same effect. He could only persuade or dissuade.

'The last time you saw your father,' he reminded her.

Her anger had died. She was practical again, crisply reciting facts. But there was something derisive in the way she spoke of her father, as if he were a joke to her – or an organism under a microscope.

'I came in and he was just leaving. I heard him talking to Mum about the route he was going to take. The A26 for Tonbridge, then the Dartford Tunnel on to the M25 and the M25 to the A12 which would take him to Ipswich.'

'Why was he telling her the route? Would she be interested? I mean, wasn't it the route he normally took?'

'I said you didn't know my father. I'd say for a start he wouldn't be much concerned about the other person's *interest*. Dad talks a lot about cars and driving, roads, that sort of thing. I'm not interested but he talks to me about it. The car's a person to him, a woman, and she's got a Christian name. He calls her Greta. Greta, the Granada, you see.'

'So your father left and your mother went to Pomfret and you stayed here on your own studying?'

Was he imagining that hesitation, that brief wary flare in her eyes?

'That's right. I don't go out in the evenings at the moment. I haven't time.' She smiled again, this time with great artificiality. 'I heard they'd found his car.'

'In the process of being dismembered for its wheels and its radio.'

'Cannibalised,' she said, and she laughed the way her mother did. 'Poor old Greta.'

186

Could he have a look round the rest of the house? Notably through Williams's papers and clothes? Joy put up no objection. The television clack-clacked through the floor and the pop music thumped and droned through the wall. In the book of rules of human behaviour he kept in his head one of the first laws was the one about who got which bedroom. The British middle class mostly lived in three-bedroomed houses, one big bedroom, one slightly smaller, one little. In a family of parents, son and daughter, the daughter invariably got the second bedroom and the son the tiny one, irrespective of seniority. It was one aspect of life (the women's movement might have said if they'd noticed it) in which the female had the advantage over the male. Presumably it came about because girls from the first were conditioned into being more at home, more centred on home things and being confined within walls. In which case the women's movement wouldn't like it so much. But it was the girl in this household who had the smallest bedroom, even though her brother was now away most of the time. Of course, it might be that she had chosen this arrangement, but somehow he didn't think so.

He opened the door of the second bedroom and looked inside. There was a newish pine bedroom suite, two bright Afghan rugs, a fringed bedcover that was recognisably one of Marks and Spencer's designs. It looked as if someone with not much taste or money had done her best to make a 'nice' room of it and the sole personal touch its occupant had contributed was to hang a map of the world on the wall opposite the bed.

The main bedroom was like his own in size and proportions. The walls were even painted in the same colour as his own, Sevenstar emulsion Orange Blossom. There the resemblance ended. The Williamses slept in twin beds, each narrower than the standard three feet, he thought. He could tell hers was the one nearest the window by the nightdress case on it, quilted peach satin in the shape of a scallop shell. The rest of the furniture consisted of a wardrobe, dressing table, dressing-table stool, chest of drawers and two bedside tables all in some dark reddish wood with a matt finish and with rather bright gold chrome handles. There was also a built-in cupboard.

Wexford looked first in the drawer of the bedside cabinet between Williams's bed and the door. He found a box that had once held cufflinks but was now empty, a comb, a tube of antiseptic skin cream, an unused toothbrush, a packet of tissues, a tube of throat pastilles, two safety pins, several plastic collar stiffeners, a half-full bottle of nasal drops and an empty pill bottle labelled 'Mandaret. One to be taken twice daily. Rodney Williams'.

In the cupboard part of the cabinet were two paperback novels of espionage, an unused writing pad, a current British passport in the name of Mr R. J. Williams, a clean handkerchief initialled 'R' and two electric shavers.

The wardrobe contained Joy's clothes, a collection that had an unwashed, uncleaned smell about it with a whiff of camphor and some kind of disinfectant. Rodney Williams's clothes were in the cupboard. An overcoat, a sheepskin jacket, a plastic mac, two hip-length showerproof jackets, a shabby sports jacket and a new one, four suits, two pairs of slacks. All the clothes were good, all of much better quality than Joy's. Not a large wardrobe, Wexford thought, looking into the linings of coats and feeling in pockets. In the side compartments were underwear, pyjamas, on the floor three pairs of shoes and a pair of sandals. Whatever Rodney Williams had spent his surplus money on it wasn't clothes. Unless he had taken more with him than Joy or Sara knew. Maybe he had secreted a couple of bulging suitcases in Greta's boot during the course of the day.

The dining room, you could see, they hardly ever used. A light-coloured polished table stood in the dead centre of it with four light-coloured wooden chairs with moquette seats around it. A sideboard with an empty Capo da Monte bowl on it nearly filled one wall and opposite this was a mahogany roll-top desk, perhaps a hand-down from a parent and certainly the nicest piece of furniture in the house. French windows, at which hung curtains of mustard-coloured rep – a favourite shade with Joy Williams – gave onto the back garden, a quarter acre of grass surrounded by close-board fencing and relieved by two small apple trees on which the blossom glimmered palely in the dusk. It didn't look as if the grass, several inches long now, had been mown since Williams did it five weeks before.

The desk wasn't locked. Wexford rolled back the top. There

wasn't much inside. Writing paper, not the headed kind, envelopes, a bottle of ink in a cardboard box from which it had never been removed and never would be, a box of drawing pins, a glass jar of gum, a roll of Scotch tape. In one of the drawers was nothing but old Christmas cards, in the other a receipted electricity bill, a pocket calculator and a broken ballpoint pen.

If Williams had meant to go away for good wouldn't he have taken his passport?

He looked through the pigeonholes but found no cheque books, used or in use. Joy probably kept hers in her handbag. He went back to her. She was still watching television and now the programme was the everlasting serial *Runway* in which his daughter Sheila played the stewardess heroine. Had, in fact, played her for the last time the previous week. But this was a secret known to no one but her own family as yet. No newspaper had so far got hold of the story that a major air disaster would in the autumn end the career of Stewardess Charlotte Riley for ever.

Joy Williams didn't know it. If she knew Sheila was his daughter – and surely she must – she gave no sign. He had the curious experience of standing beside her while they both watched his daughter attempting to placate an ill-tempered passenger. Then he did what Crocker recommended – or nearly so. If he didn't go so far as to pull out the plug he did switch off the set. She blinked at him.

'Does your husband possess a typewriter, Mrs Williams?'

'A typewriter? No.'

'Is he still taking Mandaret?'

She nodded, looking at the blank screen as if she expected it spontaneously and without benefit of electricity to spring into cinematic life.

'It's a form of methyldopa, isn't it? A drug for high blood pressure?'

'He's had blood pressure for two or three years.'

'I found an empty Mandaret container in his bedside cupboard. I suppose he took a supply with him?'

'He wouldn't forget them. He didn't like to miss a day on them. He always took one when he got up and one with his tea.'

189

'I take it he had a bag with him? A suitcase? Something to put his clothes in?'

Again she simply nodded.

'What was he dressed in?'

'Pardon?'

'What clothes was he wearing when he left here to drive to Ipswich?'

It was plain she couldn't remember. She looked blank – and she looked bored. Wexford understood in that moment that she didn't love Rodney Williams, hadn't perhaps loved him for years. His presence or absence as a life companion were matters of indifference to her but his financial support and the status he gave her were not. Or were her feelings more subtle and diffuse than that? Of course they were. Feelings always are. There is never a simple clear analysis of a woman's reaction to her husband or his to her.

He pressed the point he had made.

'Sort of fawn trousers,' she said, screwing up her face with the effort of it. 'Cavalry twill, they're called. A dark blue pullover. Is his raincoat upstairs?'

'A plastic mac?'

'No, he's got a good raincoat. It's nearly new. He must have taken that. I expect he had a jacket in his bag too. He's got a brown suede one.'

'Did he like a wet or dry shave?'

'Pardon?'

'Did he use a razor with shaving cream and water?'

'Oh, yes. He couldn't get on with those electrics. He'd tried but he couldn't get on with them.'

And that accounted for the Remington and the Phillips upstairs. She was staring miserably at the blank, grey, shiny screen. Wexford felt it was cruel to deprive her of her solace, like keeping a dumb hungry dog from its plate of Kennomeat. He asked her for her sister's name and address and then he switched the television on again. She looked at him as if she thought him completely mad but she said nothing and her eyes were compelled back to the screen and to Sheila, dressing now in a hotel bedroom for an evening out with the Boeing 747 captain in Hong Kong.

Wexford walked home, thinking about Williams and

money. What had he done with all that money? Even after tax and other deductions, after the stingy allotment to his household of £500 a month, he would have been left with at least £12,000 a year. He'd had a company car. It didn't go on cars. The passport, which was seven years old, showed a single visit to Majorca. It didn't go on foreign holidays. Of course, he had to keep his son Kevin at Keele and pay for his keep. He wouldn't get much of a grant on his salary . . .

And then, suddenly, Wexford understood what had been bugging him for the past hour. It had been a Thursday evening when Williams had left. Kevin Williams always phoned home on Thursday evenings. And that Thursday was certainly the first since he had returned to university after the Easter vacation. Yet his mother, who plainly adored him, who waited excitedly for his call and spoke proudly of his devotion to duty in regularly phoning at that time, had gone out on that particular Thursday evening and for no more pressing or life-enhancing appointment than a visit to her sister.

If she had visited her sister.

And how about his clothes? Was she lying when she said he had taken only a jacket and a raincoat with him? Or didn't she know? Somehow he couldn't imagine Williams leaving his car in Arnold Road and then humping huge bulging suitcases the quarter of a mile to Myringham station. Why go to Myringham anyway when, if he wanted to catch a train to London, Kingsmarkham station was eight miles nearer?

The following week the clothes, or some of them, turned up.

5

A lonely country road links Kingsmarkham with Pomfret. Once Forest Road, Kingsmarkham, is past, the only houses to be seen are those few up on the hillsides crowned by Cheriton Forest. The forest is always rather dark and forbidding as coniferous forests are. On the horizon stands an obelisk, a needle of stone, placed there by some local magnate a hundred and fifty years ago.

Almost the last building in Kingsmarkham is the police station. On the other side of the High Street Cheriton Lane runs down to the buildings and courts of the Kingsmarkham Tennis Club, and half a dozen other narrow roads compose a small residential web. The gardens of houses in Forest Road back onto open fields, and fields traversed by a footpath lie between the club grounds and the town. The street lamps stop two hundred yards on the Pomfret side of the police station and after that there is an isolated one to light the bus stop.

Roughly halfway between the towns, at the point of no return, is the bus stop with bus shelter. The shelter was put there because there are no trees at this point to break the wind or provide cover from the rain. And on this night it was raining as it had been for many nights. The fine rain swept across the meadows in grey sheets.

The last bus from Pomfret to Kingsmarkham was due at 10.40. It came ten minutes late, rolling along not too fast through the rain, sending up fountains of spray onto the grass verges. The stop where the bus shelter was was a compulsory one, not a request, so the bus pulled in to make a token stop and prepared to pull out again, for there was no one waiting. A shout from a woman passenger sitting in a front nearside seat alerted the driver. He had already taken off the brake but he put it on again and the bus shuddered to a halt.

'There's a person crawling on the pavement!'

Here, where the shelter was, the lay-by was bordered by a few yards of pavement. The driver got down. Two or three of the passengers, disobeying the driver – who was he to tell them? – got down. There was no conductor on those single deckers. The rain was coming down in torrents, needles of it pounding the surface of the lay-by, the kerb, and the sodden bundle that crawled and whimpered with blood coming from its chest.

At first the driver had thought it a wounded dog. But the passenger was right, it was a man. It crawled up to the driver and rolled over at his feet.

Next day, on the other side of Kingsmarkham, the Forby side, a firm called Mid-Sussex Waterways began dragging a pond. Green Pond Hall had stood empty for years but at the end of the previous January a buyer had been found for it and the purchase was completed by April. The grounds contained the pond and a stream and the new owner intended to turn the estate into a trout farm.

If the proper definition of a lake is a sheet of water covering the minimum of one acre, Green Pond was just too small to fit the requirement. But as a pond it was very large. It wasn't stagnant, for the small fast stream flowed through the middle of it, disappearing into a pipe which passed under a path and gushing out through a spout on the other side to fall away down to the Kingsbrook. In spite of this the pond was shallow and coated with the thick green slime of blanket weed. The purpose of the dragging was to clean it, increase its depth and rid the water of the algae Mid-Sussex Waterways believed might be caused by an influx of the nitrates which had been applied as fertiliser to the nearby meadows.

In the net, after the dragging, were found a wire super-market basket minus its handle, a quantity of glass bottles, jars and light bulbs, the silencer part of a car exhaust system, wood in the form of twigs and chopped lengths, stones among which were flints and chalk pebbles, a rubber boot, a Pyrex casserole dish, chipped and cracked, a metal door handle and lock, a pair of scissors and a dark burgundy-coloured travelling bag.

The bag was coated with green slime and thin, fine-grained black mud, but when the clasps were undone and the zip unfastened it was seen that only water had penetrated the seams of the bag, soaking but hardly discolouring the clothes inside, the topmost of which was a brown suede blouson.

It was a piece of luck, Wexford thought, that William Milvey, the boss of Mid-Sussex Waterways, had found money inside the bag, £50 in fivers rolled up and fastened with a rubber band. If it had contained nothing but clothes, and damaged clothes at that, it was probable he would have tossed it into the pit which had been dug out by a mechanical digger for the purpose of receiving the rubbish caught in the dragnet. Money, Wexford had often noticed, has this kind of electric effect on people. Many a man who thinks himself honest, on finding an object bought with money will keep the object but not the money itself. It is as if the adage 'Finders keepers' applies to things but never to money, which has its own aura of sacredness, of being absolutely the preserve of him who has earned it.

But even so, Wexford might never have heard of the existence of the bag were it not for a kidney donor card which was in the breast pocket of the blouson and which was signed R. J. Williams.

William Milvey knew who R. J. Williams was. He lived next door but one to him in Alverbury Road.

This fact it took Wexford some half-hour to find out. He questioned Milvey thoroughly about the bag. Had he seen it in the pond before he saw it in the net? Well, yes, he thought he had, now Wexford came to mention it. He fancied he had. At any rate he thought he could remember seeing a brownish-red lump of something up against the bank of the pond nearest to the path and the Kingsbrook. No, he hadn't touched it or attempted to pull it out. The dragnet had pulled it out.

Milvey was a shortish thick-set man with the heavy build and big spread hands of someone who has done manual work for most of his life. He looked about fifty. The discovery of the bag seemed disproportionately to have excited him – or his excitement appeared disproportionate to Wexford at first.

'Fifty quid in it,' he kept saying, 'and that good jacket.'

'Did you see anyone about the grounds of Green Pond Hall?'

'Some fella up to no good, d'you mean?'

'I meant anyone at all.'

'We didn't have sight nor sound of no one.'

There might have been marks of car tyres on the drive in from the Forby Road or on the track that ran round the lower bank of the pond, the constant rain had turned these surfaces to mud, but any tracks there were had been obliterated by the heavy tyres of Mid-Sussex Waterways' mechanical digger.

Milvey simply couldn't remember if there had been any tyremarks on the track. They had the other man in and asked him, but he couldn't remember either.

'Fifty quid,' said Milvey, 'and that good jacket. Just chucked away.'

'Let me have your address, will you, Mr Milvey? I'll very likely want to talk to you again. Home or business.'

'They're one and the same. I operate from home, don't I?' He said this as if it were a fact he would have expected Wexford to know, and adding his address, used the same patient, mildly surprised tone. 'Twenty-seven Alverbury Road, Kingsmarkham.'

'Are you telling me you live next door but one to Mr Williams?'

Milvey's expression, though bland and innocent, had become a little uncomfortable. 'I reckoned you knew.'

'No, I didn't know.' Vaguely now Wexford recalled reading a planning application made to the local authority for permission to erect a garage – more a hangar really – large enough to house a JCB in the garden of 27 Alverbury Road. The area being strictly residential, the application had naturally been rejected. 'You must know Mr Williams then?'

'Pass the time of day,' said Milvey. 'The wife has a chat with Mrs Williams. My girl's in the same class at school with their Sara.'

'Mr Williams is missing,' said Wexford flatly. 'He's been missing from home for the past month and more.'

'Is that right?' Milvey didn't look surprised but he didn't say he knew either. 'Fifty quid in notes,' he said, 'and a jacket worth three times that.'

Wexford let him go.

'It has to be a coincidence,' Burden said.

'Does it, Mike? It would be a hell of a coincidence, wouldn't it? Williams disappears because he'd done something or someone's done something to him. His overnight bag is dumped in a pond and who should find it but the guy who lives two doors down the street from him? I haven't read any John Buchan for – well, it must be forty-five years. But I can remember in one of his books the hero's car breaks down and the house he calls at for help just happens to be the home of the master anarchist. A bit later on the hit man who's sent to get him turns out to be a burglar he's recently successfully defended in court. Now that's fiction and strictly for persons below fifteen, I'd say. But this that you call coincidence is comparable to those. Have you had any coincidences of that magnitude in your life?'

'Both my grandmothers were called Mary Brown.'

'Were they really?' Wexford was temporarily distracted. 'You never told me that before. And did they come from the same part of the country?'

'One from Sussex and one from Herefordshire. I bet you the odds against that happening are a lot longer than against Milvey finding Williams's bag. You look at it and you'll see it's not that much of a coincidence. If it had been buried, say, or stuck in a hollow tree and Milvey had found it, that would be something else. But it was in a pond and Milvey's in the pond-dragging business. Once it got in the pond and the pond was due to be dragged – which whoever put it there wouldn't know, of course – the chances would be that Milvey *would* find it. You want to look at it like that.'

Wexford knew there was more to it than that; he couldn't dismiss it in the easy way Burden did. Milvey's behaviour had been a shade odd anyway and Wexford was sure he hadn't told all he knew.

'How long do you think the bag's been in the pond?'

It was on the floor between them, deposited on sheets of newspaper, its contents, which Wexford had already examined, now replaced.

'Since the night he went, I suppose, or the next day.'

Wexford didn't go along with that either but he let it pass for the time being. As well as the brown suede blouson there was a raincoat in the bag, a trendy version of a Burberry, the fifty pounds, a toothbrush, tube of toothpaste and disposable razor wrapped up in a pair of underpants, a bottle of Monsieur Rochas cologne and a pair of brand-new socks with the label still on them. The underpants were a young man's Homs, pale blue and white, the socks dark brown, an expensive brand made of silk.

It was the kind of packing a man would do for an over-night stay somewhere, not for three nights, and the pants and socks and cologne seemed to indicate a night not spent alone. Or had there been more articles in the bag which had been removed? This could surely only have been done to prevent identification of the bag's owner. In that case why leave the donor card in the blouson pocket? 'I would like to help someone to live after my death', it stated somewhat naively in scarlet and white, and on the reverse side Rodney Williams had requested that in the event of his death any part of his body which might be required should be used in the treatment of others. Underneath this was his signature and the date a year past. The next of kin to contact was given, as might have been expected, as Joy Williams with the Alverbury Road phone number.

Men's natures were a mass of contradictions, there was no consistency, and yet Wexford marvelled a little that a husband and father could deliberately and ruthlessly deceive his wife over his income and pursue a course of skinflint meanness to her and his children yet want to donate his body for transplants. It would cost him nothing though, he would be dead after all. Was he dead?

'We're going to have to start looking for him. I mean really looking. Search the grounds of Green Pond Hall for a start.'

Burden had been pacing the office. He had taken to doing this lately and his restless pacing had a stressful effect on anyone he happened to be with, though he himself hardly seemed aware of what was going on. Twice he had been to the window, twice back to the door, pausing once to perch briefly on the edge of the desk. Now he had reached the window again where he stopped, turned and stared at Wexford in irritable incredulity.

197

'Search for *him*? Surely it's plain he's simply done a bunk to escape the consequences of whatever it is he's done.'

'All right, Mike. Maybe. But in that case what *has* he done? Nothing at Sevensmith Harding. He's as clean as a whistle there. What else could he have done? It's just possible he could be involved in some fraud that hasn't yet come to light but there's a strong case against that one. He got out. The only reason for that would be that discovery of the fraud was imminent. In that case why hasn't that discovery been made?'

Burden shrugged. 'Who knows? But it may just be a piece of luck for Williams that it hasn't been.'

'Why hasn't he come back then? If the outcome of this fraud has blown over why doesn't he come home? He hasn't left the country unless he's gone on a false passport. And why bother with a false passport when he'd got one of his own and no one started missing him till three days after he'd gone?'

'Doesn't it occur to you that leaving one's clothes on the river bank is the oldest disappearing trick in the world?'

'On the beach, I think you mean, not on the shores of a pond where the water's so shallow that to commit suicide you'd have to lie on your face and hold your breath. Besides, that bag has been in the pond only a couple of days at most. If it had been there since Williams went it'd be rotting by now, it'd stink. We'll send it over to the lab and see what they say but we can see what they'll say with our own eyes and smell it with our own noses.

'Williams is dead. This bag of his tells me he is. If he had put it into the pond for the purpose of making us think he was dead he'd have done so immediately after he left. And the contents would have been different. More identification, for instance, no scent and powder blue knickers. And I don't think the money would have been in it. He would have needed that money, he would have needed all the money he could lay hands on. There's no reason to think he could easily spare fifty pounds – whatever he's done he hasn't robbed a bank.

'He's dead and, letter and phone call notwithstanding, he was dead within an hour or two of when his family last saw him.'

* * *

Next day the searching of Green Pond Hall grounds began. The grounds comprised eight acres, part woodland, part decayed overgrown formal gardens, part stables and paddock. Sergeant Martin led the search with three men and Wexford himself went down there to have a look at the dragged pond and view the terrain. It was still raining. It had been raining yesterday and the day before and for part of every day for three weeks. The weather people were saying it would be the wettest May since records began. The track was a morass, the colour and texture of melted chocolate in which a giant fork had furrowed. There were other ways of getting down to the pond but only if you went on foot.

At three he had a date at Stowerton Royal Infirmary. Colin Budd had been placed in intensive care but only for the night. By morning he was sufficiently recovered to be transferred to a side room off the men's surgical ward. The stab wounds he had received were more than superficial, one having penetrated to a depth of three inches, but by a miracle almost none of the five had endangered heart or lungs.

A thick white dressing covered his upper chest, over which a striped pyjama jacket had been loosely wrapped. The pyjama jacket was an extra large and Wexford estimated Budd's chest measurement at thirty-four inches. He was a very thin, bony, almost cadaverous young man, white-faced and with black, longish hair. He seemed to know exactly what Wexford would want to know about him and quickly and nervously repeated his name and age, gave his occupation as motor mechanic and his address, a Kingsmarkham one where he lived with his parents.

'Tell me what happened.'

'This girl stuck a knife in my chest.'

'Now, Mr Budd, you know better than that. I want a detailed account, everything you can remember, starting with what you were doing waiting for a bus in the middle of nowhere.'

Budd had a querulous voice that always sounded mildly indignant. He was one of those who believes the world owes him elaborate consideration as well as a living.

'That's got nothing to do with it,' he said.

'I'll be the judge of that. I don't suppose you were doing anything to be ashamed of. And if you were what you tell me will be between you and me.'

'I don't know what you're getting at!'

'Just tell me where you'd been last evening, Mr Budd.'

'I was at snooker,' Budd said sullenly.

What a fool! He'd made it sound at least as if he was having it away with a friend's wife in one of the isolated cottages on the hillside.

'A snooker club?'

'It's on Tuesday evenings. In Pomfret, a room at the back of the White Horse. It's over at ten and I reckoned on walking home.' Budd shifted his body, wincing a bit, pulling himself up in the bed. 'But the rain started coming down harder, I was getting soaked. I looked at my watch and saw the ten-forty bus'd be along in ten minutes and I was nearly at the stop by then.'

'I'd have expected a motor mechanic to have his own transport.'

'My car was in a crunch-up. It's in dock having a new wing. I wasn't doing no more than twenty-five when this woman come out of a side turning . . .'

Wexford cut that one short. 'So you reached the bus stop, the bus shelter. What happened?'

Budd looked at him and away. 'There was this girl already there, sitting on the seat. I sat down next to her.'

The bus shelter was well known to Wexford. It was about ten feet long, the seat or bench inside two feet shorter. 'Next to her?' he asked. 'Or at the other end of the seat?'

'Next to her. Does it matter?'

Wexford thought perhaps it did. In England at any rate, for good or ill, for the improving of social life or its worsening, a man of honourable intent who goes to sit on a public bench where a woman is already sitting will do so as far away from her as possible. A woman will probably do this too if a woman or man is already sitting there, and a man will do it if another man is there.

'Did you know her? Had you ever seen her before?'

Budd shook his head.

'You spoke to her?'

'Only to say it was raining.'

She knew that already, Wexford thought. He looked hard at Budd. Budd said, 'I said it was a pity we were having such a bad

200

May, it made the winter longer, something like that. She pulled a knife out of her bag and lunged it at me.'

'Just like that? You didn't say anything else to her?'

'I've told you what I said.'

'She was mad, was she? A girl who stabs men because they tell her it's raining?'

'All I said was that normally at this time I'd have had my vehicle and I could have given her a lift.'

'In other words, you were trying to pick her up?'

'All right, what if I was? I didn't touch her. I didn't do anything to frighten her. That was all I said, that I could have given her a lift home. She pulled out this knife and stabbed at me four or five times and I cried out or screamed or something and she ran off.'

'Would you know her again?'

'You bet I would.'

'Describe her to me.'

Budd made the mess of that Wexford thought he would. He didn't know whether she was tall or short, plump or thin, because he only saw her sitting down and he thought she had a raincoat on. A thin raincoat that was a sort of pale colour. Her hair was fair, he did know that, though she had a hat on or a scarf. Bits of blonde hair showed under it. Her face was just an ordinary face, not what you'd call pretty. Wexford began to wonder what had attracted Budd to her in the first place. The mere facts that she was female and young? About twenty, said Budd. Well, maybe twenty-five or six. Pressed to be more precise, he said she could have been any age between eighteen and thirty, he wasn't good on ages, she was quite young though.

'Can you think of anything else about her?'

A nurse had come in and was hovering. Wexford knew what she was about to say, he could have written the script for her – 'Now I think that's quite enough. It's time for Mr Budd to have his rest . . .' She approached the bed, unhooked Budd's chart and began reading it with the enthusiastic concentration of a scholar who has just found the key to Linear B or some such.

'She had this sack with her. She grabbed it before she ran off.'

'What sort of sack?'

201

'The plastic kind they give you for your dustbin. A black one. She picked it up and stuck it over her shoulder and ran off.'

'I think that's quite enough for now,' said the nurse, diverging slightly from Wexford's text.

He got up. It was an extraordinary picture Budd's story had created and one which appealed to his imagination. The dark wet night, the knife flashing purposefully, even frenziedly, the girl running off into the rain with a sack slung over her shoulder. It was like an illustration in a fairy book of Andrew Lang, elusive, sinister and other-worldly.

6

What had Burden meant when he said this amniocentesis had discovered something to worry Jenny? Wexford found himself brooding on that. Once or twice he had woken in the night and the question had come into his mind. Sitting in the car, being driven to Myringham, he saw a woman on the pavement with a Down's Syndrome child and the question was back, presenting itself again.

He didn't like to pursue it with Burden. This wasn't the sort of thing you asked a prospective father about. What small defect was there a father wouldn't mind about but a mother would? It was grotesque, ridiculous, there was nothing. Any defect would be a tragedy. His mind ranged over partial deafness, a heart murmur, palate or lip deformities – the test couldn't have shown those anyway. An extra chromosome? This was an area where he found himself floundering in ignorance. He thought of his own children, perfect, always healthy, giving him no trouble really, and his heart warmed towards his girls.

This reminded him that he had the National Theatre's programme brochure for the summer season in his pocket. Sheila was with the company and this would be the first season she had top lead roles. Hence the disengagement from further work on *Runway*. He got out the programme and looked at it. Dora had asked him to decide which days they should go to London and see the three productions Sheila was in. For obvious reasons it always had to be he who made those kind of decisions.

The new Stoppard, Ibsen's *Little Eyolf*, Shelley's *The Cenci*.

Wexford had heard of *Little Eyolf* but he had never seen it or read it, and as for *The Cenci*, he had to confess to himself that he hadn't known Shelley had written any plays. But there it was: 'Percy Bysshe Shelley' and the piece described as a tragedy in five acts. Wexford was making tentative marks on the programme for a Friday in July and two Saturdays in August when Donaldson, his driver, drew into the kerb outside Sevensmith Harding.

Miles Gardner had been watching for him and came rushing out with an umbrella. It made Wexford feel like royalty. They splashed across the pavement to the mahogany doors.

Kenneth Risby, the chief accountant, told him Rodney Williams's salary had been paid into the account Williams had with the Pomfret branch of the Anglian-Victoria Bank. From that account then, it would seem, Williams had each month transferred £500 into the joint account he had with Joy. Risby had been with the company for fifteen years and said he could recall no other arrangement being made for Williams, either recently or in the days when he was a sales rep. His salary had always gone to the Pomfret bank, never to Kingsmarkham.

'We've heard nothing,' Miles Gardner said. 'Whatever he meant by the PS to that letter he hasn't been in touch.'

'Williams didn't write that letter,' Wexford reminded him.

Gardner nodded unhappily.

'The first time we talked about this business,' Wexford said, 'you told me someone phoned here saying she was Mrs Williams and that her husband was ill and wouldn't be coming in. Would that have been on Friday, April the sixteenth?'

'Well, yes, I suppose it would.'

'Who took the call?'

'It must have been one of our telephonists. They're part-timers. I can't remember whether it was Anna or Michelle. The phone call came before I got in, you see. That is, before nine-thirty.'

'Williams had a secretary I suppose?'

'Christine Lomond. He shared her with our assistant sales director. Would you like to talk to her?'

'Not yet. Maybe not today. It's Anna or Michelle I want. But which one do I want?'

'Michelle, I expect,' said Gardner. 'They tend to swop shifts a bit but it's usually Michelle on mornings.'

It had been, that Friday, and it was today. Michelle was a very young, very pretty girl with a vividly made-up face. The room where the switchboard was, not much more than a cupboard, was stamped with her personality (or perhaps Anna's) and there was a blue cineraria in a pot, a stack of magazines, a pile of knitting that had reached the bulky stage, and on the table in front of her, hurriedly placed face downwards, the latest diet paperback.

It was clear that Michelle had already discussed that phone call exhaustively. Perhaps with Anna or with Christine Lomond. Williams's disappearance would have been the talk of the office.

'I get in at nine,' she said. 'That's when the phone calls really start. But the funny thing was there weren't any that morning till Mrs Williams phoned at about twenty past.'

'You mean till someone phoned who *called* herself Mrs Williams.'

The girl looked at him. She shook her head quite vehemently. 'It was Mrs Williams. She said, "This is Joy Williams."'

Wexford let it go for the time being.

'What exactly did she say?'

'"My husband Mr Williams won't be coming in today." And then she sort of hesitated and said, "That's Mr Rodney Williams, I mean, the marketing manager." I said there was no one else in yet and she said that didn't matter but to give Christine the message he'd got flu and wouldn't be in.'

Whoever it was, it hadn't been Joy. At that time Joy didn't know her husband was Sevensmith Harding's marketing manager. Wexford had thanked Michelle and was turning away, diverting his mind to the matter of the firm's stock of typewriters, when he stopped.

'What makes you so sure the woman you spoke to was Mrs Joy Williams?'

'It just was. I know it was.'

'No, let me correct that. You know it was a woman who *said* she was Mrs Joy Williams. She had never phoned here before, had she, so you couldn't have recognised her voice?'

'No, but she phoned here afterwards.'

'What do you mean, afterwards?'

'About three weeks later.' The girl spoke with exaggerated patience now, as if to a very confused or simple-minded person. 'Mrs Joy Williams phoned here three weeks after her husband left.'

Of course. Wexford remembered that call. It was he who had advised Joy to make it.

'I put her through to Mr Gardner,' Michelle said. 'I was a bit embarrassed, to be perfectly honest. But I know it was the same voice, really I do. It was the same voice as the woman who phoned that Friday morning, it was Mrs Williams.'

He picked up the girl at the roundabout where the second exit is the start of the Kingsmarkham bypass. She was standing on the grass verge at the side of the roundabout, holding up a piece of cardboard with 'Myringham' printed on it. Brian Wheatley pulled in to the first exit, the Kingsmarkham town-centre road, and the girl got into the passenger seat. Then, for some unclear reason, perhaps because he had already pulled out of the roundabout and it would not have been easy to get back into the traffic, Wheatley decided to continue through the town instead of on the bypass. This wasn't such a bad idea anyway, the anomaly being that the bypass which had been built to ease the passage of traffic past the town was often more crowded than the old route.

Wheatley was driving home from London where he worked three days a week. It was about six in the evening and of course broad daylight. He had moved to Myringham only two weeks before and was still unfamiliar with the byways and back-doubles of the area. The girl didn't speak a word. She had no baggage with her, only a handbag with a shoulder strap. Wheatley drove through Kingsmarkham, along the High Street, and became confused by the sign-posting. Instead of keeping straight on he began to think he should have taken a left-hand turn some half a mile back. He therefore – on what he admitted was a lonely and secluded stretch of road – pulled into a lay-by and consulted his road map.

His intention to do this, he said, he announced plainly to the girl. After he had stopped and switched off the engine he was obliged to reach obliquely across her in order to open the glove compartment where the map was. He was aware of the girl giving a gasp of fright or anger, and then of a sharp pain, more like a burn than a cut, in his right hand.

He never even saw the knife. The girl jumped out of the car, slamming the door behind her, and ran not along the road but onto a footpath that separated a field of wheat from a wood. Blood was flowing from a deep cut in the base of Wheatley's thumb. He tied up his hand as best he could with his handkerchief but shock and a feeling of faintness made it impossible for him to continue his journey for some minutes. Eventually he looked at his map, found himself nearer home than he had thought, and was able to drive there in about a quarter of an hour. The general practitioner with whom he had registered the week before was still holding his surgery. Wheatley's wife drove him there and the cut in his hand was stitched, Wheatley telling the doctor he had been carving meat and had inadvertently pressed his hand against the point of the carving knife. Whether or not the doctor believed this was another matter. At any rate he had made no particular comment. Wheatley himself had wanted to tell him the truth, though this would have meant police involvement. It was his wife who had dissuaded him on the grounds that if the police were called the conclusion they would reach would be that Wheatley had first made some sort of assault on the girl.

This was the story Wheatley told Wexford three days later. His wife didn't know he had changed his mind. He had come to the police, he said, because he felt more and more indignant that this girl, whom he hadn't touched, whom he had scarcely spoken to except to say he was going to stop and look at his map, should make an unprovoked attack on him and get away with it.

'Can you describe her?'

Wexford waited resignedly for the kind of useless description furnished by Colin Budd. He was surprised. In many ways Wheatley did not seem to know his way around but he was observant and perceptive.

'She was tall for a woman, about five feet eight or nine. Young, eighteen or nineteen. Brown hair or lightish hair, shoulder-length, sunglasses though it wasn't sunny, fair skin —

I noticed she had very white hands. Jeans and a blouse, I think, and a cardigan. The bag was some dark colour, black or navy blue.'

'Did she give you the impression she lived in Myringham? That she was going home?'

'She didn't give me any sort of impression. When she got into the car she said thanks – just the one word "thanks", otherwise she didn't speak. I said to her that I thought I'd drive through the town instead of the bypass and she didn't answer. Later on I said I'd stop and look at the map and she didn't answer that either, but when I reached across her – I didn't touch her, I could swear to that – she gave a sort of gasp. Those were the only sounds she made, "thanks" and a gasp.'

The same girl as attacked Budd, one would suppose. But if Wheatley were to be believed, while there was some very slight justification for the attack on Budd, there was none for this second stabbing. Could the girl possibly have thought that the hand which reached across to open the glove compartment intended instead to take hold of her by the left shoulder? Or lower itself onto her knee? There was something ridiculous about these assaults, and yet two meant that they were not ridiculous at all but serious. Next time there could be a fatality.

Or had there been one already?

The manager of the Pomfret branch of the Anglian-Victoria Bank bore an extraordinary resemblance to Adolf Hitler. This was not only in the small square moustache and the lock of dark hair half covering Mr Skinner's forehead. The face was the same face, rather handsome, with large chin and heavy nose and small thick-lidded eyes. But all that would have passed unnoticed without the moustache and the lock of hair, so that it was impossible to avoid the uncomfortable conclusion that Mr Skinner was doing it on purpose. He knew whom he looked like and he enhanced the resemblance. Wexford could only attribute one motive to a bank manager who wants to look like Hitler – a desire to intimidate his clients.

His manner, however, was warm, friendly and charming. All those, and implacable too. He could not consider either letting Wexford look into Rodney Williams's bank accounts or disclose any information about their contents.

'Did you say accounts plural?' said Wexford.

'Yes. Mr Williams has two current accounts here – and now I've probably said more than I should.'

'Two current accounts in the name of Rodney Williams?'

Skinner was standing up with his head slightly on one side, looking like Hitler waiting for Franco's train at Hendaye. 'I said two current accounts, Chief Inspector. We'll let it go at that, shall we?'

One for his salary to be paid into, Wexford thought as he was driven away, and the other for what? His Kingsmarkham household expenses were drawn from the Kingsmarkham account which he fed with £500 a month from Pomfret account A. Then what of account B? His wife didn't know of the existence of account A anyway. It alone was sufficient to keep his resources secret from her. Why did he need a third current bank account?

They were searching for him now on the open land, partly wooded, that lay between Kingsmarkham and Forby. But so far, since the discovery of the bag in Green Pond, nothing further had come to light. He's dead, Wexford thought, he must be.

Burden had been in Pomfret, talking to the Harmer family, Joy Williams's sister, brother-in-law and niece. John Harmer was a pharmacist with a chemist's shop in the High Street.

'They say Joy was with them that evening,' Burden said, 'but I wouldn't put that much credence on what they say. Not that they're intentionally lying – they can't remember. It was seven weeks ago. Besides, Joy often goes over there in the evenings. More or less to sit in front of their television instead of her own, I gather. But I suppose she's lonely, she wants company. Mrs Harmer says she was definitely there that evening, Harmer says it must be if his wife says so and the girl doesn't know. You can't expect a teenage girl to take much notice of when her aunt comes.'

Wexford told him what he had learned from the telephonist at Sevensmith Harding. 'Of course, the girl may be mistaken about the voices or she may have persuaded herself they were the same voice in order to get more drama out of the situation. But it's more than possible that the woman who phoned Sevensmith Harding the day after Williams left to say he was ill and the woman who phoned three weeks later to inquire as to

209

his whereabouts are one and the same. And we know the second time was Joy. Now Joy was very keen to have me look for her husband when he first disappeared, but later on much less so – indeed, she was obstructive. That first time I talked to her she said nothing about having gone out herself that evening. That was only mentioned the second time. Joy is devoted to her son Kevin. Her daughter is nothing to her, her son everything . . . What on earth's the matter?'

Burden's face had set and he had gone rather pale. He had taken a hard grip on the arms of his chair. 'Nothing. Go on.'

'Well, then – her son always phones on Thursday evenings and that particular Thursday was the first one he had been back at college. Wouldn't a devoted mother have wanted to know all those things mothers worry about in such circumstances? Did he have a good journey? Was his room all right? Had he settled in? But this devoted mother doesn't wait in for his call. She goes out – not to some important engagement, some function booked months ahead, but to watch television at her sister's. What does all this suggest to you?'

Having struggled successfully to overcome whatever it was that had upset him, Burden forced a laugh. 'You sound like Sherlock Holmes talking to Watson.' Since his second marriage he occasionally read books, a change in him Wexford couldn't get used to.

'No,' he said, 'more "a man of the solid Sussex breed – a breed which covers much good sense under a heavy silent exterior".'

'I wouldn't say "silent". Was that from Sherlock Holmes?'

Wexford nodded. 'So what do you make of it?' he said more colloquially.

'That Joy is somehow in cahoots with her husband. There's a conspiracy going on. What for and why I wouldn't pretend to know but it's got something to do with giving everyone the impression Williams is dead. He left that evening and she went out later to meet him away from the house. Whatever they were planning was done away from the house because it had to be concealed from the daughter Sara as much as from anyone else. Next morning Joy rang Sevensmith Harding to say her husband was ill. Of course, it's nonsense to say she didn't know that he was their marketing manager and the extent of his income. Next he or she typed that letter on a *hired* typewriter. She probably did that, not knowing what he called Gardner and making the mistake of addressing him as "Mr Gardner". The abandoned car, the dumped bag of clothes were all part of a plan to make us think him dead. But the increased police attention frightened Joy, she wanted things to go more at her pace. Hence the obstructiveness. I said I didn't know why but it could be an insurance fiddle, couldn't it?'

'Without a body, Mike? With no more proof of death than a dumped travelling bag? And if you wanted people to think you were dead, aren't there half a dozen simpler and more convincing ways of doing it?'

'You feel the same as me then? You don't think he's dead?'

'I know he's dead,' said Wexford.

Next day he was proved right.

It looked like a grave. It was in the shape of a grave, as clearly demarcated as if a slab of stone lay upon it, though Edwin Fitzgerald did not at first see this. In spite of its shape he would have passed it by as a mere curiosity, a whim of nature. It was the dog Shep who drew his attention to it.

Edwin Fitzgerald was a retired policeman who had been a dog handler. He lived in Pomfret and had a job as a part-time security guard at a factory complex on Stowerton's industrial estate. The dog Shep was not a trained dog in the sense of being police-trained – as a 'sniffer', for instance. Fitzgerald had bought him after his last dog died – a wonderful dog that one, more intelligent than any human being, a dog that understood every word he said. Shep could only follow humbly in that dog's footsteps and was often the subject of unfavourable comparisons. He didn't understand every word Fitzgerald said, or at any rate behaved as if he didn't.

On this particular morning in June, a dry one, the first really fine morning of the summer, Shep disregarded all Fitzgerald's words, ignored the repeated 'Leave it, sir' and 'Do as you're told' and continued his frenetic digging in the corner of what his master saw as a patch of weeds. He dug like a dog possessed. Indeed, Fitzgerald informed him that he was a devil, that he didn't know what had got into him. He shouted (which

211

a good dog handler should never do) and he shook his fist until he saw what Shep had unearthed and then he stopped.

The dog had dug up a foot.

Fitzgerald had been a policeman, which had the double advantage of having taught him not to be sickened by such a discovery and not to disturb anything in its vicinity. He attached Shep's lead to his collar and pulled the dog away. This took some doing as Shep was a big young German Shepherd intent on worrying at the protruding thing for some hours if possible.

As far as Fitzgerald could see, now he had got the dog clear, the foot was still attached to a limb and the limb probably to a trunk. It was inside a sodden, blackened, slimy shoe caked with mud, and about the ankle clung a bundling of muddy wet cloth, once the hem of a trouser leg. Shep had dug it out from one of the corners of this curious little plot of ground. All around, on this edge of the meadow, grew tall grass ready to be cut for hay, high enough to hide the dog when he plunged in among it, but the rectangle – seven feet by three? – which Shep had found in there and had dug into was covered closely and in a neat rather horticultural way with fresh green plants. Weeds they were, but weeds attractive enough to be called plants, red campion, clover, speedwell, and they covered the oblong patch as precisely as if they had been sown there in a seed bed.

The grass which surrounded it, gone to seed, bearing light feathery seed heads of brown and greyish-cream and silvery-gold, hid it from the sight of anyone who kept to the footpath. It took a dog to plunge in there and find the grave. A day or two of sunshine, Fitzgerald thought, and the farmer would have cut the hay, cut those weeds too without a thought. Shep was a good dog after all, even if he didn't understand every word Fitzgerald said.

He retraced his steps to the branch of the lane that led to Myfleet and hurried down the hill to his bungalow where he phoned the police.

7

From the Pomfret road a narrow lane winds its way up into the hills and to the verge of the forest. All down the hedges here grows the wayfarer's tree with its flat creamy bracts of blossom, and beneath, edging the meadows like a fringe of lace, the whiter, finer, more delicate cow parsley. There are houses, Edwin Fitzgerald's among them, approached by paths, cart tracks or even smaller narrower lanes, but the lane gives the impression of leading directly to the obelisk on the hill.

It is like downland up here, the trees ceasing until the forest of conifers begins over there to the east, chalk showing in outcroppings and heather on the chalk. And all the way the obelisk looming larger, a needle of granite with its point a tetragon. The road never reaches it. A quarter of a mile this side it swerves, turns east and divides, one fork making for Myfleet, the other for Pomfret, and soon there are meadows again and the heath is past. It was in one of these meadows, close to the overhang of the forest, traversed by a footpath leading from the road to Myfleet, that the discovery had been made. Over to the west the obelisk stabbed the blue sky, catching a shred of cloud on its point.

The grave was in a triangle formed by the wood, the lane and the footpath, in a slightly more than right-angled corner of the field. It was near enough to the forest for the air to smell resinous. The soil was light and sandy with an admixture of pine needles.

'Easy enough to dig,' said Wexford to Burden. 'Almost anyone not decrepit could dig a grave like that in half an hour. Digging it deep enough would have taken a little longer.'

213

They were viewing the terrain, the distance of the grave from the road and the footpath, while Sir Hilary Tremlett, the pathologist, stood by with the scene-of-crimes officer to supervise the careful unearthing. Sir Hilary had happened to be at Stowerton when Fitzgerald's call came in. By a piece of luck he had just arrived at the infirmary to perform a postmortem. It was not yet ten o'clock, a morning of pearly sunshine, the blue sky dotted with innumerable puffs of tiny white cloud. But every man there, the short portly august pathologist included, had a raincoat on. It had rained daily for so many weeks that no one was going to take the risk of going without; no one anyway could yet believe his own eyes.

'The rain made the weeds grow like that,' said Wexford. 'You can see what happened. It's rather interesting. All the ground here had grass growing on it, then a patch was dug to receive *that*. It was covered up again with overturned earth, the weed seeds came and rain, seemingly endless rain, and what grew up on that fertile patch and that patch only were broad-leaved plants. If it had been a dry spring there would have been more grass and it would all have been much less green.'

'And the ground harder. If the ground hadn't been soft and moist the dog might not have persisted with its digging.'

'The mistake was in not digging the grave deep enough. It makes you wonder why he or she or they didn't. Laziness? Lack of time? Lack of light? The six-foot rule is a good one because things of this kind do tend to work to the surface.'

'If that's so,' said Dr Crocker, coming up to them, 'why is it they always have to dig so far down to find ancient cities and temples and so forth?'

'Don't ask me,' said Wexford. 'Ask the dog. He's the archaeologist. Mind you, we don't have any lava in Sussex.'

They approached a little nearer to where Detectives Archbold and Bennett were carrying out their delicate spadework. It was apparent now that the corpse of the man that lay in the earth had been neither wrapped nor covered before it was buried. The earth didn't besmear it as a heavier clayey soil might have done. It was emerging relatively clean, soaking wet, darkly stained, giving off the awful reek that was familiar to every man there, the sweetish, fishy, breath-catching, gaseous stench of decomposing flesh. That was what the dog had smelt and liked and wanted more of.

'I often think,' said Wexford to the doctor, 'that we haven't much in common with dogs.'

'No, it's at times like this you know what you've always suspected, that they're not almost human at all.'

The face was pale, stained, bloated, the pale parts the colour of a dead fish's belly. Wexford, not squeamish at all, hardened by the years, decided not to look at the face again until he had to. The big domed forehead, bigger and more domed because the hair had fallen from it, looked like a great mottled stone or lump of fungus. It was that forehead which made him pretty sure this must be Rodney Williams. Of course, he wasn't going to commit himself at this stage but he'd have been surprised if it wasn't Williams.

Sir Hilary, squatting down now, bent closer. Murdoch, the scene-of-crimes officer, was beginning to take measurements, make calculations. He called the photographer over but Sir Hilary held up a delaying hand.

Wexford wondered how he could stand that stink right up against his face. He seemed rather to enjoy it, the whole thing, the corpse, the atmosphere, the horror, the squalor. Pathologists did, and just as well really. It wouldn't do if they shied away from it.

The body was subjected to a long and careful scrutiny. Sir Hilary looked at it closely from all angles. He came very close to touching but he did not quite touch. His fingers were plump, clean, the colour of a slice of roast pork. He stood up, nodded to Murdoch and the photographer, smiled at Wexford.

'I could have a poke-about at that after lunch,' he said. He always spoke of his autopsies as 'having a poke-about'. 'Not much doing today. Any idea who it might be?'

'I think I have, Sir Hilary.'

'I'm glad to hear it. Saves a lot of hassle. We'll smarten him up a bit before his nearest and dearest come for a private view.'

Joy Williams, Wexford thought. No, she shouldn't be subjected to that. He felt the warmth of the mounting sun kind and soft on his face. He turned his back and looked across the sweep of meadows to the Pomfret road, green hay gold-brushed, dark green hedgerows stitched in like tapestry, sheep on a hillside. All he could see was that face and a wife looking at it. This horrid image doth unfix my hair and make my seated heart knock at my ribs . . .

It occurred to him that the nearest point on the main road to this place was the bus stop where Colin Budd had been attacked. Did that mean anything? The lane that passed within yards of the burial place met the road almost opposite the bus stop. But Budd had been stabbed weeks after this man's death. The brother-in-law might do the identification instead. John Something, the chemist. John Harmer.

He seemed a sensible man. Younger than Williams by five or six years, he was one of those tailored people, a neat, well-made, smallish man with regular features and short, crisply wavy hair. He had closed up his dispensary and left the shop in the care of his wife.

Having taken a deep breath, he looked at the body. He looked at the face, his symmetrical features controlled in blankness. He wasn't going to show anything, not he, no shock, disgust, pity. You could almost hear his mother's voice saying to a small curly-headed boy: Be a man, John. Don't cry. Be a man.

Harmer remembered and was a man. But he might have said with Macduff that he must also feel it like a man, for his face gradually paled until it became as sickly greenish white as the corpse's. His stomach, not his will, had betrayed him. Or threatened to. He came out into the air, into the sunshine, away from charnel-house corpse rot, and smelt the summer noonday, and the bile receded. He nodded to Wexford, he nodded rather more and longer than was necessary.

'Is that your brother-in-law, Rodney Williams?'

'Yes.'

'You are quite certain of that?'

'I'm certain.'

Wexford had thought of asking him to be the bearer of the news to Joy but he had quickly seen Harmer wouldn't be a suitable, let alone a sympathetic, messenger. He went himself, walking to Alverbury Road, thinking as he walked. There wasn't much he personally could do until the pathologist's report came and the lab had been over Williams's clothes.

With distaste he recalled the bloodied mass of cloth that had wrapped the wounds. He felt glad now he had had the lab go over that car so carefully and at a time when it looked as if Williams might have been guilty of some misdemeanour and have done a moonlight flit.

Those crumbs of plaster in the boot could be vital evidence. At first he had supposed they derived from some routine of Williams's work. But Gardner had told him there was never a question of Williams having handled the stuff he sold. More likely the truth was that those plaster crumbs had been caught up in the folds of that bloodstained cloth and the body itself had been in the boot of the car . . .

In the front garden of 31 Alverbury Road someone had mown the bit of lawn and cut the privet hedge. It looked as if both these tasks had been performed with the same pair of blunt shears. Rodney Williams had been in one respect domestically adequate – he had kept his garden trim.

Sara opened the front door to him. He hadn't expected her to be there and he was a little taken aback. He would have preferred breaking the news to her mother alone. The school term wasn't yet over but A-levels were and with those examinations behind her there was perhaps nothing for her to go to school for.

She had on a white tee-shirt, pure unrelieved white, short-sleeved and showing felt-tipped pen drawings on her arms and hands, the snake again in green, a butterfly with a baby face, a raven woman with aggressive breasts and erect wings, some-how obscene on those smooth golden arms, childish and rounded.

'Is your mother in, Sara?'

She nodded. Had the tone of his voice told her? She looked sideways at him, fearfully, as they went down the short passage to the kitchen door.

Joy Williams anticipated nothing. On the table at which she was sitting were the remains of lunch for two. She looked up with a mildly disagreeable inquiring glance. They had been eating fish fingers with baked beans – an infelicitous mixture, Wexford thought. He could tell the constituents of their lunch by the quantity of it Sara had left on her plate. Joy had been reading a women's magazine of the royalty-sycophantic-crocheted-tea-cosy kind which was propped against a bottle of soy sauce, pathetic import surely of Sara's. What does a daughter do for her mother in a situation such as this? Go to her and put an arm round her shoulders? At least stand behind her chair? Sara went to the sink, stood with her back to them, looking out of the window above it at the grass and the fence and the meagre little apple trees.

Wexford told Joy her husband had been found. Her husband's body. More than that he couldn't tell her, he knew no more. The girl's shoulders twitched. Mrs Williams leaned forward across the table and put her hand heavily over her mouth. She sat that way for a moment or two. The whistling kettle on the stove began to screech. Sara turned round, turned the gas off, looked at her mother with her mouth twisted up as if she had toothache.

'D'you want a coffee?' Joy said to Wexford.

He shook his head. Sara made the coffee, instant in two mugs, one with a big 'S' on it and the other with the head of the Princess of Wales. Joy put sugar into hers, one spoonful, then after reflection, another.

'Shall I have to see him?'

'Your brother-in-law has already made the indentification.'

'John?'

'Have you any other brothers-in-law, Mrs Williams?'

'Rod's got a brother in Bath. "Had", I should say. I mean he's still alive as far as I know and Rod's not, is he?'

'Oh, Mum,' said Sara. 'For God's sake.'

'You shut your mouth, you little cow!'

Joy Williams screamed it at her. She didn't utter any more words but she went on screaming, drumming her fists on the table so that the mug bounced off and broke and coffee went all over the strip of coconut matting on the floor. Joy screamed until Sara slapped her face – the doctor already, the cool head in an emergency. Wexford knew better than to do it himself. Once he'd slapped a hysterical woman's face and later been threatened with an action for assault.

'Who can we get hold of to be with her?' he asked. Mrs Milvey? He thought of Dora and dismissed the thought.

'She hasn't any friends. I expect my Auntie Hope will come.'

Mrs Harmer that would be. Hope and Joy. My God, he

218

thought. Although the girl was sitting beside her mother now, holding her hand, while Joy leaned back spent, her head hanging over the back of the kitchen chair, the tears silently rolling out of her eyes, he could see that it was all Sara could do to control her repugnance. She was almost shaking with it. The need to be parted, the one from the other, was mutual. Sara, no doubt, couldn't wait for those exam results, the confirmation of St Biddulph's acceptance of her, for October and the start of term. It couldn't come fast enough for her.

'I'll stay with Mum,' she said, and there was stoicism in the way she said it. 'I'll give her a pill. She's got Valium. I'll give her a couple of Valium and find something nice for her on the TV.'

The ever ready panacea.

It was too late for lunch now. He and Burden might have something in the office, get a sandwich sent down from the canteen. He had said he'd see the press at 2.30. Well, young Varney of the local paper who was a stringer for the nationals . . .

There was a van on the police station forecourt marked TV South and a camera crew getting out of it.

'They've been up at the forest getting shots of the grave and Fitzgerald and the dog,' Burden said, 'and they want you next.'

'Good. I'll be able to put out an appeal for anyone who may have seen that car parked.' A less encouraging thought struck Wexford. 'They won't want to make me up, will they?' He had never been on television before.

Burden looked at him morosely, lifting his shoulders in a shrug of total indifference to any eventuality.

'It's not the end of the world if they do, is it?'

There was no time like the present, even a present that would end in ten minutes with his first ever TV appearance.

'What's happened to end your world, Mike?'

Burden immediately looked away. He mumbled something which Wexford couldn't hear and had to ask him to repeat.

'I said that I supposed I should tell you what the trouble is.'

'Yes. I want to know.' Looking at Burden, Wexford noticed for the first time grey hairs among the fair ones. 'There's something wrong with the baby, isn't there?'

'That's right.' Burden's voice sounded very dry. 'In Jenny's

opinion, mind you. Not in mine.' He gave a bark of laughter.
'It's a girl.'

'*What?*'

Wexford's phone went. He picked up the receiver. TV
South, the *Kingsmarkham Courier* and two other reporters
were downstairs waiting for him. Burden had already gone,
closing the door quietly behind him.

8

She was laying the table with their wedding present glass and silver. The lace cloth had been bought in Venice where they went for the first holiday after their honeymoon. Domesticity had delighted her when, as soon as she knew she was pregnant, she gave up teaching. It was the novelty, of course, being at home all day, playing house. Since then she had grown indifferent, she had grown indifferent to everything. Except to the child, and that she hated.

Sometimes, walking about the house after Mike had gone to work, pushing the vacuum cleaner or tidying up, the tears fell out of her eyes and streamed down her face. She cried because she couldn't believe that she who had longed and longed for a baby could hate the one inside her. All this she had told to the psychiatrist at their second session. She had listened to her in almost total silence. Once she said, 'Why do you say that?' and once 'Go on', but otherwise she simply listened with a kind interested look on her face.

Mike had suggested the psychiatrist. She had been so surprised because Mike usually scoffed at psychiatry that she said yes without even protesting. It was somewhere to go anyway, something different to do from sitting at home brooding about the future and her marriage and the unwanted child. And inevitably crying, of course, when she remembered as she always did what life used to be – when the days seemed too short, when she was teaching history to sixth formers at Haldon Finch, playing the violin in an orchestra, taking an advanced art appreciation course.

Jenny despised herself but that changed nothing. Her self-pity sickened her.

The sound of his key in the door – time-honoured heart stopper, test of love sustained – did nothing for her beyond bringing a little dread of the evening in front of them. He came into the room and kissed her. He still did that.

'How did you get on with the shrink?'

She resented the haste he was in. He wanted her cured, she felt, so that life could get back to normal again. 'What do you expect? A miracle in two easy lessons?'

She sat down. That always made her feel a little less bad because the bulge was no longer so apparent. And, thank God, the child was still, not rolling about and kicking.

'Don't let him give you drugs.'

'It's a woman.'

She wanted to scream with laughter. The irony of it! She was a teacher and this other woman was a psychiatrist and Mike's daughter Pat was very nearly qualified as a dentist, yet here she was reacting like a no-account junior wife in a harem. Because the baby was a girl.

He gave her a drink, orange juice and Perrier. He had a whisky, a large one, and in a minute he would have another. Not long ago he hadn't needed to drink when he got home. She looked at him, wishing she could bring herself to touch his arm or take his hand. An apathy as strong as energy held her back.

'Mike,' she said, and said for the hundredth time, 'I can't help it, I wish I could. I have tried.'

'So you say. I don't understand it. It's beyond my understanding.'

In a low voice, looking down, she said, 'It's beyond mine.' The child began to move, with flutters only at first, then came a hearty kick right under her lower ribs, giving her a rush of heartburn. She cried out, 'I wish to God I'd never had the thing done. I wish I'd never let them do it. They shouldn't have told me. Why did I let them? If I'd been ignorant I'd have gone on being happy, I'd have had the baby and I wouldn't have minded what it was, I'd have been pleased with any healthy baby. I didn't even specially want a son, or I didn't know I did. I didn't mind what it was, but now I know what it is I can't bear it. I can't go through all this and all through having it and the work and the pain and the trouble and a lifetime of being with it, having it with me, for a *girl*!'

He had heard it all before. It seemed to him that she said it every night. This was what he came home to. With slight variations, with modifications and changed turns of phrase, that was what she said to him on and on every evening. Until she grew exhausted or wept or slumped spent in her chair, until she went away to bed – earlier and earlier as the weeks passed. In vain he had asked why this prejudice against girls, she who was a feminist, a supporter of the women's movement, who expressed a preference for her friends' small girls over their small sons, who got on better with her stepdaughter than her stepson, who professed to prefer teaching girls to boys.

She didn't know why, only that it was so. Her pregnancy, so long desired, at first so ecstatically accepted, had driven her mad. The worst of it was that he was coming to hate the unborn child himself and to wish it had never been conceived.

The wine bar was dark and cool. The restoration of an old house in Kingsmarkham's Queen Street had revealed and then opened up its cavernous cellars. The proprietor had resisted the temptations of roof beams, medieval pastiches, flintlocks and copper warming pans and simply painted the broad squat arches white, tiled the floor and furnished the place with tables and chairs in dark-stained pine.

Wexford and Burden had taken to lunching at the Old Cellar a couple of times a week. It had the virtue of being warm on cold days and cool on hot ones like this. The food was quiche and salad, smoked mackerel, coleslaw, pork pie, quiche, quiche and more quiche.

'What did they serve in these places before quiche caught on? I mean, there was a time not long ago when an Englishman could say he'd never heard of quiche.'

'He's always eaten it,' said Wexford. 'He called it cheese and onion flan.'

He had the morning papers with him. The *Kingsmarkham Courier* was a weekly and wouldn't be out till Friday. The national dailies had given no more than a paragraph to the discovery of Rodney Williams's body and had left out all the background details he was sure Varney had passed on to them. The *Daily Telegraph* merely stated that the body of a man had been found in a shallow grave and later identified as Rodney John Williams, a salesman from Kingsmarkham in Sussex. Nothing about Joy, his children, his job at Sevensmith Harding or the fact that he had been missing for two months. True, they had put him, Wexford, on TV but only on the regional bit that came after the news and then only forty-five seconds of the half-hour-long film they'd made.

The corpses of middle-aged men weren't news as women's were or children's. Women were always news. Perhaps they would cease to be when the day came that they got their equality as well as their rights. An interesting speculation and one which reminded him . . .

'You were going to tell me but we were interrupted.'

'It's not that she's anti-girls usually,' Burden said. 'For God's sake, she's a feminist. I mean, it's not some stupid I-must-have-an-heir thing or every-woman's-got-to-have-a-son-to-prove-herself. In fact I think she secretly thinks women are better than men – I mean cleverer and more versatile, all that. She says she doesn't understand it herself. She says she had no feelings about the child's sex one way or the other, but when they told her, when she knew, she was – well, dismayed. That was at first. It's got worse. It's not just dismay now, it's hatred.'

'Why doesn't she want a girl?' Wexford remembered certain sentiments expressed by his daughter Sylvia, mother of two sons. 'Is it that she feels women have a raw deal and she doesn't want to be responsible for bringing another into the world?' By way of apology for this crassness, he added, 'I have heard that view put.'

'She doesn't know. She says that ever since the world began sons have been preferred over daughters and now it's become part of race memory, what she calls the collective un- conscious.'

'What Jung called it.'

Burden hesitated and then passed over that one. 'She's mad, you know. Pregnancy has driven her mad. Oh, don't look at me like that. I've given up caring about being disloyal. I've given up damn well caring, if you must know. Do you know what she says? She says she can't contemplate a future with a daughter she doesn't want. She says she can't imagine living for twenty years, say, with someone she hates before it's born. What's my life going to be like with that going on?'

'At the risk of uttering an old cliché, I'd say she'll feel differently when the baby's born.'

'Oh, she will? You can be sure of that? She'll love it when it's put into her arms? Shall I tell you what else she says? That she never wants to see it. We're to put it up for adoption immediately without either of us seeing it. I told you she was mad.'

All this made Wexford feel like a drink. But he couldn't start drinking at lunchtime with all he'd got ahead of him. Burden wasn't going to drink either. Judging by the look of him some mornings, he saved that up for when he got home. They paid the bill and climbed up the stone steps out of the Old Cellar into a bright June sunshine that made them blink.

'She's seeing a psychiatrist. I pin my faith to that. Me of all people! I sometimes wonder what I've come to, saying things like that.'

Sir Hilary Tremlett's report of the results of the post-mortem had come. To decipher the obscurer bits for Wexford, Dr Crocker came into the office as Burden was departing. They nearly passed each other in the doorway, Burden long-faced, monosyllabic. The doctor laughed.

'Mike's having a difficult pregnancy.'

Wexford wasn't going to enlighten him. The other chair had been pushed under the desk. He shoved it out with his toe.

'He says here he found three hundred and twenty milligrammes of cyclobarbitone in the stomach and other organs. What's cyclobarbitone?'

'It's an intermediate-acting barbiturate – that means it has about eight hours' duration of effect – a hypnotic drug, a sleeping pill if you like. The proprietary brand name would be Phanodorm, I expect. Two hundred milligrammes is the dose. But three hundred and twenty wouldn't kill him. It sounds as if he took two tablets of two hundred each.'

'It didn't kill him, though, did it? He died of stab wounds.'

Wexford looked up to see the doctor looking at him. They were both thinking the same thing. They were both thinking about Colin Budd and Brian Wheatley.

225

'What actually killed him was a wound that pierced the carotid.'

'Did it now? The blood must have spouted like a fountain.'

'There were seven other wounds in the neck and chest and back. A lot of stuff here's about fixed and mobile underlying tissues.' Wexford handed the pages across the desk, retaining one. 'I'm more interested in the estimate he makes of the proportions of the knife. A large kitchen knife with a dagger point, it would seem to have been.'

'I see he suggests death occurred six to eight weeks ago. What d'you reckon? He took two sleeping pills and someone did him in while he was away in the land of nod? If it happened as you seem to think soon after he left his house at six that evening, why would he take sleeping pills at that hour?'

'He might have taken them,' said Wexford thoughtfully, 'in mistake for something else. Hypertension pills, for instance. He had high blood pressure.'

While the doctor was reading Wexford picked up the phone and asked the telephonist to get him Wheatley's number. Wheatley had said he worked in London on only three days a week so there was a chance he might be at home now. He was.

'I didn't think you showen much interest,' he said in an injured way.

That one Wexford wasn't going to answer. It was true anyway. They hadn't shown all that much interest in a man getting his hand scratched by a girl hitchhiker. Things had taken on a different aspect since then.

'You gave me a detailed description of the girl who attacked you, Mr Wheatley. The fact that you're a good observer makes me think you may have observed more. Will you think about that, please, and try and remember everything that happened? Principally, give us some more information about what the girl looked like, her voice and so on. We'd like to come and see you.'

Mollified, Wheatley said he'd give it some thought and tell them everything he could remember and how about some time that evening?

The doctor said, 'It couldn't have happened inside a car, you know, Reg. There'd have been too much blood.'

'Perhaps in the open air?'

'And tied his neck up in a Marks and Spencer's floral-printed teatowel?'

'It doesn't say that there!'

'I happened to notice it when the poor devil was resurrected. We've got one like it at home.'

The phone rang. The telephonist said, 'Mr Wexford, there's a Mrs Williams here wanting to talk to someone about Mr Rodney Williams.'

Joy, he thought. Well.

'Mrs Joy Williams?'

'Mrs Wendy Williams.'

'Have someone bring her up here, will you?'

The sister-in-law? The wife of the brother in Bath? When you don't know what to do next, Raymond Chandler advised writers of his sort of fiction, have a man come in with a gun. In a real-life murder case, thought Wexford, what better surprise visitor than the mysterious Wife of Bath?

He looked up as Burden re-entered the room. Burden had been going through the clothes found on Williams's body: navy blue briefs – very different from the white underwear in the cupboard in Alverbury Road – brown socks, fawn cavalry-twill slacks, blue, brown and cream striped shirt, dark blue St Laurent sweater. The back pocket of the slacks had contained a cheque book for one of the accounts with the Anglian-Victoria at Pomfret (R. J. Williams, private account), and a wallet containing one fiver, three £1 notes and two credit cards, Visa and American Express. No car keys, no house keys.

'He probably kept his house keys on the same ring as his car keys,' Burden said. 'It's what I do.'

'At any rate, we'll get at that bank account now. The doctor here says there was a teatowel wrapped around his neck. To staunch the blood presumably.'

There came a knock at the door. Bennett came into the room with a young woman, not anyone's idea of a Wife of Bath.

'Mrs Wendy Williams, sir.'

She looked about twenty-five. She was a pretty girl with a delicate nervous face and fair curly hair. Wexford asked her to sit down, the doctor having sprung to his feet. She slid into the chair, gripping the arms of it, and jumped as Crocker passed behind her on his way to the door. Burden closed the door behind him and stood there.

'What did you want to see me about, Mrs Williams?'

She didn't answer. She had fixed him with a penetrating stare and her tongue came in and out, moistening her lips.

'I take it you're Rodney Williams's sister-in-law? Is that right?'

She moved her body back a little, hands still tight on the chair arms. 'What do you mean, his sister-in-law?' She didn't wait for a reply. 'Look, I . . . I don't know how to say this. I've been so . . . I've been nearly out of my mind.' Mounting hysteria made her voice ragged. 'I saw in the paper . . . a little bit in the paper and . . . Is that, that *person* they found . . . ? Is that my husband?'

9

It was seldom he could give people reassuring news. He was tempted to say no, of course not. The body has been identified. She was holding on to the arms of the chair, rubbing her fingers up and down the wood.

'What is your husband's name, Mrs Williams?'

'Rodney John Williams. He's forty-eight.' She spoke in short jerky phrases, not waiting for the questions. 'Six feet tall. He's fair going grey. He's a salesman. It said in the paper a salesman.'

Burden stared, then looked down. She swallowed, made an effort against panic, an effort that concentrated on tensing her muscles.

'Could you . . . please, I have a photo here.'

Her hands, unlocked from the chair, refused to obey her when first she tried to open the bag. The photograph she handed to Wexford fluttered, she was shaking so. He looked at it, unbelieving.

It was Rodney Williams all right, high domed forehead, crack of a mouth parted in a broad smile. It was a more recent picture than the one Joy had and showed Williams in swimming trunks (flabby hairless chest, spindleshanks, a bit knock-kneed) with this girl in a black bikini and another girl, also bikini'd but no more than twelve years old. Wexford's eyes returned to the unmistakable face of Williams, to the head you somehow wanted to slap a fringed wig on and so transform it.

She was waiting, watching him. He nodded. She brought a fluttery hand up to her chest, to her heart perhaps, froze for a moment in this tragic pose. Then her eyelids fell and she sagged sideways in the chair.

Afterwards he was to think of it as having been beautifully done but at the time he saw it only as a genuine faint. Burden held her shoulders, bringing her face down onto her knees. Picking up the phone, Wexford asked for a policewoman to come up, Polly Davies or Marion Bayliss, anyone who was around. And someone send a pot of strong tea and don't forget the sugar basin.

Wendy Williams came out of her faint, sat up and pressed her face into her hands.

'You are the wife of Rodney John Williams and you live in Liskeard Avenue, Pomfret?'

She drank the tea sugarless and very hot, at first with her eyes closed. When she opened her eyes, and they met his he noticed they were the very clear pale blue of flax flowers. She nodded slowly.

'How long have you been married, Mrs Williams?'

'Sixteen years. We had our sixteenth wedding anniversary in March.'

He could hardly believe it. Her skin had the clear bloom of an adolescent's, her hair was baby-soft and the curl in it looked natural. She saw his incredulity and in spite of her emotion was flattered, a little buoyed up. He could tell she was the sort of woman to whom compliments, even unspoken ones, were food and drink. They nourished her. A faint, tremulous smile appeared. He looked again at the photographs.

'My daughter Veronica,' she said. 'I got married very young. I was only sixteen. That picture was taken three or four years back.'

A bigamist he had been, then. Not a common or garden wayward husband with a girlfriend living in the next town, not a married man with a sequence of pricey mistresses, but your good old-fashioned true blue bigamist. There was no doubt in Wexford's mind that Wendy Williams had as good-looking a marriage certificate as Joy's and if hers happened not to be valid she would be the last to know it.

That, then, was why he had taken no change of clothes with him. He had those things in his other home. And more than that, much more. Wexford now saw the point of those bank accounts: one for his salary to be paid into and two joint accounts to be fed from it, one for each household, R. J. Williams and J. Williams; R. J. Williams and W. Williams. There had been no need to assume a different name on his second marriage – Williams was common enough to make that unnecessary. He had been like a Moslem who keeps strictly to Islamic law and maintains his wives in separate and distinct dwellings. The difference here was that the wives didn't know of each other's existence.

That Williams had had another wife, what one might call in fact a chief wife, was something this girl was going to have to be told. And Joy was going to have to be told about her.

'Can you tell me when you last saw Mr Williams?' Not calling him 'your husband' any more was the beginning of breaking the news.

'About two months ago. Just after Easter.'

This wasn't the time to ask her to account for that eight week gap. He told her he would come and see her at home that evening. Polly Davies would look after her and see she got home safely.

Something had at last happened to distract Burden temporarily from his private troubles. His expression was as curious and as alerted as a little boy's.

'What did he do at Christmas?' he said. 'Easter? What about holidays?'

'No doubt we shall find out. Other bigamists have handled it. He probably had a Bunbury as well.'

'A *what*?'

'A nonexistent friend or relative to provide him with alibis. My guess is Williams's Bunbury was an old mother.'

'Did he have an old mother?'

'God knows. Creating one from his imagination wouldn't have been beyond his capacity, I'm sure. You know what they say, a mother is the invention of necessity.'

Burden winced. 'That night he left Alverbury Road, d'you think he went to his other home?'

'I think he set off meaning to go there. Whether he reached it is another matter.'

Fascinated by Williams's family arrangements, Burden said,

'While Joy thought he was travelling for Sevensmith Harding in Ipswich he was with Wendy and while he was with Joy Wendy thought he was where?'

'I don't suppose she knew he worked for Sevensmith Harding. He probably told her a total lie about what he did.'

'You'd think he'd have got their names muddled – I mean called Wendy Joy and Joy Wendy.'

'There speaks the innocent monogamist,' said Wexford, casting up his eyes. 'How do you think married men with girlfriends manage? Wife and all get called "darling".'

Burden shook his head as if even speculating about it was too much for him. 'Do you reckon it was one of them killed him?'

'Carried his body and stuck it in that grave? Williams weighed a good fifteen stone or two hundred and ten pounds or ninety something kilos or whatever we're supposed to say these days.'

'It might have been Wendy made that phone call.'

'You reckon her voice sounds like Joy's?'

Burden was obliged to admit that it didn't. Joy's was monotonous, accent-free, uninflected; Wendy's girlish, rather fluting, with a faint lisp. Wexford was talking about voices, about the rather unattractive but nevertheless memorable quality of Joy's voice when his phone rang again.

'Another young lady to see me,' he said to Burden, putting the receiver back.

'Bluebeard's third wife?' It was the first attempt at a joke he had made in two months.

Wexford appreciated that. 'Let's say a fan, rather. Someone who saw me on the telly.'

'Look, why don't I take Martin and get on over to Wheatley? Then I'll be able to come to Wendy's with you tonight.'

'OK, and we'll take Polly along.'

The girl walked into his room in a breeze of confidence. She was seventeen or eighteen and her name was Eve Freeborn. Apposite names of the Lady Dedlock-Ernest Pontifex-Obadiah Slope kind that Victorian novelists used are in real life less uncommon than is generally supposed. That Eve Freeborn was aptly named Wexford came quickly to under-

232

stand. She might have been dressed and cast for the role of Spirit of Freedom in a pageant. Her hair was cropped short and dyed purple in parts. She wore stretch jeans, a check shirt and thongs.

The story she told Wexford, sitting with legs wide apart, hands linked, forearms making a bridge from the chair arms to rest her chin on, was delivered in a brisk and articulate way. Eve was still at school, had come there straight from school. President of the debating society no doubt, he thought. As she turned her hands outwards, thumbs on her jaw, he noticed the felt-tipped pen drawing on her wrist, a raven with a woman's head, and then as she moved her arm the shirtsleeve covered it.

'I realised it was my duty as a citizen to come to you. I delayed just long enough to discuss the matter with my boyfriend. He's at the same school as me – Haldon Finch. In a way he's involved, you see. We have the sort of relationship where we believe in total openness.'

Wexford gave her an encouraging smile.

'My boyfriend lives in Arnold Road, Myringham. It's a single-storey house, number forty-three.' Opposite Graham Gee who had reported the presence of poor old Greta, Wexford thought. 'His mother and father live there too,' said Eve in a tone that implied enormous condescension and generosity on the part of the boyfriend in allowing his parents to live in their own house. 'The point is – and you may not believe this but it's the honest truth, I promise you – they don't like him having me to stay the night with him. I mean, not me personally, you could understand that if they didn't like me, but any girl. So what we do is I come round after he's gone to bed and get in the window.'

Wexford didn't gape at her. He merely felt like doing this. He couldn't resist asking, 'Why doesn't he come to you?'

'I share a room with my sister. Anyway, I was telling you. I went round to his place around ten that Thursday night. There wasn't all that much space to park and when I was reversing I went into the car behind. I just bashed the wing of it a bit, not much, it wouldn't have had to have a new wing or anything, but I did think it was my duty to take responsibility and not just leave it, so I . . .'

'Just a moment. This was the night of April the fifteenth?'

233

'Right. It was my boyfriend's birthday.'

And a charming present he must have had, Wexford thought.

'What was this car you went into?'

'A dark blue Ford Granada. It was the car you asked about on TV. I wrote a note and put it on the windscreen, under a wiper. Just with my name and address on and phone number. But it blew away or got lost or something because the car was still there a long while after that and the driver never got in touch with me.'

At ten that night. Greta the Granada had been there at ten but how long had it been there?

'Just as a matter of curiosity, whose car were you driving?'

'My own,' she said, surprised.

'You have your own car?'

'My mother's technically. But it comes to the same thing.'

No doubt it did. They were amazing, these young people. And the most amazing thing about them was that they had no idea previous generations had not behaved as they did. People got old, of course, became dull and staid, they knew that, but in their day surely teenage girls had slept with their boyfriends, appropriated their parents' cars, stayed out all night, dyed their hair all colours of the spectrum.

He thanked her for her help and as she got up he saw the little drawing or tattoo again. He realised that he didn't know which of the local schools Sara Williams attended. And there remained the as yet unknown quantity, Veronica Williams . . .

'Do you know a girl of your own age called Sara Williams? Is she perhaps at school with you?'

He was positive she hadn't made the connection before, was making it now for the first time. 'Do you mean Sara is the daughter of this man who was murdered?'

'Yes. You go to the same school?'

'No, we don't,' she said carefully, 'but I know her.'

Wheatley lived on an estate of new houses on the Pomfret side of Myringham. They had been built, Burden recalled, by a company so anxious to sell their houses that 100 per cent mortgages had been guaranteed with them and a promise given to buy a house back for its purchase price if after

234

two years the occupier were dissatisfied. The place had a raw look, oddly cold in the June sunshine. Wheatley's pregnant wife came to the door. A child of about three, a girl, was behind her, holding on to her skirt. Burden registered the fact of the pregnancy and the sex of the child with his heightened sensitivity to such matters and then he thought that his wife's pregnancy might have affected Wheatley's attitude to the girl he picked up. For instance, he might be sexually frustrated. Burden knew all about that. Wheatley too might have exaggerated the purity of his attitude towards the girl because he dared not risk the possibility of his pregnant wife finding out he was capable of putting his hand on other women's knees — or, in this instance no doubt, on other women's breasts.

The third bedroom of this very small house had been turned into a study or office for Wheatley. He was on the phone but rang off within seconds of Burden's and Martin's arrival. Yes, he had remembered some more about the girl. He was sure he could give them a more detailed description. There was no question of his remembering more of what the girl had said to him because she hadn't said any more. 'Thanks' and a gasp had been the only sounds that had come from her.

'I told you she was tall for a woman, at least five feet nine. Still in her teens, I'm sure. She had dark brown shoulder-length hair with a fringe, very fair skin and very white hands. I think I can remember a ring, not a wedding or engagement ring or anything, but one of those big silver rings they wear. I wouldn't call her pretty, not a bit.' Was that a sop to the wife who had come quietly into the room, carrying the little girl? 'Sunglasses, a dark leather shoulder bag. She had blue denim jeans on and a grey cardigan. She was thin — really skinny, I mean.' Another matrimonial sop. 'And underneath the cardigan she had a tee-shirt on. It was a white tee-shirt with a crazy picture on it — some sort of bird with a woman's head.'

'You didn't mention that before, Mr Wheatley.'

'I didn't mention the ring before or what colour her clothes were. You asked me to think about it and I thought about it and that's what I remember. You can take it or leave it. A white tee-shirt with a bird on it with a woman's face.'

* * *

235

'I don't believe it!'

She stared at Wexford, her mouth open in an appalled sort of way, her eyelids moving. She brought her hands up and scrabbled at her neck.

'I don't believe it!' Now there was defiance in her tone. Then, by changing one word, she showed him she accepted, she understood that what he had told her was true. 'I *won't* believe it!'

Polly Davies was with him, sitting there like a good chaperone, silent but attentive. She glanced at Wexford, got a nod from him.

'I'm afraid it's true, Mrs Williams.'

'I don't – I don't have a right to be called that, do I?'

'Of course you do. Your name doesn't depend on a marriage certificate.' Wexford thought of Eve Freeborn. There was a world between her and Wendy Williams, though a mere fourteen years, less than a generation, separated them. Would Eve know such a thing as a marriage certificate existed?

'Mrs Williams,' said stalwart Polly, 'why don't you and I go and make some coffee? We'd all like coffee, I'm sure. Mr Wexford will want to ask you some questions but I know he'd like you to have time to get over the shock of this.'

She nodded and got up awkwardly as if her bones were stiff. A glazed look had come across her face. She walked like a sleepwalker and no one now would have mistaken her for a twenty-five-year-old.

Burden shrugged silently as the door closed behind them and subsided into one of his typical morose reveries. Wexford had a look round the room they were sitting in. The house was newer than the Williams home in Kingsmarkham, a small 'town house' with an integral garage, built probably in the late 1960s. Wendy was a thorough, meticulous and perhaps fanatical housekeeper. This was a through room with a dining area and it had very recently been redecorated in gleaming white with an undertone of palest pink. One of the colours in the Sevensmith Harding 'Ice Cream' range? The carpet was deep strawberry pink, some of the furniture mahogany, some white canework, cushions in various shades of pink and red. It was tasteful, it was a far cry from the stereotyped shabbiness of Joy's home, but somehow it was also uncomfortable, as if everything had been placed there – hanging baskets, little tables, red Venetian glass – for effect rather than for use.

He remembered that a young girl also lived here. There were no signs of her. But what sign did he expect or would he recognise if he saw it? She had been twelve in the picture . . .

'My daughter is sixteen now,' Wendy said when the coffee was brought. A slightly defiant note came into her voice as she added, 'She was sixteen three weeks ago.'

Her gaze fell. He did some calculations, remembering what she had said about her wedding anniversary taking place in March. So Williams had 'married' her three months before the child was born. He had had to wait until she reached the legal age for marrige.

'Where were you married, Mrs Williams?'

'Myringham Registry Office. My mother wanted us to have a church wedding but – well, for obvious reasons . . .'

Wexford could imagine one very obvious reason if she had been six months pregnant. The nerve of Williams, a married man, 'marrying' this child, as she had been, a mere dozen miles from his home town! The wedding to Joy, Dora had told him, had been at St Peter's, Kingsmarkham, the bride in white slipper satin . . .

Wendy was thrusting a paper at him. He saw it was her marriage certificate.

In the Registration District of Myringham, at the Registry Office. Rodney John Williams, aged thirty-two. In some respects, at any rate, he had been honest. Though he could hardly have distorted those facts. They had been on his birth certificate. A Bath address, his brother's probably, his occupation sales representative. Wendy Ann Rees, aged sixteen, Pelham Street, Myringham, shop assistant. The witnesses had been Norman Rees and Brenda Rees, parents presumably, or brother and sister-in-law.

He handed it back to her. She looked at it herself and her tongue flicked out to moisten her lips. For a moment, from the way she was holding it, he thought she was going to tear the certificate across. But she replaced it in its envelope and laid the envelope on the low white melamine table that was close up against the arm of her chair.

She pressed her knees together and folded her hands in her

237

lap. Her legs were very good with elongated slim ankles. To come to the police station she had worn a grey flannel suit with a white blouse. He had a feeling she was a woman who attached importance to being suitably dressed. The suit was changed now for a cotton dress. She was the type who would 'save' her clothes, not sit about in a straight skirt or risk a spot on white silk. In her sad wistful look youth had come back into her face.

'Mrs Williams,' he began, 'I'm sure you won't mind telling me how it was you weren't alarmed when your husband was away for so long.'

She did mind. She was reluctant. Patience, simply waiting quietly, succeeded with her where pressing the point might not have.

'Rodney and I . . .' She paused. It was always 'Rodney' with her, Wexford noted, never 'Rod'. 'We – we quarrelled. Well, we had a very serious quarrel. That must have been a few days after Easter. Rodney spent Easter with his mother in Bath. He always spent Christmas and Easter with her. He was an only child, you see, and she's been in an old people's home for years and years.'

Wexford carefully avoided looking at Burden. Wendy said, reminded by her own explanation, 'Has she been. . . ? I mean, has anyone *told* her?'

Enigmatically, Wexford said that had been taken care of. 'Go on please, Mrs Williams.'

'We quarrelled,' she went on. 'It was a very private thing we quarrelled about. I'll keep that to myself if you don't mind. I said to him that – well, I said that if he – if *it* didn't stop, if he didn't promise me faithfully that never – well, I said I'd take Veronica away and he'd never see us again. I – I struck him, I was so angry, so distressed, I can't tell you – well, he was angry too. He denied it, of course, and then he said I needn't trouble about leaving him because he'd leave me. He said he couldn't stand my nagging any more.' She lifted her head and looked Wexford straight in the eye. 'I did nag him, I'll be honest about it. I couldn't bear it, never seeing him, him always being away. We'd never had a single Christmas together. I always had to go to my parents. We hardly ever had a holiday. I used to *beg* him . . .' Her voice faltered and Wexford understood that

238

realisation was dawning. She was beginning to see what the real reason was for those absences. 'Anyway,' she said, making an effort at control, 'he – he calmed down after a while and I suppose I did too. He was going away again and he was due back on the Thursday – the fifteenth, that is. I was still very sore and upset but I said goodbye to him and that I'd see him on Thursday and he said maybe I would and maybe he'd never come back, so you see, I – when he didn't come back I thought he'd left me.'

It wasn't a completely convincing explanation. He tried to put himself in her shoes. He tried to think how he would have felt years ago when he and Dora were young if they'd had a row and she, going away to visit her sister, say, had told him maybe she wouldn't come back. Probably such a thing had actually happened. It did happen in marriages, even in excellent ones. But if she hadn't come back on the appointed day, if she'd been a couple of hours late even, he'd have started going out of his mind with worry. Of course, much depended on the seriousness of the quarrel and on the reasons for it.

'Tell me what happened that Thursday.'

'In the evening, do you mean?'

'When he didn't come.'

'I was at work. Thursday's our late night. I didn't tell you, did I? I'm manageress of the fashion floor at Jickie's.'

He was surprised. Somehow he had taken it for granted she didn't work. 'In Myringham?' he asked. 'Or the Kingsmarkham branch?'

'Oh, Kingsmarkham. In the Precinct.'

Jickie's was Kingsmarkham's biggest department store and the largest area of the Kingsbrook Shopping Precinct was given over to it. Doubtless Rodney Williams had taken care never to accompany Joy when she went shopping there for a jumper or a pair of tights on a Saturday afternoon. Had he risked walking arm in arm down Kingsmarkham High Street during shopping hours? With his son or daughter in the car, had he risked parking in the precinct car park? It was a tightrope he had walked and no doubt, for such is the nature of people like him, he had enjoyed walking it, but he had fallen off at last. Because of the tightrope or for some entirely different reason?

'We stay open till eight on Thursdays but I can never get away till nine and it takes me a quarter of an hour to get home. When I did get back Veronica was here but Rodney hadn't come. I thought there was still a chance he might come but he didn't and then I knew. Or I thought I knew. I thought he'd left me.'

'And in all the weeks that followed,' Burden put it, 'you weren't anxious? You didn't wonder what could happen to you and your daughter if he didn't come back?'

'I'd be all right financially without him. I've always had to work and now I'm doing quite well.' There was a note of self-esteem in the little soft voice now. Inside the white and pink and fair curls and underneath the lisp and diffidence, Wexford thought there might be a core of steel. 'We had a ninety per cent mortgage on this house and up till five years ago it was all Rodney could do to keep us. He got promotion then and things were easier but I kept on working. I needed a life of my own too, he was away so much.'

'Promotion?' hazarded Wexford, feeling his way.

'It's quite a small company and they haven't been doing too well lately – bathroom fittings and furniture, that sort of thing. Rodney was made sales manager for this locality.'

Polly Davies picked up the tray and took it away into the kitchen. Wexford thought how easy it was to imagine Rodney Williams – or his idea of Rodney Williams – in his other home but next to impossible to imagine him here. Seated at that glass-topped dining table, for instance, with its bowl of pink and red roses or in one of those pink chintz armchairs. He had been a big coarse man and everything here had a daintiness like a pink shell or the inside of a rose.

'I have to know what you quarrelled about, Mrs Williams.'

Her tone became prissy, very genteel. 'It has nothing whatsoever to do with Rodney's death.'

'How do you know?'

She looked at him as if this were unfair persecution.

'How could it be? He got killed because he picked up someone hitching a lift and they killed him. Something like that . . . It's always happening.'

'That's an interesting guess but it's only a guess, isn't it? You've no evidence for it and there's plenty of evidence against

240

it. The car being returned to Myringham, for instance. A phone call was made to your husband's employers and a letter of resignation sent to them. Do you think that phone call was made by some homicidal hitch-hiker?'

She sat rigid, keeping her eyes obstinately averted. Polly came back.

'Are you all right, Mrs Williams?'

A nod. An indrawn breath and a sigh.

'What did you quarrel about?'

'I could refuse to tell you.'

'You could. But why take a stand like that when what you tell us will be treated in the strictest confidence? Ask yourself if it's so awful that we won't have heard it before. And don't you think that if you don't tell us we may come to think it something worse than it really was?'

She sat silent. She wore an expression like someone who expects at any moment to see something nasty and shocking on television. It was an anticlimax when she said almost in a whisper. 'There was another girl.'

'You mean your husband had a woman friend he'd been seeing?'

' "Seeing",' she said, 'I like that expression – "seeing". Yes, he'd been seeing a woman friend. That's one way of putting it.'

'How would you put it?'

'Oh, like that. The way you do. What else does one say? Something crude, I suppose.' The repressive lid suddenly jumped and let out a dribble of resentment, of bitterness. 'I thought no one else but me would ever matter to him. I look young, don't I? I'm pretty enough, I don't look my age. People say I look eighteen. What was the matter with him that he . . . ? Yes, we quarrelled about that. About a girl. I wanted him to promise me it would never happen again.'

'He refused?'

'Oh, he promised. I didn't believe him. I thought it would start up again when he got the chance. I couldn't stand it, I didn't want him if he was going to do that. I was glad when he didn't come back. Don't you see? I was *glad*.'

'I'll have to have this girl's name.'

Quick as a flash: 'I don't know her name.'

'Come now, Mrs Williams.'

241

'I don't know it. He wouldn't tell me. Just a girl. What does it matter?'

She had said too much already, she was thinking. He could read that, plain in her face, the look in her eyes of being appalled at her own indiscretion. At that moment, before he could say any more, the door opened and a young girl came in. Just before this happened there had been a sound downstairs and footsteps on the stairs – the living room was on the middle floor – but it had all taken place very quickly, within a few seconds. And now, without warning, the girl was here among them.

What first struck Wexford was that although she was not so tall and her hair was shorter she looked exactly like Sara Williams. They might have been twins.

10

Her hair was the same pale fudge colour, not curly but not quite straight either, the tips just touching her shoulders. Brown eyes, ellipse eyebrows, small straight nose, fine white skin sprinkled with freckles. Rodney Williams's high domed forehead and his small narrow mouth. But instead of jeans she wore a summer dress with white tights and white sandals. She stood in the doorway looking surprised at the sight of them, a little more than just startled.

Wendy Williams was taken aback.

In a flustered way she said, 'This is my daughter Veronica,' and to the girl, 'You're home early.'

'Not much. It's after nine.'

The voice was her mother's, soft and slightly affected but without the lisp. It was quite unlike Sara's abrupt uninflected tones. Recovering poise Wendy said to her, 'These are police officers. They'll only be a few minutes.' She lied fluently, 'It's to do with trouble at the shop. You won't mind leaving us alone for a bit, will you, darling?'

'I'm going to have a bath anyway.'

Closing the door with the sort of precision her mother might use, she went off up the spiral staircase that was the core of this house.

'I don't know why she's so offhand with me lately. This past year . . .'

Wexford said, 'You haven't told her?'

'I haven't seen her. She always goes to her friend's straight from school on a Tuesday. Or so she says, she's so secretive . . .'

243

'Which school, Mrs Williams?'

'Haldon Finch Comprehensive. I'll tell her about her father after you've gone. I suppose I shall have to tell her what he was – a bigamist, with another wife somewhere. It won't be easy. I don't know if you appreciate that.'

Wexford, when interrogating, would allow any amount of digression but never total distraction. Those he questioned were obliged to come back to the point sooner or later. It was hard on them for often they believed they had escaped. The leash had snapped and freedom was surely there for the taking, but the hand always came down and snatched up the broken end.

'We were talking about this woman friend your husband had. He may have gone to her on the night he died.'

'I don't know any more about her!'

Fear had come into her voice now. It was what many would have called caution or apprehensiveness but it was really fear.

'You called her a girl. You implied a young girl.'

A panicky jerky rapid way of speaking – 'A young single girl, very young, that's all I know. I told you, I don't know any more!'

Wexford recalled the overtures Williams had once made to Sylvia. When Sylvia was fifteen. Was it something like that that Wendy had implied when she asked so pathetically if she didn't still look young? That she at thirty-two to his forty-eight might not be young enough for him?

'Do you mean she's young enough to live at home with her parents?'

A nod, painful and perplexed.

'What else do you know of her, Mrs Williams?'

'Nothing. I don't know any more. Do you think I wanted him to talk to me about her?'

That was reasonable enough. At first he thought she was lying when she said she was ignorant of the girl's name. Now he was less sure. How often had he heard people say, 'If my husband (my wife) were unfaithful to me I wouldn't want to know', and when they were forced to know, 'I don't want to hear anything about it?' The knives of jealousy are honed on details.

The question he sensed she would hate but which must be asked he had saved till last.

'How did you know it was happening at all? How did you know of her existence?'

He had been wrong. She didn't mind. She didn't mind because her answer was a lie that she had been rehearsing in her mind, silently and busily while they talked, waiting for the past half-hour for the question to come.

'I had an anonymous letter.'

Eventually he would get at the truth. It could wait.

'Now, Mrs Williams, your daughter . . .'

'What about her?' Very quick and defensive.

'I shall want to talk to Veronica.'

'Oh no, not that. Please.'

'When you have told her and she has had a day or two to get over the shock.'

'But why?'

'Her father has been murdered. He was due to come here and she was here, alone here. It's possible he did come and she was the last person to see him alive.'

'He didn't come here. She would have told me.'

'We'll see, Mrs Williams. We shall also want to look over this house, particularly at any of your husband's personal property.'

'We keep coming back to these young girls,' Burden said.

'And to ravens with women's faces.'

'That too. Budd and Wheatley were both attacked by a young girl – not very seriously, either of them, but they were attacked and the assault was with a knife. Rodney Williams liked young girls – I mean, he seems especially to have liked them very young – and he had a very young girlfriend. He died as the result of a knife attack, he was stabbed to death. Now Wheatley says the girl who attacked him was wearing a white tee-shirt with a design on it of a sort of bird with a woman's head . . .'

'And Sara Williams,' said Wexford, 'possesses just such a tee-shirt and has a poster with a similar motif on her bedroom wall.'

'Does she? You're kidding.'

'No. It's true. And Eve Freeborn has a raven with a woman's head tattooed or drawn on her left wrist, and since the sun came out, Mike, and women aren't bundling themselves up in cardigans and jackets I've seen no less than five girls around Kingsmarkham and Pomfret wearing white tee-shirts with ravens with women's faces on them. How about that?'

'God, and I thought we were really getting somewhere. It's like that bit in Ali Baba and the Forty Thieves when the woman says he'll know the right oil jar because it'll have a cross on it and when he gets there someone's put crosses on all the oil jars.'

'You've been reading again. Or going to pantomimes. It looks to me as if these raven-harpy pictures are the motif or symbol of some sort of society or cult. Latter-day anarchists or some sort of spurious freedom fighters.'

'Animal Rights?' said Burden doubtfully.

'It could be, I suppose. The implication being that the animal – or in this case bird – has the feelings and rights of a human being? The poster Sara Williams has in her bedroom has some letters on it as well as the picture. An acronym, I think, a, r, r, i, a, Arria.'

'Animal Rights something or other?'

'There was a woman called Arria, in Roman history, I seem to remember. I'll try and find out. If it's animal rights, Mike, you would expect its members to make their attacks on people who in their view were being cruel to animals. Factory farmers, for instance, or masters of foxhounds. I don't suppose Wheatley keeps calves chained up in boxes in his back garden, does he? We'll ask Sara. But first I want to leave her and Joy to get over the shock of Williams having another wife and another child.'

'You've told them.'

'Yes. It was the money aspect that seemed to mean most to Joy. She had been deprived in order that he could maintain another household. She gave that bitter laugh of hers. If I'd had to live with that laugh it would have got horribly on my nerves.'

'How's Martin getting on with his typewriter inquiries?'

Wexford threw the report across the desk. It was no Sevensmith Harding machine that had been used to type Williams's letter of resignation. All the typewriters in use in the Myringham office were of the sophisticated electronic kind.

Neither of the Williams households contained a typewriter of any sort. The Harmers had a typewriter in the two-storey flat over the shop where they lived and both Hope Harmer and her daughter Paulette used it. It was a small Olivetti, an electric machine.

'His new young lady typed that letter,' Burden said. 'Find her and we find the typewriter.'

'Find her and it won't matter whether we find the typewriter or not.'

Sergeant Martin had also been to Bath.

There, it seemed, Rodney Williams had had his origins. On an estate of houses some few miles outside the city, in a house very like the one Rodney had bought for his second bride, lived his brother Howard. It was Howard's address that appeared on Wendy's marriage certificate.

His parents had also once lived in Bath but his father had died when he was a child and his mother when Rodney was twenty-seven. That dead mother Rodney in his calculating way had used to his advantage. No doubt he had told Wendy that old Mrs Williams disapproved of his marriage to a young girl, would never wish to meet her, but the good son would be obliged to pay the occasional duty visit . . .

The brother seemed honest and straightforward. There was very little contact between him and Rodney. Years ago, fifteen or sixteen at least, some of Rodney's mail had been sent to his address by mistake. He had simply sent it on. Communications from the registrar at the time of the marriage to Wendy, Wexford thought. Howard Williams was also a salesman and on 15 April he had been in Ireland on business for his firm.

Joy hadn't told him of his brother's death. He had seen it in the papers and seemed to have reacted with calm indifference.

Wendy Williams's home was on the outskirts of Pomfret and a mile from the Harmer's shop. Had the relative nearness of his in-laws to his second and bigamous home worried Williams? Had he only agreed to buy a house there to placate Wendy or gratify some wish of hers? Or did he see this sort of risk as just part of the tightrope walk?

Between the estate and the nucleus of the town, that which not long ago *was* the town, lay the sports grounds of the

247

Haldon Finch Comprehensive School, playing fields, tennis courts, fives courts, running track. The Haldon Finch, though new and an example of the new education with its two thousand pupils of both sexes housed in no less than six buildings, was as much 'into' games as any public school of the past. You might get ten O-levels but you were nothing if you weren't good at games.

At 5.30 in the afternoon twelve girls were playing tennis on the courts adjacent to Procter Road.

'It must be a match with another school,' Burden said. 'They start after school's finished.'

He and Wexford were in the car, on their way to see Veronica Williams. Donaldson had taken a short cut, or at least a traffic-avoiding cut, and they had found themselves amid this complex of sports fields.

'We'll get out and watch for a minute or two.'

Burden got out, though demurring.

'It makes me feel funny standing about watching girls. I mean, you ask yourself – *they* ask *them*selves – what sort of blokes would do that?'

'What would you think if you saw two middle-aged women watching young men playing squash?'

Burden looked sideways at him.

'Well, nothing, would I? I mean, I'd think they were their mothers or just women who liked watching sport.'

'Exactly. Doesn't that tell you something? Two things? One is that, whatever the women's movement says, there is a fundamental difference between men and women in their attitude to sex, and the other that this is an area in which women might claim – if it's occurred to them – to be superior to us.'

'It's changing though, you have to admit. Look at all those clubs up north where men do strips for women audiences.'

'The attitude is still different. Men go to strip shows and gawp in a sort of seething silence.'

'Don't women?'

'Apparently women laugh,' said Wexford.

One of the tennis players was Eve Freeborn. He spotted her from the purple slick in her hair. Her partner was a thin dark girl, their opponents a big heavily built blonde and another thin dark girl, this one wearing glasses. This four was on the court nearest to the road. Wexford could see enough of the other two courts and the other four couples only to be sure that Sara Williams was not among them. Sara didn't attend the Haldon Finch, of course – that would have been too great a risk even for Rodney Williams – but if this was a match six of the girls must come from another school. Seated on the three umpire chairs were three young women who had the look of games teachers.

He was aware at once that no one was playing very well. Had the standard deteriorated since the days when he had watched Sylvia and Sheila playing tennis? No, it wasn't that. It was television. These days you saw tennis played on TV. Top championships week after week, it seemed, here or in Europe or in America, and it spoiled you for the real thing, the local article. A pity really. It made you irritated at how often they missed the ball. Eve Freeborn had a good hard service. She would have served aces – only they were always on the wrong side of the line. Her opponent in the glasses was the worst player of the twelve, slow on her feet with a weak service and a way of scooping the ball up into the air, making it easy prey for Eve's slamming racket.

'Two match points,' said Burden, who had been attending more closely to the progress of the set.

Eve served a double fault. One match point. She served again, weakly, and the blonde shot it back like an arrow down the tramlines. The umpire announced deuce. Eve served another double fault.

'Van out,' said Wexford.

'My God, but that shows your age. That's what they said at tennis parties in the thirties.'

The umpire corrected him by saying crisply that the score was 'advantage Kingsmarkham'. So it was Kingsmarkham High who were the visitors here, once a grammar school, now private and fee-paying, no longer state-aided.

Kingsmarkham won the game. They changed ends, the girls paused by the umpire's chair and wiped faces and arms, drank Coke out of cans. Eve was standing only a few yards from Wexford. The little flame-coloured badge he had till now seen only as an orange spot near the neckline of her white tee-shirt

249

showed itself at closer quarters to be a badge. He could make out spread wings on it and the letters ARRIA. Eve didn't or wouldn't look at him. Perhaps he wasn't recognisable out of his office, in shirt-sleeves. He peered more closely. The umpire got down from her chair and came to the wire fence. She was a stocky, muscular young woman with a cross face and flashing eyes. In a voice full of crushed ice she said, 'Was there something you wanted?'

Wexford inhibited all the possible replies, improper, provocative, even mildly lecherous, that sprang to mind. He was a policeman. Anyway, Burden got in first with the flasher's classic caught-before-the-act answer.

'We were just looking.'

'Well, perhaps you'd like to get on with whatever you're supposed to be doing.'

'Move along, Mike,' said Wexford.

They went quickly to the car. The games mistress glared after them.

'Do they still call them that?'

'Call them what? Games mistresses?' Burden was silent for a moment. Then he said, screwing up his face, 'I'll tell you when my new daughter's eleven. If she gets to exist. If she gets to be eleven. If she and I are together when she does.'

'It's not as bad as that.'

'No? Maybe not. Maybe it's she and I that'll be together and not Jenny and I.'

Things must be bad with Burden for him to burst out with that in Donaldson's hearing. Not that Donaldson would say a word. But he would hear and he would think. Wexford said nothing. He watched Burden's face close up, the eyes grow dull and the mouth purse, the frown that was hardly ever absent re-establish itself in a deep double ridge. The car drew away. He looked behind him and saw Eve leaping to achieve her best volley of the match.

'Veronica was supposed to be playing in a tennis match,' said Wendy Williams, 'but of course she was too upset. She hasn't been to school today and I had to take the day off. I had to tell her her father had another wife and family. It was bad enough telling her he was dead.'

The second Mrs Williams, whom Wexford had at first thought of as rather sweet and gentle, he now saw had other sides to her nature, among them a rather unpleasant habit of laying the blame for her misfortunes on whomsoever else might be present.

'I told her everything and at first she wouldn't speak and then she became very distressed.' The soft little voice trickled round the phrases. The eyes opened wide and wistful, like a Pear's Soap child seeing distant angels. Wexford had the disturbing thought that perhaps she had cultivated all this because Williams had fancied little girls. 'You'll be gentle with her, won't you? You'll remember she's only sixteen? And it's not just that she's lost her father, it's worse than that.'

No question here of being sent up to the girl's bedroom. Veronica would come down. And Wendy would be there. He supposed Veronica must have been the missing tennis player for whom the dark girl not wearing glasses had substituted. While he was speculating Veronica came in, walking diffidently, a dead look still on her face. She had been crying but that was a long while ago now. Her eyes were dry and the lids pale, but a puffiness remained. Nevertheless she had dressed herself carefully for this encounter, as had her mother. Such things, which would have been lost on many men, never escaped Wexford. Wendy was in a black cotton dress with big sleeves that was a little too becoming to qualify as true mourning and Veronica in a pink pleated skirt, sweat shirt with a gold V on it and pink and white running shoes. Probably Wendy got their clothes from Jickie's at a discount.

'This is Chief Inspector Wexford and Inspector Burden, darling. They want to ask you one or two questions. Nothing difficult or complicated. They know what a bad shock you've had. And I shall be here all the time.'

For God's sake, she's not ten, Wexford thought. The girl's dull staring look disconcerted him.

'I'm sorry about your dad, Veronica,' he began. 'I know you're feeling unhappy and you'd probably like to be left alone. But your mother's told you what's happened. Your father isn't simply dead. He was killed. And we have to find out who killed him, don't we?' A not unfamiliar doubt assailed him. Did they? *Cui bono?* Who would be satisfied, avenged,

251

recompensed? He was a policeman and it wasn't for him to think such thoughts. Not a hint of them was in his tone. He looked at the girl and wondered what had been going on in her mind all those weeks her father was missing. Had she believed, like her mother, that he was with another woman? Or had she accepted his absence as she must have accepted all his other absences when he was allegedly away travelling for his firm or paying filial visits in Bath? She was no longer looking at him but down at the floor, her head drooping like a tired flower on a stalk.

'Do you think we could go back to April the fifteenth?' he said. 'It was a Thursday. Your mother expected your father home that evening but she had to stay on late at work. You were here though, weren't you?'

The 'yes' came very quietly. He might not have understood it for what it was if she hadn't nodded as well.

'What did you do? You came home from school when – at four?' He too was talking to her as if she were ten, but something in her attitude, her bowed head, feet crossed, hands in lap, seemed to invite it. Again that nod, the head lifted a little to make it. 'And then what happened? What sort of time did you expect your father to come?'

She murmured that she didn't know.

'We never knew what time to expect him,' Wendy said. 'We never knew. It might have been any time.'

'And did he come?' said Wexford.

'Of course he didn't! I've told you.'

'Please, Mrs Williams, let Veronica answer.'

The girl was shy, nervous, perhaps also unhappy. She was certainly in shock still. But suddenly she made an effort. It was as if she saw that there was no help for it, she was going to have to talk, she might as well get it over. Sara's tortoiseshell brown eyes looked into his and Sara's Primavera lips parted with a quiver.

'I had tea. Well, a Coke and some stuff Mummy left me in the fridge.' Yes, Wendy for all her own youth was the kind of woman who would be smotheringly protective, even to the extent of preparing meals in advance for a sixteen-year-old as if she were an invalid. Veronica said, 'I'd asked my friend round – the one whose place I was at when you came before –

252

but she rang up and said she couldn't come. She said I could go to her.'

'But you wanted to wait in for your father?'

She was no Sara, no Eve Freeborn. She turned her head and looked to her mother for help. It came, as no doubt it always did.

'Veronica had no need to wait in for Rodney. I've told you, we never really thought he'd come at all.'

' "We", Mrs Williams?'

'Well, I don't really know what Veronica thought. I hadn't said anything to her then about the possibility of our splitting up. I was waiting to see what would happen. But the point is Veronica had no need to wait in for him and I wouldn't have . . . well, she's got her own life to lead.'

What had she been going to say when she broke off and made that extraordinary statement about this little creature's obviously nonexistent independence?

'You went out then?'

'I went to my friend's. I didn't stop there long. We played records. I wanted her to come out for a coffee but she couldn't, she was baby-sitting with her brother. She's got a brother who's only two. That was why she couldn't come over to me.'

'So you went back home. What time?'

'I didn't go straight home. I had a coffee on my own at Castor's. I got home about nine and Mummy came in ten minutes after.'

'You must have been disappointed your father wasn't there.'

'I don't know,' she said. 'I didn't think about it,' and surprisingly, for this wasn't really at issue, 'I don't mind being alone. I like it.'

'Well, my goodness,' said Wendy, not letting that one pass, 'you're never left alone if I can help it. You needn't talk as if you'd been neglected.'

Wexford asked the name of the friend and was told it was Nicola Tennyson and given an address that was between here and the town centre. No objection was put up by Wendy to their examining such of his personal property as Rodney Williams had in this house. It left Wexford with the feeling that this was because she rather wanted them to see over her house,

253

its cleanliness, its elegant appointments and the evidence of her skill as housekeeper.

Here, at any rate, was the rest of Williams's wardrobe. It was interesting to observe how he had kept his more stylish and 'in' clothes for this household. Jeans hung in the gilt-decorated white built-in cupboard, Westerner shirts, a denim suit and another in fashionably crumpled stone-coloured linen mixture. There were two pairs of half-boots and a pair of beige kid moccasins. And the underwear was designed for a younger man than the part-time occupant of 31 Alverbury Road.

'He was two different men,' Wexford said.

'Perhaps three.'

'We shall see. At any rate he was two, one middle-aged, set in his ways, bored maybe, taking his family for granted, the other young still, even swinging – take a look at these underpants – making the grade with a young wife, living up to this little bandbox.'

Wexford looked around him at the room, thinking of Alverbury Road. There were duvets on the beds here, blinds at the windows, a white cane chair suspended from the ceiling, its seat piled with green, blue and white silk cushions. And the bed was a six-foot-wide king-size.

'He probably called it the playpen,' said Burden pulling a face.

'Once,' said Wexford.

In this house Williams had had no desk, only a drawer in the gilt-handled white melamine chest of drawers. This had been Wendy's house, no doubt about it, the sanctum where Wendy held sway. Girlish, fragile, soft-voiced though she might be, she had made this place her own, feminine and exclusive – exclusive in a way of Rodney Williams. He had been there on sufferance, Wexford sensed, his presence depending on his good behaviour. And yet his behaviour had not been very good even from the first. There had always been the travelling, the Bunbury of a mother, the long absences. So Wendy had made a home full of flowers and colours and silk cushions in which he was allotted small corners as if – unconsciously, he was sure it was unconsciously – she knew the day would come when it would be for herself and her daughter alone. Wexford looked inside the drawer but it told him little. It was full of the kind of papers he would have expected.

Except for Williams's driving licence with the Alverbury Road address.

'He was taking a risk leaving that about,' said Burden.

'Taking risks was his life. He took them all the time. He enjoyed the high wire. Anyway, suspicious wives read letters not driving licences.'

There were bills in the drawer, the counterfoils from credit-card chits, an American Express monthly account. Which address had that gone to? Yes, this one. It fitted somehow. Visa and Access were the workaday cards, American Express more cosmopolitan, more for the playboy. No doubt it was Wendy who paid the services' bills from the joint account. There was none in the drawer, only a rates demand, a television rental account book, an estimate from Godwin and Sculp, builders, of Pomfret, dated 30 March for painting the living room, and an invoice from the same firm (stamped *Paid*) for renewal of a bathroom cistern. Under this lot lay Rodney's joint account cheque book, a paying-in book for the joint account, and a small glass bottle, half full of tablets, labelled 'Mandaret'.

On this the top floor of the house were two more bedrooms and a bathroom. Veronica's room was neat as a pin, white with a good deal of broderie anglaise about it and owing much to those magazines articles prevalent in Wendy's own child-hood on how to make a dream bedroom for your daughter. No doubt poor Wendy had never had a dream bedroom of her own, Wexford thought, and he sensed that her youth had been nearer to that of Sara. No posters here, no home-made mobiles and no books either. It was designed for a girl who would do nothing in it but sit in the window seat looking pensive and wearing white socks.

The spiral staircase, a contraption of hideous discomfort and danger to all but the most agile, went through the middle of the house like a screw in a press. Down on the ground floor was a shower room, a separate lavatory, the third door on that side opening into the integral garage, and at the end of the passage a room the width of the house that opened through french windows onto patio and garden roughly the size of a large dining table. The room, that might have been for dining in or a study for Rodney Williams if he had been allowed one, was plainly devoted to Wendy's interests. She had a sewing machine in it and a knitting machine, an ironing board set up with two irons on it, one dry and one steam, and there were clothes everywhere, neatly hung or draped, sheathed in plastic bags.

Mother and daughter were still sitting upstairs at the glass-topped table. Wendy had taken up some sewing, a handkerchief or possibly a traycloth into which she was inserting tiny stitches, her little finger crooked in the way it used to be said was vulgar to hold a teacup. Veronica nibbled at dry roasted peanuts out of a foil packet. The dry kind it would be, the other sort tending to leave grease spots. They were both as tense as compressed springs, waiting for the police to go and leave them alone.

'Have you heard of a society or club called ARRIA?' Wexford said to Veronica.

The spring didn't leap free of its bonds. There was no shock. Veronica merely nodded. She didn't screw up the empty peanut packet but flattened it and began folding it very carefully, first into halves, then quarters.

'At school?'

She looked up. 'Some of the girls in the sixth and seventh years belong to it.'

'But you don't?'

'You have to be over sixteen.'

'Why girls?' he said. 'Haldon Finch is co-ed. Don't any boys belong?'

She was a normal teenager really. Underneath the prissy looks, the shyness, the Mummy's girl air, she was one of them. The look she gave him seethed with their scorn for the cretinous incomprehension evinced by adults.

'Well, it's all women, isn't it? It's for women. They're – what d'you call it? – feminists, militant feminists.'

'Then I hope you'll keep clear of it, Veronica,' Wendy said very quickly and sharply for her. 'I hope you'll have nothing to do with it. If there's anything I really hate it's women's lib. Liberation! I'm liberated and look where it's got me. I just hope you'll do better than I have when the time comes and find a man who'll really support you and look after you, a nice good man who'll – who'll *cherish* you.' Her lips trembled with emotion. She laid down her sewing. 'I wasn't enough of a woman for Rodney,' she said as if the girl wasn't there. 'I wasn't enough of a girl. I got too hard and independent and – and *mature*, I know I did.' A heroic effort was made to keep the tears in, the break out of the voice, and a victory was won. 'You just remember that, Veronica, when your turn comes.'

Sergeant Martin was handling the complaint though, as he told Wexford, he hadn't much to go on. Nor had any harm been done – yet.

'A Ms Caroline Peters who's a physical education instructor at the Haldon Finch Comprehensive,' Martin said. 'Miz not Miss. She got very stroppy, sir, when I called her Miss. I called her an instructress too and had a job getting my tongue round it but that wasn't right either. She says two men were hanging about watching the girls playing a tennis match. Acting in a suspicious manner, she says. Came in a car which was parked for the express purpose of them getting out to watch. Voyeurs she called them. Afterwards she asked the girls if any of them knew the men but they denied all knowledge.'

Thank you Miss Freeborn, thought Wexford.

'Leave it, Martin. Forget it. We've better things to do.'

'Leave it altogether, sir?'

'I'll handle it.' A note to the woman or a phone call explaining all, he supposed. She had a right to that. She was a good conscientious teacher acting in a responsible manner. He mustn't laugh – except later perhaps with Burden.

There had been much food for thought picked up on his visits to Liskeard Avenue. And there had been something to make him wonder, something that was neither a piece of information nor the germ of an idea but entirely negative.

Wasn't it extraordinary that during those visits, those long talks, and during his initial interview with her, Wendy Williams had shown not the slightest interest in Rodney's other family? She had asked not a single question about the wife she had supplanted but not replaced, nor about the children who were siblings by half-blood of her own Veronica. Because she was inhibited by intense jealousy? Or for some other reason more germane to this inquiry?

257

11

Kevin Williams looked more like his mother than his father. He wouldn't have been recognisable as Veronica's half-brother. The genetic hand-down which was so distinctive a feature in Sara and Veronica had missed him and his forehead was narrow with the hair growing low on it. His manner was laconic, casual, indifferent.

Wexford, who had Martin with him, had interrupted what seemed to be a family conclave. For once the television was off, sight and sound. Joy Williams introduced no one but her son and this introduction she made proudly and with abnormal enthusiasm. Wexford was left to deduce that the woman and the girl who sat side by side on the yellow sofa must be Hope Harmer and her daugher Paulette.

Mrs Harmer, though plumper, fairer and better cared for than her sister, looked too much like her for her identity to be in doubt. She was a pretty woman and even in the present crisis she looked pleased with life. But the girl – to use an expression favoured by Wexford's grandsons – was 'something else again'. She was beautiful with a beauty that made Sara and Veronica merely pretty young girls. She reminded Wexford of a picture he had once seen, Rossetti's portrait of Mrs William Morris. This girl was dark and her face had the same dark glow as the face in the picture, her features the same symmetry and her large dark eyes the same other-worldly soulfulness. When he asked her if she was who he thought she was she raised those dark grey dreaming eyes and nodded, then returned to what she had been looking at, a magazine that seemed entirely devoted to hairstyles.

Kevin's term had ended the day before and he had come straight home. Not to stay, though, he made clear to Wexford when they were alone in the stark dining room. He owed it to his mother to stay a few days, but next week he intended to stick to the plan he had made months before of going down to Cornwall to stay with a friend and later he would be camping in France. He seemed astonished when Wexford asked him for the address of the Cornish friend.

'We'd rather you didn't leave the country at present.'

'You can't keep me here. My father's death has nothing to do with me.'

'Tell me what you did on the evening of Thursday, April the fifteenth.'

'Was that when he died?' The casual manner had grown sullen. He was his mother in truculent mood all over again.

'I'll ask the questions, Kevin.'

It wasn't said roughly, but nevertheless the boy looked as if no one had spoken like that to him before. His low forehead creased and his mouth pouted.

'I only asked. He was my father.'

In his tone, that of contrived, badly acted sentiment, Wexford suddenly understood that no one in this household had cared a damn for Rodney Williams. And they hadn't in the other household either. People didn't care for him for long. In this area he had, at any rate, got his deserts.

'What happened that evening? What did you do?'

'Phoned home, I suppose,' he said, careless again. 'I always do on Thursdays or my mother goes bananas.'

'You phone from college?'

'No, the phones are always out of order or it's a hassle finding one that's free.' Kevin seemed to have decided he might as well give in to Wexford's questioning if not with a good grace. 'I go out to phone. Well, two or three of us do. To a pub. I phone home and transfer the charge.'

'You'll remember that Thursday if I tell you it was the first Thursday after you got back to college from the Easter vacation.'

The boy thought about it, seeming to concentrate. Wexford had no doubt he had known perfectly well all along.

'Yeah, I do remember. I phoned home around eight,

eight-thirty – I don't reckon you want to know to the minute, do you? My mother was out. I talked to Sara.'

'That must have surprised you, your mother being out when you phoned.'

'Yeah, it was unusual. She thinks the sun shines out of my arse, as you've maybe noticed.' He jerked his shoulders in an exaggerated shrug. 'Unusual,' he said, 'but not unknown.'

More indignation came when Wexford asked for the names of Kevin's companions on the trip to the pub where the phone was. But it was hot air, pointless obstructiveness. The names were forthcoming after some expostulation.

'How did you get on with your father?'

'There was no communication. We didn't talk. The usual sort of situation, right?'

'And your father and Sara?'

The reply came sharply. It was incredible. It was exactly the reply a boy of Kevin's age might have made a hundred years before – or, according to literature, might have made.

'You can leave my sister out of this!'

Wexford tried not to laugh. 'I will for now.'

He found Joy and her sister questioning Martin in depth about Wendy Williams. The girls, the two cousins, had gone. Martin was answering in monosyllables and he looked relieved when Wexford came in. Joy broke off at once and, having seen he was alone, said, 'Where's my son?' as if Wexford might have arrested him and already stowed him away in a police car.

This would be his first encounter with Miles Gardner since the discovery of Rodney Williams's body. He and Burden waited for him in the managing director's office. The panelled room was dim and shadowy in spite of the bright day outside. A copper pot filled with Russell lupins stood on the windowsill. Wexford picked up the desk photograph of Gardner's family and looked at it dubiously.

'I suppose I'm sensitised to adolescent girls,' he said. 'I see them everywhere.'

'Just remember what the games mistress said.'

'I don't think I'm in danger, though they're a very pretty lot we're in contact with. One can almost see Williams's point of view.'

'He was just a dirty old lecher,' said Burden, apparently forgetting Williams had been a mere three years his senior.

'The primrose way to the everlasting bonfire.'

Gardner came in, apologising for having kept them waiting. He began on some insincere-sounding expressions of sorrow at Williams's demise which Wexford listened to patiently and then cut short.

'If you're free for lunch we might all go over to the Old Flag.'

But this was something Gardner, regretfully, couldn't manage. 'I've promised to give my daughter lunch, my youngest one, Jane. She's got the day off school to go for an interview at the university here. A bit of an ordeal, she's a nervous kid, so I bribed her with the offer of a slap-up lunch.'

The University of the South was situated at Myringham. Another eighteen-year-old then . . .

'She should get a place,' Gardner said, and with a kind of rueful pride, 'There go our holidays abroad for the next three years.'

Wexford said he would like to talk to Christine Lomond, and in the room that had been Williams's if possible. Gardner took him there himself, up in the small slow lift. There were two desks and two typewriters, a Sierra 3400 and an Olympia ES 100. But this place was 'clean' as far as typewriters went. Martin had seen to that. The girl who came in was fresh-paint glossy in a suit of geranium-red linen, dark green cotton blouse, green glass rhomboid hanging on a chain and on her left wrist a watch with a red and green strap. Her hair had been touched with what his daughter Sylvia assured him were called 'low lights', though Wexford couldn't quite believe this and thought she must have been having him on. Christine Lomond's fingernails were the brilliant carmine of the latest Sevenshine front-door shade Pillarbox ('A rich true red without a hint of blue, a robust high gloss that stands up ideally to wind and weather'). They scuttled over the filing cabinet like so many red beetles.

Wexford had asked her to see what she could find him as samples of Williams's own typing, any report, assessment, rough notes even, he might have brought to the office with him. She said she was sure anything of that sort would have been handwritten, and it was two or three handwritten sheets that she produced for him, and then several more which she told him had probably been typed on the Olympia machine but using a different daisywheel, thus altering the typeface. Wexford was particularly interested because there seemed to him to be a flaw in the apex of the capital A.

The experiment, however, showed nothing but his own ignorance of typewriters or at any rate of recent technological advances made in typewriters. The red-tipped white fingers whipped a sheet of paper into the machine, switched it on, switched if off, whipped out the daisywheel, inserted another, and rapidly produced a facsimile of the first four lines of Williams's sales forecast for the first three months of the year.

'It's getting a bit ragged,' Christine Lomond said. 'We need a new wheel,' and she pulled the damaged one out and dropped it into the wastepaper basket.

'Where do you live, Miss Lomond?'

'Here. In Myringham. Why?' She had a rather abrupt manner, of the kind that is usually called 'crisp'.

'Did you like Mr Williams?'

She was silent. She seemed affronted, having anticipated perhaps nothing more than an investigation of papers and machines. How old was she? Twenty-six? Twenty-seven? She could be a good deal less than that. The heavy make-up and elaborate hairstyle aged her.

'Well, Miss Lomond?'

'Yes, I liked him. Well, I liked him all right. I didn't think about liking or disliking him.'

'Would you think back, please, and give me some idea of what you were doing on the evening of April the fifteenth?'

'I can't possibly remember that far back!'

Her eyelids flapped. They were a gleaming laminated sea blue ('Delicate turquoise with a hint of silver, ideal for that special ceiling, alcove or display cabinet').

'Try and pinpoint it,' said Burden, 'by thinking of what you were doing next day. That was the morning someone phoned to say Mr Williams was ill and wouldn't be in. Does that help?'

'I expect I was at home on my own.'

She didn't sound defensive, guilty, afraid. She sounded

sullen, as if the clothes and the make-up, the 'grooming' had not been effective.

'Do you live on your own or with someone?'

Surely the most innocent of questions. She pounced on it as surely as if those red nails had seized and clutched.

'I certainly do not live with someone! I was at home on my own watching the TV.'

Another one. What had they done in the old days before the cathode conquest? He ought to be able to remember pre-television alibis but he couldn't. I was reading, sewing, putting up shelves, fishing, listening to the radio, out for a walk, in the pub, at the pictures? Maybe.

Unwillingly, even grudgingly, she gave them her address. She admitted to possessing a typewriter, an old Smith Corona, though not a portable, and insisted it was in her parents' house in Tonbridge and she had never had it with her in the Myringham bedsit.

Downstairs in the reception area they encountered a young girl undressing. Or so to Wexford's astonished eyes it at first appeared. She was talking to the telephonist (Anna today) and in the act of pulling a cotton dress off over her head. Long slim legs in white tights, pale blue pumps with curly heels, and yes, a skirt which dropped to its former just-above-the-knee length when the garment, evidently a middy blouse, was off. Underneath it was a white tee-shirt. Her back was to Wexford. She kicked off the blue pumps, sending one flying across the room and leaving no doubt in the mind of an observer that this was a cathartic shedding of a hateful costume after an ordeal was over

'Jane,' said Anna in a warning tone, 'there are some . . .'

She spun round. On the front of the tee-shirt were printed the letters ARRIA.

The first thing that struck Wexford about the house in Down Road, Kingsmarkham, was that there was no question of any of its occupants being obliged to share a bedroom. It was a very large, castellated, turreted, balconied Edwardian pile. Most houses like it had been converted into flats but not this one. A single family inhabited it and its (at least) eight bedrooms. Yet Eve Freeborn had given him the reason for going to her boyfriend in Myringham instead of his coming to her that she shared a bedroom with her sister. Perhaps she hadn't a sister either. He would soon see.

At first he thought the girl who opened the front door to him *was* Eve. After all, the fact that this one had green hair meant nothing. They changed their hair colour these days as fast as they used to change their lipstick. A second look told him they weren't even identical twins. Twins, yes, fraternal twins with the same build of body and the same eyes. That was all. God knew what colour their hair really was. They had probably forgotten themselves.

The house smelt faintly of marijuana. An unmistakable smell that was like woodsmoke blended with sweet cologne.

'Eve?' Eve's sister said with incredulity. 'You want to see Eve?'

'Is that so difficult?'

'I don't know really . . .'

He had shown her his warrant card. After all, she was a young girl and it was evening. She shouldn't admit un-identified men into the house. But she was looking at it as if it were a warrant for her arrest. He felt impatient.

'Perhaps I should fill in a form or produce a sponsor.'

'Oh, no, come in. I'm sorry. It's just that . . .'

She had an irritating way of leaving her sentences unfinished. He followed her into the hall, darkly panelled like the offices of Sevensmith Harding, and up a big elegant winding staircase with a gallery at the top. The marijuana smell was fainter but it was still there. What astonished him about the house was the aura of the sixties that pervaded it. On the wall here was a poster (albeit a glazed and framed poster) of John Lennon seated at a white grand piano. A vase stood on a side table filled with dried grasses and shabby peacock's tail feathers. And hanging up as an ornament, not because it had been left there by chance, was an antique red silk dress embroidered with gold, its red and its gold tattered and shredded by time and moths. He said, 'Are your parents at home?'

'They've got a flat in London. They're there half the time.'

Impossible to tell if she minded or was glad. Those parents need not be more than forty themselves, he thought, and Mother might be less. Eve's twin said, 'Perhaps you'd better wait here. I'll just see if . . .'

All the bedroom doors were open. Only they weren't bedrooms, not exactly. Each one, as far as he could see, had the look rather of a bedsit, with chairs and tables and floor cushions and a couch or divan with an Indian bedspread flung artlessly over it, posters on the walls and postcards pinned up higgledy-piggledy. He sat down to wait in a rocking chair that had its rockers painted red, black and white and a dirty lace veil draped over its back, and wondered how to explain this mysterious house.

Then he understood. It wasn't the girls who were living in the past, who were twenty years out of date, or purposely living in an anachronism. Those parents had been young in the sixties, had revelled probably in that new inspiring freedom, and now the spirit of the sixties, the flavour, the mores would never leave them. Not the girls but the parents were the marijuana users. He would have to do something about that . . .

How long was she going to keep him waiting?

He got up and went out into the passage. There was no one about. But from somewhere he could hear the sound of female voices – a sound that was not in the least like the twittering of birds, strong earnest talk rather than a murmuration. A staircase led to the attic floor but it wasn't from up there that the voices came.

There was a burst of laughter, some sporadic clapping. He walked down the passage towards the sound, came out into another smaller, squarer landing, a map of the heavens painted on its ceiling by a trained but unsure hand. An amateur astrologer who had been to art school, he thought, which brought the sixties once more to mind. As he stood there, doubtful of the wisdom of bursting into a room full of women, the door opened and two girls came out. They stopped in the doorway, looking at him in astonishment. One was unknown to him, the other was Caroline Peters, physical training instructor.

Before anyone spoke Eve Freeborn came out of the room, shouldering her way past the two who blocked the doorway. She was once more in the pelvis-crusher jeans but this time with a purple satin blouse to match her hair. Caroline Peters, on the other hand, was dressed exactly like a boy – or like boys used to dress before punk apparel came to stay: blue jeans, brown leather jacket, half-boots; no make-up, hair cropped in a crewcut.

'Sorry,' Eve said. 'Have you been waiting long?'

'*They* kept *us* waiting,' said Caroline Peters with the maximum venom, 'for four thousand years.'

She had recognised him and wasn't pleased. Or had he been recognised for what he was in addition to being a policeman – a man? Wexford had never before personally encountered the kind of militant feminist who advocates total separatism. Enlightenment broke upon him.

'Have I by any chance interrupted a meeting of ARRIA?'

'It's over,' said Eve. 'It's just over.'

'We wouldn't have permitted interruption.'

Wexford looked at Caroline Peters. 'Don't go yet, please. I'd like to talk to you too.'

She lifted her shoulders, went back into the room. Eve waved a hand at the other girl, a pretty, sharp-faced redhead.

'This is Nicky.'

Inside the room, another, larger, bedsit hung with striped bedspreads on ceilings and walls like a Bedouin tent, half a dozen more girls were standing about or preparing to leave. Sara Williams was there and her cousin Paulette, the two of them talking to Jane Gardner, and all of them wearing ARRIA tee-shirts. A black girl, thin and elegant as a model, sat crosslegged on a floor cushion.

Eve said to the company, 'I don't remember what he's called,' as if it hardly mattered, 'but he's a policeman.' She pointed at one girl after another: 'Jane, Sara, Paulette, Donella, Helen, Elaine, and Amy, my sister, you've met.'

Caroline Peters pushed her hands into the pockets of her leather jacket.

'What is it you want?'

'I'd like to know more about ARRIA for a start.'

'For a *start* it was *started* by me and a like-minded woman, a classical scholar now at Oxford.' She paused. 'Arria Paeta,' she said, 'was a Roman matron, the wife of Caecina Paetus. Of course she was obliged to take his name.' Wexford could tell she was one of those fanatics who never miss a trick. 'Ancient

Rome was known for its gross oppression and exploitation of women.' Teacher-like, she waited for his comments.

They came – perhaps to her surprise. 'The Emperor Claudius,' said Wexford who had done his homework, 'ordered Paetus to commit suicide but he proved too cowardly, so his wife took the sword and plunging it into her own heart, said, "See Paetus, it does not hurt . . ." '

'You've been reading Graves!'

'No. *Smith's Classical Dictionary*.' The girl called Nicky laughed. 'But I don't know what the letters stand for,' he said.

'Action for the Radical Reform of Intersexual Attitudes.'

'A case of making the nym fit the acronym? Or is it a deliberate obscuration?'

'Perhaps it is.'

'How many schools are involved?'

It was Eve who answered him. 'Kingsmarkham High, Haldon Finch, St Catherine's . . .' but Caroline Peters interrupted her.

'I teach at Haldon Finch. ARRIA had its inception just over a year ago at St Catherine's. We admitted as members only those women over sixteen, those in fact in the sixth and seventh years. I'm glad to say it had an immediate appeal – how could an organisation designed expressly for women, designed to give men no quarter – be otherwise?' She turned on him a glacial look of distaste and it gave him a most unpleasant feeling. He didn't belong to a minority, there was no way he could be categorised into a minority, yet the sensation she gave him was of doing so and of an oppressed one at that. 'Our very well-organised propaganda machine,' she said, 'spread the good news through the other schools in the area and we soon had considerable cells at Pomfret College of Further Education and Kingsmarkham High.' The good news, he thought, the 'gospel' no less. She astonished him by saying, 'We now have a membership of just over five hundred women.'

He suppressed the whistle he wanted to give. What must the local population of seventeen- and eighteen-year-old girls be? All of them, including those who had left school, could surely hardly amount to more than a couple of thousand and that meant 25 per cent in ARRIA. Why, they could almost start a revolution!

'All right, you've got badges, you've had tee-shirts printed, you hold meetings, but what do you *do*?'

Caroline Peters answered readily. 'Basically, have as little contact with men as possible. Defy men by intellectual and also by physical means.'

He pricked up his ears at that. She wasn't carrying a bag but she had pockets. Most of the other girls had bags. He hadn't got a warrant and, almost more to the point, hadn't a woman with him to carry out a search.

'We have a constitution and manifesto,' she said. 'I expect there's a copy about and I see no objection to your having one. Would you women agree to that?' There was a murmur of assent, some of it amused. 'But I must point out that our aim isn't to meet men on equal terms. It isn't to come to a truce or compromise with them nor to reach that uneasy détente which in past revolutions has sometimes come into being between a proletariat and a bourgeosie. As Marx said in another context: Philosophers have tried to explain the world. The point surely is to change it. Good night, everyone.' She went out of the room, closing the door with a somewhat sinister quietness behind her.

Silence. The black girl, Donella, cast up her eyes, rolling sloe-brown pupils in moon-white whites. Eve said, 'By physical means, she only meant self-defence stuff. It's compulsory when you join to take a self-defence course, karate or judo or tai chi or whatever.'

'Personally,' said Donella, 'I think that's one of the things that attracts people – the sport, you know.'

'You may have noticed, there've been three times as many evening courses in martial arts started since ARRIA began. That's in response to increased demand, that's ARRIA.'

Nicky had spoken with pride, not aggressively. She made a swift chopping movement with one arm. Wexford, a large man over six feet tall, felt relieved he wasn't on the receiving end of that blow. It was true about the judo and karate courses, he had remarked on it himself to Burden, pleased that women were at last taking steps to defend themselves against the muggings and rapes which in the past few years had so disproportionately increased.

'All right,' he said, 'that's for self-defence. How about

aggression? I don't suppose anyone's going to admit to carrying an offensive weapon?'

Nobody was. They didn't look scared or guilty or even alert. He fancied he saw wariness in one or two faces.

'I'll give you a copy of the constitution,' Eve said. 'There's nothing private about it. Everyone's welcome to know what we do, men as well as women. Do you have daughters?'

'They're a lot older than you.'

She looked at him in a not unkindly way, assessing. 'Well, they would be, wouldn't they? You can't be too old for ARRIA, though.'

The constitution was typed and photocopied. He noted that there were no flaws in the apexes of the capital As or the ascenders of the lower-case ts. It went into his pocket to be read at leisure. Sara Williams, he observed, was watching his every movement. The big fair girl called Helen he now realised had been Eve's partner in the tennis match. He said to Eve, 'If everyone is in fact going I'd like to talk to you alone for five minutes.'

The brisk policeman's tone replacing the one of easy jocularity seemed to jolt her. She pushed fingers through the purple crest of hair.

'OK, if that's the way you want it. Everybody out, right?' She gave a hiccuping giggle. 'Home, women!'

Amy said, 'Well, I think I'll just . . .' and drifted vaguely towards the door.

They all began to take their leave in ways peculiar to young girls, whether feminists or reactionaries. Helen and Donella closed in upon each other with a tight bear hug which ended in giggles and heads subsiding on each other's shoulders. Sara wrapped her arms round herself and moved across the floor with vague dancing steps. Jane humped her bag, filled with ARRIA constitution sheets, as if it weighed a ton, making agony faces. Nicky was lost in a dream that seemed to turn her into a sleepwalker so that she neither paused in her exit nor spoke but merely raised a languid flapping hand in farewell as she passed through the doorway.

Alone with Eve, Wexford said, 'You've been telling me lies.'

'I have not!'

'Why did you tell me your boyfriend couldn't come here

269

because you had to share a bedroom with your sister? This is an enormous house and as far as I can see your parents mostly aren't here anyway. But you told me lack of space – and you implied lack of privacy – stopped him coming here.'

'Well,' she said, a sly look in her eyes, 'I can explain that. You'll see the answer in our constitution actually. Rule 4.'

He pulled the constitution out of his pocket. Here it was, Rule 4. 'Women' – not ARRIA members, he saw, but always 'women' as if the society contained the world's entire female population – 'Women shall avoid the company of men wherever possible but should their presence be required for sexual, biological, business or career purposes, it is expedient and desirable for women to go to them rather than permit them to come to us.'

'But why?'

'Caroline and Edwina – she's the classical one who's at Oxford – they said it smacked of the sultan visiting his harem. You've got to think it through, you know. When you do you can see what they mean.'

'So that's why you went to your boyfriend in Arnold Road? You required his presence for sexual or even biological purposes?'

'Isn't that why women usually require men?'

'There are other ways of putting it. More aesthetic ways, I'd say. Maybe more civilised.'

'Oh, *civilised*. Men made civilisation and it's not up to much, is it? It's no big deal.'

He left it. 'Did you know Sara Williams was the daughter of the murdered man whose car you saw in Arnold Road?'

'Not then I didn't. I do now. Look, I only know her through ARRIA and I didn't know her father. For all I knew, she mightn't have had a father.'

He accepted that. 'Miss Peters didn't tell me much about this society of yours, did she? Only that it's a wildfire movement, it's caught on in all the local schools. How about the – what shall I call it? – esoteric stuff? How do you join? Do you pay a subscription? Is there any sort of ritual – like freemasons, say?'

'We don't need money,' she said, 'so there's no sub. Where would they get it from anyway? Most of our members are still at school. They'd have to get it from their fathers and that's

270

out. See Rule 6 and dependence. The only thing that costs us is the photocopying, only it doesn't because Nicky does it on her dad's Xerox in the night, when he's asleep.'

There was an irony there but Wexford didn't point it out. 'Anyone can join?'

'Any woman over sixteen who's not married. Obviously a married woman has already capitulated. Anyway, it wouldn't be possible for her to keep to the rules.'

'That would let my daughters out.'

She ignored him. 'I'm a founder member. When we started there was a lot of really wayout stuff going on. Edwina wanted initiation ceremonies, sort of baptisms of fire if you can imagine.'

'What sort?'

He was deeply curious. At the same time he was afraid she would soon realise she was spending too much time unnecessarily in the society of a man. She considered his question in thoughtful silence. She was not a pretty girl. But perhaps this didn't matter in these days when beauty was no longer at a premium. She had one of those chinless faces, long-nosed, full-lipped, but with creamy delicate skin. A frown creased, or rather crumpled, her forehead. Creasing was for older people. Eve's frown was like the bunching of a piece of cream velvet.

'Some of the others went along with her ideas,' she said. 'I mean, she was a radical feminist. For instance, she used to say we couldn't make revolution on Marxist principles on account of Marx having been a man. She said sexuality was politics and the only way to get freedom was for all women to be lesbians. Any hetero behaviour was collaborating with the enemy. Even Caroline Peters never went as far as that.'

'You were going to tell me about initiation.'

Eve seemed reluctant to reach the subject. 'They actually formed a splinter group over it. Sara, the one whose father was murdered, she was one of them and Nicky Anerley was another. One of the things they objected to was being educated along with the other sex. They wanted schools and colleges run by women and with women teachers. Of course, it would be best, it's the ideal if you know what I mean, but it's a bit fantastic.'

'Particularly as it's only in very recent years that women

have gained admission to certain men's colleges, notably at Oxford.'

'That's beside the point. This would be a question of getting the men out altogether. Edwina and the rest of them who were at mixed schools wanted to go on strike until they agreed not to admit boys. But Caroline wouldn't have that. I suppose she was afraid of losing her job.'

'And that's what caused the rift in the party?'

'Well, partly. This was all last summer and autumn. It more or less stopped when Edwina went up to Oxford in October and the others drifted back. I may as well tell you. It was all a sort of fantasy anyway. Edwina said in order to prove herself a true feminist a woman ought to kill a man.' Eve looked at him warily. 'I don't mean everyone who joined ARRIA was to have to kill a man to get to be a member. The idea was for groups of three or four to get together and . . .

'But that's not an initiation ceremony really, is it? I could tell you about some of those if you want.'

12

With inscrutable face Jenny Burden sat reading ARRIA's manifesto. She was past the stage now of prettifying disguises of her pregnancy. It was beyond disguise and her condition didn't flatter her. Younger than her years though she had always looked, she now appeared too old to be having a baby. Her face was not so much lined as lacking in its former firmness, caverns hollowed out under the eyes and chin muscles sagging. She had no lap now so she held the flimsy sheets against a book propped up on the table in front of her.

But Wexford could tell by Burden's pleased expression that he was content to see his wife making even this small effort to escape from the apathy that had settled on her as the psychotherapy she was having progressed. No longer in revolt, no longer violent in her hatred of the child, she had become resigned. She waited in hopeless passivity. When Wexford arrived she had taken his hand, put up her face for a kiss, inquired in a limbo voice after Dora and the girls. And he had thought: when the baby is born she could go completely mad, enter a schizophrenic world and pass the rest of her life in hospital. She wouldn't be the first to whom such a thing had happened.

Still, now she was reading ARRIA's constitution, and apparently reading every word with care. Wexford wouldn't talk about the Williams case in her presence and Burden knew that. Suddenly she began reading aloud.

'Rule 6: With certain limited exceptions, no woman shall be financially dependent on a man. Then they list the exceptions. Rule 7: All women shall take a course in some martial art or self-defence technique. Rule 8: All women shall carry a permitted weapon for self-defence, i.e. ammonia spray, pin, penknife, pepper shaker, etc. Rule 9: No member shall marry, participate in the bourgeois concept of becoming 'engaged' or share accommodation with a man in a cohabiting situation. Rule 10 . . . Do you want Rule 10?'

'Oh, I have read it,' Wexford said. 'It is heresy!'

She didn't recognise the quotation. 'You're bound to think that way, aren't you? Perhaps I should have read all this before I met you, Mike.'

He took the blow with a physical flinch.

'ARRIA didn't exist then. It was around earlier this year before I gave up work, though. I always wanted to get hold of their manifesto but no one would even talk to me about it. I was a married woman, you see.'

'I suppose I was lucky to get it,' Wexford said.

Burden was making an effort to recover from the pain she had given him. 'I want to hear Rule 10.'

'All Right. Rule 10: Women wishing to reproduce should select the potential father for his physique, health, height, etc., and ensure impregnation in a rape or near-rape construct.'

'In a *what*? What the hell does that mean?'

Wexford said, 'Margaret Mead says men of the Arapesh fear rape of women just as women in other cultures fear rape by men.'

'The mind boggles.' By this, Wexford knew, Burden meant he would dearly have loved to inquire further into the mechanics and techniques but was hampered by inhibition. 'The trouble is surely that most of this was written by lesbians like Edwina Klein and Caroline Peters. It doesn't seem to cater for women who actually *love* men – and those are surely in the vast majority.'

Jenny looked coldly at her husband. 'In the sort of explanation bit that comes after the rules, it says the authors realise women may feel affection for men and even – I quote – "what is termed sexual love" but it is necessary that something must be given up for the cause. Other women in the past have denied themselves this indulgence and been amply compensated. It goes on: "After all, what does this so-called 'love' amount to when a woman sets it against its concomitants:

gross exploitation, pornography, degradation, career prohibition or curtailment, rape, father-daughter incest and the still-persisting double standard?" '

'It doesn't seem to bear much relation to our own home lives, does it?' said Burden.

Jenny had tears in her eyes, Wexford saw. They shone there, unshed. 'Revolutionaries are always extreme,' she said. 'Look at the Terror of 1793, look at Stalinism. If they're not, if they compromise with liberalism, all their principles fizzle out and you're back with the status quo. Isn't that what's happened to the broader women's liberation movement?'

The men looked at her with varying expressions of doubt and dismay. Burden had gone rather pale.

'If these girls,' said Jenny, 'can accomplish just a fraction of what they're setting out to do, if they can begin to make people see what "inequitable arbitration" really amounts to, perhaps – perhaps I shan't so much mind my daughter being born.'

This time she didn't break down into tears. 'I know you want to talk. I'll leave you.' She turned to her husband, kissed his forehead, carried herself clumsily to the door. There was no dignity there and no beauty because the child that made her heavy was unwanted . . . Burden put out one finger to touch the ARRIA manifesto like someone steeling himself to make contact with something he has a phobia about.

'I feel it threatens me, all this. I'm frightened of it.'

'It's good that you're honest enough to admit it.'

'Do you really think there's anything in this killing a man stuff?'

He had done so at first. It had seemed the obvious answer and for a moment or two the only possible answer. At that point his whole tone towards Eve had changed. He had been dancing lightly with her and then, suddenly, the music stopped and he seized hold of her. That was what it was like. Of course, he had frightened her with his quick rough questions . . .

'But nobody ever did it! It was a fantasy – like group sex or something. Like an orgy. You think about what it would be like, you fantasise, but you don't *do* it.'

'Many do.'

'Well, OK, that wasn't a very good comparison. The point is fantasy doesn't become reality, the two don't mix.'

'Don't they? Isn't that what a psychopath is? Someone who confuses fantasy with reality?'

She had insisted, with the panic of someone who realises she has said too much, that Edwina Klein's idea had been hers alone, even the splinter group had opposed it. Knives next. He had gone on to ask her what was meant by 'permitted weapons'. Did this category include knives? Not *real* knives, she said, and she had looked at him as a child might, round-eyed, afraid of something it doesn't understand.

'It's tempting,' he said to Burden, 'to think of a group of those ARRIA girls grabbing hold of poor old Williams like the Maenads with Orpheus and doing him in on the Lesbian shore.'

Burden looked at him, mystified. 'Shall we have a beer?' he said.

'Good idea.

> ' "Malt does more than Milton can
> To justify the ways of God to man." '

'You're right there,' Burden said feelingly.

He came back with two cans and two tankards on a tray. Poor chap, Wexford thought, he's had enough. And how curious it was that these dramatic things happened to Burden, who was such an ordinary, unimaginative, salt-of-the-earth person. The prototype surely of Kafta's man to whom who, though he shut himself up in his room, hid himself, lay low, life nevertheless came in and rolled in ecstasy at his feet. Whereas for him, Wexford, nothing much came along to disturb his private peace. Thank God for it!

'Just the same,' he said, 'we're going to have our work cut out checking out every one of ARRIA's members. There are said to be five hundred of them, remember.'

'The girl who stabbed Budd may not be the same girl who stabbed Wheatley who may not be the same girl as the one that killed Williams, but on the other hand they may be one and the same.'

'Right,' said Wexford. 'But don't let's talk of the "one" that killed Williams. No girl on her own could have carried his body into that car and then carried it out again and buried him.'

'The way I see it, we have to think of it along these lines. On the one hand we have the radical feminists of whom we know (a) that the notion of killing a man was at any rate considered by them and (b) that they are required by their own rules to carry offensive weapons. We also know that Wheatley certainly and Budd probably were stabbed by ARRIA members. We've been told too that Williams, pursuing his well-known tastes, had a very young girlfriend. Now is this girlfriend a member of ARRIA?'

'Whatever the ARRIA rules may say,' said Wexford, 'we know members do have to do with the opposite sex. Look at Eve climbing in through her boyfriend's window. She hasn't made the supreme sacrifice of giving up men. And if you want to kill a man what better way of doing it than in what ARRIA would probably call a libido-emotional construct – in other words a love affair?'

Burden finished the last of his beer. In the next room Jenny had put a record on, Ravel's *Pavane on a Dead Infanta*. 'Who said that about malt and Milton?'

'Housman. His life was ruined by an unrequited love.'

'Blimey. Why ravens?'

'In ARRIA's logo, d'you mean? They're predatory birds, aren't they? No, I suppose not. Harsh-tongued? I really don't know, Mike. At any rate, they're not soft and submissive. The collective noun for them is an "unkindness". An Unkindness of Ravens. Appropriate, wouldn't you say? In their attitude to the opposite sex anyway. They stab at us with knives rather than beaks.'

'Not without provocation, of course.'

'That's true. Budd on his own admission tried to get fresh with the girl who attacked him. He may have got fresher than he says. Wheatley says he didn't get fresh at all but I'm not inclined to believe him. They made passes and got themselves stabbed. Makes you wonder what Williams did, doesn't it?'

As Wexford walked home he thought about what he had had to do as a result of his visit to the Freeborns' house. Sergeant Martin and Detective Bennett had paid a follow-up call and this morning Charles Freeborn, the girls' father, had appeared at Kingsmarkham Magistrates' Court charged with possessing

277

cannabis and with permitting cannabis to be smoked upon his premises. Bennett, who detected the stuff in a positively cat-and-mouse way – or cat-and-catmint way – had begun a methodical search of the big overgrown garden, starting at the conservatory, following the crazy-paving path through a copse of unpruned dusty shrubs. This path curved all round the perimeter of the garden, winding its way between ghosts of flowerbeds where a few attenuated cultivated plants thrust their heads through a matting of bindweed, ground elder and thistles. A gate in the fence at the garden's foot afforded a shortcut into a path to the High Street. Bennett had been wondering if he was getting obsessional imagining *Cannabis sativa*, which requires sunlight and space, might ever flourish here when he suddenly came upon the only tended flowerbed in the whole half acre.

He was nearly back at the house again, the stifling, shadow-spreading trees behind him. A neat rectangular clearing had been made in the shaggy grass here, the soil well watered, weeded, and the bed bordered with bricks. Martin had declared the vigorous young plants to be seedling tomatoes but Bennett knew better. Infra-red light is essential to the Indian hemp if its effect when ingested is to be the characteristically hallucinogenic one, and these plants were basking in it, for their bed was in the only part of the garden to enjoy day-long uninterrupted sunshine.

Wexford pondered, not for the first time, on the ethics of going into someone's house for a check and a chat, while there detecting a forbidden drug and immediately, scarcely with a qualm, taking steps to prosecute the offender. One's host *in absentia*, so to speak. Of course he was right, *it* was right. He was a policeman and that came first. That must always come first or chaos would come instead . . .

By the time the schools broke up towards the end of July Wexford's men had vetted and cleared something like 50 per cent of the ARRIA membership. Tracking them down was the difficulty, for Caroline Peters denied the existence of a list of members. Why should a list be needed when there was no subscription, and dates and venues of meetings were passed on by grassroots?

Paulette Harmer, Williams's niece, a sixth-form-college student, was cleared. She had been out with her boyfriend, to whom she would become engaged at Christmas – thereby abrogating ARRIA membership? – on the evenings Budd and Wheatley were stabbed, and at home with her parents and her aunt Joy on 15 April. Eve Freeborn, before going to her boyfriend in Arnold Road, had spent the evening at home with her parents and her sister. This alibi also accounted for Amy. Neither could be cleared of the Budd and Wheatley stabbings. Nor could Caroline Peters who, however, had been at a meeting in London on the evening of the 15th. The redheaded Nicky turned out to be Nicola Anerley and not the Nicola Tennyson who was Veronica Williams's friend. She had been at a party on 15 April, Helen Blake's eighteenth birthday party, which had also been attended by another twelve members of ARRIA, all of whom Wexford was able to discount as far as the murder of Williams was concerned.

Jane Gardner he questioned himself. She was the right age, pretty and lively, an active member of ARRIA. He owed it to the cordial relationship he had had with her father to go himself and not send Bennett, say, or Archbold.

Miles was at home, had made a point evidently of being at home. He was affronted and preparing to be bitterly offended. He and his tall wife were in the drawing room (walls of Sevenstar Chinese yellow, black carpet, *famille jaune* porcelain) and Wexford was shown in by the cleaning lady masquerading as a maid. They spoke to him, he thought, in the aghast tones of parents asking a headmaster why he intends to expel their daughter from his school. Pamela Gardner called him 'Mr Wexford' though it had been 'Reg' in the past. Since she had no means of summoning the cleaning lady except by shouting, she went to fetch Jane herself.

'This is so entirely unnecessary,' Gardner said in a hard voice.

Wexford said it was routine and felt like a cop in an ancient Cyril Hare detective story.

The girl came in smiling and perfectly at ease. Then he had to ask the parents to go. They did but with a very ill grace. At first Pamela Gardner pretended she didn't understand what he meant. Light dawned, then came incredulity, lastly disgusted acceptance. She took her husband's arm as if the very cornerstones of their home life had been threatened.

'Did you get a university place?' Wexford asked Jane as soon as they were alone.

'Oh yes, thanks. We met before, didn't we? At Dad's office? I never thought I would actually. I'd even enrolled at secretarial college in London just in case. My school doesn't have a commercial department.'

There came back to him a recollection of this girl changing her clothes in full view of the street. In 'Dad's office'. And when she had turned round to see him looking at her she hadn't turned a hair.

'Did you know Rodney Williams, Jane?'

'I'd met him. At the office. Dad introduced us. He had a lot of charm, you know.' She smiled, reminiscently, a bit sadly. 'He could make you feel you were the only person there worth talking to.'

It struck Wexford that this was the first person he had spoken to with a good word to say for Rodney Williams. She spoiled it a little.

'I expect he was like that with all girls of my age.'

Was she an enthusiastic member of ARRIA? Had she been in the splinter group? Did she carry a weapon? Where had she been when Budd was stabbed, when Wheatley was stabbed, when Williams was killed? Yes to the first and second questions, an indignant no, wide-eyed and law-abiding, to the third. A baby-sitting alibi for 15 April, a visit to her newly married sister for a Budd alibi, no memory of what she had been doing on the evening of the Wheatley stabbing. Apropos of none of this, surprising her with what seemed inconsequential, he said, 'Which schools do have commercial departments?'

'Haldon Finch, Sewingbury Sixth Form.' She gave him an earnest look. 'Dad's really upset that you suspect me.'

'There's no question of that. This is routine.'

'Well . . .' Suddenly she was the good daughter, dutiful, compliant, obedient. 'He and Mummy are dead against you taking my fingerprints.'

'You' presumably implied the Mid-Sussex Constabulary or did she think he had come armed with pads and gadgets? The

280

cleaning lady showed him out, her apron changed for rather smart dungarees. There was no sign of Miles or Pamela. Donaldson drove him back to Kingsmarkham and dropped him outside his own house. Dora, dressed up, was on the phone to Sylvia.

He passed close by her and touched her cheek with his lips. She responded to the kiss, mouthed something about getting a move on, went on talking to Sylvia. He went upstairs, changed into what he called his best suit, grey like the others but the latest and least shabby. When he retired he would never wear a suit again – not even to the theatre.

In the train he told Dora about the Gardners and said he had a feeling they wouldn't be asked to any more garden parties. She said that didn't matter, did it? She didn't care. And he shouldn't care either, he should relax, especially tonight.

'I wish I'd read the play.'

'You haven't had time.'

'You can always make time for things you want to do,' he said.

As it was he didn't even know what *The Cenci* was about and of its history only that it had for a long time been banned from the English stage. He and Dora, on holiday in Italy, had seen Guido Reni's portrait of Beatrice Cenci in the Galleria Nazionale in Rome, though he wouldn't have connected that with the play but for Sheila's saying it would be reproduced in the programme. It would have been a good idea to have read the play – or to have read Moravia's *Beatrice Cenci*, a novel that might be more entertaining.

The play threatened at first not to entertain at all. Shelley, Wexford thought to himself while aware he was no informed critic, wasn't Shakespeare. And wasn't he, in writing this sort of five-act tragedy in blank verse, some two hundred years out of date? Then Sheila came on, not looking like the portrait but with a small cap on her golden hair and dressed in white and grey, and he forgot everything, even the play, in his consuming pride in her. She had a peculiar quality in her acting, which critics as well as he had remarked on, of bringing clarity to obscure or periphrastic lines, so that her entrances always seemed to let light in upon the arcane. It was so now, it continued to be so . . . He saw and understood. The plot and

281

purpose of the play began to unfold themselves for him and Shelley's style ceased to be an anachronism.

The effect on Dora was less happy.

She whispered to Wexford while they were having a glass of wine during the interval, 'There's more to it than I can see, I know that. It's not just that they can't stand the old man's harshness any longer, is it? I mean, why did Sheila come tearing in screaming about her eyes being full of blood?'

'Her father raped her.' Wexford realised what he had said and corrected himself. 'Count Cenci raped his daughter Beatrice.'

'I see. Oh yes, I do see. It's not made very clear, is it?'

'I imagine Shelley couldn't afford to spell it out. As it was, it must have been the incest theme that got the play banned.'

While waiting for the curtain to go up on Act Four he read the essay on the historical facts on which the play was based which had been written for the programme by an eminent historian. Beatrice, her stepmother and her brother had been put to death for the murder of Count Cenci. They really had. It had all happened. Guido had painted the portrait while Beatrice was in prison. Later they had tortured her to extract a confession.

It wasn't the kind of piece, he decided, that one would ever want to see again or read or remember a line from. When it was over they went backstage. They always did. Sheila, though in jeans and sweater now, still had a mask of gleaming white paint on her face and her hair top-knotted for execution as when she had cried:

'. . . Here, Mother tie
My girdle for me . . . My Lord,
We are quite ready. Well, 'tis very well.'

Going home, Dora fell asleep in the train. Wexford found his mind occupied with the prosaic subject of typewriters.

It was the caretaker of the Haldon Finch Comprehensive School, primed by a phone call from the County Education Department, who showed them round. Wexford had been inside the school before, years ago when the nucleus of these buildings had been the old county high school. Incorporated into it now were the buildings next door, a former clinic and health centre, as well as a vast new assembly hall and the glass, concrete and blue-slate complex of classrooms, music room and concert hall, with the sports centre a gilt-roofed rotunda that the sun set ablaze.

'It reminds me,' Wexford said to Burden, 'of a picture I once saw of the Golden Temple at Amritsar.'

But the commercial department had no new building to house it. It was pushed away into three rear classrooms at the top of the old high school, as if the education authority had half-heartedly accepted the recent remark of a government minister that shorthand and typing were no part of education and should not be taught in schools. Wexford followed Burden and the caretaker up a remarkable (and remarkably battered) Art Deco marble staircase and along a wide vaulted passage. The caretaker unlocked and opened the double doors into the commercial department. These too were Art Deco, with parabolas and leaves in green ironwork on their frosted glass. The old high school had been built in 1930 and the classrooms inside looked as if they had received no more than one coat of paint since then. They were shabby, typically green and cream, with a view of rooftops and a brick well full of dustbins.

It was in the farthest room that the typewriters were. Wexford asked himself what he had expected. The latest in word processors? Obviously here the country's resources were mainly devoted to science and sport. Nor presumably would ARRIA encourage its members towards a secretarial career. There was not an electric typewriter among the machines and some of them looked older than the building itself. Burden, walking between the tables, had a piece of paper in his hand, probably with the faults of the typewriter they were looking for written on it. As if he couldn't remember without that! A break in the head of the upper-case A and the ascender of the lower-case t, a comma with a smudged head.

He felt a small flicker of excitement when he spotted the first of the Remington 315s.

'Can you type?'

'Enough to test these,' said Burden and impressed Wexford by getting to work and using all his fingers.

Nothing wrong with the A, and t and the comma on the first one. Burden slipped his paper into the roller of the second. The capital A wasn't all it might have been but neither was the B or the D or a lot of others. The lower-case faces and the comma seemed unflawed. He tried the third machine, the caretaker watching with the fascinated awe of one who expects the litmus paper to turn not red but all the colours of the spectrum. This typewriter, however, seemed without faults. It produced the best-looking copy so far. There was only one more. Burden slipped his paper in and this time, instead of 'Now is the time for All good men to come to the Aid of the party', typed 'A thousand ages in Thy sight are like an evening gone'. If he had been a Freudian, Wexford thought, he would have wanted to know why. Perhaps it was just done to astonish the caretaker. Anyway, whatever the reason, this wasn't the machine Rodney Williams's letter of resignation had been typed on.

'That's it then.'

'Show my four samples to the experts. We could be wrong.'

'We're not wrong. These are all the typewriters the school has?'

'Apart from them as has gone away to be serviced.'

'Now he tells me,' said Wexford.

'There's always some go away in the summer holidays. It's never the lot of them. They go in, like, rotation.'

'Do you know how many have gone and where?'

The caretaker didn't know the answer to either question. No more than, say, five, he thought. He had never heard the name of any firm which might be servicing the machines or seen a van arrive to take them away.

'We must be thankful,' Wexford said as they came out of the school, 'that at least it's an old manual portable we're looking for and not one of the modern kind with a golfball or daisywheel.'

'A what or a *what*?'

'Let's say with a detachable typeface that our perpetrator could simply have taken out and thrown away.'

School might have broken up but sport went on. Half a dozen boys in shorts and tee-shirts were running laps round the biggest playing field and on the tennis courts a doubles game and a singles were in progress. The umpire seats were empty but Caroline Peters was there in the role of coach, and as they approached the wire fencing Wexford saw that what he had supposed to be a singles match was in fact instructor and instructed, the pupil here being Veronica Williams.

The four doubles players were Eve and Amy Freeborn, Helen Blake and another girl he had never seen before. So there were actually seventeen- and eighteen-year-olds in this corner of Sussex he had never seen before? He was beginning to think he knew them all by sight and usually by name too. He and Burden went over to the fence and watched, as they had done that previous time. Caroline Peters glared but didn't come over to admonish. She knew who they were now.

It was clear from the first that Veronica was streets ahead of the other players, though two years younger than any of them. She was the best tennis player Wexford had ever seen on a local court. This time the discrepancy between what he saw on TV and what he saw at home did not seem quite so wide. She was a strong, lithe, fast player with a hard accurate backhand and a powerful smashing action. When Caroline Peters made her serve her service was as hard as Eve's but the balls struck the court well inside the line.

The doubles players changed ends. Eve looked in Wexford's direction and then ostentatiously away. Loyalty to the father he had had charged with possessing cannabis, he supposed. He had been getting a lot of stick of that kind lately. All part of a policeman's lot, no doubt. Veronica returned Caroline Peter's lob with a hard transverse drive which Caroline ran for but couldn't reach. It was a mystery, Wexford thought, where somebody got that kind of talent from. You couldn't imagine that finicking Wendy playing any sort of game or even walking more than half a mile, while Rodney Williams had been out of condition for years. Did the other Williams family play games? There had been a tennis racket up on Sara's bedroom wall, he remembered. Of course, the probable answer was that any healthy young girl keen on tennis could be coached to the standard of Veronica Williams. She was already sixteen. It was already too late for her to begin competing in anything much more significant than inter-school matches.

The girl whose face and name he didn't know served a double fault. One more of those and the set would be lost. She served one more of those and threw her racket down in the kind of petulance she wouldn't have known about if she hadn't watched Wimbledon on TV. Wexford and Burden walked back to the car.

'Have we got anything on the fingerprints found in Williams's car yet?' Burden asked.

'They took about sixty prints,' Wexford said, 'all made by nine people. By far the greater proportion were made by one man and they've more or less established that man was Williams.'

'I don't suppose his fingers were in very good shape after being in the ground for nine weeks.'

'Exactly. They matched the car ones to prints in his bedroom – well, bedrooms – of course. The other prints were made by two unknown men, and may well belong to whoever began the dismantling of Greta, by Joy, Wendy, Sara, Veronica, and two more women or girls who might be friends of the wives and daughters – or who might not. The steering wheel had been wiped.'

'Much what you would expect really,' said Burden.

Nicola Tennyson, Veronica's friend, was thrilled to have her fingerprints taken. She was unable to remember much about 15 April. Certain it was that she had been baby-sitting her brother that evening and Veronica had come in, but she couldn't remember times. Veronica and she were often in each other's homes, she said.

One of the two unidentified sets of fingerprints on Greta turned out to be hers.

13

Wheatley said that the woman who stabbed him had been more than commonly tall. Budd said that because he had only seen her sitting down he couldn't tell her height. That wasn't strictly true. He had seen her running off with the sack over her shoulder. The sack was the only thing he could really remember, that and the fact she had blonde hair. The girl who attacked Wheatley had 'brown or lightish' hair. She was eighteen or nineteen. Budd thought his assailant was twenty. Or twenty-five or -six. Or any age between eighteen and thirty.

In each case their wounds had been made with the blade of a large penknife. Not necessarily the same penknife, though. Not necessarily the same woman. Wexford asked himself what had been in the sack. He didn't think Budd had invented the sack. Budd wasn't endowed with enough imagination for that. There had been a sack all right, a black plastic dustbin liner. What had she been carrying it for and why?'

It had been pouring with rain. Those plastic sacks were very good for keeping things dry. Keeping what dry? The bus stop was the nearest one to the place where they'd found Rodney Williams's body. But he had been dead six weeks by the night Budd was attacked. Wendy Williams wasn't particularly tall but she was blonde and she looked much younger than she was. To Budd she might seem in her early twenties.

She had begun a fortnight of her annual holiday. Wexford thought to himself that she might be spending the major part of it at Kingsmarkham Police Station. He went with the car to fetch her.

Veronica was in the raspberry-ice-cream living room, seated at the glass-topped table, turning the pages of *Vogue*. He thought she looked like a teenage girl in a French film of the sixties. He hadn't seen many French films of the sixties but nevertheless the impression was there in Veronica's bandbox look, the beautifully cut, newly washed, pageboy hair, the clothes – primrose pinafore dress, starched white blouse, blue bootlace tie, white ankle socks, sky-blue sandals – that were just a little too young for her, the expression on her face that was 99 per cent innocence and 1 per cent calculation.

'I saw you playing tennis the other day.'

'Yes, I saw you too.'

Why the wary look suddenly, the shade of unease across that naivety?

'You're very good.'

She knew that already, she didn't need to be told. A polite smile and then back to *Vogue*. Wendy Williams came down the spiral staircase, walking slowly, giving him a voyeur's look if he had wanted it of shapely legs in very fine pale tights all the way up to a glimpsed border of cream lace. He wasn't looking, but out of the corner of his eye he saw her hold her skirt down as if he had been.

She had dressed up. Women these days didn't bother with fancy dressing except for special occasions, except when it was fun. That was general, not just the ARRIA view of things. For going down the cop shop, Wexford thought, you went in the jeans and shirt you wore around the house. But this was something that hadn't yet got through to Wendy Williams and maybe never would. She probably didn't possess a pair of jeans. And Veronica's would be the designer kind with Vidal Sassoon or Gloria Vanderbilt on the backside. Wendy had a pretty cotton dress on, the kind that needs a lot of ironing, a wide black patent belt to show she still had an adolescent waist and red wedge-heeled shoes that pinched where they touched.

The car filled with her perfume. Estée Lauder's White Linen, decided Wexford, who was good on scent. He made up his mind to take her up to his office, not into one of the interview rooms.

'You haven't told me much about this girlfriend of your husband's, Mrs Williams,' he said when they were there.

'I've told you all I know. I've told you it was a very young girl and that's all I know.'

'I don't think so,' he said. 'There's more if you search your memory.'

A secretive look was closing up her face. Why? Why should she want to conceal this girl's identity from him?

'I wish I'd never mentioned any girl to you!' Exasperated. The tone of a mother to a child who keeps nagging her about a treat she has promised him.

'You had an anonymous letter, you said.'

She hesitated. She opened her mouth to begin an explanation. He cut her short.

'You didn't keep it though. You burned it.'

'How did you know?'

'Mrs Williams, let me tell you what I do know. First, it's only in books that people burn anonymous letters. In real life they may not care much for them, they may even recoil from them in disgust, but they don't burn them. Most people don't have fires any more, for one thing. Where would you burn something?'

She didn't say anything. A sullen crushed look made her almost ugly.

'People who get anonymous letters may not like looking at them. Usually they put them away in a drawer in case or until we want to see them. Or there's the dustbin. You read somewhere that the requisite thing to do with an anonymous letter was burn it, didn't you? In a detective story probably. The truth is you never received one.'

'All right, I didn't.'

'Hasn't anyone told you you mustn't tell lies to the police?'

He hadn't spoken harshly. His tone was almost bantering. It was mockery, even as mild as this, she couldn't stand. She flushed and her mouth set mulishly.

'I didn't tell lies. There was a girl.' Perhaps she could see he wasn't going to say anything for a moment or two. 'He was perverted about young girls, that's what it amounted to and it ruined my life.' Her voice rose, edgy and plaintive. 'I thought he was in love with me when we first met. I thought he loved me but now I know he just fancied me because I was young. And when Veronica was coming he had to marry me. Well, *marry*. It's easy to marry, isn't it? You can do it over and over again.

'I never had any life. I never had any youth. Do you know something? I'm thirty-two and I've never so much as been taken out to dinner in a decent restaurant by a man. I've never been abroad. I've never had a thing to wear that didn't come discount from Jickie's. I never even had an engagement ring!'

He asked her how she knew of the girl's existence. Just at this point Marion came in with coffee on a tray, three unprepossessing cheese sandwiches and three custard-cream biscuits. Wendy looked at the sandwiches and shook her head in a shuddery genteel sort of way.

He repeated the question.

'Rodney confessed.'

'Just like that? Out of the blue? You didn't suspect anything but he confessed to you he had a young girlfriend?'

'I told you.'

'Why did he confess? Was he intending to leave you for her? As in fact you thought he had done?'

That made her laugh in the way someone does who has knowledge of a secret you will never guess. He persisted and she looked exasperated, answering that she had told him already. She ate nothing, he ate a sandwich, leaving the rest for Marion, who had a hearty appetite. Afterwards, he thought, Wendy Williams would probably tell people she was kept at the police station for hours and not given a thing to eat or drink.

He asked her once more about 15 April. The evening. What time had she left Jickie's to drive home to Pomfret? All the staff at Jickie's had been questioned by Martin and Bennett and Archbold. They had forgotten. Why should they remember that particular evening? One of the girls on the fashion-floor pay desk said that if Mrs Williams hadn't actually left the building before nine, that would have been very late for her. On Thursdays she usually left as soon after eight as possible and had been known to leave at 7.30.

Wendy insisted she left at nine. She stuck to that. He left it. He said there was something he had to ask her. Seeing that her husband consistently neglected her and for two months she believed he had finally left her, had she formed a friendship with any other man?

290

'It would be a natural and normal thing to you. You're a very young woman still. You said yourself that you felt life and youth had been denied you.'

'Are you suggesting I was having a – a relationship with someone?'

'It would be very understandable.'

'I think that's disgusting! That's really immoral. I've got my daughter to think of, haven't I? I've got Veronica to set an example to. Just because Rodney behaved in that horrible way, that's no reason for me to do the same. Let me tell you, I've always been absolutely faithful. I've never looked at another man, it would never have entered my head.'

He was beginning to know her and her protests. He said not another word on that one but thought the more. It was afternoon now and Burden would be setting in motion their prearranged plan. It might not work, of course – and if it did what would it show or prove? He didn't even know if he expected it to work.

In the meantime he questioned her about her life, her feelings, her reactions. Still she hadn't said a word about the other Williams family. She was prepared to acknowledge Rodney Williams had married her bigamously while ignoring the existence of his first or true wife. You would have expected her natural curiosity to get the better of her. Was she rising above such human failings? That was a possible explanation.

'Mrs Joy Williams,' he said deliberately, 'has a son and daughter. Her daughter and Veronica are very much alike. Do you have any feelings about these people?' He was aware he sounded like a psychotherapist, though any interrogating policeman was one of those. But nevertheless he made a slight correction. 'Aren't you interested in knowing something about them?'

'No.' Once more she had flushed. She looked mulish. 'Why should I be? They're nothing to me. Rodney can't have cared much for them.'

'Why do you say that?'

She made a little gesture with her hands to indicate that the answer was obvious. Wexford said that was enough for today and he'd organise a car to take her home. They went down in the lift, timing it perfectly, for as the lift came to a stop and the doors opened Burden came walking across the black and white

291

checkerboard floor towards it with Joy Williams beside him. Wexford spoke to Burden for the sake of stopping and saying something. The two women stood there, Joy staring at Wendy, Wendy contemplating the wall ahead of her as if it were the most fascinating example of interior decor since the cave paintings of Trois Frères.

They presented a contrast, pathetic and grotesque. It was almost too marked to be quite real. They were like a cartoon for an old-fashioned advertisement, the wife who doesn't use the face cream, floor polish, deodorant, stock cubes, and the wife who does. Joy had a cardigan on over a cotton dress with half its hem coming down. All her shoes had a curious way of looking like carpet slippers though they weren't. Wendy swayed a little on her high heels, craning her neck and putting on a winsome look. Wexford smelt a gush of White Linen from her, perhaps because she was sweating. The irony was that both these women had been rejected.

Burden and Joy went into the lift. The doors closed.

'Do you know who that woman was?'

'What woman?' said Wendy.

'I'm not talking about Detective Bayliss. The woman who has just gone up in the lift with Inspector Burden.'

She raised her eyebrows, moved her shoulders.

'That was Mrs Joy Williams.'

'His wife?'

'Yes,' said Wexford.

'She looked about sixty.'

Upstairs Burden was asking Joy about the phone call, the letter of resignation. Why had she gone out on the evening of 15 April instead of remaining at home to await her son's phone call?

'I can't be always at his beck and call,' she said, her voice full of bitterness. 'It's all one to him whether I'm there or not. He's his father all over again – indifferent. I've done everything for him, worshipped the ground he walked on. Might as well not have bothered. Do you know where he is now? In Cornwall. On holiday. That's all it means to him that his mother's a widow.'

It could just be true. It could just be that she had at last seen the results of spoiling a son. A quarrel, Burden thought, the day before Kevin returned to university. He could hear the things that would have been said – all right, just wait till next time you want something; you phone, my lad, but don't count on me being here . . . Yet there had been no sign since then of adoration flagging.

'Do you know who that woman was with Chief Inspector Wexford?'

'I can guess.' The harsh clattering laugh. 'Cheap little tart. I don't admire his taste.'

He asked her if Sara had a boyfriend. Incredibly, she said she didn't know. It was plain she didn't care. Hatred came into her eyes when her daughter's name was mentioned.

'And after all I've done for her,' said Joy as if their discussion had been on the subject of the host of services she had performed for Sara and the girl's ingratitude. Burden had her driven home. He felt as if he had been brought up against a wall, the solid brick an inch from his face.

Carol Milvey was not a member of ARRIA but she was eighteen years old and lived next door but one to Joy Williams. And it was her father, the boss of Mid-Sussex Waterways, who had found Rodney Williams's travelling bag in Green Pond, a coincidence which had never been explained. Sergeant Martin saw her. The interview was a brief one, for Carol Milvey had been ill in bed with tonsillitis on 15 April and had taken two days off school.

A further ten members of ARRIA were cleared, both for 15 April and the evening on which Brian Wheatley had been stabbed in the hand. It was August now and people were beginning to go away on holiday, ARRIA members surely included. The Anerley family and their daughter, the red-headed Nicola, had been in France since the end of the school term and were not expected back until 12 August. On this date too Pomfret Office Equipment Ltd were due to reopen after two weeks' holiday closure, a southern version of North Country wakes weeks, as Wexford remarked. If the type-writers missing from Haldon Finch were serviced in the neighbourhood it was with Pomfret Office Equipment they had to be. No other firm of typewriter engineers admitted to knowledge of their whereabouts.

The commerce department at Sewingbury Sixth Form College had been checked out. They had microcomputers, ACT Apricots, as well as four dedicated word processors, and their typewriters were ten highly sophisticated Brother machines. Kingsmarkham High School had one typewriter only in the building and that in the school secretary's office.

Kevin Williams came back from Cornwall and left again with six like-minded students to camp in the Channel Islands. The Harmers with Paulette's boyfriend went to North Wales for a week, leaving an Indian pharmacist and his wife, both highly qualified but jobless, in charge of shop and dispensary. Sara went nowhere. Sara stayed at home, awaiting no doubt the A-level results due the second or third week of the month, after the degree results and before the O-levels.

'I can't help wondering if there'll still be A-levels when this new baby of ours grows up,' said Burden. Nowadays he talked gingerly and awkwardly about the coming child but as if its birth were a certainty and its future more or less assured. 'I'll be an old man by the time she wants to go to university. Well, I'll be in my sixties. I'll be retired. Do you remember filling in those grant forms? Getting one's employer to vouch for one's earnings and all that? Still, by then they'll do it all on a computer, I suppose, a kind of twenty-first-century Apricot.'

'Or an Apple,' said Wexford. 'Why do computer makers call their wares after fruit? There must be some unexpected Freudian explanation.' A glazed look of boredom blanked Burden's face. 'Talking of unexpected explanations,' Wexford said quickly, 'do you realise there's one aspect of this case we've given no thought to? Motive. Motive has scarcely been mentioned.'

Burden looked as if he were going to say that the police need not concern themselves with motive, that perpetrators in any case often stated motives that seemed thin or incredible. But he didn't say that. He said hesitantly, 'Aren't we concluding Williams was killed in what ARRIA would call self-defence?'

'Surely the difficulty there is that if we assume – which we are doing – that the woman or girl who made the phone call and wrote the letter was Williams's girlfriend, why should she need to defend herself against him? Budd and Wheatley were attacked because they made sexual advances. But this girl, being his girlfriend, presumably welcomed his sexual advances.'

Burden said in his prudish way, 'That might depend on their nature.'

'You mean they were sadistic or he wanted to wear one of her nightdresses? We've no evidence Williams was funny in that way. And aren't you forgetting something? It looks as if this murder was somewhat premeditated. Williams was given a sleeping drug before he was stabbed. I don't see my way to accepting a theory that one day Williams suggested to his girlfriend that they have sex in this new naughty way, whereupon she substitutes a sedative for his blood-pressure pill and when he's asleep stabs him eight times with a French cook's knife.'

'Then what motive do you suggest?'

'I don't. I can't see a girlfriend killing him to be rid of him because surely all she had to do was give him the out, tell him to go back to his wife or wives. And although a girl could have killed him on her own, she couldn't have disposed of his body on her own. A girl with a jealous husband or boyfriend? ARRIA members don't have husbands. ARRIA members aren't supposed to get sufficiently involved with men for a triangular jealousy situation to arise. But is she an ARRIA member? Does she exist?'

'If one could only read the book of fate,' said Burden, unaware that he was quoting and no longer thinking about the Williams case anyway.

'If this were seen,' said Wexford, 'the happiest youth, viewing his progress through, would shut the book and sit him down and die . . .'

He went home to fetch Dora and the two of them went to see Sheila in *Little Eyolf* at the Olivier.

14

Pomfret Office Equipment Ltd was open for business by 9.30 on the morning of 12 August. It was a shopfront with a big storage shed behind. The business was run by two men called Ovington, father and son. Edgar Ovington, the father, acknowledged at once that his firm serviced typewriters for the Haldon Finch Comprehensive School. The machines were usually attended to during the long summer holiday. His son had fetched the Haldon Finch machines the day before term ended, 26 July.

Wexford and Burden followed him into the shed at the back. It was full of typewriters, manuals, electric and electronic machines. They stretched away, rows of them ranked on slatted shelves, all labelled with tie-on luggage labels. Ovington pointed out the Haldon Finch typewriters, three on the lower shelf, two on the upper. The label on each said: H. Finch. Three portable Remington 315s, two Adler Gabrielle 5000s. Burden gave Ovington a condensed explanation of why they were looking for a particular typewriter and what made it particular. He asked for a sheet of paper. Ovington broke open a packet of 70-gramme white bond and peeled off two sheets from the top.

A flaw in the upper-case A, the ascender of the lower-case t and the head of the comma smudged. Burden slipped a sheet of paper into the roller of the first machine and typed a few lines from 'O God Our Help in Ages Past', the only hymn he knew by heart. No flaws. No flaws in the second machine either.

'You haven't put a new typeface on any of these machines?' Wexford asked.

'I haven't so much as touched them yet,' said Ovington.

Burden tried the third Remington. It was perfect, a better face than the others had, its need of servicing apparent only in the tendency of one or two of the keys to stick.

'These were the only typewriters fetched from the Haldon Finch Comprehensive School?'

'That's right. I label everything the minute it comes in to be on the safe side.'

'Yes, I see. So there's no possibility one of these machines could accidentally have been returned to a private customer?'

'It wouldn't go to a private customer if it was labelled Haldon Finch, would it?' said Ovington truculently.

He was a dour, prickly, suspicious man, always on the lookout for slurs anyone might cast on his ability or efficiency. Burden's request to try out any other Remington 315s there might be among the two hundred or so machines in the shed started him arguing and might have held them up but for the arrival, smiling and anxious to please, of the son, James Ovington. He was a tall, big-built young man with a toothy smile and a head as bald as an egg.

'Help yourselves. Be my guest.' The big white teeth glared as the lips stretched. 'Would you like me to have a sample of typing done from every machine here?' He meant it too, there was no sarcasm.

'We'll do it,' said Burden. 'And it's only the 315s we're interested in.'

Two more stood on the shelves besides the three he had tested. 'Sufficient is Thine Arm alone,' he typed, 'And our defence is sure'. Nothing wrong with that one. 'The busy tribes of flesh and blood With all their cares and fears, Are carried downward by the flood, And lost in following years.' No flaws.

'Thanks for your help,' said Wexford.

James Ovington said it was his pleasure and smiled so widely that his dragon-seed teeth threatened to spill out. His father scowled.

'It's going to be in a ditch somewhere or a pond,' said Burden.

'Not in Green Pond, anyway. Or Milvey would have found it.' Wexford was reminded again of the as yet unexplained

297

coincidence. The connecting link between Milvey and Rodney Williams wasn't Carol Milvey, for Carol Milvey had been ill with tonsillitis on the evening of Williams's death. So what was it? Connecting link there must be. Wexford refused to believe that it was by pure chance that Milvey had discovered his neighbour's overnight bag in Green Pond.

And coincidence became remarkable beyond any possible rational explanation, entering the realms of magic or fantasy, when a call came in from Milvey himself next day to say he found not the typewriter but a long kitchen knife, a French cook's knife, in a small ornamental pond on the Green Pond Hall estate.

The three ponds in the old water garden, now a wilderness, had been silted up with soil and fine sand washed down by springs from Cheriton Forest. Wexford's men had cleaned out those ponds during their search of the estate but since that time a further silting-up had taken place. The prospective trout farmer had called Mid-Sussex Waterways in once more to attempt to find a solution to the problem of the clogged water course.

Had the knife been placed there since the police search? Or had it been washed down from a hiding place upstream? It was a large knife, the handle of ivory-coloured plastic six inches long, the blade nine inches, a right-angled triangle with the hypotenuse the cutting edge. It had a sharp and vicious-looking point. There were traces of grey mud in the rivet sockets of the handle but not a streak or pinpoint of rust anywhere. Wexford had the knife sent to Forensics at Stowerton. The Milvey link was still a mystery to him. He confronted Milvey across his desk, at a loss for what to ask him next. The wild thought entered his head that Milvey and Joy Williams might have been lovers. It was too wild – not fat dull Milvey and draggle-tailed Joy. And if Milvey were involved in Williams's death, why should he produce the weapon?

He found himself reduced to saying, 'You do see, don't you, Mr Milvey, that this situation and your position in it is a very mystifying one. The man who lives next door but one to you is murdered. You find first the bag he had with him when he disappeared, then a knife that in all probability is the murder weapon.'

'Somebody,' said Milvey who didn't seem to see the point, 'had to find them sooner or later.'

'The population of Kingsmarkham is somewhere in the area of seventy-eight thousand souls.'

Milvey stared at him with bull-headed stupidity. At last he said with truculence, 'Next time I find something I reckon will help the police with their inquiries I'll keep quiet about it.'

While Forensics were testing the knife against Williams's wound measurements Sergeant Martin with Bennett and Archbold made inquiries as to its provenance. They listed thirty-nine shops and stores in the area where similar knives were sold. Only Jickie's however, stocked that particular brand of French cook's knife.

'Wendy Williams may work there,' Wexford said, 'but everyone shops there. We do. You do. Martin's asking the staff in the hardware department if they can remember anyone recently buying a French cook's knife. You know how far that'll get us. Besides, they've stocked the things for the past five years. There's no reason to believe the knife was bought specifically to kill Williams. In fact, the chances are it wasn't.'

'Yes, we're still at square one,' Burden said.

'You're being faint-hearted. Come and spend an afternoon among the typewriters. I've a hunch I want to put to the test.'

Ovington senior was on his own. He tried at first to fob them off with pleas of pressure of work. Wexford suggested gently that this might be construed as obstructing the police in the course of their enquiries. Ovington, grumbling under his breath, led them once more into the shed at the back of the shop.

Walking between the rows, Wexford examined the labels tied to the machines.

'You always use this method of labelling?'

'What's wrong with it?'

'I didn't say there was anything wrong with it. I don't think it's very clear, that's all. For instance, what does "P and L" stand for?' He pointed to the labels on a pair of Smith Corona SX 440s.

'Porter and Lamb on the estate,' said Ovington gruffly. He meant the industrial estate at Stowerton.

'And TML?'

'Tube Manipulators Limited.'

'And you know absolutely what those initials – I might say codes – mean when you're returning machines? You know that "P and L" stands for Porter and Lamb and not, for instance, for Payne and Lovell, the hardware people in the High Street here?'

'We don't do any work for Payne and Lovell.' Ovington looked astonished.

'I think you understand me though. With this system of labelling mistakes could be made. I'll come to the point. "H. Finch" is rather a rough and ready way of indicating the Haldon Finch Comprehensive School.'

'It serves its purpose.'

'Suppose you had a customer called Henry Finch. What would stop his machine getting mixed up with the Haldon Finch ones?'

'We don't have a customer called Henry Finch, that's what.'

Burden said sharply, 'D'you have any customers called Finch?'

'We might have.'

It was the curious reply, or a version of it, Wexford had so often heard witnesses give in court when they did not want to commit themselves to a positive 'yes'. 'I might have', 'I may have done'. Ovington, in his greasy old suit, open-necked shirt, his chin pulled back into his neck and his lips thrust forward, looked shifty, guilty, suspected and suspicious, truculent for the mere sake of truculence.

'I'd like you to check, please.'

'Not Henry,' said Ovington. 'Definitely not. A lady. Not an H at all.'

'You're wasting my time, Mr Ovington.'

He was enjoying it, with sly malice. 'We did some repairs on a Remington for her a while back. Not a 315 though.' At last, scratching his head, 'I could look in the book.'

'This could be it,' Wexford said when he and Burden were alone for a moment. 'They could have got mixed up and sent the wrong one back.'

'Wouldn't she have noticed?'

'She might not be a regular typist. She might not have used the machine since its return.'

He began looking at labels on all the typewriters on the lower shelf on the left-hand side. P and L, E. Ten (what could that mean?), TML, HBSS, H. Finch, J. St G, M. Br ... Ovington came back with a ledger.

'Miss J. Finch, 22 Bodmin Road, Pomfret. She collected the machine herself on July the twenty-sixth.' He slammed the book shut as if he had just proved or disproved something to his triumphant satisfaction.

July 26. The day the Haldon Finch machines were collected and brought here, Wexford thought. Did all this mean anything or nothing? Were the girlfriend and the girlfriend's typewriter after all sitting pretty somewhere in London or Brighton?

Neither he nor Burden knew where Bodmin Road was.

'You know something?' Burden said. 'Wendy Williams lives in Liskeard Avenue and Liskeard's a place in Cornwall. Bodmin's the county town of Cornwall. It may be just round the corner.'

'We'll look it up as soon as we get back.'

It was just round the corner. Liskeard Avenue, Falmouth Road, Truro Road, with Bodmin Road running crossways to connect them all.

'She was practically a neighbour of his,' Burden said, sounding almost excited. 'An ARRIA member, I bet you. Here she is on the Electoral Register. Finch, Joan B.'

'Wait a minute, Mike. Are we saying – are we assuming rather – that a Haldon Finch typewriter was collected by her in error or that it's her own typewriter she has, that this is the machine we're looking for, and we've stumbled upon her not by deduction but by pure luck?'

'What does that matter?' Burden said simply.

Twenty-two Bodmin Road was a small purpose-built block of four flats. According to the doorbells, J. B. Finch lived on the first floor. However, she was not at home either in the afternoon or at their two further calls at seven and eight in the evening. Wexford had been home an hour when a call came through to him to say a fourth man had been stabbed, this time in the upper arm, not a serious wound, though there had been considerable loss of blood.

The difference was that this time his cries were heard by two policemen sitting in a patrol car in a lay-by on the Kingsmarkham bypass. It was after sunset, the beginning of dusk. They had found the victim of the attack lying half across a public footpath, bleeding from a wound near his shoulder. While they were bending over him a girl came out from among the trees of the woodland on the north side of the path, announced her name as Edwina Klein and handed them a penknife from which she had wiped most of the blood.

15

ARRIA expected a show. Its members were in Kingsmarkham Magistrates' Court in force. Wexford had never seen the small wood-walled area that passed for a public gallery so full. Caroline Peters was there and Sara Williams, redhaired Nicola Anerley, Jane Gardner and the Freeborn twins, Helen Blake and Donella the black girl, the tennis player who wore glasses and the tennis player who did not.

It was to be a test case of course. Wexford had guessed all of it pretty well before he talked to Edwina Klein. She had not exactly been an *agent provocateur*. It was a terrible world we lived in if a woman who chose to walk alone along a field path at dusk could be called that. But the truth was that Edwina had set out to walk there, and to do so evening after evening since she came down from Oxford at the end of June, in the expectation of being attacked. She had been frank and open with him, hiding nothing, admitting, for instance, that it was she who while home for a weekend had been Wheatley's assailant. For this reason he had decided not to oppose bail. She would talk freely to him again, she had promised and, with a faith that would have set the Chief Constable's hair standing on end, he believed her.

With Caroline Peters a founder member of ARRIA, she was a thin straight girl of medium height, fiercely intelligent, a pioneer and martyr. She was dressed entirely in black, black trousers, black roll-neck sweater, her hair invisible under a tightly tied black scarf. A raven of a woman, the only colour about her the tiny orange ARRIA badge pinned on near her left shoulder.

What did the girls in the public gallery expect? Something like the trial of Joan of Arc, Wexford supposed. All were ignorant of magistrates' court procedure, all looked disbelieving when in five minutes it was all over and Edwina committed for trial to the crown court. The charge was unlawful wounding. She was released on bail in her own surety of £1000 and for a similar sum in that of an elderly woman, her great-aunt, not old enough to have been a suffragette but looking as if she might regret having missed the chance.

The ARRIA contingent filed out, muttering indignantly to each other. Helen Blake and Amy Freeborn picked up the orange banner with a woman-raven on it that they had been obliged to leave outside. The others fell in behind them and what had been a group became a march. 'We shall overcome,' they sang, 'we shall overcome some day.' They marched behind the banner up to the police station forecourt and across it and out into the High Street.

Joan Finch was sixty-five years old, perhaps more. Wexford wasn't surprised. There must be few women called Joan under fifty, and even fifty years ago Joan was becoming an old-fashioned name. It was Burden who had built so much on the chance of her being the girl they were looking for.

She took them into the poky little den, designed for surely no more than luggage storage, where she worked, and showed them the typewriter, a big manual Remington at least as old as herself. Fingers today would flinch at that iron forest of keys that took so much muscle power to fell it.

As Ovington had told them, she had collected it from Pomfret Office Equipment on 26 July. There was no doubt at all that it was hers. It had been her mother's before her and seemed as much of a family heirloom as any clock or piece of china.

Of sole significance to Wexford and Burden was the fact that it wasn't a Remington 315 portable machine. This was something Miss Finch seemed unable to grasp. She insisted on sitting down at the typewriter and producing for them a half page of men coming to the aid of the party and quick brown foxes. The Ovingtons had done a good job. There wasn't a flaw or an irregularity to be seen.

They had lunch at the little bow-fronted wine bar two doors away. Pamela Gardner was at a corner table lunching with a woman friend. She looked through Wexford with a contemptuous stare. Her daughter had bounced along that morning, singing as heartily as anyone and a good deal more loudly, waving to him as if they were old friends. Edwina Klein was coming to the police station at 2.30 to talk to him. It was no part of the conditions of her bail that she should do this but he felt sure she wouldn't fail him. Burden said, 'Only three weeks to go now.' He was talking of the coming baby. 'They say it'll be on time. They don't really know though.'

'There's more they don't know than they ever let on.'

Burden picked at his quiche. 'She had the heartburn at the beginning and I'm getting it now.' He was pale, bilious-looking.

'We'll see if the Harmers can supply you with an indigestion remedy.'

The Pre-Raphaelite head of Paulette could be seen through the window of the dispensary where she was evidently helping her father. It was Hope Harmer who served Burden. She seemed discomfited by their visit, unable perhaps to realise that policemen too have private lives and are as liable to bodily ills as anyone else.

'Did you have a good holiday?' Wexford asked her.

'Oh, yes, thank you, very nice. Very quiet,' she added as people do when describing their Christmas celebrations as if to admit to liveliness and merriment were to deny respectability. 'All good things come to an end though, don't they? We could have stayed away another week only my daughter's expecting her A-level results. They're due any day.'

Sara Williams must also be on tenterhooks then . . . 'Another would-be doctor in the family?'

'No, no. Paulette's hoping to follow in her daddy's footsteps.'

She was all bright placatory smiles, accompanying them to the door when they left like an old-fashioned shopkeeper. Wexford walked into the police station just before 2.30. Edwina Klein was waiting for him, shown upstairs to his room, and he felt relief at the sight of her in spite of his confidence that she would keep her word. With her, seated in the other visitor's chair, like a chaperone, was the aunt.

Wexford was surprised. He had seen Edwina as the very epitome of independence, of self-reliance.

'I happen to be a solicitor as well as an aunt.'

'Very well,' said Wexford, 'but this won't be an interrogation, just a talk about various aspects of this case.'

'That's what they all say,' said the aunt whose name was Pearl Kaufmann. In appearance she was rather like Virginia Woolf in her latter days, tallish, thin, long-faced, long-nosed, with a full mouth. She wore a navy blue silk dress, mid-calf length, and clumpy white sandals that made her feet look large.

Edwina was still in the black she had worn in court but with the roll-necked sweater changed for a sleeveless black tee-shirt that was better suited to the heat of the day. The ARRIA badge had been transferred to this. Edwina had sunglasses on which turned her face into an expressionless mask.

'He treated me exactly as if I was a prostitute,' she had said to him of Wheatley at that earlier conversation. The black glasses hadn't covered her eyes then. They had been bright with eagerness, with earnestness, with the zeal of youth. 'Not that there's anything wrong with being a prostitute. That's OK, that's fine if that's where you're at. It's just the way men *assume* . . .'

'Only some men.'

'A lot. He didn't even talk to me. I tried to talk to him. I asked him where he worked and where he lived. When I asked him where he lived he gave a strange sort of laugh as if I'd said something *wrong*.'

'Why did you ask him for a lift? To provoke exactly the sort of situation that arose?'

'No, I didn't. Not that time. I admit I did last night but it was different with the man in the car. I'd had a lift from London to Kingsmarkham and the guy couldn't take me any farther.' She seemed to consider. 'It was because of what happened in the car that I decided to try walking in the forest and see.'

'You'd better tell me what happened in the car, hadn't you?'

'He pulled into a lay-by. He did talk then. He said, "Come on, we'll go in the wood." I didn't know what he meant, I really didn't. Do you know what he thought? He thought I wanted paying first. He said, "Will ten pounds do?" And then he touched me.' Edwina Klein laid her right hand on her left breast. 'He touched me like I'm doing now. Like it was a tap or a switch. He didn't try to put his arms round me or kiss me or anything. It was just offering to pay and feeling the switch. I took out my knife and stuck it in his hand.'

There had been no aunt present when she talked to him then and no black circles to take the character from her face. Her manner now was more subdued, less indignant. Her experience of the court had perhaps chastened her. She waited almost meekly for him to begin questioning her. Miss Kaufmann sat looking at Wexford's wall map with simulated interest.

'Have you stabbed any other men?' he said abruptly, knowing the remark would be objected to.

Edwina shook her head.

'We won't mind about that, Mr Wexford.' It seemed highly suitable to the aunt's manner and appearance that she should use this obsolete Victorian phrase. She elucidated with something more contemporary. 'We'll forget you said that.'

'As you please,' said Wexford. 'When the police use *agents provocateurs* – as, for example, in the case of a policewoman sitting in a cinema where a member of the audience is suspected of assaulting women – the public, particularly the public of your sort of persuasion, gets up in arms. There's an outcry when a young policeman deliberately uses a public lavatory frequented by homosexuals. In other words, it's not all right for them to do this in the interests of justice but it's all right for you to in the mere interest of a principle. There's a rather crude name for what you did and were, isn't there?'

He had been too mealy-mouthed, too gentlemanly, he quickly saw.

'A pricktease,' she said flatly. The aunt didn't move an eyelid. 'I didn't do that. I didn't do anything but go for a walk in a wood. I wasn't provocatively dressed.' Scorn came into her voice now and she lifted up her head. 'I wouldn't be! I had jeans on and a jacket. I never wear make-up, not ever. The only thing I did to provoke anyone was *be* there and be a woman.'

'I think my niece is saying,' said Miss Kaufmann dryly, 'that it isn't possible to be a woman in certain places with impunity. She was out to prove this and she did prove it.'

307

He let it go. He left it. He felt the force of what the two women said and he knew it was true, and that this was an instance of a policeman knowing that the opposing argument is sounder than his own but of having to stick to his own just the same. That all women who intended to go about by themselves at night should learn self-defence techniques seemed to him the best answer. The alternative was that men's natures should change and that was something which might slowly happen over centuries but not in years or even decades. He wrote busy nothings on the sheet of paper in front of him to fill thirty seconds of time and keep them temporarily silent. At last he lifted his head and looked at Edwina Klein. For some reason, perhaps because his eyes were naked, she took off her glasses. Immediately she looked earnest again, and very young.

'You know the Williams family, I think?'

She was prepared for this. Somehow she knew that this was what she was really there for. Her answer surprised him.

'Which Williams family? There are two, aren't there?'

'There may be two hundred in this neighbourhood for all I know,' he said sharply. 'It's a common name. I'm talking about the Williams family that live in Alverbury Road, Kingsmarkham. The girl is called Sara. She was in court this morning. I think you know her.'

She nodded. 'We were at school together. She's a year younger than I am.'

'Did you know Rodney Williams, the dead man?'

She was very quick to reply. Miss Kaufmann looked up as if warningly. 'Him and Mrs Williams, yes. Sara and I used to do ballet together.' She smiled. 'Believe it or not.' Miss Kaufmann cast up her eyes as if she could hardly believe it. 'They'd come for Sara or one of them would. I remember him because he was the only father who ever came. Sometimes he'd come and sit through the whole class.'

Watching pubescent girls in little tutus, thought Wexford, or more likely leotards these days.

'You asked me which family I meant,' he said.

'I slightly know the other one.' She lifted her shoulders. 'Veronica Williams looks exactly like Sara.'

He felt a tightening of nerves. She might be a link between

the two families. She was the only person he had yet talked to who knew – or admitted to knowing – both sets of Williamses.

'You were aware that they were half-sisters then? You knew Williams was their father?'

'No. Oh no. I suppose I thought – well, I didn't think about it. I honestly don't know, really. Perhaps that they might be cousins?'

'When did you last see Rodney Williams?'

'Years ago.' She was becoming nervous, frightened. It meant nothing, it was evidence only of her realisation that she had been brought here to face one sort of ordeal and, that over, was being subjected to another of an unexpected kind. 'I haven't seen him for years.'

'Then how do you know Veronica?'

No dramatic *crise de nerfs* and no hesitation either. 'I played tennis against her. When I was at school.'

'She's three years younger than you.'

'OK. Sure. She was a sort of child prodigy. She was in Haldon Finch's first six when she was under fourteen.'

It was all reasonable, more than plausible. She had been in Oxford the night Rodney Williams died, having gone up early, a week before her term began. She had told him so last evening and told him, in grave and careful detail, whom to check this with. Bennett was in Oxford checking now but Wexford had little doubt Edwina hadn't lied to him.

'You knew both families,' he said now, 'but you didn't know, so to speak, they were one family? You didn't know Rodney Williams was the father of Veronica as well as of Sara and Kevin?'

'Kevin? I've never even heard of him before.'

'Sara's older brother.' He decided to be entirely frank with her. Miss Kaufmann sat watching him, an acid twist to her mouth. 'They didn't know of the existence of the others,' he said. 'The Pomfret family didn't know of the existence of the Kingsmarkham family and the Kingsmarkham family didn't know of the existence of the Pomfret family until quite a while after Rodney Williams was dead. So if you knew, that must mean you also knew Rodney Williams was a bigamist or at least a married man maintaining two households. And if you knew that how did you know it?'

'I didn't.'

The cool negative disappointed him. He had felt on the brink of a breakthrough. But she qualified it.

'I didn't know. I said they looked alike, I'd noticed that, and I remember once saying to my aunt that they must be cousins.' Edwina looked at Miss Kaufmann and Miss Kaufmann nodded in a rapid impatient way. 'I didn't know either of them well,' Edwina said. 'You've got to remember that. I'd never spoken more than a few words to Veronica. And Mrs Williams, that's the real wife, I've seen her about but she's forgotten who I am or something, and as far as the other one goes I was just a customer.'

He had nothing else to ask her. She hadn't stabbed Brian Wheatley and Peter John Hyde, her assailant in the wood, but he was certain she hadn't killed Williams. If a woman had done that she would have needed a second to help her.

'That's all then, thank you, Miss Klein.'

She got up and walked slowly and gracefully to the door, holding herself erect but with her head slightly bowed. They had the same figure, the same walk, this aunt and niece, though fifty years separated them. What would become of Edwina Klein now? It was inevitable she would be found guilty. Would her college have her back? Or was her whole future spoiled? Had she blown it for the sake of a lost cause? At the door, just before he opened it for her, she said, 'There's one thing. You said the Pomfret Williamses and the Kingsmarkham Williamses didn't know about each other. For the sake of setting the record straight, that's not right.'

The excitement was back, drying his throat. 'What do you mean?'

'What I say. They did know about each other.'

He took his hand from the door and leaned against it like someone barring egress. But Edwina Klein stood there willingly, looking a little puzzled, the aunt bored but patient.

'How do you know that?'

'Because I've seen them together,' she said.

Relief ran over him like sweat. He felt cool and lightheaded with it. She was aware now that she had told him something

310

revelatory, unguessed at, and her face, close to his, was full of alert inquiry.

'Whom did you see together?' he asked her.

'Those two women. I saw them in the Precinct Café in Kingsmarkham having coffee together.'

'When? Can you remember when?'

If it were a week ago or even a month ago it meant nothing.

'Last Christmas, I think. It must have been Christmas or Easter for me to have been at home. The only weekend I've been home was when *Wheatley* gave me that lift.' Edwina put infinite scorn into the pronunciation of his name. 'It wasn't then and it wasn't Easter. I know it can't have been because there was snow on the ground.'

'Snow fell,' said Miss Kaufmann, helpful now her niece was not directly threatened, 'during the first week of January.'

'It must have been then,' said Edwina.

She smiled, as if pleased to have been of help at last. He knew she hadn't lied.

16

As Wexford opened the gate of 31 Alverbury Road the postman was coming down the path, a wad of mail fastened with a rubber band in his left hand. None of it apparently was for 29 and his next call was at Milvey's, two doors down. Watching him, Wexford suddenly understood how Milvey came into the case. There was no coincidence at all, it was all simple and logical, only he had been putting the cart before the horse . . .

He rang the bell. As he did so St Peter's clock struck nine. It was Sara who opened the door and so quickly he knew she must have been standing directly behind it. She was holding a paper.

'Two As and a B,' she said, and smiled with gratification.

She had spoken as if the sole purpose of his call had been to hear about her A-level results. Before she closed the door she must have seen the police car outside with Donaldson at the wheel and Marion Bayliss in the back.

'Congratulations,' Wexford said. 'Where's your mother?'

She didn't answer. She might not have heard for all the notice she took.

'St Biddulph's told me they'd take me with three Bs or two Bs and an A, so this is rather better.'

Frenetic excitement was in the girl's eyes, an excitement that was manic and all the more disconcerting for being under such tight control. He had seen her as a Botticelli girl, mild-faced, tranquil, with a spring-like innocence. Primavera should not tremble with triumph nor Venus's eyes glitter.

'I'm going to phone my cousin Paulette, find out how she did.'

To crow a little? Or to be kind? Joy Williams came out from the kitchen, dressed as he had never seen her before. He hadn't told her but perhaps she had guessed she would be meeting Wendy again. Or Wendy herself had told her the evening before? He was prepared for that. He rather hoped they realised he knew of their prior acquaintance. Joy wore a clean, tidy skirt and blouse. She had washed her hair and smudged lipstick on her mouth, in the uncertain slapdash way women do who seldom wear it and somehow feel ashamed to do so. Probably she always dresses up when she and Wendy meet, he thought. There would be rivalry there even if they were allied in a common hatred of Williams. Besides, an alliance would not mean they actually *liked* each other . . .

Sara could be heard on the phone. 'Have they come? Well?' Not much of a bedside manner. He imagined her talking in that hectoring way to a patient. A hard, neurotic little go-getter, he thought her, without an atom of concern for the mother whom the police suspected of murdering her father.

'That's not bad though, is it?' she was saying. 'It's not as if you need As or even Bs.'

Patronising. Somewhat lofty. The pharmacist, of course, was the poor man's doctor, or the doctor for the faint-hearted. 'I'll ask the chemist to give me something for my throat.' Or my head, back, cystitis, bleeding, lump in the breast . . . He took Joy out and closed the front door behind them.

Sergeant Martin and Polly Davies brought Wendy in. The evening before she had been in tears of vexation at missing a day's work but that she could have refused to come – that the police were still in a position only to ask and persuade – seemed no more to have occurred to her than to Joy. They were not blessed with lawyers for aunts. The senior wife – the Sultana Valideh – was already seated in the interview room when Wendy was brought in, the expressionless face averted, the dark brown animal eyes staring past her at the window.

Wendy wore a printed smock dress, Kate Greenaway-like, in a Laura Ashley print, at the neck and wrists frills tied with bows. She had white tights on and white shoes. While the sergeant and Polly stood by (Polly told Wexford later) Wendy had taken her daughter Veronica in her arms and hugged her in a highly emotional way, bringing a fresh rush of tears. Veronica had looked very taken aback. But Wendy had pressed her close to her, stroking her hair, almost as if she expected never to see her again. And Polly, who was a reader of romantic period fiction, said it was like Marie Antoinette setting off in the tumbril.

'Farewell, my children, for ever! I am going to your father.'

Now all that remained as evidence of this scene was the swollen pinkness of Wendy's face. She gave Wexford a piteous look. She would have preferred Burden to interrogate her, she found him more sympathetic than this elderly, hard, sardonic man, but Burden wasn't there. He was in Alverbury Road in conversation with Mrs Milvey.

Wexford said, and he seemed to be addressing either or both of them, 'Which of you first found out the other existed?'

It was Wendy who answered. Her voice was even more fretful than usual. 'I don't understand what you mean.'

'I'll put it another way. When did you first discover Rodney Williams had a wife? And you, Mrs Williams, when did you find out your husband had "married" again?' He put very audible inverted commas round that past principle. 'Well?' he said. 'I know you haven't been truthful with me. I know you knew each other. The question is when did you first know?'

'I never knew she existed till you told me.' Joy spoke in her weary lifeless way. 'When you told me my husband was a bigamist on top of all the rest.'

'All what "rest", Mrs Williams?'

'Lying to me about his job for a start.'

Wendy murmured something.

'I'm sorry, Mrs Williams, I didn't catch that.'

'I said "having other women". I meant that's what the rest was, having other women.'

'He never had other women,' said Joy. She was responding to Wendy's prompting but she wasn't speaking to her. It was Wexford she was addressing. 'He had *her* but he never had others.'

'Let her delude herself if she wants,' said Wendy to no one in particular, lifting her shoulders and smiling very faintly.

'When did you first meet her, Mrs Williams?' Wexford was finding it a shade awkward, their both sharing the name. He

314

got up and came round the table to address the words specifically to Wendy. Joy burst out, 'You've no business to call her that! She's no right to that name. She's Miss Whatever-she-used-to-be. You call her that!'

'The manners of a fishwife,' said Wendy. 'She's as common as dirt. No wonder he came to me.'

'Nasty little bitch! Look at her, dressed up like a kid!'

They're staging it, Wexford thought, they must be. It's all set up for my benefit, rehearsed as like as not. He called the two women quietly to order.

William Milvey was at home that day. The offices of Mid-Sussex Waterways were in his house and he was awaiting the visit of the VAT inspector. That was who he thought Burden was and for some moments they talked at cross-purposes, having one of those conversations so amusing to hearers and so frustrating to the participants.

Their hearer in this case was Mrs Milvey, a big-built lady, very ready with her laughter. She laughed merrily at their discomfiture. But Burden's troubles were quickly over. After that all went smoothly and it turned out to be as Wexford had supposed.

'The wife's a director of our company just as much as me,' Milvey said importantly. 'And naturally she knows the ins and outs of the business equally to what I do.'

'I have to know where he's going to be every day in case there's phone calls,' said Mrs Milvey, who was less pompous than her husband. 'The fifteenth of April? I'll have a look in the book, shall I, Bill?'

At this point the VAT inspector did arrive, a man in his early twenties by the look of him, carrying a briefcase. Milvey seemed reluctant to absent himself from the more interesting (and perhaps less alarming) examination but he was obliged to go. He took the VAT man into his office and closed the door. Mrs Milvey smiled comfortably at Burden.

'From Easter right up till the end of April they was working up Myringham way,' she said, referring to the ledger she was holding. 'They never started on Green Pond till a month later.'

'Are you sure?'

'Positive. No doubt about it. It's down here in black and

315

white. Green Pond, May the thirty-first. Besides, I remember it all now. Bill had a job lined up for the end of May, a big drainage job over to Sewingbury, and the chap cancelled at the last minute. But as luck would have it, this trout farm chap at Green Pond had been given his name and he rung up and said could he drag the pond? Well, Bill happened to be free on account of the cancellation. Must have given the trout farm fella a bit of a surprise, him saying yes, I'll start prompt on Monday.'

The office door opened again and Milvey put a hand out for his book. His wife gave it to him.

'Did you tell anyone?'

'I expect so. There was no secret about it, it was open and above board. You like to have a bit of news to tell folks, don't you? Now you're wanting to know if I told my neighbour Mrs Williams, aren't you?'

'Did you?'

'I never knew a thing about her husband then, mind you. I met her going down to the shops. Bill was getting the van out. I said something like, Monday he'll be doing a job at Green Pond Hall. There's going to be a trout farm, did you know? Something like that.'

'But you definitely told her your husband would be dragging the pond on Monday, May the thirty-first?'

'I couldn't see it would do any harm, could I?'

Had it? Wexford hadn't been entirely correct in his supposition, which was that Mrs Milvey had told Joy the pond had already been dragged or was not to be dragged until a much later date. But this gave a different – and incomprehensible – look to things. If Joy had known Green Pond was to be dragged on the following Monday, the pond into which she had dumped her husband's travelling bag, wouldn't she have retrieved it during the weekend? The alternative possibility was that she had hidden it elsewhere and only put it in Green Pond when *she knew it was to be immediately dragged*. Why should she do such a thing, why behave so absurdly?

This was a hunch of Wexford's that had gone awry. Burden was on his way to put the second one to the test. They seemed no nearer, as far as he could see and in spite of Edwina Klein's revelation, to breaking the case. Next week he would probably start his paternity leave . . .

Bald-headed James Ovington, the son, was alone in charge of Pomfret Office Equipment. His ingratiating smile was as broad as ever. Burden noticed a new mannerism, a nervous way he had of rubbing his hands together. At any rate, the dour and obstructive father was nowhere around.

'Now can I help? Tell me what I can do.'

'You have a method of labelling your machines here,' said Burden. 'Not exactly a code, a kind of speedwriting. Last time we were here we noticed one labelled "E. Ten". I wondered what that stood for. It wasn't a Remington 315, of course, we'd have pounced on it if it had been. This is a kind of shot in the dark and I daresay I'm not making myself too clear.'

'It's clear enough you want to know what "E. Ten" stands for and that's easy.' Nevertheless, he hesitated and Burden wondered why a shade of unease seemed to cross his face.

'Eric Tennyson,' Ovington said. 'That's who it is, that's who "E. Ten" stands for.'

Second time lucky . . . 'I don't suppose you know if he has a daughter called Nicola?'

'Well, I do know as a matter of fact. The answer's yes.'

Veronica Williams's friend, her home the house to which Veronica regularly went on Tuesdays. But the typewriter labelled 'E. Ten' wasn't a Remington 315. Unless . . .

'An Olivetti,' said Ovington. 'They've got another machine. I don't rightly remember what. She types stuff for people, I mean does it for a living.' The uneasy look was back again. 'I may as well tell you,' he said as if about to make a confession of something that for a long while had weighed heavily on him. 'They're friends of mine. I knew I ought to tell you last time you were here.'

'But why shouldn't they be friends of yours, Mr Ovington?'

'Well . . . They're friends of Mrs Williams too. I mean the Mrs Williams whose husband got killed, the one you're making inquiries about. I mean that's where I met her, in their house.'

'Are you trying to tell me something, Mr Ovington?'

This fresh smile, a forced straining of the muscles, turned his face into a gargoyle. He rubbed his hands briskly, then clasped them behind his back to prevent a repetition of the gesture. Light from the shallow overhead lamps in the shed shone with

317

a yellow gleam on the hairless head. Why were the heads of bald men compared to eggs? Ovington's head more than anything resembled a polished pebble.

'What is it you're saying, Mr Ovington?'

'I've been getting friendly with her. With Mrs Williams. There was nothing wrong, I don't mean that. I met her at Eric's and we'd have a drink sometimes, go for a walk, that sort of thing. When it looked as if that husband of hers had finally – well, when it looked as if he'd gone for good, I – I hoped things could get more serious.' He spoke jerkily, floundering, hopelessly unable to handle the situation he had got himself into. 'There was nothing *wrong*. I'd like to repeat that.'

Burden thought irrelevantly that Wendy Williams must be attracted to bald men, first Rodney with his exaggerated forehead, naked as an apple, then this pebble-head.

'But I thought,' Ovington said earnestly, 'that it would be wrong of me – disloyal, you know – to deny the relationship at this juncture, sort of deserting the sinking ship when you hear the cock crowing, if you get my meaning.'

More or less Burden did get it. He thought of the joy Wexford would have in that gloriously mixed metaphor. Now for the Tennysons. Half an hour later he was in their house on the Haldon Finch side of Pomfret, being told by Mrs Tennyson that her daughter was camping in Scotland till the end of the month but could she help him?

Her husband had fetched the repaired and serviced Olivetti from Pomfret Office Equipment three days before. Yes, she had her small portable for use when the other one was away for its annual overhaul. She showed it to him: a Remington 315.

Burden stuck the sheet of paper she gave him into the roller. 'A thousand ages in Thy sight, Are like an evening gone . . .' A flaw in the apex of the capital A, the ascender of the lower-case t, the head of the comma . . .

'I'd never seen her in my life till you had us meet here.'

That was Wendy. Joy said nothing.

'I put it to you that you'd known each other for a long time. I suggest it was like this: Mrs Joy Williams came into Jickie's as a customer one day and in conversation you discovered the link between you. This happened a year ago. You've been in touch with each other ever since.'

Joy gave one of her cold rattling laughs that had something in it of the cackle of a game bird.

'If I'd known about her why should I pretend I didn't?' said Wendy.

Joy answered. She didn't exactly address Wendy, she hadn't yet done that except to abuse her, but she made her first statement not inimical to the other Mrs Williams.

'If her and me knew each other he thinks we might have murdered Rod.'

'I'm more likely to have murdered *her*,' said Wendy in a lofty voice. She looked down and noticed a ladder in her pale milk-coloured tights. It crept up the outside of her right leg like a millipede. Joy noticed it too. She fixed her eyes on the slowly mounting run and her mouth moved. It was nearly a smile.

Wexford said, looking at Joy, 'Someone phoned Sevensmith Harding on Friday, April the sixteenth, to say Rodney Williams was ill and wouldn't be coming to work. The girl who took the call isn't in much doubt that it was your voice, Mrs Williams.'

'She doesn't know my voice. How could she, whoever she is? Aren't you forgetting, I didn't know Rod worked there?'

The door opened and Burden put his head round. Wendy was licking her finger and dabbing at the ladder with her wet fingertip, dabbing as it happened in vain, for the ladder quite suddenly crept another half-inch. It was this which might have occasioned Joy's rattle laugh. Wexford got up and went out of the room, leaving the two women with the two women detectives.

Burden had sent his typing sample to the forensics lab. He told Wexford the substance of his interview with Mrs Tennyson. She had typed no letter of resignation herself and no one had asked her to do such a thing. Wendy Williams she had known for years, though her acquaintance with Rodney had been slight. Their daughters were the same age, were at school together, were 'best friends'.

'Could Wendy have typed it?' Wexford asked him. 'I mean, could she have had access to this machine? If this killing was premeditated, and it looks as if it was, she could have typed that letter days or even weeks before.'

'The Tennyson woman shuts herself up in a room she uses as an office and types for three or four hours a day. As a regular thing she uses the Olivetti and the Remington isn't even kept in there. It's usually in a cupboard in the hall unless the husband Eric wants it or the daughter Nicola uses it to type a school essay. Apparently, they're allowed to do that at the Haldon Finch. Could you credit it?'

'It seems a sensible and harmless practice,' said Wexford. 'Was Wendy ever alone in that house?'

'Early in April she came to call for Veronica, take her home or something. It was dark or late or she was passing. Anyway, the two girls were still out and Mrs Tennyson was typing something. She left Wendy alone for at most ten minutes, she says, until she finished off what she was doing.'

'Wendy would have to know the machine was there. She would have to have paper. But I agree it goes a long way to answering the question of how and where the letter was typed. As to typewriters, what better than to use one that was normally kept shut up in a cupboard? It was by the merest luck that we got on to it.' He listened while Burden told him about Ovington. 'Is that a motive, Mike? We keep coming back to that, the lack of motive. But if Wendy wanted to marry Ovington . . .'

'Who did Joy want to marry?'

'Yes, OK, I see your point. If they did it they did it together and Joy wouldn't be likely to help murder Rodney so that Wendy could marry someone else.' Wexford brought his fist to his forehead and drummed against it. 'I'm a fool! There's no motive. If Wendy knew about Joy she also knew she wasn't married to Rodney, so there was no legal bar to her marrying someone else . . . What about the knife, the weapon we're never going to prove *was* the weapon beyond a doubt? It could have been Joy's or Wendy's.'

'Wendy works at Jickie's and Jickie's stock those knives.'

'Wendy works there but the whole neighbourhood shops there.' Wexford thought for a moment. 'Among the stuff we found in Rodney Williams's bedroom in Liskeard Avenue,' he said, 'was an estimate from a firm of decorators for painting

Wendy's living room. When we saw that room it had obviously been painted very recently. By that firm? By another? By Wendy herself? I think we ought to find out, don't you?'

Burden looked at him. They were both thinking that Rodney Williams had been stabbed to death. One of the knife thrusts had pierced the carotid. 'Yes, I do,' he said.

The day was very warm and close, a heavy, sultry, almost sunless day of the kind that only comes as August wanes. For the few moments he and Burden were in his office, the window open and the half-closed blinds swaying slightly in a hint of breeze, he had kept his jacket off. Now he put it on again and went back downstairs to the interview room where the two women were.

17

A picture of Joy and Wendy leaving Kingsmarkham Police Station was on most front pages of the national press next day. The more sensational of the newspapers managed to give the impression that they were not leaving but entering and that readers would not be too wide of the mark in concluding they had never left. Joy had her hand up over her face, Wendy looked piteously into the cameras, a distraught waif in her little-girl smock. The ladder in her tights was cruelly evident. Burden stood by, cool and rather aloof in a newish suit.

'You look young and handsome,' said Jenny at the breakfast table. 'You look so thin!' She shifted her huge weight, pushing back her chair.

'It's the worry.'

'I expect it is, poor Mike.' She put up her arms and hugged him. It was now only possible for her to do this while sitting down. He held her and thought, It may still be all right, we may still survive.

He went out before nine into a morning that was anything but fresh, a grey, sultry, sticky day. The sky was a flat, very pale grey with the sun a puddle of white glowing through it. This was the kind of day, he thought, that only England knows. Fifty of them can compose a summer.

How many builders and decorators were there in Pomfret? In Kingsmarkham? Not just the established firms but the one-man bands, the man who works in his spare time for money in the back pocket? With luck the Pomfret Williamses had availed themselves of the services of the firm who sent Rodney the estimate.

He didn't go to the police station first, so he was not present when Hope Harmer phoned to say her daughter was missing, had not been home all night or reappeared that morning.

John Harmer was in his dispensary and business was as usual. That is, when customers wanted soap or disposable razors instead of a prescription made up he came out and served them. He refused to believe anything had happened to his daughter. She was a grown woman well able to take care of herself as her prowess at that judo stuff evinced. Her absence probably had something to do with this women's movement nonsense.

Paulette's mother had come to work but only perhaps because of the pressures put on her by her husband. It was from there that she had phoned, the culminating act of a scene between them, Wexford guessed. She was in a piteous state. Hope Harmer was a woman whom it suited only to be happy. She was easily content and in contentment her plump, fair good looks bloomed. Unease affected her as it does an animal, drawing her face, freezing her features, mysteriously making bright hair lank and placid eyes stark with fear.

Wexford had Martin with him, the two of them top brass for the mere matter of a missing girl – but circumstances alter cases.

'My husband says what do I expect when I let her go out with her boyfriend at all hours and stay the night at his place. But they all do it these days and you can't be different. Besides they're engaged and I always say if you really love each other . . .'

She was talking for the sake of talking but her voice faltered. She began twisting her hands.

'Did Paulette go out with her fiancé last night?'

'No, he's in Birmingham. He had to go to Birmingham for his firm.'

Not for the first time Wexford marvelled at how illogical human thinking can be.

'But she did go out? Where did she go?'

'I don't know. She didn't say. She just went out at about seven.'

Martin said, 'You didn't want to know where she was going?'

'Want to know! Of course I wanted to know. If I had my way I'd know where she was every minute of the day and night. I mean I didn't ask her, I'd forced myself to that. When she was younger her father used to say: I want to know where you're going and who with but once you're eighteen you're legally grown-up and you can do what you like. Well, she's eighteen and she remembered that and my husband remembers it and he stops me asking and Paulette wouldn't answer anyway.'

The poor woman was wretchedly caught between husband and daughter, and bullied, doubtless, by both – or had she been happy to have decision-making taken out of her hands?

'Tell me what happened later on. Of course you didn't wait up for her?'

'I would have. I knew Richard was in Birmingham, you see. John said he wasn't having me get in a hysterical state. He took a sleeping pill and he made me take one.'

Presumably sedatives were unlimitedly on tap *chez* Harmer . . .

'This morning I – well, I left her bedroom door open before I went to sleep. That way – if it was shut, you see, I'd know she'd come in. I – I had to make myself open my own bedroom door and look. Her door was still open, it was such a shock, I . . . Well, I went to look, in case she'd come in and left her door but, of course, she hadn't. John still wasn't alarmed. Somehow I couldn't make him see that if Richard was in Birmingham Paulette couldn't have been with him . . .'

Mrs Harmer burst into raging tears. Instead of falling forward onto her arms to cry she lay back, let her head hang back and wailed. Martin went into the dispensary and fetched John Harmer. He came in looking cross and harassed. The noise his wife was making had the effect of causing him to put his hands over his ears in the manner that does nothing to block out sound but indicates that the sound is in some way distasteful or irritating.

'She'd better have a Valium. That'll help her pull herself together.'

'What she had better do, Mr Harmer,' said Wexford, 'is get off home. And you had better take her. Never mind the shop.'

* * *

324

Godwin and Sculp had not done Wendy Williams's decorating but they knew who had — a man who had once worked for them, who had left to set up in business on his own and who undercut them, Burden was told, at every opportunity. Running Leslie Kitman to earth was less simple. He had no wife and his mother was no Mrs Milvey to have his precise location at her fingertips. She gave Burden five possible addresses at which her son might be found: a farmhouse between Pomfret and Myfleet, a block of flats in Queen Street, Kingsmarkham, a cottage in Pomfret, and two houses on new estates outside Stowerton. Kitman was at none of them but the second Stowerton household told Burden he might just be lucky and find him in — Liskeard Avenue.

And it was there, three houses away from Wendy Williams's, that Burden discovered Kitman on top of a ladder. The house was like Wendy's, grey bricks and white weatherboard and picture windows. Kitman was painting a top-floor window frame. When Burden, standing at the foot of the ladder, shouted up who he was, Kitman launched immediately into a catalogue of reasons for not renewing his car tax. Burden hadn't even noticed his car, still less that the tax disc showed an expiry date of the end of June. At last, though, Kitman was made to understand and he came quickly down the ladder, his brush dripping white paint onto the lawn beneath.

The evening before Wendy Williams had spent in bed where she had retired, worn out, as soon as she returned from the police station. Veronica had brought her tea and bread and butter. It was all she ever seemed to fancy when upset. Joy Williams had also been at home with her daughter. At any rate they had been in the same house, Sara in her room as usual, Joy watching television and intermittently struggling to complete the form of application for a grant that would take Sara through medical school. And although it was a Thursday evening there had been no phone call from Kevin who extended this courtesy to his mother only when he was at college and not while junketing around holiday resorts.

These were the alibis Wexford was given by his two principal suspects. Richard Cobb came back from Birming ham in the course of the afternoon and furnished Wexford with a very detailed and apparently satisfactory account of where he had been the night before. Police in Birmingham would help with a check on that. By six Paulette hadn't come home and Wexford knew she never would, he felt in his bones she wouldn't.

The day was sultry and overcast. For hours the thunder had been growling and rumbling and gradually a wind had risen, a dry gusty wind that did nothing to lower the temperature. It still remained hot and stuffy. Wexford and Burden sat in Wexford's office. A search for Paulette hadn't begun yet. Where would one search?

'The lines I'm thinking along,' said Wexford, 'are that Paulette Harmer procured the Phanodorm with which Rodney Williams was sedated. She was in a position to do that, she could easily have done it. I'm wondering if she lost her nerve and told someone – well, Joy – she was going to admit it before we found out.'

'Of course, there's another possibility . . .' Burden left the suggestion suspended.

Wexford looked abstractedly out of the window. It was time to go home but he had no inclination to go. The weather, the atmosphere, the late day, hung heavy with expectation. The thunder, of course, was a threat in itself, a sign of imminent storm, yet it seemed to contain some kind of emotional menace as well, as of looming tragedy.

'Tell me about Kitman,' Wexford said. 'In detail.' Burden had already given him an outline of his talk with the painter.

'He started doing that job for Wendy on April the fourteenth. There was paper on the walls, he said, and he had a job stripping it off. He was doing it all through the fourteenth and the fifteenth and he still hadn't finished by the time he knocked off on the fifteenth.'

'Should have used Sevensmith Harding's Sevenstarker, shouldn't he?' said Wexford and quoting, ' "The slick, sheer, clean way to strip your walls." '

'Maybe he did. He says the room was still furnished but he had covered the pieces of furniture up with his own dustsheets. When he came back in the morning – the morning of Friday the sixteenth, that is – some of the sheets were off and folded up. But that was also on the morning of the fifteenth and other mornings, I gather. Wendy and Veronica were to some extent still living in that room.'

'Did he notice anything else that Friday morning?'

'A stain on the wall is what we want, isn't it? A great bloodstain? And blood all over his dustsheets? There wasn't anything like that or if there was he didn't notice or can't remember. The walls were splashed and marked and patchy anyway, you can imagine. And on the sixteenth he covered up whatever might have been there by putting his first coat of paint on. Sevenstar emulsion, no doubt. One thing he did notice, though, and I didn't ask him about this, he volunteered it. Apparently it's been vaguely preying on his mind ever since. One of the dustsheets wasn't his.'

'*What?*'

'Yes. I thought that'd make you sit up. He has a few dustsheets he takes about with him. Some of them are old bed sheets and there are a couple of curtains and a candlewick bedspread too. Well, according to him, when he left on the fifteenth all seven of his sheets were covering the furniture and part of the carpet. Next morning he came in to find that three of the sheets had been taken off the furniture and were folded up on the floor. He thought nothing much of it but later he noticed that one of the folded sheets wasn't his. It was newer than his and in better condition.'

'Did he ask Wendy about it?'

'He says he did. On the Saturday. She told him she knew nothing about it. And what did it matter to him, after all? He had the right number of dustsheets. You don't go to the police because someone has taken one of your dustsheets and substituted another. But he wondered about it, he says. It niggled him is the way he puts it. Are we going to have those two women back?'

'Of course we are.'

It was Friday, the last Friday in the month. ARRIA met on the last Friday of the month, Wexford thought. No, the last Thursday. It was two months ago yesterday that he had gone to the Freeborns' house and interrupted a meeting.

He picked up the phone and spoke to John Harmer. Paulette's father was anxious now, no longer calm and scathing. He said his wife was asleep. Heavily sedated, Wexford guessed.

'The place is crawling with police,' said Harmer.

Wexford replied dryly, 'I know.'

He thought it an unfortunate way of describing the initial search he had mounted in the environs of the Harmers' home. The man's breathing at the other end of the line was audible. His voice had been rough and shaky. If insulting the police helped him, well . . .

'I can't tell you I don't think this a serious cause for concern, Mr Harmer. I'm very sorry. I think you should prepare yourself for bad news. Perhaps it would be best to say nothing to your wife as yet.'

'I'm not likely to wake her up and tell her you think her only child's dead, am I?'

Wexford said a polite goodbye and rang off. Harmer's rudeness gratified him a little. It was more than excusable in the circumstances and at least it showed Harmer wasn't the unfeeling husband he had thought him. Tomorrow morning they would widen the search for Paulette. By then he might have some idea of where and how to widen it.

A few drops of rain struck the windows, needles on the glass. The thunder thudded and cracked over Myringham way. Martin and Marion Bayliss brought the two Mrs Williamses in and Wexford went down to the interview room to confront them. Wendy in her Jickie's suit, hair freshly set – in Jickie's hairdressing department? – was in tears, dabbing at her eyes with a pink tissue. Joy had never looked so down at heel, broken sandals on her bare feet, a button missing from her button-through creased cotton dress, a scarf tied round her head. She looked like a refugee, such as have passed in streams across Europe at frequent times in modern history. Her face was grey and drawn.

Burden came in and sat beside him. The room had got so dark they had to have the light on. Still it wasn't really raining. When no one attempted to comfort Wendy and no offers of cups of tea were made she stopped crying. Rather defiantly, she produced the box of pink tissues from her bag and set it on the table in front of her.

'Was Paulette Harmer the girl your husband was seeing?'

328

Wexford addressed the question to both women. It was awkward. It seemed to treat polygamy as a legal state. Joy gave a dry cackle, more than usually scornful. Wendy said she didn't know who Paulette Harmer was, she had never heard of her.

'Who was it then?'

'He didn't have a young girlfriend,' said Joy. 'He didn't have any girl.' She nodded at Wendy. 'Unless you count her. And that's not the word I'd use for her.'

Wendy sniffed and pulled a tissue out of the box.

'Well, Mrs Williams?' Wexford said to her.

'I told you, I don't know.'

'On the contrary, you told me you knew there was one. This very young girl living around here with her parents – you never heard of her, she doesn't exist?'

Wendy looked at Joy. Their eyes met. For the first time Wexford thought he sensed a rapport between them. Then Wendy turned sharply away and shook her head violently.

'Rodney Williams was attracted by young girls,' Wexford said. 'You're an example yourself, Mrs Williams. How old were you when you and he met? Fifteen? Is that why you invented a young girlfriend for him? You knew it was in his nature?'

'I didn't invent it.'

He was suddenly aware of a change taking place in Joy. She was shaking with emotion. Her hands held the table edge. Rain had begun to patter on the windows. Burden got up and closed the fanlight. Joy leaned forward.

'Has Sara been talking to you?' she said.

It was on the tip of his tongue to say he would ask the questions. But he didn't say it. He felt his way. 'It's possible.'

'The little bitch!'

How was it that he sensed that the two women were at last united by some common bond? And that bond wasn't the dead man. The noise of the rain was intense now, a crashing cloudburst. He thought, they did know each other. The Klein girl was telling me the truth. They were close in a conspiracy and they're back in it again, the acting is over . . . He turned to Joy and it was as if his approaching, ultimately fixed gaze lit the fuse.

She spoke in a raucous throaty voice.

'You may as well have it. It wasn't young girls he was attracted to, not *any* young girls. It was his own daughter.'

18

It happened, it wasn't even uncommon. Lately it had been the modish subject for the pop sociology paperback. Yet that father-daughter incest might be a motivating factor in this case had not crossed Wexford's mind. Afterwards he was to ask himself *why* it hadn't crossed his mind, knowing his mind and the way it worked, but now in the interview room with the two women across the table from him he could only recall *The Cenci* and Beatrice – his own daughter playing Beatrice – running onto the stage crying:

'O world! O life! O day! O misery!'

That should have told him. Wendy had covered her face with her hands. Joy stared at him, her lips sucked in. A bead of saliva had appeared at the left corner of her mouth. She put her hand out for one of Wendy's tissues, tentatively, cautiously, watching Wendy, like an old dog approaching the food bowl but uncertain as to what the young dog will do. Wendy took her hands down. She didn't speak. She gave the tissue box a little push in Joy's direction. Burden sat, wearing his stony, contemptuous look.

Wexford was framing a question. Before he could utter it Joy spoke.

'She came and told me. Her own mother! His own wife! She said he'd come into her bedroom in the middle of the night. He said he was cold, he never seemed to get warm since we'd slept in twin beds. That's what he said to her. He said she could make him warm. Why didn't she scream out? Why didn't she run away? He got into bed with her and did it to her. I'm not going to repeat the word she used, they all use it for *that*. It was while I was asleep. I was asleep and he was doing that with his own daughter.'

She laughed. The sound was drier than ever with more of a rattle in it but it was a laugh. She looked at Wendy and directed the laugh at her. And, Wexford thought, she may have been in cahoots with her, she may have told her all this before in womanly confidence, in sisters-under-the-skin conspiracy, but she enjoys telling it now – in our presence, a public triumphant putdown.

Like the therapist to whom he had compared himself, he would let her talk without interruptions, without breaking in to question. If she would talk. The pause endured. Wendy looked away and at the screen of water, curiously claustrophobic, the rain was making down the panes. She had pushed her fingers so hard into the skin of her face that they left pink pressure marks. Without prompting, Joy went on.

'She waited till he'd gone to work and then she told me. I was ironing her a blouse for school.' Insult had been thus added to injury, she implied. The father's rape would have been less offensive to the mother if the news had been imparted to her while she was ironing a shirt for Kevin. 'She burst right out with it. There wasn't a question of being tactful, mind, of – well, breaking it gently. He was only my husband. It was only my husband she was telling me about being unfaithful to me.' The laugh came again, but a ghost of it this time. 'I wouldn't listen to her. I said, don't tell me, I don't want to hear. I put my hands over my ears.'

A rejecting gesture not unknown in the Harmer-Williams families, Wexford thought. He nodded at Joy, feeling it was necessary to give some sign.

'I put my hands over my ears,' she said again. 'She started shouting at me. Didn't I care? Wasn't I upset? I answered her then. I said of course I was upset. No mother wants to hear her daughter's like that, does she? I said to her, You spread that about and you'll split us all up, your father'll go to prison and what are people going to think of me? What's Kevin going to say to them at college?'

332

Burden said quietly, 'What did you mean by that, Mrs Williams, your daughter was "like that"?'

'It's obvious, isn't it? I'm not saying he wasn't weak.' A glance for Wendy and a quick withdrawal of the eyes. 'Well, we know he was. But he'd never have done that without . . .'

She stopped and looked at Wexford. He remembered when he had first talked to Sara and her mother had sent him up to her bedroom saying she wouldn't object – 'Rather the reverse if I know her.'

'Encouragement?' he said flatly.

She nodded impatiently. 'Putting her arm round him, trying to get his attention. She wasn't *ten*. I said to her, you're not ten any more. Sitting on his knee – what did you expect? Now the least you can do is keep quiet about it, I said, think of my feelings for a change.'

'When did all this happen?'

'It was before Christmas. I know it was because I remember saying that she'd picked a fine time, hadn't she, just when we were all going to be together for Christmas.'

Wendy, whose face had been impassive, winced slightly. Had she realised at last where and how Rodney Williams spent his Christmases? It was soon after that, probably in the first week of January, Wexford recalled, that Edwina Klein had seen the two women together.

'Did you tell anyone?' Burden asked.

'Of course I didn't. I wasn't going to broadcast it.'

He turned on Wendy. 'When did she tell you? Or should I say warn you?'

Wendy had looked shocked by none of this. Not even surprised. But she shook her head. 'She never did.'

'Come on, Wendy . . .' Wexford had solved the names problem at last. 'Joy found out you existed, sought you out especially to tell you what Rodney was really like. To tell you, in fact, to have a care to your own daughter.'

'Tell her?' said Joy. 'Why should I care?'

'Wendy,' Wexford said more gently, almost insinuatingly, 'you're not going to tell us you didn't know about Rodney and his daughter Sara. You're not going to make believe what we heard just now was all news to you. You couldn't have looked less surprised than if I told you it was raining. Joy came into

333

Jickie's, didn't she, and told you who she was? I'll make a guess at the week before Christmas. How did she know who you were? She'd seen Veronica in the street and spotted the resemblance to Sara – a likeness no one could mistake . . .'

That they were surprised now, both of them, he couldn't doubt. He had been wrong there then. Never mind. There were other ways – following Rodney, seeing him and Wendy together, a host of ways.

'You met at Jickie's, went on to meet again after Christmas. No doubt there were many meetings . . .'

Wendy jumped up, eyes full of tears, grabbing a handful of tissues.

'I want to talk to you alone! Just you and me quite alone!'

'Surely,' said Wexford.

He got up. Burden didn't wait for them to leave the room before starting on Joy with his questions. When did she first suspect Rodney had a second home? Did she ever ask him? Joy was laughing at this second suggestion when Wexford closed the door. He took Wendy upstairs to his own office. The rain had abated, was now merely trickling, slipping, spilling, down the washed gleaming glass. Twilight hadn't yet begun and the sky was a clear grey, light from cloud-coated sunshine. Wendy stumbled a little going into the room. He thought it might be unwise to touch her, even to the extent of steadying her. She held on to the door frame and shot him a look of grievance.

In the chair he held out for her she sat down gingerly, treating herself as if she had become fragile. She had turned into a convalescent, tentatively putting out feelers to the world. Her shoulders she was keeping permanently lifted.

'What did you want to say to me, Wendy?' He had dropped the 'Mrs Williams' altogether now.

She whispered it, sustaining the invalid image, a broken woman, wan-faced, such as might fittingly inhabit the Castle of Petrella and be called Lucretia.

'The same as what she said.'

'I'm sorry, Wendy. You must make yourself plainer than that.'

'It was the same for us. The same as what she said. Or – well, it would have been. I mean, he would have done but he went away and got himself killed.'

334

Light penetrated. 'You mean Rodney also made advances to Veronica? Only, if I interpret what you're saying correctly, it was merely advances?'

She nodded, tears splashing now, wads of tissues held to her eyes like swabs.

'Before Joy warned you or afterwards?'

A shrugging, then a shaking, of the whole body. Make-up scrubbed off with that cheapest and most readily available cleanser, tears, Wendy presented to Wexford a youthful, naked, desperate face.

'He had been a little more attentive to her, had he, than we in our society expect of a father to a teenage daughter? Did she tell you or did you see? Kissed her and said it was good to be alone with her and you out of the way?'

She jumped up. 'Yes, yes, yes!' she shouted.

'So on April the fifteenth, although you didn't think there was much chance of Rodney coming back, you encouraged your daughter to go out so as not to be alone with him? You told her not to run the risk of being alone with him but to stay out until you came home?'

Guilt was heavy on her face now, driving away indignation. He felt she was on the brink of a confession.

'Or did you send her out so that *you* could be alone with Rodney — you and Joy?'

The air was sharply clear, the rain past, the sky two shades of blue, a dark clean azure and the smoky blue of massed cloud. Nine o'clock and growing dark. Water lay in glassy pools, reflecting the sky. There was an unaccustomed coolness, almost a nip in the temperature. Before morning there would be more rain. Wexford could see it in the clarity and smell it in the atmosphere. He walked from the police station and kept on walking, just to get away from the enclosing four walls, the stuffiness, the millions of uttered words, the weariness of lies.

People used to tell him when they needed an alibi — now they cited television — that they had been for a walk. They didn't know where, just for a walk. He hadn't believed them. Everyone knew where they had been on a walk. Now he thought he might not be able to say where he had been tonight. His progress was aimless, though not slow, a fairly brisk marching in the fresh cold air, a thinking walk to dwell on what had passed.

So inconclusively. So unsuccessfully. He had wrung those two women, turned the handle and ground them through the rollers. Joy had laughed and Wendy had wept. He had kept on repeating over and over to himself: Edwina Klein saw them together. Why should she lie? Why should she invent? He had to let them go at last. Wendy was near collapse – or feigning it beautifully.

It was clear, the whole case, Burden said. A motive had at last emerged. Joy killed out of bitterness and jealousy, Wendy out of fear Rodney would serve Veronica the same way as he had served Sara. An unfortunate verb in the circumstances, but perhaps not inept . . . A conspiracy laid just after Christmas, brooded over through the early spring, hatched out in April. Murder in the room that would be decorated tomorrow. Staunch the blood with Kitman's dustsheet, realise too late what you have used.

It must have happened that way, there was no other. Perhaps they hadn't intended to kill, only confront him jointly, threaten and shock. But the French cook's knife had been handy, lying on the table maybe. That didn't explain drugging him with Phanodorm. The knife Milvey had found? Its blade matched the width and depth of the wounds. So would a thousand knives.

He was in Down Road, under the dripping lime trees. Perhaps, all along, he had known he was making his way here. The big old houses, houses that could justly be called 'piles', seemed sunken tonight in dark, still, sodden foliage. A dark green perfume arose from grass and leaf and rain-bathed flowers. Somewhere nearby a spoilt dog, left alone for the evening, vented its complaints in little bitter whimpering wails. Wexford opened the gate to the Freeborns' house. Lights were on, one upstairs and one down. The dustmen had been that morning, long before the rain started, and left the scattering of litter they didn't bother to remove from places where the occupants failed to tip lavishly. A sodden sheet of paper, pasted by rain onto the gravel, bore the ARRIA logo and a lot of printing it was too dark to read.

Both twins came to the door. He approved their caution.

Once more they were alone in the house, left to their own devices, the switched-on parents far away at some veteran hippies' haunt. Both had pale blue hair tonight, pink stuff on their eyelids, otherwise the nearly identical faces were bare. And identical on both faces was dismay at the sight of him. Eve spoke.

'Do you want to come in?'

'Yes, please.' The house no longer smelt of marijuana. That was one thing he had achieved, a dubious success. The girls seemed not to know where to take him. They stood in the hall. 'There was a meeting of ARRIA last night,' he said. 'Where was it? Here?'

'They're mostly held here,' said Amy.

'And it was here last night?'

'Yes.'

He pushed open a door and switched a light on. It was a huge living room, floor cushions making islands on parquet that hadn't been polished for two decades, a divan with thrown over it something that might have had its origin in Peru, the only chair a wicker hemisphere hanging from the ceiling. French windows, uncurtained, gave onto what seemed an impenetrable wood.

He sat in the hanging chair, refusing to be alarmed by its immediate swinging motion.

'Who was at the meeting?'

They exchanged glances, looked at him. 'The usual crowd,' said Amy, and conversationally, 'It's always the same lot that turn up, isn't it?'

The names he ran through got a nod at every pause. 'Caroline Peters? Nicola Anerley? Jane Gardner? Paulette Harmer?' Eve nodded. She nodded in the same way as she had at the other names. 'Edwina Klein?'

There must have been a note of doubt in his voice.

'Yes, Edwina was here. Why not?'

'Why not indeed. And why not Sara Williams, come to that?'

'Sara didn't come,' said Amy. 'She had to stay home with her mother.'

So John Harmer hadn't been so far out when he suggested his daughter's disappearance had something to do with this 'women's movement nonsense'.

337

'What time did the meeting end?'

'About ten,' said Amy. 'Just about ten.' She had forgiven him if her sister never would. She had altogether put off that distant manner. 'Someone told me today that Paulette didn't go home all night and . . .' She left the sentence hovering.

'You never told me,' Eve said sharply.

'I forgot.' Amy turned her eyes back on Wexford. 'She was a bit late. She didn't say why. Edwina brought her aunt – not to join, just to see what went on, though she's eligible of course, never having married. It was good seeing someone old who'd had principles and stuck to them.'

'I have fought the good fight,' said Wexford. 'I have run a straight race. I have kept the faith.'

'That's right. That was exactly it. How did you know?'

He didn't answer her. The Authorised Version was unknown to them, lost to their generation as to the one before, a dusty tome of theology, in every way a closed book.

'Was Paulette alone when she left?'

'The meeting was upstairs.' Eve was chilly and unbending but she had spoken. 'We didn't see people out. They went downstairs and let themselves out. Paulette left with Edwina and her aunt.'

'They may have left together,' said Amy, 'but they didn't go off together. I looked out of the window and saw Edwina and her aunt getting into the aunt's car and Paulette wasn't with them.'

'What's out there?' Wexford said abruptly. He pointed at the long windows beyond which was visible only a mass of foliage.

'The conservatory.'

Amy opened the doors, swung them open and put her hand to a switch. Unconventional the Freeborn family might be; they were not feckless. The old domed conservatory, its upper panes of stained glass, claret and green in an Art Nouveau design of tulips, was full of dark green leafy plants, some of which looked subtropical, all demanding ample water and getting it. It must cost a fortune to heat in winter, Wexford thought, coming closer, entering the conservatory and spotting an orchid or two, the velvety mauve trumpet of a *brunfelsia*.

Eve, without being asked, flooded the garden beyond with light. Touching another switch brought on arc lamps, one on the conservatory roof, another in the branches of an enormous ilex. The garden, so-called, hardly deserved floodlighting. It was a wilderness of unmown grass, wild roses, brambles, the occasional hundred-year-old tree. And it was huge, the kind of garden whose owners might justly say they were never overlooked. Shrubs that appeared dense black at this hour made an encircling irregular wall round its perimeter.

'We don't any of us go in it much,' said Amy. 'Except as a shortcut to the High Street. And when it's muddy or whatever . . .' Another sentence was left hanging. She went on vaguely, 'Dad's keen on the conservatory. It's him that grows the plants.'

The *Cannabis sativa*, thought Wexford, but hardly in here. You needed infra-red light for that and plenty of it. He opened the door into the garden, a glass door of slender green and white panels. The cold damp air breathed water in suspension at him. He noticed a path among the grass, pieces of crazy paving let into what had once been turf, was now wet hay. The girls weren't coming with him. Eve wound her arms round her body, hugging herself against the cold. Amy breathed on the glass and with her fingertip began drawing a raven with a woman's face. Wexford went down the path. The arc lamps reached no further than thirty feet or so. He took his torch out of his pocket and switched it on.

The path led to the gate in the far fence, he thought. That was what Amy meant by a shortcut to the High Street. First it wound through a copse of dark shrubs, laurels, rhododendrons, all glistening and dripping with water. He was curiously reminded of walking in a cemetery. Cemeteries were like this, untended often, places of ornamental shrubs, funereal trees, like this without flowers, unlike this with gravestones.

He came upon the fence and the gate quite suddenly, almost bumping into the gate which was in a break in the untrimmed hedge that followed the line of the close-boarding. From here the backs of other big houses could just be seen, two of them with yellow rectangles on black that were lights in their windows. The light didn't reach here and no moon had appeared. The path curved its way all round the garden. He followed its ellipse, returning on the right-hand side. Bamboo here, half dead most of it, a mass of canes. Then something prickly that caught at his raincoat. He pulled and heard the tearing sound. Turn the torch on it to see what had happened . . .

Turn the torch into the midst of this circle of briar roses, brambles with wicked thorns – onto an outflung arm, a buried face, a logo and acronym, red on white cotton – ARRIA and the raven-woman.

It was more like a cemetery here than he had supposed . . .

19

The scene-of-crimes officer. Dr Crocker. Sir Hilary Tremlett fetched out of his bed and wearing a camelhair coat over pyjama top and grey slacks. Burden as neat and cool as at mid-morning. And the rain coming down in summer tempests. They had to rig a sort of tent up over the body.

She had been strangled. With a piece of string or cord perhaps. Wexford himself could see that without reference to Dr Crocker or Sir Hilary. The photographer's flash going off made him blink. He didn't want to look at her any more. It sickened him, though not with physical nausea, he was far beyond that. No pharmacology degree now, no marriage to Richard Cobb, no full flowering of that strange beauty that had been both sultry and remote.

The girls worried him, Eve and Amy, alone in that house with a young girl, a contemporary, dead in the garden. Marion Bayliss had tried to reach their parents but they were at none of the phone numbers the twins could produce. Neighbours shunned the Freeborns. With the families immediately next door they weren't even on speaking terms. Eve thought of Caroline Peters and it was she who came to the house in Down Road and stayed for the rest of the night. Wexford crawled into bed at around three. There was a note for him from Dora which he read but did not mark or inwardly digest: 'A man called Ovington keeps phoning for you.' She was deeply asleep and in sleep she looked young. He lay down beside her and the last thing he remembered before sleeping himself was laying his hand on her still-slender waist.

* * *

'She'd been dead about twenty-four hours,' said Crocker, 'which is about what you thought, isn't it?'

When you don't get enough sleep, Wexford thought, it's not so much tired that you feel as weak. Though perhaps they were the same thing. 'Strangled with what?' he asked. 'Wire? Cord? String? Electric cable?'

'Because it's easily obtainable and pretty well impossible to break I'd guess the kind of nylon cord you use for hanging pictures. And where were your suspects – Crocker looked at his watch ' – thirty-six hours ago?'

'At home with their daughters, they say.'

Wexford began going through the statement Burden had taken from Leslie Kitman, the painter. A description of the missing dustsheet was gone into in some detail. Useless now, of course. It was four months since that dustsheet, concealed in a plastic bag, had been removed by the council's refuse collectors. And the knife as likely as not with it. Somehow he couldn't believe in Milvey's knife, he couldn't take two Milvey coincidences . . .

The walls had been stained and pitted, Kitman said. He couldn't remember if the stains had looked any different on the morning of 16 April from the afternoon of 15 April. Some of the holes, he thought, might have been filled in by someone else. He had made good some of the cracks and holes with filler which, when it dried, left white patches. On 16 April and the morning of the 17th he had lined the walls with wood-chip paper and on the Monday following begun painting over the paper.

Was he going to have those women in again? One of them had killed the girl the night before last. To keep her from confirming their guilt in the matter of the Phanodorm. Only one of them or both? Joy could easily have known where she would be and that she left by the shortcut to the High Street where she would catch the Pomfret bus.

Burden was late. But then he too had been up and on the go since early yesterday morning, finally getting to bed even later than Wexford. To be up after midnight, thought Wexford, is to be up betimes. He had always liked that, only no one knew what 'betimes' meant any more, which rather spoiled the wit of it. Thinking of going to bed reminded him of Dora's note and he was about to pick up the phone and get hold of Ovington when Burden walked in.

He didn't look tired, just about ten years older and a stone thinner. He was wearing his stone-coloured suit with a shirt the same shade and a rust tie with narrow chocolate lines on it. Might be going to a wedding, thought Wexford, all he needed was a clove carnation.

'Jenny's started,' he said. 'I took her to the infirmary this morning at eight. There's not going to be anything doing much yet awhile but they wanted her in promptly.'

'You'd better start your leave as from now.'

'Thanks. I thought you'd say that. I must say these babies do pick their moments. Couldn't she have waited a week? She's going to be Mary, by the way.'

'After your grandmothers, no doubt.'

But the coincidence he had related to Wexford had slipped Burden's memory. 'Do you know that never crossed my mind? Perhaps Mary Brown Burden then?'

'Forget it,' said Wexford. 'It sounds like an American revivalist preacher. Keep in touch, won't you, Mike?'

Later in the day, with luck, the pathologist's report on Paulette Harmer would come and also perhaps something from Forensics on the murder weapon. He had Martin go to a magistrate and swear out a warrant to search the Williams home in Liskeard Avenue, and he wasn't anticipating any difficulties in getting it. In the meantime he had himself driven to the other Williams home. He didn't feel up to walking, whatever Crocker might advise.

Sara was mowing the front grass with one of those small electric mowers that cut by means of a line wound on a spool and are principally intended for trimming edges. As he got out of the car the motor whined and stopped cutting and the girl, crimson with bad temper, up-ended the flimsy machine and began tugging furiously at the line. He heard a hissed repetition of the word Joy disliked so much that she had used of her father's assault.

'Fuck, fuck, fuck, fuck!'

'If you do that with the current switched on,' Wexford said, 'one day you're going to cut your hand off.'

She cooled as rapidly as she had become incensed.

343

'I know. I've promised myself I'll always switch it off before I fiddle with it. But these god-damned things never work for long.' She pulled prongs out of socket to oblige him and smiled. An ARRIA tee-shirt today, identical to the one on dead Paulette. 'This is the fourth of these spools we've had this summer. Do you want to see my mother?'

As yet she couldn't know about Paulette. He remembered her thinly veiled boasting to her cousin on the phone and he didn't think she would much care. Nor would she much care when her mother was arrested for the murder. But perhaps it was natural for victims of incest not to care much about anything. He felt a wrench of pity for her.

'I want to talk to you first.'

The garage, now there was no car to occupy it, had become a toolshed and repository for rather battered garden furniture. Sara indicated a deckchair to Wexford. For her part she sat down on an upturned oil drum and set about struggling with the stubborn spool. This looked as if it might go the way of its fellows, three of which lay on a shelf next to a dozen half-used Sevenstar paint tins. He supposed she was busying herself so as not to have to look at him while he talked to her about her father.

At his first mention of incest, a tactful broaching of what her mother had told him, she didn't flush but turned gradually white. Her skin, always pale, grew milk-like. And he noticed a phenomenon, perhaps peculiar to her. The fine gold down on her forearms erected itself.

He asked her gently when it had first happened. She kept her head bent, with her right hand attempting to rotate the spool while with her left forefinger and thumb she tugged at the slippery red line.

'November,' she said, confirming his own ideas. 'November the fifth.' She looked up and down again quickly. 'There were only two times. I saw to that.'

'You threatened him?'

She hesitated. 'Only with the police.'

'Why didn't you tell your brother? Or did you? I have a feeling you and your brother are close.'

'Yes, we are. In spite of everything.' She didn't say in spite of what but he thought he knew. 'I *couldn't* tell him.' Like a

344

different girl speaking, her face turned away, 'I was ashamed.'

And she hates her mother, so it was a pleasure to tell *her*? She gave a final tug and the line came through, far too much of it, yards of loosely-coiled scarlet flex.

Kevin was indoors, having unexpectedly arrived that morning by means of some comfortless and inefficient transport. He was lying spent, exhausted, dirty and unkempt, on the yellow sofa, his booted feet up on one of its arms. Joy had answered Wexford's knock with refreshments for Kevin in her hands, a trayful of sandwiches, coffee, something in a carton that was ice cream or yoghurt. Wexford shut the door on him, hustled Joy into the kitchen. She was dressed exactly as she had been the day before, even to the headscarf – had she tied it on to run to the shops for Kevin-provender? – and gave the impression of having never taken her clothes off, of sleeping in them. He told her, quite baldly, about Paulette, but she knew. John Harmer had phoned her while Sara was in the garden. Or that was the explanation she gave Wexford for knowing. He said he would want her later at the police station, she and Wendy. He would send a car for her.

'What's my son going to do about his evening meal?'

'Give me a tin opener,' said Wexford, 'and I'll teach him how to use it.'

She didn't observe the irony. She said she supposed he could have something out of a tin for once. At least she didn't suggest his sister might cook for him, which was an improvement (if that was the way you looked at things) on twenty years ago.

The next stop was Liskeard Avenue, Pomfret. Martin had got his warrant and was there with Archbold and two uniformed men, PC Palmer and PC Allison, Kingsmarkham's only black policeman. A tearful Wendy was trying to persuade them it wouldn't be necessary to strip the paper off her living-room walls.

At the glass table sat Veronica. Evidently she had been at work on the hem of a white garment that lay in front of her but had laid down her needle when the policemen arrived. Wexford thought of the girl in the nursery rhyme who sat on a cushion and sewed a fine seam, feeding on strawberries, sugar and cream. It must have been her dress which suggested it to him with its pattern of small wild strawberries and green

345

leaves on a creamy ground. Tights again, dark blue this time, white pumps. Another thing that made those girls look alike was the way neither of their faces showed their feelings. They were the faintly melancholy, faintly smug, nearly always impassive faces of madonnas in Florentine paintings.

Wexford's daughter Sylvia had a cat which uttered sound-less mews, going through the mouth-stretching motion of mewing only. Veronica's 'hello' reminded him of that cat, a greeting for a lip-reader, not even as audible as a whisper. Wendy renewed her appeals as he came in, now making them to him only.

'I'm sorry, Wendy. I understand your feelings. We'll have the room redecorated for you.' Or for someone, he thought but didn't say aloud. 'And there'll be as little mess as possible.'

And it really was Sevensmith Harding's Sevenstarker they intended to use for the job, four large cans of it, each labelled in red italic script that this was the slick, sheer, clean way to strip your walls. Wexford found himself hoping this wasn't too gross an exaggeration.

'But what for?' Wendy kept saying, at the same time, curiously enough, picking up ornaments and pushing them into a wall cupboard, loading a tray.

'That I'm not at liberty to say,' said Wexford, falling back on one of the stock answers of officialese. 'But there's plenty of time. Please clear the room yourself if you want to.'

In silence Veronica picked up her sewing. She threaded her needle, using a small device manufactured for that purpose, and slipped a pink thimble onto her forefinger.

'She's doing the hem of her tennis dress. She's playing in the women's singles final at the club this afternoon.' Wendy spoke in tragic tones, only slightly modified by a faint proud stress on the word 'club'.

Kingsmarkham Tennis Club, presumably, or even Mid-Sussex. 'We shan't stop her,' Wexford said.

'You'll upset her.' She drew him into the kitchen, through the already open doorway. 'You're not going to say anything to her about you-know-what? I mean you're not going to go into it?'

'I'm not a social worker,' he said.

'Nothing actually happened anyway. I saw to it nothing happened.'

Impossible though, not to see Rodney Williams, hitherto no more than liar and con-man, as some sort of monster. To make a sexual assault on one daughter was heinous enough, but almost immediately to have designs on her younger half-sister?

'Of course, you wouldn't have suspected anything *might* happen if Joy hadn't warned you.'

'How many times do I have to tell you I never saw the woman till you – introduced us?'

'Something you haven't told me is how you knew Rodney made sexual advances to Veronica. He didn't tell you but you knew. Veronica was the young girl living at home with her family you led us a wild goose chase about, wasn't she?' He closed the door between the rooms and leaned against it.

Wendy nodded, not looking at him.

'How did you know, Wendy? Did you see something? Did you notice something in his behaviour when he thought you weren't looking? Was that after or before Joy warned you?'

She mumbled, 'I didn't see anything. Veronica told me.'

'*Veronica?* That innocent child in there who's more like twelve than sixteen? That child you've very obviously sheltered from every exposure to life? She interpreted her father's affectionate kisses, his arm round her, his compliments, as sexual advances?'

A nod. Then a series of vehement nods.

'And yet you say "nothing actually happened". By that I take it you mean there was no more than a kiss and a touch and a compliment. But she – *she* – saw this as an incestuous approach?'

Wendy's response was characteristic. She burst into tears. Wexford pushed up a stool for her to sit on and found a box of tissues, never a difficult task in that house. He returned to the living room where the carpet was now covered with sheets and from which Veronica had disappeared. Allison was daubing the walls with Sevenstarker, Palmer already at work with a metal stripping tool. The hunch he had about what was under that paper was probably crazy, but besides that it was just possible an analysis of old plaster might show traces of Rodney's blood. And might not. Anyway, it was work for

347

Leslie Kitman. He could come in next week and put it all back again at the expense of the Mid-Sussex Constabulary.

The rain had started again. That would put paid to Veronica's match in the afternoon as neither the Kingsmarkham Tennis Club nor the Mid-Sussex County at Myringham had covered courts. Wexford, back in his office though it was Saturday, noted the time. Twelve-thirty. Getting on for three hours since Mike had been in and announced the imminence of his new daughter. Well, it was too soon yet to expect much, early days.

Something kept nagging at the back of his mind, something that Wendy had said. About the tennis match, he thought it was. But she hadn't said anything except that Veronica would be playing that afternoon. Why did he have this curious feeling then that in what she said lay the whole answer to this case? He often had feelings like that about some small thing then when a case was about to break, and the small thing always turned out to be vital and his hunch seldom wrong. The difficulty was that he didn't know what he had a hunch about.

All the available men he had were either at Wendy's taking her room apart or else, the far greater number of them conducting a house-to-house in Down Road and interrogating every girl who had been at the ARRIA meeting. A mood of loneliness and isolation enclosed him. Dora had gone to London and to stay the night with Sheila in Hampstead. His elder grandson Robin would be nine today, his birthday party due to begin three hours from now. Crocker played golf all day on Saturdays. Wexford would have liked to sleep but he found it hard to sleep in the daytime. What the hell was it Wendy had said? What *was* it? Tremlett was probably still at work on that poor girl's body ... She had got Phanodorm for Joy and threatened to tell that she had. Well, not threatened, warned rather that she would have to, she would be scared not to. Joy had given Rodney the Phanodorm, substituting it for his blood-pressure pills, and it took just the time of a drive to Pomfret to act. Follow him by bus to Wendy's. He's asleep when you get there and you look at him and remember what he's done to you by way of what he's done to your daughter. Married another woman too, like a bloody sheikh. And the other wife goes along with you, though you hate her. It's her daughter at risk now since you told her where his tastes lie. Why let him ever wake up again? If there's a mess she says the room's going to be decorated tomorrow. And if you hide the body for long enough . . .

In the morning phone the office, say he's ill, disguising your voice a bit. She'll type his letter of resignation for you, she's got access to a typewriter in a friend's house that no one's going to trace. You're both in it equally, you and she, the two wives of Rodney Williams, for better for worse, till death parts you. She stabbed him too, though you gave him the sleeping pill. You and she together carried the body down that crackpot spiral staircase, through the doorway into the integral garage. Laid him in the car with his travelling bag. She drove because you never learned, but you did most of the grave digging. Soiling your hands never bothered you the way it did her. Two wives, in it together equally, and whom murder has joined let no man put asunder.

Wexford had got himself under Joy's skin and he very nearly finished this internal monologue with one of her awful laughs. The chances were Burden wouldn't phone before evening. And then surely he'd phone him at home. He drove to the Old Cellar and had himself a slice of quiche, broccoli and mushroom, a pleasant novelty, one small glass of Frascati to go with it – it was Saturday, after all, though with nothing to celebrate – and then back again to the estate where the streets were named for Cornish towns, Bodmin, Truro, Falmouth, Liskeard. A cold grey rain fell steadily. They were back to the weather they had had between Rodney Williams's disappearance and the discovery of his body.

In Wendy's living room considerable progress had been made. Three walls were more or less stripped. It wasn't what Wexford would have called slick, sheer and clean but it wasn't bad. Martin had got hold of someone from Forensics, a shaggy girl in navy all-in-ones, who nevertheless had the air of an expert and was painstakingly scraping samples of brownish plaster off the walls.

Wendy was downstairs in her sewing-ironing-laundry room or whatever, cutting patterns out of magazines. For therapy, no doubt. Veronica was with her, Miss Muffet on a velvet pouffe. No match for her today as he had predicted. He

349

suddenly remembered his threat to send a car for Joy 'later' and the crisis over Kevin's dinner this had precipitated. Well, it would have to be much later . . . Or tomorrow. Or every day on and for ever. No, he mustn't think that way.

Wendy had changed her dress for a linen suit. Perhaps she had been going to watch her daughter play, for Veronica, as though not resigned to cancellation until the last moment, was in her tennis whites, pleated miniskirt – who could imagine her in shorts? – and a top almost too well finished to be called a tee-shirt.

'I suppose they'll postpone it till Monday night,' said Wendy in a high rather mad voice, 'and that means half the spectators won't come.'

Down the spiral staircase came the expert with her case of samples, the scraper still in her hand.

'I think I'm going to be sick,' whispered Veronica.

Her mother was all care, all solicitude, jumping up, hastening her to the ground-floor bathroom.

Wexford went back upstairs. Archbold had gone. The expert had gone. Martin was drinking tea from a flask and the other two Coke from cans while they waited for the Sevenstarker on the fourth wall to do its stuff. Wexford felt something very near a qualm. The room, which had been a shell-pink sanctuary, was a nasty mess. A shambles, Martin called it, but a shambles, meaning a slaughter house, was just what Wexford thought it had been used for, the reason for this destruction. Suppose he was wrong? Suppose the killing of Rodney Williams had taken place elsewhere?

Too late now.

The police's loss would be Kitman's gain. It is the business of the thinking man, he paraphrased, to give employment to the artisan.

'Let me have one of those, will you?' he said to Martin, pointing to the scrapers. The white patches of plaster among the brown were the areas Wendy herself had filled before Kitman began papering.

It wouldn't budge the white plaster.

'Want me to have a go, sir?' Allison produced what Wexford thought might be a cold chisel.

'We'll all have a go.'

350

It made Allison's day. He had never before distinguished himself in any way since joining the force two years before. Sometimes he thought — and his wife — that they had only taken him on because he was black and not because he was suitable or any good. They were inverted race snobs. For weeks everyone had bent over backwards to treat him with more kindness, courtesy and consideration than they would show, for instance, to a millionaire grandfather on his deathbed. That had worn off after a while. He was a bit lonely too in Kingsmarkham where only his wife, his kids and two other families were West Indian like him. But today paid for all that. It was what made him in his own eyes an officer of the law.

'Sir, I think I've found . . .' he began.

Wexford was there beside him like a shot. Under his eyes Allison dug in carefully, thanking his stars he'd remembered to put his gloves on. The object was stuck in the fissure wrapped up in newspaper, plastered over. He chipped and dug and then put his hand to it, looking at Wexford, and Wexford nodded.

The knife didn't clatter out. It was unveiled as reverently as if it were a piece of cut glass. They all looked at it lying there on its wrappings, clean as a whistle and polished bright as a long prism in a chandelier.

20

Wexford had them with him all day Sunday and Monday morning's papers said an arrest was imminent. But Wexford wanted the two women, not just one, Joy as well as Wendy. Charging Wendy with Rodney Williams's murder was an obvious act. The knife buried in her living-room wall had a blade which exactly matched the knife wounds on the body and it was wrapped in part of the *Daily Mail* of 15 April. Still, he wanted Joy as well and Joy had no apparent connection with the crime. The only evidence he had was a witness who claimed to have seen the two women together and a voice on the phone that was probably hers.

Joy also had an alibi. Wendy didn't. All day long nails were going into Wendy's coffin, or at least the shades of the prison house were closing about her. Until Ovington came. That is, until Ovington's second visit.

Alone in the house, eating a junk food supper, Wexford got a call from Burden late on Saturday evening. Jenny's labour hadn't exactly been a false alarm but it had gradually subsided during the day. They were keeping her in, though, and considering some method of induction . . .

'You wanted her to wait a week,' said Wexford nastily. 'You'd better come back to work.'

He phoned Ovington first thing in the morning. Never mind about Sunday and all that. By the time Ovington arrived at the police station he and Sergeant Martin and Polly Davies had Joy and Wendy in an interview room, the demented refugee and the broken doll. The curious thing was they had come closer to each other. In appearance, that is. There had been a

352

sort of blending, and he thought of Kipling's hedgehog and tortoise, combining to make an armadillo. Joy and Wendy hadn't gone that far, but anxiety and harassment had done their work on the younger woman and the older had smartened herself up, perhaps because her son was back. At any rate the headscarf was gone and she had proper shoes on. But Wendy's make-up was stale, she had hairs all over the shoulders of her black cotton dress and the ladder that sprang in her tights didn't fidget her.

He left them to go and talk to Ovington. Smiling as usual, absurdly ingratiating, he could hardly have persuaded even the most gullible to believe him, certainly not a hard-headed policeman.

'She was with you on April the fifteenth?' Wexford said. 'She came to your place after work for a drink? Why hasn't she so much as mentioned this to me?'

'She doesn't want anyone to know she was seeing me while her husband was still alive.'

This was in character. Wifely virtue was one of the aspects of the image Wendy liked to present. That didn't mean Ovington's story was true. Ovington was trying it on, a kind, stupid man with a misplaced idea of duty. Absently Wexford thanked him for coming. Then, as he was going back to the Williams wives, it occurred to him Ovington might have been in it with Wendy instead of Wendy with Joy. In that case who had made the phone call?

Wendy was crying. She said she was cold. It was true that the weather had turned very cold for the time of year but she should have been prepared for that, sacrificed vanity and brought a coat. He thought of all the places in the world and all the policemen in them where Wendy would have been allowed to shiver, where the temperature would have been lowered if possible, a little hypothermia encouraged. You couldn't call it torture, cooling someone into admissions . . .

'Get her something to put on,' he said to Polly.

He took them through the incest again and he got more stories full of holes. Joy hadn't believed Rodney would do that, yet she insisted Sara had led him on, insisted too that he would have gone to prison if she had breathed a word. Wendy now said Veronica had told her Rodney had started coming into her bedroom to kiss her good night and it wasn't 'nice'. That, said Joy, forgetting her former statement, was just how it had begun with Sara. Polly came back into the room with a grey knitted garment, something from Marks and Spencer's range for old ladies – God knows where she found it – which Wendy put on with a show of reluctance.

Sandwiches were brought in to them at lunchtime, one lot corned beef, the other egg and cress. Not exactly the Sunday joint, two veg and Yorkshire pudding. By that time Wexford had taken them through 15 April and was getting on to last Thursday night. Wendy had forgotten her coat but not her box of tissues, shades of peach this time. She sat snivelling into handfuls of them.

Just before three Joy broke at last. She started to howl like a dog. She rocked back and forth in her chair, howling and drumming her fists on the table. Wexford stopped the proceedings and sent for a cup of tea. He took Wendy into the interview room next door and asked her about Ovington. Rather to his surprise she agreed without much reluctance that she had been in Ovington's flat on 15 April from about 7.45 until about 9.15. Why hadn't she said so before? She gave the reason Ovington had given for her. They had hatched this up together, Wexford thought.

'I thought I might as well tell you,' she said with an aplomb that almost staggered him. 'I didn't before because you've all got minds capable of anything. But there's been so much real dirt dug up I don't think my innocent little friendship amounts to much.'

What did any of it weigh against that knife in the wall?

Late in the afternoon Burden walked in, looking a hundred years old.

'For God's sake,' said Wexford. 'I wasn't serious.'

The truth was Burden didn't know how otherwise to pass the time. He started on Joy, trying to break her alibi. But the tea had done wonders for her. She stuck to her story about watching television at the Harmers' and after half an hour of that had the brainwave that might have struck her days ago. She didn't have to talk at all if she didn't want to. Nobody had charged her with anything.

Unfortunately, by this time Wendy was back in the room with her and heard what she said.

Through her tears she smiled quite amicably at Joy. 'Good idea. I'm not talking either then. Pity I didn't think of it before.'

Joy uttered one last sentence. 'It was me thought of it, not you.'

United in silence, they stared at Wexford. Why not charge them both? With murdering Rodney Williams and, if he couldn't make that stick, with murdering Paulette Harmer? Special court in the morning, a remand in custody . . . Archbold came in and said there were three people to see him. He left the silent women with Burden and Martin and went down in the lift.

James Ovington was sitting there with his taciturn father and an elderly woman he introduced as his mother. Somehow Wexford had never thought of Ovington *père* as having a wife but, of course, he would have; James Ovington must have come from somewhere. He only looked like a waxwork. More so than ever this afternoon, his complexion fresher, his cheeks pinker, his smile flashing.

'My parents want to tell you something.'

That was one way of putting it. They didn't look as if they had any desire beyond that of going home again. Wexford asked them to go up to the first floor with him to his office but Mrs Ovington said she'd rather not, thank you, as if any suggestion of going upstairs in the company of men was indecent. They compromised with an interview room. Mrs Ovington looked disparagingly about her, evidently thinking it wasn't very cosy. James Ovington said, 'What were you going to tell the chief inspector, Dad?'

Nothing, apparently.

'Now you know you were willing to come here and tell him.'

'Not willing,' said Ovington senior. 'If I must I must. That's what I said.'

'Is this something about Mrs Wendy Williams, Mr Ovington?' prompted Wexford.

Very slowly and grudgingly Ovington said, 'I saw her.'

'We both did,' said Mrs Ovington, suddenly brave. 'We both saw her.'

355

Wexford decided patience was the only thing. 'You saw her, yes. When was this?'

James opened his mouth to speak, wisely shut it again. His father pondered, at last said, 'She's got a car. She'd parked it outside the shop on the yellow line. That don't matter after half six. We never saw her go in.'

Silence fell and endured. Wexford had to prompt.

'Go in where?'

'My son's place, of course. What else are we talking about? He's got the bottom flat and we've got the top, haven't we?'

'Up four flights,' said his wife. 'Wear the old ones out first, that's what it is.'

'We saw her come out,' said Ovington. 'Out of our front window. Round a quarter past nine. Tripped over and nearly fell in them heels. That's how Mother come to see her. I said, Here, Mother, look at this, them heels'll have her over.'

'It was April the fifteenth!' said James, unable to contain himself any longer.

'I don't know about that.' His father shook his head. 'But it was the first Thursday after Easter.'

That night he went to bed early and slept for nine hours. He didn't let himself think about the two women, Joy with no evidence against her, Wendy exonerated by the Ovingtons. They had been sent home with the warning that he would very likely want them back again on Monday morning. Old Ovington hadn't been lying but still his story didn't militate against the possibility that while Joy had done the deed in Wendy's house Wendy had later met her in time to help her dispose of the body, the clothes and the car.

In the morning he awoke clear-headed and calm. Immediately he remembered what it was Wendy had said to him. It had been when she told him Veronica was to play in a tennis singles final. The significance was in what it reminded him of, and now he remembered that too and as he did so everything began to fall gently and smoothly into place, so that he felt like one recalling and then using the combination of a safe until the door slowly swings open.

'But what a fool I've been,' he said aloud.

'Have you, darling?'

356

'If I'd got on to it sooner maybe that poor girl wouldn't have died.'

'Come on,' said Dora. 'You're not God.'

The phone was ringing as he left the house. It was Burden but Wexford wasn't there to answer it and Dora spoke to him.

A report on the postmortem, rushed through by Sir Hilary Tremlett, was awaiting Wexford. He went through it with Crocker beside him. Strangling had been with a fine powerful cord and whatever this was had left a red staining in the deep indentation it had made around the victim's neck.

'The nylon line from the spool of an electric edge trimmer,' said Wexford.

Crocker looked at him. 'That's a bit esoteric.'

'I don't think so. Joy Williams has three such spools in her garage and one of them, unless I'm much mistaken, will be empty.'

'Are you going to go there and check that?'

'Not just at the moment. Maybe later. Do you think it wrong to encourage a child to inform against its immediate family?'

'Like what happens in totalitarian societies, d'you mean? Or what I suppose happens. Extremists always believe the means are justified by the end. It depends what you mean by immediate family too, I mean, against a parent is a bit grim. That sticks in one's throat.'

'Drugging a man and stabbing him and burying the knife in a wall sticks in one's throat too.' Wexford picked up the phone and put it down again. 'I've got two women to arrest,' he said, 'and the way things are I'll never make the charges stand up. When do the schools go back?'

Crocker looked a little startled at this apparent *non sequitur*. 'The state schools – that is, the older kids – sometime this week.'

'I'd better do it today if I'm to catch her without her mother.' He lifted the phone again, this time asked for an outside line. It rang for so long he began to think she must be out. Then at last Veronica Williams's soft, rather high voice answered, giving the number in all its ten digits. Wexford spoke her name, 'Veronica?' then said, 'This is Chief Inspector Wexford of Kingsmarkham CID.'

'Oh, hallo, yes.' Was she afraid or did she always answer the phone in this cautious breathless way?

'Just one or two things to check with you, Veronica. First, what time is your match tonight and where is it?'

'Kingsmarkham Tennis Club,' she said. 'It's at six.' She gathered some courage. 'Why?'

Wexford was too old a hand to answer that. 'After that's over I'd like to talk to you. Not you and your mother, just you alone. All right? I think you have quite a lot of things you'd like to tell me, haven't you?'

The silence was so heavy he thought he'd gone too far. But no. And it was better than he had hoped. 'I have got things to tell you. There are things I've *got* to tell you.' He thought he heard a sob but she might only have been clearing her throat.

'All right then. When you've finished your match come straight here. D'you know where it is?' He gave her directions. 'About ten minutes' walk from the club. I'll have a car to send you home in.'

She said, 'I'll have to tell my mother.'

'By all means tell your mother. Tell anyone you like.' Did he sound too eager? 'But make sure your mother knows I want to see you alone.'

The enormity of what he was doing hit him as he put the phone down. Could anything justify it? She was a sixteen-year-old girl with vital information for him. The last teenage girl with vital information for him had been strangled before she could impart it. Was he sending her to the same death as Paulette Harmer? If Burden had been there he would have told him everything but with the doctor he had reservations.

'You're not going round there, then?' Crocker said, a little mystified as much by Wexford's expression as by the cryptic phone conversation.

'That's the last thing I must do.'

Later, when the doctor had gone, Wexford thought, I hope I have the nerve to stick it out. Pity it's so many hours off. But the advantage of an evening match was that afterwards it would soon be dark . . . Advantage! She would be phoning her mother now at Jickie's to tell her, he thought, and somehow – hopefully – persuading Wendy not to come with her. He would have that girl watched every step of the way.

358

The phone rang.

He picked it up and the telephonist said she had a Miss Veronica Williams for him. What a little madam she was giving her name as 'Miss'!

'I could come and see you now,' the childish voice said. 'That might be easier. Then I wouldn't have to upset Mummy. I mean I wouldn't have to tell her I don't want her with me.'

He braced himself. He hardened his heart. 'I'm too busy to see you before this evening, Veronica. And I'd like you to tell your mother, please. Tell her now.'

If she called back, he thought, he'd relent and let her come. He wouldn't be able to hold out. Would she recognise Martin? Archbold? Palmer? Certainly she'd know Allison. But would it matter if she did recognise them? He'd be there himself anyway. There was no way he was going to let her take that ten-minute walk in the half-dark from the club down a lane off the Pomfret Road to the police station, especially in the case of her following his directions and taking the footpath across one and a half fields.

The phone rang again. That's it, he thought. I can't keep it up. I'll go round there and she'll tell me and that'll be evidence enough . . . He picked up the receiver.

'Inspector Burden for you, Mr Wexford.'

Burden's voice sounded strange, not really like his voice at all.

'It's all over. Mother and baby are doing fine. Jenny had a Caesarean at nine this morning.'

'Congratulations. That's great, Mike. Give my love to Jenny, won't you? You'd better tell me what Mary weighed so I can tell Dora.'

'Eight pounds nine ounces, but it's not going to be Mary. We're changing just one letter in the name.'

Wexford didn't feel up to guessing. Jenny's persuaded him into something fancy against his better judgement, he thought.

'Mark, actually,' said Burden. 'I'll see you later. Cheers for now.'

21

A woman had once been found murdered on that very footpath.* They would all have that in their minds, even Palmer and Archbold who hadn't been there at the time, who had probably still been at school. As Veronica Williams still was. Had she ever heard of the murder? Did people still talk about it?

That woman had lived in Forest Road, the last street in the area to bear the postal address Kingsmarkham. The Pomfret boundary begins there, though it is open country all the way to Pomfret in one direction and nearly all the way to Kingsmarkham Police Station in the other. The tennis club, however, is not in Forest Road but in Cheriton Lane which runs more or less parallel to it on the Kingsmarkham side. Smallish meadows enclosed by hedges cover the few acres between the club and the town, and the footpath runs alongside one of these hedges, at one point skirting a little copse. It emerges into the High Street fifty yards north of the police station and on the opposite side.

Wexford had Martin and Palmer in a car in Cheriton Lane, would station himself and Archbold in the copse, Loring among the spectators at the match, Bennett to start walking from the High Street end, Allison to follow her at a discreet distance.

'One black man'll look very like another to her, sir,' Allison had said. 'That mightn't be so in a city but it is out here.'

'Don't tell me Inspector Burden and I look alike to you.'

* See *A Sleeping Life*.

360

'No, sir, but that's a question of age, isn't it?'

Which puts me firmly in my place, thought Wexford. Burden was in his office, sitting beside him, anxious to take part in the protection-of-Veronica exercise. Can't keep away from the place for more than five minutes, Wexford had grumbled at him. At least Burden had supplied a diversion in the lull of the long afternoon.

'I don't understand how they could make a mistake over the sex like that. God knows I don't know much about it, but if a man has an XY chromosome formula and a woman XX surely they must always have it from embryo to old age?'

'It's not that. It's like this. In an amniocentesis they extract cells from the amniotic fluid the foetus is in. But occasionally they make a mistake and once in about ten thousand times they take cells from the mother not the child. And even then they aren't always going to know their error. Because if the child does happen to be a girl . . . In this case, though, I gather someone's head is going to roll.'

'It caused a lot of unnecessary misery.'

'Misery, yes,' said Burden, 'but maybe not unnecessary. Jenny says it's taught her a lot about herself. It's taught her she's not what you might call a natural feminist and now she has to approach feminism not from an emotional standpoint but from what is – well, right and just. We didn't know, either of us, what a lot of deep-rooted old-fashioned prejudices we had. Because I felt it too, you know, I also wanted a son though I never said. It's taught us how much we've concealed from the other when we thought we were frank and open. All this has been – well, not far from – what does Jenny call it? – Guided Confrontation Therapy.'

With difficulty Wexford kept a straight face. 'So long as now you've got a son you don't wish it was a girl.' He said 'you' but he meant Jenny whom he thought the kind of woman for whom the unattainable grass might always be the greener.

'Of course not!' Burden exclaimed, looking very sour. 'After all, as Jenny says, what does it really matter so long as it's healthy and has all its fingers and toes?'

This was a cliché Wexford didn't feel he could compete with. Now Burden was here how would he feel about taking part in the Veronica watch? Not much, said Burden, he had to be back at the hospital. Then Wexford thought it might start raining. If it rained the match would be cancelled and in all probability Veronica would simply take the bus to the police station from Pomfret.

But the sky lightened round about 5.30. He wondered what those two women were thinking. How had they reacted to being left all day to their own devices? Unless the match was over in two straight sets Veronica could hardly expect to leave the club before seven. Should he fill in the time by seeing what he could get out of Kevin Williams? But he didn't really want to get anything out of him. He knew it all already. Why not simply go and watch the match?

It hadn't occurred to him to ask himself – or anyone else for that matter – if the tournaments of the Kingsmarkham Tennis Club were or were not open to the public. And it wasn't until he walked through the doors of the clubhouse that the question came into his mind. But a hearty elderly man with the air of a retired Air Force officer who said he was the secretary welcomed him with open arms. They loved spectators. If only they could get more spectators. It provided such encouragement for the players.

He had already spotted Martin and Archbold sitting in the car a discreet distance from the gates. Now if Veronica saw him, as it was most likely she would do, his best course would be to leave. Then, later, she wouldn't fail to follow. The great thing was not to give her a chance to speak to him. Therefore, to the bar, a refuge which was also the last place to which a sixteen-year-old competitor was likely to retreat before a match. The secretary, seeing him headed in that direction, trotted up to say that as a non-member he wasn't allowed to purchase a drink but if he would permit a drink to be bought *for* him . . . ? Wexford accepted.

The bar was semicircular, with a long curved window offering a view of three of the club's nine hard courts. Wexford had a half of lager, the club like most places of its kind being unable to provide any sort of draught beer or 'real ale'. The secretary talked rather monotonously, first about the bad public behaviour of certain international tennis stars, then their own disappointment at Saturday's rain and the enforced cancellation of this singles final. There would have been more spectators on a Saturday, he said sadly. In fact, nine people had actually come along – he had counted – but had had to be turned away. Of course, they were most unlikely to come back tonight. Wexford had the impression that if any of them had turned up the secretary would have bought them drinks too.

It got to six, to ten past. She's not going to come, Wexford thought. Then an umpire arrived and climbed up into the high seat. Five canvas chairs and a wooden bench had been arranged for a possible audience. It looked as if they would remain empty but after a while two elderly women with white cardigans over their tennis dresses came and sat down and at the same time, approaching by the path that led from the farther group of six courts, Loring sauntered up. In sound English fashion the women sat in the canvas chairs on the left-hand end of the row and Loring at the extreme right-hand end of the bench. Colin Budd should have been so wise.

Veronica and a taller, older, altogether bigger girl appeared outside the court and let themselves in by the gate.

'Well, best get out there and give them some moral support,' said the secretary, rubbing his hands together.

It was certainly cold. A gust of wind whipped across the court, tearing at Veronica's short pleated skirt. In classic style they began with a knock-up.

'I don't think I will,' said Wexford. 'D'you mind if I watch from in here?'

The secretary was terribly disappointed. He gave him a look of injured reproach.

'You mustn't buy any drinks, you do know that, don't you? And you're not to serve him, mind, Priscilla.'

Loring, his jacket collar turned up, was smoking a cigarette. The secretary appeared, running up to the two women, and sat beside them. The knock-up, in which Veronica had had the best of it, was over and the match began.

Dark would come early because the day had been so dull. Wexford wondered if the light would hold long enough for the match to be played to the finish. Veronica, whose service it was, won the first game to love but had a tougher time when her opponent came to serve.

'You can have a drink if you like,' said Priscilla. 'I work it like this. I give it to you for free and next time a member buys me a drink I'll charge yours up to him. I'm a total abstainer actually but I don't let on to this lot.'

Wexford laughed. 'Better not, thanks all the same.'

'Suit yourself.' She came over and stood beside him and watched.

Three games all. It looked as if it would go on and on and then quite quickly it was all over, Veronica having won her own two service games and broken her oponent's.

'She's a little cracker, that kid,' said Priscilla. 'Strong as a horse. She's got arms like whipcord.'

It was twenty to seven and the edge of dusk. Veronica won the first two games but the other girl was fighting back for all she was worth. Perhaps she had never played against Veronica before. At any rate, it had taken her all this time to find her weakness but she had found it at last. Veronica couldn't handle long swift diagonal drives to her forehand, though backhand presented her with no problems. It was half a dozen of those forehand drives that won her opponent the next game and the next and the next two until she was leading 4–2. The light had grown bluish but the white lines on the court were still clearly visible, seeming to glow with twilight luminosity.

And then it was as if Veronica mastered the craft of dealing with those hard cross-court strokes. Or, curiously, as if some inspiration came to her from an external source. Certainly it was not that she had spotted him or had recognised Loring, whom she had never previously seen. But a charge of power came to her, a gift of virtuosity she had not known before. She had never before played like this, Wexford was sure of it. For a brief quarter of an hour she played as if she were on the centre court at Wimbledon and was there not by a fluke but by a hard-won right.

Her opponent couldn't withstand it. In that quarter hour she gained only four points. Veronica won the set by 6 games to 4 and thus secured the match. She threw her racket into the air, caught it neatly, ran to the net and shook hands with her opponent. Wexford said good night to Priscilla and left the way he had come, having watched the players go into the pavilion where the changing rooms were. Loring was still sitting on the bench.

Allison he spotted as soon as the footpath entered the field. He was lying very still in the long grass by the hedge and mostly covered by it. But Wexford saw him without giving any sign that he had done so. He was pretty sure Veronica wouldn't. The path wound on parallel to the hedge, then began to skirt the copse.

The false dusk hung still, suspended between light and dark. If it had been much darker no prudent young girl would have dared walk this way. Veronica Williams, of course, in spite of the impression she gave, was not a prudent young girl.

The air was still and damp and the grass moist underfoot. Wexford made his way along the path, under the high hedge, certain as he had been all along that Veronica's assailant would wait for her in the copse. Archbold had been there since 5.30 to be on the safe side. It was too late now for Wexford to join him without taking the risk of being seen. As it was, by staying to watch the match, he was taking a chance of spoiling the whole plan. Ahead of him a maple tree in the hedge spread its branches in a cone shape, the lowest ones almost touching the ground. He lifted them, stood against its trunk and waited.

By now it was 7.30 and he had begun to wonder if she would come after all. Though members had been thin on the ground there might have been some plan to fête her in the clubhouse. Hardly with drinks though. And she would have got out of it, she needed to see him as much as he her. Then he remembered she was her mother's daughter; it would take her longer than most girls to change her clothes, do her hair. She might even have a shower. Wendy was the sort of woman who would get a dying person out of bed to change the sheets before the doctor comes.

He stood under his tree in the silent dusk which was growing misty. Occasionally it was possible to hear in the distance a heavy vehicle on the Kingsmarkham to Pomfret road. Nothing else. No birds sang at this season and this hour. He could see the path about ten yards behind only and perhaps fifty yards ahead and it seemed to him then the emptiest footway he had ever contemplated. Allison would get rheumatism lying there on the damp ground, the cold seeping into his bones. Archbold, wrapped in his padded jacket, had probably fallen asleep . . .

She appeared quite suddenly. But how else could she have come but noiselessly and walking quite fast? She didn't look afraid though. Wexford saw her face quite clearly for a moment. Her expression was – yes, innocent. Innocent and trusting. She had no knowledge that there was anything to fear. If Sara, her half-sister, was a Florentine madonna, she was a Medici page, her small face grave and wistful in its gold-brown frame of bobbed hair and fringe. She wore her pink cotton jeans, beautifully pressed by Mother, her pink and white running shoes, a powder blue and white striped anorak that hung open over a white fluffy pullover, and she was carrying her tennis racket in a blue case. Wexford took all this in as she passed him, walking quickly.

He didn't dare come out. She might look back. Instead he dropped down into the field at the other side of the hedge. There had been a crop growing here, wheat or barley, but the grain had been cut and all that remained was a stubble that looked grey in this light. He ran along the hedge side, some few feet above the footpath. A long way ahead now he could just see the top of her head bobbing along. She had reached the corner of the copse.

There was a barbed-wire entanglement here that threatened to bar his passage, the spaces between the wires too narrow to squeeze through, the top wire too high to sling a leg over without terrible detriment to trousers. There was nothing for it but to retrace steps, pass through the hedge and clamber up the bank onto the footpath. She was too far away to see him even if she did look back. He jumped down, rounded the bend in the path, but now, though the copse was in full view, he couldn't see her at all.

His heart was in his mouth then. If she had met her assailant and gone into the wood, if Archbold truly had gone to sleep . . . He left the path and plunged into the copse. It was dark and dry in there, a million needles underfoot from the firs and larches. He ran through the trees and met Archbold head on.

'There's no one here, sir. I haven't seen a soul in three hours.'

'Except her,' said Wexford breathlessly.

'She just walked past. She's on her own, heading for the High Street.'

He came out of the wood on the Kingsmarkham side, Archbold behind him. She was nowhere to be seen, the hedges too high, the foliage on the trees too thick and masking. And then he forgot discretion and catching a murderer and ran along the path in pursuit of her, afraid for her and for himself. A moment before he had been praying Bennett wouldn't appear, walking from the Kingsmarkham end, and spoil it all. Now he hoped he would.

There was one more field and that low-lying, the path passing diagonally across it and then running beside a hedge at right angles to the road. No sign of Bennett. Because he had seen her? Or seen her attacker? Would he be capable of that in this fast-fading light? The meadow was grey and the hedges black and the air had the density of fallen cloud. Through the mist you could just see a light or two from cars on the Pomfret road, behind that an irregular cluster of pale lights that was probably the police station.

She was nowhere. The meadow was empty. There was a movement just discernible on the far side of it, where the path met the hedge. She had crossed the diagonal and come to the last hundred yards, her pale clothes catching what light there was so that she gleamed like a night moth. And like a night moth fluttered along against the dark foliage.

Wexford and Archbold didn't take the diagonal. They dared not risk being seen. They kept to the boundary hedge, though there was no path here, and Archbold, who was thirty, outran Wexford who felt that he had never run so hard in his life. All the time he could see the pale fluttering moth moving down there, homing on the stile that would bring her to the wide grass verge of the Pomfret road.

She never reached it. The fluttering stopped and there was something else down there with her at the bottom of the field where the dead elms stood, their roots a mass of underbrush, of brambles and nettles and fuzzy wild clematis. The something or someone else had come out of that and barred her way. He thought he heard a cry but he couldn't be sure. At any rate it was no scream but a thin shriek of – surprise perhaps. He cut the corner, running hell for leather, his heart pounding fit to burst, running the way no man of close on sixty should run.

And Archbold got there only just first. It was strange that the knife should catch a gleam on it even in this near darkness. Wexford saw the gleam and then saw it drop to the ground. Archbold was holding Veronica who had turned her face into his chest and was clinging to his coat. He went up to the other himself. She made no attempt to run. She clasped her hands and hung her head so that he couldn't see her face.

In that moment Bennett materialised, so to speak. He came out of the dark, running. Sara Williams looked up then with an expression of faint dull surprise.

'Take them both,' said Wexford. 'They'll be charged with the wilful murder of Rodney Williams.'

22

'It was they, not their mothers, who knew each other,' Wexford said. 'Edwina Klein told me but I misinterpreted what she said. "Those two women knew each other," she said to me. "I saw them together." I took her to mean Joy and Wendy. Joy and Wendy were women and Sara and Veronica were girls. Except that to a militant feminist founder member of ARRIA all females are women. Just as they are,' he added, 'to organisers of sports events. It's the women's singles even if both players are fifteen.'

Burden and the doctor said nothing. They were all sitting in Burden's grass widower's house, drinking Burden's grass widower's instant coffee. It was over. A special court for one and a special juvenile court for the other and the two girls had been committed for trial. Afterwards the press had caught Wexford, a camera crew springing out of their van with the agility of the SAS, and once again he would be on television. Looking a hundred years old, he thought, after being up half the night talking to Sara Williams. People would phone in suggesting it was time he retired.

'They met at a tennis match, of course. The second time I met Sara I noticed she had a tennis racket up on her bedroom wall. She wasn't anywhere near Veronica's standard, not in the high school's first or second six. She just scraped into their reserve. Still, one day she was called on to play and she met Veronica as her opponent. What happened then? I don't know and she hasn't told me. I'd guess that one of the other girls there commented that they looked alike and seeing they had the same surname, were they cousins? It was up to one of them to probe further and one of them did. Sara, probably. After that it wouldn't have been hard to find out, would it? "Look, I've got a photo, this is my mum and dad . . ."'

'Something of a shattering experience, wouldn't you say?' said the doctor.

'Also I think an exciting one.'

'That's a superficial way of looking at it,' said Burden. 'I'd almost say unfeeling. Both those girls were lonely, Veronica sheltered and smothered, Sara neglected, no one's favourite. Wouldn't it have been both shattering and immensely *comforting* to find a sister?'

The sensitivity which had developed in Burden late in life always brought Wexford a kind of affectionate amusement. It was so often misdirected. It resembled in a way those good intentions with which hell is paved.

He picked his words carefully. They were strong words but his tone was hesitant.

'Sara Williams doesn't have normal feelings of affection, need for love, loneliness. I think she would be labelled a psychopath. She wants attention and she wants to impress. Also she wants her own way. I imagine that what she got from her half-sister was principally admiration. Sara has an excellent brain. Intellectually, she's streets ahead of Veronica. She's a strong, powerful, amoral, unfeeling solipsist with an appalling temper.'

Crocker's eyebrows went up. 'You're talking about an eighteen-year-old who was raped by her own father.'

Wexford didn't respond. He was thinking about what the girl had said to him, presiding at the table in the interview room with Marion Bayliss at one end, himself opposite and Martin facing Marion. But Sara Williams had presided, holding her head high, describing her feelings and actions without a notion of defending herself.

'My sister looks just like me. I used to feel she was another aspect of me, the weaker, pretty, feminine part, if you like. I wanted ultimately to be rid of that part.'

Solipsism, according to the Oxford dictionary, is the view or theory that self is the only object of real knowledge or the only real thing existent.

'Why didn't you tell your parents you and Veronica had met?'

'Why should I?'

Her cool answers took the breath away.

'It would have been the natural thing to confront your father with what you had found out.'

She was honest in her way. 'I liked having the secret. I enjoyed knowing what he thought I didn't know.'

'So that you could hold it over him?'

'Perhaps,' she said indifferently, bored when the discussion was not totally centred on herself.

Was that what she had had to threaten him with in the matter of the incest? Was that how she had stopped it?

'You prevented Veronica from telling her mother?'

'She did what I told her.'

It was uttered the way a trainer speaks of an obedient dog. The trainer takes the obedience for granted, so effective are his personality and technique, so unthinkable would an alternative reaction be. Wexford thought Crocker and Burden would have had to hear and see Sara to appreciate all this. He couldn't even attempt to put it across to them. 'The two girls met quite often,' he went on. 'Sara even went to Veronica's home when Wendy was at work. Veronica came to admire her extravagantly. She followed her, she would have obeyed her in anything.'

'Would have?'

'Did. Psychiatrists call what overtook them *folie à deux*, a kind of madness that overtakes two people only when they are together and through the influence of each on the other. But in all such cases you'll always find one party who is easily led and one who is dominant.' Wexford digressed a little before returning to the point. 'Looking back, I don't think Sara Williams has ever addressed a sentence to me that didn't begin with "I" or wasn't about herself.'

He went on, 'The coming and going between the Williams homes led to a pooling of information. For instance, Sara had believed her father was a sales rep with Sevensmith Harding for the Ipswich area. Veronica thought he was a rep with a bathroom fittings company. They took steps to find out the truth and did. It's over a year now since they found out what Rodney really did, what his position was, and discovered – via some research into marketing managers' earnings on Sara's part – what his actual salary was.

'Sara also warned Veronica of their father's – proclivities. That, of course, is how Wendy came to fear an incest attempt. Not because she witnessed anything herself or because Veronica put two and two together from a kiss and a cuddle but because Sara told Veronica what to expect and Veronica passed it on without disclosing her source. One way and another Sara made Veronica into a very frightened girl. A very bewildered and confused girl. Think of her situation. First she discovers her father has a legal wife and a grown-up family, next that he could never have in fact married her mother and she must be illegitimate. Necessarily, therefore, he's deceitful and a liar. He doesn't even have the job he says he has. Worst of all, he has raped his other daughter and will certainly have the same designs on her. No wonder she was frightened.

'Telling Wendy her fears of a sexual attack had the effect only of causing trouble between her mother and father. Did Wendy accuse Rodney and Rodney hotly deny it? Almost certainly. The quarrel was at any rate bad enough to make Wendy believe Rodney would leave her but fear that if he didn't Veronica would be in danger. So we see that the reason she didn't want Veronica to stay in on the evening of April the fifteenth was that if Rodney did come back she would be alone with her father – and this would be the first time she would be alone with him after the disclosure was made.

'But Veronica had another confidante and friend now, apart from her mother. She had Sara. And Sara absolutely justified the faith she put in her. Sara had a good idea for diverting Rodney's attention from his daughter, diverting his attention from everything, in fact. Substitute sleeping pills for his blood-pressure tablets. It was something that could only be done once though and in an emergency.

'Now on April the fifteenth, however much their mothers may have been in ignorance, Sara and Veronica knew that when Rodney left Alverbury Road he would drive straight to Liskeard Avenue. So Sara herself made the exchange of tablets, two only remaining in the container. Don't forget we found an empty Mandaret container in Alverbury Road and a half-full one in Liskeard Avenue. Rodney took his two Mandaret as he thought, leaving the empty container in his bedroom, and drove to Pomfret. No doubt he began to feel drowsy on the way.'

372

'But these were Phanodorm, supplied by Paulette Harmer?' said the doctor.

'I suppose they were supplied by her. It seems most likely. But Paulette didn't die because she illicitly provided a sleeping drug. She died because the turn events were taking made her concentrate her mind on the evening of April the fifteenth, made her remember in fact what had really happened. What she remembered was her mother speaking to her aunt Joy on the phone that evening and making some remark about being glad Kevin had settled in back at college. And she was going to tell us because she knew from the papers and television and her parents' conversation how strong was the suspicion against her aunt. She knew very well her aunt had been at home that evening, in at eight to receive Kevin's phone call and still in at eight forty-five to receive her mother's.'

The girl should have been strewing flowers or rising from the waves in a cockleshell. The face was bland, innocent and somehow secretive. Even now there was a tiny self-satisfied smile. Her hair was scraped back tight from that high forehead but wisps had come free and lay in gold tendrils on the white skin.

'I got a phone call from Veronica. It was just to tell me he'd gone to sleep like I said he would. I said I'd come over.'

He had interrupted her to ask why.

'I just thought I would. I wasn't going to get a chance like that again, was I?'

He stopped himself asking her what she meant. Her eyes seemed to enlarge, her face grow blanker.

'I saw him sleeping there and I thought, I've got him in my power. I thought of the power he had over *me*. I started to get angry, really angry.'

'And Veronica?'

'I didn't think about Veronica. I suppose she was there. Well, I know she was. I said to her, "We could kill him and stop all of it." I told her to get me a knife. I wasn't serious then, it was fantasy. I was angry and I was excited – high like when you've had a drink.'

Folie à deux. Was Veronica excited too? He wouldn't get much about another's feelings out of this girl.

373

'I took the knife out of her hands and took off the cardboard guard that was on it. I went up to my father who was lying on the settee and I started playing around, waving the knife over him, pretending to stick it in him. I could tell he was sound asleep. I was making Veronica laugh because I was doing all this stuff and he was just oblivious of it. I don't remember what made me stop playing. I was so excited and high I don't remember. But that's how it was. One minute it was fantasy and the next it was for real.'

She looked down at the table at Marion and then the other way at Martin. It was as if she were gathering the attention of her audience. Once more her eyes met Wexford's in a steady gaze.

'I raised the knife and stuck it in his neck, right in hard with both hands. I'd made him wake up then and make noises, so I stabbed him a few more times to stop the blood spraying like that. I'm going to be a doctor so I knew the blood would stop when he was dead . . .'

It took Wexford, hardened as he was, a moment or two to collect words.

'Did Veronica stab him?'

'I gave her the knife and told her to have a go. I'd made a big wound in his neck and she stuck it in there and then she went off and was sick.'

'Completely mad,' said Burden. 'Bonkers.'

'Perhaps. I'm not sure. Let's not get into defining psychosis.'

'What happened next?' said the doctor.

'The room was covered for the most part in dustsheets. Rodney had come in half asleep, climbed the stairs and lain down on the settee which had a dustsheet over one end. The end, incidentally, where he laid his head. It was this sheet, the property of Leslie Kitman, which received most of the blood. Some went on an area of wall from which the paper had been stripped that day. Sara washed the wall and wrapped Rodney's head up in the dustsheet. Veronica, recovered and very much under orders from Sara, washed the knife and then had the idea of plastering it into the wall. This was the first weird too-clever thing the girls did. There were others. There were fissures in the walls needing to be filled in and in the garage was a packet of filler. Also in the garage was Rodney's car, Greta the Granada, which Sara, though not Veronica, was able to drive. They rolled up the dustsheet and wrapped two of Wendy's Marks and Spencer's teacloths round Rodney's neck. Having cleaned up the room, they carried Rodney down the spiral staircase, through the door from the hall into the garage and put him into the boot of the car. On their way out in the car they deposited the dustsheet in the dustbin. It was about seven-thirty.'

'Then,' said Burden, 'how did Kevin manage to speak to his sister when he phoned Alverbury Road at eight o'clock?'

'He didn't. He spoke to his mother. And, of course, he and Joy were both well aware it was his mother he had spoken to. They lied to protect Sara. Oh, I know Joy hasn't much affection for Sara but she was her daughter. Once she began to think about it she saw that Sara might have had something to do with Rodney's disappearance. At first she genuinely thought he had left her and she got me in to advise her. But then things changed. I think I know why. On my advice, she phoned Sevensmith Harding and they told her *she* had spoken to them on Friday, April the sixteenth, to explain Rodney was ill. Now Joy no doubt at first thought this a mere mistake but they had been so sure it was her voice. Joy knew someone whose voice sounded very like hers – her own daughter.

'Don't forget that she knew how Sara felt towards her father on account of the incest. She also knew Sara had been out of the house for hours on the evening of April the fifteenth. So she told us and got Kevin to agree – no difficulty there, he distrusts the police and is close to his sister – that it was she who had gone out and Sara who had been at home to take the phone call. Was there collusion with Sara? I doubt it. There was no real communication between her and her mother. My guess is Joy said it might be wiser to arrange things this way and Sara agreed with just a nod and a "yes" probably.'

'You're painting a picture of a self-sacrificing maternal type,' said the doctor, 'which doesn't at all accord with our concept of Joy Williams. Rather like the old story of the mother pelican tearing at its own breast to feed its young – and just as much of a myth.'

'No. Joy quite rightly believed there was no real risk in it for her. She thought it impossible we could arrest the wrong person. Her trust must have been sorely put to the test these past few days.'

Always happier on circumstantial details, Burden said, 'So the two girls took Williams's body up to Cheriton Forest and dug a grave for him with his own snow shovel?'

'A shallow grave because, having killed him, Sara didn't want it to be too long before the body was discovered. She wanted a couple of weeks to pass only, rightly believing that this was the sort of time which would be just about right to blur the evidence. In fact, things didn't go her way and it was two months before the body was found.

'I turned over and over in my mind the complication of the Milvey coincidence. But now it has come out quite clearly. There is no coincidence. Sara and Veronica hid Rodney's travelling bag – in the forest probably – hoping it would be found within, say, the next few days. But as it happened, no one found it. Then one day Mrs Milvey happened to say to Joy in Sara's hearing that Milvey would be at Green Pond next day, dragging the pool. Sara retrieved the bag and dumped it in the pool in time for Milvey to find it next day.'

'But why did she want the body found? What difference could it make to her?'

'I'll come to that later.'

'I don't see why go to all the trouble of phoning Sevensmith Harding and forging a letter to delay discovery and then later try to accelerate it. Incidentally, I take it it was Sara who made the phone call? Her voice is very like Joy's.'

'She made the phone call and Veronica typed the letter. At her friend Nicola Tennyson's house, on Nicola's mother's typewriter.

'They buried the body, hid the travelling bag, and Sara drove Veronica back to Pomfret to be sure she got home before Wendy did. That was at about nine. Wendy, of course, didn't get home until nine thirty, being out doing some mild courting with James Ovington. Sara drove to Myringham and dumped the car in Arnold Road where no more than half an hour later it was seen and indeed bumped into by Eve Freeborn. If Sara had been a bit later and Eve a bit earlier those two members of ARRIA would have encountered each other and made our task a lot easier. But by the time Eve came Sara was on the bus for home.

'In the morning she shut herself in the living room and made the phone call before she went to school. Of necessity it was a very early call and she was lucky there was someone there to receive it. And that, I think, accounts for all the circumstances of the murder of Rodney Williams.'

Burden picked up the tray.

'Does anyone want more coffee?'

Neither did. Wexford said it was nearly beer time, wasn't it? The doctor frowned at him and he deliberately looked away, out into Burden's bright, neat garden, the flower borders like chintzy dress material, the lawn a bit of green baize. The sunshine was making Jenny's yellow chrysanthemums nearly too bright to look at. Burden opened the french windows.

'The sad thing,' said Crocker, 'is that all this is going to make it next to impossible for Sara Williams to make a career in medicine.'

Burden looked at him. He said sarcastically, 'Oh, surely St Biddulph's will overlook a little matter like stabbing her father to death with a carving knife.'

'You don't think it justification then, and more than justification, for a girl to make a murderous assault on the father who has raped her and shows signs of meting out the same treatment to her younger half-sister? Don't you think any judge or jury would see this as an extenuating circumstance?'

It was Wexford who answered him. 'Yes, I do.'

'Right, then there's not going to be any question of years of imprisonment, is there? She'll never have the dubious distinction of being a GP like your humble servant here, but at least there won't be punishment in the accepted sense.'

'I wouldn't be too sure of that.'

'On account of the planning and the covering of tracks, do you mean?'

'She killed Paulette Harmer,' Burden said.

'She did indeed but that wasn't what I meant. You see, Rodney Williams never committed incest with his elder daughter. He never showed signs of committing incest with his younger daughter. And I very much doubt if he ever sexually assaulted anyone, even in the broadest meaning of that term.'

23

Crocker had caught on quickly. Wexford left it to him to explain. The doctor began outlining Freud's 'seduction theory' as expressed in the famous paper of 1896.

Thirteen women patients of Freud claimed paternal seduction. Freud believed them, built on this evidence a theory, later abandoned it, realising he had been too gullible. Instead, he concluded that little girls are prone to fantasise that their fathers have made love to them, from which developed his stress on childhood fantasy and ultimately his postulation of the Oedipus Complex.

'You're saying it was all fantasy on Sara's part?' Burden said. 'She's not exactly a *little* girl.'

'Nor were Freud's patients little girls by the time they came to him.'

Wexford said, 'I think Sara had a daughter's fantasy about her father. When she was older she read Freud. She read books on incest too – they're all there in her bedroom. There's a mention of father–daughter incest in the ARRIA constitution. Did she read that too or did she write it? At any rate, *in her mind* she was heavily involved with her father, far more involved with him than he was with her.'

'How do you know the seduction didn't really take place? Men do commit incest with their daughters. I mean, how could Freud have known one of those thirteen wasn't fantasising but telling the truth?'

'I can't answer that,' Wexford said, 'but I can tell you it never happened to Sara. She isn't the kind of girl to whom it happens. She isn't ignorant or obtuse or cowed or dependent.

This seduction, or apparent seduction, followed a classic pattern as laid down in the books. The girl doesn't struggle or fight or scream. She doesn't want to make a disturbance. At the first opportunity she tells her mother and her mother reacts with rage, reproaches, accusations of the girl's provocative behaviour. Now Joy, as we might expect, fitted beautifully into the classic pattern. But Sara? If it had really happened wouldn't Sara, a leading member of ARRIA, a militant feminist, have fought and screamed? She was very handy with a knife, wasn't she? And she's the last person to care about making a disturbance in a household, either emotional or physical. As for telling her mother – Sara tell her mother? There's been no real communication between them for years. She despises her mother. If she'd told anyone it would have been her brother Kevin. No, there was no seduction, for if there had been she would have kept the experience secret to use against her father, not come running with it to Joy.

'It was Sara who stabbed Colin Budd, of course. It happened, if you remember, the night before Milvey started dragging Green Pond. Sara retrieved the bag after dark, went up to the forest to do it and put the bag inside a plastic sack. When Budd came along she was waiting to catch the bus that would take her to the other end of Kingsmarkham, near enough to the Forby road and Green Pond Hall. The last thing she wanted was Budd taking an interest in her. Besides, she had indoctrinated herself to be always on the watch for sexist approaches. What was she doing but going about her private business? And this man has to treat her as if her primary function in this world was to be an object for his diversion and entertainment. No doubt she also lost her nerve. She stabbed him with a penknife.'

'If it was all fantasy,' said Burden, reverting to the analysis of Sara Williams's character, 'why did she warn Veronica? Why warn her of something that would never happen?'

'You're supposing fantasy is something "made up", so therefore something the fantasiser herself doesn't believe in?'

'Well, does she? Did Sara convince herself?'

'Yes and no. She's admitted to me nothing ever happened. On the other hand, I wouldn't be surprised if tomorrow she says it did and believes it herself. Having this secret to communicate, this awful and horrifying secret, must have much increased her ascendancy over Veronica. It enhanced her power. Veronica was very frightened of her, you see, full of admiration, awe almost, but even before the killing of Rodney becoming unnerved by the whole set-up.'

Wendy had been sent for and for once had been calm, sensible, steady. He had considered the atmosphere of his office more relaxing than one of those stark interview rooms. Marion and Polly were seated side by side and Veronica a little apart from everyone until Wexford came in. Little Miss Muffet and the great spider who sat down beside her. Only there was no frightening her away. It would be a long time now before Veronica Williams could get away.

She was very pale. Her hair, he noticed, was a couple of inches longer than when he had first seen her, six inches longer than the crop of the beach photograph. Had she been growing it in imitation of her idol and model Sara? He had asked her when she first met her half-sister.

'It was September.' Her voice was so soft he had to ask her to repeat it. 'September – a year ago,' she said.

'And you met how often after that? Once a week? More?'

Very quietly, 'More.'

He extracted from her the information that they constantly spoke on the phone. It was like a game sometimes, Sara phoning and saying she would be in Liskeard Avenue in five minutes, she phoning Sara to say if Sara was careful not to be seen she could come and watch Rodney and Wendy watching *her* play tennis.

'It stopped being a game, though, didn't it? On April the fifteenth it stopped?'

She nodded and her body convulsed in an involuntary shiver. Wendy said, 'Why did you always do everything she said? Why did you tell her everything?'

How could she answer that?

'You told her you were coming here to confess your part in it, didn't you, Veronica?' Wexford spoke very gently.

Her eyes went to Wendy. 'I thought the police would arrest my mother.'

A small spark of triumph on Wendy's doleful face. In these

unbelievable circumstances her years of devotion were rewarded . . .

Wexford surfaced from his reverie to see Burden depositing three beer cans in front of them from a tray laden with the kind of junk food he lived on while Jenny was away.

'Wake up!'

'Sorry.'

'Look, if there was no incest and therefore no renewed assault from Rodney to be feared, if there was no threat to Veronica, what was the motive for killing him? All through this case we could never come up with any sort of solid motive. Or are you saying a psychopath doesn't need a motive – at any rate not a motive understood by normal people?'

Wexford said slowly, 'I've suggested to you that there was a good deal of calculation in Sara's behaviour, some of it of an apparently incomprehensible kind. Her original concealment of the body, for instance, and later her anxiety for it to be found. I've also made it clear – rather to your joint disapproval, I think – that I don't feel much sympathy towards Sara. And this is because I feel she had no justification for what she did.

'She had a motive all right, and as calculated and coldblooded a motive as any poisoner polishing off an old relation for his money.'

'But Rodney didn't have any money to leave, did he?' Burden objected.

'Not so's you'd notice, though the manager of the Anglian-Victoria has shown me how a nice little bit was accumulating in the account from which the two joint accounts were fed. Enough, anyway, for him to recommend that Rodney put it into investments. Still, it wasn't for a possible inheritance that Sara killed him, though money was her motive.'

'Not a cash gain though, I think,' said the doctor.

Wexford turned to Burden. 'You raised this very subject not long ago, Mike. That was when you thought you were going to have a daughter – and that's relevant too. You talked about her going to university and applying for government grants. Do you remember?'

'I suppose so. I don't see where the relevance comes in.'

'Sara wants to be a doctor,' said Wexford. 'Well, *wanted* to be, I should say. It was a driving ambition with her. And increasingly hard though this is becoming, she knew she had the ability to get into medical school. Her parents, however, discouraged her. And it must have looked to her at that stage as if this was a classic case of opposition to daughter's ambitions simply because she was a daughter and not a son, because in fact she was a woman. On Joy's part it probably was. Very likely she wouldn't have cared for Sara to achieve greater success and have a more prestigious profession than Kevin.

'At first this parental opposition didn't much worry Sara. I'm speaking, of course, about this time last year. Sara remembered her brother getting a place at Keele and the form of application for a grant coming from Sussex County Council Education Committee to her father. At the time she didn't take much notice. Certainly she didn't see the completed form. But she knew that the greater the parental income the smaller the grant would be and that with the form there came a form of certificate of parental employment the parent's employer had to complete detailing his gross salary, overtime, bonus or commissions and his taxable emoluments. Now, Mike, you'll recall that certificate in your own case and sending it to the Mid-Sussex Constabulary when you applied for grants for John and Pat?'

Burden nodded. 'I'm beginning to see the light here.'

'Twelve months ago Sara met Veronica. Gradually, when the shock of that encounter began to recede, when it provided the solution to certain unexplained anomalies, shall we say, Sara saw the cold reality for what it was. Her father might talk about not wanting his daughter to be a doctor for aesthetic reasons, for reasons of suitability, she would get married and her education be wasted, et cetera. He might talk that way but the reason behind the talk was very different. Finding that he had lied both to her mother and Veronica's about what his position and his earnings were, she had taken steps to discover what he did and what he earned. Now she understood. If he filled in the grant application form for her he would have to declare to the Sussex County Council that his income was not £10,000 a year but two and a half times that, and there would be no way he could deceive the authority as he had deceived

382

her mother because his employers, Sevensmith Harding, would have to complete the certificate of parental income from employment.

'Now according to the grants department's contribution scales, a parent earning £10,000 per annum would have to contribute to medical school costs only something in the region of £470 but a parent earning £25,000 a sum of nearly £2000. Rodney had two homes and two families, he was already paying out this sort of sum for Kevin at Keele – remember he had to tell the grants department the truth, whatever he told his wives – and Sara could see the way the wind was blowing. She could see there was no way he would part with £2000 a year for her benefit. And when she asked him point blank if he would fill in the form when it came he told her he wouldn't – she would never make a doctor and he was doing her a kindness in not encouraging her.'

'What a bastard,' said Crocker.

Wexford shrugged. 'The mistake is ours when we deceive ourselves about parent–child relationships. When we keep up the belief that all parents love their children and want what's best for them.'

'Surely, though, if Sara had talked about this at school or discussed it with some sympathetic officer at the grants department, a way could have been found for her to get a grant, bypassing Rodney? There must be many cases where a parent withholds consent and won't complete a grant application.'

'Probably. But Sara is only eighteen. And remember that to have done what you suggest she would have to reveal that her father was a liar and a cheat, that he deceived her mother, that he was a bigamist. And how long would all this take? Would it mean her waiting a year? And what of her place at St Biddulph's, a teaching hospital where places are like gold dust and where they keep a reserve list bursting with applicants dying to be accepted? What she decided on instead was, first, persuasion and if that failed, blackmail.'

'She told him that if he didn't consent to fill in the form she'd tell Joy about Wendy and get Veronica to tell Wendy about Joy?'

'She was *going* to tell him that. She had a bit of time though.

383

She hadn't even sat her A-levels. The grant form wouldn't come till July. And she also had the incest. Of course, it had never taken place but Joy thought it had, Veronica was scared stiff it had. If all else failed she might be able to use it as another weapon in the blackmail stock-pile. That was why she was pleased to see how effective her warnings had been in Veronica's case. Veronica was beginning to be afraid of the affectionate attention Rodney paid her. Veronica didn't want to be alone with him and if she had to be she wanted him disarmed and immobilised. Sara saw to that with the Phanodorm, and increased Veronica's fear by the seriousness of taking such a step.

'But how much simpler, after all, to kill him! And there he was, lying asleep, the potential destroyer of her future. Kill him now, in this room which will soon be made pure and immaculate, cleansed of all signs of violent death. Rid the world of him, seize your opportunity. And perhaps it would also be a heroic act. Hadn't there almost been a clause in the ARRIA constitution demanding a man's death as qualification for entry? Veronica will help because Veronica also hates him now and is mortally afraid of him . . .

'But suppose they never find the body? Suppose the weeks go by and July comes and August and with them the grant application and you can't fill in the section that says "Father, if deceased the fact should be stated . . ." because only you and Veronica know he is deceased? You have finished your A-levels and the time is going by – the moment has come to take steps for that body to be found without more delay.'

'You might say,' said Crocker, 'that the murder was both coolly premeditated and carried out on an impulse.'

'You might. Because of what Sara is, a highly complex personality, this was all kinds of a murder. A ritualistic killing – remember that Veronica was required to stab him too. A revenge killing – Sara had more than half-convinced herself and wholly convinced Veronica of the reality of the incest. When she stabbed Rodney she was a woman out of classical myth, she was Beatrice Cenci. It was an *experimental* killing, a kind of vivisection, carried out by Sara the scientist, to see if it would work, to see if it could be done. It was murder from disgust, from disillusionment. Rodney, whom she had once worshipped, was just a squalid bigamist with another daughter, a copy of herself, he loved as much or more than he had ever loved her. But above all, in spite of all those other factors, it was murder for gain, carried out so that she might satisfy her ambition at all costs. All in all, I don't think that's the sort of person I'd care to have as my family physician, still less performing surgery on me and mine. So perhaps Rodney was right when he told Sara she was an unsuitable candidate for medical school. Who knows? Perhaps it wasn't simply meanness with him, he wasn't quite the bastard you make out. Perhaps he sensed in that daughter of his, without ever examining his conclusions, traits in her character that were abnormal, that were destructive, and it was to these he referred when he said she would never make a doctor.'

Wexford got up.

'I shall call it a day,' he said. 'I shall go to the wife of my bosom the same as I ought to go.'

Burden began tidying the room, putting things on a tray. 'And tomorrow the wife of my bosom comes home to me.' He looked pleased, satisfied, hopeful, as if there had been no five months' long disruption of his happiness. 'One of her old pupils at Haldon Finch went in to see her and the baby. An ARRIA member. She told Jenny the raven bit means they're cleaning up the carrion men have left behind in the world. We did wonder.'

'Ah,' Wexford paused in the doorway. 'Something I nearly forgot to tell you. About Williams's young girlfriend . . .'

They looked at him. 'Williams didn't have a young girl-friend,' Burden said.

'Of course he did. She had nothing to do with his death, nothing to do with this case, so she hardly concerned us. But a man like Williams – it was in his nature, inevitable. Both his wives knew it, they sensed it. Probably he'd always had a young girlfriend, a succession of them.

'This one – hers were the other set of prints on the car. No wonder she said her dad didn't want me to take them. They met at Sevensmith Harding, of course. In the office.'

'Jane Gardner . . . '

'That's who he had his date with on April the fifteenth in Myringham. Join her for her baby-sitting, then spend the night

385

together at the Cheriton Forest Hotel. Why else did he have a bag with him with a single change of underwear and a toothbrush and toothpaste? But the sleeping pills overcame him as he was driving through Pomfret, and instead of going on to meet Jane he was just able to make it to his own house. What she thought was that he'd stood her up. Then, when he disappeared, that he'd gone off with another woman. I had a word with her this morning and she admitted it – no more need to conceal it now we'd made an arrest.'

'What put you on to her?'

'I don't know. Guesswork. She was the only person I ever spoke to who had a good word for Rodney Williams.'

Wexford let himself out, closing Burden's blue front door behind him.

THE
VEILED ONE

For Simon

1

The woman was lying dead on the floor when he came in. She was already dead and covered up from head to toe but Wexford only knew that afterwards, not at the time. He looked back and realised the chances he had missed but it was useless doing that – he hadn't known and that was all. He had been preoccupied, thinking of an assortment of things: his wife's birthday present that was in the bag he carried, modern architecture, yesterday's gale which had blown down his garden fence, this car park that he was entering from the descending lift.

Even the lift was not as other lifts elsewhere, being of rattling grey metal undecorated except by graffiti. Irregular printing from whose letters the red paint had dripped like trails of blood, informed him that someone called Steph was 'a diesel dyke'. He wondered what that meant, wondered too where he could look it up. The lift was going down. Into the bowels of the earth, he thought, and there was something intestine-like about this place with its winding passages and its strictly one-way direction. Perhaps, though, it was better to excavate for this purpose than to erect above the ground, especially as any extraneous building would inevitably have been in the style of the shopping centre itself – ramparts, perhaps, or the walls of a city, some quaint attempt at a reconstruction of the Middle Ages.

He had just come from the Barringdean Centre, the new shopping complex built to look like a castle. That was the style modern planners thought suitable on the outskirts of an ancient Sussex town where nothing genuinely medieval remained. Perhaps that was why. Anyway the centre looked less like a real castle than a toy one, the kind you have to assemble from a hundred plastic bits and pieces. Shaped like a capital 'I', it had four towers on the ends and a row of little turrets along its length. Looking back at it, he half-expected bowmen to appear at the Gothic windows and arrows to fly.

But inside all was of the late twentieth century, only to be expressed in eighties words – amenities, facilities, enclaves and approaches. A great fountain played in the central concourse, its waterspouts almost reaching but not quite touching the pendent chandelier of shards of frosted glass. Wexford had entered at this point by the automatic doors and approach from the glass covered way. He had gone up the escalator where a breath of spray stung his fingers on the hand-rail, realised at the top that the shop he sought must be downstairs after all – was not Suzanne the hairdresser who also sold wigs and leotards, or Linen That Shows or Laceworks – and went down again by the escalator to the Mandala. This was a set-piece in the area at the other end with potted plants in concentric circles – brown chrysanthemums, yellow chrysanthemums, white poinsettias and those plants with cherry-like orange fruit that are really a kind of potato. The crowds were thinning out; it was getting on for six when the centre closed up. Shop assistants were weary and growing impatient and even the flowers looked tired.

A Tesco superstore filled the whole crosspiece of the 'I' on both floors at this end, British Home Stores the other. Between them was Boots the Chemist with W. H. Smith facing it, the Mandala in between. Down a side passage that led from the main above-ground car park, children still played on a fat zebra made of black and white leather, a hi-tech climbing frame, a dragon on wheels. Wexford found the shop where Dora, a week ago, had pointed out to him in the window a sweater she liked. Addresses it was called, with the chocolate shop next to it and a wool and crafts place Knits 'n' Kits on the other side. Wexford was not a man to hesitate or deliberate over a matter like this. Besides, Demeter the health-food shop opposite was already closing and the jewellers next to it were lowering the fancy gilt latticework bars inside the window.

He went into Addresses and bought the sweater, the transaction taking four minutes.

By now shoppers were being hustled out, even Grub 'n' Grains the café having someone suspiciously like a bouncer on its door. And the lights were dimming, the leaping spouts of the fountain slowing . . . subsiding, until the ruffled surface of the pool into which it played became glasslike. Wexford sat down on one of the wrought-iron benches that were ranged along the aisle. He let the crowd make its way out through the various arteries that led from this central column and then he too left by the automatic doors into the covered way.

A great exodus of cars from the above-ground car parks was under way. At the far end he looked back. Flags flew from all the turrets along the centre's spine, red and yellow triangular pennants which had fluttered all day in the tail-end of the gale but drooped now in the stillness of a dark, misty evening. Slits of light still showed in the narrow pointed-topped Gothic windows. Wexford found himself alone here at the entrance to the underground car park, the only evidence of those hordes of shoppers being their abandoned trolleys. Hundreds of these jostled each other in higgledy-piggledy fashion, and would no doubt remain here till morning. A notice informed their users that the police took a serious view of those who allowed a shopping trolley to obstruct the roadway. Not for the first time, Wexford reflected that the police had more important things to do – though how much more important he was only to realise later.

The planners had decreed that this car park must be subterranean. He came into the lift and the stairs by way of a metal door whose clanging reverberations could still be heard as the lift descended. Wexford heard its echoes and at the same time feet pounding up the stairs, the feet of someone running hard; that was something else he remembered later. Down here it was always cold, always imbued with an acrid chemical smell as of metal filings awash in oil. Wexford stepped out of the lift at the second of four levels and came into the wide aisle between the avenue of pillars. Most of the cars were gone by now and in their absence the place seemed more desolate, uglier, more of a denial. Of course it was foolish and fanciful to think like this – a denial of what, for instance? The car park

393

merely served a purpose, filled a need in the most practical utilitarian way. What would he have had instead? White paint? Murals? Tiles on the wall depicting some episode of local history? That would have been almost worse. It was irrational that the place reminded him of a picture it did not in the least resemble – John Martin's illustration of 'Pandemonium' for *Paradise Lost*.

His car was parked at this end. He didn't have to walk the length of the place – under the low concrete ceiling, between the squat uprights, into the wells of shadow – but merely cross over to the bays along the left-hand wall. There was an echo down here and the sound of his footsteps rang back at him. If his powers of observation, in general so sharp, were less acute than usual, at least he noticed the number of cars that remained and their makes and colours. He saw the three between him and the middle of the car park where one ramp came up and another went down: one on the left, a red Metro, and diagonally opposite it on the right, parked side by side, a silver Escort and a dark blue Lancia. The woman's body lay between these two, closer to the Escort, concealed by a shroud of dirty brown velvet which made it look like a heap of rags.

Or so they told him afterwards. At the time he saw only the cars, the colours of their bodywork not entirely drained by the cold strip lights but muted, made pale. He lifted the boot-lid and put inside it the dark blue bag with 'Addresses' stamped on it in gold. As he closed it a car went by him, a red car going rather too fast. There were more red cars than any other colour, he had read somewhere. Motorists are aggressive and red is the colour of aggression. He got into the car, started it and looked at the clock. This was something he always did quite naturally, looked at the clock when he started the ignition. Seven minutes past six. He put the automatic shift into drive and began the climb out of the earth's bowels.

On each level the way out wound round half the floor-space at the opposite end from where the lift and stairs were, wound round anticlockwise and turned right up the ramp to the next level. He passed the three cars – the two on the left first, then the red Metro. Of course he didn't look to the right where the woman's body was. Why should he? His exit route took him round the loop, on to the straight on the other side. Not a car remained here; the bays were empty. He climbed up to the first level, looped round and out into the night. There might have been cars remaining on that level, but he hadn't noticed and he could only remember the red Vauxhall Cavalier with a girl in the driving-seat facing him as he came up the ramp. She pulled out and followed him, impatient to be off and exceed the speed limit. Teenage girls at the wheels of cars were worse than the boys these days, Burden said. Wexford emerged into the open air, up the ramp. Most of the shoppers were gone; it was ten past six, they closed the centre at six and only the last stragglers remained, moving towards cars in the above-ground parking areas. The girl overtook him as soon as she could.

Wexford had pulled in and slowed to allow her to do so and it was then that he saw the woman emerge from the glass-covered way. He observed her because she was the only person to approach the car park and because she wasn't hurrying but walking in a controlled, measured fashion threading her way between the trolleys, fending off with her foot one that rattled into her path. She was a small, slender, upright woman in coat and hat carrying two bags of shopping, both red Tesco carriers. The metal door clanged behind her and he drove on across the wide nearly empty car-less space where the mist hung as a glaucous clouding of the air, out of the exit gates and half a mile on into Castle Street and the town. The traffic lights in the High Street outside the Olive and Dove turned red as he approached. The handbrake on, he looked down at the evening paper he had bought before he drove to the centre but so far had not even glanced at. His own daughter's famous face looked back at him, affording him only a mild jolt. Pictures of Sheila in the papers weren't unusual. Seldom, however, were they accompanied by revelations of this sort. There was another photograph beside the portrait; Wexford looked at that one too and with lips pursed drew in a long breath. The lights slipped through amber into green.

The Barringdean Shopping Centre was on the outskirts of Kingsmarkham but nevertheless within the town. It had been built on the site of the old bus station when the new bus station was put up on the site of the old maltings. Everyone went shopping there and the retailers in the High Street suffered. By day it was a hive of bees buzzing in and swarming out, but at night the centre was left to its fate – two break-ins during its first year of life. Apart from the security men and store detectives within the centre itself, there was a caretaker who called himself the supervisor and who patrolled the grounds or, more usually, sat in a small concrete office next door to the car-park lift-shaft, reading the *Star* and listening to tapes of *Les Misérables* and *Edwin Drood*. At six-fifteen each evening David Sedgeman performed his last duty of the day as Barringdean Shopping Centre supervisor. He put the trolleys into some sort of order, slotting one inside another to form long articulated carriages, and closed the gates of the pedestrian entrance in Pomeroy Road, fastened the bolts and attached the padlock. These gates were of steel mesh in steel frames and the fence was eight feet high. Then Sedgeman went off home. If anyone remained about the grounds, they had to leave by the traffic exit.

The residents of Pomeroy Road had benefited from the removal of the bus station. It was quieter now that no buses turned in and departed from six in the morning until midnight. Instead there were all the shoppers coming and going, but soon after six they had all left. On the opposite side of the street short terraces of Victorian houses alternated with small blocks of flats. Directly facing the gates, in one of these houses, Archie Greaves lived with his daughter and son-in-law. He spent a large part of his days sitting in the downstairs bay window watching the people; it was far more entertaining for him now than in the bus station era. He watched the people go into the phone box just outside the gates on the right-hand side and some of them must have seen him watching them, for more than once he had been approached, accosted by a tap on the window and asked for change for the phone. He watched the shoppers arrive and the shoppers leave; it amused him to make a mental note of arrivals and check on their departure. He recognised certain regulars and because he was a lonely man – his daughter and her husband out all day – thought of them almost as his friends.

This evening was misty. It had got dark very early and by six was black as midnight, the mist very apparent where lights caught it and made a greenish shimmer. The gutters of Pomeroy Road were clogged with fallen leaves, the plane trees almost bare. Beyond the open gates lamps lit the car parks that were fast emptying and in the shopping centre building itself, where the turrets were silhouetted black like the teeth of a saw against the streaked cloudy purple of the sky, the lights were beginning to dim. Before many more minutes had passed by, they would all have gone out.

Pedestrians had been coming out sporadically ever since Archie first went to sit there at four o'clock. His breath clouded the glass and he rubbed it with his jacket sleeve, taking his arm away in time to see someone running out of the gates. A young man it was – a boy to him – empty handed, going as if all the devils in hell were after him. Or store detectives, Archie thought doubtfully. Once he had seen a woman running with people pursuing her and he guessed she had been shoplifting. This boy he had never seen before; he was a stranger to him and he passed out of sight under the plane trees into the misty dark.

Archie hadn't put a light on because he could see better sitting in darkness. An old-fashioned electric fire made a glow in the room behind him. No one was pursuing the boy – perhaps he had only been in a hurry. The people who were leaving at a more leisurely pace had looked at him without much curiosity and, like Archie, expected to see retribution coming. But the darkness absorbed them as well. He saw a car come up out of the mouth of the underground park and then another. The lights that illuminated the shopping centre turrets went out. Then Archie saw David Sedgeman appear from behind the angle of the concrete wall with the padlock keys in his hand. Because of the mist and because Archie hadn't put his light on, Sedgeman had to peer to see the pale blur of the old man's face and then he nodded and raised his hand. Archie gave him a salute. Sedgeman closed the gates, looped the chain through the steel mesh, fastened and locked the padlock. Then he shot both bolts, one at the bottom and another a foot above his head. Before he went back, he gave Archie another wave.

This was the signal for Archie to get moving. He got up and went to the kitchen where he made himself a mug of tea with a tea-bag and took two chocolate chip cookies out of the biscuit tin. No potatoes to peel tonight because his daughter and her husband would be out at a friend's son's engagement party. There would be no cooked supper for Archie, but at his age he preferred little snacks of tea and biscuits and bits of chocolate anyway. Back in the front room he put the television on, though he had missed most of the six o'clock news and the bit he got was all about the trial of terrorists and some actress damaging Ministry of Defence property. He didn't turn it off but just turned down the sound and switched on the central light. Archie had read somewhere that watching television in the dark turns you blind eventually.

The light was also on in the phone box now. It came on at six-thirty when the box hadn't been vandalised and the lamp smashed as sometimes happened. Archie sat on the window seat once more, one eye watching the street and another the screen, hoping something more cheerful would come on soon. By now the shopping centre was in darkness, though two lamps were still alight in the open-air car parks. A middle-aged man, one of the neighbours, came along with his dog which lifted its leg against the red metal door of the call box. Archie felt like banging on the window but knew it would do no good. Dog and owner went off into the mist while Archie drank his tea, ate the second biscuit and wondered whether he should get himself a third or wait an hour. Weather forecast now; he couldn't hear it, but he could see by all those little clouds and whirly lines that it was going to be the mixture as before.

Outside was silence, darkness, mist which moved and cleared and rolled sluggishly back, which the lights – half-obscured by plane-tree branches – turned to a watery, acid-green phosphorescence. The darkness was deep in the tarmac desert, nothing visible but two islanded spots of light and now these also went out . . . one, two . . . leaving blackness that met a dark grey but luminous sky. Only the lamps of Pomeroy Street and a ray or so from the mouth of the underground car park faintly lit the area behind the gates. And into this a little woman walked from behind the concrete wall, having perhaps come from the car-park lift, Archie thought. She walked a few yards in one direction to stare into the blackness, then she turned and gazed towards the gates and him. She seemed to be looking to see if there was anyone about, or looking for someone or something. There was anger, repressed and contained, revealed in the slow deliberate way she moved – he could tell that even in the dark.

She might have a car in there and be unable to get it started. There was nothing he could do and now she had gone again, the wall cutting her off from his view. Archie switched off the television, for he could stand no more of what had appeared silently on the screen – starving Africans with pot-bellied dying babies, more of those people that he in his impotence and penury could not aid. He looked back at the empty stillness outside. Fetching the third biscuit might be postponed for an hour or so. He had to find ways to fill up his evening, for he couldn't very well go to bed until nine which was more than two hours away. The chances were that nothing more would happen out there until eight next morning when the shopping centre opened, nothing at all except cars passing and maybe a couple of people coming to use the phone box. He was thinking this, reflecting on it, when the woman appeared again, walking now in the stalking single-minded fashion of a cat homing in on its prey.

When she came up to the gates, she got hold of them as if expecting they would open, as if the padlock would fall apart and the bolts slide back. Archie got to his feet and leaned forward on the window sill. The woman was much too short to reach the top bolt; she seemed now to have realised that the padlock was fastened and the key gone, and she began to rattle the gates. Her eyes were not on him but on the phone box, which was only a few yards from her but tantalisingly outside those gates.

She shook the gates more and more violently and they clanged and rattled. Anyone could see it was useless doing that because of the bolts and the padlock, and Archie began to wonder, because of the sudden and violent change in her demeanour, if she wasn't quite all there, if she were a bit mad . . . crazy. His reaction to anything like that would usually be to ignore it, to shut his eyes or go away. But it was the phone box she wanted; all this frenzy was on account of not being able to reach the phone box. There were always the neighbours – let someone else attend to it, someone younger and stronger. Only no one ever did. Archie sometimes thought a person could be murdered in Pomeroy Street in full view, in broad daylight, and no one would do anything. The woman was shouting now – well, screaming. She was stamping her feet and shaking the gates and roaring at the top of her voice, yelling things Archie couldn't make out but which he heard all right when he put his cap on and his raincoat round his shoulders and was making his way out on to the pavement.

'The police! The police! I've got to get the police! I've got to phone. I've got to get the police!'

Archie crossed the road. He said, 'Making all that fuss won't help. You calm down now. What's the matter with you?'

'I've got to phone the police! There's someone dead in there. I've got to phone the police – there's a woman and they've tried to cut her head off!'

Archie went cold all over; his throat came up and he tasted tea and chocolate. He thought, my heart, I'm too old for this. He said feebly, 'Stop shaking those gates. Now, come on, you stop it! I can't let you out.'

'I want the police,' she shrieked and fell to lean heavily against the gates, hanging there with her fingers pushed through the wire mesh. The final clang reverberated and died away, as she sobbed harshly against the cold metal.

'I can go and phone them,' Archie said and he went back indoors, leaving her sagged there, still, her hands hooked on the wire like someone shot while trying to escape.

2

The phone rang while he was in the middle of going through it all with Dora. Supper had been eaten without enthusiasm and the bag containing Dora's birthday sweater lay unregarded on the seat of a chair. He had turned the evening paper front-page downwards but – unable to resist the horrid fascination of it – picked it up again.

'Mind you, I knew things weren't going well with her and Andrew,' Dora said.

'Knowing one's daughter's marriage is going through a bad patch is a far cry from reading in the paper that she's getting a divorce.'

'I think you mind about that more than about her coming up in court.'

Wexford made himself look coolly at the newspaper. The lead story was the trial of three men who had tried to blow up the Israeli Embassy and there was something too about a by-election, but the page was Sheila's. There were two photographs. The top picture showed a wire fence – not unlike the fence that surrounded the shopping complex he had recently left, only this one was topped with coils of razor wire. The modern world, he sometimes thought, was full of wire fences. The one in the picture had been mutilated and a flap hung loose from the centre of it, leaving a gaping hole through which a waste of mud could be seen with a hanger-like edifice in the middle of it. From the darkish background in the other photograph his daughter's lovely face looked out, wide-eyed, apprehensive, to a father's eye, aghast at the headlong rush of events. Wisps of pale curly hair escaped from under her woolly cap. The headline said only: 'Sheila Cuts the Wire'; the story beneath told the rest of it, giving among all the painful details of arrest and magistrates' court appearance the surely gratuitous information that the actress currently appearing in the television serialisation of *Lady Audley's Secret* was seeking a divorce from her husband, businessman Andrew Thorverton.

'I would have liked to be told, I suppose,' Wexford said. 'About the divorce, I mean. I wouldn't expect her to tell us she was going to chop up the fence round a nuclear bomber base. We'd have tried to stop her.'

'We'd have tried to stop her getting a divorce.'

It was then that the phone rang. Since Sheila had been released on bail, pending a later court appearance, Wexford thought it must be her at the other end. He was already hearing her voice in his head, the breathy self-reproach as she tried to persuade her parents she didn't know how the paper had got that report about her divorce . . . she was overcome . . . she was flabbergasted . . . it was all beyond her. And as for the wire-cutting . . .

Not Sheila though. Inspector Michael Burden.

'Mike?'

The voice was cool and a bit curt, anxiety underlying it, but he nearly always sounded like that. 'There's a dead woman in the shopping centre car park, the underground one. I haven't seen her yet, but there's no chance it's anything but murder.'

'I was there myself,' Wexford said wonderingly. 'I only left a couple of hours ago.'

'That's OK. Nobody thinks you did it.'

Burden had got a lot sharper since his second marriage. Time was when such a rejoinder would never have entered his head.

'I'll come over. Who's there now?'

'Me – or I will be in five minutes. Archbold. Prentiss.' Prentiss was the scene-of-crimes man, Archbold a young DC. 'Sumner-Quist. Sir Hilary's away on his hols.'

In November? Well, people went away at any old time these days. Wexford rather liked the eminent and occasionally outrageous pathologist, Sir Hilary Tremlett, finding Dr Basil Sumner-Quist less congenial.

402

'There's no identification problem,' said Burden. 'We know who she is. Her name's Gwen Robson, Mrs. Late fifties. Address up at Highlands. A woman called Sanders found her and got hold of someone in Pomeroy Street who phoned us.'

It was five past eight. 'I may be a long time,' Wexford said to Dora. 'At any rate I won't be back soon.'

'I'm wondering if I ought to phone Sheila.'

'Let her phone us,' said Sheila's father, hardening his heart. He picked up the bag with Dora's present in it and hid it at the back of the hall cupboard. The birthday wasn't until tomorrow anyway.

The car-park entrance was blocked with police cars. Lights had appeared from somewhere, the place blazed with light. Someone had shot the linked shopping trolleys across the parking area to clear a space and trolleys stood about everywhere but at a distance, like a watching crowd of robots. The gates in the fence at the pedestrian entrance in Pomeroy Road stood wide open. Wexford pushed trolleys aside, spinning them out of his way, squeezed between the cars, opened the lift door and tried to summon the lift. It didn't come, so he walked down the two levels. The three cars were still there – the red Metro, silver Escort and dark blue Lancia – but the blue one had been backed out of its parking slot up against the wall and reversed into the middle of the aisle, no doubt to allow room for pathologist, scene-of-crimes officer and photographer to scrutinise the body that lay close up against the offside of the silver Escort. Wexford hesitated a moment, then walked towards the group of people and the thing on the concrete floor.

Burden got to his feet as Wexford approached and Archbold who had old-fashioned manners, nodded and said, 'Sir!' Sumner-Quist didn't bother to look round. The fact that he happened at that moment to move his shoulder so that the dead woman's face and neck were revealed was, Wexford thought, purely fortuitous. The face bore the unmistakable signs of someone who has met her death by strangulation. It was bluish, bloated, horrified, and the mark on her neck of whatever was responsible for her asphyxiation was so deep that it had more the appearance of a circular cut, as if the blade of a knife had been run round throat and nape. Blazing lights in a place usually feebly lit showed up all the horror of her and of her surroundings – stained and discoloured concrete, dirty metal, litter sprawling across the floor.

The dead woman wore a brown tweed coat with fur collar and her hat of brown and fawn checked tweed with narrow brim was still on her grey curly hair. Apparently small and slight, she had stick-like legs in brown lacy tights or stockings and on her feet brown lace-up low-heeled walking shoes. Wedding and engagement rings were on her left hand.

'The Escort's her car,' Burden said. 'She had the keys to it in her hand when she was killed. Or that's the way it looks, the keys were under the body. There are two bags of groceries in the boot. It looks as if she put the bags in the boot, closed the boot-lid, came round to unlock the driver's door and then someone attacked her from behind.'

'Attacked her with what?'

'A thin length of cord, maybe. Like in thuggee.' Burden's general knowledge as well as sharpness of intellect had been enhanced by marriage. But it was the birth of his son, twenty years after his first family, that had made him abandon the smart suits he had formerly favoured for wear even on occasions like this one. Jeans were what the inspector had on this evening, though jeans which rather oddly bore knife creases and contrasted not altogether happily with his camel-hair jacket.

'More like wire than a cord,' Wexford said.

The remark had an electric effect on Dr Sumner-Quist who jumped up and spoke to Wexford as if they were in a drawing room, not a car park, as if there were no body on the floor and this were a social occasion, a cocktail party maybe: 'Talking of wire, isn't that frightfully pretty TV girl who's all over the paper this evening your daughter?'

Wexford didn't like to imagine what effect the epithet 'TV girl' would have had on Sheila. He nodded.

'I thought so. I said to my wife it was so, unlikely as it seemed. OK, I've done all I can here. If the man with the camera's done his stuff, you can move her as far as I'm concerned. Myself, I think it's a pity these people don't go cutting the wire in Russia.'

Wexford made no reply to this. 'How long has she been dead?'

'You want miracles, don't you? You think I can tell you that after five minutes' dekko? Well, she was a goner by six, I reckon. That do you?'

And he had been here at seven minutes past . . . He lifted up the grubby brown velvet curtain that lay in a heap a few inches from the dead woman's feet. 'What's this?'

'It was covering the body, sir,' Archbold said.

'Covering it as might be a blanket, do you mean? Or right over the head and feet?'

'One foot was sticking out and the woman who found her pulled it back a bit to see the face.'

'Yes – who was it found her?'

'A Mrs Dorothy Sanders. That's her car over there, the red one. She found the body, but it was a man called Greaves in Pomeroy Street phoned us. Davidson's talking to him now. He found Mrs Sanders screaming and shaking the gates fit to break them down. She went raving mad because the phone box is outside the gates and she couldn't get out. Diana Pettit took a statement from her and drove her home.'

Still holding the curtain, Wexford tried the boot-lid of the red Metro. There was shopping inside that too, food in two red Tesco carriers and a clear plastic bag full of hanks of grey knitting-wool done up with string like a parcel. He looked up at the sound of the lift, an echo from it or reverberation or something; you could always hear it. The door to the lift had opened and a man appeared. He was walking very diffidently and hesitantly towards them and when his eyes met Wexford's he stopped altogether. Archbold went up to him and said something. He was a young man with a pale heavy face and dark moustache and he was dressed in a way which while quite suitable for a man of Wexford's own age, looked incongruous on someone of – what? Twenty-one? Twenty-two? The V-necked grey pullover, striped tie and grey flannel trousers reminded Wexford of a school uniform.

'I've come for the car,' he said.

'One of these cars is yours?'

'The red one, the Metro. It's my mother's. My mother said to come over and bring it back.'

His eyes went fearfully to where the body lay, the body that was now entirely covered by a sheet. It lay unattended –

pathologist, photographer and policeman having all moved away towards the central aisle or the exits. Wexford noted that awe-stricken glance, the quick withdrawing of the eyes and jerk of the head. He said, 'Can I have your name, sir?'

'Sanders, Clifford Sanders.'

Burden asked, 'Are you some relation of Mrs Dorothy Sanders?'

'Her son.'

'I'll come back with you,' Wexford said. 'I'll follow you; I'd like to talk to your mother.' He let Clifford Sanders, walking edgily, pass out of earshot and then said to Burden, 'Mrs Robson's next-of-kin. . . ?'

'There's a husband, but he hasn't been told. He'll have to make a formal identification. I thought of going over there now.'

'Do we know who that blue Lancia belongs to?'

Burden shook his head. 'It's a bit odd, that. Only shoppers use the car park – I mean, who else would want to? And the centre's been closed over two hours. If it belongs to the killer, why didn't he or she drive it away? When I first saw it I thought maybe it wouldn't start, but we had to move it and it started first time.'

'Better have the owner traced,' said Wexford. 'My God, Mike, I was in here, I saw the three cars, I drove past her.'

'Did you see anyone else?'

'I don't know, I'll have to think.'

Going down in the lift, he thought. He remembered the pounding footsteps descending, the girl in the red Vauxhall following him, the half-dozen people in the above-ground parking areas, the mist that was visible and obscuring but really hid nothing. He remembered the woman carrying the two bags coming from the covered way, strolling, languidly kicking the trolley aside. But that was at ten past six and the murder had already taken place by then . . . He got into the car beside Archbold. Clifford Sanders in the red Metro was waiting a few yards along the roadway while a uniformed officer – someone new that Wexford didn't recognise – trundled the scattered trolleys out of their path.

The little red car led them along the High Street in the Stowerton direction and turned into the Forby Road.

Archbold seemed to know where Sanders lived, in a remote spot down a lane that turned off about half a mile beyond the house and parkland called 'Sundays'. In fact it was less than three miles outside Kingsmarkham, but the lane was narrow and very dark and Clifford Sanders drove even more slowly than the winding obscurity warranted. Thick, dark, leafless hedges rose high on either side. Occasionally a pulling-in place revealed itself, showing at least that passing would be possible if they met another vehicle. Wexford couldn't remember ever having been down there before, he doubted if it led anywhere except perhaps finally to the gates of a farm.

The sky was quite black, moonless, starless. The lane seemed to wind in a series of unnecessary loops. There were no hills for it to circumvent and the river to flow in the opposite direction. No longer were any pinpoints of light visible in the surrounding countryside. All was darkness but for the area immediately ahead, illuminated by their own headlights, and the twin bright points glowing red on the rear of the Metro.

But now Clifford Sanders' left-hand indicator was winking. Plainly, he was the kind of driver who would signal his intention to turn a hundred yards before the turning. A few seconds elapsed. There were no lights ahead, only a break in the hedge. Then the Metro turned in and Archbold followed, guided by the red tail-lights. With a kind of amused impatience Wexford thought how they might be in some Hitchcock movie, for he could just make out the house – a house which probably looked a lot less disagreeable by daylight but was now almost ridiculously grim and forbidding. Behind two windows only a pallid light showed. There was no other light either by the front door or about the garden. Wexford's eyes grew accustomed to the darkness and he saw that the house was biggish, on three floors, with eight windows here in the front and a slab of a front door. A low flight of steps without rails led up to it and there was neither porch nor canopy. But the whole façade was hung, covered, clothed in ivy. As far as he could see it was ivy, at any rate it was evergreen leaves, a dense blanket of them, through which the two pale windows peered like eyes in an animal's shaggy face.

A garden surrounded the house – grass and wilted foliage at any rate, extending at the back to a wooden fence. Beyond that only darkness, fields and woods, and over the low hill the invisible town which might as well have been a hundred miles away.

Clifford Sanders went up to the front door. The bell was the very old-fashioned kind which you ring by turning a handle back and forth, but he had a key and unlocked this door, though when Wexford started to follow him he said in his flat chilly tone, 'Just a minute, please.'

Mother, evidently, had to be warned; he disappeared and after a moment or two she came out to them. Wexford's first thought was how small she was, tiny and thin; his second that this was the woman he had seen entering the underground car park as he had left it. Within moments then she had found the body that he had missed. Her face was very pale, as near a white face as you could find, very lined and powdered even whiter, a young girl's scarlet lipstick unbecomingly coating her mouth. She was dressed in a brown tweed skirt, beige jumper, bedroom slippers. Did her recent discovery account for the curious smell of her? She smelt of disinfectant, the apparent combination of lime and thymol which hospitals reek of.

'You can come in,' she said, 'I've been expecting you.'

Inside, the place was bleak and cavernous; carpets and central heating were not luxuries that Mrs Sanders went in for. The hall floor was quarry-tiled, in the living room they walked on wood-grain linoleum and a couple of sparse rugs. There was scarcely an ornament to be seen – no pictures, only a large mirror in a heavy mahogany frame. Clifford Sanders had seated himself on a very old, shabby horsehair sofa in front of a fire of logs. He now wore on his feet only grey socks; his shoes were set in the hearth on a folded sheet of newspaper. Mrs Sanders pointed out – actually pointed with an extended finger – precisely where they were to sit: that armchair for Wexford, the other section of the sofa for Archbold. She seemed to have some notion of rank and what was due to it.

'I'd like you to tell me about your experience in the Barringdean Centre car park this evening, Mrs Sanders,' Wexford began. He forced himself to shift his eyes from the newspaper on which his daughter's face looked out at him from between the pair of black lace-up brogues. 'Tell me what happened from the time you came into the car park.'

Her voice was slow and flat like her son's, but there was something metallic about it too, almost as if throat and palate were composed of some inorganic hard material. 'There isn't anything to tell. I came up with my shopping to get my car. I saw something lying on the ground and went over to look and it was . . . I expect you know what it was.'

'Did you touch it?'

'I pulled back the bit of rag that was over it, yes.'

Clifford Sanders was watching his mother, his eyes still and blank. He seemed not so much relaxed as sagging from despair, his hands hanging down between his parted legs.

'What time was this, Mrs Sanders?' Wexford had noted the digital watch she wore.

'Exactly twelve minutes past six.' To account for her leaving the shopping precinct so late, she gave an account of a contretemps with a fishmonger, speaking in a measured level way – too measured. Wexford, who had been wondering what her tone reminded him of, now recalled electronic voices issuing from machines. 'I came up there at twelve minutes past six – and if you want to know how I can be sure of the time, the answer is I'm *always* sure of the time.'

He nodded. Digital watches were designed for people like her who, prior to their arrival on the scene, had to make approximate guesses as to what time was doing between ten past six and six fifteen. Yet most of them were speedy people, always in a hurry, restless, unrelaxed. This woman seemed one of those rare creatures who are constantly aware of time without being tempted to race against it.

She spoke softly to her son. 'Did you lock the garage doors?'

He nodded. 'I always do.'

'Nobody always does anything. Anybody can forget.'

'I didn't forget.' He got up. 'I'm going into the other room to watch TV.'

She was a pointer, Wexford saw, a finger-post. Now the finger pointed into the hearth. 'Don't forget your shoes.'

Clifford Sanders padded away with his shoes in his hand and Wexford said to Dorothy Sanders, 'What were you doing between twelve minutes past six and six forty-five when you managed to attract the attention of Mr Greaves in Queen Street?' He had registered very precisely the time of the phone

409

call Greaves made to Kingsmarkham Police Station: fourteen minutes to seven. 'That's half an hour between the time you found the body and the time you got down to the gate and . . . called out.'

She wasn't disconcerted. 'It was a shock. I had my shock to get over and then when I got down there I couldn't make anyone hear.'

He recalled Archbold's account, albeit at third hand. She had been screaming and raving inside those gates, shaking them 'fit to break them down' because the phone box was on the other side. Now the woman looked at him coldly and calmly. One would have said no emotion ever disturbed her equilibrium or altered the tone of the mechanical voice.

'How many cars did you see parked at that time on the second level?'

Without hesitation she said, 'Three, including mine.'

She wasn't lying; perhaps she hadn't been lying at all. He recalled how when he had passed through the second level there had been four cars parked there. One had pulled out, the one driven by the impatient young girl, and followed him fretfully. That had been at eight or nine minutes past six . . .

'Did you see anyone? Anyone at all?'

'Not a soul.'

She would be a widow, Wexford thought, nearly pensionable, without any sort of job, dependent in many ways and certainly financially dependent on this son who no doubt lived not far away. Later on, he reflected that he couldn't have been more wrong.

A wave of disinfectant smell hit him and she must have seen him sniffing.

'Coming in contact with that corpse,' she said, looking at him with steady, unblinking eyes, 'I had to scrub my hands with antiseptic.'

It was years since he had heard anyone use the word corpse. As he got up to go, she crossed to the window and began to draw the curtains. The place smelt like an operating theatre. The better to observe Clifford's arrival with the car, Wexford supposed, the curtains – of brown rep, not velvet – had been left drawn back. He watched her pull them together, giving each an impatient tug. Attached to the top of the door into the room was one of those extendable brass rails made to accommodate a draught-excluding curtain. No curtain, however, hung from it.

Wexford decided the time was not ripe to ask the question that came to his lips.

It had fallen many times to Michael Burden's lot to be the bearer of bad tidings of a particular kind, to break the news of a spouse's death. He, whose own first wife had died prematurely, flinched from this task. And it was one thing to have to tell someone, for instance, that his wife had died in a road accident; quite another that her murdered body had been found. No one knew better than Burden that the majority of those who are murdered have been done to death by a near relative. The chances are that a murdered wife has been murdered by her husband.

It was only a few moments before Wexford's arrival that he had looked inside the dead woman's handbag. After the first photographs had been taken and the dirty brown velvet curtain lifted from the body, her handbag had been revealed lying under her, half concealed by her thigh. More photographs were taken, Sumner-Quist came and at last he was able to free the bag from where it lay and, holding it in gloved hands, undo the clasp and look inside. It was a standard cache of documents: driving licence, credit cards, dry-cleaning bill, two letters still in their envelopes. Her name and address presented themselves to him before he had even noted the other contents of the bag – chequebook, purse, pressed powder, packet of tissues, ballpoint pen and two safety-pins, Gwen P. Robson, 23 Hastings Road, Highlands, Kingsmarkham KM10 2NW. One of the envelopes was addressed to her as Mrs G. P. Robson, the other to Mr and Mrs R. Robson.

It might not be a shock to Robson; part of Burden's job was to observe whether it was a shock or not. He silently framed the words he would use as the car climbed the long hill that led up to the Highlands estate. All this had been countryside when Burden first came to Kingsmarkham, heathy hillsides crowned with woods, and from the top of this incline by day you had been able to see the ancient landmark called Barringdean Ring. It was very dark tonight, the horizon defined only by an occasional point of light, and the circle of oaks was invisible. Nearer at hand Highlands was cozily lit. This was the way Gwen Robson had no doubt intended to come home, driving the silver Escort, entering Eastbourne Avenue and soon turning left into Hastings Road.

Burden had been here only once before, though the estate had been put up by the local authority some seven years ago. Street trees and garden trees had grown up and matured: the first newness of the houses had worn off and they looked less as if built from playbox bricks by a giant's child. Smallish blocks of flats no more than three storeys high alternated with terraced or semi-detached houses, and opposite the block in which No. 23 was located stood a row of tiny bungalows designed as housing for the elderly. Not too far a cry from the old almshouses, thought Burden, whose wife had made him a lot more socially conscious than he used to be. On the doorstep of the Robsons' house stood a rack made for holding milk-bottles; it was of red plastic-covered wire, surmounted by a plastic doll in a white coat with 'Thank you, Mr Milkman' in red letters under it and a clip to hold a note in its outstretched hand. This absurd object made Burden feel worse, indicative as it was of domestic cheerfulness. He looked at DC Davidson and Davidson looked at him and then he rang the bell.

The door was answered very quickly. Anxious people fly to doors, to phones. Their anxiety, of course, may not be brought about by the obvious cause.

'Mr Robson?'

'Yes. Who are you?'

'Police officers, Mr Robson.' Burden showed his warrant card. How to soften this? How to ease it? He could hardly say there was nothing to be alarmed about. 'I'm afraid we have very serious news. May we come in?'

He was a smallish, owl-faced man, rather overweight; Burden noticed that he used a stick even to bring him this short distance. 'Not my wife?' he said.

Burden nodded. He nodded firmly, his eyes on Robson. 'Let's go in.'

But Robson, though they were in the hall now, stood his ground. He leant on his stick. 'The car? A car accident?'

'No, Mr Robson, it wasn't a car accident.' The bad part was

412

that this could all be fake, all acting. He might have been rehearsing it for the past hour. 'If we could go into your . . .'

'Is she – is she gone?'

The old euphemism. Burden repeated it. 'Yes, she's gone,' and he added, 'She's dead, Mr Robson.'

Burden turned and walked through the open doorway into the well-lit, warm, over-furnished living room. A fire of gas flames licking beautifully simulated smokeless fuel looked more real than the real thing. The television was on, but more indicative of Robson's recent tension was the clock patience game laid out on a small appropriately round marquetry table in front of the armchair with its indented seat and crumpled pink silk cushions. Only a murderer who was also a genius would have dreamt up that one, Burden thought.

Robson had turned very pale. His thin-lipped mouth trembled. Still upright but leaning heavily on the stick, he was shaking his head in a vague, uncomprehending way. 'Dead? Gwen?'

'Sit down, Mr Robson. Take it easy.'

'Would you like a drink, sir?' DC Davidson asked.

'We don't drink in this house.'

'I meant water.' Davidson went off and came back with water in a glass.

'Tell me what happened.' Robson was seated now, no longer looking at Burden, his eyes on the circle of playing cards. Absently he took a minute sip of water.

'You must prepare yourself for a shock, Mr Robson.'

'I've had a shock.'

'Yes, I know.' Burden shifted his gaze and found himself looking at the framed photograph on the mantel-shelf of a very good-looking girl who rather resembled Sheila Wexford. A daughter? 'Your wife was killed, Mr Robson. There is no way I can make this easier to hear. She was murdered and her body was found in the Barringdean Shopping Centre car park.'

Burden wouldn't have been surprised if he had screamed, if he had howled like a dog. They came upon all sorts in their job. But Robson didn't scream; he merely stared with frozen face. A long time passed, a relatively long time, perhaps nearly a minute. He stared and passed his tongue over the thin lips, then he began mumbling very rapidly.

413

'We were married very young; we'd been married forty years. No children, we never had chick nor child, but that brings you closer; you're closer to each other without them. She was the most devoted wife a man ever had; she'd have done anything for me, she'd have laid down her life for me.' Great tears welled out of his eyes and flowed down his face. He sobbed and wept without covering his face, sitting upright and holding the stick with both hands, crying as most men only cried when they were very young children.

3

'It looks as if she was garrotted.'

Sumner-Quist's voice sounded pleasurably excited as if he had rung up to impart a piece of gossip: that the Chief Constable had run off with someone else's wife, for instance.

'Did you hear me? I said she was garrotted.'

'Yes I heard,' Wexford said. 'Good of you to tell me.'

'I thought you might go for a tasty little titbit like that before I let you have the full report.'

Extraordinary ideas some people have about one's tastes, Wexford thought. He tried to assemble in his mind what he knew about garrotting. 'What was it done with?'

'A garrotte,' Sumner-Quist chuckled cheerfully. 'Search me what kind. Home-made, no doubt. That's your problem.' Still laughing, he told Wexford that Mrs Robson had met her death after five-thirty and before six and had not been sexually assaulted. 'Merely garrotted,' he said.

'It used to be a method of execution,' Wexford said when Burden came into the office. 'An iron collar was attached to a post and the victim's neck placed inside. The mind boggles a bit when you start thinking how they *got* the victim's neck inside. Then the collar was tightened until asphyxiation occurred. Did you know this method of capital punishment was still in use in Spain as late as the 1960s?'

'And we thought it was only bull-fighting they went in for.'

'There was also a more primitive implement consisting of a length of wire with wooden handles.'

Burden sat on the edge of Wexford's rosewood desk. 'Haven't I read somewhere that if you were up for burning by

415

the Inquisition the executioner would garrotte you for a small fee before the flames got under way?'

'I expect that was where the wire-with-wooden-handles type came into its own.'

He wondered digressively if Burden's jeans were the kind called 'designer'. They were rather narrow at the ankle and matched the inspector's socks that were probably of a 'denim blue' shade. Unconscious of this rather puzzled scrutiny, Burden said, 'Is Sumner-Quist saying that's what was used on Gwen Robson?'

'He doesn't know, he just says "a garrotte". But it has to have been something of that kind. And the murderer has to have had it with him or her, ready-made, all prepared – which when you come to think of it, Mike, is pretty strange. It argues unquestionably premeditated murder, yet in a situation where no one could have forecast the prevailing conditions. The car park might have been full of people, for instance. Unless our perpetrator carries a garrotte about with him as you or I might carry a pen . . . I don't think we can say much more about that until we get the full forensic report. In the meantime, what's the sum total of our knowledge of Gwen Robson?'

She was fifty-eight years old, childless, a former home help in the employment of Kingsmarkham Borough Council but now retired. Her husband was Ralph Robson, also a former Borough Council employee, retired two years before from the Housing Department. Mrs Robson had been married at eighteen and she and her husband had lived first with his parents at their home in Stowerton, later on in a rented flat and then a rented cottage. Their names high on the borough housing list, they had been allocated one of the new houses at Highlands as soon as they were built. Neither was yet eligible for the state retirement pension, but Robson derived a pension from the local authority on which they had contrived to live in reasonable comfort. For instance, they had managed to run the two-year-old Escort. As a general rule they took an annual holiday in Spain and had been prevented from doing so this year only by Ralph Robson's arthritis, which was seriously affecting his right hip.

All this had been learned both from Ralph Robson himself

and from his niece Lesley Arbel, the original of the photograph
that had so much reminded Burden of Sheila Wexford.

'This niece – she doesn't live with them, does she?'

'She lives in London,' Burden said, 'but she spent a lot of
time down here with them. More like a daughter than a niece, I
gather, and an unusually devoted daughter at that. Or that's
how it appears. She's staying with Robson now – came as soon
as he told her what had happened to his wife.'

According to Robson, his wife had been in the habit of doing
their weekly shopping every Thursday afternoon. Up until six
months ago he had always gone with her, but his arthritis had
made this impossible. On the previous Thursday, two days
before, she had gone out in their car just before four-thirty. He
had never seen her again. And where had he been himself
between four-thirty and seven? At home alone in Hastings
Road, watching television, making himself tea. Much the same
as Archie Greaves, Wexford thought, whom he had been to see
earlier that morning.

A policeman's dream of a witness, the old man was. The
narrowness of his life, the confined span of his interests made
him into a camera and tape device for the perfect recording of
incidents in his little world. Unfortunately, there had not been
much for him to observe: the shoppers leaving, the lights
dwindling and going out, Sedgeman closing and locking the
gates.

'There was this young chap running,' he said to Wexford. 'It
was just on six, a minute or two after. There were a lot of
people leaving, mostly ladies with their shopping, and he came
running from round the back of that wall.'

Wexford followed his gaze out of the window. The wall in
question was the side of the underground car-park entrance
beside which stood a small crowd of ghoulish onlookers.
There was nothing to see, but they waited in hope. The gates
stood open, an empty food package rolled about the tarmac
propelled by gusts of wind. The pennants on the turrets
streamed in the wind, taut and fluttering. I was there, Wexford
thought, almost with a groan, I came out of there at ten past
six and saw – nothing. Well, nothing but the Sanders woman.

'I reckoned he was in trouble,' Archie Greaves said. 'I

417

reckoned he'd done something he shouldn't and been spotted and they was after him.' The man was so old that his face as well as the skin of his hands were discoloured with the liver spots that are called 'grave marks'. He was thin with age, his knitted cardigan and flannel trousers baggy on a bony, tremulous body. But the pale blue eyes, pink-rimmed, could see like those of someone half his age. 'He was just a boy with one of them woolly hats on his head and a zip-up jacket and he was running like a bat out of hell.'

'But there was in fact no one after him?'

'Not as I could see. Maybe they got fed up and turned back, knowing as they wouldn't catch him.'

And then he had seen Dorothy Sanders who was later to scream and rattle the gates, walking up and down searching the car parks for something or someone, her anger contained but her affronted indignation vibrating as later a demented terror was to stream from her, making Archie Greaves shiver and shake and fear for his heart.

An incident room had been set up in Kingsmarkham Police Station on Thursday night to receive calls from anyone who might have been in the Barringdean Shopping Centre underground car park between five and six-thirty. The local television station had broadcast an immediate appeal for possible witnesses to come forward and Wexford had managed to get a nationwide appeal on that night's ten o'clock news going out on the network. Calls started coming in at once – before the number to call had even disappeared from the screen, Sergeant Martin said – but of these the great majority were well-meant but misleading or ill-meant and misleading, or were deliberate attempts to deceive. A call came from a young woman called Sarah Cussons who identified herself as the driver of the Vauxhall Cavalier which had followed Wexford's out of the car park, and another from a man beside whose car Gwen Robson had parked her silver Escort. He had seen her drive in and was able to give her time of arrival at the centre as about twenty to five.

Throughout Thursday night the calls continued to come in, many of them from drivers of cars parked on all the levels who had seen nothing untoward. They were interviewed just the same. Early on Friday morning came a call on behalf of the owner of the blue Lancia. Mrs Helen Brook, nine months pregnant, had gone into labour while in the health-food shop in the shopping centre at about five on the previous evening. An ambulance had been called and she had been taken to the maternity wing of Stowerton Royal Infirmary.

None of the obviously genuine and well-intentioned callers was able to describe anyone else they had seen while parking or fetching their cars, though plenty of fantastic descriptions came in from those jokers who enjoy teasing the police. Two assistants from the Barringdean Centre shops phoned in to say they had served Gwen Robson, one just before five and the other, Linda Naseem – a checkout assistant at the Tesco supermarket – half a hour later. But by that time two of Wexford's officers were at the shopping centre questioning all the shopworkers, and Archbold had interviewed the man in charge of the fish counter in the Tesco superstore who confirmed he had had a row with a woman answering Dorothy Sanders' description 'at around six when they were closing up'. All that did was confirm her time of coming into the car park which Wexford could confirm himself.

That same morning Ralph Robson made a formal identification of his wife's body; the neck had been discreetly covered during this ordeal. He hobbled in on his stick, looked at the horror-stricken face from which some of the blue colour had faded, nodded, said, 'Yes,' but didn't cry this time. Wexford had not seen him on that occasion, hadn't yet seen him. He had interviewed David Sedgeman, the car park supervisor, himself. The man should have been a valuable witness, yet he seemed to have seen nothing or to have registered nothing he had seen. He could recall waving to Archie Greaves because he did this every evening, and for the same reason could recall locking the gates. But his memory offered him no worried woman or running man, no fast-driven car or suspicious escaper. Everything had been normal, he said in his dull way. He had locked the gates and gone home just as he always did, collecting his own car from where he always left it in a bay in one of the open-air parking areas.

The November air felt raw and the sky was a leaden grey. A reddish sun hung over the roof-tops, not very high in the sky

419

but as high as it would get. Burden had on a padded jacket, a pale grey Killy, warm as toast and turning him from a thin man into a stout one. His wife was away, staying with her mother who was convalescent after an operation, and that disturbed Burden, making him jumpy and insecure. He would spend tonight with her and their little son in his mother-in-law's house outside Myringham, but what he really wanted was his own family back home with him in his own house. His face took on a look both irritable and cynical as Wexford spoke.

'Did Robson strike you,' Wexford said in the car, 'as the sort of man who would sit himself down and with deliberation fashion a wire implement with a handle at each end for the express purpose of garrotting his wife?'

'Now you're asking. I don't know what sort of a man that would be. He had no car, remember, his wife had the car. The centre's a mile away from Highlands . . .'

'I know. Is the arthritic hip genuine?'

'Even if it isn't, he had no car. He could have walked, or there's the bus. But if he wanted to murder his wife, why not do it at home like most of them do?'

Wexford couldn't keep from laughing at this insouciant acceptance of domestic homicide. 'Maybe he did, we don't know yet. We don't know if she died in that car park or the body was only dumped there. We don't even know if she drove the car.'

'You mean Robson himself may have?'

'Let's see,' said Wexford.

They had arrived at Highlands and Lesley Arbel opened the front door to them. She didn't remind Wexford of his own daughter; to him she bore no resemblance to Sheila. He saw only a pretty girl who struck him at once as being exceptionally well-dressed, indeed almost absurdly well-dressed for a weekend of mourning in the country with one's recently bereaved uncle. She introduced herself, explained that she had not waited until the prearranged time for her visit but had come on Friday morning.

'My uncle's upstairs,' she said. 'He's lying down. The doctor came and said he was to get as much rest as he could.'

'That's all right, Miss Arbel. We'd like to talk to you too.'

'Me? But I don't know anything about it. I was in London.'

420

'You know about your aunt. You can tell us something of what sort of a person she was, better than your uncle can.'

She said in a rather pernickety way, 'That's right, he's my real uncle. I mean, my mother was his sister; she was my aunt because she married him.'

Wexford nodded, aware that his impatience showed. Mentally he cautioned himself against deciding too soon that a witness was irredeemably stupid. She took them into the Robsons' brightly furnished living room where a conflict of textile patterns dazzled Wexford — flowers on the carpet, flowers of a more formal design on the curtains, trees and fruits on the wallpaper, a rug with a sunburst pattern. The flames of a gas fire licked indestructible coals. The girl sat down and her own face smiled over her shoulder out of a silver frame. His question astonished her.

'These curtains, are they new?'

'Pardon?'

'Let me rephrase it. Were there ever different curtains at these windows?'

'I think Auntie Gwen once had red curtains, yes. Why do you want to know?'

Wexford made no answer but watched her while Burden asked about the telephone call her uncle had made to her on Thursday evening. Her clothes were remarkable, somehow evoking the unreal elegance of actresses in Hollywood comedies of the thirties, as sleek and as unsuitable for the wear and tear of living. A bunch of gold chains that looked too heavy for comfort hung against her cream silk shirt between the lapels of the coffee-coloured silk jacket. Crimson-nailed hands lay in her lap and she lifted one to her face, touching her cheek as she replied to his questions.

'You intended coming down for the weekend on Saturday as you often did?'

She nodded.

'But your uncle phoned you himself on Thursday evening and told you what had happened?'

'He phoned me on Thursday, on Thursday night. I wanted to come then, but he wouldn't have that. He had one of the neighbours, a Mrs Whitton, with him so I thought he'd be all right.' She looked from one to the other of them. 'You said you wanted me to talk about Auntie Gwen.'

'In a moment, Miss Arbel,' Burden said. 'Would you mind telling me what you were doing yourself on Thursday afternoon?'

'What do you want to know for?' She was more than astounded; her manner was affronted as if she had encountered insolence. Her long elegant legs, the feet encased in high-heeled cream leather pumps, drew close together, were pressed together. 'Why ever do you want to know that?'

Perhaps it was pure innocence.

Burden said blandly, 'Routine questions, Miss Arbel. In a murder inquiry, it's necessary to know people's whereabouts.' He attempted to help her along. 'I expect you were at work, weren't you?'

'I went home early on Thursday, I wasn't very well. Don't you want me to tell you about Auntie Gwen?'

'In a moment. You went home early because you weren't well. You had a cold, did you?'

A vacuous stare was turned on Burden, but perhaps not entirely vacuous for it seemed to contain an element of earnestness. 'It was my PMT, wasn't it?' she said as if she were famous for this disorder, as if all the world was aware of it. Wexford doubted if Burden even knew what those initials stood for, and now the girl seemed equally dubious. Frowning, she leaned towards Burden. 'I always have PMT and there's not a thing they can do about it.'

At this point the door opened and Ralph Robson came in, leaning on his stick. He had a dressing gown on, but with a shirt and a pair of slacks underneath it. 'I heard voices.' His flat but beaky face was turned on Wexford with a puzzled look.

'Chief Inspector Wexford, Kingsmarkham CID.'

'Pleased to meet you,' Robson said, sounding anything but pleased. 'You coming here has saved me a phone call. Maybe one of you can tell me what's become of the shopping?'

'The shopping, Mr Robson?'

'The shopping Gwen got on Thursday, as was in the boot of the blessed car presumably. I can see I can't have the car back yet awhile, but the shopping's a different story. There's meat in those bags, there's a loaf and butter and I don't know what else. I don't say I'm poor, but I'm not so rolling in money as I can just let that lot go, right?'

Self-preservation or a tenacity for life overcame grief. Wexford knew this, but it never ceased mildly to surprise him just the same. It might be that this man felt no grief; it might be that he was responsible for his wife's death, but it might only be that he had ceased to feel much emotion for anyone or anything. That sometimes happened to people as they aged and Wexford had noticed it dispassionately but with an inner shiver. Yet Burden said he had wept when first told.

'We'll get it back to you later today,' was all Wexford said.

He had carefully gone over the contents of the shopping bag himself before having the perishable items placed in one of the police canteen fridges. There had been nothing among them to excite much interest: mostly food, but things from the chemist as well - toothpaste and talcum powder – and from the British Home Stores four lightbulbs; all of these contained in a BHS bag, indicating perhaps that she had stopped there first. Mrs Robson's handbag, which would also soon be returned and which Burden had first looked into in the car par, contained her purse with twenty-two pounds in it, plus some small change and a chequebook from the Trustee Savings Bank. The credit cards were a Visa and the card which the Barringdean Shopping Centre supplied for its patrons. Her handkerchief and the two folded tissues were unused. The letters which had provided the police with her identity and address were from a sister in Leeds and the other – scarcely a letter in any sense – an invitation to a Christmas fashion show at the shop where Wexford had bought Dora's sweater.

'Are you missing a brown velvet curtain, Mr Robson?'

'Me? No. What do you mean?'

'A curtain which might have been kept in the boot of your car for the purpose, say, of covering up the windscreen in frosty weather?'

'I use newspaper for that.'

Lesley Arbel said suddenly, 'Could you eat a bit of lunch, Uncle? A little something light?'

He had sat down and was leaning forward in the chair, pressing one hand on his thigh in what seemed genuine pain, his face twisted with it. 'There's nothing I fancy, dear.'

'But you're not still having those pills, are you? The ones that upset your tummy?'

'Doctor took me off the blessed things. There's some they don't suit, he said; they can give you ulcers.'

'You've got arthritis, have you, Mr Robson?'

He nodded. 'You listen,' he said, 'and you can hear the hip joint grind.' To Robson's evident agony there came a shift of bone in socket and Wexford did hear it, heard with dismay an unhuman ratchet-like sound. 'It's a bit of bad luck for me that I'm allergic to the painkillers. Got to grin and bear it. I'm in line for one of those replacement ops, but there's a waiting list round here of up to three years. God knows what sort of state I'll be in in three years. It'd be a different story if I could have it done private.'

This was no news to Wexford, that hip replacements could be carried out almost at once if the patient were prepared to pay but that the waiting time for National Health Service surgery might be very protracted. The unfairness of this was not lost on him, but he was more intent on trying to assess the genuineness of Robson's disability. He turned his eyes towards the girl and she looked at him artlessly, her face a beautiful blank.

'Where do you work, Miss Arbel?'

'*Kim* magazine.'

'Could you give me the address, please, and your own address in London too? Do you live alone or share?'

'I share with two other girls.' She sounded peevish, muttering the north-west London address. '*Kim*'s office is at Orange-tree House in the Waterloo Road.'

Wexford had only once seen the magazine when Dora had bought it for the sake of some mail-order bargain it featured. A semi-glossy weekly, it had seemed aimed at a not very youthful market but at the same time making little provision for women past forty or so. The issue Wexford had seen had carried articles he thought dreary but which the magazine itself vaunted as controversial and lively, under such headings as: 'Is it OK to be a Lesbian?' and 'Your Daughter Your Own Clone?'

'Could you eat some scrambled egg, Uncle, and a little thin bread and butter?'

424

Robson shrugged, then nodded. Burden began speaking to him of Mrs Whitton, the neighbour who had come to sit with him before Lesley Arbel arrived. Had he seen anyone, spoken on the phone to anyone, while his wife was out?

Lesley got up, said, 'Well, if you'll just excuse me . . .'

While Robson told Burden about the Hastings Road neighbours, speaking in a wretched halting monotone and separating virtually every sentence from the next with a phrase to the effect that Gwen had known them all better than he did, Wexford left the room. He found Lesley Arbel standing in front of an electric stove, a printed teatowel rather than an apron tied round her waist to protect the coffee silk skirt. Two eggs reposed in a bowl, a beater beside them, but instead of preparing her uncle's lunch she was examining her face in a handbag mirror and painting something on to it with a small, fat brush.

As soon as she saw Wexford she put brush and mirror away with extreme haste, as if this rapid manoeuvre would some-how render the prior activity invisible. She broke open the eggs, not very skilfully, got a piece of shell into the bowl and had to pick it out with a long red nail.

'Why would anyone want to murder your aunt, Miss Arbel?'

She didn't answer him for a moment, but reached up into a cabinet for a plate and put a cruet on to the tray she had laid with a cloth. Her voice when it came was nervous and irritable. 'It was some crazy person, wasn't it? There's never any reason for murders, not these days. The ones you read about in the papers, they're all people who say they don't know why they did it or they've forgotten or had a blackout or whatever. The one who killed her will have been like that. I mean, who would have wanted to kill her for a reason? There wasn't any reason.' She turned away from him and started beating the eggs.

'Everybody liked her?' he said. 'She wouldn't have had enemies?'

In her left hand she held the pan in which butter was smoking too strongly, in her other the bowl with the egg mixture. But instead of pouring one into the other, she stood with the two vessels poised. 'It's a laugh really, hearing you talk like that. Or it would be if it wasn't such a tragedy. She was a wonderful, lovely lady – don't you understand that? Hasn't anyone told you? Look at Uncle Ralph, he's heartbroken, isn't he? He worshipped her and she worshipped him. They were just a lovely couple, like young lovers right up to when this happened. And this'll be the death of him, I can promise you that – this'll be the end of him. He's aged about twenty years since yesterday.'

She swung round, tipped the eggs into the pan and began rapidly cooking them. Wexford had the curious feeling that for all the apparent sincerity of her words what she was really trying to do was impress him with a kind of caring competent maturity – an ambition that went wrong when she seemed to realise that though the eggs were cooked she had forgotten about the bread and butter. Rather harassed by now, she cut doorsteps of bread and covered them with wedges of butter chipped from the refrigerated block. He opened doors for her, feeling something very near pity without exactly knowing what he pitied her *for*. The apron improvised from a teatowel fell off as she teetered into the living room on her stilt heels. But even so, as she passed the small wall mirror which hung between kitchen and living-room doorways, she was unable to resist a glance into it. Balanced on her pointed toes, holding the tray, flustered, she nevertheless took the opportunity of a narcissistic peep at her own face . . .

Robson was lying back in his armchair and had to be jolted out of his half-doze. This his niece did not only by propping him up with a cushion behind him and plumping the tray down on his lap, but also with the rough and somehow shocking, 'He asked me if Gwen had enemies! Can you credit it?'

Dull, bewildered eyes were lifted. Incredibly came the mumble, 'He's only doing his job, dear.'

'Gwen,' she said, and sentimentally, 'Gwen that was like a mother to me.' Suddenly her manner sharpened. 'Mind you, she wasn't soft. She had principles, very high principles, didn't she, Uncle? And she knew how to speak her mind. She didn't like that couple living together, the ones next-door-but-one, whatever they're called, the people that run a business from home. I said times had changed from when she got married, but it didn't make any difference. I mean, everyone does that

426

now, I said. But she wouldn't have it, would she, Uncle?'

They were all looking at her, Robson as well. She seemed to realize how animated her manner had been for one so recently bereaved and she flushed. Not much real love there, Burden thought, and said, 'Now we'd like to take a look round the house. Is that OK?'

She would have argued but Robson, having eaten almost nothing, pushing away his plate, nodded and waved one hand in an odd gesture of assent. Wexford wouldn't have bothered with the house; there was nothing relevant to Mrs Robson's life or death he expected to find. He was already half-adhering to the girl's view, that some badly disturbed person had killed Gwen Robson for no better reason than that she was there and a woman, unprepared and frail enough. However, he made his way into the bedroom she had shared with Robson and saw everywhere signs of domestic harmony. The bed was unmade. On an impulse aimed at no particular enlightening discovery, Wexford lifted up the flatter and less rumpled of the pillows and found underneath it Mrs Robson's nightdress just as it must have been folded and tucked away by her on Thursday morning . . .

A framed photograph showed her as she had once been, her hair dark and plentiful, mouth widely smiling, plumper than now. She was seated and her husband was looking over her shoulder, perhaps to give an illusion of the greater height he had not possessed. The books on her bedside cabinet were two novels of Catherine Cookson, on his the latest Robert Ludlum. On the dressing table a small container of Yardley 'Chique' perfume stood between his hairbrush and a pincushion in which were pinned three brooches. A surprising number of pictures covered the walls: more framed photographs of the two of them, a framed collage of postcards, sentimental mementos of their own holidays, cat and dog pictures perhaps cut from calendars, a cottage in a flowery garden embroidered by someone – perhaps Gwen Robson herself.

The curtains in the room were as floral as this picture. In spite of her sober style of dressing, she had liked bright colours – pinks and blues and yellows. She might have worn brown, but she would not have furnished her house with it. A neatly stacked pile of *Kim* magazines occupied half the top of a long

427

stool and on top of these lay last night's evening paper. Did that mean that the night after his wife had been murdered Robson had taken the evening paper up with him for his bedtime reading? Well, why not? Life must go on. And no doubt he had been given sleeping pills, had needed something to read while waiting for the drug to take effect. Wexford just glanced at the lead story and the photograph of the barrister Edmund Hope, as handsome and striking-looking as any of the Arab bombers he was prosecuting, then he turned away to study the view.

Beyond the window the Highlands estate presented a panorama of itself she must often have seen while standing here: Hastings Road where the house was, Eastbourne Road leading down to the town, Battle Hill mounting to the crown of the estate, pantiled roofs deliberately placed at odd angles to one another to give the illusion of some little hillside town in Spain or Portugal – coniferous trees bluish, dark green and golden-green because conifers are cheap and grow swiftly, winding gravel paths and concrete paths, windows dressed in Austrian blinds, looped-up festoons and frills, one solitary resident only to be seen: an elderly, very stout woman in long skirt and multi-coloured jacket who was breaking into pieces the end of a loaf of bread and putting them on to a bird-table in a garden diagonally opposite. The house she returned to was the first of those past the row of old people's sheltered housing. She looked back once at where Mrs Robson had lived, as anyone must look who lived here or came into this street. That was human nature. Her eyes met Wexford's and she immediately looked away. It was rather as Lesley Arbel had quickly put away her mirror and brush, as if this would negate the past act.

Wexford said, 'We may as well go. We'll give Mrs Sanders a ring and get her down to the station.'

'You wouldn't prefer to go to her?'

'No, I'd prefer to give her a bit of trouble,' said Wexford.

4

It was spread out on the table in the interview room – a curtain that had once been handsome, of a rich thick-piled tobacco-brown velvet, lined and weighted at the two corners of its lower hem. But splashed across the centre of it was a large dark stain, a stain which might have been blood but which Wexford had already ascertained was not. Other stains had since been superadded; there was certainly an impression that the original splashings had ruined the curtain as a curtain, and that since the occurrence which had led to them any further damage to the velvet had been of no account.

Dorothy Sanders looked at it. Her eyes flicked and as she looked back at Wexford he noticed for the first time that they were of a curious pale fawn colour.

'That's the curtain that used to hang up on my door.' And then, after a long blank stare at Wexford had elicited no particular reaction, 'It's still got the hooks in it.'

He continued to stand and watch her, his face expressing nothing, but now he gave a small reflective nod. Burden was frowning.

'Where did you get it?' she said. 'What's it doing here?'

'It was covering Mrs Robson's body,' Burden said. 'Don't you remember?'

The change in her was electric. She jumped back, retracting arms and hands as if it were offal or slime her fingers had touched. Her face flushed darkly, her lips sucked in. She put a hand to her mouth – a characteristic gesture, he thought – and then flung the hand away, aware of what it had been in contact with. He had a glimpse then of how this slow, deliberate

429

woman could become a screaming demented creature, and for the first time he understood that the old man called Archie Greaves might not have been exaggerating.

'You've touched it before, Mrs Sanders,' he said. 'You pulled it back to look at her face.'

She shuddered, her arms stretched out and shaking as if she could shake off her hands and so get rid of them.

'Come and sit down, Mrs Sanders.'

'I want to wash my hands. Where can I go and wash my hands?'

Wexford didn't want her to run away, but as he picked up the phone DC Marion Bayliss tapped on the door and came in. She began on a routine question and he nodded assent and said, 'Would you take Mrs Sanders to the ladies' loo, please?'

Dorothy Sanders was brought back after about five minutes, calm again, stony-faced and with more red lipstick on her mouth. He could smell the police station liquid soap ten feet away.

'Have you any suggestions, Mrs Sanders, as to how your curtain came to be covering Mrs Robson's body?'

'I didn't put it there. The last time I saw it was in a . . .' she hesitated, went on more carefully, '. . . a room in my house. Folded up. In an attic, they call them attics. My son may have gone up there; he may have wanted it for something, though he'd no business . . . without me saying he could.' A grim look cramped her features.

This hadn't occurred to Wexford as a possibility before, but it did now. 'Does your son live with you, Mrs Sanders?'

'Of course he lives with me.' She spoke as if, though it were possible there were some very few grown-up children who through general viciousness or perhaps being orphans lived apart from their parents, such situations were rare enough to provoke incredulity and even disgust. She spoke as if Wexford were a depraved ignoramus to suppose otherwise. 'Of course he lives with me. Where did you think he lived?'

'Are you sure this curtain was in a room in your house? It couldn't have been in the boot of your car?'

She was no fool. At least, she was sharp enough.

'Not unless he put it there.' The identity of 'he' was evident enough. She thought, reasoned, nodded her head. This was not one of those women, Wexford thought with a kind of grim amusement, who even at the cost of their own lives would protect a child, criminal or otherwise – the kind who hid a wanted son or lied when questioned as to his whereabouts, who regarded a son not so much as an extension of herself but as a precious superior. 'I expect he did put it there,' she now said. 'I'd sent through my catalogue for a proper nylon cover for the car. Nylon or fibreglass or one of those things.' Mail order she meant, Wexford decided. 'I'd sent for it a good two months ago, but they take their time, these people. I expect he couldn't wait.'

She looked up at him, making him perform one of those about-turns in his assessment of human nature. For a moment he felt he knew nothing; people and their ways were as much a mystery as ever they had been. She looked human, at least she spoke in a human way. 'He's not like me, he hasn't got much patience. He can't help it. I expect he thought he'd just take that curtain and use it when we had the cold spell. You can't be kept waiting about for ever, can you?' She looked down at her watch, drawn to this recorder of time's passage by her references to its delays. Her wrist was like a bundle of wires, thinly insulated.

Burden had been pacing up and down. He said, 'It's your car but your son uses it?'

'It's my car,' she said. 'I bought it and paid for it and I'm the registered owner. But he has to go to work, doesn't he? I let him use it to go to work and then if I want to go shopping, he can take me and pick me up. He's got to have transport.'

'What does your son do, Mrs Sanders?'

She was one of those who expect their private arrangements to be intimately known by others, to need no elucidation, yet who show affront when those others reveal a knowledge gained by sensitivity or intuition. 'He's a teacher, isn't he?'

'You tell me,' Burden said.

She curled her nostrils in disgust. 'He teaches in a school for children who can't pass their exams without extra coaching.'

A crammer's, Wexford thought. Probably Munster's in Kingsmarkham High Street. It surprised him a little and yet – why not? Clifford Sanders, he thought in the light of his new knowledge, would be one of those who lived at home while they attended university, going to and fro by bus. It would be interesting to find out if he was right there.

'Part-time,' she said, and astonished them both by saying in the same level, indifferent tone, 'He's inadequate in some ways.'

'What's wrong with him? Is he ill?'

Her old harshly censorious manner was back. 'They call it ill nowadays. When I was young, they called it lacking character.' A dark flush moved into her cheeks, mottling them. She was dressed in green today, a dark dull green, though her shoes and gloves were black. When the blush faded, the dull seaweed green seemed to show up the pallor of her skin. 'That's where he was, wasn't he, when he was supposed to be coming for me in the car park? He'd been to this psychiatrist. They call them psychotherapists; they don't have any qualifications.'

'Mrs Sanders, are you telling me that your son was in the Barringdean Centre car park when you were?'

Emotions warred behind the blush, the succeeding pallor, the muffling screen of green and black. She had not meant to let that out. Protecting her son was not as unknown to her as Wexford had at first believed: he could even see that in an intense, self-disgusted, incredulous way she loved her son, but perhaps she had not been able to resist that dig at a profession she disapproved of. She spoke with extreme care now, the pace of the voice electronically slowed to make understanding easier.

'He should have been there but he was not. He had come in, the car was there, but he . . .' she paused, breathing deeply, '. . . was not.' An abrupt halting explanation followed. At first, when she saw the car and a body, she had thought it was Clifford lying there dead. She couldn't see the body because it was covered up and believing it to be Clifford, she pulled back the brown velvet covering. It wasn't Clifford, but it had been a great shock just the same. She had had to sit in her car and rest, recover herself. Clifford had been going to pick her up as he always did on Thursdays, always. It was an unvarying arrangement, though the school time might vary. She looked at her watch as she said this. Clifford brought her to the shopping centre, went to his session with the psychotherapist, returned to pick her up. She didn't drive. This Thursday they had arranged for him to be in the car park on the second level by six-fifteen. On her arrival she had had her hair done at Suzanne's on the upper floor of the centre – another inflexible arrangement – shopped, come back to the car park at twelve minutes past six.

After the shock of finding the body, after she had recovered somewhat – Wexford found this frailty of hers rather hard to believe in – she had gone up to look for Clifford. She had walked about looking for him, a statement that was confirmed by Archie Greaves. At last she had gone to the pedestrian gates . . .

'I broke down,' she said, giving each word equal monotonous weight.

'Where was your son, then? No, you needn't answer that, Mrs Sanders. You tell him we're interested and we'll have a talk with him later. We'll all take a break and he can do some thinking. How's that?'

She moved towards the door. Someone would drive her home. Her manner had in it something of the sleepwalker, or as if almost everything she thought and felt – perhaps momentous or amazing things – she kept veiled. She was so thin and wiry you would expect her to be a brisk woman, Wexford thought, but she was as languid as some slippery, rotund sea creature. Burden said as soon as she had gone, 'Is she saying he's potty?'

'I should think that depends on how strict you are and –' Wexford looked up at Burden with a half-smile, 'how out of date. Apparently he can hold down a job and drive a car and carry on a normal conversation. Is that what you mean?'

'You know it isn't. He sounds very much like a candidate for Lesley Arbel's psychopath role to me.'

' "The outstanding feature is emotional immaturity in its broadest and most comprehensive sense. These people are impulsive, feckless, unwilling to accept the results of experience and unable to profit by them . . ." ' Wexford faltered for a moment, then went on, ' ". . . sometimes prodigal of effort but utterly lacking in persistence, plausible but insincere, demanding but indifferent to appeals, dependable

433

only in their constant unreliability, faithful only to infidelity, rootless, unstable, rebellious and unhappy." '

Burden gaped a bit. 'Did you make that up?'

'Of course I didn't. It's David Stafford-Clark's definition of a psychopath – or part of it. I learned it by heart because I thought it might come in useful, but I can't say it ever has.' Wexford grinned. 'I liked the prose too.'

The expression on Burden's face rather indicated that he didn't know what prose was. 'I think it's very useful. It's good. I like that bit about dependable in their constant unreliability.'

'Oxymoron.'

'Is that another mental disease?' When Wexford only shook his head, Burden said, 'That bit you quoted – is it in a book? Can I get it?'

'I'll lend you my copy. I expect it's out of print; it must be twenty years since I read it. But you can't apply that to Clifford Sanders, you know. You've hardly talked to him.'

'That can be remedied,' said Burden grimly.

It was dark as Wexford drove along the street where he lived and approached his own house. A car was parked on his garage drive, Sheila's Porsche. He felt a tiny dip of the heart and immediately reproached himself. He loved his daughters dearly and Sheila was his favourite, but for once he wouldn't be elated to see her. A quiet evening was what he had looked forward to; it might be the last for a long time, for he had no faith in Burden's forecast of the straightforwardness of this case. And now it would be given over not only to talk, but talk on serious matters.

Irritation of a different kind succeeded this initial flash of dismay. She had parked her car on the garage drive because she supposed him to be home already, even supposed this to be his day off as it should have been, and expected his car to be inside the garage. Now he would have to leave it out in the street. Unburdening her heart to her mother would have taken priority over everything. He could imagine her saying every ten minutes or so how she must rush out and move the car before darling Pop got home . . .

Thinking like that cheered him, made him smile to himself, hearing with his mind's ear her enchanting, slightly breathless voice. He would say nothing, he resolved, of the wire-cutting, the reports of her coming divorce; he would utter no word of reproach, certainly no intimation of disappointment or upset, would cast on her no grave looks. He touched the Porsche lightly on its long, gleaming, nearly horizontal rear window as he passed it. Did she go to demonstrations in that? Well, it was only a small Porsche and black at that . . . Would she come and kiss his cheek or would she hang back? There was no knowing. He went in the back way, into the hall from the kitchen, hung up his coat, hearing her voice from the living room – hearing the voice of Beatrice Cenci, Antigone, Nora Helmer and now Lady Audley – falter and fall silent. He went into the room and immediately she was rushing to him and in his arms

Over her shoulder he saw the small satirical smile on Dora's face. He hugged Sheila and as she relaxed, distanced her with his arms stretched and said, 'Are you OK?'

'Well, I don't know,' she giggled. 'Not really. I'm not really OK. I'm in an awful mess. And Mother's being very sniffy. Mother's being horrible, actually.'

Her rueful smile showed him this was only half-meant. Foolish this was, he knew it every time, but when he looked at her like this he could never help admiring afresh the beautiful, fair, sensitive face that would with luck defy time, the long, pale, soft hair, the eyes as clear as a child's and as blue, but not a child's. There was no wedding ring on her left hand, but often she wore no rings, just as she nearly always kept her fancy clothes for public or publicity appearances. The jeans she wore were shabby compared with Burden's. She had on a blue sweater of a similar shade and a string of wooden beads.

'Now you're home, darling,' said Dora, 'we can all have a drink. I'm sure I need it. In fact . . .' she looked from one to the other with a certain tact, with a knowledge that they might care for two minutes alone together, '. . . I'll get it.'

Sheila fell back into the chair she had jumped out of. 'Aren't you going to ask me why? Why, why, why everything?'

'No.'

'You have a blind faith in the rightness of everything I do?'

'You know I don't.' He was tempted to say of the husband she had left, 'I liked Andrew,' but he didn't say it. 'What are we talking about, anyway? Which of your sensational acts?'

435

'Oh, Pop, I had to cut the wire. It wasn't done hysterically or without thinking or for publicity or in defiance or anything. I *had* to do it. I've been psyching myself up to it for ever so long. People take notice of what I do, you see. I don't just mean *me*, I mean anyone in my position. They kind of say, "If Sheila Wexford does it there must be some meaning to it, there must be a point if a famous person like her does it."'

'What happened?' He was genuinely curious.

'I bought a pair of wire-cutters in a DIY place in Covent Garden. There were ten of us, all members of PANDA – Players Anti-Nuclear Direct Action – only I was the only well-known one. We went to a place in Northamptonshire called Lossington and we went in three cars, mine and two others. It's an RAF station where they have obsolete bombers. The importance of the place doesn't matter, you see, it's the gesture . . .'

'Of course I see,' he said a little impatiently.

'There was this bleak plain with a couple of concrete huts and some hangers and grass all round and mud and a wire fence gone rusty – miles of it, and high enough not to lose tennis balls if you were playing inside. Well, we all stood up against the wire and each of us cut a bit and a great flap of wire came down, then we went to the nearest town and the police station and walked in and told them what we'd done and . . .'

Dora came in with their drinks on a tray – beer for Wexford, wine for herself and her daughter. Having heard the last words, she said, 'You might have given a little more thought to your father.'

'Oh, Pop, the first idea was for us to cut the wire at RAF Myringham, but I stood out against that because of you, because it was on your patch. I did think of you. But I had to do it, I *had* to – can't you understand?'

His temper for an instant got the better of him. 'You're not Antigone, however much you may have played her. You're not Bunyan. Don't keep saying you *had* to do it. Do you really believe your cutting the wire round an obsolete bomber station or whatever is going to lead to a total ban on nuclear arms? I don't like them, you know, I don't believe anyone likes them; I'm afraid of them. When you and Sylvia were little I used to be – oppressed with fear for you. And if they've kept the peace for

436

forty-five years, that doesn't mean a thing; it certainly doesn't mean they'll keep it for ninety. But I know better than to suppose this kind of thing is going to affect government.'

'What else can we do?' she said simply. 'I often think I don't believe that either, but what else can we do? They all think that banning Cruise missiles solves everything, but they're getting rid of less than ten per cent of the world's arsenal. The alternative is apathy, is pretending everything's solved.'

'You mean that "for evil to triumph",' Wexford said, ' "it is only necessary for good men to do nothing"?'

But Dora followed sharply with, 'Or do you mean that between the early warning and the bomb going off you'll have ten minutes in which to congratulate yourself on not being an ostrich?'

Sheila sat up, was silent for a while. It was as if what her mother said had not touched her, had gone unheard. Then she said very quietly, 'If you're a human being, you have to be against nuclear weapons. It's a . . . a sort of definition. Like . . . like mammals suckle their young and insects have six legs. The definition of a human being is one who hates and fears and wants to be rid of nuclear weapons. Because they're the evil, they're the modern equivalent of the devil, of Antichrist – they are all we'll ever know of hell.'

After that, as he remarked to Dora while Sheila made a mysterious secret phone call, there didn't seem any more to be said. Or not for the present. Dora sighed. 'She says Andrew's right wing and only interested in capitalism and he doesn't have an inner life.'

'Presumably she knew that before she married him,' Wexford said.

'She isn't in love any more and that always makes a difference.'

'It's not so much a depraved society that we live in as an idealistic one. People expect to remain in love with their partners all their lives or else break up and start again. Are you still in love with me?'

'Oh, darling, you know I love you very much, I'm devoted to you, I'd be lost without you, I –'

'Exactly,' said her husband, laughing, and he went outside to get himself another beer.

* * *

437

Nothing had been said about Sheila staying the night. She had arrived at four and in the usual course of things would have started back for London at about nine. It was less than an hour's drive. But the phone call she had made changed her mind, or so it seemed. She came back into the room looking pleased, looking happier than she had since Wexford arrived home, and announced that if they didn't mind – this with the self-confidence of the always-beloved child to whom parents' 'minding' was unknown – she would stay until tomorrow, she might even stay until after lunch tomorrow.

'Mother's the only person I know who still cooks roast beef and Yorkshire pudding for Sunday lunch.'

Wexford thought that asking her where she was living now could hardly be construed as interference, but he resisted saying how much he had liked the house in Hampstead.

'I had to move out, didn't I? I couldn't go on living in Downshire Hill, in Andrew's house that he'd paid for, and turn him out. Someone told him it was worth two million.' She sat down on the floor, hugging her knees. 'I can't cope with that kind of money. I've got this flat in Bloomsbury, Coram Fields, and it's OK, it's really quite grand.' She flashed a smile at her father. 'You'll like it.'

Dora had the *Radio Times* on her lap. 'Nearly time for Lady Audley. I don't want to miss it, so if you don't like watching yourself I'll have to send you to bed.'

'Oh, Mother. Do you really imagine I haven't seen it? I don't mind watching it again with you, but of course I saw a preview. Look, I must rush outside though and move my car so that Pop can put his in. No, I'll move mine and put his in. It doesn't matter if I miss the beginning of –'

'I'll move the cars,' Wexford interposed. 'We've got five minutes. Keys, please, Sheila.'

She fished them out of her jeans pocket. His car was a little wide for the garage and he had made his offer less out of altruism than for fear of getting the new Montego scraped. Dora switched on the television. The wind had dropped and the night was dark and quiet, rather misty, each streetlamp a yellow blur. Between his garden and the empty site next door that had never been built on, the fence was sagging, in places laid flat on the flowerbed where the wind had felled it. The last

438

few leaves on the cherry tree in his front lawn had been shrivelled by early frost and still clung to the nearly bare branches. Leaves lay everywhere, dark and wet, a blackened coating on path and pavement. Someone had found a child's Fair Isle glove on this mat of leaves and laid it on top of the low wall. The street was deserted. In a bay window opposite, between dark evergreen shrubs standing like sentries, between open curtains, he saw the blue glow of a screen suddenly flooded with colour and his daughter's face filling it in close-up.

Sheila hadn't locked the Porsche. Wexford opened the door and got into the driving-seat. It was an irony that his much cheaper and less prestigious car had automatic transmission, while this one had a manual gearbox. Presumably Sheila preferred it that way. The Montego had been his for only six months and it was the first automatic car he had ever possessed, but even so he was coming near to forgetting about letting in clutches and shifting handles. So much so that when he switched on the ignition he failed to notice she had left the car in bottom gear. It jumped – being a powerful sports car it bounded like a spirited horse – and stalled. Wexford grinned to himself. So much for his conviction that he was the more careful driver. Another two inches and the Porsche would have hit his garage doors.

He moved the gear lever into neutral and switched on the engine once more. His foot on the clutch pedal, he was moving the lever into reverse when he became aware of a feeling of unparalleled strangeness, an unaccountable sensation of being more than usually alert and alive. It was as if he were young again, a young man with the vigour and carefree nature of youth. Some strengthening elixir seemed to surge through his veins. On this damp, dark night when he was tired at the end of a long hard day, he was visited with a renewal of youth and power, a springiness in muscle and nerves like a young athlete's.

All this was momentary. It came in a flash that was also a piercing ray of enlightenment. Did he hear anything? The ticking mechanism as of a clock – or was that imagination, some vibration in his brain? The thrusting gear slid into the reverse position, made contact, and without knowing why, without a pause for reasoning, he flung open the car door and precipitated himself with all his force horizontally out as the roar came behind him, the earthquake, the loudest most violent explosion he had ever known.

It happened simultaneously, all of it – the bomb going off, the leap from the doomed car, the fierce blinding pain as he struck his head on something cold and upright and hard as iron . . .

5

After Dorothy Sanders had been driven home, Burden meant
to go to the Irelands' house at Myringham. But he would be
too late now to see his son put to bed, too late to enjoy (as
Wexford, quoting, had once expressed it) '. . . those attrac-
tions by no means unusual in children of two or three years
old; an imperfect articulation, an earnest desire of having his
own way, many cunning tricks and a great deal of noise.' His
wife didn't expect him until later and the house would be full
of visiting relatives.

Instead, after a lapse of ten minutes or so and without giving
any warning of his intention, he followed Dorothy Sanders.
Something in her son's appearance and manner told him this
wasn't the kind of young man who went out on Saturday
nights. And indeed it was Clifford himself who opened the
door to him. His was a shut-in face, mask-like and inexpressive, with a pudginess about the features. He spoke
lifelessly, showing no apparent surprise at another visit from a
policeman. Burden was rather curiously reminded of a dog
owned by a former neighbour of his. The owner had been
inordinately proud of its submission, its total obedience, the
subservience with which it had responded to his severe
training. And one day, without warning, without any
apparent prior change in its character, it had savaged a child.

Clifford, however, seemed to have the right idea and was
leading Burden into that back room to which, on the
inspector's previous visit with Wexford, he had retreated to
watch television, when his mother opened the living-room
door and said in her slow harsh voice to come in, as there could

be nothing the policeman had to say to her son which she couldn't hear.

'I'll have a word with Mr Sanders on his own for the time being, if you don't mind,' Burden said.

'I do mind.' She was rude in a way that wasn't even defiant; it was uncompromising, straight rudeness, with a straight look into her interlocutor's eye. 'There's no reason why I shouldn't be there. This is my house and he'll need me to get his facts straight.'

Clifford neither blushed nor turned pale; he did not even wince. He simply stared ahead of him as if thinking of something deeply sad. Long, long ago Burden had learned that you do not let the public get the better of you. Lawyers, yes, inevitably sometimes, but not the untrained public.

'In that case, I'll ask you to accompany me to the police station, Mr Sanders.'

'He won't go. He's not well, he's got a cold.'

'That's unfortunate, but you leave me no choice. I've my car here, Mr Sanders. If you'd like to get your coat on? It's a nasty damp night.'

She yielded, going back into the room she had come from and slamming the door with calculation, not from temper. Burden resisted the hackneyed maxim that bullies give way if you stand up to them, but he had found nevertheless that it was usually true. Would Clifford profit by his example? Probably not. It had gone too far with him; he needed help of a more expert kind. And it was of this that Burden first asked him when they were seated in the bleak dining room, furnished only with table, hard upright chairs and television set. On one wall hung a mirror, on another a large dark and very bad painting in oils of a sailing vessel on a rough sea.

'Yes, I go to Serge Olson. It's a sort of Jungian therapy he does. Do you want his address?'

Burden nodded, noted it down. 'May I ask why you go to . . . Dr Olson, is it?'

Clifford, who showed no signs of the cold his mother claimed for him, was looking at the mirror but not into it. Burden would have sworn he was not seeing his own reflection. 'I need help,' he said.

Something about the rigidity of his figure, his stillness and

442

the dullness of his eyes stopped Burden pursuing this. Instead he asked if Clifford had been to the psychotherapist on Thursday afternoon and what time he had left.

'It's an hour I go for, five till six. My mother told me you knew I was in the car park – I mean, that I put the car there.'

'Yes. Why didn't you tell us that at first?'

He shifted his eyes, not to Burden's face but to the middle of his chest. And when he answered Burden recognised the phraseology, the manner of speech, as that which people in therapy – no matter how inhibited, reserved, disturbed – inevitably pick up. He had heard it before. 'I felt threatened.'

'By what?'

'I'd like to talk to Serge now. If I'd had some sort of warning I'd have tried to make an appointment with him and talk it through with him.'

'I'm afraid you're going to have to make do with me, Mr Sanders.'

Burden was apprehensive for a moment that he was to be confronted with total silence against which even an experienced detective can do little. Sounds from Mrs Sanders could now be heard. She was in the kitchen moving about, making an unnecessary noise by putting crockery down heavily and banging instead of closing cupboard doors. Whatever she was doing it seemed to be contrived to disturb. He winced at the sound of something breaking as it fell from her hands on to a stone floor. And then he heard another sound – he had got up to stand by the window – and this was far distant, the dull roar of an explosion. He stood quite still, his ear to the glass, listening to the reverberations die away. But he thought no more of it once Clifford began to speak.

'I'll try and tell you what happened. I should have told you before, but I felt threatened. I feel threatened now, but I'd be worse if I didn't tell you. I left Serge's place and I drove to the car park to pick up my mother. I saw there was a dead person lying there before I parked the car. I went to look at it – when I had parked the car, I mean – because I meant to call the police. You could see the person had been killed; that was the first thing you could see.'

'What time was this?'

He shrugged. 'Oh, evening. Early evening. My mother

wanted me there at a quarter past six. I think it was before that; it must have been, because she wasn't there and she's never late.'

'Why didn't you call the police, Mr Sanders?'

He looked at the picture on the wall, then at the dark shiny window. Burden saw his reflection in it, impassive, one would have said devoid of feeling.

'I thought it was my mother.'

Burden turned his eyes from the reflected image in the dark glass. 'You what?'

With patience, in a heavy, almost sorrowful way, Clifford repeated what he had said. 'I thought it was my mother.'

And she had thought it was her son. What was the matter with the pair of them that each expected to find the other dead? 'You thought Mrs Robson was your mother?' There was a slight resemblance between the two women, Burden thought wonderingly – that is, to a stranger there might be . Both were of an age, thin, grey-haired, dressed in the same kind of clothes of the same sort of colour . . . but to a son?

'I knew it wasn't really my mother. Well, after the first shock I knew. I can't explain what I felt. I could tell Serge, but I don't think you would understand. First I thought it was my mother, then I knew it wasn't and then I thought someone was doing it to . . . to mock me. I thought they had put it there to get at me. No, not quite that. I said I couldn't explain. I can only say it made me panic. I thought this was an awful trick they were persecuting me with, but I knew it couldn't be. I knew both things at the same time. I was very confused – you don't understand, do you?'

'I can't say I do, Mr Sanders. But go on.'

'I said I panicked. My "shadow" had taken me over completely. I had to get out of there, but I couldn't just leave it lying there like that. Other people would see it like I had.' Dark colour had come into his face now and he held his hands clasped tightly. 'I had an old curtain in the boot of the car I'd used to cover the windscreen in cold weather. I covered it up with that.' Suddenly he shut his eyes, screwing them up as if to drive away the sight, to blind himself. 'It wasn't covered, you understand, when I found it, not when I found it. I covered it up and then I went away, I ran away. I left the car and ran out of the car park. Someone was in the lift, so I ran up the stairs. I went home, I ran out into the street at the back and then home.'

'It didn't occur to you then that you'd meant to phone the police?'

The eyes opened and he expelled his breath. Burden repeated his question and Clifford said, with a tinge of exasperation now, 'What did it matter? Someone would phone them, I knew that. It didn't have to be me.'

'You went out by the pedestrian gates, I suppose.' Burden remembered Archie Greaves' evidence, the running 'boy' he had taken for a scared shoplifter. And he remembered what Wexford had said about the sound of feet pounding down the car park stairs. That had been Wexford in the lift. 'Did you run all the way home? It's getting on for three miles.'

'Of course I did.' The voice held a tinge of contempt.

Burden left it. 'Did you know Mrs Robson?'

The blank look was back, the colour returned to normal – a clay pallor. Clifford had never once smiled; it was hard to imagine what his smile would be like. 'Who's Mrs Robson?' he said.

'Come now, Mr Sanders. You know better than that. Mrs Robson is the woman who was killed.'

'I told you I thought it was my mother.'

'Yes, but when you realised it couldn't be?'

He looked Burden in the eyes for the first time. 'I didn't think any more.' It was a devastating remark. 'I told you, I didn't think, I panicked.'

'What did you mean just now by your "shadow"?'

Was it a pitying look Clifford Sanders gave him? 'It's the negative side of personality, isn't it? It's the sum of the bad characteristics in us we want to hide.'

Not at all satisfied with what he had been told, finding the whole of this man's behaviour and much of his talk incomprehensible and even sinister, Burden resolved just the same to pursue it no further until the next day. It was at this point, though, that his determination began to take shape, a decision to get to the bottom of Clifford's disturbed mind and whatever motives had their source there. His behaviour was immensely suspicious; and more than that – disingenuous. The man was

445

trying to make him, Burden, look a fool; he thought himself the possessor of an intellect superior to a policeman's. Burden was familiar with this attitude and the reaction it produced in himself – the chip on his shoulder, as Wexford called it – but he could not be persuaded that it was unjustified.

In the living room now, he talked to a rigid and sullen Dorothy Sanders, getting nowhere in his attempts to discover if Mrs Robson had been known to the family. Clifford brought in a basket of coal, fed a fire which did little to raise the temperature in the room, went away and returned with soap-smelling hands. Both mother and son insisted Mrs Robson had been unknown to them, but Burden had the curious feeling that though Dorothy Sanders' ignorance was genuine, her son was lying, or at least evading the truth for some obscure reason of his own. On the other hand, Clifford might have killed without motivation, or without the kind of motivation that would be understandable to a rational man. For instance, suppose he had not found a dead body and thought it was his mother's, but had seen a woman who had suggested to him his mother in her worst aspects and for this reason had himself killed her?

After leaving them, Burden drove further down the narrow road which he now remembered – though there was nothing to show it – was called Ash Lane. The Sanders' house therefore was very likely Ash Farm. But as this passed through his mind and as he was thinking that they seemed to have no neighbours, he came to a bungalow set a little way back from the road which proclaimed itself as Ash Farm Lodge on a rustic board attached to wrought-iron gates. This he could see in his headlights. The bungalow itself was in darkness but as he paused, the engine running and the headlights beam undipped, a light came on in the house and a man appeared at the window.

Burden reversed and began turning the car, a lengthy process in that narrow defile. When he was once more pointing in the direction of Kingsmarkham he glanced to his right and with a start – more a jolt than an actual shock – he saw that the man had come outside and was standing on the doorstep looking at the car, his hand clutching the collar of a cowed-looking retriever. By now the whole place – with the two barns and tall silo behind it, plainly the present farmhouse – blazed with light. Burden drove off. He wouldn't have been surprised to hear a shotgun let off behind him, or to see the dog frenziedly pursuing the car. But nothing happened, there was only darkness and silence and an owl calling.

The news about Wexford reached Burden in a peculiarly horrible way. It was due to his own haste and keenness, he afterwards realised, behaving like some young ambitious copper instead of enjoying his day of rest. Of course, the point was that it would hardly have been a day of rest with Jenny's demanding mother and the Ireland aunts, and Jenny running up and down stairs. Even if he had glanced at the Sunday paper before he left Myringham, he would only have read commentaries on the latest dramatic developments in the Israeli Embassy trial; there would have been nothing in it about the car bomb. The explosion had happened too late in the evening for that. And because the house was full of guests, no one had looked at television on Saturday night.

He phoned Ralph Robson before he left, but it was Lesley Arbel who answered, who agreed to his coming though telling him she couldn't think why as they had absolutely nothing more to tell him. Driving up the hill to Highlands, he told himself it was a pointless interview he had ahead of him, as the obvious thing was to wait until the next day and consult the Social Services department of Kingsmarkham Council. They might keep no records of those for whom their past home helps had worked, but they were more likely to put forward ideas and suggestions than Ralph Robson was.

The invalidism his niece fostered still kept the widower in his dressing gown. He seemed to have aged even in this short time, to hobble more painfully and be more bent. He sat by the gas fire with on his lap a little circular tray fancifully printed with wild birds in improbable colours, on which reposed a cup of tea and a plate of sugar-frosted biscuits. Burden had hardly been taken into the room by the girl – who this morning was dressed in a pink silk outfit, a kind of trouser suit with sarong top and harem pants, and very high-heeled pink shoes – when there came a ring at the doorbell and another visitor arrived. Lesley Arbel had no scruples about showing in the newcomer,

447

though she must have been aware that Burden expected a private interview with her uncle. It was the neighbour opposite he and Wexford had seen from the window who had called, a Mrs Jago as far as Burden could gather from the mumbled introduction Robson made.

The reason for the visit seemed to be the usual one at a time of bereavement. She had come to see if there was anything she could do – any shopping, for instance, that she could get on the following day when Lesley Arbel had gone. Burden wasn't much interested in her, noticing only that she was a large stout woman, puffily overweight, dark and florid, and with a strong accent that suggested Central Europe to him. At least she seemed to have the tact or the good sense to realise Burden wanted privacy, and she left again as soon as Robson had said he would take up her offer and would she mind coming in again on the following morning?

The front door had scarcely closed and Lesley Arbel passed the hall mirror with an inevitable glance into it, when Robson said, 'It's time they did something for us. It's their turn, the lot of them. When you consider what my wife did for everyone in this blessed street, never spared herself, nothing was too much trouble. She'd only to hear someone was a bit under the weather and she'd be round seeing what she could do. Especially the old folks. I reckon she did more good on her own than all those so-called social services people. Isn't that right, Lesley?'

'She did a lot more good than my agony aunt,' Lesley said. 'Well, she was sort of agony aunt herself, wasn't she? I used to call her that – joking, of course.'

Mystified, Burden echoed her words. 'Your agony aunt?'

'People brought her their troubles, didn't they?' It was Robson who answered for her. 'She works,' he said in a rather proud way, 'for the agony aunt on the magazine. For *Kim*. It's the problem page – you know, all those letters from readers about their troubles that the agony aunt answers. Lesley's her assistant.'

'Secretary, Uncle.'

'A bit more than a blessed secretary to my way of thinking. More a right hand. I thought you know all that,' he said to Burden.

'No,' Burden shook his head. 'No, I didn't know. Your aunt – I mean your real aunt, Mrs Robson – I understand she'd been a council home help. Can you remember the names of some of the police she worked for?'

He addressed this question as much to Robson as his niece and Robson immediately took exception to it. 'Home helps don't work for people. They don't have employers, they have clients. They're more civil servants really.'

With an effort at patience Burden accepted this. He had to listen while Robson made out a case for his wife's having carried out her civil servant's function in the home of (it sounded like) every elderly, sick or deprived person in greater Kingsmarkham. Individual names, though, he couldn't recall. He enumerated the tasks his wife had performed gratuitously for the neighbours, and by association this recalled shopping to him and from here the two bags of groceries which the police still retained. With a slightly scathing edge to his voice, he said, 'I suppose you'll say you've got too much on your plates with last night's trouble to worry about a minor matter like that.'

'Last night's trouble?'

'The car bomb. One of your blokes got blown up, didn't he?'

Lesley Arbel said, 'The one that was here with you – or that's how I understood it from the TV. I'm sure it was his name they said.'

Practice at not showing one's feelings comes in useful. And it is true that shock stuns. Burden remembered now the dull and distant explosion he had heard on the previous evening while standing up against the french windows in the Sanders' dining room. Some sense of dignity, some knowledge that it would be wrong and a matter for later regret to do so, stopped him inquiring any more from Robson and his niece. But he was numbed with shock too, getting up almost mechanically, making routine remarks, the replies to which he found afterwards that he had totally forgotten. He was aware too – and this he did remember – of their faces looking at him curiously and with a mild, perhaps only imagined, malice.

Robson said something more about his groceries, something about wanting them before he gave his neighbour Mrs Jago a shopping list, and then Burden had made his escape, was

449

keeping himself from running to his car until the door had closed on Lesley Arbel's pink silk and high heels. He ran then.

Wexford's house was about as far from Highlands as it was possible to be, yet still be situated in Kingsmarkham. It wasn't wasting time, it was to calm himself, to make him a safer driver, that he went first into the phone box at the foot of the hill only to find it vandalised and the lead pulled from the wall. The second phone box he tried was the kind which, along with its fellows in the railway-station entrance, could only be operated with a Telecom card. Burden got back into the car, the palms of his hands damp and sliding on the steering wheel. He turned into Wexford's street with the feeling that he hadn't really breathed for five minutes; he seemed to have been holding his breath until his throat closed up. Yet all the time he was clinging to the hope that Robson and his niece might somehow be mistaken. Now he 'found the difference' as Wexford could have quoted to him, 'between the expectation of an unpleasant event, however certain the mind may be told to consider it, and certainty itself.'

The sight of Wexford's house came as a second shock, and one not dulled by the first.

The garage was no longer there. The room over the garage was no longer there. The whole area between what remained of Wexford's house – the basic three-bedroomed structure – and the open ground next door was a heap of rubble, bits of car body, branches and twigs, shreds of fabric, twisted metal, broken glass. The side of the house from which the garage and the room above it had been torn was open to the weather – fortunately this morning mild and dry – and no attempt had yet been made to shroud in tarpaulins the gaping rooms in one of which a bed could be seen, in the other a picture hanging crooked on blue wallpaper. Burden sat in his car with the window down and stared at it. He stared in horror at the devastation and at the garden now revealed beyond, where fruit trees held leafless boughs against a tranquil pale blue sky.

In the middle of the front lawn the stout cherry tree still retained its branches – even, incredibly, some of its frostbitten leaves. And the lavender hedge which Wexford had so frequently in the past weeks promised to trim back as soon as he had the time was mostly still there, while looking as if the

450

passage through it of a heavy missile had crushed some of it to the ground. The front wall was still there and undamaged, a child's woollen glove lying on one of the piers; Burden couldn't imagine how it came to be there. He looked back again at the wreck of the house, at what seemed to him only half or less of a house remaining. Then, slowly, he got out of the car and walked towards the front door, though he knew there could be no one living there now. If either of them survived, there could be no one there now . . .

He found himself numbed where he stood, paralysed and quite unable to think how next to act, when a man came out of the house next door, the house Wexford called next door though it was separated from his by a narrow open space that no one had ever been able to decide was large enough for a building site.

He said to Burden, 'How is he? Is he. . . ?'

'I know nothing. I didn't even know . . .'

It was as if the street had been watching for him, took him necessarily for the bringer of news. A woman came out from opposite, a couple with a small child from further down on the same side.

The man next door said, 'He was in the car, his daughter's car. Sheila, you know. It was a hell of a bang, like the bombs in the war. I can just remember the war. My wife and I, we came out and there was smoke and you couldn't see a thing. I said to phone the police first thing and I did, but someone else had done it already. The ambulance got here like a shot. I must hand it to them, they didn't waste time. But we couldn't see what happened, only that they took someone away on a stretcher and then it was on the late-night news on telly about Mr Wexford and a car bomb, but they didn't know much, they couldn't tell you much.'

'He was lying on the lawn there,' said the woman with the child. 'He was lying there unconscious.'

'He was blown out of the car,' said her husband. 'It was the most amazing thing. We were watching Sheila in her serial and we heard this terrific bang and it was here, it was her car . . .'

'Where are they now, Sheila and her mother?' Burden asked.

'Someone said they went to the other daughter, wherever she lives.'

451

Burden said no more. Shaking his head, aware that he held one hand pressed against it as if it ached, he went back to his car and started the engine.

6

His dream was of cherry trees, notably the one George Washington was said to have chopped down and then been unable to tell a lie about when questioned by his father. A white cherry though, presumably that was, like the ones he had seen in a picture somewhere that were planted along the shores of the Potomac. Because of Washington's particular affinity with cherry trees? It must be. Probably those pink double cherries whose flowers looked as if made from crêpe paper weren't invented then. The one in his garden had been given him a year after he moved into the house by his father-in-law and he had never liked its papery blossoms and unnatural weeping branches, though he had liked his father-in-law very much. The tree was pretty for one week of the year, around the end of April . . .

He wasn't dreaming any more; this was more in the nature of a reverie. In some cherry-growing areas they put scarecrows in the trees, and in others sewed together sheets of netting large enough to protect the fruit from birds. Not that his tree was the kind that ever bore fruit but was sterile, those bright fluffy blossoms falling and leaving not a trace behind. He was aware now of a dull ache in his head above the forehead, a pain unaccountably associated with cherry trees. And yet not unaccountably . . . no. He opened his eyes, said to anyone who might be there, though for all he knew no one was, 'Did I hit my head on the cherry tree?'

'Yes, darling.'

Dora was sitting at his bedside and round the two of them the curtains were drawn. He tried to sit up but she shook her head, putting out her hand.

'What time is it?'

'About eleven. About eleven on Sunday morning.' She read what was passing through his mind. 'You haven't been unconscious all this time; you came round in the ambulance on the way here. You've been asleep.'

'I don't seem to remember anything except hitting my head on the cherry tree. Oh, and taking a sort of flying leap for some unknown reason . . . maybe from the front doorstep? I can't think why.'

'There was a bomb,' she said, 'underneath the car. It wasn't our car, it was Sheila's. Something you did set it off – I mean, whoever had driven it would have set if off.'

Wexford digested that. He couldn't remember; he wondered if he ever would. Dora and Sheila had been watching television and he came into the front garden for something and leapt into the darkness as a man who flies in a dream might, but the tree was in his way . . . Dora, though, was saying he was in a car, Sheila's car.

'I was in a car?'

'You went out to move Sheila's car and put ours away.'

'The bomb was meant for Sheila?'

She said unhappily, 'It looks like that. Well, it must have been. You mustn't distress yourself, you're supposed to rest.'

'I'm all right. I've only had a bang on the head.'

'You've got cuts and bruises all over you.'

'It was meant for Sheila,' he said. 'Oh God, thank God I drove it. Oh, thank God! I don't remember, but I must have driven it. Am I in the Infirmary? In Stowerton?'

'Where else? The Chief Constable's downstairs and he wants to see you. And Mike's dying to see you; he thought you were dead. It was on television about you. Lots of people thought you were dead, darling.'

Wexford was silent, digesting it. He wouldn't think about Sheila at the moment and how near she had been to death, he wouldn't think of that yet. A sense of humour began creeping back.

'One thing, we shan't have to have the fence done,' he said and then he went on, 'A bomb. Yes, a bomb. Have we got any house left?'

'Well, you mustn't distress yourself. A bit more than half a house.'

Burden was temporarily in charge of the Robson case. It was his belief that Wexford would be off for at least a fortnight, though Wexford himself said that a day or two would do it. That was what he said to Colonel Griswold, the Chief Constable, whose sympathy was conveyed in incredulity that Wexford could remember nothing about the bomb and unreasonable anger against Burden for going away for the night without telling anyone.

'I'll make them let me go home tomorrow,' he told Burden.

'I shouldn't – not if I'd got your home to go to.'

'Yes. Dora says there's only about half of it left. I never liked that garage extension: I said it was jerry-built. No doubt that's why it fell down. I understand that people in our sort of situation usually go and live in a caravan.'

He had a large bandage round his head. Cuts on his left cheek were dressed with a white plaster. The other side of his face was turning black – before Burden's very eyes, it seemed. Sheila came in while he was still there and threw her arms round her father until he groaned in pain. And then the bomb expert from the Myringham Division of the Serious Crimes Squad came to question him and he and Sheila were obliged to leave. Now Burden, with Sumner-Quist's medical report in front of him, had to make up his mind whether it would be good for Wexford to be shown it later in the day. He would probably ask for it anyway, thus taking the power of showing it or withholding it out of Burden's hands.

In fact, there wasn't much in it Burden didn't already know. The time of Mrs Robson's death was as firmly fixed as it ever could be at between five-thirty-five and five-fifty-five. And death had taken place on the spot where the body was found. She had died of asphyxiation as the result of a ligature being applied to her neck. Sumner-Quist went on to suggest that the ligature – he never once here used the term 'garrotte' – was of wire probably in some kind of plastic coating, minute particles of such a substance having being found in the neck wound. This substance, presently being subjected to lab analysis, was more likely flexible polyvinyl chloride or polyvinyl chloride in combination with one of the polymers such as styrene acrylonitrile.

Burden winced a bit at these names, though he had a pretty good idea of the kind of stuff meant; no doubt it was much like the substance that insulated the lead on his desk lamp. It was suggested that the ligature had a handle at each end which the perpetrator must have grasped in order to secure a purchase on it and avoid cutting his or her own hands.

Gwen Robson had been a strong and healthy woman, five feet one inch tall, weight one hundred and ten pounds. Sumner-Quist estimated her age at three years less than what it had been in fact. She had never borne a child, suffered surgery of any sort. Her heart and other major organs of the body were in sound condition. She had lost her wisdom teeth and three other molars, but otherwise her teeth were present and healthy. If someone hadn't come up behind her in a car park with a garrotte, thought Burden, she would very likely have lived another thirty years; she would long have outlived that arthritic, prematurely aged husband.

The Home Help Service was administered by the County Council, not the local authority, Burden soon discovered. It functioned from one of those bungalow buildings that house administrative officers in the grounds of once great private houses all over England. The great house in question was called Sundays on the Forby Road near the junction with Ash Lane. It had until recently been in private hands and, approaching it, Burden remembered the pop festival which had been held there back in the seventies and the murder of a girl during that festival. A huge sum had been spent on the purchase, causing anger among local ratepayers. But Sundays had been bought and these ugly single-storey buildings soon put up in the environs of the house. The mansion itself, though in part offices, was also available as a conference centre and for courses. Burden noted that a course in word processing was due to begin that day. His appointment was with the Home Help Supervisor, but it was her deputy who met him and began telling him pessimistically that they could give him very little help. Their records went back only three years and Mrs Robson had been gone for two. The Deputy Supervisor could remember her, but the Supervisor herself had been in her present post less than two years. She produced for Burden a list of names, with addresses, of those men and woman who had been Gwen Robson's 'clients'.

'What does a cross after a name indicate?'

'It means they've died,' she said.

Burden saw that there were more crosses than otherwise. On an initial glance no name or address leaped out significantly.

'What did you think of Mrs Robson?' he asked. This was Wexford's technique and although Burden did not altogether approve of it, he thought he might as well give it a go.

The reply came slowly, as if a good deal of thought and calculation was going into it. 'She was efficient and very reliable. A great one for phoning in, if you know what I mean. She'd warn you by phone if she was going to be even ten minutes late.'

Burden, irrepressibly, saw again the resemblance between the dead woman and Dorothy Sanders. Here was a new point of similarity – a shared obsession with time – but what he wanted was a meeting point, a location at which she and Clifford Sanders might have come into collision.

'I don't want to speak ill of her. That was a dreadful way to die.'

'It won't go any further,' said Burden, hope springing. 'What you say to me will be treated in confidence.'

'Well, then, she was a terrible gossip. Of course I didn't have that much to do with her, and to tell you the truth I used to avoid having much contact with her, but it seemed to me sometimes that she liked nothing better than finding out some poor old dear's private trouble or secret or whatever and spreading it round this place. Starting off always of course with that old one about it being within these four walls and she wouldn't say it to anyone else and so forth. I don't say there was any harm in it, mind, I don't say there was malice. As a matter of fact it was all done quite sympathetically, though she was a bit moralistic. You know the kind of thing – how wicked it was to have a baby without being married, how unfair on the child, and people living together not knowing the rewards of a happy marriage.'

'There doesn't seem much in that,' Burden said.

'Probably not. She was a great talker, she never stopped talking, and I don't suppose there's much in that either. I'll give her one thing, she was devoted to her husband. She was one of those women who are married to perfectly ordinary men and go about saying how wonderful they are – one in a million – and how lucky they are to have got a man like that. I don't know whether it's sincere, or if they're trying to make out they've got an exceptional marriage or what. I remember her going on in here one day about someone she knew who'd had a Premium Bond come up. If that happened to her, she said, the first thing she'd do would be to buy her husband some special kind of car – I don't know what, a Jaguar maybe – and then she'd take him on holiday to the Caribbean. Anyway, you've got your list; it's the best I can do, and I hope it's of some help.'

Burden was disappointed. He wasn't sure what he had expected – some name on the list, perhaps, to tally with that of a witness in the case or with someone he had talked to in connection with it. As it was, because he had gone so far, everyone whose name was here would have to be seen. Archbold or Davidson could do that. Among those whose names were followed by a cross Burden noted that of a man who had lived in the sheltered housing at Highlands opposite the Robsons' own home: Eric Swallow, 12 Berry Close, Highlands. But what could that signify? The only difference between Eric Swallow and the others was that he was a 'client' who happened to have lived on the other side of the street from his home help.

The alibi of Clifford Sanders was the next important question of Burden's day. He saw from his notes that Clifford had told him he had left the psychotherapist Serge Olson at six p.m. Queen Street, where Olson had his premises in the flat over the hairdressers, was metered and except on Saturday mornings there were usually meters available. Burden, due to see Olson at half-past noon, stood in Queen Street observing that now, late on a Monday morning, three of the twelve meters were vacant. Clifford could easily have been in his car and away by two minutes past six if he left Olson at six. The worst of the Kingsmarkham rush-hour traffic would have been over by then and he could have got into the Barringdean Shopping Centre car park with ease by ten-past six. But there was no way, if he was telling the truth, that he could have been there before five minutes to six.

Briefly calling in at the police station, Burden had phoned Stowerton Royal Infirmary to be told that Wexford was 'satisfactory and comfortable', a formula that conveys to the nervous caller the imminence of death. Burden had wasted no more time on the Infirmary, but phoned Dora at her elder daughter's. They had said that if Wexford continued to make good progress he could leave the hospital on Thursday. Wexford said he was going out tomorrow. Bomb experts were at the house, sifting through rubble, and until they were finished nothing could be done about clearing up the mess. Burden was early for his appointment and he walked up and down looking in the windows of the newly refurbished Midland Bank, the shoe boutique and the toy-shop, but thinking about the bomb and wondering if it had really been meant for Sheila. Why would anyone want to blow up Sheila? Because she had cut the wire round a Ministry of Defence air base?

Burden strongly disapproved of the Campaign for Nuclear Disarmament and Greenpeace and Friends of the Earth and 'all those people'. This was one of the few issues on which he and his wife disagreed, or on which his wife had not won him over to her point of view. He thought they were all cranks and anarchists, either misguided or in the pay of the Russians. But it was quite feasible that other cranks, equally if not more reprehensible, might try to blow them up. Such a thing had been attempted – and indeed had succeeded – in the case of the Greenpeace vessel in the South Pacific. On the other hand, suppose some enemy of Wexford's – even if it were not too far-fetched, someone involved in the Robson case – knew that when Sheila stayed with him he was always in the habit of moving her car in order to put his own away? Whether or not this was true Burden was unsure but he thought it likely, knowing his chief. It had been a dark, misty evening. Would it have been possible to creep unseen across the wasteland and fasten that bomb to the underside of the Porsche? Burden found he knew very little about bombs.

The hairdressers was called Pelage which Wexford, who had looked it up out of curiosity, said was a collective noun for the fur, hair or pelt of a mammal. It had been open only six months and the interior décor was very hi-tech, resembling nothing so much as the inside of a computer. But the building in which it was housed was as ancient as anything in this part of Kingsmarkham High Street and the narrow steep staircase up which Burden made his way was a good hundred and fifty years old. By the look of the worm-holes in the treads, it wouldn't endure much longer. If the woman descending hadn't been as thin as Burden they would have had difficulty in passing one another, for neither had been prepared to retreat. At the top a door was slightly ajar. There was no bell, so Burden pushed open the door and walked in, calling out, 'Hallo!'

He was in an ante-room, unfurnished but for floor cushions and something folded up to large suitcase size which reminded him of a mobile bench he had once borrowed for pasting wallpaper on, but was more likely to be a massage table. The ceiling was painted rather ineptly with signs of the zodiac and on the walls hung strange posters – one of a pair of boots with no legs in them but with distinctly separate toes and toenails, which Wexford could have told him was from a Magritte painting, and another of cats in cloaks and boots riding white horses. Burden remembered what Clifford Sanders had told him about his feelings and thought that this was what he felt here; he felt threatened.

A door at the opposite end of the room opened and a man came out in a very unhurried way. He stood just outside the door with his arms folded. He was a short man and extremely thickset without being fat; great breadth of shoulder and width of hip and thigh were not matched by a big belly. His hair – 'pelage', Burden could not help thinking – was dark and curly, long and thick as a woman's, growing low over his forehead, linked by brown curly sideburns to his round bushy beard which itself was linked to a dense and rather more gingery moustache. Very little face showed, no more than a surprisingly fine-pointed nose, thin lips and a pair of dark eyes like those of a fierce animal.

On the phone Burden had given his full name, but Olson extended his hand and said, 'Come in here, Michael – or is it Mike?'

Burden had an old-fashioned and (his wife said) ridiculous

460

antipathy to being called by his christian name except by friends. But he was aware too of how foolish it made him look to stand on his dignity with a contemporary, so he merely shrugged and followed Olson into . . . what? A consulting room? A therapy room? There was a couch and it was so much like the famous one in the Freud museum in London that Burden and Jenny had been to, even to the scattered oriental rugs, that he was sure a deliberate attempt at duplication had been made. Apart from the couch the room was cluttered with cheap ugly furniture and hung with posters, including an anti-nuclear one which pictured a devastated glove and above it a quote from Einstein: 'The unleashed power of the atom has changed everything except our modes of thinking and thus we drift towards unparalleled catastrophe.' This obscurely reminded Burden of Wexford and recalled to him with how much more of an open mind his chief would have approached this man . . . yet, how could you, at his age, conquer your prejudices?

Olson had sat down at the head of the couch, no doubt a customary position for him. He gazed at Burden in silence, again probably a habitual pose.

Burden began, 'I understand Mr Clifford Sanders is a patient of yours, Dr Olson.'

'A client, yes.' There it was again, that word. Patients, customers, guests – all in his contemporary world had become clients. 'And I'm not a doctor,' Olson went on.

This immediately recalled to Burden indignant articles he had read about purveyors of various forms of psychiatry being permitted to practise without medical degrees. 'But you have some sort of qualification?'

'A psychology degree.' Olson spoke with a kind of calm economy. It was as if he would attempt to justify nothing, explain nothing; there he was, to be taken or left. Such a manner always gives an impression of transparent honesty and therefore made Burden suspicious. It was time for Olson to ask him precisely what it was that Burden wanted to see him about – they always did ask at this point – but Olson didn't ask, he merely sat. He sat and looked at Burden with a calm, mild almost compassionate interest.

'I am sure you have your own code of professional conduct,'

461

Burden said, 'so I won't – at any rate, at this stage – ask you to divulge anything you may have diagnosed in Mr Sanders' . . . personality.' He frankly thought he was being magnanimous and rather resented Olson's faint smile and inclination of the head. 'It's a more practical matter I'm concerned with – the times of Mr Sanders' last appointment with you, in fact. Now as I understand it, he had a five o'clock appointment for a one-hour session and left you at six?'

'No,' said Olson.

'No? That isn't so?'

Shifting his gaze with what seemed perfect control, Olson turned his eyes on to the grey and cratered globe and the Einstein prediction. 'Clifford,' he said, 'comes at five as a general rule, but sometimes I've had to ask him to change and I did that last Thursday. I was giving a lecture in London at seven-thirty and I wanted to allow myself more time.'

'Do you mean to say Mr Sanders didn't come to you last Thursday?'

Olson was perhaps a man who would always smile indulgently at needless consternation. His smile was slight and a little sad. 'He came. I asked him to come half an hour earlier and in fact he came about twenty minutes earlier. And he left me at five-thirty.'

'Do you mean five-thirty, Mr Olson? Or with time for various parting remarks and fresh appointments and so on, would that be nearer twenty to six, say?'

Olson took off his watch, laid it on the table beside him and, indicating it, said, 'At five-thirty I pick up my watch and tell the client – in this case, Clifford – that time's up and I'll see him next week. There are no parting remarks.'

Jenny, Burden's wife, had been in analysis during her pregnancy. Had it been like this? Burden realised he had never exactly asked her. If you lay on that couch – did you? or wasn't it for lying on? – if you talked to this man, then, and opened your heart and spoke of your inmost secrets, he would be like an enormous impersonal ear . . . Burden, without liking or trusting him, suddenly understood that this of course was what was required.

'So Clifford Sanders left here at five-thirty sharp?'

Olson nodded indifferently; there was no question of

Burden's disbelieving him. He said, 'You went to London? Where were you . . . lecturing?'

'I left here at six and walked to the station to get the six-sixteen train that arrives at Victoria at ten-past seven. My talk was on projection-making factors and I gave it before an audience of members of MAPT – that is, the Metropolitan Association of Psychotherapists – at the Association's premises in Pimlico. I went there by taxi.'

The man seemed to have perfect assurance. Burden looked closely at him and said, 'Can you think of any reason, Mr Olson, why Clifford Sanders should have told us that his appointment with you was from five until six and that he left here at six?'

He's going to tell me he was threatened, Burden thought. He's going to talk about threats and defensiveness and projection. Instead, Olson got up and, moving to a very untidy desk which had perhaps once been a kitchen table, slowly turned the pages of an appointment book. He seemed to be examining some particular entry with care. Then he glanced at his watch and some inner reflection made him smile. He closed the book and still standing up, turned to face Burden.

'You may not know this, Michael. You may never have considered what a powerful figure time is in the human psyche. It might not be too presumptuous to suggest he could be another Jungian archetype in the collective unconscious. Certainly for some he can be an aspect of the Shadow.'

Burden stared at him with a failure of understanding as deep as disgust.

'Let's call him Time with a capital T,' said Olson. 'He has been depicted as a god in a chariot with wings and even been given a personification as Old Father Time – I expect you've come across that. Some people seem to be enslaved by time, by this old man with a skull for a face and a scythe in his hand, by this god in the winged chariot hurrying by behind them. They are his servants and they become very worried – very anguished, indeed – if they are not there, all present and correct, to bow down to him and do his bidding. But there are others, Michael, who hate time. They fear him and because this dread is so great and so omnipresent, they have no recourse but to drive him back into the unconscious. He is too

463

frightening and so they banish him. The result of course is a total lack of knowledge of him, a world in which he is absent. His hours and half-hours for them pass uncounted. These are the people – and we all know them – who can never get up in the morning and at night are always astonished that it should be three or four by the time they get to bed. To be on time for a date entails for them an almost superhuman effort. Their friends get to know this and invite them to come half an hour earlier than the party begins. As for a memory of time – to ask them to have any kind of accurate record is almost an act of violence.'

Burden blinked a little. He had seized on a point though.

'Are you telling me that these regular five o'clock appointments with Clifford Sanders were in fact made for four-thirty?'

Olson nodded, smiling.

'But I thought you said he had the five p.m. appointment?'

'I said that he *comes* at five; that isn't quite the same thing.'

'So last Thursday when you phoned him you must have asked him to come at four?'

'And he came about ten minutes late. That is, as I said, he came at about four-forty.' A genuinely good-humoured smile now broke across Olson's face. 'You're thinking I'm dishonest with my poor clients, aren't you, Michael? I'm pandering to their neurosis in a way perhaps that robs them of their basic human dignity – is that it? But I have to live, too, you see, and I have to recognise Time as a figure in my life. I can't afford to waste half an hour of him any more than one of his most abject slaves.'

Neither can I, thought Burden, getting up to take his leave. To his dismay, as he showed him out Olson laid an almost affectionate arm across his shoulder.

'You won't resent a lesson, I'm sure, Mike.'

Burden looked at him, then at the couch, and recovered some of his aplomb. He said with an edge of sarcasm, 'I expect it makes a change for you to talk.'

At first Olson frowned, then his face cleared. 'That's for the Freudians, the silent listening therapist. I talk quite a lot; I help them along.' He had the happy man's simple, unclouded smile.

It looks very much as if it was intended for your daughter, the

464

Serious Crimes Squad man from Myringham said. You say your daughter hadn't given you any prior warning of her intention to visit you? She hadn't given me any prior warning, Wexford said. I don't know about my wife, I didn't ask. You'll have to ask my wife. We have asked her, Mr Wexford, and no – your daughter's visit was a complete surprise to her.

What made the bomb go off?

You were about to back the car, weren't you? You were going to back it out of the garage drive in order to put your own car in, your wife says. We think it was activated by reverse gear – triggered off by putting the gear into reverse. You see, your daughter says she never had the Porsche in reverse between getting into it outside her London flat and arriving at your home about an hour and a half later. And one can see, sir, that there would have been no occasion for her to use the reverse gear.

The bomber wasn't bothered, you can see that. It didn't bother him whether the bomb went off five minutes after she started and outside the Great Ormond Street Hospital for Sick Children, for instance, or down here on Sunday afternoon when she was backing out to go off home. It was all the same to him as long as she was in the driving-seat.

As long as she was in the driving-seat . . . Wexford lay in bed thinking about it. They got him up at four and made him have his tea with a lot of other men seated round a table in the middle of the ward. Some bomber had tried to kill Sheila and had failed – but he wouldn't stop, would he, because he had failed once? He would try again and again. It might be because of her anti-nuclear activities, but on the other hand it might not. Freaks and oddballs were envious of the famous, the successful, the beautiful. There were even people who equated actors with the parts they played and who were capable of seeing Sheila as Lady Audley, a bigamist and murderess. For that she must be punished, for her beauty and her success and her lack of morals; for acting a treacherous wife and for being one . . .

How was he going to live and go about his daily work with that ever-present fear of an assassin stalking Sheila? The newspapers were full of it; he had three daily papers lying on his bed, all of them speculating with a kind of merry cynicism

465

as to what particular terrorists might have it in for Sheila. How was he going to stand all that?

Sylvia came after she had fetched her son Robin from his choir practice and then Burden came at evening visiting, full of the Robson medical report, his theories about Clifford Sanders as perpetrator, Gwen Robson as arch-gossip and ferreter out of secrets in the home help sorority and a curious interview he had had with a psychiatrist.

'This stuff about some people being unpunctual – because that's really what it amounts to – doesn't really affect the issue. Sumner-Quist gives the latest time at which Mrs Robson could have been killed as five to six. Clifford could easily have got there before five to six. Without hurrying he could have got there by a quarter to.'

Wexford made an effort. 'Intending to meet Mrs Robson there? You're saying it was premeditated? Because to keep in with your theory he certainly couldn't have encountered her by chance. He wouldn't have gone to that dreary car park to sit there for half an hour and wait for his mother. Or are you saying he was so lost to time that he didn't know whether it was a quarter to or half-past?'

'Not me,' said Burden, 'Olson the shrink. Anyway, I don't go along with that. I think Clifford has a perfectly normal attitude to time when he wants to have. And why shouldn't it have been premeditated? I don't believe Clifford thought or imagined or fancied or however you like to put it that Gwen Robson was his mother. Anyone would have to be a total banana truck to do that. And if he wanted to kill his mother, he could do that at home. No, the motive is likely to be a good deal more practical than that, as motives usually are.' He looked defiantly at Wexford, waiting for argument, and when none came went on, 'Suppose Gwen Robson was blackmailing him? Suppose she found out some secret about him and was holding it over him?'

'Like what?' said Wexford, and even to Burden his voice sounded weary and uninterested.

'He could be queer – I mean gay – and afraid of Mum finding out. I mean, that's just a possibility since you ask.'

'But you haven't established any sort of link between them, have you? There's no evidence they knew each other. It's the kind of situation in which a son would only know a woman of her age if she were a friend of his mother's – and she wasn't. It's not as if Clifford has ever been in the market for a home help; he's not a housebound octogenarian or some bedridden invalid. And while Mrs Robson *may* have been a blackmailer, have you any actual evidence that she was?'

'I will have,' Burden said confidently. 'Inquest in the morning. I'll give you a complete run-down on what's happened this time tomorrow.'

But Wexford seemed no longer to be following what he said – to be distracted by some action of his neighbour in the next bed, and then by the arrival of a nurse with a drugs trolley – and Burden, looking at him with slightly exasperated sympathy, thought how true it was that patients in hospital rapidly lose all interest in the outside world. The ward and its inmates, what they had for lunch and what sister said, these things are their microcosm.

The inquest opened and was adjourned, as Burden had expected. It could hardly have been otherwise. Evidence was taken from Dr Sumner-Quist, who was again making very free with the term 'garrotte'. And a lab expert was able to treat the coroner to some very abstruse stuff about polymers and long-chain linear polyesters and a substance called polyethylene terephthalate. It was all by way of discovering what the wire of the garrotte had been coated in and Burden wasn't much wiser when the expert had finished, though he gathered it all amounted to grey plastic.

Robson was not in court. There was no reason for him to have attended. Clifford Sanders and his mother were both there; Clifford due for a drubbing from the coroner, Burden thought, for his curious action in covering up the body and running away. But the first witness of all was Dorothy Sanders, who went into the box with deliberate self-assured deportment – having dressed herself, no doubt by chance, in clothes very like those found on the dead woman, even to the lacy brown stockings.

The man who had evidently come with them and who now sat beside Clifford he recognised as the farmer he had seen in Ash Lane, and who had come out on to the doorstep with his dog to stare after Burden's departing car.

7

Houses without women – Burden could always recognise them. It was not that such places were particularly dirty or uncared-for, but rather that the absence of a woman's hand showed in an asymmetry, a placing of objects in bizarre ways, clumsy makeshifts. The kitchen of Ash Farm Lodge – a large kitchen, since the bungalow had obviously been purpose-built for a farmer – was like that: the table littered with account books and pamphlets, a pair of boots standing on a magazine on top of the oven, a dishcloth spread out to dry on the back of a Windsor chair, a twelve-bore shotgun suspended from what was originally a saucepan rack.

The man Burden had seen in court said his name was Roy Carroll. He looked about fifty, perhaps more. His hands were particularly large, red and calloused, and the skin of his face was a darkly-veined red. The dog lay curled up not in a basket but a large drawer. Burden had the feeling that before it dared wake up it would have to indicate in some canine way a request for permission to do so.

Carroll was brusque and uncouth. He had admitted Burden to the house in a grudging fashion and his replies to questions were hardly fulsome, a 'Yes' and a 'No' and a 'Yes' and other grunted monosyllables. He knew 'Dodo' Sanders, he knew Clifford Sanders; he had lived in this house since it was built. When was that? Twenty-one years ago.

'Dodo?' Burden queried.

'That's what they called her, her husband and that. His mum. Dodo they called her, that's what I call her.'

'You're friends?'

'What does that mean? I know her, I've done odd jobs for her.'
Burden asked him if he was married.

'Never you mind that,' Carroll said. 'I'm not now.'

Gwen Robson? He had never heard of her until her death was on television. He had never had a home help in the house. Where was he on the previous Thursday afternoon? Carroll looked incredulous at being asked. Out shooting, he said, getting a rabbit for the pot. This time of the year he was out shooting most days at dusk. Burden noticed something that was interesting but surely of no importance. The magazine the boots stood on was a copy of *Kim*, the last kind of reading matter to associate with a man of Carroll's sort. It brought to mind the poster in Olson's room, the one with the boots that had five toenailed toes but no legs in them, and unaccountably he shuddered.

A weekday morning and Clifford very likely at work. Burden phoned Munster's, the school which ran crash courses for A levels, and asked to speak to Mr Sanders. He wasn't even sure Clifford worked there, but it turned out to have been an intelligent guess. Mr Sanders was teaching. Could they take a message? Wexford would have treated this more delicately, Burden knew that, but he didn't see why he should be tender towards the feelings of someone who was probably a layabout and certainly a liar, who was very probably homosexual, who had mixed-up feelings of confusion between his mother and dead women and was a psychopath anyway. He asked the woman who answered the phone to give Clifford Sanders a message that Detective Inspector Burden had called and would like him to come to the police station and ask for him as soon as his class was finished.

In the meantime, he made an application for a warrant to search the Sanders' house in the expectation of finding something in the nature of a garrotte somewhere. Of course he could simply have asked Mrs Sanders' permission to search, most people don't refuse this request, but he felt that she would. While he was waiting for Clifford he suddenly remembered Robson's shopping bags, so he summoned DC Davidson to find them, locate their contents and have the lot taken round to Highlands. The bags were red Tesco carriers and Burden had had intensive enquiries made at the Tesco store in the Barringdean Shopping Centre. Dressed in brown clothes similar to those worn by Mrs Robson, Marian Bayliss had retraced her possible steps through the centre. One of the checkout assistants remembered her passing through on the previous Thursday and put the time at about five-thirty. Burden began re-reading DC Archbold's report.

Linda Naseem knew Mrs Robson by sight, indeed knew her well enough to comment on the weather and ask after her husband. Gwen Robson was a regular shopper in the store and almost always came in on a Thursday afternoon, but what most interested Burden about this evidence was that Linda Naseem claimed to have seen Mrs Robson in conversation with a girl. This encounter, she said, took place immediately after Mrs Robson had paid and received her change, and when she was standing at the end of the checkout counter putting the goods she had bought into a carrier.

Describe the girl? She had been attending to her next customer and she hadn't taken much notice. Indeed, she hadn't seen the girl's face at all, only her back and the back of her head. She had been wearing a beret or some sort of hat. When Mrs Robson finished packing her bag, she and this girl went off together. At least, they went off. Linda Naseem couldn't absolutely say they went together.

Clifford came to the police station about half an hour after Burden had made his phone call; Munster's School was only about two hundred yards down the High Street. Burden's own office was rather a pleasant, comfortable place where any visitor might have felt he was paying a social call, so Burden didn't take him in there but into one of the interview rooms at the back on the ground floor. The walls were bare, painted the colour of scrambled eggs, and the floor was of grey vinyl tiles. Burden motioned Clifford into one of the grey metal chairs and himself sat down opposite him at the plastic-topped yellow table.

Almost without preamble, he began, 'You told me you didn't know Mrs Robson. That wasn't true, was it?'

Clifford looked truculent to Burden, his dull face sullen. He wasn't showing any obvious symptoms of fear as he spoke in his slow, monotonous voice. 'I didn't know her.'

There was a point in any interrogation or enquiry when

470

Burden simply changed from using a suspect's surname and style to his or her first name. Wexford asked permission before he did this, but Burden never did. Using people's surnames and styles, in his opinion, was very tied up with feeling respect for them. This was why he needed to be called 'Mr' himself. He would have said he reached a stage when he lost respect for the person he was questioning and therefore pushed them a few rungs down the ladder of his esteem. If we had a language – where you could tutoyer and vouvoyer, said Wexford, you'd start thouing them.

'Now, Clifford, I'll be honest with you. Frankly, I don't yet know where you met her or how you knew her, but I know you did. Why not tell me and save me the trouble of finding out?'

'But I didn't know her.'

'When you say that, you're not helping yourself or deceiving me. All you're doing is wasting time.'

Clifford repeated doggedly now, 'I did not know Mrs Robson.' He laid his hands on the table and contemplated them. The nails were closely bitten, Burden noticed for the first time, this gave them the look of a child's hands, pink and pudgy.

'All right, I can wait. You'll tell me in your own good time.'

Did he really take that phrase literally or is he sending me up? Burden wondered. Not a gleam of humour showed on the round blank face when Clifford said, 'I don't have my own good time.'

A change of subject and Burden said, 'You must have been in that car park well before six. Mr Olson has told me you left him not at six but at five-thirty. You must have been there by five-forty-five at the latest. Would you like to know when Mrs Robson died? It was between five-thirty-five and five-fifty-five.'

'I don't know what time I got there,' Clifford said, speaking very slowly. 'It's no use asking me about times. I don't wear a watch, perhaps you've noticed.' He raised his arms in what Burden saw as an effeminate gesture, exposing plump white wrists. 'I don't think I went straight to the car park. I sat in the car and thought about what I'd been saying to Serge. We'd been talking about my mother; hardly anyone calls my mother by her first name any more, not now, but when they did they called her Dodo. It's short for Dorothy, of course.'

471

Burden said nothing, perplexed as to whether he was being teased or whether Clifford generally talked to strangers like this.

'Dodos are large flightless birds, now extinct. They were all killed by Portuguese sailors on Mauritius. My mother isn't a bit like that. Serge and I talked about a man's anima being shaped by his mother and my mother having a negative influence on me. That can express itself in the man having irritable depressed moods, and when I was sitting in the car I thought about that and went back over it all. I like to do that sometimes. The car was on a meter and there was ten minutes to run. And I got out and fed the meter some more.'

'So you do take note of time sometimes, Clifford?'

He looked up and turned on Burden a troubled gaze. 'Why are you asking me questions? What do you suspect me of?'

'Suppose I said you went straight to the shopping centre, Clifford. Isn't that what you did? You parked the car in the car park and then you went in to the shopping centre and ran into Mrs Robson, didn't you?'

'I've told you the truth. I sat in the car in Queen Street. You ought to tell me what you suspect me of doing.'

'Perhaps you'd better go and sit in your car and think about that one,' said Burden, and he let him go.

Such mock naïvety angered him. Dodos, indeed, flightless birds! What was an anima anyway, or come to that a negative influence? Grown men didn't naturally behave and talk like children, not men who were teachers and had been to universities. He was suspicious of the childlike stare, the puzzled ingenuousness. If Clifford was sending him up, he would be made to regret it. In the morning they would search that house. Burden couldn't help thinking how satisfying it would be to have the case all wrapped up before Wexford was back at work.

Sheila, Wexford discovered on being driven from hospital to his other daughter's house, was staying at the Olive and Dove, Kingsmarkham's principal hostelry. There was no room for her as well at Sylvia's, where her parents now occupied the only spare room.

'Anyway, I expect she feels it's easier to have her boyfriend there.'

There was rivalry between the two sisters of a never-quite-expressed kind. Sylvia cloaked her envy under the complacency of a happily married mother of sons. If she would have liked what her sister had – success, fame, the adoration of a good many people, lovers past and in the future – her covetousness was never explicit. But comments were made; a virtue was made of necessity. There was a tendency to talk about fame and money not bringing happiness and show-business people seldom having stable relationships. Married at eighteen, Sylvia would perhaps have liked at least a memory of lovers and the consciousness of something attempted, something done. Sheila, more open about her views, frankly said how nice it must be to have no worries, no fear of the future, reading in a leisurely way for an Open University degree, to be dependent on a loving husband. She meant she would have liked the children, Wexford sometimes thought. Sylvia was waiting for him to ask for enlightenment, but he kept his enquiry to himself until she had gone to fetch the boys from school.

'I know there's someone,' Dora said. 'She was phoning someone she called Ned just before you went out and set that bomb off.'

'Thanks very much,' said Wexford. 'You make it sound as if I put a match to a fuse.'

'You know what I mean. When she comes over this evening, we can ask her about him.'

'I wouldn't ask her,' said Wexford.

But Sheila phoned to say she wasn't coming, that she was postponing her visit to her father until the following morning. Something had come up.

'Come down, I should say,' Sylvia said. 'Come down on the London train. I suppose he's an actor or a Friend of the Earth or both.'

' "Those who find ugly meanings in beautiful things," ' said her father austerely, ' "are corrupt without being charming." ' He returned to the copy of *Kim* magazine he had found lying about.

Sylvia had told them she took it occasionally and had supplied the little defensive explanation people in Jane Austen's day thought they had to give for reading novels. It

473

was something to pass the time; you could pick it up and put it down; some of the stories were of a really high standard. Wexford liked the name of the magazine which seemed to him very avant-garde and appealing, for he confessed to himself that a part of him still lived in a world of *Home Knits* and *Modern Mother*. He turned to the page of enquiries from worried readers.

The 'agony aunt' Lesley worked for was a woman of the name, or alias, of Sandra Dale. At the head of the page was a photograph of her, a plump middle-aged woman with fair curly hair and a sympathetic expression. Two of the letters were featured in bold-face type. One didn't appear at all, only the answer to it: T.M., Basingstoke: Practices like this may seem fun and I can understand they please your boyfriend, but is it worth risking your whole future sexual happiness? One day when you are married or in a permanent relationship, you may bitterly regret habits you can't break but which are keeping you from true fulfilment.'

Wexford wondered if the purpose of this sort of thing was simply the titillation of readers. It would be a very strong-minded or deeply inhibited *Kim* reader who didn't speculate as to the nature of T.M.'s unbreakable habits. Very likely it was Robson's niece who had typed all these replies, having taken them down at Sandra Dale's dictation.

'There's a piece in there about Sheila,' Sylvia said, 'and some quite nice photos from the TV series.'

He turned to look at pictures of Sheila in a white ball-gown, in her Victorian lady's black street dress and bonnet. The last instalment of *Lady Audley's Secret* was showing that evening; it would be repeated on Saturday, but who knew where they would be on Saturday? Neil wanted to watch a programme about finance on another channel and his elder son Robin was trying to persuade his mother to let him stay up and see Auntie Sheila. Rather surprisingly, Sylvia came down on her mother's side and in favour of watching this final episode. Had Neil forgotten they wouldn't be able to see the repeat because they were going out to dinner on Saturday night?

Neil lost and Robin lost. The little boy had come down for the third time in his pyjamas and was standing wistfully in the doorway. Wexford suddenly knew he wasn't going to be able to watch; he had re-read the novel while Sheila was rehearsing for the television adaptation, and he knew very well what was to happen to Lady Audley tonight: she was to be cast into the continental insane asylum. The way he felt, he would be unable to bear seeing Sheila even acting that stuff, to see her manhandled and screaming . . .

His head ached and he was tired. He got up and took the little boy's hand and said he was going to bed, too, so he would come up with Robin. The introductory music, melancholy-sweet, followed them softly up the stairs and then someone closed the door.

It was a dangerous feeling, this excitement born of hunting down a quarry – or born, rather, of creating a quarry fit to be hunted. Burden knew he was doing this and that it would be wise to pause and take stock. He did pause, briefly, and reminded himself how important it was not to tailor facts to fit a theory. On the other hand, he was growing very sure that Clifford Sanders was guilty of this crime. All he must be careful to do was to avoid pushing witnesses. Guide them, yes, but not give them enthusiastic shoves. In a frame of mind he told himself was cool and unbiased, he went very early in the morning to Highlands. There he got a surprise; as he turned into Hastings Road, he saw Lesley Arbel come out of Robson's house and approach his car, the silver Escort which was parked at the kerb. Burden pulled up behind the Escort.

'Not back at work, Miss Arbel?' he asked.

She was dressed with extreme severe formality in a black suit, white tie-necked blouse, black transparent seamed stockings and very high-heeled black patent shoes. With her glistening chestnut-coloured hair and painted eggshell face, she reminded Burden of one of those 'grown-up' dolls little girls have for birthday presents and which come with their own fashionable wardrobe.

'I'm not at work this week. I'm doing a course in word processors.'

'Ah,' said Burden. 'That would be the one at Sundays.'

'The Sundays Conference Centre, yes. The company has given me two weeks off to take the course and it happened to be very convenient to stay with Uncle.' She put a hand in a sleek black glove on the car door, remembered something. 'Uncle's got a bone to pick with you. Those bags of stuff you sent over, he said the piece of beef had gone off. It smelt disgusting, he said. I never saw it – he'd wrapped it up and put it in the bin before I ever got home.'

Taken aback, Burden had no rejoinder, but at that moment another car drew up and parked on the opposite side of the street. The woman called Mrs Jago came down to her front gate as a little girl of about three and a young woman got out of the car; there appeared to be another, bigger child sitting in the passenger seat. The visitor, though thin as a reed, was sufficiently like Mrs Jago as to leave no doubt this was a daughter. A mass of dark curly hair, rather resembling Serge Olson's but longer and glossier, covered half her back. The child, who also had long curly hair, ran to her grandmother and was taken up in her arms, where she clung to the massive bosom like a limpet to a domed, shiny, seaweed-clothed rock.

Ralph Robson was a long time coming to the front door. Burden could hear his stick making muffled thuds on the carpet. By the time the door opened, the two little girls and their mother had once more driven off. Robson was more than ever owl-like this morning, his nose apparently beakier, his mouth pursed, his eyes round and cross. A sports jacket of brindled brown tweed enhanced the effect and the hand on the stick gripped like a bird's claw round a twig. Burden was prepared for an exchange of courtesies, but Robson plunged straight into the bone-picking of which Lesley Arbel had forwarded him: he wanted compensation, he wanted re-imbursement to the amount of four pounds fifty-two which was the price of the piece of spoiled sirloin.

Burden told him to put it all in writing and where to send his complaint. As soon as Robson had switched off that particular diatribe, he got on to the subject of his hip. The pain had intensified since his wife's death, it was ten times as bad as it had been a week ago and he could hear the joint grinding when he so much as shifted his position in a chair. Of course he was having to move about a lot more now that his wife was gone, she had saved him all that. There were areas in this country, he said, where you could get a hip replacement on the National Health Service in a matter of weeks. And he had heard that if you lived elsewhere they could transfer you to one of those places, but his doctor wouldn't have that – his doctor had said it couldn't be done. He had got himself to the surgery the day before, and that was what the doctor had said. It would have been different, he was sure, if he had had his wife to speak up for him.

'Gwen would have got things moving. Gwen would have told him what's what. If she'd known they could get me into some hospital on the other side of the country, she'd never have rested until she got some sense out of him. What's the use of talking now she's gone? I'm stuck with this for years maybe, until I can't stick another blessed day of it and take an overdose.'

It crossed Burden's mind that Robson was rather more than naturally obsessive about his arthritic hip. On the other hand, if you had a thing like that perhaps it would tend to exclude everything else from your existence. That physical pain might even distract you from the mental pain of losing your wife. Intent on not leading Robson (as the judges say), he asked him, once they were seated in front of the realistic blue flames, if he could remember any comments his wife might have made about her past 'clients'. Robson, as expected, immediately said it was a long time ago. Burden pressed him, which only had the effect of making him return to the subject of his hip and Gwen's remarks on what had brought it about and why he should have had arthritis when she didn't. This time Burden said he thought Robson was being obstructive and presumably he did want his wife's killer found.

'You've no business talking to me like that,' Robson said, thumping his stick on the floor and wincing.

'Then cast your mind back and try to remember what your wife said to you about these people. She was a talkative woman, I'm told; she was interested in people. You're not going to tell me she'd come home at lunchtime or in the evening and not say a word to you about the old people she'd been working for? What, she never came back and said old Mrs So-and-So kept all her money in a stocking under the bed, or old Mr Whatever had a lady-friend? Nothing like that, ever?'

Burden need not have worried about leading Robson. These

477

examples, far from stimulating him to invention or recall, seemed to provoke a truculent bewilderment. 'She never said about any old lady keeping money under the bed.'

'All right, Mr Robson,' Burden said, keeping his temper with difficulty, 'what did she talk about?'

An effort was made, as of a disused engine sparking into life with rusty wheels turning. 'There was that old boy over the road – Gwen was very good to him. She went on popping in there day after day long after she stopped working for the council. A daughter couldn't have done more.'

Eric Swallow of 12, Berry Close, Highlands, Burden thought nodding encouragingly at Robson.

'Mrs Goodrich – that was the name. She wasn't so old, but she was crippled with one of those things they just give letters to, MS of MT or something. She'd been a lovely woman, a concert pianist Gwen said. She said she'd got some beautiful furniture in her place – valuable pieces, Gwen thought, worth a fair bit.'

Julia Goodrich of Paston Avenue, since moved from the district.

'I can't remember the rest of them; there was dozens and I can't remember them by name. I mean, there was one as told Gwen she'd had three kids by three different fathers and not married to any of them. That really upset Gwen. And there was an old boy as hadn't nothing but his pension, and used to give Gwen five-pound notes just for cutting his blessed toenails. She gave him a lot of her time, she'd be a good hour with him . . .'

'Someone gave your wife five pounds to cut his toenails?' Burden was intrigued and imagined Wexford's reaction to this bizarre picture. Was some sexual titillation or even satisfaction involved? Surely there must have been.

'There was nothing wrong in it,' Robson said, on the defensive at once. 'He just took his socks off and sat there and she did his nails with clippers. He never touched her, she wasn't that sort. His feet were spotless, she said, clean as a baby's. And there was someone else – I can't remember names – as she gave a regular bath to. He was getting over some illness; he wasn't old, but he couldn't stand the district nurses bathing him and he said Gwen was as gentle as his own nanny when he was a little kid.'

Don't lead him, Burden said to himself. You must take your chance.

'Wait a minute, I've thought of a name: an old spinster called Miss Mac-something.'

'Miss McPhail,' said Burden, thinking this justified. Robson didn't seem interested in how he knew; like a lot of people, he took a degree of omniscience in the police for granted. They only asked questions to catch you out or for their own amusement. 'Miss McPhail of Forest Park.'

'That's her. She was wealthy, had a big house that was going to rack and ruin for want of looking after, and a blessed great garden. This young boy used to come in and do a bit to the garden in his college holidays. She wanted Gwen to come and work full-time for her. No thanks, Gwen said, I've got a husband to see to. I'll give you a hundred pounds a week, she said, and this was four years ago. You're joking, Gwen said, but she said no, that's what she'd give her to be her full-time cook and companion . . . and I reckon Gwen was tempted, only I put my foot down.'

Robson shifted his weight in the armchair and this time Burden thought he heard the hip joint grind. He heard something and saw Robson's face contort. Then Robson said, 'Is that all, then? Got enough, have you?'

Burden didn't answer but got up to go. Miss McPhail was dead now, he reflected as he was leaving, hers was one of the names on the list with a cross after it. Passing his own home, he went in to use the phone and check up on Wexford's recovery, then continued to Ash Farm where a search had been in progress for the past two hours. Clifford wasn't there. Burden hadn't expected him to be, but Dorothy Sanders was waiting for him, her face tragic with woe, her eyes staring.

'They said two hours was the maximum. They said two hours at the outside, and they started at nine.'

'It's only ten-past eleven, Mrs Sanders,' said Burden, who should have known better.

'Why do people say these things and not stick to them?'

'They won't be long now. They'll put everything back as they found it; we do make a point of that.'

479

He made his way upstairs to Davidson and Archbold on the first floor. Archbold pointed up the narrow flight of stairs which lead to the top storey and said the rooms up there were stuffed with old furniture – rubbish, junk, the accumulation of years. Going through all that had delayed them. Burden decided to investigate outside, where Diana Pettit had gone to search the garage and a kind of toolshed attached to the rear fence. He made his way along the passage that must lead to a kitchen and a back way out. Dorothy Sanders had her face pressed against the window, watching the search. Her back was rigid and her arms flexed and she was perfectly still, reacting to his arrival with not the faintest twitch of her body. Burden went out by the back door.

Beyond the Ash Farm ground – you could hardly call it a garden – farmland, drowned in rain, stretched away in all direction. There was no other house in sight. A hill shaped like a camel's hump cut off the view of Kingsmarkham and heavy clouds rested on the ridge of it.

Diana looked round when Burden came in and said, 'There's nothing here, sir.'

'That depends on what you're looking for, Diana. I suppose you've been told what you're looking for?'

'A garrotte, though I'm not very sure what that is.'

Burden put his hands into the box of tools. It was one of those metal boxes divided into sections on two levels, in which the upper drawers can be drawn outwards by a kind of concertina motion. He picked out two objects, saying, 'These would answer the purpose very well.'

480

8

Diana Pettit and DS Martin both told Burden these were the kinds of things to be found in every toolbox in every garden shed. You might as well find a hammer or screwdriver in such a place and call it an offensive weapon. Everybody had a spool of plastic-covered wire and a great many people a garden line for making straight edges. Burden said he didn't; he had never even seen a garden line before. Was DC Pettit sure that's what it was?

Two metal pegs, ring-headed, were linked by a length of twine. The twine was merely knotted on to the pegs and a piece of the plastic wire might well have temporarily replaced it, thus making a serviceable garrotte. He took the things away, getting Diana to give Dorothy Sanders a receipt for them. The wire went to the lab for analysis and comparison with the particles of plastic found in Gwen Robson's neck wound. With a similar length of plastic wire which he had been out to buy tied to the iron pegs, Burden shut himself up in his office and practised garrotting first the angled lamp and then one of the legs of his desk. Neither was the right size for a human neck.

Next morning Linda Naseen, who had Wednesdays off, was back on her checkout. Burden went to talk to her himself. It was exactly a week today since Gwen Robson had come in here, having parked her car underground on the second level, and walked under the glazed covered way to the Barringdean Shopping Centre, arriving inside at about four-thirty. The next three-quarters of an hour were easily accounted for: a little window-gazing and the purchase of two items from Boots, where an assistant remembered her. The toothpaste and

481

talcum powder had been in one of the carriers with the groceries and the light-bulbs from British Home Stores. No one remembered her in there, but that was to be expected. She had probably entered Tesco at about ten-past five, taken a trolley or perhaps only a basket and begun walking round the store picking out items from her list. Clifford Sanders at that time had certainly still been with Olson. Burden saw that he was putting Gwen Robson's visit to the store too early; it was far more likely that she had not gone into Tesco until twenty-past five. That way she wouldn't have reached the checkout until five-thirty-five or maybe a little later.

There were five girls on the Tesco checkouts. Burden was looking for an Indian and three of the girls appeared to be of vaguely Indian origin. He went up to one of them and she pointed down the line to where a small, slight girl of ethereal fairness, white-skinned and flaxen-haired, was changing the spool in her till. As he approached her, he noticed her wedding ring. Of course she was called Naseem because she was married to a Moslem from the East or Middle East. Burden reprimanded himself for jumping to conclusions as he knew Wexford would have admonished him. It was inexcusable in someone of his experience.

She took him into a side room or office marked 'Private' on the door.

'You knew Mrs Robson by sight, I think?' he began.

She nodded, looking slightly apprehensive.

'What time did you say she passed through your checkout last Thursday?'

She hesitated. 'I know I did tell the other policeman five-fifteen, but I've thought about it since and it could have been later. I remember looking at my watch and seeing twenty to six and thinking good, only half an hour to go. We close at six, but they're still going through after that.'

'How much later?' Burden asked.

'Pardon.'

'How long after you had seen Mrs Robson did you look at your watch and see five-forty?'

'I don't know. It's ever so hard to say, isn't it? Ten minutes?'

Ten minutes or five minutes, thought Burden, or even two

482

minutes. He asked her about the girl she had seen Mrs Robson talking to – was she quite sure it was a girl?

'Pardon,' she said again.

'If you only saw the back of this person, who was in any case wearing a hat and presumably a coat or jacket as well, how did you know it was a girl and not a boy – a man, that is?'

She said slowly, as if reorganizing impressions and conclusions, 'Well, I just sort of knew – I mean I think it was. Oh, yes, of course it was. She had a hat on – a beret, I think.'

'It could have been a man, couldn't it, Mrs Naseem?'

'That just wasn't the impression I got,' said Linda Naseem.

Burden didn't ask her any more. Looking back on the interview, he felt he had been in the role of counsel who breaks down a witness's evidence by subtle questioning, leaving the jury to draw very firm conclusions from her uncertain replies. There had been no jury in Tesco's, but if there had been he had no doubt its members would have been thoroughly convinced of this fact: that on the previous Thursday Gwen Robson had been seen in the store talking to a young man at twenty minutes to six. He wandered back into the wide gallery of the lower level and stood in the Mandala concourse. It was all red and white poinsettias today and some sort of dark blue flower. Why these signs of patriotism on November 26? Probably those were simply the flowers the florist had most of.

Burden had a look in Boots, paused to examine the window of Knits 'n' Kits which today was full of tapestry canvases printed with dog and cat faces, glanced across at Demeter with its display of water filters and air ionisers. None of the assistants in any of these shops remembered seeing Gwen Robson. The fountain was playing, shooting up its jets of water to splash the lowest prisms of the chandelier. Burden went out through the main car-park exit, from the dry warmth and air-freshener smell of the place into a cutting wind.

How long was he going to have to wait for a result from the lab? Several days probably. A phone call to Wexford's daughter's home obtained the engaged signal. Burden took his improvised garrotte out of the desk drawer and practised flexing his hands round the pegs. One possibly got a better purchase by putting one's fingers through the rings and gripping the handles that way. He needed something more closely resembling a human neck than the desk leg. Into his mind's eye came an urn-shaped plant-pot container made of white polystyrene cunningly contrived to look like marble. DC Polly Davies had left it behind, with instructions as to the proper care of the cyclamen it contained, when she took her maternity leave and it had ended up in Wexford's office, the cyclamen long perished. The stem of that urn would be just about the right size and with a similar flexibility.

Still holding his garrotte, Burden went up in the lift and along the corridor. The office door was slightly ajar and he pushed it open and went in. Wexford was sitting behind the desk, hunched up, wrapped in his old tweed overcoat. His head was plastered up and the bruises on his face had turned a sickly yellow-green. The small grey eyes that turned on Burden and his improvised weapon had a glassy look, atypically apprehensive, but his opening remark wasn't uncharacteristic.

'So it was you all along.'

Burden grinned. 'I've made this up and I was going to try it out on your plant-pot. Don't look like that; it's quite a reasonable idea.'

'If you say so, Mike.'

'What are you doing here, anyway? You're supposed to be off till the end of the week.'

'This is the end of the week,' Wexford said, shifting in his seat and flexing bruised hands. 'I've been reading all this stuff.' Every report made on the case so far had been sent up and lay on the desk in front of him. Burden, who loved reporting every interview in detail and even recording his own thoughts, had typed screeds. 'There are some quite interesting bits. I like Mrs Robson getting five quid for cutting the old boys' toenails.'

'I thought you would.'

'It makes me wonder how much of that sort of thing there was. This bath business, for instance. It's a fascinating line of enquiry.' Burden raised an eyebrow. Not quite certain what Wexford meant and somewhat repelled by the image, he picked the mock-marble urn off the window-sill and set about strangling it with his garrotte. Wexford watched him speculatively. 'There are a lot of things I'd like to know which no one seems to have bothered with much,' he said. 'Lesley Arbel, for instance. Where was she last Thursday afternoon? We don't seem to know, though we do know that Gwen Robson was seen talking to a girl at five-thirty.'

'That was a man and it was five-forty,' said Burden, pulling on his handles, feeling the polystyrene crack and split, the wire digging into the spongy white flesh-like substance.

'I see. It would be a help to know why she was always down here and what she found so compelling about that not very exciting couple.' Wexford had picked up the only photograph they had of Gwen Robson – the snapshot, much blown-up, which the *Kingsmarkham Courier* had used. ' "One of those characteristic British faces," ' he quoted, ' "that once seen are never remembered." '

'Those Sanderses say they don't remember her; both of them say they never saw her before. But I just know Clifford knew her, I feel it in my bones.'

'For God's sake give over doing that, Mike. I'm not squeamish, but it turns me up. Her home help visits are another interesting thing. You note how she never seems to have spent much time with those who had little or nothing to give. I wonder what old Mr Swallow had on offer, the one who lived opposite. Did she cut his toenails too – and did she perhaps have some particularly erotic technique with the scissors?'

'It's rather disgusting, isn't it?'

Wexford grinned, lifted his shoulders.

'Is it important?' Burden put the garrotte into his pocket and came to sit on the edge of the rosewood desk. When Wexford made no reply to this but only sat there looking bemused, he said, 'You don't look well, you know. I doubt if you should be here.'

'I'm going to have a quiet day,' Wexford told him. 'I'm going to see how many cups of tea I can drink between two and five this afternoon.' Enlightening Burden, he added, 'it seems to me we haven't chatted up Robson's neighbours nearly enough.'

But he went on sitting there after Burden had gone. If he hadn't put his hand to the radiator and felt it almost too hot to handle, he could have sworn the central heating had gone wrong. Without the comfort of his old overcoat, he would have been freezing. Sheila was back in London; he hadn't wanted her to go, but of course he hadn't said a word. What he would have liked was to shut her up somewhere for ever and stand guard over the door. But she had gone back to London in a rented car, back to the flat by Coram Fields that those people – whoever they were – those bombers, terrorists, fanatics – very well knew she occupied. Sylvia had the radio on most of the day, so Wexford got to hear every news bulletin, and every time he braced himself to hear the sentence that would start, 'An explosion . . .' That was why he had come back to work so soon really.

Bomb experts from Scotland Yard had come down to talk to him and the Myringham man had been back. Wexford had wanted to know what they were doing to protect Sheila and they had given him plenty of sturdy reassurance, only he wasn't reassured. He knew he wouldn't have felt so frightened if Sheila had been living with her husband, though that was illogical enough. If anyone had told him he would actually be glad to hear that his daughter was living with a man while married to someone else, he wouldn't have believed them. But that was how he felt now. It would comfort him to know that Sheila had that man Ned, whoever he might be, around night and day. What would comfort him most, of course, was what his son-in-law Neil advocated.

'Get her to stop doing acts of criminal damage. Take away her wire-cutters, or better still get her to make a public statement of guilt and her intention not to do it again.'

Surprisingly, it was Dora who countered, 'Would you have much respect for her if she did a thing like that?'

'Being alive's more important than respect, I should say.'

'Of course she won't do that,' Wexford had said. He was almost cross. 'She can't deny her principles, can she? She doesn't think she's guilty; she thinks the law's wrong – the law itself is guilty, if you like.'

Sylvia looked askance. 'Rather a strange commentary from a policeman, surely, Dad?'

He hadn't said any more. Apart from finding some way out of this anxiety, of making Sheila safe, he wanted more than anything to avoid a flaming row with Sylvia and Neil. The Chief Constable had said something to him on the phone yesterday about the loan of a police house until his own was repaired – well, largely rebuilt, and at the pace at which builders worked nowadays that would be a year hence.

At any rate it was peaceful here. It was quiet and the cold he felt wasn't real. He had to 'struggle against a great tendency to lowness', as he put it to himself, and he went up to the canteen to get some lunch. Working his way through hot soup, hamburger and chips, comforting if not healthy food, he faced the prospect of getting into a car again and driving it. Neil had brought him to work and dropped him outside the gates. Donaldson, his driver, would take him up to Highlands. But sooner or later he was going to have to overcome the great barrier of inhibition that reared up between him and the driving-seat and wheel of a car. He would have to conquer the paralysis he felt would descend upon his left hand as it tried to close over a gear shift, even in his case an automatic shift. Last night he relived in a dream the explosion he thought he had no memory of, but had said nothing about it to anyone, not even Dora.

Patterns of life had changed subtly but radically during the years since Wexford had first become a policeman interviewing witnesses. In those early days all the men were out at work and all the women at home. Split-shift working, the advance in women's education and freedom, self-employment and of course unemployment had changed all that. He was not much surprised, at the first house where he called after leaving the car and Donaldson, to be admitted by a young man with a baby in his arms and a child of about three clinging to the legs of his jeans.

This was John Whitton, student and father of two, whose wife was a systems analyst in a full-time job. It was she who had spent time with Ralph Robson while he awaited the arrival of his niece. The house inside had that curious faint smell which all who have themselves been parents recognise – that of a compound of milk, infants' digestive processes, ammonia and talcum powder. This young parent had lived next door but one to Gwen Robson for three years since his marriage when the local authority had allocated him and his wife a house at Highlands, but he assured Wexford that their acquaintance had been slight. Knowing her to be a council home help and with a reputation for philanthropy (his own

487

word), they had once ventured to ask her if she would baby-sit for them.

'Our regular sitter had let us down and it was a special occasion. As a matter of fact it was our third wedding anniversary, and Rosemary was expecting this one any day. We knew it would be months before we got out in the evening again. I asked Mrs Robson and it wasn't that she wouldn't do it; it was the amount she wanted paying. We couldn't run to that, living on one salary; we couldn't give her three pounds an hour. It wasn't as if Scott ever wakes in the evening – it would have been twelve quid for just sitting about watching telly.'

It was a long shot but Wexford thought he might as well try it, he asked John Whitton about the previous Thursday. Had he seen Ralph Robson during the course of the afternoon, preferably about four-thirty? But Whitton shook his head. He had been at home, for his wife had the car that day, but it was a busy time for him with the children's tea to get and both of them to be bathed. He couldn't even recall having seen Gwen Robson go out.

Next door, between the Whittons and Ralph Robson, lived the couple Mrs Robson had so disapproved of, Trevor Morrison and Nicola Resnick. They were both in the house from which they ran a mail-order secondhand-book business which Wexford guessed was of a rather precarious kind. Here the first of that anticipated tea was offered, though of the herbal sort – crimson liquid with a floral-labelled bag floating in it. Wexford accepted a coarse, dark brown crunchy biscuit. Nicola Resnick, though young and liberated-looking in jeans and boots and Guernsey, turned out as much of a gossip as ever her grandmother could have been.

'She tried to get that old boy opposite to make his will in her favour. He used to tell everybody about the money he'd got in the bank. He was about a hundred, wasn't he, Trev?'

'He was eighty-eight when he died,' Trevor Morrison said.

'Yes, well, ancient. You see, he was always whingeing about not being able to manage, especially his fuel bills in the winter. And he liked to use his phone. He'd got this daughter in Ireland or somewhere and he liked to phone her; no good waiting for her to phone him, he used to say. Well, I said to him you ought to apply for supplementary benefit. Why not? You've got a right to it and I believe in getting everything you're entitled to. These old people are proud but it's just pointless, that sort of pride. You work all your life, you've got a right to anything the state will let you have. But it wasn't that with him. It's no good me applying, he said to me, I've got money in the bank and I'll have to tell them; I've got more than three thousand in the Trustee Savings Bank and when I let on about that, no way are they giving me benefit. And it was true.'

'This is Mr Eric Swallow we're talking about?' Wexford asked, making a valiant effort to drink his hibiscus tea.

'Old Eric, yes. I don't think I ever knew his other name, did you, Trev? Anyway, he used to tell everyone about this three thousand in the bank; he used to boast about it. And I heard him say his daughter was counting on getting that but she mustn't think it was automatic; it was his money to do what he liked with. Mind you, he was whingeing about her at the time, he hadn't had a word from her for weeks.'

'What was this about a will?'

'It must have been a year ago or more – at least that. She'd given up being a home help, but she was in and out over the road every day. I was sitting here working on our catalogue and Trev was here too when she came to the door and asked if we would witness some document old Eric had got. It was quite a surprise – I mean, I'd hardly spoken to her before that and she'd ignore me if she saw me in the street. She said he had to sign this form and he needed two witnesses. And then do you know what she said? That we'd be better not being married, not being connected with each other! I was amazed. Well, I thought maybe it was something to do with this supplementary benefit and I was going to go, but Trevor asked Gwen what it was and all she said was it was nothing we need worry about, just a form. Well, naturally, that wasn't good enough for Trev and he said we had to know what we were signing before we went over there, and then she said it was Eric's will.'

'And that put me off quite a bit, as you can imagine,' said Trevor. 'It smelt, if you know what I mean.'

'That's absolutely right, it smelt. Anyway, I just said we were a bit busy and to count us out. Gwen said that was OK; she'd soon find someone and anyway her neice would be down the next night. I expect you know that niece, don't you, the one that looks like she was modelling clothes?'

It was all interesting enough, and would have been useful if Gwen Robson had been suspected of murder and Eric Swallow and any of these other old people had been her victims. But it was she who had been the victim. Wexford asked his question about Ralph Robson's movements and Nicola Resnick was able to tell him that she had heard sounds from next door late on Thursday afternoon. The wall between the houses was thin and you could hear the click of lights being switched on and off, the thump-thump of Robson's stick and of course the television.

How could she particularly remember last Thursday?

Robson had had the children's programme *Blue Peter* on, she told him. That began at five-past five and was followed by a health programme about trace elements as food supplements. Nicola Resnick was interested in that and she had switched on her own set though Robson had his so loud she need scarcely have bothered.

Thursday afternoon once more, a week since the killing. Seven days ago Clifford Sanders had entered Queen Street from the High Street in his mother's car and parked it on the left-hand side on a meter, inserting into the slot, if he were to be believed, the forty pence that would ensure him one hour's parking. But it was already twenty minutes to five when he arrived, so that when he left Olson ten minutes on the meter still remained to run. And he had sat out those ten minutes, brooding on the things he had talked about to Olson, all that Dodo rubbish. Not that Burden believed that for a moment.

He went into all the shops on both sides of this part of Queen Street, the grocer's, a fishmonger, a fruiterer, a wine-shop, two cheap clothes boutiques and Pelage the hairdressers. No one remembered seeing Clifford Sanders sitting in a car on the meter outside Pelage. The difficulty was that the red Metro was regularly parked on one of those meters on a Thursday afternoon, so it was hard to sort out when it had been there and when it hadn't, and when Clifford had been sitting in it and when he had not. One of the stylists at Pelage was very definite about having sometimes seen him sitting in the car in the driving seat, just sitting there as if lost in thought, not reading or looking out of the window or anything.

From the cover of the wine supermarket window, Burden watched Clifford arrive at ten minutes to five. There was no meter free and he drove as far as where Castle Street cut across, then turned and came slowly back. By now someone was pulling out so Clifford waited, moved the Metro into the space, got out of the car and locked it. The day was damp and very cold and he wore a grey tweed overcoat and grey knitted hat pulled down well over his ears. From a distance, Burden had to admit, he looked not so much like a girl as an old woman. He put a couple of coins into the meter, which must still have had time to run from the previous insertion. Then he came quite slowly across the road as if he had all the time in the world instead of being, as was in fact the case, nearly twenty-five minutes late for his appointment. Burden felt a sneaking admiration for Serge Olson's technique in deliberately naming a time for this client half an hour in advance of the five o'clock when he knew he would arrive.

After Clifford had disappeared into the entrance at the side of Pelage, Burden went off along Castle Street to have a cautionary word with a jeweller he suspected of being a fence. Then into a call box to phone his wife and say he might be late but not very late – say around eight-thirty. A cup of tea and a cake in the Queen's Café and it was two minutes to six when he came back down Queen Street. An icy rain had begun to fall and the dark was the darkness of midnight, though brilliantly illuminated here by dripping, fuzzy yellow and white lights that turned the pavements a gleaming dirty gold and silver. Snowflakes started appearing among the silvery rods of rain.

Clifford came out of Olson's door at two minutes past six. He wasn't hurrying, but he was moving a good deal faster than when he had arrived. Burden sheltered from the rain and Clifford's view in the doorway of the green-grocer's; they were closing up and people kept pushing past him to carry in trays of chicory and aubergines. Clifford got into the car without even glancing at the meter; he started up and was away as the hands of Burden's watch moved to five-past six.

Wexford had read and heard about people seeing on someone

491

else's arm the brand mark of the concentration camps, but he had not had that experience himself; and he didn't have it now – Dita Jago on this cold afternoon having her arms covered by a woolly garment that was itself a work of art; a knitted tapestry of greens and purples, rich reds and jewel blues. But when he glanced enquiringly at the great pile of manuscript which lay on the table in this strange cluttered room, the perhaps orderly muddle of notebooks and loose leaves, scrawled-on envelopes and works of reference, she had nodded to him.

'My great work,' she said. A smile made the remark a modest one. 'My memoirs of Oswiecim.'

'Auschwitz?' he said.

She nodded and, lifting up the topmost sheet of manuscript, turned it over so that only a blank side showed.

9

The room was of the same size and shape as the one in which he had talked to Robson and his niece; as the room Trevor Morrison and Nicola Resnick used as their office; as John Whitton's nursery. It was on the other side of the street and faced the opposite way, but the main difference from all those others lay in its rich clutter, the abundance of curious interesting things, the piles of books and papers and the adornment of its walls which was like nothing Wexford had ever seen before.

Unless you looked out of the window – seeing the trim little roadway, the trees in the pavement grass plots, the semi-detached houses – you might have believed yourself anywhere but on a local authority housing estate outside an English country town. What the walls were papered or painted with it was impossible to say, for they were covered all over with hangings which to Wexford had at first looked like lavish and elaborate embroideries but which, on examining them more closely, he saw to be knitted. Dora's efforts at what has been called 'the common art', resulting in jumpers for grandsons, at least told him that much. But this knitting was in all colours of the spectrum, those colours subtly matched and contrasted, creating abstract designs of immense complexity as well as pictures that in the execution of their strong primitive imagery reminded him of the paintings of Rousseau. In one a tiger crept through a jungle of green fronds and dark fruit-laden branches: in another a girl in a sarong walked with peacocks. The biggest, which covered the whole of one wall and had evidently been constructed in panels, was Chinese rather than tropical and showed a green landscape with little temples on the summits of hills and a herd of deer browsing between the woodland and the lake.

She was smiling at his wonderment. He only knew she was the creator of all this by the piece of work now in progress, another jungle picture taking shape from a circular needle, which lay on a round table beside Venetian glass animals and painted porcelain eggs. She had completed perhaps half of it.

'You're a busy woman, Mrs Jago,' he observed.

'I like to keep occupied.' Her accent was a rather unfamiliar guttural, Polish perhaps or Czech, but the English itself was grammatically and syntactically flawless. 'I have been writing my book for two years now and it's nearly done. God only knows if anyone will ever publish such a book, but I wrote it for my own satisfaction, to get it all down on paper. And it's true what they say.' She smiled at him again. 'Get it down, write it out and it's no longer such a terrible thing to remember. It doesn't cure but it helps.'

'The writer is the only free man, as someone said.'

'Whoever that someone was knew what he was talking about.'

She sat down facing him and picked up her knitting. Supplied with hibiscus tea by Nicola Resnick and Earl Grey by a Miss Margaret Anderson – who claimed never to have spoken to Mrs Robson or heard of her until she was dead – Wexford was rather relieved that Mrs Jago offered him no refreshment. Her fingers worked skilfully, moving with assurance a complex mass of coloured threads, selecting one, taking two or thee stitches with it, abandoning this first shade and joining in another. Plump and tapering these fingers were, the wedding ring cutting deeply into the flesh. She was a mountain of a woman, yet somehow neither gross nor ungainly, her legs shapely with fine ankles and small feet in tiny black pumps. Remains of a gipsyish beauty showed in her full, pink-cheeked face. Her eyes were black, bright and in their cobweb wrinkles like jewels in a fibrous nest. Hair that was still dark was drawn back with combs into a large glossy bun.

'You came in and offered to do some shopping for Mr Robson,' he began. 'That makes me think you must have known them fairly well.'

She looked up at him and the fingers were momentarily stilled. 'I didn't know them at all. I wouldn't be far wrong if I said that was only the second time I'd ever spoken to him except to say good morning.'

Wexford was disappointed. His hopes of this woman, though quite unjustifiable, had been high. Something about her made him feel she was essentially truthful.

'He was a neighbour,' she said. 'He'd lost his wife. She had been killed in a horrible way and it was the least I could do.' She remembered his name, though she had only briefly seen his warrant card. 'It was no trouble to me, Mr Wexford. I'm no Good Samaritan. My daughter takes me shopping or does it for me.'

'You may not have known him but you knew her, didn't you?'

She came to the end of her row, turned the linked needles. 'Hardly. Will you believe me if I tell you that was the first time I'd ever been in their house? Let me tell you something. I don't want you to waste your time on someone who can tell you very little. When I came out of the camp, they put me in a hospital the army ran. There was a man there, a soldier who was a ward orderly, and he fell in love with me. God knows why, for I was a skeleton and my hair had all fallen out.' She smiled. 'You wouldn't think that to see me now, would you? And I used to long and long to put on weight like they said I must. Well, this man – Corporal Jago, Arthur Jago – he married me and made me an Englishwoman.' She pointed to the pile of manuscript. 'It is all in the book!' Her knitting resumed, she said, 'But though I have tried I have never become very English, Mr Wexford. I have never quite learned to get on with the English way of always pretending everything in the garden is lovely. Do you understand what I mean? Everything in the garden is *not* lovely. There is a snake in the bush and worms under the stones and half the plants are poisonous . . .'

He smiled at the image she created.

'For example, Mr Robson – that poor man – he will say that what is to be will be; perhaps it is all for the best, life must go on. And Miss Anderson down the street who found a man who wanted to marry her at last when she was sixty years old . . . when he died a week before the wedding, what does she say?

495

Maybe it was too late, maybe they'd both have regretted it. I cannot do with this.'

'But these are the tenets of survival, Mrs Jago.'

'Perhaps. But I cannot see that you survive any less if first you cry and rage and show your feelings. At least, it isn't my way and I am not comfortable with it.'

Wexford, who would have been quite happy to continue with this exploration of English emotion or lack of it, nevertheless thought it was time to move on. Weariness had come to take hold of him and his headache was back, a tight band wound around above the eyes. It was a piece of luck, sheer serendipity, that made him speak the name of the old man who had lived a few houses away in Berry Close.

'Eric Swallow,' he said. 'Did you have the same slight acquaintance with him?'

'I know who you mean,' she said, laying the knitting in her lap. 'That was rather amusing, but nothing to do with poor Mrs Robson being killed. I mean it couldn't be anything, really.'

'All right. But if it's amusing I'd like to hear it. There's little enough in this business to make us laugh.'

'The poor old man was dying. That isn't funny, of course. If I were English I would say maybe it was a merciful release, wouldn't I?'

'Was it?'

'Well, he was very old, nearly ninety. He had a daughter but she was in Ireland and she wasn't young, naturally. Mrs Robson used to do a lot for him; I mean, after she stopped being a home help and getting paid for it, she still went in there nearly every day. In the end when he got so that he couldn't get out of bed, they took him away and he died in hospital . . .'

Wexford had had his eyes on the great landscape tapestry, but the sound of a car door slamming made him turn his head and them almost immediately the doorbell rang. Mrs Jago got up, excused herself and went out into the hall with a surprisingly light, springy tread. Voices could be heard, the clamorous treble of children. Then the front door closed again and Mrs Jago came back with two little girls: the younger of them, though too big to be carried, was in her arms; the other, who looked about five or six and who wore a school uniform of navy coat, yellow and navy scarf and felt hat with stripey band, walking by her side.

'These are my granddaughters, Melanie and Hannah Quincy. They live in Down Road, but sometimes their mummy brings them to me for an hour or two and we have a nice tea, don't we, girls?' The children said nothing, appearing shy. Dita Jago put Hannah down. 'Tea is all ready and we shall have it at five sharp. You can tell me when it is three minutes to five, Melanie; Mummy says you can tell the time now.'

Hannah went immediately to the table where the painted eggs and glass animals were. And though the older child had a book to read and had opened it, she was keeping a sharp cautionary eye on her sister's handling of the fragile things. Wexford, from personal experience, knew only too well the advantages and the pitfalls of that particular relationship, the stresses created in infancy that lasted a lifetime.

Dita Jago was placidly knitting once more. 'I was telling you about old Mr Swallow. Well, one afternoon – a Thursday I think it was, a year ago or a bit more – the front-door bell rang and there was Mrs Robson. She wanted me to come into Mr Swallow's with her and be a witness to something. In fact, she wanted two people and she'd seen my daughter's car outside, so she knew Nina was here. I found out afterwards that she had already been to a couple who live on the other side. He's called Morrison, I don't know her name, but anyway for some reason they wouldn't do it.

'As I've said, I don't suppose I'd ever spoken more than two words to her and she'd never met Nina. I had to introduce them. But that didn't stop her asking us both to go down there and witness this form.'

'Hannah, I'm going to be very cross if you break that little horse,' said Melanie.

A struggle ensued as the elder granddaughter did her best to prise from her sister's fingers a blue glass animal. Hannah stamped her foot.

'Grandma is going to be very unhappy if you break it. Grandma will cry.'

'No, she won't.'

'Give it to me, please, Hannah. Now do as you're told.'

'Hannah will cry! Hannah will scream!'

497

Shades of Sylvia and Sheila ... Dita Jago intervened, drawing the younger child – who was by now carrying out her threat – on to her lap. Melanie looked mutinous, frowning darkly.

'Birds in their little nests should agree,' Mrs Jago said, not without irony, Wexford thought. She stroked the little girl's mane of dark curly hair. 'We thought it was something to do with the money he wanted to get from the what-do-you-call-it? DH-something – the supplementary benefit. There are always forms, aren't there? Anyway, we went down to Mr Swallow's with her and when we got there we found him asleep in bed. Mrs Robson was a little bit put out. My daughter said what was this form and had he already signed it? Well, you could see Mrs Robson didn't want to say. She said she'd wake Mr Swallow up; it was important and he'd want her to wake him.'

Hannah, her crying over, placed one thumb in her mouth and opening the other fist, showed her sister the blue glass horse, clenching her hand as soon as Melanie made a pounce for it.

Melanie turned away loftily. 'Five minutes to five, Grandma,' she said.

'All right. I said to tell me when it was three minutes to. Anyway, the piece of paper we had to sign was lying there on the table face-downwards. I mean we thought that's what it was and we were right. Nina just picked it up and took one look – what do you think it was?'

Wexford had a pretty good idea, but he decided not to steal Mrs Jago's thunder and merely shrugged.

'It was a will, made out on a will form. Nina didn't get to read it because Mrs Robson snatched it away, but we could guess what was on it. It would have been leaving his money to Mrs Robson. Three thousand pounds, he used to boast he had; everyone here knew that. And she was after it – she liked money, there was no doubt about that. Well, we both shied away like anything. We told each other afterwards no way, absolutely not. Suppose that daughter had brought it up in court and we'd had to go there and say we'd signed it?'

'What was Mrs Robson's reaction to that?'

'Three minutes to five, Grandma,' Melanie said.

'I'm coming, darling. She didn't like it, but what could she do? I couldn't help having a laugh when we were outside. I heard later she went trying other people down the street, but she never struck lucky; she couldn't get anyone but her niece. It was only a few days after that they took Mr Swallow away and when he died there wasn't a will and his daughter got his money – being his real heir, you see, as was quite right. Now I must keep my promise to these children.'

Mrs Jago put the child on the floor and the knitting on the table and got up. 'You will stay for tea? We have Grandma's version of *sachertorte*.'

Wexford thanked her but shook his head. He had told Donaldson to come back for him at five and he thought of the deep pleasure of leaning back in the car and closing his eyes. Hannah had crept quietly to the table and replaced the little horse amongst the other animals with precision, with perfectly coordinated delicate fingers, her eyes all the while on her sister, her lips not quite smiling. It reminded him of Sheila playing all those years ago with a china ornament which Sylvia (though no one else) had forbidden her to touch. And Sheila had teased like this little one, peeping over a defiant shoulder with the faintest Gioconda smile.

'Of course, to do her justice she didn't want money for herself,' Dita Jago's voice interrupted his reverie. 'It was for him, it would have been all for him.' It was just as he was leaving, when they were out in the hall, that she said, 'Don't you want to know where I was last Thursday evening?'

He smiled. 'Tell me.'

'My daughter always goes shopping on Thursday afternoons and usually she takes me. But last week she dropped me off at the public library in the High Street and left the girls with me. She picked us up again at five-thirty.'

Why had she insisted on telling him that? he wondered. Perhaps merely to avoid a repetition of his visit. Or was he imagining things that the tone of her voice gave no hint of – reacting in a confused, almost fuddled, way because of the huge weariness which had overtaken him? Passing a wall mirror in the hall as he made his way out, he caught sight of his discoloured face, the bruised muzzle of a prize-fighter recovering from a bout, and turned quickly away. He was no narcissist, no lover of his own image.

The front door closed on him. Her grandchildren's demands had cut short any parting pleasantries Mrs Jago might have made. It was just before five, for her old clock had been fast, and Wexford waited for the car with the anxiety of a disabled pensioner expecting an ambulance. He had to lower himself into a sitting position on the low wall, feeling his bruised body creak. Going back to work had not been a wise idea, yet it hadn't seemed like work, more a matter of paying social calls. Mike ought to be left to himself to handle this case; he was quite capable of doing so. Someone like Serge Olson would say that he, Wexford, was at fault – only probably he wouldn't use a word like 'fault' – in being unable to delegate, in refusing to yield authority to the younger man. It was very likely a sign of insecurity, fear of seeing Mike usurp his place, even his job. Psychology, he thought, and not for the first time, often just wasn't true.

Cars passed. With a strong inner shudder, an actual shrinking, he tried to contemplate what it would be like to sit at the wheel again, start the ignition, move the shift into gear. That, of course, he wouldn't quite have to do, just manipulate from 'park' to 'drive'. But the notion of putting his hand to that lever brought a darkness before his eyes and made him hear a sound he had no recollection of hearing: the roar of the bomb. He closed his eyes, opening them to see Donaldson draw up at the kerb.

A hunch he couldn't quite believe in – it all seemed behaviour of the crassest, most unfeeling kind – led Burden to assume that Clifford Sanders was heading for the Barringdean car park. He couldn't follow him: he hadn't a car immediately to hand and, making his way there on foot, he told himself he was wasting his time. No one would do that. No one would return to the scene of so horrific a crime precisely seven days to the hour later, and there go through the same prescribed ritual. With, that is, one notable exception . . .

He entered the shopping complex by the pedestrian entrance where, a week before, Dodo Sanders had stood rattling the gates and screaming for help. But first he went into the underground car park, descending to the second level in the lift. At least Clifford hadn't parked the car on precisely the spot where it had been the week before, but perhaps he had not done so only because that particular space and those next to it and opposite were already occupied. This time the Sanders' car was at the extreme opposite end to the lift and the stairs. It was empty which meant, presumably, that Clifford was somewhere in the shopping centre.

As he had been in the previous week, thought Burden, looking at his watch by the light of the glaring greenish strip-lights. Six-twenty-two, but he, of course, had walked here and taken some time to locate the car. Clifford's appointment had been at his normal time, five o'clock, so today his date to pick up his mother would be later. Six-thirty perhaps? With the centre closing at six and usually emptied by six-fifteen, would she be prepared to wait for him? But as he was speculating along these lines, watching the last cars backed out and driven away, he heard the clang of the descending lift. Clifford and his mother came out of it and Burden watched them walk towards their car, Clifford carrying two Tesco bags and a wicker basket. Burden thought he could easily be taken for a girl at the back; it was something to do with his plump hips and the rather short steps he took. He caught up with them as Clifford was lifting the boot-lid of the Metro.

Mrs Sanders turned and cast upon him a basilisk look. She was hatless, her hair set in a rather bouffant, cloudy way which didn't suit her. The red lipstick glistened in the pale face. He had wondered what that particular colour of skin reminded him of and now he knew: raw fish, a translucent, faintly pinkish white. She was perfectly calm and her voice was cold.

'I wish I'd never told anyone about finding that dead body. I wish I'd kept quiet,' Burden had an inkling then of the icy authority she exercised over her son and had no doubt exercised since he was an infant. There was an awful precision in that tone and it was backed by a great storehouse of nervous energy. 'I'm not usually a fool. I should have had the sense to stay out of it; I should have followed his example.'

'What example was that, Mrs Sanders?' Burden asked.

Her attention was on the time by her digital watch and that indicated on the clock in the Metro which she bent down to look at. Abstractedly, she said, 'He ran away, didn't he?'

'You tell me. I've got a very good idea what it was he did, running away was only a small part of it.' While Clifford unlocked the driver's door, he said, 'You won't mind giving me a lift, will you? We can take your mother home first and then you and I will have another talk at the police station.'

Clifford didn't say anything. The only sign that he had heard was when he reached inside to release the lock on the passenger door. And on the way back to Ash Lane no one said a word. Half the carriageway of this end of the Forby Road was undergoing repairs, temporary traffic lights had been installed and a long queue of cars waited. Dodo Sanders, sitting in the front next to Clifford, pulled down her glove and lifted up her coat cuff to look at her digital watch. Why it should have been important to her to know the precise time they had left the car park and the precise time they began queueing at the lights, Burden couldn't guess. Perhaps, though, that wasn't the purpose of all this watch-gazing. It might be that she simply wanted to know the time, that all day long, every day, every five minutes, she had to know the time.

She spoke as Clifford drew up by the kerb. 'I can take the things in. There's no need to come with me.'

But he got out of the car, removed the bags from the boot and carried them up to the front door. He unlocked the door and stood back for her to pass in ahead of him. Burden understood it all. She was one of those people who say things like that but don't mean them. She was the sort who would say, 'Don't worry about me, I'll be all right on my own,' or 'Don't bother to write me a thank-you letter,' and then create hell when she got left alone or when no letter came. His mother-in-law was a bit like that, though Mrs Sanders was a thousand times worse.

Clifford got back into the driving-seat and Burden stayed where he was, in the back. He didn't care whether they talked or not; they would talk at the station. The driving was done with the slow care, the superfluous signals and excessive braking habitual to Clifford. He broke the silence as they turned in to find the last remaining parking space.

'What is it you suspect me of?'

Burden felt a reluctance to answer questions of that kind.

502

They seemed to bring him down to Clifford's level of ingenuousness and simplicity. Simple-mindedness expressed it better, perhaps. 'Let's leave that until we're inside, shall we?' he suggested.

He called up Diana Pettit and together they shepherded Clifford into that grey-tiled interview room. It was dark now, of course, had been dark for two hours, and the lights in this room were as grim and uncompromising as those in the Barringdean Centre car park, but much brighter. The central heating was on in here, though, just as it was all over the building. Police officers just as much as those they interviewed, as Burden had once told someone without irony, were often obliged to sit there for hours. The immediate warmth, a much greater heat than he enjoyed in his own home, made Clifford ask to take off his hat and coat. He was one who would ask permission before he did almost anything; no doubt asking for leave had been a requirement of right conduct dinned into him from his earliest years. He sat down and looked from Diana to Burden and Burden back to Diana, like a puzzled new boy whom school rules bewilder.

'I'd like you to tell me what you're accusing me of.'

'I'm not accusing you of anything yet,' Burden said.

'What do you suspect me of, then?'

'Don't you know, Clifford? Haven't you got a clue? What do you think it is – helping yourself out of the collection in church?'

'I don't go to church.' He essayed a faint smile and it was the first Burden had ever seen him give. The smile seemed contrived with difficulty as if a mechanical process had to be set in motion, a series of button-pressing and lever-pulling only half-remembered. It irritated Burden.

'Perhaps you stole a car then. Or nicked a lady's handbag.'

'I'm sorry. I don't know what you're getting at.'

Burden said abruptly. 'Have you any objection if I record this interview? Tape it, I mean?'

'Would it make any difference if I had?'

'Certainly it would. This isn't a police state.'

'Do as you like,' Clifford said indifferently and he watched Diana begin recording. 'You were going to tell me what I'm supposed to have done.'

'Let me tell you what I think happened. I think you met Mrs Robson inside the shopping centre, in Tesco's. You hadn't seen her for quite a while, but you knew her and she knew you – and she knew something about you you'd like kept secret. I wonder what it was. I don't know yet, I honestly don't know, but you'll tell me. I hope you'll tell me tonight.'

Clifford said in an uneven voice, 'When I first saw Mrs Robson, she was dead. I never saw her before in my life.'

'What you saw, Clifford, was your opportunity. You and she were alone and you very much wanted her out of the way . . .'

He had to remind himself that this was a man, not a boy, nor a teenager. And not simple-minded, not retarded. He was a teacher; he had a university degree. The blank, soft face looked even more spongy, but a spark showed in each dull eye. Clifford's voice squeaked. Fear or guilt of God-knows-what had done something to the vocal cords, leaving him with a eunuch's soprano.

'You don't mean you think I'd kill someone? Me? Is that what you mean?'

Not wanting to fall in with this play-acting, this vanity – for what else would explain it? – that made a man believe he could do as he pleased without fear of discovery, Burden said drily, 'He's cottoned on at last.'

Next moment he was on his feet and Diana too, stepping back from the table. Clifford had leapt up, face and lips white as if in genuine shock, his hands grasping the table edge and shaking it, vibrating it as his mother had shaken the wire gates.

'Me? Kill someone? You're mad! You're all crazy! Why've you picked on me? I never knew you meant that with all your questions, I never dreamed . . . I thought I was just a witness. Me kill someone? People like *me* don't kill people!'

'What kind do then, Clifford?' Burden spoke calmly as he lowered himself once more into his chair. 'Some say everyone's capable of murder.'

He met the other man's round staring eyes. A dew of sweat had appeared all over the putty-like skin, the pudgy features, and a drop trickled down his upper lip between the two wings of the moustache. Burden felt for him an impatient contempt. He wasn't even a good actor. It would be interesting to hear how all that would play back, that stuff about killing people. He'd play it to Wexford, see what he thought.

'Sit down, Cliff,' he said, his growing contempt making him accord the man less than the dignity of his unabridged Christian name. 'We're going to have a long talk.'

Exhausted when the car dropped him at Sylvia's, Wexford would have liked a home of his own to recover in, the sole companionship of his own wife. He had to settle for a drink, the whisky Dr Crocker strictly forbade. Someone had brought in an evening paper; a story on the front page was about a man who had all day been 'helping the police with their enquiries into the Kingsmarkham bomb outrage'. There was no picture and of course no name or description, nothing to make even tentatively possible the identification of this man who had wanted Sheila dead, who had conceived for her that particular brand of cold, impersonal, political hatred.

The boys were watching television, Sylvia trying to write an essay on the psychological abuse of the elderly.

'I know all about that,' Wexford said. 'Would you like to interview me?'

'You're not elderly, Dad.'

'I feel it.'

Dora came out and sat beside him. 'I've been to look at our house,' she said. 'The builders have been in and weatherproofed it. At least the rain can't get in. Oh, and the Chief Constable phoned, something about a house we can live in if we like. We do like, don't we, Reg?'

A leap of the heart before he started feeling ungrateful to Sylvia. 'Did he say where it is?'

'Up at Highlands, I think. I'm almost sure he said Highlands.'

10

Remorse was perhaps too strong a word; it was distaste
tempered with a hint of shame that Burden felt throughout
that weekend. He said to himself, and he even said it to his wife
who was home again with their son, that this was what the job
was about, this was police work.

'The end justifies the means, Mike?' she said.

'It's the merest idealism to deny that. Every day in everything we do, it's implicit even if we don't come out and say it.
When we were going through that bad patch with Mark and
we decided the only way was to let him cry, that two nights of
that would cure him, we were saying the end justifies the
means.'

He took the child on his lap and Jenny smiled.

'Don't teach it to him though, will you?'

He spared himself half an hour to play with Mark and eat
his lunch and then he was back at the police station in that
interview room, confronting Clifford Sanders once more. But
on the way the task behind him and the task ahead goaded
him, made him wrinkle up his nose at the nastiness of it. How
far removed from torture was it, after all? Clifford had to sit
there in that comfortless room, left alone for part of the time
for as much as an hour, food brought to him on trays by an
indifferent police constable. And it would not have been quite
so bad if Clifford had been tougher, less like a child. He looked
like a big child, a kind of fined-down Billy Bunter. A stoicism
had succeeded his bewilderment, a air of being a brave boy and
sticking it out a little longer. But here Burden told himself he
was being a fool. The man was a man, educated, neurotic

506

perhaps but sane, simply lacking character and strength of mind. And look what he had done. The facts spoke for themselves. Clifford had been in the shopping centre, had been seen with Mrs Robson, had a garrotte in his possession, had run away.

Was it likely that he had found the body, covered it up because it looked like his mother and then fled? Nobody behaved like that outside the pages of popular psychiatry. All that stuff which Serge Olson no doubt dispensed – about neurotics choosing girlfriends because they were looking for a mother, or employers as father-figures, or being put off sex because you'd seen your mother in her underwear – that was strictly for the books and the couch as far as Burden was concerned. And he was a fool to let himself feel a sneaking pity for Clifford Sanders. The man had meant to kill Mrs Robson and had succeeded. Hadn't he gone specifically to meet her armed with a garrotte?

Probably his self-doubt was due solely to his failure so far to find the link between Clifford and Gwen Robson. He knew there must be a link and once he had found it, he would no longer be a prey to this unprofessional and certainly un-familiar guilt. Facing Clifford again, with Archbold there to assist in this renewed interrogation and the tape recorder on, Burden reminded himself that the police had interviewed Sutcliffe the 'Yorkshire Ripper' nine times before he was arrested. And in the intervening time Sutcliffe had murdered his final victim. It would be a fine thing if Clifford Sanders were to kill again because he, Burden, had been squeamish.

He lowered himself slowly into the chair. Clifford, who had been gnawing at a fingernail, snatched his hand from his mouth as if he suddenly recalled nail-biting was something he must not do.

Burden began, 'Has your mother ever been ill, Clifford?'

An uncomprehending look. 'What do you mean?'

'Was she ever ill so that she had to stay in bed? When she needed someone to look after her?'

'She had what-do-you-call-it once. Like a kind of rash, but it aches.'

'He means shingles,' Archbold said.

'That's right, shingles. She had that once.'

507

'Did a home help come in to look after her, Clifford?'

But this approach led nowhere. Dodo Sanders had been confined to bed for more than a few hours throughout the whole of Clifford's life. Burden abandoned this line of enquiry and carefully took Clifford through the sequence of events from the time he left Olson until he ran from the car park out of the pedestrian gates. Clifford got in a hopeless muddle with the times, saying he had got to the centre at five-thirty, later changing it to ten-past-six. Burden knew he was lying. Everything was going according to his expectations and the only surprising thing which happened was when Clifford corrected him over the use of his name.

'Why have you stopped calling me Cliff? You can call me that if you like, I don't mind. I like it.'

Awaiting him in his office was a lab report on that spool of plastic-covered wire. There was a great deal of technical detail – Burden found himself back among the polymers – but the plain fact easily sorted out was that the shreds of substance found in Mrs Robson's neck wound were quite different from the stuff coating the wire in Clifford Sanders' tool-box. Well, he had been wrong. That might only mean, of course, that Clifford had disposed of the wire he used for his garrotte – thrown it in the river or, more safely, stuck it in his own or someone else's dustbin. In the meantime Clifford could sweat for a day or two. Wexford was his immediate concern, Dr Crocker had strictly forbidden the Chief Inspector to return to work at the office and to see him Burden had to drive up to Sylvia's house.

'At any rate I shall be on the spot,' Wexford said. 'I'm going to be living up at Highlands. How about that?'

Burden grinned. 'That's right. There are two or three police houses. When are you moving in?'

'Don't know yet,' Wexford said, glancing through the paperwork Burden had brought him. 'I don't think the person – a useful genderless word – that the checkout girl saw talking to Mrs Robson was Clifford Sanders at all. I think maybe it was Lesley Arbel. But I'll tell you where I agree with you – when you say Mrs Robson was a blackmailer. I think so too.'

Burden nodded eagerly. He was always disproportionately pleased when Wexford approved some suggestion of his.

'She liked money,' he said. 'She was near enough prepared to do anything for money. Look at all that stuff you told me about the old man's will. She was running up and down the street searching for witnesses to a will under which she was to be the sole beneficiary. We may laugh about her bathing someone and cutting some other old man's toenails, but weren't those normally distasteful tasks undertaken for a very inflated payment? There's probably more of that sort of thing we haven't yet uncovered.'

'Mrs Jago says she did what she did all for her husband. There's an implication that this makes it all right, exonerates her. I imagine that was precisely the way Gwen Robson saw it herself.'

'Why did Ralph Robson specifically need money anyway?' Burden asked. 'Has anyone queried that one? I mean, if I said I needed money I'd really mean Jenny and Mark and me, my family. And you'd mean you and Dora, surely?'

Wexford shrugged. 'We've looked at her bank account at the TSB. She had rather a lot in it; I mean more than one would have expected. Robson has his own personal account and they've no joint savings. But Gwen Robson had something over sixteen hundred pounds and that could be the fruits of blackmail. Your idea is that Gwen Robson had evidence Clifford had done something reprehensible and was blackmailing him?'

Burden nodded. 'Something like that. And the worm finally turned. Clifford's pretty worm-like in most respects, I'd say, so why not in that one too?'

'What could Clifford have done? It would surely have to be an earlier murder. Nobody cares much about sexual irregularities these days.'

Burden's face indicated that he did. 'Gwen Robson cared about them.'

'Yes, but you can't imagine that the cramming school would – or Dodo Sanders, come to that. It would be hard to assign any sort of moral convictions to her. She strikes me as a person who has never heard of ethics, still less ever thought she needed views about them.'

Burden wasn't interested. 'I'll find out what it was,' he said. 'I'm working on it.' He studied Wexford's face: the bruises

509

that were fading, the cut that might or might not leave a permanent scar. 'They had to let that chap go, the one they thought was your bomber. It was on the news this morning.'

Wexford nodded. He had had a phone call about it and a long talk had ensued, culminating in a request to take part in a conference at Scotland Yard. Dr Crocker had sanctioned this with the utmost reluctance and there was no way he would have agreed had he known Wexford intended to drive there. When Burden had gone, Wexford wrapped himself up, adding a scarf of Robin's that was hanging in the hall in case Dora or Sylvia should come home early and see him. His car was on the garage drive and he noticed for the first time – no one had told him – how scarred the bodywork was by chips of flying glass. He got into the driving-seat, feeling that this was unfamiliar, a strange thing to be doing, an act he hadn't performed for a long time.

Closing the door, he thought he would just rest for a moment or two, sit there holding the ignition key. Now if this were a thriller, he thought, a television drama maybe, and he an unimportant character or even a villain, he would put the key in and turn it and the car would blow up. He tried to laugh at that but couldn't, which was absurd, because he had no memory of the explosion and the bangs he thought he heard were not memory but the invention of his imagination. Go on, jump, he said, pushing himself along the plank, easing to the edge of the springboard. He took a breath, pushed the key in, turned it. Nothing happened; the engine didn't even start. Well, why would it? Dora had left it in 'drive'. He moved the automatic shift before he realized what he was doing, the terrible step that was going to be his crossing point.

Because there was nothing now but to go on, he turned the ignition key.

Burden was walking down the High Street, occasionally looking into shop windows already decorated for Christmas, when he saw Serge Olson coming towards him. The psycho-therapist wore a check tweed jacket, its collar of mock fur turned up against the sharp east wind.

He greeted Burden as if they were old friends. 'Hallo, Mike, good to see you. How are you?'

Taken aback, Burden said he was fine and Serge Olson asked if he was making much progress. This wasn't a question Burden was accustomed to being asked by those he thought of as the public and he couldn't help thinking it a shade impertinent. But he make a non-committal, vaguely optimistic reply and then Olson surprised him very much by announcing that it was too cold to stand about and why didn't they go into the Queen's Café for a cup of tea? Burden realised at once that Olson must have something he at least thought important to tell him. Why else would he made such a suggestion? For all his use of Burden's Christian name, the two men had met only once before and then strictly on a policeman-and-witness basis.

But when they were seated at a table, instead of imparting secrets of the consulting room, Olson began to talk only of the recent Arab bombers' trial, the huge sentences meted out to the three guilty men and the threat made by some allied terrorist organization to 'get' the prosecuting counsel. Burden was at last moved to ask what it was in particular that Olson had wanted to talk to him about.

The fierce bright animal eyes gleamed. There was an incongruity here, for Olson's voice was always calm and leisurely and his manner placid. 'Talk to you about, Mike?'

'Well, you know, asking me in here for a cup of tea, I thought there must be some specific thing . . .'

Olson shook his head gently. 'Perhaps I might say Clifford Sanders could be a killer in certain circumstances? Or that his manner was very odd when he left me that evening? Or that men of twenty-three who live at home with their mothers must be psychotic by definition? No, I wasn't going to say any of those things. I was cold and I fancied some good hot tea I didn't have to brew up myself.'

Unwilling to let it go at that, Burden said, 'You really mean you weren't going to say any of that?' Olson's head shook more rapidly. 'Surely it is odd a man living with his mother, even if she's a widow. Mrs Sanders isn't what one would call old.'

Olson said nearly incomprehensibly, 'Have you ever heard of the Fallacy of Enkekalymmenos?'

'The what?'

'It means "the veiled one" and it goes something like this. "Can you recognise your mother?" "Yes." "Can you recognise this veiled one?" "No." "This veiled one is your mother. Hence you can recognise your mother and not recognise her."'

There was something veiled about Mrs Sanders. Her own face was a kind of veil, thought Burden, surprised by his own imagination. But in a brusque policeman-like way he said, 'What's that got to do with Clifford?'

'It's got something to do with all of us and our parents, and with knowing and unknowing. Over the entrance to the oracle at Delphi were the words. "Know thyself" and I'm talking about a very long time ago. In the two or three thousand years since then, have we heeded that advice?' Olson smiled and, leaving a moment for his words to sink in, added, 'She's not a widow either.'

'She's not?' This was firmer, better charted terrain. Burden checked his sigh of relief. 'Clifford's father's still living, then?'

'She and her husband were divorced years ago when Clifford was a child. Charles Sanders' people were farmers and that house had been in his family for generations. He was living there with his parents when he married. Putting it bluntly, his wife Dorothy was the family servant who came in daily to clean for them. It's not known what the parents thought about that. Obviously Clifford doesn't know. You needn't look like that, Mike, I'm not being a snob. It's not her menial status that set me wondering so much as – let's say her unattractive personality. I suppose she was good-looking and in my job I've learned that in nine cases out of ten that's enough. Five years later, he left them and he gave up the house to his wife and son.'

'What about the grandparents?' Burden asked.

Olson, who had eaten two elaborate iced cakes and a slice of fruit loaf, began brushing crumbs out of his beard with a green and yellow paper napkin. 'Clifford remembers them, but only just. He and his mother had his grandmother living with them when the father left. The grandfather had just died. There wasn't much money, and Charles Sanders doesn't seem to have supported them. It was a hard, lonely sort of life. I've never been to the house, but I imagine it's a bit grim and remote. She went out cleaning, did a bit of dressmaking and I'll

512

give her credit were it's due; she insisted on Clifford's going to university – the University of the South, that is, at Myringham – though he had to live at home and take jobs in the holidays. I don't doubt she was lonely and fancied she needed him with her.'

Burden got up to pay. He felt curiously grateful that after his earlier incomprehensible remarks, Olson had managed to avoid jargon and Greek words and talk like anyone else. But something amongst what the psychotherapist had said touched a chord in his mind, set a vibration twanging.

'I invited you,' Olson said, 'but if you'll guarantee the ratepayers will foot the bill I'll give in gracefully.'

'What was that you said about Clifford taking holiday jobs?'

'The usual sort of thing, Mike, only even that kind of job is harder to come by these days. Unskilled labour, a bit of gardening, shop work.'

'Gardening?' Burden said.

'I believe he did have one job like that. He told me about it at some length – largely because he hated it, I suspect. He's not keen on an outdoor life and nor am I for that matter.'

There wasn't a chance, Burden thought. You didn't get your wishes coming true like that . . . 'You don't remember the name, I suppose?'

'No, I don't. But it was an old spinster woman in a big house in Forest Park.'

11

Waiting in reception, Wexford felt the guilt that comes from disobeying a doctor's orders. It was really a fear of being found out, of Dora or Crocker or Burden discovering that he hadn't gone straight to Scotland Yard. In fact, he probably wouldn't have phoned this woman, have come here, if he hadn't been buoyed up by his own success at starting that car, at driving that car, at eventually driving himself to the station in it. Better to think of this as his reason than his anxiety over the slow progress which was being made on the case. Curious looks were no longer levelled at his face; the discolouration had nearly gone. The cut was one he might have made while shaving – if he had been drunk, for instance, or all his life up to now had worn a beard. The Bomb Squad people when he presented himself, would hardly believe he had been the victim of an explosion. But first there was this alibi to check and some curiosity, perhaps pointlessly aroused, to satisfy.

The brighter coloured of the two receptionists, the one with orange curls, kept assuring him that Sandra Dale wouldn't keep him a moment, then no more than one minute, finally that she was on her way. Meanwhile Wexford contemplated *Kim* covers pinned up on the carpeted walls, photographs recording various *Kim* functions, a framed certificate or diploma commemorating the award to *Kim* of something or other. Someone touched him lightly on the shoulder.

'Mr Wexford?' He started easily but she didn't seem to notice. She was a young girl, not in the least like the picture in the magazine. 'I'm Rosie Unwin,' she said, 'Sandra Dale's assistant. Would you like to come this way, please? I'm sorry to have kept you.'

They went down passages and up in a lift and then up a flight of stairs and along another passage. At least it wasn't open plan, one of those office complexes where it is impossible to shut oneself away. Rosie Unwin opened a door at the end of the corridor and Wexford saw a woman seated at a desk who was scarcely more like her own photograph than her assistant was. She got up and put out her hand.

'Sandra Dale.' She hesitated. 'It really is my name.'

'Good morning, Miss Dale.'

The photograph was purposely designed to make her look older, plumper, more motherly – or 'aunty'. Wexford didn't think this woman was much over thirty; to him she seemed a young girl, slender, long-legged, with a broad-browed round face and soft blonde hair. The picture made her into someone to be trusted, confide in, someone wise whose advice one could rely on. She asked him to sit down, herself retreating once more behind her desk. The other girl came into the room after him and stood looking not altogether confidently at a visual display unit where amber-coloured letters and geometric figures danced.

'Lesley's not here,' Sandra Dale said, 'but perhaps you knew that? She's away doing a course in working those things and I'm left to manage as best I can.'

'It's you I want to talk to,' Wexford said, 'and perhaps Miss Unwin too.'

The office was large and extremely untidy, though perhaps there was method underlying the apparent disorder. Letters lay all over Rosie Unwin's desk, face-upwards, and Wexford wondered if they could be of the kind he had read in Sylvia's copy of *Kim* but decided not. He wasn't able to read any of them and those he could see were nearly all handwritten. Another pile filled Sandra Dale's in-tray. She read his mind – or rather misread it.

'We average about two hundred letters a week.'

He nodded. There was a little library of works of reference and two shelves of books: a medical dictionary and an encyclopaedia of alternative medicine, a dictionary of psychology, Eric Berne's *A Layman's Guide to Psychiatry and Psychoanalysis*. Rosie Unwin pressed a key and the screen emptied of its dancing figures.

'Would you like coffee?' Wexford had accepted before she added, 'It'll be instant and it comes in Styrofoam.'

He said to Sandra Dale. 'You'll have heard about the woman who was murdered in Kingsmarkham – you know she was Lesley Arbel's aunt?'

'I haven't seen Lesley since it happened. I know about it of course. Lesley's been very brave, I think – very gallant, carrying on with the course – considering Mrs Robson was more like a mother to her.'

'Didn't she have a mother of her own?'

She looked sideways at him, not slyly but perhaps rather mysteriously. 'You'll say she was only my secretary, but I know a lot about her. We all know a lot about each other in here. Sometimes I think the way we work is a bit like a kind of ongoing encounter group. It must be the effect of our . . . our clients.' There it was, that word again. 'Their problems – they bring things up in our own lives, I guess. Lesley wouldn't mind my telling you that her mother abandoned her when she was twelve and her aunt and uncle just took her over. She was already at boarding school so they didn't adopt her, but she was almost as much their daughter as if they had.' The phone on her desk whistled and she picked up the receiver, murmured into it, 'Yes, yes . . . right,' and said to Wexford, 'Excuse me just one moment. Rosie will be with you right away.'

But for a few minutes he was left alone. Curiosity that had nothing much to do with the case in hand impelled him to read the topmost letter on Rosie Unwin's desk. He didn't even have to get out of his chair, only lean to one side. Eyesight lengthens as age comes on and Wexford thought his had become about as long as anyone's could. Holding a book at arm's length was no longer any use to him. His arms were too short.

'Dear Sandra Dale,' he read, 'I know this is awful and horrible and I am disgusted with myself, but I can't pretend about it any longer. The fact is that I am experiencing very powerful sexual feelings towards my own teenage son. I think I am in love with him. All the time I struggle against these feelings of which I assure you I am deeply ashamed, but just the same . . .'

He had to stop and sit up straight again as Rosie Unwin came in with the coffee, but not before he had noticed that

516

there was an address on the letter and it was signed. Strange. He had somehow assumed most letters would be anonymous.

'About point nought-nought-one per cent,' she said when he spoke these thoughts aloud. 'And most people send us a stamped addressed envelope too.'

'How do you make your selection? The ones you decide to print, I mean?'

'We don't pick the most bizarre,' she said. 'That one you were reading, that wasn't typical. You *were* reading it, weren't you? Everyone who comes in here reads the letters; they can't resist it.'

'Well, I admit I was. You wouldn't print that, though?'

'Probably not. That's for Sandra to decide, and then if there's any query it would be the editor's decision – I mean the editor of *Kim*.'

'Like going to a higher court,' Wexford murmured.

'Sandra picks out those she things will have the widest appeal or impact – let's say common problems, the most human if you like. We'd only print the reply to that one from the woman who fancies her own son. We'd say, "To W.D., Wiltshire," and then write our reply. I mean we do draw the line. Can you believe it, we had a letter last week from someone asking us what the protein content of semen was . . . it's about somewhere.'

Wexford was saved from replying by the return of Sandra Dale. He waited until she was seated again, then asked her, 'So you last saw Lesley when? On Thursday November 19?'

'That's right. She didn't come in on the Friday, she phoned in and told me about her aunt, though I knew then, mind you: I recognized the name. And on the Monday – Monday the twenty-third, that is – she started the computer course. It was a bit of luck, it you can call it luck in the circumstances, that the course happened to be in the same town where her uncle lives.'

'She left here on Thursday afternoon, did she? What time would that have been – five? Five-thirty?'

Sandra Dale looked surprised. 'No, no, she took the afternoon off. I thought you knew.'

Wexford smiled neutrally.

'She finished at one. It was something about having to go down to Kingsmarkham to register for the course. She'd filled in one of the forms wrongly, something like that; she tried to phone the place, but their phone was out of order. Well, according to her it was. I'll be frank with you: I wasn't terribly pleased. I mean, I'd got to do without my secretary for a fortnight as it was, and all for the sake of doing our page on a word processor instead of a typewriter which had always suited us perfectly well.'

Wexford thanked her. This was not at all what he had expected to hear. He had hoped only to pick up from the agony aunt's department some useful pointers to Lesley Arbel's character. Instead he had been handed a smashed alibi.

Rosie Unwin said as he was leaving, 'I hope you won't mind my asking, but are you any relation to Sheila Wexford?'

He was always being asked that, so he ought not to have experienced that clutch at the heart. 'Why do you ask?' he responded rather too quickly.

She was taken aback. 'Only that I admire her very much. I mean, I think she's beautiful and a great actress.'

Not that she had heard something awful on the news, or been told of Sheila's fatal injuries . . . death . . . on breakfast television . . .

'She's my daughter,' he said.

They liked him now, they were all over him. He should have told them the minute he came in, he thought. He waited for one of them – the younger, surely – to tell him as most people sooner or later did that Sheila didn't look much like him, inferring really not so much lack of resemblance as the discrepancy between her beauty and his . . . well, lack of it. But they were tactful. They didn't say anything about wire-cutting either. He went off through the labyrinthine building with Rosie escorting him, talking of Sheila all the way, then they were taking his identification disk from him and signing him out. In half an hour's time he had an appointment at Scotland Yard for another session with the Bomb Squad, and he thought he might as well walk at least part of the distance. So he made his way across Waterloo Bridge, beneath which the river lay sluggish as oil and above him not only the sun but the sky itself was invisible.

It was three days since he had last seen Clifford Sanders and in that time Burden's enquiries had confirmed most satisfactorily that he had indeed worked as a gardener for Miss Elizabeth McPhail at Forest House, Forest Park, Kingsmarkham. Her neighbours remembered him and one of them also remembered Gwen Robson's visits. What he would have liked was to have found someone who had seen them together, talking to each other. Perhaps this was a lot to expect. Beyond a doubt, Gwen Robson had received her offer of employment as Miss McPhail's full-time housekeeper four years ago. Clifford was twenty-three and four years previously would have been a year into his university course. Burden considered his strategy. Clifford would be at work now, at Munster's; he worked all day on Tuesdays until five. He would be tired when he got home and it would do no harm for him to find Burden there waiting for him, anxious for another talk either there in the back of beyond or down at the police station once more.

Davidson drove the two of them down the long lane that went past Sundays Park. At ten to five it was already dark and pockets of fog made very slow, cautious driving essential. The ivy-clad façade of the house loomed up out of the misty dark, looking alive, looking like a gigantic square bush or a surrealist nightmare of a tree. All the leaves hung limp and gleaming, dewed with water-drops. The car headlamps alone showed him the dark glistening mass, for not a light was showing amongst the coat of foliage. What did Dorothy Sanders do there all day – her son having taken the car and no bus stop nearer than Forby or Kingsmarkham, both at least two miles distant? Once a week Clifford took her to the Barringdean Shopping Centre, had his hour-long session with Olson, went to pick up his mother. What friends did she have, if any? How well did she really know Carroll the farmer? Each, it would seem, had been deserted by a partner; they were not far removed from each other in age . . .

The door opened and she was standing there. 'You back again? My son's not here.'

Burden remembered what Wexford had said about it being hard to associate her with ethics, with any moral sense. He was aware of something else, too, something he would never have thought of himself as sufficiently sensitive to feel – a coldness emanating from her. It was hard to think of her as having a normal body temperature, warm blood. And as he reflected these things, the whole passing rapidly through his mind as he stood on the doorstep, he felt also how very much he would hate to have to touch her, as if her living flesh would feel like rigor mortis.

She would think it was the icy air that made him shiver. He said, 'We'd like a few words with you, Mrs Sanders.'

'Shut the door, then, or the fog will get in.' She spoke of the fog as if it were some sort of elemental or ghost, always waiting outside for a chance unwise invitation.

Her face was thickly and whitely powdered, the lips painted a waxy red, her head tied up tightly in a brown-patterned scarf so that no hair showed. She was dressed in her favourite brown, jumper and skirt, ribbed tights, flat tan-coloured shoes. Following her into the living room, burden noticed how thin and upright she was – her hips narrow, her back flat – so that it was something of a shock to see her frontal aspect reflected in the big mahogany-framed mirror, her stringy neck and the deep lines on her forehead. It was cold in there and, whatever she had said about keeping the fog out, it seemed already to have penetrated. A damp chill touched Burden's skin, the only heat in the room concentrated in the few feet around the coal fire. He glanced at the empty mantelpiece of dark grey flecked marble, the chest of drawers and cabinet in a rather dull dark wood, their surfaces equally bare.

'May we sit down?' She nodded. 'Your son worked as a gardener for a Miss McPhail of Forest Park, I believe. That would have been while he was at university?'

She detected criticism Burden had not meant to imply. 'He was a grown man. Men should work. I couldn't keep him; the grant he got didn't cover everything.'

Burden said simply, 'Mrs Robson worked as a home help for Miss McPhail.'

The words were hardly out of his mouth before he realized Dodo Sanders was going to do it again. Once more she was going to register incomprehension at the name of Robson. Robson? Who's Mrs Robson? Oh, that woman, that one who was murdered, the one whose body I found, that one. Oh yes, of course. She said none of these things but she looked them all, nodding when Burden reminded her as if recollection had come tardily.

'He didn't know her,' she said evenly in her robot's mechanical voice.

'If you didn't know her, or know she worked there, how can you know that?'

She showed no sign of awareness at having betrayed herself or her son. 'She was in the house and he was in the garden; you said that. She wouldn't go into the garden and he wouldn't go into the house. Why should he? It was a big garden.'

Burden left it and allowed a silence to fall before saying, 'Have you ever let the upstairs rooms in this house?' He asked because the idea of the furniture up there intrigued him in an awesome kind of way. He remembered Diana Pettit talking about all that furniture impeding them in their search.

'Why do you ask?' The robot was talking again, its microchip tone giving each word equal weight.

'Frankly, Mrs Sanders, the place is barely furnished down here and cluttered upstairs – or so I understand.'

'You're welcome to look at it if you want.' It was a cordial turn of phrase she used, but not uttered in a cordial way. So might the wolf in Red Riding Hood have said that its teeth were all the better to eat you with. The dome-like bluish eyelids half closed once more, the head went back and Dodo Sanders said, 'My son is coming now.'

Light from the Metro turning in at the gates trickled across the ceiling and down the walls. The woman didn't speak again; she seemed to be listening, to be straining in fact to hear something. There came the distant sound of a wooden door closing, a bolt being shot. Visibly she relaxed, sinking a little from the waist. Clifford's key in the lock was succeeded by the sound of Clifford's feet being vigorously wiped. He must have known by the presence of the car that Burden was here and he didn't hurry; he even pushed the door open very slowly. He entered the room, looked at Burden and Davidson without giving any sign of recognition, without speaking, and walked towards the single empty chair like someone under hypnosis.

But before he had sat down his mother did an astonishing thing. She spoke Clifford's name, just the bare Christian name, and when he turned to look slowly in her direction she leaned her head to one side and lifted her cheek. He moved towards her, bent down and planted an obedient kiss on the floury white skin.

'Can we have a talk, Cliff?' Burden found himself speaking with undue heartiness, as he might have done to a boy of ten or so who has had a fright, who requires jollying along. 'I'd like to talk to you about Miss McPhail. But first we're going upstairs to take a look round the attics.'

Clifford's head turned, his eyes rested momentarily on his mother and moved away. It wasn't exactly a glance requesting permission, more a look of incredulity that such a step might be allowed, had apparently already been sanctioned. Dodo Sanders got to her feet and they went upstairs – all four of them went. It had been a farmhouse once, so the first flight of stairs was handsome and wide, the second which led to the attics narrow and too steep to climb without grasping at banisters. At the top Burden saw closed doors all round him, smelt a cold mustiness, the smell of neglect, and an uncomfortable memory of past dreams came to him – of secrets and things hidden in lofts, of a hand coming out of a cupboard and a disembodied smiling face. But he wasn't imaginative as Wexford was. He put his hand up to a wall switch and a light of low wattage came on; then he opened the first door.

Mother and son stood behind him, Davidson behind them. The room was crammed with furniture and pictures and ornaments, but these were not arranged in any sort of order and the framed paintings were all stacked against walls. Pieces of china and books lay on the seats of chairs, cushions in a heap in the corner. None of it looked valuable, certainly not antique or even of curiosity value but dating from the twenties and thirties, a few pieces older and with turned legs and piecrust edges. Downstairs everything was clean and any assessment of Dodo Sanders' character must have included her housewifely qualities, but up here there had been no sweeping and dusting. No vacuum cleaner had been lugged up the narrow stairs. Cobwebs hung from the ceilings and gathered in the corners in fly-filled traps. Because this was in the country, in a quiet place not much frequented by motor vehicles, the dust was not thick and flocculent, but dust there was: a thin, soft powdering on every surface.

The next room was the same, except that there were two bedsteads in there and two flock mattresses and feather-beds, bundles of pink satin eiderdowns and counterpanes tied up with string, sausage-shaped bolsters covered in ticking, rolled blankets, home-made wool rugs in geometric patterns and home-made rag rugs in concentric circles of faded colours. And there were more pictures, but this time they were photographs in gilt frames.

Burden took a few steps inside this room, picked up one of the photographs and looked at it. A tall man in tweed suit and trilby hat; a woman also wearing a hat, her dress shawl-collared and with a long flared skirt; a boy between them in a school cap, short trousers, knee socks, the group redolent of the mid-thirties. Man and boy closely resembled each other; it might have been Clifford's face he was looking at, the same pudginess, the same thick lips and even the same moustache, the same inexpressive eyes. But there was something in those people that Clifford lacked, an air in all of them of . . . what? Superiority was to put it too strongly. A consciousness of social position and social duties? Still carrying the framed picture, Burden looked into the other two attics while Davidson and Clifford and his mother silently followed him. Here was more furniture, more rolled-up rugs and water-colours mounted on gold paper framed in gilt, more books and china animals, but gilded pink Lloyd Loom chairs as well and a Susie Cooper teaset tumbled on a pile of cushions embroidered with flower gardens and country cottages. It was all rather dirty and shabby and practically valueless, but none of it was sinister or suggestive of the supernatural, none of it was the stuff nightmares are made of.

What had happened? Why was it all up here? He asked himself this as they descended. It wasn't as if the furnishings downstairs were superior to this or newer; nor that there was so much furniture downstairs that the surplus had found its way up here. Indeed, it was inadequate and Burden had come to the conclusion that mother and son must eat their meals from plates on their laps. He could imagine them with TV dinners or dehydrated messes, bought to save trouble. What he couldn't picture was this woman cooking the sort of food anyone would want to eat.

'Those are my grandparents and my father,' Clifford said, putting out his hand for the photograph.

Dorothy Sanders issued an order to him as if he were a schoolboy like the one in the picture. 'Take it upstairs, Clifford; put it back where it's kept.' Burden would have been more astonished to witness a protest on Clifford's part, a hesitation even, than to see what in fact happened – automatic obedience as he went immediately up to the attics.

'I'd like you to tell me a bit about your relationship with Mrs Robson, Cliff,' Burden said when they were all downstairs once more.

'His name's Clifford. It was my name ... and he doesn't have relationships,' his mother said.

'I'll rephrase that. Tell me about when you first met her and what you talked about. It was at Miss McPhail's, wasn't it?'

Dorothy Sanders had withdrawn down the passage towards the kitchen regions. Clifford looked rather blankly at Burden and said he had once done gardening for Miss McPhail. He too seemed to have forgotten who Mrs Robson was; Burden reminded him and asked him if he ever went inside the Forest Park house – to have a cup of tea or coffee for instance, or to bring flowers in.

'There was a cleaning lady used to give me tea, yes.'

'That was Mrs Robson, wasn't it?'

'No, it wasn't. I don't remember her name; I never heard her name. It wasn't Mrs Robson.'

His mother came back and Clifford looked at her, childlike, as if for help. She had been washing her hands and reeked of disinfectant. To rid herself of contamination from all that furniture, or from that of the two policemen?

She said, 'I've already told you she was in the house and he was in the garden. I've told you he didn't know her. You people don't seem to understand plain English.'

'All right, Mrs Sanders, you've made your point,' Burden said. He wasted no more time on her and looked away. 'I'd like you to come back to the police station with me, Clifford. We can get a clearer picture of things there.'

Clifford went with them in his docile way and they drove back to town. He sat at the table in the interview room and looked across it first at Burden and then at DC Marian Bayliss.

524

His eyes went back to Burden, then were lowered towards the tiny geometric pattern on the table-top. In a low voice, not much more than a mumble, he said, 'You're accusing me of murdering someone. It's incredible, I still can't accept what's happening to me.'

Much of the skill of a policeman in interrogation lies in knowing what to ignore as well as what to seize on. Burden said quietly, 'Tell me what happened when you first got to the shopping centre and met Mrs Robson.'

'I've already told you,' Clifford said. 'I didn't meet her, I saw her dead body. I've told you over and over. I drove down into the car park on to the second level and I was going to park the car when I saw this person lying there, this dead person.'

'How did you know she was dead?' Marian asked.

Clifford leaned forward on his elbows, holding on to his temples. 'Her face was blue, she wasn't breathing. You're beginning to make me feel what happened isn't true, that it wasn't that way. You're changing the truth with all this until I don't know any more what happened and what didn't. Maybe I did know her and I forgot. Maybe I'm mad and I killed her and forgot. Is that what you want me to say?'

'I want you to tell me the truth, Clifford.'

'I've told you the truth,' he said and then, looking away for a moment, twisting in his chair, he directed a curiously appealing gaze on Burden. His voice was the same, a fairly resonant adult male voice, but the tone was that of a child of seven. 'You used to call me Cliff. What stopped you? Was it Dodo stopped you?'

Afterwards, when he looked back, Burden thought it was at this point that he abandoned his theory of Clifford's being as sane as he and understood that he was mad.

12

Leaning over the garden gate, the new resident of Highlands surveyed the estate that would be his home for at least the next six months. It was one of those days that sometimes occur even in December, a clear sunny day of cloudless skies and a gradually falling temperature. The frost to come that night would silver all the little grass verges and turn everyone's miniature conifers into Christmas trees. On the hill behind Wexford's new home Barringdean Ring sat like a black velvet hat on a green cushion. The sky blazed silvery azure. At the bottom of Battle Lane he could see where Hastings Road turned off and make out the roof of Robson's house and the Whittons' and Dita Jago's. It was high up here, the highest point of Highlands, so that he could even see the cluster of latter-day almshouses that made up Berry Close.

The removal van, newly arrived with half the furniture from the bombed house, blocked any view he might have had of the town. Sylvia had taken the boys to school, then come with the van driver to help her mother move in. Wexford thought he would walk to work and then if he couldn't face walking home Donaldson could bring him. Dora would need their car. He went back in and said goodbye to her, looking round the bare, bleak little house, trying not to prejudge what living in these cramped quarters would be like, the neighbours and their noisy children separated from these rooms only by thin dividing walls, the strips of gardens partitioned by wire fences. More wire fences! Never mind, they were lucky to have somewhere, lucky not the have to go on living with Sylvia . . . and he reproached himself for the ungrateful thought as his kind, busy daughter came in carrying a crate of his favourite books.

The air was nippy and the sunshine warm, but sun hung low on the horizon and the shadows were long. His route down into the town took him along Hastings Road and into Eastbourne Drive. There was no one about, the streets empty of people and nearly empty of cars. This was the last day of Lesley Arbel's word-processor course, but no doubt she would spend the weekend with her uncle. It was more than two weeks since Gwen Robson's death, nearly as long since someone had tried to kill Sheila. His cuts and bruises were nearly healed, his strength returning. He had several times driven his car, felt quite calm and assured at the wheel. The bomb experts kept on coming to him or getting him to go to them, pursuing their interminable questions. Try to remember. What exactly happened after you got into the car? Who are your enemies? Who are your daughter's enemies? Why did you jump out of the car? What warned you? He could recall none of it and believed those lost five minutes lost for ever. It was only in the night-time, in dreams, that he relived the explosion – or rather, instead of reliving what he couldn't remember, conjured up new versions for himself in some of which he died or Sheila died or the world itself disappeared and he hung suspended in a dark void. But last night, instead of the roar of the bomb he had heard thin reedy music and instead of Sheila's body, he had seen wheels spinning in the darkness, circles that shone and glittered and were filled with geometric patterns . . .

Striving to dispel these ideas and look at things rationally occupied his thoughts until he reached the police station. Once there, he somehow knew before he enquired that Burden had Clifford Sanders with him and Archbold in one of the interview rooms. Late in the morning Burden came out but kept Clifford there alone, sending in coffee and biscuits. Wexford couldn't tell what Clifford looked like after this continuous ordeal but Burden was haggard, his face pale and tense and his eyes exhausted.

'You were talking about the Inquisition,' Wexford said. 'About executioners taking payment to garrotte the condemned before they were burnt at the stake.'

Burden nodded, slumped in his chair, his strained face

rather ghastly in the pale, bright light from the sun.

'You said you'd read about it. Well, I've read of Inquisitors suffering as much as their victims, of the strain wearing them out and brainwashing them till they get like you. It's watching the torture that does it; you have to be a very special sort of person to be able to watch torture and not be affected by it.'

'Clifford Sanders isn't being tortured. I had doubts about that earlier on, but I don't any more. He's being put through a fairly heavy interrogation but not tortured.'

'Not physically perhaps, but I don't think you can separate mind and body like that.'

'He isn't kept awake artificially; he isn't under bright lights or kept on his feet or starved or denied a drink. He isn't even here all the time; he goes home to sleep. I'm going to send him home today, now; I've had enough for today.'

'You're wasting your time, Mike,' Wexford said mildly. 'You're wasting your time and his because he didn't do it.'

'Excuse me if I differ from you there. I differ from you most strongly.' Burden sat up revived, indignant. 'He had the motive and the means. He has strong psychopathic tendencies. Remember that book you lent me with that piece in it about psychopaths? The Stafford-Clark? "The outstanding feature is emotional instability in its broadest and most comprehensive sense . . ." Let me see, how does it go on? I haven't got your memory. ". . . prodigal of effort but utterly lacking in persistence, plausible but insincere, demanding but indifferent to appeals, dependent only in their constant unreliability . . ."'

'Mike,' Wexford interrupted him. 'You haven't got any evidence. You've trumped up what you've got to suit yourself. The single piece of evidence you do have is that he saw the body and instead of reporting it, ran away. That is absolutely all you've got. He didn't know Gwen Robson. He was a gardener in a place were she popped in sometimes in her home-help role, and he may once or twice have said hello to her. He wasn't seen talking to her in the shopping centre. He doesn't and didn't possess a garrotte or anything that could be made into a garrotte.'

'On the contrary, he has a hard and fast motive. I can't yet prove it, but I'm convinced he committed a crime in the past which Gwen Robson discovered and started blackmailing him over. Blackmailers don't succeed for long with psychopaths.'

'What crime?'

'Murder, obviously,' Burden said on a note of triumph. 'You suggested that yourself. You said no one would care about some sex thing, it had to be murder.' His voice grew tired again as he suppressed a yawn. 'Who, I don't know, but I'm working on it. I'm probing into his past. A grandmother maybe? Even Miss McPhail herself. I'm having Clifford's past looked into for signs of any remotely possible unexplained deaths.'

'You're wasting your time. Well, not your time – ours, the public's.'

This was an accusation to which Burden was particularly sensitive. He was beginning to look angry as well as tired and his face grew pinched as it always did when he was cross. He spoke coldly. 'He met her by chance in the shopping centre, she asked for more money and after he had followed her down into the car park, he killed her by strangling her with a length of electric lead he was carrying in the boot of the car along with the curtain. This he took with him and threw away on his way home.'

'Why cover the body and run away?'

'You can't account for inconsistencies of that sort in a psychopath, though probably he thought that if he covered the body it might not be found for a rather longer time than if he left it exposed. Linda Naseem saw him talking to Mrs Robson. Archie Greaves saw him running away.'

'Mike, we know he ran away, he admits that himself. And it was a girl with a hat on that Linda Naseem saw.'

Burden got up and walked the length of the room, then came back to lean on the edge of Wexford's desk. He had the air of someone who is bracing himself to say something unpleasant in the nicest possible way. 'Look, you've had a bad shock and you're still not well. You saw what happened when you came back to work too soon. And for God's sake, I know you're worried about Sheila.'

Wexford said dryly but as pleasantly as he could, 'OK, but my mind's not affected.'

'Well, isn't it? It would be only natural to think it was – temporarily, that is. All the evidence in this case points to

Clifford and, moreover, not a shred to anyone else. Only for some reason you refuse to see that, and in my opinion the reason is that you're not right yet, you're not over the shock of the bomb. Frankly, you should have stayed at home longer.'

And left it all to you, Wexford thought, saying nothing but aware of a cold anger spreading through him rather like a draught of icy water trickling down his gullet.

'I shall break Clifford on my own. It's only a matter of time. Leave it to me, I'm not asking for help – or advice, come to that. I know what I'm doing. And as for torture, that's a laugh. I haven't even approached anything the Judges' Rules would object to.'

'Maybe not,' Wexford said. 'Perhaps you should remember the last lines of that passage you like so much defining a psychopath, the bit about the ruthless and determined pursuit of gratification.'

Burden looked hard at him, looked in near-disbelief, then walked out, slamming the door resoundingly.

A quarrel with Mike was something that had never happened before. Disagreements, yes, and tough arguments. There had been the time, for instance, when Mike had lost his first wife and gone to pieces and later had that peculiar love affair – Wexford had been angry with him then and perhaps paternalistic. But they had never come to hurling abuse at each other. Of course he hadn't meant to infer that Mike was a psychopath, or had psychopathic tendencies or anything of that sort, but he had to admit it must have sounded like that. What had he meant then? As with most people in most quarrels, he had said the first hurtful, moderately clever thing that came into his head.

Some of the things Mike had said he was sure were right. In his assessment of the character of Gwen Robson he was right. She would do a great deal for money, almost anything, and what she had done had led to her death. He knew that and Burden knew it too. But he had chosen the wrong person from among her possible . . . what? Clients? Perhaps that was the best word even in this context. Clifford Sanders was not Gwen Robson's murderer.

Wexford looked out of the window and saw him being

shepherded out to one of the cars. Davidson was about to drive him home. Clifford neither trudged nor shuffled, he didn't walk with he head bowed or his shoulders hunched, yet there was something of desperation in his bearing. He was like one caught in a recurring dream from which to awaken is to escape, but which will inexorably return the next night. Fanciful nonsense, Wexford told himself, but his thoughts persisted in dwelling on Burden's chosen perpetrator as Davidson drove out of the forecourt and on to the road, and all that could be seen of Clifford Sanders was his solid heavy-shouldered shape through the rear window, his round cropped skull. What would he go home to? That cold, dictatorial woman, that house which was big and bare and always chilly and where, according to Burden, everything that might have made it comfortable was stored away up in the attics. Useless to ask why he stayed. He was young and fit and educated; he could leave, make a life of his own. Wexford knew that so many people are their own prisoners, jailers of themselves, that the doors which to the outside world seem to stand open they have sealed with invisible bars. They have blocked off the tunnels to freedom, pulled down the blinds to keep out the light. Clifford, if asked, would no doubt say, 'I can't leave my mother, she's done everything for me, brought me up single-handed, devoted her life to me. I can't leave her, I must do my duty.' But perhaps it was something very different he said when alone with Serge Olson.

Wexford might not have gone to Sundays that day, might have sat in his office for a long time brooding over his quarrel with Burden, but a call came through from a man called Brook, Stephen Brook. The name meant nothing, then recall came with a recollection of the blue Lancia and a woman who had gone into labour while in the shopping centre. Brook said his wife had something to tell the police and Wexford's thoughts went at once to Clifford Sanders. Suppose this woman wanted to tell him something that would put Clifford entirely beyond suspicion? She might know him. It could, with some exaggeration, be said that in a place like Kingsmarkham everyone knew everyone else. It would bring him considerable satisfaction to have Clifford exonerated and might also heal

531

the breach between himself and Burden – without if possible Burden's losing face.

The Brooks lived at the Forby Road end of town, their home a flat in the local authority housing area of the Sunday's estate. From the window of their living room Sunday's Park could be seen – its hornbeam avenue, its lawns and cedars, the cars of those taking the word-processor course parked at the side of the big white house. This small room was very warm and Mrs Brook's baby lay uncovered in a wicker cradle. The Brooks' furniture consisted of two battered chairs and a table and a great many small crates and boxes, all of them covered or draped with lengths of patterned material and shawls and coloured blankets. There were posters on the walls and dried grasses in stoneware mustard jars. It had all been done at the lowest possible cost and the effect was rather charming.

Mrs Brook was all in black. Dusty black knitted draperies was the way Wexford would have described her clothes if he had had to do so. She wore wrinkled black and white striped stockings and black trainers, and a very curious contemporary madonna she looked when she lifted the baby and, unbuttoning black cardigan and black shirt, presented one round white breast to its mouth. Her husband – in jeans, shirt and zipper-jacket uniform – would have appeared more conventional if he had not dyed his spiky hair to resemble the bird of paradise flower, a tropical blue and orange. Their modulated Myringham University accents came as a slight shock, though Wexford told himself he should have known better. Both of them were about the age of Clifford Sanders, but how different a life they had made for themselves!

'I didn't tell you before,' Helen Brook said, 'because I didn't know who she was. I mean, I was in hospital having Ashtoreth and I didn't really think much about all that.'

Ashtoreth. Well, it sounded pretty and was just another goddess like Diana.

'I mean, it was all a shock really. I meant to have her at home and I was all set to do that. Squatting, you know, not lying down which is so unnatural, and three of my friends were coming to perform the proper rites. The people at the hospital had been really angry at me for wanting to have her the natural

532

way, but I knew I could prove to them my way was right. And then of course they caught me. It was almost as if they set a trap to get me into hospital, though Steve says not – they couldn't have.'

'Yeah, that's paranoia, love,' said Stephen Brook.

'Yes, I just started these labour pains – how about that? I was in Demeter and these pains just started.'

'In what?' Wexford said before he remembered this was the Barringdean Centre's health food shop. Briefly, it had sounded like some obstetrical condition.

'In Demeter,' she said again, 'getting my calendula capsules. And I sort of looked up and through the window and I saw her outside talking to this girl. And I thought I'll go out and show myself to her and I wonder what she'll think – the way she used to go on saying she hoped I'd never have children, that was all.'

'He doesn't know what you're on about, love.'

Wexford nodded his assent to this as Helen Brook shifted the child to her other breast, cupping the soft downy head in her hand. 'Saw whom?' he asked.

'That woman who got killed. Only I didn't know; I mean, I didn't know what her name was. I just knew I knew her, then when we read in the paper that she'd been a home help and where she lived I said to Steve, that's the woman who used to look after the lady next door to Mum. I was in Demeter and I recognized her, I hadn't seen her for yonks. You see, she'd heard about the way Steve and I got married and she was all peculiar about it.'

'The way you got married?'

'Well, Steve and I didn't go to a register officer or a church or anything on account of our beliefs. We had a very beautiful ceremony at Stonehenge at dawn, with all our friends there. I mean, they won't let you go up into the stones like Mummy said you used to, but it was very beautiful just being able to see Stonehenge. Steve had a ring made of bone and I had a ring made of yew wood and we exchanged them, and our friend who's a musician played the sitar and everyone sang. Anyway, the council let you have a flat even if you don't get married the official way. Mum told the lady – what was she called, Gwen? – Mummy told her that, but she was still really sniffy and when she saw me that's what she said. She said I hope you don't have children, that's all. Well, that was two years ago and I hadn't seen her since and then I did see her talking to this girl outside Demeter. They went off into Tesco's together and I was going to follow them and kind of say, look, how about that? And then I had this terrific pain . . .'

She sat there, smiling blandly, the baby Ashtoreth now recumbent in her lap and subsiding into sleep. Wexford asked her to describe the girl.

'I'm not very good at describing people. I mean it's the way they are inside that counts, isn't it? She was older than me but not all that much, and she had dark hair that was quite long and she was wearing the most amazing clothes; that's what stuck in my memory, her amazing clothes.'

'Are you saying she was smartly dressed?' Wexford understood at once that he was using very outdated terms and Helen Brook looked puzzled. She leaned forward as if she had misheard. 'Her clothes were particularly elegant?' he corrected himself, and added, 'New? Beautiful? Fashionable?'

'Well, not specially new. Elegant – that might be the word. You know what I mean.'

'Was she wearing a hat?'

'A hat? No, she wasn't wearing a hat. She had lovely hair; she looked lovely.'

A young woman ought to be able to judge the style of a contemporary. What she had told him had confirmed Linda Naseem's evidence – or had it? Hats, after all, can be temporarily taken off. If this were the same girl both she and Helen Brook had seen, it meant that Gwen Robson had met her in one of the aisles of the shopping centre and presumably walked through the Tesco supermarket with her, the two of them then leaving together for the underground car park. If it was the same girl . . .

It is rare to recognize someone at the wheel of a car. Generally, it is the car we recognize, then look quickly to identify the driver. Silver Escorts attracted Wexford's attention at present, as did red Metros, and a closer look at the one approaching showed him Ralph Robson in the driving-seat. So Lesley Arbel was without transport today . . .

'Turn round,' he said to Donaldson. 'Take me to Sunday's.'

When they arrived, people were coming down the steps of the Regency mansion; the course had come to an end. There were as many men as women and most of them were young. Lesley Arbel, emerging from the open double entrance doors, stood out conspicuously from the rest by her looks and her clothes. Wexford, who when he first met her had been reminded by her sleek dressing of actresses in the early days of the talking cinema, now again recollected those thirties' films. Only in them was it possible to capture such a scene, where there was no room for doubting who where extras and who the star. But because this was not a film and Lesley Arbel no confident movie queen swanning on celluloid, her appearance was a little ridiculous by contrast with all those in tweed coats and anoraks and jackets over tracksuits. She even came rather awkwardly down those steps, her heels so high as to throw her off-balance.

The Kingsmarkham bus passed along the Forby Road, stopping opposite the gates and Sundays Lodge, and it was no doubt this bus she meant to catch. But her heels and the long tight black skirt restricted her steps and she was making very slow strutting progress towards the avenue when Wexford put his head out of the car window and asked if they might give her a lift home. It was more than a surprise, it seemed a shock, and she jumped. He had a feeling that if more comfortably shod, she would have made a run for it. However she came cautiously up to the car. Wexford got out, opened the rear door for her and she got awkwardly in ahead of him, ducking her head and holding on to her small black grosgrain hat.

'I thought we might have a talk in private,' he said. 'Without your uncle, I mean.'

She was too nervous to speak and sat with her hands in her lap, staring at Donaldson's broad back. Wexford noticed that her nails – which had protruded a good half-inch from her fingertips – had been filed down and were unpainted. Donaldson began to drive slowly down the avenue, between the lines of leafless hornbeams. The sun had just set and all the trees made a black tracery against a spectacular crimson sky.

Wexford said quietly, 'You didn't tell me you were in Kingsmarkham on the day your aunt was killed.'

She responded quite quickly and it was as if the question had been of no great significance. So might she have replied if a friend had reproached her for failing to make a promised phone call.

'No, I was upset and I forgot.'

'Come now, Miss Arbel. You told me you left Orangetree House early because you weren't feeling well.'

She muttered, 'I *wasn't* feeling well.'

'Your illness didn't prevent your coming to Kingsmarkham.'

'I mean I forgot it might be important where I was.'

She had been frightened, but she wasn't frightened now; this must mean he had not asked the question she feared to hear. 'It's very important where you were. I understand you came here to check that you were on this course that was to start the following Monday?' She nodded, relaxing a little, her body less rigid under the stiffly padded shoulders of her pink and black striped jacket. 'That can be verified, you know, Miss Arbel.'

'I did check up on the course.'

'You could have done that by phone, couldn't you?'

'I did try but their phones were out of order.'

'And then you went to meet your aunt in the Barringdean Centre.'

'No!' He couldn't tell if it was a cry of denial through fear of discovery or simple astonishment that such a meeting could have been suspected. 'I never saw her, I never did! Why would I go there?'

'You must tell me that. Suppose I told you that you were seen by at least one witness?'

'I'd say they were lying.'

'As you were lying when you told me you were ill on November 19 and went home early from work?'

'I wasn't lying. I thought it wasn't important just coming down here to look at a form and check up and then go back again. That's all I did. I never went near the Barringdean Centre.'

'You came and went by train?'

She gave an anxious nod, falling into his trap.

'You were very near the centre then, considering the pedestrian entrance is in the next street to Station Road.

536

Wouldn't it be right to say you returned to the station from Sundays and, remembering your aunt would be in the Barringdean Centre at that time because she always was, you went in and met her in the central aisle?'

It was a vehement, tearful denial she made, but again Wexford had the feeling that whatever she was afraid of it was not this; it was not fear of having been seen with her aunt half an hour before her death that frightened her. And to his astonishment she suddenly exclaimed miserably, 'I'll lose my job!'

This seemed almost an irrelevancy, at least a minor matter compared with the enormity of Gwen Robson's death. He let her go, opening the door for her when the car stopped in Highlands outside her uncle's house. For a few moments he stood there, watching the house. Behind drawn curtains the lights were already on. She had gone up the path at a hobbling run and was fumbling with her key when Robson opened the door to let her in. It was closed very rapidly. Now for the long evening, Wexford thought; the making of tea and perhaps scrambled eggs, the chat about the day she had passed and he had passed, complaints about his arthritis and sympathy from her, the relief of television. What had people in that situation done before television? It was unthinkable.

Was it all out of the kindness of her heart? Was it that she had truly loved her aunt and now loved and pitied her uncle? A saint, an angel of mercy – that she must be to remain here for yet another weekend when London and her own home and friends were available to her, when there were three trains an hour to take her there. But Wexford didn't think she was an angel of mercy; she hadn't impressed him even as being particularly kind-hearted. Vanity and self-absorption don't generally go with altruism – and what was the meaning of that final impassioned cry?

Dita Jago's daughter had called to collect her little girls and Wexford said to Donaldson, 'You can take the car back and knock off if you like. I'll walk home from here.'

A momentary surprise crossed Donaldson's face, then he remembered where home now was. Wexford strolled across the road. The Highlands lights were not the gentle amber lamps of the street where his own house was but the harsh white kind, glass vases full of glare borne on concrete stilts. They stained the dark air with a livid fog and turned people and their clothes reptile colours, greenish and sour brown and sallow white. Melanie and Hannah – what was their name, Quincy? – looked tubercular, their lively dark eyes dulled and their red cheeks pallid. Their mother was wearing one of her own mother's brilliant knitted creations, a sweater that probably had as many colours as a Persian carpet, a skirt of thick gathered folds on which the intricate stripes, no doubt of rich and varied shades, undulated like shadows in the wind . . . only it all looked brown and grey in that light.

Nina was her name? As Wexford asked himself that, he heard Mrs Jago call her by it and Nina Quincy, having settled her children in the back of the car, went up to her mother, put her arms round her and kissed her. Strange, Wexford thought; they see each other every day . . . Mrs Jago waved as the car departed; a shawl wrapped her shoulders today, a tapestry-like square with a fringed border. It seemed to suit her monumental shape, the heavy-featured face with its load of bunched coils of hair, better than contemporary dress. She acknowledged Wexford calmly.

'You're living up here now, they tell me.'

He nodded. 'How are the memoirs?'

'I haven't been doing much writing.' She gave him that look peculiar to people who have something to confide but don't know if this is the right confidant. Should I? Shouldn't I? Will I regret it once the words are out? 'Come in a moment and have a drink.'

A chat with a neighbour on the way home. A sherry. Why not? But it wasn't sherry she gave him, far from it. A kind of schnapps probably, Wexford thought: icy-cold, sweetish and unbelievably strong. It made his eyebrows shoot up, it made him feel as if his hair stood on end.

'I needed that,' she said, though there had been no alteration in her pleasant friendly manner, no gasp of relief.

The pile of manuscript was precisely where it had been when he was last in this room, a hair lying across the top of the title page. He was sure that hair had been there last time. If Mrs Jago had not been writing she had been knitting, and the jungle landscape had grown several more inches from the long curled needle, palm trees now sprouting fronds and a sky appearing. The germ of an idea pushed a shoot into his mind.

'Did Gwen Robson know you were writing this book?'

'Mrs Robson?' It sounded like a measure, if not of her indifference to her dead neighbour, of the degree of acquaintance she had had with her in life. A remoteness was implied that Wexford found himself not quite believing in. 'She was only once in this house; I don't suppose she noticed.' Wexford thought for a moment that she was going to sneer, to add that Gwen Robson wasn't the kind to read books or be interested in them. But instead she said, in such sudden contrast as to be shocking, 'My daughter and her husband have parted. "Split up" is what they say, isn't it? I hadn't any idea of it, I hadn't any warning. Nina just came in this afternoon and said their marriage was over. My son-in-law left this morning.'

'My daughter's parted from her husband too,' Wexford said.

She said, rather sharply for her but with some justice perhaps, 'That's different, though. A famous actress, rich, with a wealthy husband, always in the public eye . . .'

'Only to be expected, do you mean?'

She was too old and experienced to blush; it was more a wince she gave. 'I'm sorry, I didn't mean that. It's only that Nina's got the two girls and it's terrible for the children. And women left on their own to bring up children, they lead a miserable existence. She earns so little from her job, it's only part-time. He's leaving her the house, he'll have to support them, but – if only I could see why! I thought they were so happy.'

'Who knows what goes on in other people's marriages?' said Wexford.

Leaving her, he set off to walk up the hill. Wexford's Third Law, he thought, ought to be: always live at the foot of a hill, then you'll be fresh for climbing it in the morning. It was quite a steep haul up and all the way he could see his new home ahead of him, glowering uncompromisingly from the crown of the hill. There was no garage, so his car stood outside with Sylvia's behind it and behind that another unidentifiable one that might be a neighbour's. The removal van had gone. He wasn't out of breath as he opened the gate (wooden in the wire fence) and walked up to the front door. I must be quite fit, he was thinking as he turned his key in the lock, opened the door and had his ears at once assaulted by the voice of Sylvia – shrill, cross, loud, easily penetrating these thin walls: 'You ought to think of Dad! You ought to think how you're putting his life in danger with your heroics!'

13

The other car must have been Sheila's, rented or else a replacement for the Porsche. Both sisters were standing up, glaring at each other along the length of the room. It was a very small room and they seemed almost to be shouting into each other's faces. There was a door into the hall and another door into the kitchen and as Wexford came in through one Dora entered by the other, accompanied by the two little boys.

Dora said, 'Stop it, stop shouting!'

But the boys were indifferent. They had come in to secure a pocket calculator (Robin) and a drawing block (Ben), and they proceeded to forage for these items in diminutive school briefcases, undeterred by the slanging match going on between their mother and their aunt. Their reaction would have been different if this had been parents quarrelling, Wexford thought.

He looked from one young woman to the other. 'What's going on?'

Sylvia's reply was to throw up her hands and cast herself into an armchair. Sheila – her face flushed and her hair looking wild and tangled, though this might have been by design – said, 'My case comes up on Tuesday week, in the magistrates' court. They want me to plead guilty.'

'Who's "they"?'

'Mother and Sylvia.'

'Excuse me,' Dora said. 'I didn't say I wanted you to do anything. I said you ought to think about it very seriously.'

'I have thought about it. I hardly think of anything else and I've discussed it with Ned exhaustively. I've discussed it with him because he's a lawyer as much as . . . well, my boyfriend, or whatever you call it. And it isn't doing our relationship a lot of good, to tell you the truth.'

Robin and Ben gave up the search and carried their cases outside to the kitchen. Tactfully, Ben closed the door behind him.

It was as if this freed Sylvia to speak openly and she said in a hard, unsympathetic way, 'What she does is her own business. If she wants to stand up in court and say she's not guilty, that governments are guilty for breaking international law or whatever – well, she can do that. And when she gets fined and refuses to pay the fine, she can go to prison if that's what she likes.'

Wexford interrupted her. 'Is that what you're going to do, Sheila?'

'I have to,' she said shortly. 'There's no point otherwise.'

'But it's not just her,' Sylvia continued. 'It's all the rest of us she involves. Everyone knows who she is, everyone knows she's your daughter and my sister. What's that going to do for you as a police officer, having a daughter go to prison? This is a democracy and if we want to change things we've each got a vote to do it with. Why can't she use her vote and change the government like the rest of us have to?'

Sheila said tiredly, 'That's the biggest cop-out of all. If you had a hundred votes all to yourself down in this neck of the woods you couldn't change anything, not with a sitting Member with a sixteen-thousand majority.'

'And that's not the worst,' Sylvia went on, ignoring this. 'The worst is that when those people who tried to bomb her know what she thinks, when she gets up and says it in court, they're going to have another go, aren't they? They nearly got you by accident last time and maybe this time they really will. Or maybe they'll get you on purpose – or one of my children!'

Wexford sighed. 'I've been drinking schnapps with a lady of my acquaintance.' He glanced at Dora and gave her the ghost of a wink. 'I rather wish I'd got the bottle with me.' How wrong of me it is, he thought, that I love one of my children more than the other. 'I suppose you've got to do what you've got to do, as the current phrase has it,' he said to Sheila, but as he got up and made for the kitchen door – made for the beer he trusted was in the fridge – it was Sylvia on whose shoulder he laid a caressing hand.

'Not all that current, Pop,' said Sheila.

Things calmed down. At any rate, Sylvia soon left to take her sons home and cook her husband's supper. Then Sheila and her parents went out to eat, no one yet feeling comfortable in what Dora called 'this horrid little house'. Sheila talked moodily about Ned not wanting it known that someone in his position was consorting with someone in hers, though she didn't explain what his position was and Wexford, true to his principles, wouldn't ask.

'When peace is so beautiful,' Sheila said, 'and what everyone wants, why do they treat workers for peace like criminals?'

Passing the police station on their way back from the restaurant in Pomfret, Wexford saw a light on in one of the interview rooms. Of course there was no real reason to suppose that Burden was in there with Clifford Sanders, yet he did suppose it with a chilling sense of unease. Forgetting Sheila and her troubles for a moment, he thought: I shall be embarrassed when I next see Mike, I shall feel awkward and therefore shall postpone that meeting. What am I going to do?

Burden had not meant to recall Clifford to the police station. His intention had been to call off his dogs for the duration of the weekend and let his baited creature make a partial recovery. The metaphor was his wife's, not his, and he reacted with some anger to it. He now regretted discussing the case with Jenny and wished he had stuck to the principle (never much honoured in the observance) of not taking his work home.

'I've had the same sentimental rubbish at work,' he said. He would normally have said 'from Reg', but he was too angry with Wexford even to want to think of him by his Christian name. Burden had a Victorian attitude in this area, rather in the manner of those fictional heroines who called a man William while they were engaged to him and Mr Jones after they had broken it off. 'I don't understand all this sympathy with cold-blooded killers. People should try thinking of their victims for a change.'

'So you've said on numerous previous occasions,' said Jenny, not very pleasantly.

That did it. That sent him back to the police station after his dinner and Archbold to the Forby Road to fetch Clifford again. He used the other ground-floor interview room this time, the one at the front where the window gave on to the High Street, where the tiles were shabby black and tan (like an ageing spaniel, said Wexford) and the table had a brown-checked top with a metal rim.

For the first time Clifford didn't wait for Burden to begin. In a resigned but not unhappy voice, he said, 'I knew you'd fetch me back again today. I sensed it. That's why I didn't start watching TV; I knew I'd only be interrupted in the middle of a programme. My mother knew too; she's been watching me, waiting for the doorbell to ring.'

'Your mother's been asking you about this too, has she, Cliff?'

Again Burden reflected how much like an overgrown schoolboy he looked. The clothes were so much the conventional wear of a correct well-ordered teenager at a grammar school in, say, the fifties, as to seem either a mockery or a disguise. The grey flannel trousers had turn-ups and were well-pressed. He wore a grey shirt – so that it could be worn two or three days without washing? – striped tie, grey hand-knitted V-necked pullover. It was plainly hand-knitted, well but not expertly, the hand of the imperfectly skilled evident in the neck border and the sewing up. Somehow Burden knew it had to be Mrs Sanders' work. He already had an idea of her as a woman of many activities, but who did none of them well; she would not care enough to do things well.

Clifford's face was its usual blank, revealing no emotion even when he spoke those surely desperate sentences. He said, 'I may as well tell you. I tell you all the truth now, I don't hide anything, I hope you believe that. I may as well tell you that she says I wouldn't be questioned like this day after day, on and on, if there wasn't something in it. She says I must be that sort of person, or you wouldn't keep getting me down here.'

'What sort of person would that be, Cliff?'

'Someone who would kill a woman.'

'Your mother knows you're guilty then, does she?'

Clifford said with curious pendantry, 'You can't know something that isn't true; you can only believe it or suspect it.

544

She says that's the sort of person I am, not that she thinks I killed anyone.' Pausing, he looked sideways at Burden in what the latter thought of as a mad way, an unbalanced way. It was a sly, crafty look. 'Perhaps I am. Perhaps I am that sort of person. How would you know till you did it.'

'You tell me, Cliff. Tell me about that sort of person.'

'He would be unhappy. He'd feel threatened by everyone. He'd want to escape from the life he had into something better, but that better would only be fantasy because he wouldn't be able to escape really. Like a rat in a cage. They do these psychological experiments; they put a piece of glass outside the open door of the cage and when the rat tries to get out it can't because it bumps into the glass. Then when they take the glass away it could really get out but it won't, because it knows it gets hurt bumping itself on the invisible thing outside.'

'Is that yourself you're describing?'

Clifford nodded. 'Talking to you has helped to show me what I am. It's done more for me than Serge can.' He looked into Burden's eyes. 'You ought to be a psychotherapist yourself.' To Burden's ears it was a slightly mad laugh that he gave. 'I thought you were stupid, but now I know you're not. You're not stupid; you've opened up places in my mind for me.'

Burden wasn't sure he knew what this meant. Like most people, he didn't like being called stupid even though the term was immediately revoked. But he had a feeling that Clifford would be even franker if they were alone and so he sent Archbold away, ostensibly to fetch coffee from the canteen. Clifford was smiling again, though there was nothing pleased in that smile, nothing happy.

'Are you taping all this?' he asked.

Burden nodded.

'Good. You've shown me what I'm capable of. It's frightening. I'm not a rat and I know I can't break the invisible wall, but I can force the person who put it there to break it.' He paused and smiled, or at any rate bared his teeth. 'Dodo,' he said. 'Dodo, the big bird. Only she's not, she's a little pecking bird with claws and a beak. I'll tell you something; I wake up in the night and think what I'm capable of, what I could do, and I want to sit up and scream and yell – only I can't because I'd wake her up.'

545

'Yes,' said Burden, 'yes.' He didn't much care for this sudden feeling he had of being in waters that were too deep for him. He had had enough too and would have liked to send Clifford home. Not very vigorously he asked, 'What are you capable of?'

But Clifford made no answer to this. Archbold came in with the coffee and at a nod from Burden left the room again. Clifford went on, 'At my age I oughtn't to need my mother. But I do. In a lot of ways, I rely on her.'

'Go on,' said Burden.

But Clifford sidetracked, saying, 'I'd like to tell you about myself. I'd like to talk about me. Is that all right?'

For the first time Burden felt . . . not fear, he would never have admitted this was fear – but apprehensiveness perhaps, a tautening of muscles, the cautionary chill of being alone with a mad person.

However, he only said, 'Go on.'

Clifford spoke dreamily. 'When I was young – I mean really young, a little boy – we lived with my father's parents. The Sanders family had lived in our house since the late seventeen-hundreds. My grandfather died and then my father's and mother's marriage came to an end. My father just walked out on us and they were divorced and we were left with my father's mother. Mother put her into an old people's home and then she moved everything out of the house that reminded her of my father and his people; she moved all the furniture and the bed linen and the china upstairs into the attics.

'We hadn't any furniture, only mattresses on the floor and two chairs and a table. All the carpets and the comfortable chairs were upstairs, locked away. We never saw anyone, we hadn't any friends. My mother didn't want to send me to school, she was going to teach me herself at home. Dodo! Imagine! She'd been a cleaner before she got married – Dodo, the maid. She hadn't any qualifications to teach me and they caught her and at last they made her send me to school. She'd walk me into Kingsmarkham every morning and come and fetch me every afternoon. It's nearly three miles. When I grumbled about walking, do you know what she said? She said she'd push me in my old pushchair. I was six! Of course I walked after that; I didn't want the others to see me in a pushchair. There was a school bus, but I didn't know I could have gone on that: she didn't want me to, it was two years before I knew I could go on it and then I did. When she wanted to punish me she didn't hit me or anything; she shut me up in the attics with that furniture.'

'All right, Cliff,' said Burden, looking at his watch, 'that'll do for now.' He realized, when Clifford was silent and got up obediently, that he had spoken as a psychotherapist might: he had spoken in the manner of Serge Olson.

A confession was what he had expected from Clifford on the previous night. That confiding manner, that unprecedented free and open way of speaking, those discomforting references to his mother's nickname had seemed to herald it. All the time they seemed on the brink of the final revelation, the ultimate admission, but it had not come and Clifford had digressed into that account of his early youth which was the last thing Burden wanted to hear. But one good thing had resulted; he no longer felt guilt or much unease. Jenny had been wrong and Wexford had been wrong. Clifford might be mad, might well be the psychopath Burden had designated him, but he was not being terrorized or pushed over some edge or driven to desperation. He had been almost cheerful, talkative, in command of himself, and he had seemed – odd though this was – actually to enjoy their talk and look forward to more.

It must only be a matter of time now. Burden would have liked to discuss all this with Wexford. Best of all he would have liked Wexford in on his next session with Clifford, sitting there at the table, listening and occasionally putting a question of his own. Burden didn't feel like an inquisitor or torturer any more, but he did feel the responsibility, that it weighed heavily on his own shoulders.

In the morning Sheila made amends.

'Sylvia wanted me to apologize in court,' she said. 'Can you imagine? I'm to stand there and make a public retraction and say I'm sorry to a bunch of terrorists, plead guilty and promise not to do it again.'

'She didn't mean that,' Dora put in.

'I think she did. Anyway, I'm not apologizing to anyone except you and Pop. I'm sorry I made a row in your . . . new

547

home. Especially considering I'm kind of responsible for wrecking your old one.'

She kissed them goodbye and went off to Ned and Coram Fields. Half an hour after she had gone, Sylvia rang up to apologize for what she called 'that unnecessary scene.' Perhaps she should come over and explain what she really felt about the whole Sheila-wire-cutting situation?

'All right,' Wexford said, 'but only if you'll bring me every copy of *Kim* magazine you've got in the house.'

First of all she said she was sure she hadn't any copies; then when her father told her she was like her mother and never threw anything away, she said that she only kept them for the knitting patterns. In the afternoon she turned up with a stack too heavy to be fetched out of the car at one go and Wexford himself had to make two trips to carry them. There were more than two hundred, covering a period of something like four years. He knew that nothing except Sylvia's guilty feelings would have induced her to reveal to her father such a propensity for magazine-reading – and downmarket magazine reading at that. Dora said nothing when they were brought into the small living room, but her face registered a restrained dismay as Sylvia stacked them up into a kind of tower block between the bookcase and the television table.

Her explanation and a kind of manifesto of her views on the nuclear issue and the role of public figures in civil disobedience and non-violent direct action took a long while. Wexford listened sympathetically because he knew he would have listened to Sheila, and of course he bent over backwards to be fair to the daughter he loved less. Even thinking in those terms made him feel mean and rotten. And if she was really concerned that he might get blown up again, really worried about him and his life being in danger, he ought to go down on his knees to her in gratitude for caring that much for him. So he sat there hearing it all and nodding and agreeing or gently disagreeing, trying not to acknowledge the enormous relief, the leap of the heart when the doorbell rang and, looking out of the window, he saw Burden's car at the kerb. The odd thing was that he forgot all about being embarrassed.

Burden had Jenny with him and the little boy, Mark. If Sylvia's children had been girls – a comparable pair for instance with Melanie and Hannah Quincy – they would have immediately taken the two-year-old under their wing, talked to him and played with him with a precocious maternity. But being male they merely looked at him with bored indifference and, when adjured by Sylvia to show Mark their Lego, responded with, 'Do we *have* to?'

'I was going to ask you to come out for a drink,' Burden said, 'but Jenny says she won't have any of that sexist stuff.'

Sylvia said enthusiastically, 'Absolutely not! I quite agree.'

At the old house Wexford would have taken Burden into the dining room but there was no such place here, only a corner behind a strip of counter called a 'meals area'. But the kitchen, though small, had a table in it and two chairs which there was just room to sit in if you weren't overweight and were prepared to keep your elbows close to your sides. The big fridge dominated the room. Wexford took out two half-pint cans of Abbot.

'I'm sorry, Mike . . .' he was beginning as Burden simultaneously started to say, 'Look, I do regret saying those things yesterday . . .'

Their joint laughter was shamefaced as embarrassment gripped them.

'Oh, for Christ's sake,' Wexford said, nearly groaned it. 'Let's get it over with. I never meant you had psychopathic tendencies – I mean, would I say anything so daft?'

'No more than I meant that the accident had made you – well, lose your grip . . . or whatever it was I said. Why do we say these things? They just seem to come out before you think.'

They looked at each other, each one holding his green can of beer, each rejecting the actual use of the glasses Wexford had fetched from the cupboard. Burden was the first to break the eye contact which anyway had been only momentary. He looked down, busied himself with the can fastener and said in an uneven, hearty voice, 'Look, I want to talk to you about Clifford Sanders. I want to tell you everything he's told me and hear what you think. And then I want something I don't think you'll consent to do.'

'Try me.'

'To interview him with me – sit in at one of our sessions.'

'Your what?' said Wexford.

549

'Sorry, I mean interrogations.'

'Tell me what he's told you.'

'I could play you the tapes.'

'Not now. Just tell me.'

'He's been going on about his childhood, about that weird mother of his. He keeps calling her Dodo and laughing. I don't want to have to think him unbalanced – that is, I don't care for the idea of him getting off on the grounds of diminished responsibility – but I reckon I have to.' And then Burden told him all that had taken place at the interview of the night before, detailing what Clifford had said.

'You don't want me there,' said Wexford. 'He'll clam up if I'm there.'

'You've changed your mind, though, haven't you? You agree with me he's guilty?'

'No, I don't, Mike. Not at all. I just see that your believing it is more reasonable than I thought it was. You've no weapon that you can trace to his hand. However you may be deceiving yourself, you've no motive, and frankly I don't think you've even got opportunity. You'll never prove it; you haven't a hope unless you get him to confess.'

'That's just what I do hope for. I'm going to have another go at him on Monday.'

When they had all gone peace descended on the little house on Battle Hill, a peace however that was not entirely silent for through the thin dividing walls could be heard neighbours' noise: light-switches clicking, inane cackles of televised laughter, children's running feet, unidentifiable crashes. Wexford sat down with the new A.N. Wilson and was absorbed in it when the phone rang.

Dora went to answer it, 'If that's anyone else wanting to come and apologize, tell then I'm quite at leisure.'

But it was Sheila. He heard Dora speak her name and heard the deep concern and shock in her voice, then he was out of that chair at a bound.

She turned to him from the receiver. 'She's all right. She didn't want us to hear it on TV first. A letter-bomb . . .'

Wexford took the phone from her.

'It was there with the rest of my post. I don't know why, but

I didn't like the look of it. The police came like a shot and they took it away and did I don't know what to it and it blew up. . . !'

She started sobbing, her words no longer comprehensible, and Wexford heard a man's voice murmuring comforting things.

14

'My grandmother Sanders had some money, but she left it all to my father,' said Clifford. 'I never saw my father again. He went away when I was five; he didn't even say goodbye to me. I can remember it all quite well. He was there when I went to bed and in the morning when I woke up he was gone. My mother just said to me that my father had left us, but that I should see him quite often – that he would come to see me and take me out. But he never did come and I never saw him again. It's no wonder my mother didn't want anything about the place to remind her of him; it's no wonder she put all his family things up there in the attics.'

Involuntarily, Burden followed his glance upwards to the cracked and rather discoloured dining-room ceiling. Beyond the french windows a thin mist hung over the wintry garden, and the hill that hid the prospect of Kingsmarkham was a grey, treeless hump. It was Sunday afternoon and at a quarter-past three already growing dark. Burden had not intended to come here – had meant, as he told Wexford, to postpone any further interrogation of Clifford until the following day. But as he was finishing his lunch Clifford had phoned.

There was no reason why he shouldn't have found Burden's home number, it was there in the telephone directory for anyone to see, but Burden was astonished to get the call, astonished and encouraged. A confession was surely imminent, an intuition he had which was very much substantiated by the low, wary tone in which Clifford spoke as if he feared being overheard – and the sudden haste with which he rang off as soon as Burden said he would come. The suspicion was inescapable that Dodo Sanders had come into the room; another word and she would have guessed what Clifford was up to and surely tried to stop him.

It was Clifford who had admitted him to the house. His mother put her head round the door of what was perhaps some kind of washroom and stared, saying nothing. Her head was swathed in a towel, obviously because she had just washed her hair in spite of visiting the hairdresser three days before. But this brought to Burden's mind what Olson had said about the fallacy of 'the veiled one'. Of course he had not meant anything of this sort, that particular veiling surely referred to hidden aspects of personality or nature. The turbanned head ducked back and the door closed. Burden looked at Clifford, whose appearance was much as usual. He wore his school uniform clothes, no concession to the casual having been made for Sunday. Yet there was a subtle change in his manner, something indefinable that Burden couldn't put his finger on. Up until yesterday, he had come into Burden's presence grudgingly or with injured outrage or even straight fear. This afternoon Clifford had admitted him to the house not as one might a friend, not that, but at least as some visitor whose call was a necessary and inevitable evil, a tax inspector perhaps. Of course it must be remembered that he had come at Clifford's personal invitation.

A fire had been lit in the dining room and it was fairly warm. Burden was sure Clifford had done this himself. He had even drawn up two of the dining chairs to the fireplace – hard upright chairs, but the best he could offer. Burden sat down and Clifford launched at once into this resumed story of his life.

'Children don't question what they live on, where the money comes from, I mean. I was a lot older when my mother told me that my father had never paid her a penny. She tried to force him to pay her through the court, but he couldn't be found; he'd just deserted her and disappeared. And he had a private income, you know; I mean he had investments of his own, just enough to live on without working. She had to go out cleaning to keep us and then she made things, sort of cottage industry things – bits she knitted and sewed. I was nearly grown-up before I knew any of this. She never told me before. I was at school while she was working and of course I never guessed.'

Burden didn't know what questions to ask, so he said nothing. He just listened, thinking of his confession, pinning faith on that. The recorder was on the dining table; Clifford had placed it there himself.

'I owe her everything,' Clifford went on. 'She sacrificed her whole life to me, wore herself out to keep me in comfort. Serge says I needn't think of it like that, that basically we all do what we want and that was what she wanted. But I don't know. I mean I do know intellectually, I know he's right, but that doesn't do away with my guilt. I feel guilty about her all the time. For example, when I left school at eighteen I could have got a job; someone I knew at school, his father actually offered me an office job, but my mother insisted on my going to university. She always wanted the best for me. Of course I got the maximum grant, but I was still a drag on her; I wasn't earning money except for a bit I got from gardening for people like Miss McPhail. When I got to Myringham University I never lived in; I came back home every night.' Clifford shifted his eyes, looking quickly into Burden's and they away. 'She can't be left alone at night, you see. Not in this house, at any rate, and she always is in this house. She hasn't anywhere else to go, has she?' He made the astonishing statement with low-key carelessness, 'She's afraid of ghosts.'

Another little shiver exacerbated Burden's discomfort and he found himself nodding, murmuring, 'Yes, yes, I see.'

It was quite dark outside now. Clifford drew the brown velvet curtains, remained standing, holding the border of one of them rather too tightly and clutching it in a fist. 'I feel guilty all the time,' he said again. 'I ought to be grateful, and I am in a sort of way. I ought to love her, but I don't.' He lowered his voice, glanced at the closed door and then, bending towards Burden said in a near-whisper, 'I hate her!'

Burden just stared at him.

'My other grandmother died, the one called Clifford,' Clifford said, sitting down once more. He smiled in a slightly contemptuous way. 'My mother's mother, that was. My mother got her furniture and the money she had in the Post Office. It wasn't much, just enough to buy a secondhand car.

We got that Metro and I learned to drive. I can learn things, I'm quite good at that. Not much good at earning my living though, and I feel guilty about that too, because there's a part of me knows that I ought to be able to pay my mother back for all she did for me. I ought to – well, buy her a flat to live in where she wouldn't be afraid of the ghosts and then I could stay on alone here, couldn't I? Actually, I think I'd like that. She'd take the glass wall with her and . . .'

The door was suddenly opened and Dodo Sanders stood there in her brown clothes, flat polished lace-up shoes, the white lined face on those trim shoulders always a shock, the scarlet mouth a clown's painted gash. A fresh turban concealed her hair which under the brown-patterned scarf was perhaps done up in curlers. She looked at her son, then slowly turned her head to fix her eyes on Burden. He tried to avoid meeting those eyes but he failed.

'You're wrong if you think he killed that woman.'

Burden thought of that machine voice on his tape, wondering if it would sound more or less metallic, 'Whatever I may think, Mrs Sanders,' he said mildly, 'I'm sure I'm not wrong.'

'It's impossible,' she said. 'I should know. My instincts would know. I know all about him.'

Clifford seemed about to bury his head in his hands, but instead he sighed and said to Burden, 'Could we talk some more tomorrow?'

Burden agreed, feeling confused and helpless.

Nothing had happened to her; she was all right. The letter had been sent to 'the occupier' and perhaps had not been meant for her or indeed anyone specific – was possibly a mere wanton arbitrary missive of destruction directed at whichever tenant of the flat might have the misfortune to open it. Wexford told himself all this as he descended Battle Hill, his umbrella up against the ferocious rain of Monday morning. But he didn't believe it. Coincidence had not that long an arm.

Next week she would appear in court to be charged, he supposed, under the Criminal Damage Act of 1971, and he repeated the charge over to himself: 'That you on Thursday, 19th November, at RAF Lossington in the Country of Northamptonshire, had in your custody or under your control a pair of wire-cutters and did use them without lawful excuse to damage certain property, namely the perimeter fence belonging to the Ministry of Defence . . .' Something like that. Dora was right and Sylvia and Neil were right. She had only to make a statement in court to the effect that her action had been misguided – plead guilty, pay her fine, do no more. They would leave her alone then; they would let her live. He was tempted for a moment, seeing it briefly as such a small thing, such an easy thing to do in exchange for life and happiness, remarriage, children perhaps, a glorious career. But of course, she couldn't do it. He almost laughed out loud at the idea, walking down there through the rain, and suddenly felt a lot better.

It wasn't Ralph Robson who admitted him to the house, but Dita Jago. Wexford furled his dripping umbrella and left it in the porch.

Mrs Jago said: 'We came in to see if we could get anything for him while we're out.'

Nina Quincy was sitting in that cheerful but somehow comfortless room, having taken her daughters to school, and Robson was in an armchair on the opposite side of the fireplace. He had taken up the hunched, lopsided attitude arthritic people adopt to minimize suffering, one leg stretched out, one shoulder raised. But even so his owl's face was sharp with pain. Dita Jago's daughter provided a cruel contrast to him, not only young and beautiful but blooming with beauty and health. Her face, innocent of make-up, was rosily flushed and her dark eyes bright; dark chestnut hair fell below her shoulders in a mass of waves. She had something of the appearance of a healthy Jane Morris, but Rossetti would have resisted painting anyone as fit and flourishing as she. Both women wore garments of unmistakable Jago manufacture, the younger a tunic of dark chenille patterned all over with stylized crimson and blue butterflies. In a stiff, rather formal way her mother introduced her to Wexford.

She held out her hand, said unexpectedly, 'I must tell you how I admire your daughter. We loved her in that serial. Not much like you, is she?'

It was a little meagre voice to emanate from so much rich, colourful beauty and momentarily he marvelled that someone could look so intelligent yet in a couple of sentences reveal she was not. He acknowledged her comment with a small, dry shake of the head and turned to Robson.

'Your niece has gone back to London, has she?'

'She went last evening,' Robson said. 'I shall miss her; I don't know what I'll do without her.'

Dita Jago said with unexpected briskness, 'Life must go on. She's got her living to earn, she can't stay here for ever.'

'She got down to it and spring-cleaned the whole blessed house for me while she was here.'

Spring-cleaning in December? It was an activity, anyway, which Wexford had imagined must be obsolete. Hard, too, to picture the exquisitely dressed and coiffed Lesley Arbel brushing ceilings and washing paint. His raised eyebrows elicited more information from Ralph Robson.

'She said she might as well give the place a complete turn-out while she was here. Not that it needed it; Gwen kept it like a new pin, as far as I could see. But Lesley insisted; she said she didn't know when I'd get it done again and she was right there. She had all the cupboards out, and the wardrobes, went through Gwen's clothes and took them off to Oxfam. Gwen had a good winter coat – only bought it last year and I thought Lesley might have liked to keep that for herself, but maybe it wasn't smart enough for her.'

Wexford saw Nina Quincy's lips twitch, her eyes shift if not quite cast up as Robson went on, 'She even went up in the roof, but I said to leave that; I said you can't take the blessed Hoover up there. There was no need to lift up fitted carpets either. But when Lesley does a thing she does it thoroughly and the place is like a new pin, spotless. I shall miss her, I can tell you; I'll be lost without her.'

Nina Quincy got up. Her attitude, her look showed her as a woman easily and quickly bored, needing new sensations. She yawned and said, 'Shall we go if you've got that list?'

Wexford parted from the two women when they reached the gate. Again he marvelled at Mrs Jago's light springy tread as she made for the car under the yellow and black golfing umbrella her daughter held up over them. For no reason apparent to him at that moment, he found himself thinking of Defoe who had written his *Journal of the Plague Year* as if it were autobiography, as if he had witnessed the plague's horrors instead of being an infant at the time.

Burden was in his office, awaiting the arrival of Clifford Sanders whom Davidson had gone to fetch. Clifford had asked on the previous day if they could talk again this morning and Burden was puzzled by the request, or had been for a while after it was made. But now his hopes had rallied and his expectation of a confession was restored.

When Wexford came in he said, 'I never thought I'd see the day when the hottest suspect in a murder case started asking to help us with our enquiries.'

It was delicate ground for Wexford and he put on a look of polite interest.

'He actually wants to come here this morning. I suppose it's one way of skiving off work.'

Wexford just looked at him. 'I'll tell you an interesting thing. Lesley Arbel's been spring-cleaning Robson's house, turning out all the cupboards, been up in the roof pretending to want to vacuum-clean it, had the carpets up. What was she looking for?'

'Maybe she was just cleaning.'

'Not she. Why would she? The house was clean enough for any normal person not a fanatic already. Young girls these days aren't mad about cleaning, Mike. They don't know how to do it, or else they don't care. It would have been a different matter if she'd come down to be with Robson and found the place in a mess. Then she might have cleaned up – if she was exceptionally kind and thoughtful for her age . . . which she's not. And then there's the matter of her fingernails. Her nails were long and varnished earlier last week, but when I saw her last Friday they'd been cut short. That means she either broke a nail cleaning or thought it wiser to cut her nails before the cleaning started. And I should think she was the kind of girl who would be as proud of her long red nails as any Chinese emperor's concubine.'

'Maybe she had to cut them for the computer.'

Wexford shrugged. 'No different from a typewriter keyboard, is it? She'd been typing with long nails for years probably. No, she sacrificed her nails in order to perform the supremely generous task of cleaning her uncle's house.'

'What is it you're trying to say?'

'That she wasn't cleaning, or that the cleaning was incidental or an excuse to make to Robson. She was looking for something; she was turning the house upside down, lifting up the carpets, going up in the loft in search of something. I don't know what it was, though I've got a few ideas. I don't know if she found it, but I think the search was what brought her here and kept her here so long, not devotion to Robson. And I don't think we'll see her here again very much, either because she found what she was looking for or because she realizes she isn't going to find it. And that means it isn't in the house or that it was very cleverly hidden indeed.'

Instead of asking the obvious question, Burden said, 'We haven't searched the place ourselves. Should we?'

Wexford was hesitating when the phone rang and Burden picked up the receiver. Apparently Clifford had arrived.

'I'll have to go. What was she looking for, anyway?'

'The documentary evidence on which Gwen Robson based her blackmailing activities, of course.'

'Oh, there wasn't any of that,' Burden said breezily. 'It was all hearsay, all just what she'd heard or suspected.' He didn't wait for Wexford's reply, but went off down to the interview room on the ground floor, the one done up in shades of ancient spaniel. Rain was streaming down the window, making the glass opaque. Clifford sat at the table with a styrofoam beaker of coffee in front of him, Diana Pettit on the opposite side reading the legal page of the *Independent*. She got up and Burden gave her the sideways nod that meant to leave them with the tape recorder running. Clifford half rose and put out his hand; Burden was so surprised that he had shaken it almost before he knew what he was doing.

'Can we start?' Clifford asked eagerly.

It was difficult for Burden to handle this. For the first time in his career as a policeman he had the feeling that he had been insufficiently trained or that a branch of his training had been neglected. 'What is it you want to tell me?' he asked in a voice he knew sounded tentative and unsure.

'I'm telling you about the sort of person I am. I'm talking about my feelings.' Clifford's eyes moved and to Burden's astonishment a mischievous gleam appeared in them; it was so

559

incongruous as to be shocking. He laughed gleefully. 'I'm trying to tell you what made me do it.'

'Do it?' Burden learned forward across the table.

'Do what I do,' Clifford said blandly. 'Lead the life I do.' He laughed again. 'That was a joke. It was meant to make you think I was going to say "murder Mrs Robson". Sorry, it wasn't very funny.' Drawing a long breath he made a throat-clearing sound. 'I am a prisoner. Did you know that?'

Burden said nothing. What was there to say?

'I am my own jailer, Dodo has seen to that. Why does she want that, you ask? Some are born to be jailers. It's for power. I am the first person she has really had in her power, you see – the only one. The others resisted, they got away. Shall I tell you how she met my father? My father was quite an upper class sort of person, you know; he had an uncle who was the High Sheriff of the county. I don't know what that really means, but it's very important. My grandfather was a gentleman farmer, he owned three hundred acres of land. It was all sold when my father was young so that they could keep on living in the style they were accustomed to. A lot of Kingsmarkham is actually built on my grandfather's land.'

Looking at him with mounting exasperation, Burden felt resentful at the stupid trick which Clifford had tried to play on him, pretending he was about to make a confession. And Clifford said, annoying him still further, 'Your own house, wherever that is, is probably on a bit of land that was my family's.'

Clifford drank his coffee, clasping the small beaker in both hands and affording Burden a close-up of his cruelly bitten nails. 'Dodo came to work for my father's parents as a cleaner. That surprises you, doesn't it? Not a maid – oh, no – but a daily cleaner they had to do the rough work. They had had maids, and a chauffeur, but that was before the war. After the war they had to make do with my mother. I don't know how she got my father to marry her. She says "love" but she would. I wasn't born till they'd been married two years, so it wasn't that. Once she was married, she wanted to own the place, to be the boss and the jailer.'

'How can you know that?' Burden found himself saying uncomfortably, for he was beginning to understand what

Olson had meant with his fallacy of recognising and not recognising.

Clifford seemed to underline this when he went on, 'I know my mother. My grandfather died; he was very old and he'd been ill for a long time. As soon as the funeral was over, my father left us – the very next day it was, I can remember all that. I was five, you see. I can remember going to the funeral with my mother and my father and my grandmother. I had to go; there wasn't anyone to leave me with, it was before I started school. My mother wore a bright red hat with a little veil and a bright red coat. It was new and she'd never had it on before and when I saw her in it I thought that was what women wore to funerals – bright red. I thought it must be the correct thing because I'd never seen her in that colour before. When my grandmother came down, she was in black and I said to her. "Why aren't you in red, Grandma?" and Dodo laughed.

'Now I'm grown-up, I've sometimes thought it was wrong of my father to abandon his mother. I mean, it was wrong of him to go anyway, but doubly wrong really to leave his mother with Dodo. Of course I didn't think about that when I was a child. I never thought much about my grandmother and what her feelings were. My mother put her into an old people's home; it wasn't long after my father left, only a few days. She didn't say goodbye either, just went out and never came back. I asked my mother how she managed it – I mean, I asked years later when I was in my teens. Somebody had said how hard it was to get old people into those council homes. My mother told me about it, she was proud of it. She had a hired car come round – it was when minicabs first started – and told my grandmother they were going for a drive. When they got to this house, she took her in and just said to the matron or whoever it was that she was leaving her there and they'd have to look after her. Dodo doesn't mind what she says to people, you see; that's one of the things that gives her power. People say to her, "I've never been spoken to like that in my life" or "How dare you?" but it doesn't bother her; she just looks at them and says something else awful. She's got through the inhibition barrier, you see, the inhibition on being rude.

'My grandmother lived another ten years, all the time in that home and then in a geriatric ward. The social services tried to get my mother to take her back but they couldn't force her to, could they? She just refused to let them in the house. But before that, as soon as the minicab brought her back in fact, she moved all the furniture upstairs. Mr Carroll, the farmer – he and his wife were the only people I remember we ever saw. They weren't friends but they were people we knew, the only people. My mother got him to help her take all the furniture up into the attics and then when—'

'What's all this leading up to, Clifford?' Burden put in.

Clifford ignored him, or appeared to ignore him. Perhaps he responded only to what he wanted to hear. His eyes were on the window. The rain had slackened and the streaming water separated into trickling droplets between which a green-grey blur could be seen and a lowering overcast. But perhaps he saw nothing and the sense of sight was shut. Burden felt uncomfortable and his discomfort increased with every sentence Clifford spoke. All the time he was expecting some sort of climax or explosion, expecting Clifford to jump up and begin screaming. But for the present the man on the other side of the table seemed locked in an unnatural calm.

He went on in a lighter, more conversational tone, 'When I was disobedient or offended her in some way, she'd lock me up in one of those attics. Sometimes it would be the one with all the photos in and sometimes with the beds and mattresses. But I got to know I'd always be let out before it got dark. She wouldn't go up there in the dark because she's afraid of ghosts. I think the supernatural is the only thing my mother *is* afraid of. There are bits of our garden she won't go near after dark – well, in the daytime, too, come to that. I used to sit in the attic looking at all those faces.'

'Faces?' repeated Burden in a hollow tone.

'In the photos,' Clifford said patiently. He was silent for a moment and the inspiration came to Burden to do as Serge Olson did, to take off his watch and lay it on the table in front of him. Clifford's eyes flickered as he observed the movement. 'I used to study the faces of my ancestors and think to myself, all those ladies in long skirts and big hats and all those men with dogs and guns, all of them had just ended up in me, that's all they'd come to in the end – me. I'd watch the light fade till I couldn't see the faces clearly any more and when it happened

I knew she'd come. When she came it would be quite slowly, taking her time, and then the door would slide open and in a nice quiet pleasant sort of way, just as if nothing had happened, she'd tell me to come down and that my tea was ready.'

Burden said wearily, picking up the watch, 'Time's up, Clifford.'

He rose obediently. 'Shall I come back this afternoon?'

'You'll hear from us.' Burden almost said, 'Don't call us, we'll call you,' and then, standing alone in the room after Clifford had been taken away, asked himself with near-disbelief what he thought he was doing. Didn't he expect an admission of guilt? Wasn't that what it was all about? He went up to his office and began looking through the reports which were the result of seemingly fruitless efforts on the part of Archbold and Marian Bayliss to find evidence of unsolved murder in Clifford's past. Both grandmothers had died natural deaths, or so it seemed. Old Mrs Sanders had died after a heart attack in the council home where her daughter-in-law had dumped her; old Mrs Clifford had been found by a neighbour dead in her bed at home. Elizabeth McPhail had died in hospital after months of incapacity caused by a stroke.

Still, he must keep on questioning him – that afternoon if necessary, and next day and the day after, every day until Clifford reached the present and finally told him in that monotonous voice that he had killed Gwen Robson.

Wexford was in the Midland Bank in Queen Street. It was four-thirty and the bank had been closed to customers for the past hour. The manager had been cooperative and answered all his questions without protest. Yes, Mr Robson had an account at the branch but no, Mrs Robson – who hadn't banked there anyway – had nothing on safe deposit. Wexford hadn't really expected it. Whatever Lesley Arbel had been searching for was hidden elsewhere – or Lesley had already found it. The manager was plainly unwilling to tell him anything about Mrs Sanders' account, also at the branch, presumably because she wasn't dead.

He came out into grey drizzle, into early dusk. The greengrocer's display looked glistening wet even though the awning was up, a sheen like dew on green leaves and citrus rind. Behind the bow window of the boutique skimpy clothes in fruit-salad colours shimmered. Into the tawny-lit warmth of the wine market Serge Olson was disappearing, passing in the doorway a man who was also known to Wexford: John Whitton, Ralph Robson's neighbour. His baby nestled fast asleep against his chest in a carrying sling; the older child, muffled to the eyes in knitted wraps and quilted nylon, grasped with a gloved hand the hem of his Barber jacket, for Whitton's arms were fully occupied with his two carrier bags of wine. He looked at Wexford without recognizing him and made for the Peugeot estate car parked at the kerb. The meter had no more than a couple of minutes to run and a traffic warden was already bearing down.

Whitton put the baby into a cot on the back seat, the wine on to the floor, and had no sooner straightened up than the crying began. The three-year-old clambered in, viewing its brother or sister with that dispassionate mild interest children often show towards a younger sibling in distress. Wexford watched because he was wondering how poor Whitton was going to extricate the car without touching the one in front or the one behind, though 'touching' was hardly the word for what had recently been done to the Peugeot; its offside headlamp had been smashed and the metal surround buckled. Nevertheless he would have turned away, knowing the dreadful irritation of being watched while one is manoeuvring a car, had Whitton – now in the driving-seat – not called out to him.

'I say, would you mind awfully telling me how near I am?'

Those people who stand in front of drivers, beckoning and holding up a warning hand – Wexford had often been exasperated by them, had long ago resolved never to join their number. It was different, though, when one was invited. The car crawled forward and he signalled to Whitton to stop when within an inch of the rear mudguard of the Mercedes in front.

'You ought to make it on the next lock,' he said as Whitton reversed.

And then Whitton did recognize him, speaking above the baby's frenetic yells: 'You came to talk to me about Mrs Robson.' The engine stalled and he swore, made an effort, smiled. 'I shouldn't lose my cool like that. That's what

564

happens when you do.' A thumb cocked towards the left side of the car's bonnet indicated what he meant. 'My wife had a bit of a contretemps with a parking meter here three weeks ago.'

Wexford knew Whitton was telling him this because he was a policeman, because like so many of the public he thought all policemen, whatever branch of the force they belonged to and whatever their rank, were equally preoccupied by traffic offences. In a moment he would be defending his wife lest Wexford whipped out a notebook . . .

'Mind you, she didn't so much as scratch another vehicle, which was a miracle considering the way this young fellow in a Metro got at her.'

A polite, 'Really?' and a short preamble to saying goodbye were on the tip of Wexford's tongue. Instead he said rather quickly, though knowing it was a long shot, 'When exactly was this, Mr Whitton?'

Whitton liked talking. Without being exactly garrulous, he liked a chance to talk and naturally he would, having taken over the role long assigned exclusively to women where he was locked into a daily relationship with children too young for conversation. First, however, he reached into the back of the car and picked up the baby off the back seat, its cries at once fading to whimpers. Amused, Wexford saw that he was settling down for a long, companionable talk . . . and then he wasn't amused any more, but excited.

'Three weeks ago, as I said. Well, as a matter of fact, it must have been the day Mrs Robson was killed. Yes, it was. Rosemary had the car that day and she was picking up our fruit and veg on the way home. A quarter-to-six maybe, ten-to. . . ?'

15

It was Burden's idea to have him up in his office rather than in either of the interview rooms. He couldn't stand any more of those vinyl tiles and the blank walls and the metal rim round the table. It wasn't any less warm down there than up here, but there was a sense of chill, a feeling that draughts crept in between plaster and window frame and under the unpanelled door with its corroded metal handle. So Clifford was brought upstairs and he came in as if paying a social call – smiling, hand outstretched. Burden wouldn't have been surprised if he had asked him how he was, but Clifford didn't do that.

The blinds were down and the lights were on. They were soft lights though, coming from an angled lamp on the desk and two spots on the ceiling. Burden sat down behind the desk and Clifford in front of it, in a chair with padded seat and wooden arms which Diana Pettit pulled out for him. She was still in the room, sitting near the door, but he seemed unaware of her presence. He was wearing a different grey shirt, this one with a button-down collar, and his pullover was a darker grey with a cable pattern but errors had been made in the knitting of the cables. Burden found himself compulsively staring at one of these flaws up near the left shoulder, where the knitter in twisting the cable had passed the rib over instead of under the work.

'I'd like you to tell me about your relations with your other grandmother,' Burden began. 'Mrs Clifford, I mean, your mother's mother. Did you see much of her?'

Instead of answering, Clifford said, 'My mother's not all bad. I've given you a bad impression of her. She's really like everyone else, a mixture of bad and good, only her Shadow's very powerful. Can I tell you a story? It's a romantic story really; my grandmother Clifford told it me.'

'Go on,' encouraged Burden.

'When my mother was a little girl they lived in Forbydean, her and her mother and father. She used to go to school past Ash Farm on her bicycle and she got to know my father who was a bit younger. Well, they played together; they got to play together whenever they could, which was mostly in the holidays because my father was away at his prep school. When she was thirteen and my father was twelve, his parents found out about the friendship and put a stop to it. You see, they thought their son was a lot too good for my mother even to play with: they said a farm labourer's daughter wasn't good enough for their son. And my father didn't put up any sort of resistance; he agreed with them, he hadn't understood before, and when my mother came round next time he wouldn't speak to her, wouldn't even look at her. And then my grandmother came out and told my mother she must go home and not come any more.'

Burden nodded abstractly, wondering how long all this was going to take. It wasn't an unusual story for this part of the world at that period. Similar things had happened to his own contemporaries, forbidden for reasons of social snobbery to 'play in the street'.

Clifford went on, 'I'm really telling you this to show you the good side of my mother. I said it was romantic. Later on, you see, she went to work for them and they didn't recognize the little girl they'd prevented from playing with their Charles. And *he* didn't until she told him after he'd married her. I wonder what they all thought then?'

Burden was not sufficiently interested to hazard guesses. 'Did your grandmother Clifford come to see you when you were a child? Did you visit her with your mother?'

Clifford sighed. Perhaps he would have preferred to continue his speculations about the romantic story. 'I sometimes think I spent my childhood walking. I walked through my childhood, if you know what I mean. It was the only way to get anywhere. I must have walked hundreds of miles, thousands. My mother doesn't walk that fast but I was always breathless, trying to keep up with her.'

567

'You walked to your grandmother's, then?'

Clifford sighed again. 'When we went, we walked. There was the bus, but my mother wouldn't pay bus fares. We didn't go to my grandmother's very much. You have to understand that my mother doesn't like people and she didn't particularly like her mother. You see, my grandfather died very suddenly, then when my father walked out and my grandmother Sanders went into a home we were left alone with the house to ourselves. I think she liked that.' He hesitated, looked down at his bitten nails, said half-slyly, 'And she likes me, so long as I'm obedient. She moulded me into a slave and a protector. She made me like Frankenstein made the monster, to go wrong.' A small shrill laugh, which might have moderated those words, somehow made them the more terrible.

Burden looked at him with a kind of uneasy impatience. He was framing a question about Mrs Sanders' mother, a wild idea coming to him of Gwen Robson possibly having once been to her as a home help, when Clifford went on: 'Once when I wouldn't do what she wanted, she locked me in the attic with the photographs and she lost the key to the room. I don't know how she lost it – she never told me, she wouldn't – but I expect she dropped it down the plughole or it fell down a crack in the floor or something. She's accident-prone, you see, because she doesn't think about what she's doing; her mind's always on something else. So I expect that's how she lost the key. She's very strong even though she's small and she tried to break down the door by putting her shoulder to it, but she couldn't. I was inside, listening to her crashing at the door. It was winter and starting to get dark and she was frightened; I know she was frightened, I could feel her fear through the door. Maybe the ghosts were creeping up the stairs after her.'

He smiled, then laughed on a high shrill note, wrinkling up his nose as if in a mixture of pleasure and pain at the memory. 'She had to go and get help. I was scared when I heard her go away, because I thought I was going to be left there for ever. It was cold and I was only a little kid, in there in the half-dark with that old furniture and all those faces. She took the bulbs out of the sockets, you see, so that I couldn't put the light on. But that meant *she* couldn't put the light on either . . .' Another smile and rueful shake of the head. 'She went to get

568

Mr Carroll and he came back with her and put his shoulder to the door and burst it open. I never got put in there again, because the door wouldn't lock after that. Mrs Carroll came with him and I remember what she said; she turned on my mother and said she'd a good mind to tell the prevention of cruelty to children people, but if she did they never did anything.

'Mrs Carroll went away six months ago. She ran away from her husband – with another man, my mother said. It was Dodo who had to tell Mr Carroll. She sort of hinted to him that there was this other man and then she told him straight out. I thought he was going to attack her but people don't attack her, or they never have yet. He broke down and sobbed and cried. Do you know what I thought? What I hoped? I thought, my father left my mother and now Mrs Carroll's left her husband. Suppose Mr Carroll was to marry Dodo? That would be the best escape, wouldn't it, the cleanest way to get free? I wonder if I'd be jealous, though, I wonder if I'd mind. . . ?'

He was interrupted by a tap at the door, followed by the appearance of Archbold to tell Burden that Wexford would like to see him.

'Now, do you mean?'

'He said it was urgent.'

Burden left Clifford with Diana. Perhaps it was no bad thing to take a break here. He wasn't interested in Clifford's boyhood, but he valued the mood these reminiscences seemed to bring him to, a mood of open revelation and frankness. All these stories of his youth (which was precisely how Burden saw them) would lead Clifford, though by a crazy path, to the final incriminating outburst.

Instead of taking the lift, he walked upstairs. The door to Wexford's office stood a little ajar. Wexford was nearly always to be found either behind his desk or standing at the window thinking, while apparently contemplating the High Street. But this morning he stood abstractedly looking at the plan of greater Kingsmarkham which hung on the left-hand wall. He turned his eyes as Burden came in.

'Oh, Mike . . .'

'You wanted to see me?'

'Yes. I apologise for the interruption, but perhaps you'll see it wasn't exactly an interruption, more a breaking-off. Clifford Sanders – he didn't do it, he couldn't have done. You may as well let him go.'

Hard-faced, immediate anger starting, Burden said, 'We've been through all this before.'

'No, Mike, listen. He was seen sitting in his mother's car in Queen Street at five-forty-five on November 19th. A woman called Rosemary Whitton saw him; she spoke to him and he spoke to her.'

'She was trying to move her car,' Wexford said, 'and she hadn't much room, only a few inches each end to play with—'

With the sexism of the stand-up comic, but straightfaced and deadly serious, Burden interrupted him: 'Women drivers!'

'Oh, Mike, come on! Clifford was sitting in the car behind her and he had a couple of yards behind him. She asked him if he'd move and he told her to go away. "Leave me alone, go away," was what he said.'

'How does she know it was Clifford?'

'She gave me a good description. It was a red Metro. She's no fool, Mike; she's something rather high-powered, a systems analyst, though I confess I'm not sure what that is.'

'And she says it was at a quarter to six?'

'She was late, she was in a hurry. Women like her are always in a hurry – inevitably. She says she wanted to get home before the kids were put to bed at six. When she first got back to the car she looked at the clock – I always do that myself, I know what she means – and it was exactly five-forty-five. Which means it was a good few minutes after that by the time she'd had her slanging match with Clifford and crunched the headlight on a meter.'

'Is that what she did?' asked Burden ruminatively, his frown threatening a further attack on women at the wheel. 'Why didn't he tell me that?'

'Didn't notice, I daresay. She says he moved as soon as it was too late to matter.'

The woman's statement would now have to be checked, thoroughly investigated, and until that had been done Burden's interrogation of Clifford must be suspended. He didn't go back to the interview room. The anger and frustration which might more naturally have been vented on Wexford he wanted to splash furiously over the man downstairs. He could have put through a phone call to his own office but couldn't face explaining to Clifford, so he sent Archbold back with the message to let him go, to tell him he wouldn't be needed again.

'Where would you hide something, Mike, if you were Gwen Robson?'

Smarting from his defeat, not yet fully grasping what the result of exonerating Clifford would be, Burden said sullenly, 'What sort of something?'

'Papers. A few sheets of paper.'

'Letters, do you mean?'

'I don't know,' Wexford said. 'Lesley Arbel was looking for papers, but I don't think she found them. They're not in the bank and they're not with Kingsmarkham Safe Depository Limited – I've just tried there.'

'How do you know Lesley Arbel didn't find them?'

'When I spoke to her on Friday she was worried and unhappy. If she'd found what she turned the house out for, she'd have been over the moon.'

'I'm wondering if Clifford could have killed his other grandmother, his mother's mother. He's a very strange character altogether. He has all the salient features of the psychopath . . . What are you laughing at?'

'Leave it, Mike,' Wexford said. 'Just leave it. And leave the psychiatry to Serge Olson.'

Burden was to remember that last remark when Olson phoned him on the following morning. He had thought of very little apart from Clifford Sanders during the intervening time and everything he had done had been concerned with this new alibi. He had even interviewed Rosemary Whitton himself and, unable to shake her conviction of the relevant time, had questioned the Queen Street greengrocer. If no one in Queen Street remembered Clifford in the Metro, a good many shopkeepers recalled Mrs Whitton hitting the meter post. The manager of the wine market remembered the time: it was before he closed at six, but not much before. He had turned the door sign to 'Closed' immediately he returned from inspecting the damage. Unconvinced but obliged at any rate temporarily to yield, Burden turned his attention from Clifford Sanders to Clifford Sanders' father . . . As a temporary measure at any rate. He wouldn't speak to Clifford Sanders again for a week, and in the meantime he would root out Charles Sanders and begin a new line of enquiry there. But before he could begin, Serge Olson phoned him.

'Mike, I think you should know that I've just had a call from Clifford cancelling his Thursday appointment and, incidentally, all further appointments with me. I asked him why and he said he had no further need of my particular kind of treatment. So there you are.'

Burden said rather cautiously, 'Why are you telling me, Mr Olson – Serge?'

'Well, you're subjecting him to some fairly heavy interrogation, aren't you? Look, this is delicate ground – for me, at any rate. He's my client. I am anxious not to, let's say, betray his confidences. But it's a serious matter when someone like Clifford abandons his therapy. Mike, Clifford needs his therapy. I'm not saying he necessarily needs what I can give him, but he needs help from someone.'

'Maybe,' said Burden, 'he's found another psychiatrist. You needn't worry about the possible effects of what you call heavy interrogation anyway. That's over, at any rate for the time being.'

'I'm glad to hear it, Mike, I'm very glad.'

Putting it into words, that he had given up questioning Clifford, put things into perspective. Burden suddenly realised how much he hated being closeted with Clifford and hearing all those revelations. He would have no more of it – not until, that is, he had another positive lead. His mind made up, he looked out of the window to where they were putting lights in the branches of the tree that grew on the edge of the police station forecourt. It wasn't a Christmas tree or even a conifer, come to that, but an ash whose only distinction was in its size. Burden watched the two men at work. Putting coloured lights in the tree was his idea, later backed up by the Chief Constable, in the interest of promoting jollier relations with the public. Wexford's comment had been a derisive laugh. But surely you couldn't go on feeling antagonistic towards or afraid of or suspicious about a friendly body that hung fairylights in a tree in its front garden? This morning he felt neither jolly nor friendly, in the mood rather to snap at anyone who made jokes about the tree. Diana Pettit had already had the rough side of his tongue for suggesting that all the little lamps should be blue. When the phone rang again he picked up the receiver and said, 'Yes?' testily.

It was Clifford Sanders. 'Can I come and see you?'

'What about?' asked Burden.

'To talk.' No time was mentioned and Burden knew what Clifford was like about time. 'You made me finish early yesterday and I'd a lot more to say. I just wondered when we could start again.'

In my own good time, my lad, Burden thought. Next week maybe, next month. But what he said was, 'No, that's it. That's all. You can get back to work, get on with your life – OK?' He didn't wait for an answer, but put the phone down.

It rang again ten minutes later. By the time the younger and more intrepid of the two men had climbed to the top of the ladder and threaded the lead with bulbs on it through some of the highest branches. Burden thought how disastrous it would be, and what the media would make of it, if the man fell and got hurt. He spoke a milder 'Yes?' into the phone and got Clifford's voice suggesting in an eager, urgent tone that previously they had been cut off. Burden said that as far as he knew they hadn't been cut off. All that needed to be said had been said, hadn't it?

'I'd like to come and see you this afternoon if that's all right.'

'It's not all right,' Burden said, aware that he was back into an earlier mode of addressing Clifford – talking as if he were a child, but unable to do otherwise. 'I'm busy this afternoon.'

'I can come tomorrow morning then.'

'Clifford, I'm going to ring off now. OK, is that understood? We're not being cut off, I've finished, I can't discuss this any more. Goodbye.'

For some reason this second call disturbed Burden. It gave him a curious feeling very much like that experienced by those who, having had little to do with the handicapped, are brought into unexpected contact with someone who lolls and drools and paws at them with spastic hands. Their recoil and gasp are

573

unforgivable, are outrageous, and Burden felt a little ashamed of himself as he put the phone down sharply, as he stepped back, looking at the phone as if Clifford or something of Clifford actually lived inside the brown plastic instrument. What a fool! What was the matter with him? He lifted the receiver once more and gave instructions to the switchboard to put no more calls from Clifford Sanders through to him; furthermore, to monitor all calls that came.

It would be useless to search the house. Lesley Arbel had had two weeks in which to do that and she might be less experienced at searching than Wexford's officers were, but she had had more time and presumably a personal interest in what she was seeking – whatever that was. A will? Gwen Robson had had nothing to leave. Something that would incriminate a guilty, frightened person? Wexford couldn't imagine her blackmailing her own, surely loved, niece. And yet Lesley had been desperate to find those papers, if it was papers.

'I'll lose my job!' she had cried out to him.

It seemed quite inconsequential. At one moment he had been asking her why she had not told him she was in Kingsmarkham that Thursday; the next, she was bewailing her threatened job. He walked up the path to Mrs Jago's house and rang the bell. She came quickly to the door – large, smiling, light-footed. The smile looked a little forced but not, he thought, because he as a policeman was unwelcome.

'All alone today?' he asked.

'Nina doesn't work on Tuesday or go shopping. I saw her yesterday.' They were in the living room now, in the jungle of knitted flowers and trees, but the manuscript was no longer on the table. Dita Jago followed the direction of his eyes. 'I didn't want to see her today. I'd had enough, I didn't feel I could take any more.'

The miseries of a deserted wife, did she mean? The plaints of a young woman abandoned to bring up two children on her own? He didn't enquire. He asked her where she thought Gwen Robson would have hidden whatever it was she had to hide, but as he did so he remembered how she had disclaimed all but a bare acquaintance with the dead woman. She picked up the circular needle from which the great tropical landscape

574

hung and he saw that she had reached the sky, a blue expanse with tiny clouds. But instead of resuming her work, she sat clasping the two reinforced points of the needle in her hands. She looked at him and away.

'I knew her so little. How can I say?'

'I don't know,' he said. 'The house is the same as this one. I was thinking there might be some peculiarity, some feature of the house well known to residents but absolutely unknown to outsiders?'

'A secret panel?'

'Not exactly that.'

'Perhaps the murderer took this mysterious thing away, whatever it was. Would you like a drink?'

He shook his head rather too quickly and her eyebrows rose.

'What's become of the book?' he asked for something to say. 'You've finished it and sent it to a publisher?'

'I haven't finished it and I never will. I nearly burned it last night and then I thought – who needs emotional gestures, dramas? Just put it away in a drawer – so I did. I had such a day yesterday, it upset me so. It's a funny thing, but I'd like to tell you about it. May I? There doesn't seem to be anyone else I could tell.'

'It makes a change,' he said, 'someone wanting to tell me things.'

'I like you,' she said, and it wasn't naïve or disingenuous; it sounded simply sincere. 'I like you, but I don't really know you and you don't know me, and I doubt if we shall ever know each other much better.' A glance levelled at him seemed to ask for confirmation and he nodded. 'Maybe that's an ideal set-up for confiding.' She was silent, but her hands were still and they no longer held the needle.

'My daughter told me that she had an affair with a man – no, not an affair, not so much as that, a one-night stand, I think it's called – and she was silly enough to tell her husband about it. Not at once; she waited a long while. She should have forgotten it, put it behind her. He confessed something of his own to her, some peccadillo, and she came out with this thing of hers and instead of being as forgiving as she was, he said that changed everything – it changed all his feelings about her.'

'Like *Tess of the d'Urbervilles*,' Wexford murmured, 'and

we think times have changed. She didn't say anything of all this to you till yesterday?'

'That's right. I'd asked her if there was any hope of a reconciliation. Well, I went so far as to ask her what was the basic trouble between them. You're a parent, so you know what I mean by "went so far". They don't like questioning even when it . . . well, springs from one's real concern.'

'No,' said Wexford, 'they don't.' He considered. 'May I. . . ?' he was unusually tentative. 'Would it be possible for me . . . to read your manuscript?'

She had picked up her knitting, but now she let it fall into her lap once more. 'Why on earth. . . ?' A sudden eagerness in her voice nearly told him he was on the wrong tack, pursuing the wrong course altogether. 'You don't know any publishers, do you?'

He did, of course. Burden's brother-in-law Amyas Ireland had become a friend over the years, but he wasn't going to encourage false hopes there. Nor to tell the whole truth at this stage. 'I'm simply curious to read it.' He observed how her attitude towards the manuscript had changed since she had taken heart from confiding in him. 'Will you let me?'

Thus it was that he found himself making his way up a hill which seemed steeper than it had the evening before, carrying what felt like ten pounds' weight of paper in one of Tesco's red plastic bags. He had planned on finishing the A.N. Wilson that evening and longed to know how it ended – but this, this was important.

It was too early yet to switch on the Christmas lights in the tree, Burden thought, only December 8. However, no one showed any signs of wanting to switch them on and to passers-by they must be invisible. The evening was dark and misty. How long was it since they had seen the sun by day or, come to that, the moon by night?

There were the usual cars on the forecourt where the lamps made everything look like an out-of-focus sepia photograph. Someone had just driven up in a Metro which could have been of any colour. It meant nothing to Burden and he took his raincoat off the hook and went down in the lift. Home early for once! His little boy would still be up, bathed and powdered, running around in pyjamas; the radio on because Jenny preferred it to television; a smell of something exotic but not too exotic, one of the few examples of foreign cuisine he liked – pesto sauce, for instance, or five spices in a stir-fry being prepared for his dinner; Jenny harassed but happy in a blue tracksuit. Burden took a yearning, sensuous delight in these things. The clutter, the pretty paraphernalia of domestic life which are the aspects of marriage many married men dislike gave him intense pleasure. He never got enough of them.

He crossed the black and white checkerboard floor of the foyer and someone got up from a chair and came over to him. It was Clifford Sanders.

Clifford said, 'I've been trying to get hold of you all the afternoon. They kept saying you were busy.'

Burden's initial reaction was to turn on Sergeant Camb who stood behind the reception counter, but as he took a step towards him he remembered he had said nothing to the sergeant, or indeed to anyone, about not admitting Clifford to the police station. It hadn't occurred to him that Clifford would actually come here. Had he the right, come to that, to exclude him? He didn't know. He didn't know if he could legally keep innocent, law-abiding members of the public out. Anger against Clifford must be kept under control.

He said stiffly, 'I was busy. I'm busy now. You must excuse me, I'm in a hurry.'

The otherwise blank, childlike, pasty face seemed to have only one expression – puzzlement. A deep bewilderment left the eyes unclouded, puckered the skin of Clifford's forehead into a concentrated frown. 'But I've got a lot more to say. I've only just started; I have to talk to you.'

Not for the first time, Burden thought that if he had seen this man in the street and not known who he was, he would have thought him retarded. These were deep waters, muddied and with strange things in their depths – but was it possible to be retarded not in body or the brain but somewhere else? In the soul, the psyche? A horribly uncomfortable feeling took hold of Burden and he seemed to shrink away from the touch of his own clothes on his skin. He could no longer look into those infant's eyes, watch the working of thick, uncontrolled lips.

'I've told you, we've nothing more to say to one another.'

577

God, he sounded like someone ending a love affair! 'You've helped us with our enquiries, thank you very much. I assure you we shan't want you again.'

With that he escaped. He would have liked to run, but dignity forbade it, that and self-respect. He was aware as he walked with deliberately measured tread towards the swing doors that Camb was watching him curiously, that Marian Bayliss who had just come in had paused to stare and that Clifford still stood in the centre of the floor, his lips moving silently and his hands held up in front of him.

Burden opened the door and, once outside, ran to his car. The red Metro he had seen come in but whose colour the yellow lamps had altered was parked beside it. Impossible to draw any conclusion but that Clifford had done this purposely.

And as Burden switched on the ignition, he saw Clifford come out. He ran up, calling, 'Mike, Mike. . . !'

Burden didn't have to back. He drove straight out through the gates.

16

'He's made a transference,' Serge Olson said. 'It's a very clearly defined example of transference.'

'I don't know what that means,' Burden said. They were in Wexford's office, the three of them. The psychotherapist's face amid surrounding and intervening bushes of hair was like that of an extremely intelligent vole peering out from a frondy sanctuary. And the bright beady eyes had their fierce animal look. Burden had expected to go to him, but Olson had said he would come to the police station as he had no clients on a Thursday morning. Throughout the previous day Clifford Sanders had pursued his course of trying to speak to Burden. None of his phone calls had been put through but Burden was told, to his considerable dismay, that fifteen had been made. And Clifford had returned to the police station in time to repeat his intercepting tactic as Burden left for home.

But it was his presence on the forecourt this morning – the red Metro parked just inside the gates and Clifford patiently seated at the wheel – which had really rattled Burden. He had had enough. No sooner was he inside than he was on the phone to Olson, and Olson had been there within fifteen minutes.

'I'll try to explain, Mike,' he said. 'Transference is the term employed by psychoanalysts to describe an emotional attitude the subject develops towards his or her analyst. It can be positive or negative, it can be love or hate. I've often experienced it with clients – though not really with Clifford.' Burden's puzzled face seemed to give him pause and he looked at Wexford. 'I think you know what I mean, don't you, Reg?'

Wexford nodded. 'It's not a difficult concept. It seems natural when you think about it.'

'You mean he's got to like me? He's kind of come to depend on me?'

'Absolutely, Mike.'

Burden said almost wildly, 'But what did I do? What in God's name did I do to set something like this up? I only put him through a routine interrogation; I only questioned him the way I must have questioned thousands of suspects. No one ever did this before, they were only too glad to get shut of me and this place.'

Wexford was at the window. The red Metro was still down there, its bonnet a few inches from the trunk of the tree decorated with the lights. Clifford sat in the driving-seat, not reading, not looking out of the window, just sitting with bent head.

'People are different,' Olson was saying. 'People are individuals, Mike. You can't say that because no one ever made the transference before, no one ever would. Were you particularly gentle with him? Paternal? I don't mean paternalistic. Sensitive in your approach?' The expression in those gleaming dark eyes rather indicated Olson's doubts of such a possibility.

'I don't think so. I don't know. I just listened, I let him talk; I thought I'd be more likely to get somewhere that way.'

'Ah.' Olson gave a reflective smile. 'Listening, letting the client talk – you did what the Freudians do. Maybe he prefers a Freudian therapist.'

Suddenly it began to rain. In straight glistening rods the rain bore down on the tarmac, the roofs of the parked cars, the roof of the metro, hard enough to create immediate puddles. Wexford turned from the streaming glass with a quick, repudiating shake of the head.

'What's to be done then?' he asked.

'It's a good rule, Reg, not to yield to the subject's wishes. Part of his problem, you see, is the way in which he wants to fashion his world. But the world he makes isn't conducive to his happiness, to his adjustment. It doesn't tally with reality; it just looks easier to him. Do you understand that, Mike? If you see Clifford now, you'll be allowing him to make his world in

580

the shape he wants and people it with the people he wants. For instance, because he's lost his own father he wants to put you in his world as his father. I'd say sure, do that, if it would be best for him, but I don't think it would be. It would deepen the transference and create even greater divergencies from reality.'

'Are you suggesting I simply have someone go out there and send him home?' asked Wexford. 'I don't know why but it seems . . . irresponsible.'

Olson got up. Taking no risks with the weather, he had arrived wrapped in yellow oilskins and these he fastened and zipped round himself once more, his sharp nose sticking out from under the canary-coloured hood.

'He's a very badly disturbed human being, Reg,' he said. 'You're right there. But you and Mike, you have to understand I'm a professional. You, Mike, were kind enough to call me "doctor" when we first met and though I'm not that, I have to have professional ethics. I can't go up to Clifford and tell him to come back to me. I can't go and tell him he's got his usual appointment at five today and mind not to be late. All I can do is go and get in that car beside him, sit there as his friend and try to persuade him to confront what he sees as his relationship with you and maybe get it into a more . . . reasonable perspective.'

They both watched from the window. The increasing torrent of rain made it difficult to see. Olson's figure looked like a bright yellow bird hopping and flapping its way to a dry nest. The Metro's door shut on him and once more the rain enclosed the car in walls of water like reeded glass.

'I suppose it's sound,' Wexford said, 'that stuff about not letting him create his own world, about not giving away to him. I must confess to feeling a bit apprehensive.'

'Of what?' Burden asked almost rudely.

A car driven recklessly, a fatal accident that was only partly accident, a handful of pills washed down with brandy, a rope slung over the beam of an outhouse . . . Wexford put none of this into words. He saw the Metro begin to back, sliding slowly through sheets of water and sending up jets of spray. It turned and headed for the gates. Olson still inside.

'That's fixed him for a bit,' and Burden. 'Thank God for it! Now perhaps we can get on with some work.'

581

He shut the door rather too hard behind him. Wexford turned his back on the window and the rain and thought about the dreams he kept having of wheels spinning in space, of circles with squares inside them. Had they anything to do with the fact that the evening before and the evening before that he had been reading the manuscript of Dita Jago's concentration camp experiences? It was with him in the office today, Donaldson having come for him that morning in the car.

'Is it any good? Dora had asked.

'I don't think I'd answer that question if anyone else had asked it. But "as an offering to conjugal unreserve", frankly, not much. As a writer, she makes a fine knitter.'

'Reg, that's unkind.'

'Not when it isn't heard outside these four flimsy walls. Who am I to judge, anyway? What do I know? I'm a policeman, not a publisher's reader. It's not for its style or atmosphere that I'm reading the thing.'

In her discreet way she hadn't asked why he was reading it, any more than she had asked why he always had his nose in *Kim* magazine. She knew better than that. He turned to where he had placed a marker between the sheets. It was at a point about half-way through and the young Dita Kowiak had begun work in the Auschwitz Krankenbau – the hospital – as an orderly. Wexford should have been moved by the descriptions of emaciated patients, the administering of intracardiac injections of toxic substances, the hurling of naked corpses into trucks. Dita had survived because for a time at any rate the hospital workers were regularly fed, even if the diet of turnip soup and mouldy bread was inadequate. She told of Russian prisoner-of-war poisoned with Cyclon-B gas, the burning of five hundred corpses in the space of one hour. But instead of being affected, he felt only that he had heard all this before. She had no gift for delineating place or bringing a character to life. Her prose was wooden and repetitious and there was no impression of her own sufferings permeating the text. She might never had been there; she might have copied all this piecemeal from the concentration camp autobiographies which, after all, were legion. And perhaps she had . . .

Several times he had come to points in the narrative where pages were missing, but up till now those pages had always

582

turned up later on. The lack of numbering made things difficult. Here, however, the narrative stopped abruptly in mid-sentence, in the middle of an anecdote about a doctor at the hospital called Dehring. Wexford carefully scrutinized all the remaining pages of the manuscript, but could find no further mention of Dehring's name. There was at least one page missing, perhaps two.

But would Dita Jago have let him take the manuscript if it contained – or conspicuously did not contain – something incriminating? It would have been easy to refuse. 'I couldn't bear to have anyone read it,' would have done the trick. Or when he asked where the manuscript was, she need only have said that she had sent it away to be typed or had even, as she threatened, burned it.

Whatever efforts Serge Olson had made, they failed to have any effect on Clifford Sanders. He made five phone calls to Kingsmarkham police station in the course of the afternoon, though none of these was actually put through to Burden. Next morning there was a letter for him, sent to his home. At the police station someone else might very likely have opened any missive that came, but here Burden naturally opened his own post. This brown envelope he had at first supposed to contain the bill for fitting a new carpet in the dining room.

Clifford addressed him as Mike. This was probably Olson's doing, Burden thought. The letter began 'Dear Mike'. The writing was a child's – or a teacher's – a round, neat, admirably legible hand, upright but with the slightest tendency to a backward slope. 'Dear Mike, I have a lot I want to say to you and I think you would be interested to hear it. I know you want me to think of you as my friend, and that is how I do think of you. In fact, I don't find it easy to confide in people, but you are an exception to this rule. We really get on well together, as I am sure you will agree.' Here Burden laid down the letter for a moment and sighed. 'I do understand that other people, those in authority over you I mean, are doing everything in their power to stop our meeting, and I expect you feel threatened with the loss of your job. Therefore I suggest we arrange to meet outside your working hours. Even employers like the police surely cannot object to their officers having their own personal friends. I will phone you to-morrow . . .' Burden noticed that he mentioned no precise hour and recalled what Olson had said about Clifford's attitude towards time. 'Please tell them you expect a call from me so that if you are out they can take a message. My idea is to call on you at your home this evening perhaps or during the weekend. With best wishes. Yours ever, Cliff.'

Burden's little boy had climbed on to his lap and he stroked his hair, held him close for a moment. Suppose his Mark should grow up into such a one? How could you tell? Clifford had looked like this once, been as endearing, inspired perhaps the same breath-catching love. Only I shan't walk out on him when he's five, thought Burden. But when he tried to summon up pity for Clifford, he failed and felt only exasperation.

'I'm taking no calls from this man,' he said when he got to the police station, 'and I'd like him to be told that no messages he leaves will reach me. Right?'

After that he concentrated on the quest of the moment, finding the whereabouts of Charles Sanders. If Sanders had never paid maintenance to the wife he had deserted and she, presumably, had been too proud to ask for it, he could not be traced through the courts or social services. It wasn't an uncommon combination of names. Telephone directories and electoral registers yielded a number for Archbold, Davidson, Marian Bayliss and Diana Pettit to call on, and Archbold had run to earth a likely-sounding Charles Sanders in Manchester. Burden had plans to go up there and see him, though he wanted to get the man on the phone first, and as yet he hadn't even managed to hear the sound of his voice. Engaged signals alternated with ringing tones as if Sanders unplugged his phone between answering calls. However, he never answered Burden's.

Later in the morning when he saw the red Metro come on to the forecourt, Burden had to suppress a feeling that was not too far from panic. He was being hounded, persecuted. The anxious fears which had been building up inside him had the effect which such an accumulation sometimes does, that of heightening the powers of his imagination. He found himself envisaging a future in which Clifford Sanders dogged his footsteps, in which every time he lifted a phone receiver he heard Clifford's voice at the other end of the line, in which – worst of all – when he looked in a mirror he saw Clifford's face over his shoulder. You are a hardened, tough police officer, he told himself fiercely. Why do you let this boy shake you? Why are you rattled by it? You can keep him off, others will keep him off. Calm yourself. Ignorant as he acknowledged himself to be of the workings of the psyche, he nevertheless recognised the evidences of paranoia in Clifford's letter and now he saw them in himself. And then he recalled the precise moment when he had first recognised Clifford's madness.

A memory came to him of something he had been told by his historian wife: how going to look at the mad people in Bedlam was as popular a pastime in the late eighteenth century as safari park visiting was today. How could they? His instinct was to put himself as far from the mad as he could, to pretend they didn't exist, to build walls between them and him. Yet Clifford wasn't mad in a padded cell, straitjacket way; he was only disturbed, deprived, lonely, his thought processes some-how askew. Burden picked up the phone, arranged for Sergeant Martin to go out there and tell Clifford to leave, to tell him he was trespassing or something.

He wondered if Wexford had seen him and felt a sudden need to talk to Wexford about it, to be franker on the subject of his feelings in respect of Clifford than he had been up to now. But as he was going down, had got so far as entering the lift, he remembered that Wexford – for some mysterious reason of his own – had gone to the Barringdean Shopping Centre. Burden thought he would like a drink or even a Valium, though he hated the things and feared them. Instead he sat at his desk and briefly put his head in his hands.

The sandwich, according to the claims of Grub 'n' Grains, was 'American style', pastrami and cream cheese on rye. If he hadn't been told that it was pastrami, which he had never tasted before, Wexford would have sworn he was eating corned beef of the well-known Fray Bentos type. He had been doing a bit of crime reconstruction, mostly in his head, but the true scene of the crime seemed the right place in which to do it.

The fountain played in the left-hand concourse, its jets of

585

spray concealing the ascending and descending escalators and the entrance to British Home Stores. But opposite him Wexford could see the several clothes shops and between them and Boots the Chemist the wools and crafts shop called Knits 'n' Kits. Next door to the café was Demeter with its bakery adjacent, then a travel agent, then W.H. Smith. Wexford drank his tropical fruit cocktail, paid for his lunch and made his way up to Demeter.

The health foods store kept its herbal remedies on shelves immediately to the left of the window and Wexford soon found the calendula capsules. It was these which Helen Brook had been looking for when she saw Gwen Robson outside in the aisle between the shops in conversation with a very well-dressed girl. And here she had been taken with the first of those early labour pains which prevented her from going up to Mrs Robson and speaking to her. Wexford bent down, took a jar of capsules from the shelf and dropped it into his wire basket. Then he straightened up and looked out of the window. Boots the Chemist could be seen and, this side of it, the wools and crafts shop, with the Mandala – circles of chrysanthemums and cherry-fruited solanum today – cutting off sight of the entrances to Tesco. Gwen Robson had shopped in Boots, bought her toothpaste and talcum powder, paused to look at the Mandala flowers perhaps, and there encountered the girl Helen Brook had seen her speaking to. It must have been Lesley Arbel, Wexford thought, who – perhaps having time to spare before the departure of the London train – had come in here specifically to meet her aunt. He imagined a conversation, surprise expressed by Mrs Robson, a brief explanation from Lesley about the word-processing course, a promise perhaps that she would see her aunt on the following night. Or had it all been more sinister?

It must have been on this side of the Mandala that they had stood, for Helen Brook to have seen them. And somehow Wexford knew that if the girl were Lesley she would not have been looking at flowers but, even while talking to her aunt, would have had her eyes fixed on those shop windows to the left of her with their window displays of clothes and shoes. He looked at them himself, at the space Dora's sweater had occupied which was now filled by an extraordinary red and black frilled corselette; on the next window which was a medley of red and black and green and white shoes and boots, to the window of Knits 'n' Kits. Here a loom with a half-completed piece of work on it – a wall-hanging or rug – predominated. He thought inescapably of Dita Jago. Did she use this shop? Making his way to the door with the basket over his arm, his thoughts miles away from herbal remedies and packets of nuts, he was jolted to attention by an indignant voice.

'Excuse me, but you haven't paid for your tablets!'

Wexford grinned. That would be a fine thing, a turn-up for the book, a detective chief inspector getting done for shop-lifting. As bad as, or worse than, his daughter going to prison. But he didn't want to think about that, he wouldn't think of it. Under the resentful gaze of the shop assistant, he replaced the calendula capsules on the shelf, leaving the wire basket on the floor.

It had been there in his mind, lying under a level of consciousness, for days now . . . well, weeks. Gwen Robson had been dead three weeks. It drew him to that window. Of course he had already dimly glimpsed it, half-noticing it as he came into Demeter. The pair of knitting needles were hung in a sort of zig-zag pattern all down the right-hand side of the window, hanks of wool on the left and the loom with its half-completed achievement in between. But they weren't, strictly speaking, all pairs. Wexford went in. Better not attack the window display, he thought, not yet.

Men didn't come in here much. There were two women at the counter, one leafing through a book of patterns. Wexford found a metal stand, the kind of thing that used to be called a 'tree', with packets of needles hung all over it. He unhooked the one he wanted. Lesley Arbel might have come in her before she met her aunt. Why not? She would have known the shop was here and known what she wanted. Dita Jago too, seeking only a replacement perhaps and later finding another use . . .

With a sharp tug he pulled the circular knitting needle out of its plastic pack and held it up as one might hold a divining rod, each hand clasping the thick metal pins at each end, the long wire hanging slack between and then pulled taut. Wire and pins were coated in a pale grey plastic substance. His eye

587

caught sight of the obvious victim to experiment on – a torso in styrofoam wearing a lilac lacy jumper, with an extravagantly elongated neck on which the head was poised at an unnatural angle. Approaching it with the garrotte at the ready, he was aware of a hush in the shop, then of the three pairs of eyes fixed on him and following his moves.

Hastily, he replaced the circular needle in its packet. He had found his weapon.

17

Clifford Sanders came to Burden's house at nine in the evening. It was no surprise to Burden; he had been expecting this from the moment he got home and thinking of various ways to handle it so as to avoid a confrontation. He considered getting his wife to answer the door or asking his elder son John who had come to eat supper with them, to answer it; he thought of taking the whole family, including little Mark, out to eat. In a wild moment he even had an idea of going away for the night, booking a room in an hotel. But when the time came, he answered the door himself.

It was the first time for days that he had actually faced Clifford and spoken to him. Clifford wore a raincoat, navy blue, very like a policeman's. His face was pale, but that might have been due to the light from overhead in the porch. Behind him hung a thin greenish fog. He put out his hand.

Burden didn't take it but said, 'I'm sorry you've come all this way for nothing, but I have explained I've no more questions to ask you at present.'

'Please let me talk to you.'

The foot in the door – Clifford had taken a step forward, but Burden planted himself firmly between door and architrave. 'I have to insist you understand you can give us no more help with our enquiries. It's over. Thank you for your help, but there's nothing more you can do.' Every parent knows the expression on a child's face just before it cries: the swelling of tissues, the seeming collapse of muscles, the trembling. Burden couldn't bear it, but he couldn't cope with it either. 'I'll say good night, then,' he said absurdly. 'Good night.' And stepping back, he closed the door hard.

Retreating across the hall, standing and listening, he waited for Clifford to ring the bell. He was bound to do that – or try the knocker. Nothing happened. Burden was sweating; he felt a trickle of sweat run down his forehead and one side of his nose. Mark was in bed, Jenny and John still in the dining room at the back of the house. Burden went into the living room which was in darkness, made his way stealthily to the window and looked out. The red Metro was parked at the kerb and Clifford was sitting in the driving-seat in that accustomed pose of his, the way he perhaps passed several hours of each day. Burden was still standing there watching when the phone rang. He answered it in the dark, still looking out of the window.

It was Dorothy Sanders.

Burden was obliged to recognise the voice, for she did not identify herself or ask if she were speaking to Inspector Burden. 'Are you going to arrest my son?'

In other circumstances Burden would have made some discreet and non-committal reply. Now he was beyond that. 'No, Mrs Sanders, I'm not. There's no question of that.' A mean, despicable kind of hope took hold of him that he could get this woman on his side, enlist her aid even. But he only said, 'I don't want to see him, I've no more enquiries to make of him.'

'Then why do you keep getting him down there? Why don't you leave him alone? He's never here, I never see him. His place is at home with me.'

'I quite agree,' said Burden. 'I couldn't agree more.' As he spoke the car door opened, Clifford got out and once more came up the path towards the house. The bell ringing made a searing sound in Burden's ears, almost pain. He found himself gripping the phone receiver in a wet palm as the doorbell rang again. 'He'll be back home with you in ten minutes,' he said, screwing up his nerve, feeling anger bring a fresh flood of sweat.

'I can complain to the proper authorities, you know. I can complain to the Chief Constable – and I will.' Her tone changed and she said in a slow deliberate way, pausing between the words, 'He didn't do anything to that woman. He didn't know her and he hasn't anything to tell you.'

'Then you'd better lock him up, Mrs Sanders,' Burden said indiscreetly. He put the receiver back, heard John go to the door, a murmured exchange and then John, who had been primed, said firmly, 'Good night.'

In the dark there, Burden thought wildly of an injunction to restrain Clifford from persecuting him, of seeking out a judge in chambers, of arresting and imprisoning Clifford when he broke the order. He heard the Metro door close and listened, holding his breath, for the engine to start up. The silence seemed to endure a long time and the eventual sound of the motor turning and firing was a glorious relief. Burden didn't watch the departure of the Metro but when next he looked out of the window it was gone, the street empty, the fog thick and still and opaque as muddy water.

Returning the manuscript, he asked about the missing pages, but there were no guilty reactions and no evasions.

'I realized as soon as you'd gone,' Dita Jago said. 'I took two pages out to check something on them at the public library.' She looked at him steadily – too steadily? 'You remember I told you I was at the library on the day Mrs Robson was killed? I was checking up something about a man called Dehring.' She didn't ask if he had enjoyed reading the manuscript or what his impression was, commenting only, 'You read that far!'

While she was out of the room fetching the pages, he examined quickly the circular needle from which the great wall hanging depended. The pins at each end of the wire were of a much finer gauge then the one he had handled in the Barringdean Centre and would not have stood up to excessive pressure. But that meant nothing. Mrs Jago would have other circular needles, probably in every available size. He glanced at the sheets of paper she showed him, noting corrections made in red ballpoint. She made no comment on his interest, but as he walked down the path and glanced back he saw her watching him from the window, her expression one of benign mystification.

Ralph Robson was cleaning his car, a popular Saturday afternoon pastime at Highlands. Out here he managed without his stick, holding on to the bodywork of the car for support. Wexford said good afternoon to him and suggested

591

that the task on which he was engaged was not perhaps the wisest activity for someone in his condition.

'Who's going to do it if I don't?' Robson said belligerently. 'Who's going to give me a helping hand? Oh, it's one thing when anything like that first happens. They're all coming round. Can I do this and can I do that? That soon cools off. Even Lesley. You wouldn't credit it, would you, but I haven't seen Lesley for a whole blessed week. She hasn't so much as phoned.'

Nor will she, Wexford thought. You've seen the last of her. She either got what she wanted or knows there's nothing in it for her.

'There's one bright spot though.' Robson winced as he straightened up from rinsing out his cloth in the bucket of water. 'I'm getting my hip done. Doctor's transferring me to another what they call health area the week after next. Sunderland. I'll be getting my replacement up in Sunderland.'

The Saab passed Wexford as he began the climb up the hill, passed him and drew into the kerb ahead. His thoughts had shifted, as they mostly did these days, from the Robson case to Sheila. She was coming to stay the night; it was years since they had seen so much of her as they had in these past few weeks, and inevitably he speculated as to why this was. Because she understood and sympathised with his anxieties for her safety? Or because she was sorry for her parents having to live in this poky, uncomfortable little house? A bit of both, maybe. She got out of the passenger side of the Saab and his heart leapt with the usual old relief.

'Pop, this is Ned.'

The man in the driving-seat was young, dark, distinguished-looking. Wexford knew at once that he had seen him somewhere before. They shook hands over the seats and Wexford got into the back of the car.

'Ned's not staying, he's on the way to Brighton. He's just going to drop me off.'

'That sounds like an early warning in case we start evincing our well-known lack of hospitality.'

Ned laughed, and there was a bit of an edge to the sound. Because Wexford had said 'early warning' which had another, quite separate, significance?

'Oh, Pop,' said Sheila, 'I didn't mean that.'

'At least I hope he'll stay for a cup of tea,' Dora said when they reached the house.

'Of course I will. I'd like to.'

They had rather taken it for granted that with both daughters married all this sort of thing would be over. There would be no more suitors brought home, the sight of whom aroused dismay or resignation or hope. Sylvia indeed had married so young that before Neil there had been no more than a couple of casual boyfriends. But Sheila's men had come in a constantly changing series, until at last the chosen one, Andrew Thorverton, had surely put an end to this parade. Or so it had seemed to those naïve parents who, because of their age, inevitably regarded marriage – at any rate in their own family – as an institution of permanence. Was this Ned a prospective second husband? Sheila seemed to treat him in a rather cavalier fashion.

He had gone on his way to Brighton before Wexford found out his surname. She could go back on the train; he wasn't to trouble himself about her – that was Sheila's airy parting shot as she and her father stood in the flowerbed sized front garden watching him go.

'Nice car,' Wexford said tactfully.

'Well, I suppose. It's always having to have things done to it. I mean, that last weekend you were in the old house and I came down, it was in being seen to. I offered to lend him mine as a matter of fact, but considering what happened it was just as well he hired a car instead.'

They went back into the house. With the coming of early dusk the fog was returning. Wexford closed the front door on the dank chill outside. 'I've seen him somewhere, him or his picture.'

'Of course you have, Pop. His photograph was all over the papers when he was prosecuting those Arab terrorists.'

'Do you mean to say he's Edmund Hope? Your "Ned" is Edmund Hope the barrister?'

'Of course he is. I thought you knew.'

'I don't quite know how you could have thought we knew,' said Dora, 'considering you never introduced him. "This is Ned" doesn't convey much information.'

Sheila shrugged her shoulders. Her hair was tied back in a ponytail with a length of red ribbon. 'He's not "my" Ned. We're not together any more – just friends, as they say. We actually lived together for four whole days.' Her laugh had a hint of bitterness in it. 'It's all very well these brave statements: "I don't agree with what you say, but I'd die for your right to say it." That sort of thing doesn't amount to much when it comes to the crunch. He's like the rest of you – well, not Dad – who don't want to know me if I go to jail.'

'That's not fair, Sheila. That's very unkind and unjust. I'll never not want to know you.'

'I'm sorry, Mother – not you either, then. But Ned didn't even want other people to know he knew me. And I went along with it – can you imagine?' She came up to Wexford, who had been silent and staring. 'Pop. . . ?' Her arms were on his shoulders, her face lifted up to his. She had always been uninhibited, demonstrative, a 'touching' person. 'Is this nasty house haunted? Have you seen a ghost?'

'You actually offered to lend Edmund Hope your car for the weekend while he was in the middle of prosecuting those terrorists?'

'Don't be cross, Pop. Why not?' She made a face at him, lips protruding, nose wrinkled up.

'I'm not cross. Tell me the circumstances. Tell me exactly when and how you offered to lend him the Porsche.'

Extreme surprise made her step back and hold out actressy hands in a wide sweep. 'Goodness, I'm glad I'm not one of your criminals! Well, he'd stayed the night and when he tried to start his car in the morning it wouldn't start, so I drove him to court – the Old Bailey it was. And before I dropped him I said he could borrow my car if he wanted.'

'Could anyone have heard you say it?'

'Oh, yes, I expect so. He was standing on the pavement and I called it out after him; it was a sort of afterthought. I said something like, "You can have this car for the weekend if you like," because I knew he was supposed to be staying with some friends in Wales, and he called back thanks and he'd take me up on that. Only after that I remembered I'd said I'd come down here, and I was quite glad when he rang up in the evening and said his own car would be ready in the morning.'

Realisation came to her quite suddenly and drained the colour from her face. The white stood out round the blue irises of her eyes. 'Oh, Pop, why did I never think of that? Oh God, how awful!'

'The bomb was meant for him,' Wexford said.

'And the letter bomb too? That was during our – er, four-day honeymoon.'

'I think we'd better tell someone, don't you?' He picked up the phone, feeling an unlooked-for, absurd happiness.

The night had passed without disturbance or dreams. Burden lay awake for a long time thinking about Charles Sanders One – the Manchester one, who had eventually answered his phone and turned out to be twenty-seven years old – and Charles Sanders Two, from Portsmouth, with children of Clifford's age, a young wife and an Australian accent. But his mind was not fraught with anxieties and soon he slept heavily and uninterruptedly. The dense fog which enveloped town and countryside brought its own kind of silence, the muffled sensation less of there being no sound to hear than of deafness. Jenny was up and Mark was up on Sunday morning before he awoke to see the bedroom curtains drawn back and a fluffy whiteness pressing against the windowpanes. It was the phone ringing which had awakened him and in spite of his peaceful night, the first possible caller that occurred to him was Clifford.

Jenny must have answered it on the other phone, for the ringing stopped. Burden picked up the receiver at his bedside and to his enormous relief heard Wexford's voice. It was Wexford wanting to tell him the solution to the bomb puzzle; wanting also to come round later in the day with another solution, the answer to the mystery of the weapon Gwen Robson's killer had used. Burden said nothing about Clifford or Clifford's mother's phone call. That could wait till later, till he saw Wexford – or perhaps might never need to be told.

The morning passed with no more phone calls and no more visits. There was usually considerable traffic in Tabard Road, which was a through road, but today it was quiet, the fog keeping people at home. Was it also keeping Clifford at home, or was there another reason for his absence? Burden wondered how much his mother's power and influence over him would enable her, at her level of necessarily far less physical strength, to be his jailer.

The fog did not dissipate as it had on the preceding days, but seemed to thicken as afternoon came on. His sister-in-law Grace and her husband came to lunch, also Jenny's brother. Burden thought how awkward it would have been if the red Metro had arrived and Clifford presented himself once more at the front door, but nothing like that happened. His guests went at about four, when the fog darkened and the yellow gleams of streetlights faintly penetrated it. None of them lived far away and they had all come on foot. Watching the departure from the front window, he saw Amyas encounter Wexford just outside the gate. This was about as far as it was possible to see, and even so the figures of the two men seemed as if swathed in lightly swaying pennants of gauze.

'It was a huge relief,' Wexford said, taking of his coat in the hall. 'Yet when you come to think of it, what does that amount to? Aren't I really saying I'm glad it's someone else's child and not mine that's threatened? There but for the grace of God, in fact – which is only another way of saying, "I'm all right, Jack".'

'Edmund Hope may be all right too. It's likely they've found another target by this time. After all, it's more than three weeks ago.'

'Yes, and more than three weeks since Gwen Robson's death. How's this for a garrotte, Mike?' Wexford drew from his pocket the circular needle he had bought at the Barringdean Centre; the pins at each end were a quarter of an inch in diameter, forming tough, strong handles to hold on to. 'You're the plastics expert,' he said. 'Would this be the right sort of stuff?'

'It's the right colour. I should say it's pretty obvious a thing like this was used. Does that necessarily make it a woman who used it?'

They went into Burden's living room, where a fire had been lighted; the blaze from it lit the room with flickering yellow. Burden put up the fireguard in case Mark came in.

'This was a premeditated crime,' Wexford said, 'only in the sense, I believe, that the perpetrator had had an idea of killing

596

for some time and was waiting only for opportunity. But I don't think he or she went into that car park with the weapon at the ready. It's more likely it had just been bought in the shop where I got this one, and that means the prospective user might have bought it or someone else purchased if *for* the prospective user. In other words, it was on a shopping list, so the purchaser could have been a man or a woman.'

'And he or she,' Burden went on, 'came up into the car park looking at it perhaps? I mean, perhaps it came loose from its packaging and the purchaser was curling it up and replacing it?'

'Or the purchaser, who wasn't the prospective user and maybe had never seen such a thing before, was fascinated by such a peculiar thing. It *is* a peculiar-looking thing, Mike. The purchaser might have just been standing there unwinding it and looking at it when Mrs Robson came along.'

A car drew up outside. Its progress sounded slow, as it would necessarily have had to be in the dense fog. Burden jumped up a bit too quickly and went to the window – not Clifford, but Burden's next-door neighbour whom he could see getting out to open his garage drive gates.

'It's not too early to draw the curtains, is it?'

'I didn't know there was any prescribed time for it,' Wexford said, eyeing him speculatively.

'It seems a pity to lose the last of the light.'

The impenetrable greyness outside made nonsense of this remark. It was now impossible to see across the street, in fact to see much beyond the pavement and kerb on this side. Burden pulled the curtains across the window and was switching on a table lamp when the phone rang. He gave a nervous start which he knew Wexford had seen.

'Hello?'

His mother-in-law's voice and his wife's intermingled as Jenny picked up the bedroom extension. He couldn't control the little gasp of relief. Wexford said with quick intuition, 'Has Clifford Sanders been hounding you?'

Burden nodded. 'I think it's stopped though. He hasn't phoned or been here all day.'

'Been here?'

'Oh, yes. He was here last night, came to the door twice, but

597

I do think it's over now. Anyway,' Burden lied, 'it's not important, it's not a problem. Your Mrs Jago — do you see her as. . . ?'

Instead of answering directly, Wexford said, 'Dita Jago might very well have been one of Gwen Robson's blackmailees. She had the means to kill her. Of everyone in the case, she was the most likely to have been buying a circular knitting needle in the shopping centre that afternoon. On the other hand, she says she was in the public library, the central branch in the High Street, with her granddaughters. I jib a bit at asking those two little girls to alibi or not alibi the grandmother they're obviously fond of; I won't do it if I can avoid it, but. . .

'Anyway, the papers Lesley Arbel was looking for — and ransacked or spring-cleaned her uncle's house in the process of so doing — weren't sheets from Dita Jago's manuscript. They were photocopies of letters.'

Burden said, 'Do you mean letters Gwen Robson took or borrowed from the homes of her clients? Incriminating letters she then had copied?'

'Not quite, her niece got these letters for her. It was Lesley Arbel who made the copies to show to her aunt. Not because she thought they could be used for any criminal purpose, certainly not that, but to amuse her, I think — to entertain someone who loved gossip and took the same kind of pleasure in sexual irregularities as some of our Sunday newspapers do — gloating over matters that ostensibly they deplore.'

'Are you talking about letters to the agony aunt?'

'Of course. Lesley Arbel had easy access to them and a photocopier in the office where she worked. Some of the letters would appear in *Kim* — my God, Mike, the amount of *Kim* I've grubbed through in the past week — but most wouldn't and some, even in these days of licence, would be considered unfit for publication. And even though there's an unwritten law in the agony aunt's department that staff preserve discretion — lip service to a kind of poor woman's Official Secrets Act — it must have seemed harmless enough, what she was doing. None of it would go beyond the four walls of the house in Hastings Road . . . What is it, Mike? What's wrong?'

Burden had jumped up and stood with head lifted. 'Did you hear a car?'

598

Drily Wexford said, 'I hear a car every minute of my life when I'm not asleep. How do you escape it in this world?'

The door opened and Mark came in, followed by his mother. But Burden continued to stand transfixed, only holding out an absent hand to the child. Mark wasn't shy; he went up to Wexford, wanting the pencil he held in his hand, then the pad on which notes had been made, finally climbing on to Wexford's knees. Burden went to the window and parted the curtains with both hands. His knuckles had whitened and his shoulders drooped a little.

'Oh, not again?' Jenny said. 'He's not back again?'

'I'm afraid he is.' Burden turned back into the room and faced Wexford. 'Am I overreacting when I say I'm seriously thinking of applying for an injunction?'

Instead of answering directly, Wexford said, 'Let me go.' He lifted the little boy on to the floor, sacrificed pad and pencil to him. 'Don't get it on the carpet, or your Mum'll be after me.'

As he came out into the hall, the bell rang. Wexford let it ring again. Burden had joined him, was standing just behind him. The letter-box lid started flapping as fingers pushed at it and then the other hand pounded on the knocker. The fingers appeared under the opened letter-box lid and there was something about them and the smear marks they left on pale paintwork that made Burden draw in his breath with a rough hiss. Wexford crossed the hall and opened the door.

Clifford took a step back when he saw him. He was looking beyond Wexford's bulk and when he saw Burden he smiled. Wexford eyed him in a kind of stricken silence, for Clifford was covered with blood. His grey shirt and knitted pullover and the zipper-jacket he wore, his grey flannel trousers, his striped tie and grey socks and lace-up shoes – all were thick with blood, matted and plastered with it, and in places the blood was damp still, glistening still. And Clifford, smiling, stepped over the threshold into the hall with no one to impede him until the little boy came out of the living room and Burden, sweeping him up in his arms, shouted, 'Don't let him see. For God's sake, don't let him see!'

599

18

The driving-seat of his mother's car which had always been a curious place of refuge for Clifford, a sanctuary and scene of unimaginable cogitations, was bloodied from his clothes. Easy to make an analogy here with wombs, but Wexford shield away from that one. Though it was dark and foggy, he had the seat of the car and the blood-encrusted steering wheel covered up before it was towed away. Now they sat in the first of a convoy of police vehicles, Clifford between him and Burden, crawling through the fog. Donaldson's headlights made two green bars of radiance that petered out into the wool-like greyness after a few feet. Behind them another driver clung to Donaldson's rear lights and a third followed, all moving at about fifteen miles an hour.

Clifford had Burden to himself now, a captive therapist, and his face wore an expression that was at the same time serene and insane. At appalling cost he had got what he wanted. He talked. He spoke uninterruptedly, sometimes lifting up his bloody hands which had smeared Burden's door with stains, the bitten nails blacked with blood, turning them over and looking at them with wondering pleasure. Already he had told Burden what he had done and – insofar as his conspicuous mind understood this – why he had done it. But he repeated himself as if he enjoyed the sound of his own monotonous, now measured and almost complacent voice.

'She sent me up into the attic, Mike. She thought she could shut me in like she did when I was little. I was to go up there and fetch her down a lamp. The one in the dining room had got broken, there was a fault in the connection, and she said to

600

fetch her one of the lamps that had belonged to my grandparents. But I'm cunning, Mike, I'm cleverer than she is
basically, I've got a better brain. I knew she would rather sit in
the dark than use anything from up there. She wouldn't use a
lamp my father's mother had used.'

Burden was returning his gaze with what looked like
blankness unless you knew Burden as Wexford did and then
you understood it was controlled desperation.

'The truth was she wanted to keep me from seeing you.
When she told me she'd phoned you to complain about our
seeing each other – when she told me that, I saw red. But I
didn't show my feelings, I kept everything suppressed, I didn't
even answer her. I went upstairs like an obedient little boy. Of
course I couldn't be sure what she was up to then; I wondered
what she was at. I knew she was following me up, though, and
I said to myself, why is she following me when she's asked me
to fetch her something? If she's going to come up too, why
couldn't she have fetched it herself?'

Forcing the words out in a voice that sounded unlike his
own, Burden said, 'So what . . . what did you do, Clifford?' he
had already cautioned him. It had been a bizarre ritual taking
place in the hall of Burden's own house, Clifford pleasurably
pointing out individual bloodstains on his jacket, his shirt, his
trousers, beginning on a confession whose utterance held a
childlike innocence, while Burden mouthed in that same
strangled tone the words of the caution: 'You are not obliged
to say anything in answer to the charge but anything you do
say . . .'

Now Clifford continued in the same blithe, confiding way,
'It wasn't the attic where Mr Carroll had to break the door
down. We'd never had that door mended. The photographs
were in there. It was the one with the bedroom furniture.' He
brought his face closer to Burden's – said in an intimate way,
as to one familiar with the secrets of all hearts, 'You know
what I mean.'

Donaldson braked hard as they came suddenly up against
the headlights of a huge truck. It was carrying earth-moving
equipment, cranes and scoops that loomed dinosaur-like out
of the rolling mist. Slowly the convoy edged past it; they were
beyond Sundays now, in the narrow lane that led nowhere but

601

to the Sanders' house and the farmer's bungalow. Fog filled the channel between high hedges, hung overhead like dark fallen cloud. They weren't far from the entrance now. Donaldson crept along, stopped the car once or twice – like a dog sniffing, scenting its way to the familiar ground. And it seemed that down here in the least likely place, a low place still in the river valley, the fog had lifted a little, for a high wall of hedge was visible and a tree like a great figure with arms upraised.

Clifford hadn't once looked out of the window; Burden's face seemed the only view he required. He said conversationally, 'All those mattresses were in there, and blankets and things. I expect you remember that time I showed you. And there was a lamp there too, like she said there was. She's clever, she knows about getting her details right. But there was something she forgot. It was the wrong sort of plug, the old-fashioned sort with no earth, an old ten-amp plug with no earth. It was so absurd I could have laughed out loud, only I didn't feel like laughing then, Mike . . .'

The gap in the hedge was found and Donaldson turned in carefully. Tyres crunched on the gravel. The leafy wall of the house, a great square of dark, still, hanging foliage, reared before them. Clifford turned his head at last, gave his home an indifferent look.

'She came up behind me. She was quiet enough, but I was prepared for her. Strange, isn't it, Mike? She's a mystery, she's hidden behind a mask, and she's slow and gliding like all mysterious people. But I know her and I knew what she was going to do; it was so obvious. Her hand went down to the door handle to pull out the key and I was standing there with that old lamp in my hands—'

'Come on, Clifford,' Burden said, 'we're here.'

The air felt wet; it was just as if a cold, wet hand wiped their faces as Wexford walked up to the front door. Dr Crocker was getting out of the car behind with Prentiss, the Scene-of-Crimes man, and there was a new photographer he didn't recognise. Clifford wouldn't separate himself from Burden but stayed close to him, nearly but not quite touching him. If he had actually touched him, Burden thought he might have cried out in horror, though he would have exerted all the control he was capable of to avoid this. It was bad enough knowing some

602

of the blood adhered to his own clothes after that nightmare car journey. He knew he would have to burn everything it had touched.

Wexford asked Clifford for the front-door key and Clifford's answer was to pull out his pockets, the pockets of his jacket and trousers. They were all quite empty. He had left his ignition key in the Metro. As to the others . . .

'I must have dropped them somewhere. I've lost them. They may be somewhere in the garden here.'

Under the wet grass, among the blackened weeds beaded with waterdrops, or on the road in the gutter outside Burden's house. Wexford made the decision quickly.

'We'll force the door. Not this one, it's too heavy. A door at the back.'

It was a slow, grim procession that made its way round the side of the house to the back regions where the rear wall and shed were just visible in the light of Archbold's and Davidson's torches, but nothing beyond. The beam of light played on a back door that looked solid enough, but was less weighty than the massive studded oak barrier whose key Clifford had lost. Davidson was the biggest of them after Wexford and he was also the youngest, but it was Burden who pushed forward and put his shoulder to the door. He had energy which must be released, some act of violence he needed to perform.

Two hard runs at it and the door went down. The crash it made set Clifford laughing; he laughed merrily as they stepped over the shattered boards, the broken glass. Olson would have said, Wexford thought, that it was more than a citadel of bricks and mortar they had broken into and laid open. The flooding of the place with light brought a kind of relief, not that a really bright illumination was possible for Mrs Sanders had been mean with the electricity. It was colder in here even than outside. A little of the fog seemed to have got in as Burden recalled the woman had once warned him it would, waiting ghost-like on the threshold to slip in. The damp chill seemed to penetrate clothes and prick skin with icicles.

'Stop that laughing,' he said roughly.

His voice wiped Clifford's face clean of all amusement. It was at once grave and rueful. 'Sorry, Mike . . .'

They went upstairs, Wexford leading the way. Through

some lunatic quirk of meanness or indifference, it was impossible to turn upstairs lights on from downstairs, so that one walked out of light into a yawning darkness before a hand could reach out for the switch. The comparatively elegant staircase gave way to the steep attic flight. Wexford could see nothing at the top, only deep blackness. He put out his hand for Archbold's torch and the thin beam of light showed him a half-open door at the head of the stairs.

The light switch wasn't even on the staircase wall but up in the passage. He deliberately averted his eyes from the open door and the room until the light was on. Then he entered the room with Burden and Clifford at his heels, the others close behind. Wexford put the attic light on and then he looked.

Dorothy Sanders lay half on her back, half-sideways on one of the mattresses. A small, thin woman, composed of wire only in metaphor and fancy, she had had as much blood in her as anyone else and most of it seemed to have spilled from that fragile frame. Face and head were a mass of blood and tissue, cerebral matter and even bone chips. Her hair was lost in it, drowned in it. She lay in her own blood, dark as wine and clotted to a paste, on a mattress dyed crimson-black.

Beside the body, not flung down but set up precisely on a small round-topped bedside table, was a lamp in the art nouveau style, a sculptured lily growing from its heavy metal base, its shade composed of frayed and split pleated silk. It was a forensic scientist's ideal, this lamp, from the clots of blood and bloody hair which encrusted its base to the stain which transformed its now bent silk shade from green to an almost total dark brown.

Of them all only Clifford was unused to sights such as this, but he alone among them was smiling.

It was very late. They had done everything – what Sergeant Martin insisted on calling 'the formalities'. But the idea of going to their respective homes had scarcely entered Wexford's head, still less Burden's. Burden's face had that look of a man who has seen indelible horrors. They are stamped there, those sights, but showing themselves in the staring eyes and taut skin as the skull inside the flesh reveals itself, a symbol of what has been seen and a foreshadowing of a future.

Burden couldn't rest. He stood in Wexford's office. He just stood, keeping his eyes averted from Wexford's, then bending his head and pressing his fingers to his temples.

'You had better sit down, Mike.'

'You'll be saying it wasn't my fault in a minute.'

'I'm not a psychiatrist or a philosopher. How would I know?'

Burden moved. He held his hands behind his back, came over to a chair and stood in front of it. 'If I had left him alone . . .' He didn't finish the sentence.

'Strictly speaking, it was he who wouldn't leave you alone. You had to question him in the first place; you couldn't be expected to foresee the turn things would take.'

'Well, if I hadn't . . . rejected him then, when he wanted to talk to me. It's ironical, isn't it? First he didn't want me and then I didn't want him. Reg, could I have averted this by letting him come and talk to me?'

'I wish you'd sit down. I don't know what it is you want, Mike. Do you want the hard truth or something to comfort you?'

'Of course I want the truth.'

'Then the truth probably is – and I realise it's hard to take – that when you in your own words rejected Clifford, he felt he had to do something to draw your attention to him. And the best way to draw a policeman's attention to someone is to become a murderer. Clifford, after all, isn't sane; he doesn't have sane reactions. Of course he attacked his mother to prevent her locking him in that room, but he could have achieved that without killing her. He could have overpowered her and locked her in there himself. He killed her to attract your attention.'

'I know, I see that. I realised it when we were there . . . in that room. But he was a murderer already. Why couldn't he have admitted killing Mrs Robson? That would have attracted my attention all right. Do you think–' Burden drew in his breath, expelled it with a sigh. He was sitting down now, leaning forward and holding on to the edge of Wexford's desk with both hands. 'Do you think that's what he wanted to talk to me about when he kept on trying to see me? Do you think he wanted to confess?'

605

'No,' Wexford said shortly. 'No, I don't.'

He was anxious now to bring this conversation to a close. The question he was sure Burden was going to ask would be far better postponed till the morning. Burden was in a bad enough state as it was without this further addition to his guilty feelings. For this would be the ultimate guilt. Of course he would have to know tomorrow, he would have to know as soon as possible in the morning . . . before the special court sat. 'Mike, would you like a drink? I've got some whisky in the cupboard. Don't look like that, I don't tipple the stuff secretly – or even un-secretly, come to that. One of our . . . clients offered it to me as a bribe and because I thought it would be handy to have, I took it and gave him the current Tesco price for it. Six pounds forty-eight, I think it was.' He was talking for the sake of talking as, burbling on. 'I won't have one, though. Let me have the Clifford tapes, will you, and then I'm going to drive you home. I'll give you a stiff one and then take you home.'

'I don't want anything to drink. I shall feel like hell in the morning. If I could justify what I did, I'd feel better. If I could tell myself the only possible way we could have nailed this man was by waiting for him to commit another murder – giving him enough rope, so to speak. You say you don't think he wanted to confess?'

'I don't think he wanted to confess, Mike. Let's go home.'

'What time is it?'

'Nearly two.'

They closed the office door and walked down the corridor under the pale, steady, bleaching lights. Clifford was downstairs, at the back, in one of the cells. Kingsmarkham police station cells were more comfortable than most prisons, with a bit of rug on the floor, two blankets on the bunk and a blue slip on the pillow, a cubicle with loo and basin opening off the tiny room. Burden cast a backward glance in that direction as they came out of the lift. Sergeant Bray was on duty behind the desk with PC Savitt beside him, looking at something in a file. Wexford said good night but Burden said nothing.

For the first time, the Christmas lights were on in the tree. Burden had noticed them as something unreal in the fog, a kind of mockery, as they returned from Ash Farm bringing

Clifford with them. Either they were on a time clock which had failed to work, or someone had forgotten to switch them off. The reds and blues and whites came on for fifteen seconds, then the yellows and greens and pinks, then the lot, winking hard before the reds and blues and whites returned alone. By now the fog had almost lifted and the colours glimmered in a thin mist.

'Wicked waste of the taxpayers' money,' Burden growled.

'I haven't got my car,' Wexford said. 'It seems so long ago that I'd forgotten. I suppose I meant to drive you in your car.'

'I'll drive you.'

A town that slept, a town that might have been emptied of its folk that silent night – inhabitants who had fled, leaving a light on here and there.

Burden said, climbing up to Highlands, turning into East-bourne Road, 'I still can't see how he did it – killed Gwen Robson, I mean. He must have been in that car park by a quarter to six, met her as she came in to get her car and killed her. He would have been getting out of his mother's car and she walking up to hers. That must have been the way of it – unpremeditated, a frenzied act on the spur of the moment. He'll tell us now, no doubt.'

Wexford began to say something about the grotesqueness, the incongruity, of a young man stepping out of a car and happening by chance to be holding a circular knitting needle. They passed Robson's house – dark, all the curtains drawn – and Dita Jago's where a light was on, a red glow behind drawn crimson curtains. A cat came out of the Whittons', streaked across the road. Burden braked hard as it leapt clear, on to a wall, up a tree.

'Damned things,' said Burden. 'One shouldn't brake, one shouldn't give way to one's reflexes like that. Suppose there'd been someone behind me? It was only a cat. Look, Reg, that woman Rosemary Whitton has to be wrong. I mean, it's pretty hard for me to have to face that, because it means I was irresponsible in not consenting to talk to Clifford when he wanted me to. I took her word, of course I did. But we never really confirmed it.'

Wexford sighed. 'I did.'

'What? Took her word? I know. But she was wrong. And

607

the wine-market manager was wrong too. Rosemary Whitton must have seen Clifford ten minutes earlier and he'd gone before she hit the meter. It was a genuine mistake, but it was a mistake.'

Up Battle Hill to stop outside his gate. The house was dark; Dora had gone to bed long ago.

Wexford unclipped the seat belt. 'Wait till the morning, shall we?'

He said good night, dragged himself upstairs and fell exhausted into bed – then awoke immediately, energetically, into a prospect of sleepless hours. When they were past and he was back down there, preparing for Clifford's appearance before the magistrates, he was going to have to tell Burden the facts: that he had checked and double-checked Rosemary Whitton's statement; that he had not only checked with the wine-market manager and three occupants of flats above the wine market, but had also found the traffic warden who, arriving on the scene to examine the damaged meter, had – while talking to Rosemary Whitton – seen Clifford drive away. It had been five to six.

19

Dorothy Sanders had never been divorced; Davidson's investigation of records had established that. Nor had she needed to keep herself by the humble sewing and knitting – traditional occupations of the poor virtuous woman she had once read about in some historical romance? – which she told her son had supported them in his childhood. For during those years she had been regularly drawing on the joint bank account that was in her name and her husband's. Now that she was dead, access to that account was no longer denied to the police.

It had been fed by the interest of Charles Sanders' investments, mostly unit trusts. Over a period of eighteen years since their separation, only she had drawn on it. From the bank manager's slightly defensive manner, Wexford gathered that this perhaps curious fact had never been noticed. He was a man opposed to new technology and blamed the fault, if fault it was, on the fact that in recent years the administration of the account had been by computer. Wexford marvelled at Mrs Sanders' capacity for lying and sustained secretiveness. It made him wonder if she had ever been married to Sanders, even if Clifford was her own child, but these facts were soon established. Dorothy Clifford and Charles Sanders had been married at St Peter's, Kingsmarkham in October 1963 and Clifford born to her in February 1966.

Wexford had himself driven back to Ash Farm and he took Burden with him, insisted on it. Burden had accepted Clifford's innocence of the first crime at first with reservations and arguments, then with a deep and bitter self-reproach. It was clear to him, and this Wexford was unable to deny, that

609

the death of Dorothy Sanders had come about as the direct result of his refusal to continue the sessions with Clifford.

Burden was silent for a while. Then he said, 'I think I shall have to resign.'

'For God's sake, why?'

'If it's true that I could drive a man to murder – and it is, I did do that – I'm not fit to be a police officer. It's part of my duty to prevent crime, not provoke it.'

'So, logically, you should never have questioned Clifford in the first place. Suspecting him of the murder of Gwen Robson, you should nevertheless have ignored him because he appeared to be an unbalanced person with abnormal re-actions.'

'I'm not saying that. I'm saying that having once questioned him I shouldn't have . . . well, abandoned him to his fate.'

'You should have gone on talking to him day after day, for hours on end, session after session? For how long? Weeks? Months? What about your work? Your own sanity, come to that? Am I my brother's keeper?'

Burden took that question which Wexford had meant rhetorically – which perhaps Cain had meant rhetorically – in a literal way. 'Well, yes, maybe I am. What was the answer to it, anyway? What did whoever it was – God, was it? – say?'

'Nothing,' said Wexford. 'Absolutely nothing. Come on, forget about resigning. You're not resigning, you're coming with me to the scene of the crime.'

In gloomy silence Burden sat beside him in the car. It was a passive sort of winter's day, neither cold nor mild, the sky pale grey and clotted like porridge. Sometimes the sun appeared low on the horizon, a shiny disc of plate showing through where the gruel thinned. The shop windows in the High Street were full of pre-Christmas glitter and a huge imported Christmas tree, gift from some town in Germany no one had previously heard of but which was twinned with Kingsmark-ham, had been set up outside the Barringdean Centre. Burden remarked in a sour way about the amount it must cost to run that electronic digital arrangement at the Tesco end which announced alternately that here were gifts for all the family and that nine shopping days remained until Christmas.

'What are we coming here for, anyway?'

He meant to Ash Farm, down long winding Ash Lane, where the grass verges were grey with splashing mud and dead elms with peeling trunks awaited the axe. But the air was clear today and in the distance the outline of the hummocky hill that hid the town could be seen. Ivy-clad Ash Farm slid into view, its many eyes peeping from amongst the evergreen growth. Two police cars were parked in front of it and a policeman in uniform was on duty at the foot of the flight of steps.

'I hadn't thought of going inside,' Wexford said.

'You said we were visiting the scene of the crime.'

Wexford made no reply but nodded to PC Leonard who saluted him and said, 'Good afternoon, sir.' In spite of what he had seen on the previous evening he found it hard to realise that Dorothy Sanders, so strong and upright and confident, was dead, the metallic voice silenced for ever. And when he looked through the dark gleaming glass into the thinly furnished room where the ashes of a fire lay in the grate, he half-expected to see her there, moving across the uncarpeted floor, issuing her orders with a pointing finger. A ghost, that would have to be, and she had been afraid of ghosts, afraid of the dark and of letting fog enter the house . . .

With Burden following him and Donaldson, he walked round the house into the back garden. It was new to him, but Burden had been out there before on the day of the search, triumphantly discovering garrottes in the shed attached to the rear wall. A curious place to put a shed, wasn't it? In order to reach it, a considerable area of damp grass had to be crossed. Earth, whether turfed or not, is always wet in winter, even during dry spells. He felt his shoes sink into the squelchy softness.

Dorothy Sanders had paid less attention to her garden than to her house, but had nevertheless achieved out here a similar kind of barren neatness. There were few plants that looked cultivated, though it was hard to tell at this time of the year, and even fewer weeds. It looked as if Mrs Sanders – or Clifford, on her instructions – had watered the flowerbed areas with the kind of toxic stuff that destroys broad-leafed plants. It looked as if at some point during her life in this house she had set about destroying the garden as it must once have existed. The few trees had been savagely lopped, so that from the stumps of amputated branches new twigs grew out at strange angles. A faint pinkness had appeared in the sky, sign of sunset. It would be dusk very soon, then deeply dark. Nine shopping days to Christmas, seven long nights and seven short days to the Solstice. One day to Sheila's court appearance . . .

These short days, cut off in mid-afternoon, hindered his progress. Nature still had the upper hand . . . just. Or, rather, he couldn't be absolutely sure the expense of using powerful lights was warranted. He padded through the wet grass to the furthermost corner of the garden and there, up against the back fence, he could just make out in the distance the low roof of what must be Ash Farm Lodge, rising above screens of Leyland cypress.

'Would you like to introduce me to Mr Carroll?'

They drove down the lane in the sunset light, the last of the light. With a rattling cry, a cock pheasant rose out of the hedge on seldom-used cumbersome wings. There was the sound of a shot and then another.

'It's only Carroll,' said Burden. 'The way Kingsmarkham's become urbanised, we forget we live in the country sometimes.'

Carroll's dog came timidly to meet them. Perhaps, though, it wasn't timid – perhaps it was slyly creeping up preparatory to an attack. Wexford put out his hand to the dog and a harsh voice shouted, 'Don't touch him!'

The farmer appeared with a dead hare slung round his neck, in his left hand a pair of redleg partridges he was holding by their tail feathers.

Wexford said mildly, 'Mr Carroll? Chief Inspector Wexford, Kingsmarkham CID. I believe you've met my colleague, Inspector Burden.'

'He was this way before, yes.'

'Can we go inside?'

'What for?' Carroll asked.

'I want to talk to you. If you'd rather we didn't go into your house, you can come back to the police station with us. That will suit us just as well. It's up to you, one or the other.'

'You can come in if you want,' Carroll said.

The dog preceded them in, head down and tail between its legs. Carroll made a growling noise at it, a remarkable animal

612

noise which might have been expected to come from the dog, not its master. This was apparently the signal for it to go into its basket which it did like a hypnotic subject, curling itself into a circle and putting its head on its paws. Carroll hung up the twelve-bore, took off his boots and put them on the now stained and corrugated magazine on the oven top which was still just recognisable as a copy of *Kim*. The hare and the birds trailed bloody heads into the sink. The table was a mass of papers, chequebook and paying-in book from the Midland Bank, a VAT ledger, crumpled invoices. Wexford knew the chances of his being asked to sit down were around a hundred to one, so he had seated himself and motioned to Burden to do the same before Carroll had got his slippers on.

'Where's your wife, Mr Carroll?' Wexford began.

'What's that to you?' He didn't sit down, he stood over them. 'It's her up the road that's dead, and her boy that's potty did it. You stick to that, you see he's put away for life; that'll keep you lot busy, not coming poking into my business.'

'Rumour has it that your wife has left you,' Wexford observed.

For a moment he thought the farmer was going to strike him. Unpleasant as that would be, it would at least provide a reason for arresting him. But Carroll, having clenched his fists and put them up, stepped back, setting his teeth. Wexford decided just the same that he might feel more at an advantage on his feet. He was a bigger man than Carroll, though older.

The kitchen was rapidly growing dark. He reached for the only switch in the room and unexpectedly bright light poured from the central bulb in its incongruous shade: pink frilled cotton in the shape of a mob-cap. There were other such touches in that grim place: a battery-operated wall clock, its face a sunflower, a calender that pictured a kitten in a basket, the date May of this year. In the bright light Carroll blinked.

'It was about six months ago that she left, wasn't it? End of June?' If Carroll wouldn't answer, there wasn't much he could do. He changed tack a little. 'Tell me about your neighbour, Charles Sanders? Did you know him? Were you here when he was living here?'

Carroll growled. It was the same language he used when issuing commands to his dog, but succeeded by reasonably comprehensible English. 'His dad died. Day after the funeral he upped and left. What do you want to know that for?'

'You don't ask the police questions, Carroll,' said Burden. 'We ask you. Right?'

Another growl. It was almost funny.

Wexford said, 'He never came back. He never came back to see his son, he never contributed to his wife's support or his son's. He left his old mother in his wife's care and she dumped her in an old people's home. I'm being very frank with you, Mr Carroll, and I'd like you to do the same by us. It's eighteen years since Sanders left. You were newly married, newly arrived here. I don't think he left, I think he's dead. What do you think?'

'How should I know? It's no business of mine.'

'What did your wife think, Mr Carroll? She knew, didn't she? Somehow or other she found out about Sanders. Did she tell you what she knew, or did she keep it to herself? Maybe she told only one person?'

'What person?'

By that remark Wexford had meant to infer nothing that could in fact be of momentous significance to Carroll, but the farmer read into it more than was implied and his face grew red and seemed to swell. Although he made no immediate move, a change had come over him – a kind of concentration, a gathering and intensifying of power, enough to make Burden spring to his feet and push back the chair. It was that which did it. Carroll reached behind him for the gun on the wall, unhooked it and, stepping back, levelled it at them from a distance of about four feet.

'Put that down,' Wexford said. 'Don't be a fool.'

'I'm giving you one minute to get out of here.'

At least now they would be able to arrest him, Wexford thought. The farmer could look at them and keep his eye on the sunflower clock at the same time. One eye open, the dog watched from his basket. This was something it understood – a gun aimed, a helpless quarry. When I double up full of shot, Wexford thought ridiculously, maybe it will come and retrieve me.

Burden said, his head cocked towards the door, 'There's Donaldson coming now,' as if he heard footsteps.

614

It was a trick and it worked. Carroll turned his head and Wexford's fist shot out to catch him on the jaw. The gun went off as he fell, and in that low-ceilinged bungalow room it made an enormous noise, a noise like a bomb, a noise like the bomb in his front garden which Wexford couldn't remember hearing. The farmer rolled over and the gun dropped from his hands to clatter away across the tiles. Bits of plaster dropped from the ceiling where shot had peppered it. Smoke and a stench of gunpowder and the bewildered dog looking from side to side, beginning a helpless, forbidden barking. And then Donaldson did come, pounding up the path and throwing open the back door.

'Are you OK, sir? What happened?'

'I don't know my own strength,' said Wexford. He considered poking at Carroll with his toe, but thought better of it and heaved the man up by the shoulders. Carroll groaned, his head sagging. 'I don't suppose we've got any handcuffs in the car, have we?'

'I don't think so, sir.'

'Then we must do without, but I don't think he'll give much trouble.'

Carroll was a big man and it took the three of them to get him into the car. They shut up the dog in the kitchen and Donaldson, who was fond of dogs, gave him a bowl of water and the hare.

'That's the way to undo years of training in half an hour,' he said cheerfully.

The artifacts that lay all over the surfaces in Wexford's office – in court they would have been called 'exhibits' – included Carroll's twelve-bore, a muddied copy of *Kim* magazine, a circular knitting needle, size six, and some of the contents of the dead woman's coat pockets. There was something distressing, though scarcely pathetic, about that lipstick in its shiny gilt case, the red of a fire engine. The almost white face powder with its faint iridescence had been marketed for someone young and fair, someone like Lesley Arbel. The chequebook for the joint account was in the names of C.L. Sanders and D.K. Sanders and – at least during the lifetime of this particular book it had been used only to draw sums of cash. A hundred pounds a month was what Dorothy Sanders had drawn during the past two years. It wasn't much, it was modest, but for the past two years her income had been supplemented by Clifford's earnings.

That morning Kingsmarkham magistrates had committed him for trial on a charge of murder and remanded him in custody until the trial was due. Even Burden could see now that there could be no other murder charge for him to face, that it was impossible for him to have been guilty of the death of Gwen Robson. He had seen Clifford driven away to the remand prison at Myringham before he and Wexford left for Ash Farm and he had not mentioned him since. But now he came into Wexford's office and spoke abruptly.

'I felt I should have stood up before the magistrates and said I wanted to make a statement. I should have admitted my responsibility – well, my share in what that poor little guy did.'

' "Poor little guy", is it now? What's become of your much-vaunted principle of reserving pity for the victim?' Wexford was reading a letter, nodding from time to time as if what he read brought him a long-awaited satisfaction. He winced at the sounds that were coming from the depths of the building, a steady crash-crash-crash, and looked up at Burden irritably.

'I've let him down all along the line. I should have publicly admitted my part in what he did.'

'You'd make yourself a laughing-stock. Imagine what used to be called the press, and are now for some daft reason called the media, would make of that. Excuse me.' Wexford's phone was ringing and he picked up the receiver. 'Yes, yes, thanks,' he said. 'You've a record of that on your computer, have you? Is it possible for me to have some sort of print-out? Yes . . . yes. Someone will come down for it before the library closes. When do your close? Six-thirty tonight? That's just about an hour. All right. Thanks for your help.'

'What's that noise?' Burden opened the door a crack the better to hear the banging. When Wexford shrugged, he asked in a tone of minimal interest, 'What was all that about?'

'A woman's alibi. And another one has just fallen neatly into place. Just a matter of clearing things up really, eliminating remote possibilities. Do you remember that gale we had in the

616

middle of last month? It blew down the phone lines at Sundays and Ash Lane.'

'You think I'm a maundering idiot, don't you? It's all hot air and bullying with me, but underneath I'm weak as water. I was scared of Clifford, do you know that? When he came to my house, I was afraid to answer the door.'

'You did answer it though.'

'Why was I so set on it? Why did I make up my mind it had to be him when all the evidence was against it?'

'At any rate you admit that now.' Wexford sounded bored, languid. 'What can I say? Anything I say sounds like saying I told you so. Well, no, I might tell you to let it be a lesson to you. You'd like that, wouldn't you?' He got up and looked out of the window at the tree with its winking lights, the red, blue and white sequence, the yellow, green and pink sequence. The sky was dark but clear, a dome of deepening blue with stars. 'Mike, I truly think that if he hadn't killed her then, he would have killed her one day. Tomorrow or next week or next year. Murder's infectious too. Have you ever thought of that? Clifford killed his mother because she was there and because she was restraining him and . . . to draw your attention to him. But perhaps he also killed her because the idea had been put into his head, because he knew, if you like, that it was possible to kill people. He had seen a murdered woman he thought at first was his mother. Hoped it was his mother? Maybe. But the idea was planted, wasn't it? Others could do it, so he could do it. It infected him.'

'Do you really think so?' Burden's face was desperately hopeful, the face of a man who may drown if the flung hand can find nothing stronger than a straw. 'Do you honestly think that?'

'Ask Olson, he'll tell you. Let's go home, Mike, and make a few enquiries about our prisoner on the way.'

The phone rang again as they reached the door and Wexford went back and picked it up. The voice at the other end was so clear that even Burden heard from three yards away, 'I have Sandra Dale on the line.'

Wexford said into the phone, 'It doesn't matter, I don't need it any longer,' and after listening for a moment, 'that doesn't surprise me. You won't find it now.'

He thanked her and said goodbye and they went downstairs. PC Savitt told them that Carroll, who had been put in the cell previously occupied by Clifford, was quiet now. Dr Crocker had seen him and offered him a sedative, which Carroll had surprisingly accepted. Before that he had threatened to break the place up, though had got no further than a regular lifting up of two of the legs of the iron bedstead prior to letting them crash on to the floor.

'Could you hear him, sir?'

'I should think they could hear him in the Barringdean Centre.'

Burden stood on the steps outside the swing doors. 'It's a funny thing the way you can do something, take a determined course of action over a length of time and be absolutely sure you're right, not have a shadow of doubt. And a week later you can look back amazed at what you did, hardly able to realise it was you who did it, and wonder if anyone like that can actually be sane. I mean, I wonder if anyone like *me* can be.'

'I'm cold,' said Wexford. 'I don't want to stand about here.'

'Yes, all right, sorry. What was that you were reading?'

Wexford got into his car. 'It was the letter Lesley Arbel was searching for and Sandra Dale has been searching for, which I have been searching for and have at last found.'

'Aren't you going to tell me what was in it?'

'No,' said Wexford and he shut the car door. Rolling down the window half-way, he said, 'I would have done but you're too late, you've missed the boat. I'll tell you in the morning.' He grinned. 'I'll tell you everything in the morning.'

And he drove away, leaving Burden standing there watching the car depart, not sure if he understood quite what 'everything' implied.

20

Burden drove the car down to the second level and parked as near as he could to where Gwen Robson's body had lain nearly a month before. Every space on the level was now full and would be all day, every day, up until Christmas and beyond during the end-of-the-year sales.

Serge Olson was the first to get out of the car. He had come into the police station just as they were leaving to enquire when and how he would be permitted to visit Clifford Sanders in the remand prison, and Wexford had invited him to go with them. An Opel Kadett and a Ford Granada were now parked where Gwen Robson's Escort and the Brooks' blue Lancia had been. A Vauxhall came nosing round looking for a space and proceeded down the ramp towards the third level. But apart from themselves there were no people. It was car world, an area of car life where bodies were cars and people their brains or moving spirits. Oil and water lay in pools, car excrement, and the place smelt of car sweat.

Wexford shook himself out of fanciful imaginings and said, 'Lately we seem to have lost sight somewhat of our victim, of Gwen Robson. But if she wasn't the first to be murdered, she was at any rate the first we knew of – the first to draw our attention to this case.' Burden looked enquiringly at him, but he only shook his head.

'She brought her death on herself; she was a blackmailer. But like a lot of blackmailers she was – I won't say innocent, she was naïve. She tangled with the wrong person. And I think she justified what she was doing by the reason for which she wanted the money, which was to pay for her husband's hip replacement. If he was to have this operation on the National Health service, it was possible he would have had to wait up to three years, by which time she feared he might be totally crippled. Three or four thousand pounds would pay for the replacement to be done privately and for hospitalisation. At the time of her death, she had accumulated about sixteen hundred.' Wexford's glance took in Olson and his driver. 'Let's go into the centre, shall we?'

It was one of those freak December days that are like April; all that was missing were the leaf buds on the trees. The flags on the turrets of the Barringdean building fluttered in a light breeze and the sky was milky-blue with clouds like shreds of foam. They came out of the metal lift with its graffiti into mild sunshine.

' "This castle hath a pleasant seat," ' Wexford said dryly. And if you half-closed your eyes the centre's medieval fortress look was compounded by the trolleys tumbled about the car-park entrance and across the roadway like siege-engines abandoned by their users. 'I've already discussed this with you, Mike. We know that Lesley Arbel brought her aunt photo-copies of letters received by the agony aunt at *Kim*, the magazine she worked for, in disregard of the undertaking she had given when she got the job not to divulge or discuss the contents of such letters. Nevertheless, she did make photo-copies of certain letters and she did show them to Gwen Robson. Now Gwen Robson, being a salacious woman, was interested in a general way in what she was shown, but she was far more deeply interested in letters coming from people who lived in the neighbourhood.'

Walking along the covered way that would bring them to the doors in the middle of the central gallery, Wexford went on, 'I don't know what gave her the idea of blackmail, but it was an idea both obvious and clever. True, she might have picked up information of a damaging kind about her clients while she was working, but it was unlikely she would have been able to acquire documentary evidence. She had tried other ways of raising money, but these ways had either ceased – the old people who paid for special indulgences had died, for example – or failed, as in the case of Eric Swallow whom she was unable to induce to make a will in her favour. Blackmail

620

remained, the blackmail of women whose secrets they dared only divulge to a more or less anonymous oracle, an agony aunt.

'Two letters particularly interested Gwen Robson both because of their sensational content and the addresses of the women who had written them. One was from a Mrs Margaret Carroll of Ash Farm Lodge, Ash Lane, Forbydean, and the other . . . well, here we are half-way between Tesco and British Home Stores. Shall we go into the café for coffee, or a healthful veggie juice in Demeter?'

The dissenting voice was Olson's, who would have preferred the vegetable juice. But he gave way gracefully, only stipulating decaffeinated coffee.

'I believe,' Wexford went on, 'that Gwen Robson's black-mailing efforts had been successful up to a point, that is, her two women victims had been paying her for her silence over a period of weeks or months. No doubt because, poor things, they could raise a lump sum. Let us come to the day in question, November 19, a Thursday and four-thirty in the afternoon, the time when more of the residents of Kingsmark-ham seem to be in here than at any other. Gwen Robson arrived at four-forty, parked her car in the second level and came in most probably by the way we did, under the covered way and through the central door. Now we know what shopping she did, though not the order in which she did it, and we have no way of knowing how much window-shopping she indulged in. But we can make an intelligent guess that she started at British Home Stores where she bought her light bulbs and went on to Boots for her toothpaste and talcum powder. Let us say that brings us to five o'clock.

'Helen Brook is in Demeter next door here, buying calendula capsules. She sees Mrs Robson out of the window and at once recognises her as the busybody home help who criticised her lifestyle and said she hoped she would never have children – this presumably because she feared they would be illegitimate. Helen Brook intends to show herself to Mrs Robson as ample proof that she is indeed about to have a child, but before she can do this she actually goes into labour, or has her first labour pain. However, she has already noticed that Mrs Robson is in conversation with a very well-dressed girl.

621

Whom do we know that we should describe like that? Lesley Arbel. The Robsons' niece Lesley Arbel, whom we know to have been in Kingsmarkham that afternoon.'

The coffee came and with a slice of Black Forest cake for Burden. He must be eating for comfort. Not for the first time Wexford marvelled at the manifest untruth expressed by healthy eating experts: that if you give up sweet things, you soon lose your sweet tooth. He turned his eyes from the chocolate cake, the cream and the cherries, and looked out at the concourse where in time for Christmas a sub-aqueous arrangement of coloured lights turned the fountain jets to red and blue and rose.

'The killer had in his or her possession, or so we have supposed,' he went on, 'a circular knitting needle of some high-numbered gauge – that is with thicker pins at each end of the wire. But suppose it was Mrs Robson herself who had it, and her killer took it from her? This is possible if in her innocence she showed it to her killer. She might have been into the wool and crafts shop immediately prior to her meeting with the well-dressed girl. Why did Lesley Arbel come in here when she knew she would see her aunt on the following day anyway? She wanted the photocopies of those letters back; she was starting to regret ever leaving them in Gwen Robson's possession.

'Lesley Arbel is a narcissist, entirely self-absorbed, interested only in her appearance and the impression she makes on others. You'll have to tell me if this is a sound description, Serge?'

'Near enough,' said Olson. 'Narcissism is extreme self-love. The soul-image is not projected and a relatively unadapted state develops. A narcissist would be suspended in an early phase of psychosexual development where the sexual object is the self. The girl, does she have friends? Boyfriends?'

'We never heard of any. The only person she seems really to have liked was her aunt. How do you account for that if they don't care for others?'

'The aunt might simply be a mirror. I mean – it's Gwen Robson you're talking about, isn't it? – if Gwen Robson was much older than she and nothing much to look at, but really admired Lesley and flattered her and showed her off, that

622

would be the only kind of "friend" Lesley could tolerate. Her function would be to reflect the most flattering kind of Lesley-image. A lot of girls have that kind of relationship with their mothers – and we call those good relationships!'

'I think that was it,' said Wexford. 'I think she also liked and valued her job and was very much afraid of losing it. Not only are jobs hard to come by anyway, but she feared that if she lost her job on *Kim* for this particular reason, a flagrant breach of confidence, she would in some way be blacklisted among magazines – and for all I know she was right. She wanted those letter copies back and she wanted to be sure they had not been copied in their turn.'

'Why would she kill Gwen Robson for that?' Olson asked, his frown deepening, his eyes very bright.

'She wouldn't. She didn't. It was only after she knew her aunt was dead that she became afraid about the photocopies and took the place apart trying to find them. As far as we know Gwen Robson didn't knit: there was no evidence of her knitting in the house. And I am sure Lesley Arbel didn't. Neither of them bought a circular knitting needle on the afternoon in question. Lesley, anyway, wasn't even there. It is true, as she said, that she came to Kingsmarkham, but she came for the purpose she said she did – to make certain she was properly registered for her word-processor course. According to British Telecom the phones at Sundays were out of order all that day, the cables having been damaged by wind on the previous night. Lesley was unable to get through on the phone, so down she came. All quite clear and reasonable. Far from entering the Barringdean Centre, she went straight to the station and was on a train before her aunt left home.'

Burden objected. 'But Helen What's-her-name saw her.'

'She saw a well-dressed girl, Mike. The well-dressed girl was talking to Gwen Robson out in the Mandala concourse and the time was about five. Clifford Sanders was half-way through his session with you, Serge. Where was Dita Jago? Now from the first, I was very interested in Dita Jago. She of all possible suspects possessed the weapon – or versions and repeats of the weapon: she had in her house probably half a dozen circular knitting needles in various sizes, of small and large gauge. She is a heavily-built woman, but strong and light on her feet. Suppose she was another of Gwen Robson's blackmailees – the hold which her neighbour had over her being the fact that far from being on the receiving end, so to speak, in Auschwitz, she had in fact assisted the authorities? That afternoon we know that her daughter took her own two daughters and Dita Jago shopping, dropping her mother off at the library and presumably leaving the two children with her. But perhaps that is only an alibi concocted by the two women. Perhaps Dita went with her daughter but instead of going into the centre, preferred to sit and wait for her inside the car in the car park.'

'Would anyone prefer sitting in that car park?'

'Someone like Dita Jago might, Mike, if she had something to knit or to read – both quite likely occupations in her case. Let us say that Gwen Robson parted from the very well-dressed girl, whoever she may be, and entered the Tesco supermarket on her own where she helped herself to a trolley and began her shopping. Now your Linda Naseem, Mike, says she saw her at about five-twenty but it might have been a bit after that. Most probably it was a little before five-thirty. Again she was observed talking to a girl, but this time only the girl's back was seen. It may have been the same girl and it may not. All we know of her was that she was a girl, was slim and wearing some kind of hat. By now, Serge, Clifford is just about taking his leave of you prior to beginning his meditations in the car in Queen Street.

'If you've finished, shall we pay the bill and take a walk? You've got chocolate icing on your chin, Mike.'

'Ratepayers?' queried Olson, eyeing the chit.

'I don't see why not.' Wexford led them out into the I-shaped gallery, crossed the wide area between the line of seats and moved towards the concentric circles of flowers: poinsettias again today, fleshy-leaved kalinchoe and the Christmas cactus with spiky vermilion blossoms.

'The Mandala,' said Olson. 'Schizophrenics and people in states of conflict dream of these things. In Sanskrit, the word means a circle. In Tibetan Buddhism, it has the significance of a ritual instrument or mantra.'

Looking at the flowers but taking in Olson's words, Wexford couldn't help seeing the instrument, also circular when so manipulated, that had killed Gwen Robson. And then he remembered his own dreams after the bomb – the circular images full of patterns, kaleidoscopic designs of extreme and severe symmetry. And there was comfort in what Olson was saying: 'Its order compensates for the disorder and confusion of the psychic state. It can be an attempt at self-healing.'

They paused outside the window of the wool and crafts shop. Today the display was of canvases for tapestry work; the hanks of wool and needles had disappeared.

'Go on, Reg,' said Olson.

'Gwen Robson talks to the girl in the hat, packs her shopping into two carrier bags and leaves the centre by the Tesco supermarket exit which brings her out some two hundred yards or so to the left of the covered way. She follows the path through the car park, probably pushing her two bags in a trolley which she abandons in the trolley park at the lift-head, then goes down in the lift to the second level. It is still full of cars, the time being no more than five-forty.

'Dita Jago, sitting in her daughter's car knitting, sees her come in and also sees her opportunity. She pulls the circular needle out from her work, leaves the car, goes up behind Gwen Robson on her light feet, and, as Gwen Robson is unlocking the door of the Escort, strangles her with this highly efficient garrotte.'

'Is that really what you think happened?' asked Burden as they entered Tesco. He took a wire basket, having always in such places an uneasy feeling that to walk through without one might not be illegal but was suspect and reprehensible behaviour, likely to lead store detectives to the belief that you were up to no good. He even helped himself to a can of aerosol shoe polish. 'You really think she is our perpetrator?'

'You'll destroy the ozone layer,' Wexford said. 'You'll coat the earth in black froth – and all for the sake of shiny shoes, you narcissist. No, I don't think Dita's our perpetrator; I know she isn't. The librarian at the High Street branch of the library remembers her being there with the two little girls from somewhere around four-fifty until about five-thirty, when her daughter came back to collect her. She was checking up on facts for this book she's writing, we now know. The librarian remembers because the little girls kept asking the time; they

625

were supposed to be reading, but they kept asking their grandmother if it was half-past five yet and then they asked other people and had to be hushed. Dita Jago took out three books and the date is on the library's computer.'

Burden took his aerosol to Linda Naseem's checkout. If she recognised him she gave no sign of it, but as they passed on he looked back and saw her chattering in whispers to the girl next to her. The main exit doors slid open to let them pass through into the sunshine. There was a seat out there, just outside, with a strip of turf dividing the centre from the biggest above-ground car park. Wexford sat down in the middle of it with Olson on his left and Burden – after examining his purchase, scrutiniszng the label to see if what Wexford had said of it might be true – on his right.

Wexford said, 'We'll return to those letters. Now I knew that these particular letters would have to be out of the common run, not quite of the my-boyfriend-keeps-pressur-ising-me-to-go-all-the-way genre. They were going to be of the kind that even in these days *Kim* wouldn't care to print. The agony aunt's assistant gave me an example of this type when she said someone had enquired about the protein content of semen.'

'You don't mean it?' said Burden, horrified. 'You're joking.'

'I only wish I had that much imagination, Mike.' Wexford grinned. 'One thing I did understand – where the letter copies had gone. The killer took them out of Gwen Robson's handbag after the deed was done, that much seemed obvious. The killer's own letter and the other. One of the writers was Mrs Margaret Carroll, but Gwen Robson never blackmailed her; she had nothing to blackmail her about. So we come to the other.'

'My daughter Sylvia brought me copies of *Kim* magazine covering four years, about two hundred copies therefore. When I read through the agony aunt's pages I wasn't looking for a letter. I was looking for an answer only, because I was hoping against hope that this would be one of those appeals considered too . . . well, what? Obscene, indecent – hardly. Too open and revealing perhaps to print. But the agony aunt's reply would be printed under a heading with enough inform-ation to give me more than a clue as to who the writer was.

'There are common initials to have and highly unusual ones. I'd say mine, RW are pretty ordinary – and yours too, Mike, MB. And your wife and your elder son both with JB even more so. "JB, Kingsmarkham" wouldn't convey much, would it? But your initials, Serge, are something else; SO isn't a usual combination at all. And the combination I was looking for must be even rarer.

'Well, I found it. Take a look at this.'

He had made a copy of the relevant back page of *Kim* and he passed the original to Burden and the copy to Olson.

Burden read his aloud: ' "NQ, Sussex: I understand and sympathise with you in your dilemma. Yours is certainly a difficult and potentially tragic situation. But if there is the slightest possibility that the man you mention could be an AIDS carrier, you must see your doctor at once. Tests can be easily and quickly carried out and your mind set at rest once and for all. Feeling guilty and ashamed is pointless. Better realise that by delaying you are putting your husband, your marriage and your family life in danger. Sandra Dale." '

'Nina Quincy?' said Burden when he had finished. 'Mrs Jago's daughter?'

'The letter that was never printed was photocopied by Lesley Arbel and shown to Gwen Robson. The full name and address were on that, of course. And Gwen Robson knew at once who it was; she had met Nina Quincy in Mrs Jago's house when she was hunting for two people to witness Eric Swallow's will. She was introduced to her and noted the unusual name. Nina Quincy lives in a big house in Down Road, she has her own car. To someone like Gwen, she would appear rich and a fine potential subject for blackmail.

'And for a time, I believe, she paid up. She has a part-time job of her own, and the likelihood is that for some weeks she was giving a considerable part of her salary to Gwen. You must understand that she was worried sick. Picture what it must have been like. Her husband had been away abroad on business and she has gone to a party, drunk too much, spent the night with a man she afterwards discovered to be bisexual and actually living with someone dying of Aids. She was afraid to go to a doctor, especially as by the time she made her discovery her husband had been home for some time and they

627

had been leading a normal sex life. Or so I suppose. I haven't seen this letter because the copy of it no longer exists and *Kim*, who claim to keep all letters sent to them for a three-year-period, are unable to find either this or the Carroll letter.

'On November the 19th, Nina Quincy – who still had not consulted her doctor or said anything of this to her husband, though the reply to the letter appeared in *Kim* last May – went as usual to the Barringdean Centre, having dropped off her mother and the two children at the library, entering here at about five to five. The first shop she went to was the wool and crafts place where she bought the first item on her mother's shopping list, a circular knitting needle gauge number eight – that is, a length of plastic-covered wire with a stout peg at each end measuring perhaps a quarter of an inch in diameter. This, or something similar, would be a purchase she had often made in the past for her mother.

'Coming out of the shop, she encountered Gwen Robson by the Mandala. It wasn't very imaginative of us to conclude that someone Helen Brook thought well-dressed would also appear well-dressed to us – at least to Mike and me, a couple of conventional coppers. Helen Brook would have turned her nose up at Lesley Arbel's pencil skirts and high heels. But Nina Quincy was dressed in just the way Helen admired: elaborate tapestry knits, a patterned beret and her hair down her back, a fringed shawl no doubt, a peasant-style skirt, jacquard socks. You see how I've worked on getting my terms right. Anyway, that's well-dressed in Ashtoreth's mother's book. What did she have to say to Gwen Robson? I think she pleaded with her to ask for no more. I think she told her that it was impossible to go on paying her at this rate – fifty pounds a week or perhaps more? And we must conclude that Gwen Robson did not relent, but said something to the effect of her need being greater than Nina's and perhaps that Nina shouldn't have done what she did if she didn't expect to pay for it. She was that sort of woman, was Gwen.

'If you've sunned yourselves enough we may as well take a look at their Christmas tree, see if it's as good as ours, then we'll go underground once more.'

'Are you going to tell us,' said Olson, 'that Nina followed her while she was shopping? That sounds grotesque.'

'Not necessarily; they may have encountered each other again at the checkout. After all, whatever trouble she was in Nina did continue to lead the life of a housewife and mother; she did do her own shopping and her mother's. She had to do it and then she had her mother and her daughters to pick up at five-thirty. So, yes, we'll say they met again at the checkout and more words passed between them, only a back view of Nina and her beret being visible to Linda Naseem. But they left Tesco separately, meeting for the third time that afternoon only when they were both in the car park.

'Those white lights look a bit stark, don't you think? I prefer our rainbow effect.'

The three of them stood underneath the Norway spruce which towered to a height of thirty feet. A notice at its foot announced that Father Christmas would be in the centre to meet children every day from Tuesday December 22. The date reminded Wexford of what today's was, one week before that, and raised into the forefront of his mind Sheila's court appearance. She would have left the court some hours ago and the waiting photographers and television cameras would have departed. By now it would be in the papers. Not for her the angry hand pushed against the lens, the averted head or coat held up like a yashmak, the veil to inhibit recognition. She would want to be seen, want the whole nation to know . . . He made one of those shifts that are much a remarkable feature of man's mental processes, as if a lever were lifted and a new picture dropped into place, or a kaleidoscope shaken. With the others following, he stepped into the shade and cold of the covered way.

'We can't tell exactly what happened next,' he said, 'but Nina Quincy – having settled matters at last, having taken action and perhaps feeling relief – had got into her car and driven away. She picked up her mother and her children and took them home. The blackmail was over; Gwen Robson would never menace her again. She, however, had something left to do. Now that this particular threat was past, she had to go to her doctor and arrange to have that test.

'Well, eventually she did and the test was negative. She had nothing to fear and she knew her husband was an unforgiving man. Yet when he confessed to her some indiscretion of his own which he'd committed while he was in America, she was silly enough to tell him the whole story . . . and he left her.'

Beyond the open gates, across Pomeroy Road in his window sat Archie Greaves. Wexford put up his hand in a salute, though sure the old man wouldn't be able to see him, certainly wouldn't recognise him. But there was an answering wave from beyond the glass, the wave Archie would give to any friendly customer in the Barringdean Centre. They went down in the lift and stepped out at the second level. A car went round rather too fast, splashing oil from a puddle – a red car, of course.

'You didn't say anything about her taking the letter copies from Mrs Robson's bag,' said Burden.

'She didn't take them.'

'But someone—'

'Once she had made her decision, she had nothing to fear from that letter. She had already told Gwen Robson while they were in the centre that blackmail was pointless as she intended to go to her doctor and confess to her husband.'

There was a space now where the Robson Escort had been parked, and the space where the blue Lancia had been was empty too. Burden stood in the middle holding out his arms in rather a dramatic way, a foot on either side of the dividing white line. And in a voice made shrill by exasperated bewilderment, he demanded to know why it was then that Nina Quincy had done murder.

21

They stood for a while on the spot where Gwen Robson had died.

'You know, Mike,' Wexford said, 'I don't think we've considered sufficiently what a horrible crime this was. We've accepted it, not put it into perspective. Only a very few people would be capable of committing such a crime. What – approach a woman either from behind or face-to-face and garrotte her with a wire? Imagine the horror of it, the helpless thrashings of the victim, her struggles . . . who but one of those psychopaths you're so keen on could stand it?'

'I must say,' Olson put in, 'I wouldn't have thought a . . . well fairly sheltered ordinary middle-class sort of girl like Nina Quincy with a conventional lifestyle capable of it. But I'm not a policeman, I don't know. The affectivity might be there, but it's just that a young mother – that's the last category you'd pick on for this kind of crime. In my game, that is.'

'And in mind,' said Wexford. 'When I said that Nina Quincy felt satisfied because she had taken action, I meant only that the action she had taken was her defiance of Gwen Robson, her decision to get medical help at last. Of course, she didn't kill her, though I daresay she sometimes would have liked to, which is what I think you mean. But she didn't kill her. In order to be back in the High Street and at the library by five-thirty, she must have left the Barringdean Centre by five-twenty at the latest, and we know the earliest time at which Gwen Robson could have died was five-thirty-five.'

The acrid stench of petrol made Wexford wrinkle up his nose.

'If we want to save our lungs, we'd better get back in the car,' he said. 'Before we go into the next sequence of events, perhaps we should take a look at the couple called Roy and Margaret Carroll. We already know that the writer of the other letter was Margaret Carroll – a woman with something of a social conscience, a woman who was upset when she discovered that her neighbour was in the habit of punishing her little boy by shutting him up in cold, dark attics.'

'Do you know who they are?' Burden said to Olson. 'Neighbours of Clifford and the late Dodo Sanders? Does it mean anything to you?'

'Clifford mentioned her,' Olson said carefully. 'He said he once threatened his mother with the cruelty-to-children people.'

'That's right. She was also concerned about another aspect of the Sanders' life, though this was something she didn't begin to suspect until last summer. Strange, isn't it, how all these things erupted last summer around May and June? Her own life was none too easy, I suspect, with a husband of a kind usually called a brute – a Cold Comfort Farm kind of character, only grimly for real. He was going to have a go at us last night with a twelve-bore. Did Mike tell you?'

Olson raised his brown tufty eyebrows. 'Where is he now?'

'In custody, where I hope he'll remain for quite a while.'

'And the wife? What's happened to her?'

'She left him last summer – something else that happened then, about June, I think. The wonder was that she didn't go years ago. Well, no, I'm deceiving you and I don't want to do that. Let's say only that she seems to have left him; at any rate she disappeared. Clifford believes there was a man friend and Carroll gives the impression of believing that too. I don't. I think Margaret Carroll is dead, just as Charles Sanders is dead. A year after Roy Carroll and his wife came to live at Ash Farm Lodge, Charles Sanders died. That was why he never came back to see his little boy, why he seemed to abandon his old mother, why he contributed nothing to his son's support, why his wife was obliged to live on what she drew from their joint account – an account steadily though meagrely fed from Charles Sanders' investments – and incidently why Mike hasn't been able to find him.

632

'Let's go back, shall we? We've renewed our acquaintance with the place; we can hold what we need to in our mind's eye.'

Burden reversed the car and circled slowly towards the upward ramp. 'Is that what they're doing up there at Ash Lane, searching for Charles Sanders' body?'

'Well, the remains of it, Mike. It's eighteen years past and there won't be much left. Frankly, I don't know where to begin the search for Mrs Carroll, but there are ways of help open to us.

'You see, Mrs Carroll suspected Sanders was dead when she was in her branch of the Midland Bank and saw Dorothy Sanders drawing a cheque on a joint account. She happened to stand next to her and quite innocently saw this over her shoulder. At any rate I think so; it's an intelligent enough guess. Did other things then begin to fall into place? The sudden and quite unexpected death of Charles Sanders' father? This death immediately followed by the departure of Charles? The memory soon after of secret digging? Not enough for her to come to us – or perhaps she couldn't bring herself to the enormity of such a step. It was a pity she didn't; she might be alive today if she had.'

When the car turned into the High Street something recalled Wexford's mind to Sheila and the tribulations of her day. She or someone representing her would have phoned Dora by now. What had happened to her – an account of what had happened with pictures – would be in the evening paper. It would be on the streets by now; the London evening papers were always on Kingsmarkham streets by three and it was nearly four. The sun was setting, dyeing the sky a gold that would fade to pink and darken to dusky purple. He caught sight of a newsboard with something on it about missile treaty talks and felt a ridiculous relief because Sheila's name wasn't there. As if Sheila's court appearance, Sheila's fate must as a matter of course be the lead story.

'Mike,' he said, 'put the car on one of those meters in Queen Street, will you? I have to buy a paper.'

Her face looked at him, framed in newsprint, not smiling nor laughing, no raised hand waving at cameras. She looked frightened; her expression was grave and big-eyed. She was leaving the court and even without reading the caption it

633

didn't take a policeman's knowledge to recongnise where she was going and with whom. The headline he couldn't help reading, though he forced himself to postpone further elucidation until he was at home: 'Sheila Goes to Jail', the picture caption said. '*Lady Audley's Secret* star gets a week inside.'

The man behind the counter, an obliging, nothing-is-too-much-trouble Indian, smiled patiently at this apparently stupefied customer who didn't know you had to pay for an evening paper. He coughed discreetly. Wexford put two ten-pence pieces on the counter and crushed the paper clumsily into his pocket.

Olson and Burden were out of the car, standing outside Pelage.

'Come up to my place,' Olson said. 'I'll make you a cup of tea.'

The steep narrow staircase was a bit like the attic stairs at Ash Farm, Burden thought. But there was something cosy, something sane for all its bizarreness, about what awaited them at the top. He remembered how it had once felt threatening and now he wondered why. What had he meant? He had become a therapist himself since then – with disastrous results. His own, sometimes timid, psyche suddenly seemed less important. Wexford, who had never been up here before, saw the poster with the globe and its ruined continents, with Einstein's ominous words, and it brought home to him Sheila's fate so that he flinched. He wondered if the others had seen, decided they hadn't and anyway, so what? Olson was using spoonfuls of powdered stuff called instant tea. Inwardly Wexford laughed at himself for minding, for caring about trivia in the midst of . . . all this. He said:

'Thanks to your tapes, Mike, I know exactly what Clifford told you. Whether those tapes could be admitted now, whether you were strictly correct to make them, doesn't matter. Clifford told you he hoped his mother and Roy Carroll might get together – might even possibly marry – and he told you how all the information about Margaret Carroll having a lover, another man in her life, came to Carroll from Dorothy Sanders. It was Dorothy Sanders, the neighbour, who was in a position to see who visited Ash Farm Lodge while Carroll was out in the fields and perhaps also to see whom he went out to meet. Or so Carroll could be made to believe.

634

'Carroll is a jealous, possessive man. She inflamed his jealousy and terribly damaged his pride, but for her own sake she had to do it. Clifford was wrong when he guessed Carroll might be attracted by his mother or enjoyed her company; all he got from her was information about his wife's infidelity. When his wife disappeared he thought he knew why and who with, but the last thing he wanted was for the rest of the world to know. That was why he never reported her as missing when she disappeared last June. He preferred to keep her disappearance dark but if anyone suggested to him, as we did, that his wife might be somewhere living with another man, he went out of his mind with rage.'

Burden drank his tea as if it were the real stuff brewed from leaves in a hot, dry pot, as if the milk in it had come yesterday from a cow. 'So Carroll didn't kill her?'

'There was only one person in this case capable of committing these crimes, and that person is beyond our reach now. Retribution, if you like, or chance or misfortune has caught up with her. Only Dorothy Sanders could have killed a husband, depriving a child of its father and a mother of her son. Only Dorothy Sanders could have gone up to her victim and garrotted her with a length of wire.

'Here's the letter Margaret Carroll wrote to *Kim* last spring,' Wexford went on, holding out the photocopy to Burden. 'I went back to Ash Farm last night and found it slipped into the back of a photograph frame in one of those attic rooms. The picture, incidentally, was of a family group I take to be Charles and his parents. I wonder why she didn't burn the letter? Because something she had done murder for must be precious? Or one day to have it to show to Clifford or Carroll if a defence was needed? We shall never know. The original would have been kept by *Kim* for two years, except that Lesley Arbel saw to that when she couldn't find the copy. She destroyed both those letters as soon as she got back after her Sundays course.'

Burden read it aloud: ' "Dear Sandra Dale, I am in a terrible dilemma and cannot decide what to do. I am so worried it is stopping me from sleeping. I have good reason to believe that a neighbour of mine killed a person close to her nearly twenty years ago. The person was her husband. I won't go into what

635

made me think this after so long, but the new evidence I got made me remember certain suspicious things happening all that time ago. Her father-in-law died too and he was a healthy strong man, not old. My husband does not like the police and would be very upset I think if I had to explain all this to them, if we had police here questioning me etc. I cannot mention names here. It has taken months to screw myself up to write this. I would appreciate your advice . . ." ' He looked at Wexford. 'Did this Sandra Dale reply?'

'Oh, yes. She didn't print the letter, of course, or the reply. She wrote back very properly advising Margaret Carroll to come to us and lose no time in doing so. But Margaret Carroll didn't – too frightened of the husband, no doubt. And by then Gwen Robson had got hold of the letter through Lesley.'

Olson put in, 'But how did she know who Margaret Carroll meant by her "neighbour"?'

'She was a Kingsmarkham woman: she knew the area and knew Mrs Carroll only had one neighbour. I daresay she remembered Clifford from the Miss McPhail days. Anyway, she took herself down to Ash Farm and asked Dorothy Sanders for money – weekly payments if she liked, she didn't mind instalments – not to tell the police about the contents of the letter. By that time she was already successfully extracting payment from Nina Quincy, stashing it away for her husband's expensive op.'

'She wasn't concerned with Margaret Carroll. It wouldn't have excited her interest if she had known that Margaret Carroll had disappeared soon after Dorothy Sanders made the first payment. Besides, it was in her interest to steer clear of Mrs Carroll who, had she dreamed of what was going on, probably would have been stirred into coming to us, would have saved her own life and killed one of the geese that laid golden eggs. Dorothy Sanders made no second payment. A second payment was asked for when Gwen Robson en- countered her by chance in the Barringdean Centre that Thursday afternoon, but Dodo saw to it that it was never paid.'

Burden objected. 'But look, didn't you say you saw her come into the car park as you were leaving it at ten-past six? Gwen Robson was dead by five-to.'

'I saw her come back a second time, Mike. She had been there before.'

'She went back?' Olson said. 'When she'd committed murder? Why didn't she just leave, go home, anything?'

'She's not like other people, is she? We've already agreed on that. She didn't have their responses, their reactions, their emotions. This is what I think happened, all we'll ever know now of what did happen. First of all, it was she that Linda Naseem saw from the back talking to Gwen Robson. She had a girl's figure, we've commented on that: she looked like a girl from the back, or when you couldn't see her face and hair. Either she went with Gwen Robson into the car park – arguing perhaps, threatening even, trying to make her change her mind – or else she followed her. I lean rather towards the alternative and think she followed. You see, by then – it wasn't yet five-thirty – she hadn't finished her shopping.

'So they entered the car park more or less together. While Gwen Robson was unlocking her car Dodo went up to her and garrotted her with the circular knitting needle she had bought in the centre after she had had her hair done. Remember, we know she had been in there because she had bought the grey knitting wool which she put into the boot of the Escort in the absence of her own car. The job done, she returned to the centre.'

'But why? If she was going to report the death to us, why not do it then? Why not pretend, as she later did, that she'd discovered the body.'

'She had her shopping to finish, Mike. She only came to the centre once a week and she wasn't going to upset her routine. There was still her fish to buy and her groceries to get. Didn't I say we aren't dealing with an ordinary normal woman here? Dodo was special, Dodo was different. She had probably killed her father-in-law, she had already killed a husband, very likely with a knitting needle garrotte, and a neighbour also by the same means. Maybe she even used the garrotte afterwards to knit Clifford's sweaters. Waste not, want not! She went back to get the rest of her shopping done. It was not yet a quarter to six. Possibly she thought some other car driver would see the body, for the car park at that time would still have been half-full. However, no one did. Only Clifford did, coming in at six o'clock. He thought it was his mother, he thought the body was Mother Dodo. And he did a mad thing, a typically Clifford thing. He covered it up with a curtain from the boot of the car and then he ran away, pounding down the stairs as I was coming up in the lift, bursting out through the pedestrian gates for Archie Greaves to see.

'Dodo came back at ten-past six, so that I was permitted a sight of her emerging from the covered way, and she entered the car park as she truthfully told us at precisely twelve minutes past. One useful thing only came out of my being there, my seeing her. She was carrying two bags of shopping but not the grey knitting wool, which is how I know she had been in the car park earlier. Did she expect to find a crowd there, even the police there? By the time I saw her, she must have realised that wasn't happening. Only one thing had happened – someone had covered it up. Who? A policeman? A car driver who had gone off to get help? What? One thing was clear; it wouldn't do for her just to do nothing. Her car was there but no Clifford. If he had been there perhaps they could just have driven off, taking no action. But he wasn't and she couldn't drive. Margaret Carroll wrote about her particular dilemma. Dodo's was worse. What was she to do?'

'Wait. Think. What if the driver of the only other car on the second level turned up, the blue Lancia? Where was Clifford? Where was the man or woman who had covered the body? At least she didn't realise at that time that it was her curtain which had been used – or rather a curtain from up in her attics. She went down by the stairs or in the lift, looking for Clifford, and that was the first time Archie Greaves saw her. The second time she was screaming and raving and shaking those gates. Her nerve had broken; it was all too much, the waiting and the not knowing and . . . the silence.'

Olson nodded. He offered more tea, not seeming to notice the haste with which it was refused, then pushed his hands through the dense bush of curly hair. 'I suppose there was no real motive for those early murders? She was a true psychopath? Because if we're looking for self-interest, it was surely in her interest to keep her husband alive?'

'Oh, there was a motive,' said Wexford. 'Revenge.'

'Revenge for what?'

'Mike can tell you the story. He knows it, Clifford told him. Clifford thought it romantic; he couldn't see through the veil his mother wore. Her life had been dedicated to an act of revenge against the people who said she wasn't good enough for their son, and against the son who agreed with them.'

'She was a multi-murderer who killed dispassionately but who was afraid of her victims after they were dead. She disinfected herself to be rid of their contamination and was frightened of their ghosts.'

Burden and Olson had begun a discussion on paranoia, on infantilism and transference, and Wexford listened to them for a moment or two, smiling to himself as Burden said, 'We live and learn.'

'We live at any rate,' said Wexford and he left them, walking the few hundred yards back to the police station when he got into his own car under the Christmas lights which were already winking away on the ash tree. There he sat and read about Sheila, read the statement she had made, her refusal to pay the fine demanded on conviction – her brave, foolhardy, defiant declaration that she would do it all again as soon as she came out.

'The Chief Constable rang,' Dora said as he came into the house. 'Darling, he wants to see you as soon as possible; he couldn't get you at the office. I suppose it's about this place.'

I don't suppose so for a moment, said Wexford but to himself, not aloud. He knew exactly what it would be about and felt the crackle of the evening paper in his raincoat pocket. For some reason, for no reason, he gave Dora a kiss and she looked a little surprised.

'I don't suppose I'll be long,' he said, knowing he would be.

Dusk, nearly dark, a little before five. His route to Middleton where the Chief Constable lived took him along his old road. It would be the first time he had been there since the bomb and he knew he had consciously avoided it, but he didn't now. The sky was jewel-blue and windows along the street were full of Christmas lights. Bracing himself for the shock of devastation, he slowed as he came to the strip of open ground, the empty site. He braked, pulled in and looked.

Three men were coming out of the gate, up to a van with ladders on its roof. He saw the contractors' board, the stack of

639

bricks, the concrete-mixer covered up against the frost. He got out and stood looking, smiled to himself.

They had begun to rebuild his house.